Surviving Tomorrow

Surviving Tomorrow

EDITED BY

BRYAN THOMAS SCHMIDT

For detailed previous publication information, see page 438.

ISBN-13: 978-1-953134-01-1 hardcover
ISBN-13: 978-1-953134-02-8 paperback
ISBN-13: 978-1-953134-00-4 ebook

A 25 & Y Original   25andY.com
First Edition: October 2020

Cover Art by Luca Oleastri www.rotwangstudio.com
Cover Design by Svitlana Stefaniuk
Interior Design by Sebastian Penraeth

Published in Denver, Colorado
Printed in the United States of America 10 9 8 7 6 5 4 3 2 1

To John Schmidt and Kate Anderson
and all the other dear ones gone too soon during this pandemic.

You will always be loved and remembered.

Profits of this anthology go to benefit front line COVID-19 testing kits, Direct Relief, Global Giving, and ModestNeeds.org*. For more specific information, please go to* survivingtomorrowanthology.com/charities*.*

TABLE OF CONTENTS

INTRODUCTION I
by Peter J. Wacks

LAST BUS TO NORTH RED LAKE 1
by Martin L. Shoemaker

WINDSTREAM 13
by Andrew Mayne & Roshni "Rush" Bhatia

WHEN SYSADMINS RULED THE EARTH 23
by Cory Doctorow

CALL IT ONLY 55
by Chelsea Quinn Yarbro

FACE YOUR FURS 67
by Seanan McGuire

DALE & MABEL 75
by Scott Sigler

FLINCH 85
by K.D. McEntire

CAROUSEL 99
by Orson Scott Card

THE MONSTERS UNDERNEATH HIS BED 115
by Ken Scholes

LORD OF TIME 121
by Livia Blackburne

EVACUATION 131
by Alan Dean Foster

PURE SILVER 137
by A. C. Crispin & Kathleen O'Malley

WRITING ON THE WALL 153
by Jody Lynn Nye

BACK TO BLACK 165
by Jonathan Maberry and Bryan Thomas Schmidt

WE CAN GET THEM FOR YOU WHOLESALE 231
by Neil Gaiman

HOPIUM DEN **239**
by John Skipp

THE ULTIMATE WAGER. **247**
by Raymund Eich

BITTER HONEY. **261**
by Julie Frost

VORACIOUS BLACK **267**
by Mercedes M. Yardley

A LOVE MONSTROUSLY GRATEFUL. **271**
by C. Stuart Hardwick

THE SWEETNESS OF BITTER **289**
by Beth Cato

SIX LIL' REAPERS. **301**
A *Grim Days* Mystery
by J. Kent Holloway

IMPACT MITIGATION **319**
by Jay Werkheiser

FAIR PLAY. **335**
by Claire Ashgrove

IN THEIR GARDEN **345**
by Brenda Cooper

EMPTY NEST. **353**
by Tori Eldridge

SHOTGUN WEDDING **359**
by Peter J. Wacks

ONCE ON THE *BLUE MOON* **361**
by Kristine Kathryn Rusch

THIS IS THE ROAD. **387**
by Robert Silverberg

ACKNOWLEDGMENTS   *437*

PUBLICATION & COPYRIGHT CREDITS   *438*

BIOGRAPHIES   *440*

INTRODUCTION
by Peter J. Wacks

We find ourselves in a scared new world that is nothing like any we have experienced before. It is a stark contrast to the reality of even a year ago.

It looks different.

It smells different.

It feels different.

There are vast echoes and the sounds of birds chirping—punctuated by the sounds of sirens where we expect the rumble of urban life and the sounds of car horns punctuated ... by, well, sirens. But they are different. Sirens of isolation seem like dopplers desperately seeking anyone else out there, whereas the sirens of society were jostling noisy things—calls to move out of the way. As much as it some days seems like we are collectively facing down the apocalypse, the brightest moments can oft be found in the darkest hours.

The stories in *Surviving Tomorrow* focus on the impacts of extraordinary circumstances on the people they depict and how these people respond to these extraordinary circumstances. The great joy of reading works of speculative fiction like those included here is seeing how the writer imagines these circumstances, imagines these responses, and takes the reader on that journey of imagination.

Walking in a character's shoes can make ours seem not so heavy.

From my personal experiences as a COVID-19 survivor, I can attest to just how heavy those shoes can be. As I suffered low oxygen and energy levels, it felt like the world was closing in around me. Rage filled me because I had been so careful and caught it anyway. Anxiety filled me—if I had it, who else had I inadvertently given it to? It was an endless cycle, and I was going crazy watching the same four walls every day, every night, every moment ...

I couldn't wait till I could go outside. To experience something different. I counted the hours down … and then came the second phase crash. I got better, then worse. I imagined a million stories in those weeks—but while my brain was in a super creative mode, my body couldn't get up the energy to sit and work more than an hour or two each day. It was exhausting. I was depressed and felt more fatigue than I've ever felt before. Then I got a call, something to drag me out of my own head, my own illness … *do you want to work on an anthology to fight COVID-19?*

When we meet extraordinary circumstances in reality, it can be overwhelming—scratch that, it is overwhelming—and equally it can be empowering to respond to those around us. That is our job and our hope. To respond. To our circumstances, our neighbors, those who are ill, those who are in pain, and those who are in need.

Struck by a desire to help people as the pandemic unfolded, editor Bryan Thomas Schmidt decided to use his skills as an anthologist to raise funding for COVID-19 support by creating an anthology with two purposes—fundraising to help those in medical need, and provide readers in spiritual need with stories that would speak to them as they manage the stress of our changing social landscape. Before he even knew if he could get it published, Bryan put scores of hours into bringing this book to life.

All told, *Surviving Tomorrow* is the product of thousands of hours of artistic creation to deliver what is contained in its pages, and several hundred hours of production and development by a handful of devoted people—which speaks to the tremendous passion everyone who has touched the creation of this book has for the cause and the project. If even a fraction of that carries across the page and into your hearts, this book will be a success.

Alone we will make it through today.
Together we will survive tomorrow.
Just remember to bring a good book along for the ride.

One day at a time,
Peter J. Wacks

LAST BUS TO NORTH RED LAKE
by Martin L. Shoemaker

The Trailways bus rocked over some obstacle in the road, and Jason Cole's head bumped against the window, jolting him out of a dream. *Something about flashing lights....*

He immediately hunched down, looked around, and reached for his medical kit—which wasn't there, of course, now that he was a civilian. Then he relaxed as he saw no threat. Not that threats were likely in the middle of the Nevada desert, but instincts didn't fade so easily. It wasn't that long ago that a similar jolt in a different vehicle was a sure sign of an incoming attack.

But he wasn't in an APC in the sandbox anymore. He was in a battered old bus in Nevada, hours north and east of Reno, on the way home. Or as close to home as he had these days: North Red Lake, Nevada, population 630. The town he once couldn't wait to get out of.

Well, he'd seen the world, and now a little bit of boring North Red Lake would suit him just fine for a while.

Jason scanned the rest of the bus. It was half empty, not like before Reno. The bus had been almost full then. Now there were fewer than a dozen people, though it was difficult to tell. With the bus this empty, passengers might be laying down across rows.

Without really looking, Jason had seen that the teen girl was still next to him. She had joined him at the stop in Lake Tahoe. Before then she had sat closer to the front, not here at the rear. Up next to … Jason shook his head, trying not to judge the guy. Once upon a time, he'd been as sloppy as the civilian, some young kid in a dirty shirt with a sneer on his face. Words had been exchanged, loud enough for Jason to hear all the way back at the back of the bus, but not loud enough for him to make out. Probably the punk had hit on the teen, and not taken *No* for an answer; and so the

1

girl had moved to another seat. No doubt Jason, with his quiet demeanor and his hair still in a military cut, had been less of a threat.

Jason looked forward, and the punk was still on the bus. Maybe that's why the girl hadn't moved. They hadn't spoken to each other, but Jason was willing to be her scarecrow to keep away the punk if that was what she needed. He had a sister about that age, and he hoped somebody would take care of Marcy if the situation were reversed.

Well, he was awake now. He looked out over the desert, wondering if there were any familiar landmarks yet. They were a couple hours out from North Red Lake, but the sights and sounds were saying *home* to him.

Then a light flashed in the sky. Instinct took control, and Jason shouted, "Down!" He ducked low in the seat, pulling the teen down beside him.

Screech of brakes … Bright flash ahead … Bus bouncing … Sliding sideways … Tumbling … Someone crying for help … Crying …

Jason found himself on the roof of the bus, which had flipped completely upside down as it slid across the desert, he remembered that. Or … He had a hazy vision of *watching* it slide….

He shook his head, but that was a mistake. It hurt like a son of a bitch. But he didn't feel groggy, he had no double vision, so probably not a concussion. Maybe.

And now that he was thinking more clearly, he was sure the bus had rolled. And … crumpled. He looked along the roof, and there was a distinct bend in the middle. The bus wasn't an APC. It wasn't meant to survive….

Survive what? The light had made Jason think of a mortar, but the explosion had been a lot bigger than that. He had caught just a glimpse before the bus had tumbled. A huge white glow…. Jason looked for a window with a clear view, fearing that the next thing he'd see would be a mushroom cloud.

No, that was ridiculous. A nuke that close, they'd all be black smears on the bus roof. So not nuclear, just one hell of a lot of energy.

Then Jason felt weight on his legs, and he looked down. The girl lay face down across his legs, her legs sprawled toward the back of the bus. She was conscious, just starting to pick herself up. "What happened?" she asked.

Jason shook his head. "Not now. Hold still." The old training came back to him: *Help yourself first, or you can't help your team.* Carefully he flexed his arms. The left shoulder was sore, but he'd had worse. Next to check his legs. "Hold still," he said. "I'm going to be as gentle as I can."

Jason sat up, slid his arms under her shoulders and her legs, and guided her off him. She gave one sharp cry of pain, and he stopped. "What is it?"

"My ... ribs ..."

"Broken?" It was a dumb question. How could she know this soon? But she shook her head. "Sore. I don't think ... Try again."

Jason lifted again. The girl winced, but then got her arms underneath her, and then her knees. She crawled off his legs. "Just ... sore."

Probably from landing on his legs, maybe bashing into the seat. Ducking down had probably saved both of them from getting tossed around worse.

Now Jason was able to probe his legs. Tentatively, he rolled onto his side and bent his legs. He felt bruises, but the muscles worked. "All right," he said, "let's check you out. I'm Jason. What's your name, Miss?"

"Teri," she answered as Jason set to work. He had expected some resistance to a strange man prodding at her like this; but the girl's eyes were wide, stunned. Maybe shock?

A cut on the side of her head was bleeding, but not enough blood loss for shock as far as Jason could tell. Soon he was sure she had no broken bones. The worst she had was the cut. "We need to take care of that, Teri," he said.

"Take care what?"

Jason reached up, touched the blood in her hair, and pulled his fingers back to show them to her. Her eyes grew wide, so he said, "It's all right. Head wounds bleed a lot, but you're fine. We just need to get some pressure on it. Make a bandage somehow." He looked around.

"Here," Teri said. She tried to open the overhead compartment now under their seat, hammering on it until it gave. She pulled out her small suitcase and dug through it until she found a paper envelope with a sanitary pad.

"Good," Jason said. He ripped the paper, took out the pad, folded it into a square, and held it up against her head. "Now you hold on to this. Can you do that?"

Teri nodded. "I grew up in farm country," she said. "We learn first aid."

Jason smiled. "Farm country? Good. A good, strong farm girl can take care of herself. Now do you have any tape in there? Packing straps? We need to tie that in place."

"A T-shirt?" Teri reached in and pulled out a blue T-shirt.

"That'll work." Jason took the shirt and wrapped it over Teri's head. Then he knotted it tight around the pad. It would work for a temporary fix.

But how temporary? "Teri, find your phone and call 911. I have to see how the others are doing." It bothered Jason that in the time they'd been sitting there, he had heard nothing from the rest of the bus. And his instincts told him someone needed help.

Teri nodded, wincing a bit, and looked around until she found her purse. Jason looked toward the front the bus. He would have to crawl up there, but he could stand here. His legs ached, but no worse than a 20-mile run back in Basic.

Remembering the earlier cry for help, Jason called out, "Anybody need a medic?"

Whimpers came from the front of the bus. Someone was alive, at least.

Jason made his way forward. Six rows up he found an old lady who had spent much of the trip on her smartphone. The phone was gone now, somewhere in the wreckage of the bus. The lady lay curled atop the luggage rack and against the curve of the bus roof. Jason felt for a pulse. Her heart was beating, she seemed to be breathing, just knocked out. She hadn't been the one who had called. Jason slid her gently to rest flat on the luggage rack. He would get back to her after he had assessed the others.

Two rows up, he had to crouch. This was where the bus had flexed, as if the frame had actually snapped, and the bus had bent here.

Another two rows, and Jason had to get on his knees. He was crawling when he found the punk. The kid sat just rear of the bend, eyes glassy. Was the idiot stoned?

But then the eyes fixed on Jason, and they focused. "What the fuck?"

"Calm down," Jason said. "Are you hurt?"

"I ... think my leg's broke."

Then Jason saw blood around the right leg of the kid's jeans. That could be bad. Jason carefully touched the leg, and the punk screamed.

Jason pulled his hand away. "Sorry ... What's your name?"

"Hal ... Oh, fuck, I'm bleeding...."

"Don't worry, Hal, I'm a medic." Without a kit, but it was important to sound confident. Don't panic the patient. "We'll take care of this," Jason continued. He understood the glassy eyes now: blood loss. The kid was in and out of shock. He needed attention now.

But there were still others in the bus. Jason called back, "Teri? Any luck?"

"Zero bars, Jason," she answered. "Nothing."

Damn. No ambulance, then, and his gut told him there were more injured. "Teri, I need you to check on the other passengers, while I take care of Hal's leg here. Can you do that?" Just then a moan came from the front of the bus, and Jason added, "It's important. We've got more people hurt."

"I'm on my way."

Turning back to the kid, Jason said, "Stay with me, Hal. I need to see that leg." Jason felt for the pocket on his right thigh, and found his knife. He pulled it out, unsheathed it, and efficiently sliced away Hal's jeans leg, starting above the knee.

Ugly. As Jason had feared, a compound fracture. The bleeding wasn't arterial, or Hal would probably be dead by now. But it was steady. That was the first priority. The fracture was second.

Just then, Teri crawled up beside Jason. Her face grew pale when she looked at Hal's leg, but then she swallowed hard and looked at Jason. "That needs a tourniquet," she said.

"That's right," Jason answered. He raised one leg up over Hal's leg. "You'll have to find one. I'm busy." He pressed his knee down on Hal's inguinal canal, compressing the man's iliac artery.

Teri nodded. "I saw a first aid kit when I got on the bus. Up by the driver."

"All right!" Jason said. Things had just gotten a lot easier. "While you're getting that, check on the other passengers." Jason didn't like how quiet they were. Just a few moans, nothing more. But what was there to do?

"I … Okay," Teri said, squeezing past him and over the hump to the front of the bus.

"Stay with me, Hal." Jason checked the man's pulse. Weak, but not critical. "I know it hurts." Hal was losing his senses, starting to fade. He brushed feebly at Jason's hands, but to no effect.

Soon Jason heard a scrape and saw a large plastic box slide over the hump. "Here it is," Teri said. "I gotta go back. The driver … He's unconscious. Bleeding. And two of the students that … that …"

Jason didn't ask. The bus had flipped and rolled. They were lucky that anyone was alive.

Jason stretched back to the first aid kit, careful to keep his knee in Hal's groin as he opened the case. It wasn't Army issue, but the kit was a good substitute: bandages, splints, tape, painkillers, the works. He grabbed a tourniquet and prepped it. When it was ready, he lifted his knee, wrapped the band around Hal's thigh, and secured it. Again Hal tried to push Jason away. The pain in his leg was probably getting to him, but Jason needed him to leave the leg alone.

Jason dug into the kit and pulled out a bottle of ibuprofen. Civilian doses—candy, medics called them. But with Hal's blood loss, it wouldn't do to overdose. He gave Hal two gelcaps and managed to get the young man to swallow. It wouldn't help immediately; but the sooner started, the better.

Next Jason dug out gauze, a bandage, and a splint from the kit. He packed Hal's wound, wrapped it, and splinted the leg to immobilize it. Hal cried out, and Jason tried to sound soothing. "You're okay, Hal. We'll get you on an ambulance and evac you. The hospital will fix you up."

But with no cell service, who knew when evac might happen? If another car came by, they had to see the bus, or at least the giant hole in the road, whatever that was.

Jason would've liked to lay Hal flat, but he didn't want to move that leg at all, even splinted. He touched the thermometer to Hal's forehead. Hal's temp was low. With that much blood loss, not a surprise.

Jason's pulse was still elevated, as if the danger weren't over yet. He went back to the grandmother, trusting Teri to handle the front of the bus. The old lady was breathing regularly now. There was an ugly bruise on her temple, but there wasn't much Jason could do about that. If she had a concussion, that was another case for the hospital.

Gently Jason shook her shoulder. "Ma'am?" No response. "Ma'am, are you all right?" The old lady's eyes fluttered. "Ma'am, we've had an accident. Can you understand me?"

"Accident ... The light ..."

Jason managed a small smile. She remembered before the crash. That was a good sign. "Yes, ma'am, the light. I'm Jason Cole. I'm a medic. May I examine you?"

The woman's eyes opened. "A medic?" Then she nodded. Jason went over her, finding no obvious broken bones.

"I'm ... lying on a ridge. Can I get up?"

"Let's try, ma'am."

"It's Lydia." She shifted, using her arms to push up onto her side. She seemed to be whole except for the bruise on her head.

"All right," Jason said, helping to lift her up from the floor to a sitting position.

The woman looked around. "Holy Hannah! What happened?"

"We don't know," Jason answered. "That light you saw was some kind of ... missile or something. The shockwave knocked the bus off the road and tumbled it."

"Missile? Are we under attack?"

"There's time to worry about that later," Jason said. "How's your head?"

The woman pressed her temples carefully. "Feels like I was kicked by somebody. But ... What about the other light?"

"Other light?"

"Something ... glimmering. I saw it so clearly. Or ... am I seeing stars?"

Jason frowned. Vision problems *could* be a concussion. "Maybe. You should sit and rest."

"Have you called for help?"

Jason shook his head. "We got no signal before, but please try."

Jason crawled back to check on Hal. The man was quieter now. The ibuprofen? More blood loss? He hoped Lydia would find a signal and get them some help.

Teri had been right about the two college students who had slept in the third and fourth rows. They were gone, crushed beneath the seats in the impact. Jason thought there had been a third student before Reno, but he couldn't see the man.

Jason continued to the front of the bus, where Teri was applying pressure on the bus driver's arm. One of the gauze pads from the kit was half soaked with blood already, and she had another sitting nearby, ready if needed.

Teri looked up as Jason approached. "Some of the glass," she said, pointing up to the driver's seat. Jason was confused at first. The windshield was gone, little beads of safety glass all over the roof. Then he looked where Teri pointed, and he saw a shattered video screen. "I got it out," Teri continued, "and I put pressure on. But I think it's arterial."

"I got your back," Jason said. He fetched another tourniquet, and together they applied it.

While Teri packed the driver's arm with fresh gauze, Jason looked around. "Wasn't there another student?"

Teri looked up from the bandage. "There was some guy. He ... went outside." She nodded toward the bus door, which stood partly open.

"Outside?" Jason blurted.

Teri's eyes flashed. "I was busy, he seemed healthy. I had no reason to stop him. He acted like he didn't even hear me. He said the light was calling for help, and he slipped through the door."

"The light? But it—" Jason was going to say *But it fell;* but then he remembered Lydia's statement about *another* light. Something glimmering. Like the light in his dream....

Jason forced his way out through the bus door. The student must have been slim: Jason had to squeeze the door open wider to get through. He looked at the torn-up stretch of desert soil that marked the bus's last journey. It looked like the bus had landed almost twenty feet off the road before it had rolled and slid.

And beyond that ...

Jason had no name for what he saw, yet it gave him *deja vu*. It was a partial sphere growing out of the roadbed in the desert sands, maybe half a mile away. It glimmered, like crystals or shiny metal facets. It seemed to hum in the wind, a faint tone that Jason strained to make out. There was movement in the upper reaches, as if the sphere were growing. Closing.

And silhouetted against it was a small moving dot that might have been a man.

Then Jason heard a very faint buzzing sound, more distinct than the hum. Not from the direction of the sphere, but from overhead, and to the south. Shading his eyes against the afternoon sun, he looked up. There was just a glint to be seen, and then another, overhead and heading toward the sphere. Air Force reconnaissance drones, probably. There were bases in Nevada, and somebody had to have seen that ... thing come down.

It was their problem now. All the bus survivors had to do was wait around for rescue. With the Air Force on the scene, help had to follow.

Only long before help could arrive, that unnamed student would reach the sphere. And what then?

It took a few minutes for Jason to assure himself that Teri and Lydia had the situation inside the bus under control. Lydia was searching the overheads for water for Hal and the driver. Jason reminded them that the desert would get cold at night, and they should find cover for themselves and the patients.

Now Jason stood a hundred meters or so from the sphere. The humming was louder now, with a subsonic tone that cut straight through him, vibrating his bones. The sphere was maybe forty meters across. It seemed to be assembled of small pieces—but maybe not so small if you were closer.

And closer was exactly where Jason didn't want to be. Despite his training, Jason felt panic growing. This was outside anything the Army had prepared him for.

But closer was where he was going. The drones were gone, and Jason couldn't guess how long the next official response would take. And the student was gone as well. No sign in any direction. The only place the man could be hidden was *inside* the sphere.

The guy wasn't Jason's responsibility. Jason kept telling himself that, but he kept ignoring it. Maybe the student was injured. Concussed.

For that matter, *none* of the passengers on the bus were Jason's responsibility. An Army medic wasn't certified as a domestic first responder. There might even be legal ramifications, but Jason had ignored those. His training had overridden his caution: someone was in trouble, and he answered the call.

The call … He shivered, remembering the cry for help as the bus had crashed. A cry that had penetrated the sounds of carnage, the boom of the shock wave and the scrape of metal on rock. It gnawed at his memory now.

Jason shook his head, trying to focus. He looked closer at the sphere. His earlier impression seemed correct: the sphere was now almost completely closed, as if something were assembling it from the rocks and sand of the desert.

Jason shivered. He was a pragmatic man, not overly imaginative. That might be good for a medic, so he didn't imagine the worst in a medical crisis. But now his imagination was fired up. Whatever this sphere was, it was *not* natural, and it was beyond any military tech he had ever seen. So far beyond, he could *not* believe it came from Earth.

There. Jason had admitted it to himself: this was some alien device crashed on Earth, and now building *something*. What had happened to the student? Had the device broken the man down for building materials? Was that the fate that awaited Jason if he continued? He should just get far away and let the Air Force deal with it.

As Jason told himself this, he continued toward the sphere, as if someone else were driving his legs. As if the unnamed student were Private Ryan, and Jason were Captain Miller.

That hadn't ended well for Miller; but Jason kept going.

What had seemed like facets from afar were actually tessellated panels, thick, glassy diamonds and bars in a complicated texture. Not a geodesic dome, but reminiscent of one. There were no gaps between the panels, no sign of an entrance. Where had the student gone? Was he somehow inside?

Jason stood before the sphere, and the hum swept through him. Were the panels vibrating? He paused, but there was only one way to know. He reached his right hand out to touch the nearest panel.

The panel retreated from his touch.

Jason jerked his hand back, and the panel sprang back into place. Slowly he tried again, with the same result: the panel seemed almost *reluctant* for Jason to touch it.

Now that Jason was close, though, he could see through the panels. They were translucent, like old glass that has clouded but still retains transparency. And through the panels, distorted by the joints in the sphere, he saw an odd geometric landscape: cones and cubes and ramps. Pyramids that flexed and shrunk in an uneven rhythm. Smaller spheres rolled around, and prism-shapes slid along the desert floor, which shone like it had been converted to glass. There was a large circular pit in the middle, maybe half the diameter of the sphere, and the shapes were arrayed around it. The impression was that of some machine for which Jason could see no purpose, but he was sure it was purposeful.

And amid the strange crystal machinery, the student descended a ramp that led down into the pit. The man was barely recognizable through the many panels; but if Jason leaned close and looked through a single panel, the shape was clearly human.

How had the man gotten through? Jason saw only one thing to try. He reached his right hand forward again, and again a panel retreated; but this time Jason kept pushing. More panels were displaced, forming a glassy gauntlet around his arm.

Jason tried reaching with his left arm as well, and soon both arms were sheathed in panels. He tried various motions, but nothing he did could cause a panel to contact his skin or his clothes. He tried clapping his hands together. His palms touched, and the two gauntlets became one continuous tube; but when he pulled his palms apart, the tubes separated and sealed. Never once had his hands been truly inside the sphere.

The next thing to try took all of Jason's nerve: he stepped forward, straight into the sphere wall. And straight through. The sphere had sealed behind him, and Jason stood inside, sheathed in crystal armor. A single large, clear panel was in front of his face, giving him clearer vision than he had had outside.

The first thing Jason noticed was the silence. The humming had stopped. It was like a bug bite had stopped itching.

The second thing he noticed was moving air. Fresh air. Somehow this bubble had its own air supply.

And the third thing he noticed was the small spheres and the prisms clustering around him in some rhythmic motion, as if dancing. Or … beckoning. They moved toward him, and then toward the ramp. Then toward him, then the ramp. *What's that, Lassie? Did Timmy fall down the well?*

If this was dangerous, some sort of trap, then Jason was in too far already. He wondered at that. He was no coward, he had proven that in battles; but he normally followed orders, he didn't take the lead.

And that's what this had felt like: like he was following orders he had never clearly heard. Until this moment of silence, something had been calling him, ever since the bus had crashed. Maybe even before.

But now the decision was his. He was sure he could walk back through the sphere, run to safety, and wait for the Air Force to do their job. There was nothing stopping him. Or he could continue down the ramp, find the student, shake some sense into him, and get them both out of here.

The student. Jason hadn't noticed before: the student hadn't worn crystal armor like Jason did. Why not? And what was the purpose of the armor, besides providing fresh air?

What was the air *really* like in the sphere?

Jason walked down the ramp, driven by curiosity, but also by the echo of that subconscious call. Damn it, it *was* a call for help! Deep inside, he was sure of that.

So he descended a large spiral, nearly twenty meters across, surrounded by mobile crystalline oddities. A tall triangular prism slid along beside him, multicolored lights shifting within. Jason looked over at it. "Good girl, Lassie. Take me to Timmy."

The spiral tightened as if following the contours of the sphere beneath the desert surface. Eventually the ramp leveled off to a circular floor, ten meters down. More geometric shapes were arrayed around this space, but these glowed with small colored points like indicator lights. Many of the shapes were small hexagonal prisms, laying on their side. There were nine that he could see.

And standing among the prisms was the student. Only now, with no distortion from the panels, the man still looked indistinct. Wrong. Jason stepped forward (Lassie keeping pace), but the impression didn't change. The limbs were jointed in the wrong places. The face … The eyes were too round, the chin too pointed. This was a bad artist's rendering of a person.

The thing raised a hand, and Lassie moved between it and Jason, forcing him to stop. Then the shape pointed at the horizontal prisms, and it *shifted*. No longer even close to human, it sprouted a fifth limb from its chest, settling down to stand on three as the two "arms" elongated and added an extra joint. They looked almost as strong as the legs. The "head" sunk into the torso, and the eyes merged into a single reflective disk, larger than Jason's hand. If there was a mouth, Jason couldn't see it.

It should have been hideous. Jason wondered if he were being controlled again. This inhuman *thing* should have revulsed him.

But still he remembered the plea. Whatever this was, it wanted— *needed*—help. Or *something* did. Up close, the creature was translucent, like an excellent hologram.

And as if Jason needed more prodding, the image started to shrink. The legs shortened, thickened. The arms as well. The body shrank as well, but the eye-spot remained the same, dominating the smaller form. This smaller form was just as strange, but less intimidating.

Then the image slid sideways, straight into and through the nearest prism; and there it hovered near the top, partially visible. Other creature images appeared in the surfaces of the eight other prisms.

Jason looked at Lassie. "Those creatures are inside the prisms?" There was no way Jason could tell if the device understood; but it briefly flashed solid blue, the first time Jason had seen that color pattern. "And they need help?" Again the blue flash. "What happened?"

Suddenly the room light shifted to patterns of gold and green, flashing everywhere. The room layout changed to a different, larger space; but out of the corner of his eye, Jason could still see it as it had been. What he saw now was a larger, more elaborate hologram.

The images in the prisms divided: each now consisted of a small creature inside the prism and a larger creature placing it inside. There were thirteen prisms now, and thirteen pairs of creatures. The small creatures disappeared inside the prisms, while the larger creatures pushed the prisms together in the center of the room. The prisms touched, stopped, and then rotated onto their ends. They spun and slid and joined at their surfaces, forming a single large star-shaped block. The large creatures formed a circle, limbs joined, as the block rose, spun, and flew into the distance, slipping through a tessellated wall. It grew smaller and brighter as it flew to a bright blue dot in the distance.

Before the block reached the blue dot, the room erupted in the brightest light Jason had ever seen, forcing him to clench his eyes shut; and when he opened them again, the image was gone.

The room was back to what passed for normal. Jason looked around at the gathered prisms and spheres, and the nine prisms laying on their sides.

Nine. Jason turned to Lassie and pointed at the sky. "They didn't make it?"

The prism filled with swirling darkness, as if swallowing the light that fell upon it, then turned clear.

Jason pointed at the prisms. "And not all of them made it."

Again the dark swirl.

Jason nodded. "And they need help. And you called. And I heard it." He remembered Lydia. "*We* heard it." Blue flash.

It was a distress beacon. And a lifeboat for the survivors—the children?—of some alien expedition. They had called for help; and at some subconscious level, Jason had understood it. Maybe Teri and Lydia as well. The hum, the holographic passenger, had all been an effort to get their attention. Maybe the call triggered altruism, or maybe it simply sought it out. Maybe the lifeboat had been drawn to someone who could help.

And had killed two people in the process, maybe more. Unintended consequences. But would the authorities believe that?

Right on cue, the late afternoon desert light that filtered through the sphere flickered. Jason looked up, and through the distortion of the panels he saw two large tadpole shapes hovering overhead. Recon choppers, here to take charge of a dangerous alien object that had already killed. Unintentionally, but the Special Operations troops wouldn't know that. And these alien children would be defenseless.

But not voiceless. This was why Jason had come here. He knew that now. "Come on, Lassie, let's go talk to the Air Force."

WINDSTREAM
by Andrew Mayne & Roshni "Rush" Bhatia

W̲e let our wing packs soak up the morning light as we stand on top of the old air traffic control tower. Rusting shells of airplanes, the metal tubes people used to fly around inside, are scattered around the rubble of what remains of the airport. Vines grow around them, like ropes tying a giant to the Earth.

The wind, sweeping over the mountain range to our backs, blows across the tall grass covering the eroded tarmac like waves in a pond.

Chance catches me watching the breeze. "Pretty? Isn't it?"

"I've never seen so much grass," says Alta, her face lit up.

"Or such large snakes, I bet," Chance points to a long motion in the field, moving counter to the wind.

The grass is taller than I am, which means the snake moving through it has to be enormous. I can only imagine how much it eats each day.

"Holy cow!" Lukas exclaims, looking at the grass. "That thing must be huge."

"Wait until we go over the Valley. The grass there is taller than two of you and the snakes the size of old trains," Chance replies like a wizened old man instead of another teenager like us.

"And the titans? Will we see any of them?" Lukas asks with excitement, his eyes filled with wonder at seeing the terrible beasts as large as mountains.

Chance catches the look on my face. "Um, no. We're going to play it safe and stick to the Western range. You have to go deep into the Valley to see those."

"Oh," Lukas mumbles. "I guess it's for the best. Maybe someday we can go back."

"And sight see?" Alta gives him an odd look.

"Yeah. Is that weird?"

"Not to me," Chance replies. "You can even do a road trip across the continent."

"You'd need a road for that," I respond. "There hasn't been a solid one since before we were born. The rest look like this," I gesture to the overgrown tarmac.

Chance shakes his head. "Not true. There's still the old highway. My dad and I rode it once."

Of course he did.

"Rode it? Like in a ground caravan?" That's the only safe way to move on the ground. But even touching my foot for just a moment makes me shudder.

"No. Motorcycles."

"Motorcycles?" asks Lukas.

"Cars with two wheels," I reply.

"Not quite," says Chance. "It like a powered bicycle. You've seen one of those?"

"Yeah. Wait? Where you're on the outside? What about the monsters?" Lukas asks.

"We drove really, really fast ..." Chance replies then punches him in the shoulder.

Lukas looks up in wonder at Chance, Mr. I've Done Everything Cool In This World.

I don't know what to make of Chance's story. I've never heard of a working road more than a few miles long. After Morning Star fell, most of them were pretty wrecked up or covered in dust. The years since have only made things worse.

I tighten the buckles on my wing pack. "Well, speaking of going fast, everyone ready?"

Lukas and Alta give me the thumbs up.

Chance makes a mock salute. "Aye aye, Captain Kess."

I roll my eyes. "You have the lead. Then Lukas and Alta. I'll take the rear."

"If that's where you want to take it," Chance quips.

Lukas chuckles and Alta shakes her head in disbelief.

"You spend a lot of time on your own?" I shoot back.

"Does it show?" He gives me a grin and then steps off the platform and falls feet first, his wings still folded.

After what seems like forever, they spread apart and he shoots up into the sky, soaring above us.

Alta turns to me, "And I thought the backflip thing you and Trev do is annoying."

"Can I try?" Lukas steps to the edge.

I shrug. "If you fall we're not scraping you off the ground. The grass serpents can have you."

Lukas holds up a finger. "Excellent point."

He starts his wings buzzing and takes off much more cautiously.

Alta gives me a smile then flies after them. I give her a moment to clear the air and wait until nobody is looking then try jumping feet first.

My wings vibrate so much I'm afraid they're going to fall apart trying to slow my descent.

The ground grows closer more quickly than I expect.

At the moment I think I'm about to crash, I slow down, almost hovering, and my feet touch the top of the grass.

For a brief moment I catch the glimmer of something shiny and covered in scales just below me. It must have snuck up on us while we were sleeping. Did it sense our heat?

While I made sure the doors to the stairs were barricaded, I never thought to wonder if something could slither up on the outside of the tower.

The thought makes my knees jerk to my chest and I almost flip over, losing my balance. Fortunately, the instincts drilled into me by my Skymaster take over and I find my center.

My wings beat down a draft of air and I finally fly upwards, leaving the horrible thing hiding in the grass on the ground and gliding past the top of the control tower.

When I look up at the others, I see them looking back at me.

"I forgot to tell you," Chance says over the comm, "the snakes love to gather around the tower in the morning."

My trust issues with him are not improving.

"Come on," he shouts, ignoring the comm. "If we hurry there's something really cool I can show you when we charge our wings again!"

The grassy fields of the tarmac give way to the vine covered landscape of the lower valley. The denser vegetation, almost dark green, covers almost every square inch where the grasses haven't taken hold.

It's wetter here than the Rook where we live. Ponds and lakes fed by streams twist down from the mountains glinting like golden pools in the light of the rising sun.

I've never seen bodies of water so large. I'd like to try diving into one, but I can only imagine what horrors lay underneath.

Occasionally we spot a red skeleton of some creature, half devoured on water's edge.

People are supposed to live down there too, beneath the thick branches, in burrows they dug and the decayed tunnels Morning Star didn't annihilate.

I can't imagine what life is like in the dirt, constantly foraging for food, while hoping not to become something else's meal.

It's a mystery to me why some structures still stood, like the skyscrapers in New City, while other buildings with sturdier foundations collapsed as if they were a pile of leaves in a breeze.

Chance continues to lead us on a straight path toward the grey mountains just north of the path of the sun. In the middle, two peaks, flattened at the top, stand out like massive molars.

Traveling this route is taking us wildly off our intended course. But my reasons aren't just because of what happened in New City.

I think of the encounter we had with a Skull Rider's trained hunting drax back in the desert. That was a reminder that even the skies aren't safe.

If we were being pursued all the way from the Rook and you drew a line to New City, then it would be obvious to anyone we'd be heading towards the mountains to the north.

While my knowledge of the passes and wind streams outside the Rook's territory were as limited as my understanding of what threats lay beyond, the path I would have chosen, all things being equal, was through the Valley.

With Alta and Lukas under my wing, that seemed like the less desirable option. The air currents there blew straight up into the rising mountain range where Stratos, our destination, was located, but the unknown threats were too many and the known ones too massive.

I'd be more suspicious of Chance's intentions if he tried to convince us to fly south, towards the Skull Rider's territory, instead of away from them to the northeast.

When we met up with him back in New City, it felt a little convenient. Maybe I'm paranoid, but that's how you survive.

Sure, he hasn't said or done anything to make me suspicious, and he's kinda cute when he's not being so arrogant, but he's not from the Rook.

We fly higher, adjusting our altitude as the land begins to rise up to meet the base of the mountains.

The lush dark growth begins to give way to stones and dry rock soil where plants have a more difficult time taking hold.

On the hillsides are rows of fallen houses and broken streets not yet eroded away.

Where did the people who lived here go? Did they stay in their homes when Morning Star struck or did they retreat to the impact bunkers built to endure the crash?

My family history starts after Morning Star, like so many other people. Otherwise I would have asked.

What were their last moments like?

What would I have done?

A knot grows in my stomach when I realize my answer is obvious. I'm literally flying away from my home to safety.

Yes, it's to bring back a cure, but as difficult as it's been for us so far, my friends back at the Rook are facing an even greater threat from the sickness and the marauding Skull Riders.

All the more reason to get to Stratos as quickly as we can and bring back the cure.

The cure …

Devon, Zella, Hakai and the other flyers well enough to travel were sent off in different directions from us to search for a cure.

This implies that whatever Stratos or the other towns has may not be of any help. Our mission could be a complete waste. Whatever else I'm afraid may come next could be pointless.

To go this far and have nothing to gain …

I can't think about that.

I call out to the others. "What are your power readings?"

"Fifty percent," says Alta.

"Forty-five," adds Lukas.

Good, his battery replacement made a huge difference.

"Chance?"

"Um, I'm basically running on fumes at fifteen percent."

"When were you going to tell me that?"

"I was waiting for you to ask."

I clench my teeth in frustration. "So, should we just drop down on a mountain top here?"

"Not yet. We're almost over the summit. I can coast for a while. I've got a great spot."

At the top of the range I see his wings lock into position as he begins an unpowered glide back down.

He's a risk taker who's been lucky so far. I just hope it doesn't break while he's with us.

After another half hour of flying, Chance announces over the comm, "Here we are folks."

We pass a low rise of hills and emerge into a grassy step. At the nearest edge is a fallen city, mostly overrun with vines and brush.

Chance turns us towards a giant open bowl in the middle.

"What's that?" asks Lukas.

Chance replies, "That, buddy, is where the rock concert is."

The giant bowl is an open air arena. I stand on the edge of the stage and stare out at the thousands of empty seats.

Broken, discolored and covered with debris, I wasn't sure what they were at first. Even when Chance explained I couldn't make sense of it.

There were so many of them.

Not just thousands.

Tens of thousands.

"92,412 seats," says Lukas, standing to my right. "Give or take a few."

He wasn't just gawking, he was counting.

The floor of the arena is also covered by seats concealed by vines.

"How did they play sports here?" asks Lukas.

"They moved those chairs and the stage we're standing on wasn't here. But sports is sports. You can watch videos of that. The really special thing about this place was a rock concert," Chance explains.

"You mean where they played music?" says Lukas.

"Played music?" Chance scoffs. "Is making out with a girl just touching lips?"

"I wouldn't know," Lukas replies.

"No!" Chance holds his arms wide open and faces the arena. "A rock concert was like a living thing. 100,000 people all moving to the same beat, all singing the same thing. But it didn't make you feel small. You felt like a giant!"

I'd ask Chance how the hell he would know, but decide to drop it. Lukas is suitably enthralled and even Alta's eyes are wide open at the mental picture. Chance lowers his arms and goes off to dig through some cables.

Behind us is a twisted metal structure that once stood over the elevated platform where we landed.

Towering black boxes line the sides on either end. They resemble massive versions of the PA system we use to sound alarms.

I give them a passing look then turn my attention back to the seats.

Everyone from the Rook would fill just one tiny section.

All the people in New City might fill one level.

But the whole arena? Were that many people left in the world?

Once the earth was filled with billions of people. You couldn't fit them all in one hundred thousand places like this.

You had to go out of your way not to see people.

Now, two minutes from the Rook, or even outside of New City, there was nobody.

The world has become a lonelier place—if you're not a monster.

What was it like to stand here and see all those faces? How did they even all get inside? It must have taken days to file in and out.

And for what?

What could be so important that they would want to crowd into here? Was a concert really all that Chance made it out to be?

I'm sure in the days right before Morning Star this was used as some kind of emergency assembly place, like our town meetings at the Rook.

But before then?

I mean, I understand the concept of watching sports and entertainment, I just can't understand the scale.

I can't make out the details of one seat, how could someone notice a single performer or athlete?

Suddenly there's a loud squeal and I jump to the ground. My eyes go to the sky looking for the hunting drax.

The squelch fades and Chance's voice booms out from everywhere, louder than a thunderstorm. "I'D LIKE TO DEDICATE THIS TO MY NEW FRIENDS!"

I roll over and see him standing in front of a rusty microphone holding a strange guitar.

"What the hell are you doing?" I scream as I pick myself up.

He puts a hand over the mic and grins. "I've spent weeks getting this thing to work."

Weeks?! I realize that Chance has been here more than once before.

"You'll draw a swarm!" I scan the skies in fear.

"It's not the season around here. May I continue?" he says, hand still over the microphone.

Alta and Lukas look at me to say something. They're not sure if they should be terrified by a swarm or excited to see what Chance is about to pull off next.

Chance waves me off. "Okay then. Here's a classic rock song my dad taught me."

His fingers hit the metal strings of the guitar and there's a loud wail over the speakers.

I put my fingers to my ears.

He strikes a few chords that are mostly in tune, but nowhere near as skillful as the visiting musicians we've had back at the Rook.

"I had to learn the guitar myself!" Chance shouts over the echo of his playing.

Lukas covers his ears and yells back, "It sounds like you're still learning!"

Chance gives him a playful snarl then steps up to the microphone.

Alta hollers to me, "Is he about to sing?"

Chance nods, strums at his guitar, closes his eyes then belts out at the top of his lungs, "HEY MY LITTLE BLACKBIRD IN THE SKY!" He looks in my direction, "WHY DO YOU HAVE TO FLY SO HIGH? YOUR FEET DON'T TOUCH THE GROUND BUT YOUR HEAD NEVER REACHES THE CLOUDS."

I glance back at the stadium, afraid something is going to be attracted to the sound.

Chance keeps playing and I begin to suspect things might be running from here instead.

"HEY MY LITTLE BLACKBIRD IN THE SKY! Everybody now! WHY DO YOU HAVE TO FLY SO HIGH?! Come on!"

He waves us to the microphone.

Lukas grabs Alta by the hand and pulls her to it.

"You know it now?" asks Chance.

Lukas grabs the microphone, "YOUR FEET DON'T TOUCH THE GROUND, BUT YOUR HEAD NEVER REACHES THE CLOUDS."

Alta laughs then covers her mouth at the absurdity of the situation. Lukas pushes the microphone in front of her.

She shakes her head then finally joins in at Lukas's urging.

I roll my eyes and look out to the stadium. Just to be careful, I keep my staff gun firmly in my grip.

"Kess is protecting us from the groupies!" Chance yells.

I'm not sure if groupies are monsters or something that happens when you play really bad music.

He leads them into another song. "BABY I CAN'T LIE, BUT WE WERE BORN TO FLY!"

I tense up and then remember how when things would be the most difficult, being chased by a drax or shooting at coyax that managed to get onto one of the towers, Skymaster would often crack a joke and make us all laugh.

I roll my eyes and let my face break into a smile as they try to keep tune with what I must say, sounds nothing like any of the classic rock songs I've heard on antique records. I have a feeling the songwriter is standing ten feet from me.

The music bounces around the stadium, filling the air, immersing the empty seats.

In a flash I get what Chance was saying.

It wasn't only about the music or sports.

People came here because of the people.

They came to experience it with others.

The sight of so many people enjoying one thing was the attraction.

As my friends sing behind me, I start to mouth the words along with them. I can see myself in a crowd, at least I think I can. I close my eyes for a moment and try to imagine.

I get so caught up I don't notice the movement off to the side.

At first I think I'm just imagining that we're being watched.

Then I realize we really are.

—✳—

In the middle row of the stadium, small shapes begin to move about behind the seats. I bring my staff gun to my chest and kneel into a firing position.

I yell out over my shoulder, "Chance …!"

He gives me a nod, letting me know he sees them too, but keeps playing.

I motion for Lukas and Alta to put on their wing packs.

They leave the microphone and hurry over to strap in.

"HEY MY LITTLE BLACKBIRD IN THE SKY!" Chance belts out again.

Why is he still singing?

To heck with him.

I keep my staff gun pointed at the far end of the arena while Lukas and Alta buckle up. It's useless at this range, but it makes me feel better.

Alta finishes putting her pack on and brings me mine. "Here!" she yells over Chance's wailing.

"What is he doing?" I ask as I throw one arm, then the other through the harness while juggling the staff gun.

"I think he may be insane," she says, shrugging.

"You think?" I reply. Part of me worries that this is some kind of trap.

Lukas gets his pack in place then takes Chance's pack to the microphone.

Chance hands him the guitar and continues his singing while he straps his wings on.

Once it's secured, he grabs the guitar and starts back where he left off.

The shapes in the back begin to move towards the aisle. Still, far away, but unsettling.

Finally one emerges and I get my first look at what has been watching us. My muscles relax.

It's a child, no taller than Lukas. A girl, I think, dressed head to toe in a form fitting fabric that appears to be some kind of camouflage. There's just an opening for her face. I notice a knife at her side.

She cautiously walks down the steps, followed by seven more children, even smaller than her.

"Who are they?" I ask Chance over his ruckus.

He shrugs and covers the mic for a moment. "I don't know. They just come and watch sometimes."

"You mean you've done this before? By yourself?" Alta asks, shocked.

Chance nods his head with his playing, flicking his hair back and forth. "LET'S ALL TAKE A RIDE. PUT YOUR WORRIES ASIDE."

He strums the guitar then holds it out from his body, his arms stretched wide as he looks at the children. "Remember what I taught you?!"

The lead girl stand up nervously, then holds her hand out and starts to clap. The other children begin clapping with her.

Chance gives them a thumbs up. "This one is for you!"

He starts a rough, but upbeat melody on the guitar, then belts out, "LET ME SEE YOU SMILE! LET ME SEE YOU JUMP UP AND DOWN! LET ME SEE YOU SING THAT SONG! LET ME SEE YOU SING IT RIGHT OUT LOUD!!"

Even at this distance I can see the children's faces light up.

The smaller ones hold hands and bob their little heads with the music. Chance finishes the song then lowers the guitar. "Thank you! Thank you!"

I think we've attracted more than enough attention here. "Time to go."

Chance nods and puts his makeshift guitar back into a crate in back of the stage.

We activate our wings and take turns running and leaping off the stage into the air.

I'm the last one to go.

As I spiral over the empty seats of the stadium, building altitude, my path takes me near where the children are still sitting.

The little girl, the one who led them there, looks up at me in complete awe.

Her tiny hand waves at me.

I wave back.

"You know, Kess," Chance says over the comm, "she probably thinks you're a god."

"Where are their parents?" asks Alta.

"I don't know. I've never seen anyone other than the kids. Sometimes there are more. Sometimes less, but never any adults."

"Have you asked them?" Lukas replies.

"They never let me get close enough," Chance answers. "And I'm not sure if you noticed, but they never said a word to each other the entire time they sat there. Never."

The thought of those little children living on their own, hiding in the forgotten city, running from monsters, never saying a word, sends a chill down my spine.

I make a promise to myself. When this is all over, I'm going to do whatever it takes to make it so all the kids, not just the ones from my Rook, but these quiet ones, never have to be afraid to stand on a stage or sit in a crowd and worry about what's flying overhead or crawling through the grass.

Chance, through his buffoonery, made me realize people from the Rook and grounders, aren't that different. All it took was a badly-tuned guitar and some song lyrics that I kind of think he was making up on the spot.

As my wings take me over the mountain, for the first time since I can remember, I start to think maybe there's a glimmer of hope in the world.

WHEN SYSADMINS RULED THE EARTH
by Cory Doctorow

When Felix's special phone rang at two in the morning, Kelly rolled over and punched him in the shoulder and hissed, "Why didn't you turn that fucking thing off before bed?"

"Because I'm on call," he said.

"You're not a fucking doctor," she said, kicking him as he sat on the bed's edge, pulling on the pants he'd left on the floor before turning in. "You're a goddamned *systems administrator.*"

"It's my job," he said.

"They work you like a government mule," she said. "You know I'm right. For Christ's sake, you're a father now, you can't go running off in the middle of the night every time someone's porn supply goes down. Don't answer that phone."

He knew she was right. He answered the phone.

"Main routers not responding. BGP not responding." The mechanical voice of the systems monitor didn't care if he cursed at it, so he did, and it made him feel a little better.

"Maybe I can fix it from here," he said. He could login to the UPS for the cage and reboot the routers. The UPS was in a different netblock, with its own independent routers on their own uninterruptible power-supplies.

Kelly was sitting up in bed now, an indistinct shape against the headboard. "In five years of marriage, you have never once been able to fix anything from here." This time she was wrong—he fixed stuff from home all the time, but he did it discreetly and didn't make a fuss, so she didn't remember it. And she was right, too—he had logs that showed that after 1AM, nothing could ever be fixed without driving out to the cage. Law of Infinite Universal Perversity—AKA Felix's Law.

Five minutes later Felix was behind the wheel. He hadn't been able to fix it from home. The independent router's netblock was offline, too. The last time that had happened, some dumbfuck construction worker had driven a ditch-witch through the main conduit into the data-center and Felix had joined a cadre of fifty enraged sysadmins who'd stood atop the resulting pit for a week, screaming abuse at the poor bastards who labored 24-7 to splice ten thousand wires back together.

His phone went off twice more in the car and he let it override the stereo and play the mechanical status reports through the big, bassy speakers of more critical network infrastructure offline. Then Kelly called.

"Hi," he said.

"Don't cringe, I can hear the cringe in your voice."

He smiled involuntarily. "Check, no cringing."

"I love you, Felix," she said.

"I'm totally bonkers for you, Kelly. Go back to bed."

"2.0's awake," she said. The baby had been Beta Test when he was in her womb, and when her water broke, he got the call and dashed out of the office, shouting, *The Gold Master just shipped!* They'd started calling him 2.0 before he'd finished his first cry. "This little bastard was born to suck tit."

"I'm sorry I woke you," he said. He was almost at the data center. No traffic at 2AM. He slowed down and pulled over before the entrance to the garage. He didn't want to lose Kelly's call underground.

"It's not waking me," she said. "You've been there for seven years. You have three juniors reporting to you. Give them the phone. You've paid your dues."

"I don't like asking my reports to do anything I wouldn't do," he said.

"You've done it," she said. "Please? I hate waking up alone in the night. I miss you most at night."

"Kelly—"

"I'm over being angry. I just miss you is all. You give me sweet dreams."

"OK," he said.

"Simple as that?"

"Exactly. Simple as that. Can't have you having bad dreams, and I've paid my dues. From now on, I'm only going on night call to cover holidays."

She laughed. "Sysadmins don't take holidays."

"This one will," he said. "Promise."

"You're wonderful," she said. "Oh, gross. 2.0 just dumped core all over my bathrobe."

"That's my boy," he said.

"Oh that he is," she said. She hung up, and he piloted the car into the data-center lot, badging in and peeling up a bleary eyelid to let the retinal scanner get a good look at his sleep-depped eyeball.

He stopped at the machine to get himself a guarana/medafonil power-bar and a cup of lethal robot-coffee in a spill-proof clean-room sippy-cup. He wolfed down the bar and sipped the coffee, then let the inner door read his hand-geometry and size him up for a moment. It sighed open and gusted the airlock's load of positively pressurized air over him as he passed finally to the inner sanctum.

It was bedlam. The cages were designed to let two or three sysadmins maneuver around them at a time. Every other inch of cubic space was given over to humming racks of servers and routers and drives. Jammed among them were no fewer than twenty other sysadmins. It was a regular convention of black tee-shirts with inexplicable slogans, bellies overlapping belts with phones and multitools.

Normally it was practically freezing in the cage, but all those bodies were overheating the small, enclosed space. Five or six looked up and grimaced when he came through. Two greeted him by name. He threaded his belly through the press and the cages, toward the Ardent racks in the back of the room.

"Felix." It was Van, who wasn't on call that night.

"What are you doing here?" he asked. "No need for both of us to be wrecked tomorrow."

"What? Oh. My personal box is over there. It went down around 1:30 and I got woken up by my process-monitor. I should have called you and told you I was coming down—spared you the trip."

Felix's own server—a box he shared with five other friends—was in a rack one floor down. He wondered if it was offline too.

"What's the story?"

"Massive flashworm attack. Some jackass with a zero-day exploit has got every Windows box on the net running Monte Carlo probes on every IP block, including IPv6. The big Ciscos all run administrative interfaces over v6, and they all fall over if they get more than ten simultaneous probes, which means that just about every interchange has gone down. DNS is screwy, too—like maybe someone poisoned the zone transfer last night. Oh, and there's an email and IM component that sends pretty lifelike messages to everyone in your address book, barfing up Eliza-dialog that keys off of your logged email and messages to get you to open a Trojan."

"Jesus."

"Yeah." Van was a type-two sysadmin, over six feet tall, long pony-tail, bobbing Adam's apple. Over his toast-rack chest, his tee said CHOOSE YOUR WEAPON and featured a row of polyhedral RPG dice.

Felix was a type-one admin, with an extra seventy or eighty pounds all around the middle, and a neat but full beard that he wore over his extra chins. His tee said HELLO CTHULHU and featured a cute, mouthless, Hello-Kitty-style Cthulhu. They'd known each other for fifteen years, having met on Usenet, then f2f at Toronto Freenet beer-sessions, a Star

25

Trek convention or two, and eventually Felix had hired Van to work under him at Ardent. Van was reliable and methodical. Trained as an electrical engineer, he kept a procession of spiral notebooks filled with the details of every step he'd ever taken, with time and date.

"Not even PEBKAC this time," Van said. Problem Exists Between Keyboard And Chair. Email trojans fell into that category—if people were smart enough not to open suspect attachments, email trojans would be a thing of the past. But worms that ate Cisco routers weren't a problem with the lusers—they were the fault of incompetent engineers.

"No, it's Microsoft's fault," Felix said. "Any time I'm at work at 2AM, it's either PEBKAC or Microsloth."

They ended up just unplugging the frigging routers from the internet. Not Felix, of course, though he was itching to do it and get them rebooted after shutting down their IPv6 interfaces. It was done by a couple bull-goose Bastard Operators From Hell who had to turn two keys at once to get access to their cage—like guards in a Minuteman silo. Ninety-five percent of the long distance traffic in Canada went through this building. It had *better* security than most Minuteman silos.

Felix and Van got the Ardent boxes back online one at a time. They were being pounded by worm-probes—putting the routers back online just exposed the downstream cages to the attack. Every box on the internet was drowning in worms, or creating worm-attacks, or both. Felix managed to get through to NIST and Bugtraq after about a hundred timeouts, and download some kernel patches that should reduce the load the worms put on the machines in his care. It was 10AM, and he was hungry enough to eat the ass out of a dead bear, but he recompiled his kernels and brought the machines back online. Van's long fingers flew over the administrative keyboard, his tongue protruding as he ran load-stats on each one.

"I had two hundred days of uptime on Greedo," Van said. Greedo was the oldest server in the rack, from the days when they'd named the boxes after Star Wars characters. Now they were all named after Smurfs, and they were running out of Smurfs and had started in on McDonaldland characters, starting with Van's laptop, Mayor McCheese.

"Greedo will rise again," Felix said. "I've got a 486 downstairs with over five years of uptime. It's going to break my heart to reboot it."

"What the everlasting shit do you use a 486 for?"

"Nothing. But who shuts down a machine with five years uptime? That's like euthanizing your grandmother."

"I wanna eat," Van said.

"Tell you what," Felix said. "We'll get your box up, then mine, then I'll take you to the Lakeview Lunch for breakfast pizzas and you can have the rest of the day off."

"You're on," Van said. "Man, you're too good to us grunts. You should keep us in a pit and beat us like all the other bosses. It's all we deserve."

"It's your phone," Van said. Felix extracted himself from the guts of the 486, which had refused to power up at all. He had cadged a spare power-supply from some guys who ran a spam operation and was trying to get it fitted. He let Van hand him the phone, which had fallen off his belt while he was twisting to get at the back of the machine.

"Hey, Kel," he said. There was an odd, snuffling noise in the background. Static, maybe? 2.0 splashing in the bath? "Kelly?"

The line went dead. He tried to call back, but didn't get anything—no ring nor voicemail. His phone finally timed out and said NETWORK ERROR.

"Dammit," he said, mildly. He clipped the phone to his belt. Kelly wanted to know when he was coming home, or wanted him to pick something up for the family. She'd leave voicemail.

He was testing the power-supply when his phone rang again. He snatched it up and answered it. "Kelly, hey, what's up?" He worked to keep anything like irritation out of his voice. He felt guilty: technically speaking, he had discharged his obligations to Ardent Financial LLC once the Ardent servers were back online. The past three hours had been purely personal—even if he planned on billing them to the company.

There was sobbing on the line.

"Kelly?" He felt the blood draining from his face and his toes were numb.

"Felix," she said, barely comprehensible through the sobbing. "He's dead, oh Jesus, he's dead."

"Who? Who, Kelly?"

"Will," she said.

Will? he thought. *Who the fuck is*—He dropped to his knees. William was the name they'd written on the birth certificate, though they'd called him 2.0 all along. Felix made an anguished sound, like a sick bark.

"I'm sick," she said, "I can't even stand anymore. Oh, Felix. I love you so much."

"Kelly? What's going on?"

"Everyone, everyone—" she said. "Only two channels left on the tube. Christ, Felix, it looks like dawn of the dead out the window—" He heard her retch. The phone started to break up, washing her puke-noises back like an echoplex.

"Stay there, Kelly," he shouted as the line died. He punched 911, but the phone went NETWORK ERROR again as soon as he hit SEND.

He grabbed Mayor McCheese from Van and plugged it into the 486's network cable and launched Firefox off the command line and googled for the Metro Police site. Quickly, but not frantically, he searched for an online contact form. Felix didn't lose his head, ever. He solved problems and freaking out didn't solve problems.

He located an online form and wrote out the details of his conversation with Kelly like he was filing a bug report, his fingers fast, his description complete, and then he hit SUBMIT.

Van had read over his shoulder. "Felix—" he began.

"God," Felix said. He was sitting on the floor of the cage and he slowly pulled himself upright. Van took the laptop and tried some news sites, but they were all timing out. Impossible to say if it was because something terrible was happening or because the network was limping under the superworm.

"I need to get home," Felix said.

"I'll drive you," Van said. "You can keep calling your wife."

They made their way to the elevators. One of the building's few windows was there, a thick, shielded porthole. They peered through it as they waited for the elevator. Not much traffic for a Wednesday. Were there more police cars than usual?

"*Oh my God*—" Van pointed.

The CN Tower, a giant white-elephant needle of a building loomed to the east of them. It was askew, like a branch stuck in wet sand. Was it moving? It was. It was heeling over, slowly, but gaining speed, falling northeast toward the financial district. In a second, it slid over the tipping point and crashed down. They felt the shock, then heard it, the whole building rocking from the impact. A cloud of dust rose from the wreckage, and there was more thunder as the world's tallest freestanding structure crashed through building after building.

"The Broadcast Centre's coming down," Van said. It was—the CBC's towering building was collapsing in slow motion. People ran every way, were crushed by falling masonry. Seen through the port-hole, it was like watching a neat CGI trick downloaded from a file-sharing site.

Sysadmins were clustering around them now, jostling to see the destruction.

"What happened?" one of them asked.

"The CN Tower fell down," Felix said. He sounded far away in his own ears.

"Was it the virus?"

"The worm? What?" Felix focused on the guy, who was a young admin with just a little type-two flab around the middle.

"Not the worm," the guy said. "I got an email that the whole city's quarantined because of some virus. Bioweapon, they say." He handed Felix his Blackberry.

Felix was so engrossed in the report—purportedly forwarded from Health Canada—that he didn't even notice that all the lights had gone out. Then he did, and he pressed the Blackberry back into its owner's hand, and let out one small sob.

The generators kicked in a minute later. Sysadmins stampeded for the stairs. Felix grabbed Van by the arm, pulled him back.

"Maybe we should wait this out in the cage," he said.

"What about Kelly?" Van said.

Felix felt like he was going to throw up. "We should get into the cage, now." The cage had microparticulate air-filters.

They ran upstairs to the big cage. Felix opened the door and then let it hiss shut behind him.

"Felix, you need to get home—"

"It's a bioweapon," Felix said. "Superbug. We'll be OK in here, I think, so long as the filters hold out."

"What?"

"Get on IRC," he said.

They did. Van had Mayor McCheese and Felix used Smurfette. They skipped around the chat channels until they found one with some familiar handles.

```
> pentagons gone/white house too
> MY NEIGHBORS BARFING BLOOD OFF HIS BALCONY IN SAN DIEGO
> Someone knocked over the Gherkin. Bankers are fleeing the
  City like rats.
> I heard that the Ginza's on fire
```

Felix typed:

```
> I'm in Toronto. We just saw the CN Tower fall. I've heard
  reports of bioweapons, something very fast.
```

Van read this and said, "You don't know how fast it is, Felix. Maybe we were all exposed three days ago."

Felix closed his eyes. "If that were so we'd be feeling some symptoms, I think."

```
> Looks like an EMP took out Hong Kong and maybe Paris—realtime
  sat footage shows them completely dark, and all netblocks
  there aren't routing
> You're in Toronto?
```

It was an unfamiliar handle.

```
> Yes—on Front Street
> my sisters at UofT and i cnt reach her—can you call her?
> No phone service
```

Felix typed, staring at NETWORK PROBLEMS.

"I have a soft phone on Mayor McCheese," Van said, launching his voice-over-IP app. "I just remembered."

Felix took the laptop from him and punched in his home number. It rang once, then there was a flat, blatting sound like an ambulance siren in an Italian movie.

```
> No phone service
```

Felix typed again.

He looked up at Van, and saw that his skinny shoulders were shaking. Van said, "Holy motherfucking shit. The world is ending."

Felix pried himself off of IRC an hour later. Atlanta had burned. Manhattan was hot—radioactive enough to screw up the webcams looking out over Lincoln Plaza. Everyone blamed Islam until it became clear that Mecca was a smoking pit and the Saudi Royals had been hanged before their palaces.

His hands were shaking, and Van was quietly weeping in the far corner of the cage. He tried calling home again, and then the police. It didn't work any better than it had the last twenty times.

He sshed into his box downstairs and grabbed his mail. Spam, spam, spam. More spam. Automated messages. There—an urgent message from the intrusion detection system in the Ardent cage.

He opened it and read quickly. Someone was crudely, repeatedly probing his routers. It didn't match a worm's signature, either. He followed the traceroute and discovered that the attack had originated in the same building as him, a system in a cage one floor below.

He had procedures for this. He portscanned his attacker and found that port 1337 was open—1337 was "leet" or "elite" in hacker number/letter substitution code. That was the kind of port that a worm left open to slither in and out of. He googled known sploits that left a listener on port 1337, narrowed this down based on the fingerprinted operating system of the compromised server, and then he had it.

It was an ancient worm, one that every box should have been patched against years before. No mind. He had the client for it, and he used it to create a root account for himself on the box, which he then logged into, and took a look around.

There was one other user logged in, "scaredy," and he checked the proccess monitor and saw that scaredy had spawned all the hundreds of processes that were probing him and plenty of other boxen.

He opened a chat:

```
> Stop probing my server
```

He expected bluster, guilt, denial. He was surprised.

```
> Are you in the Front Street data-center?
> Yes
> Christ I thought I was the last one alive. I'm on the fourth
  floor. I think there's a bioweapon attack outside. I don't
  want to leave the clean room.
```

Felix whooshed out a breath.

```
> You were probing me to get me to trace back to you?
> Yeah
> That was smart
```

Clever bastard.

```
> I'm on the sixth floor, I've got one more with me.
> What do you know?
```

Felix pasted in the IRC log and waited while the other guy digested it. Van stood up and paced. His eyes were glazed over.

"Van? Pal?"

"I have to pee," he said.

"No opening the door," Felix said. "I saw an empty Mountain Dew bottle in the trash there."

"Right," Van said. He walked like a zombie to the trash can and pulled out the empty magnum. He turned his back.

```
> I'm Felix
> Will
```

Felix's stomach did a slow somersault as he thought about 2.0.

"Felix, I think I need to go outside," Van said. He was moving toward the airlock door. Felix dropped his keyboard and struggled to his feet and ran headlong to Van, tackling him before he reached the door.

"Van," he said, looking into his friend's glazed, unfocused eyes. "Look at me, Van."

"I need to go," Van said. "I need to get home and feed the cats."

"There's something out there, something fast-acting and lethal. Maybe it will blow away with the wind. Maybe it's already gone. But we're going to sit here until we know for sure or until we have no choice. Sit down, Van. Sit."

"I'm cold, Felix."

It was freezing. Felix's arms were broken out in gooseflesh and his feet felt like blocks of ice.

"Sit against the servers, by the vents. Get the exhaust heat." He found a rack and nestled up against it.

```
> Are you there?
> Still here—sorting out some logistics
> How long until we can go out?
> I have no idea
```

No one typed anything for quite some time then.

Felix had to use the Mountain Dew bottle twice. Then Van used it again. Felix tried calling Kelly again. The Metro Police site was down.

Finally, he slid back against the servers and wrapped his arms around his knees and wept like a baby.

After a minute, Van came over and sat beside him, with his arm around Felix's shoulder.

"They're dead, Van," Felix said. "Kelly and my s—son. My family is gone."

"You don't know for sure," Van said.

"I'm sure enough," Felix said. "Christ, it's all over, isn't it?"

"We'll gut it out a few more hours and then head out. Things should be getting back to normal soon. The fire department will fix it. They'll mobilize the Army. It'll be OK."

Felix's ribs hurt. He hadn't cried since—since 2.0 was born. He hugged his knees harder.

Then the doors opened.

The two sysadmins who entered were wild-eyed. One had a tee that said TALK NERDY TO ME and the other one was wearing an Electronic Frontiers Canada shirt.

"Come on," TALK NERDY said. "We're all getting together on the top floor. Take the stairs."

Felix found he was holding his breath.

"If there's a bioagent in the building, we're all infected," TALK NERDY said. "Just go, we'll meet you there."

"There's one on the sixth floor," Felix said, as he climbed to his feet.

"Will, yeah, we got him. He's up there."

TALK NERDY was one of the Bastard Operators From Hell who'd unplugged the big routers. Felix and Van climbed the stairs slowly, their steps echoing in the deserted shaft. After the frigid air of the cage, the stairwell felt like a sauna.

There was a cafeteria on the top floor, with working toilets, water and coffee and vending machine food. There was an uneasy queue of sysadmins before each. No one met anyone's eye. Felix wondered which one was Will and then he joined the vending machine queue.

He got a couple more energy bars and a gigantic cup of vanilla coffee before running out of change. Van had scored them some table space and Felix set the stuff down before him and got in the toilet line. "Just save some for me," he said, tossing an energy bar in front of Van.

By the time they were all settled in, thoroughly evacuated, and eating, TALK NERDY and his friend had returned again. They cleared off the cash-register at the end of the food-prep area and TALK NERDY got up on it. Slowly the conversation died down.

"I'm Uri Popovich, this is Diego Rosenbaum. Thank you all for coming up here. Here's what we know for sure: the building's been on generators for three hours now. Visual observation indicates that we're the only building in central Toronto with working power—which should hold out for three more days. There is a bioagent of unknown origin loose beyond our doors. It kills quickly, within hours, and it is aerosolized. You get it from breathing bad air. No one has opened any of the exterior doors to this building since five this morning. No one will open the doors until I give the go-ahead.

"Attacks on major cities all over the world have left emergency responders in chaos. The attacks are electronic, biological, nuclear and conventional explosives, and they are very widespread. I'm a security engineer, and where I come from, attacks in this kind of cluster are usually viewed as opportunistic: group B blows up a bridge because everyone is off taking care of group A's dirty nuke event. It's smart. An Aum Shin Rikyo cell in Seoul gassed the subways there about 2AM Eastern—that's the earliest event we can locate, so it may have been the Archduke that broke the camel's back. We're pretty sure that Aum Shin Rikyo couldn't be behind this kind of mayhem: they have no history of infowar and have never shown the kind of organizational acumen necessary to take out so many targets at once. Basically, they're not smart enough.

"We're holing up here for the foreseeable future, at least until the bioweapon has been identified and dispersed. We're going to staff the racks and keep the networks up. This is critical infrastructure, and it's our job to make sure it's got five nines of uptime. In times of national emergency, our responsibility to do that doubles."

One sysadmin put up his hand. He was very daring in a green Incredible Hulk ring-tee, and he was at the young end of the scale.

"Who died and made you king?"

"I have controls for the main security system, keys to every cage, and passcodes for the exterior doors—they're all locked now, by the way. I'm the one who got everyone up here first and called the meeting. I don't care if someone else wants this job, it's a shitty one. But someone needs to have this job."

"You're right," the kid said. "And I can do it every bit as well as you. My name's Will Sario."

Popovich looked down his nose at the kid. "Well, if you'll let me finish talking, maybe I'll hand things over to you when I'm done."

"Finish, by all means." Sario turned his back on him and walked to the window. He stared out of it intensely. Felix's gaze was drawn to it, and he saw that there were several oily smoke plumes rising up from the city.

Popovich's momentum was broken. "So that's what we're going to do," he said.

The kid looked around after a stretched moment of silence. "Oh, is it my turn now?"

There was a round of good-natured chuckling.

"Here's what I think: the world is going to shit. There are coordinated attacks on every critical piece of infrastructure. There's only one way that those attacks could be so well coordinated: via the internet. Even if you buy the thesis that the attacks are all opportunistic, we need to ask how an opportunistic attack could be organized in minutes: the internet."

"So you think we should shut down the internet?" Popovich laughed a little, but stopped when Sario said nothing.

"We saw an attack last night that nearly killed the internet. A little DoS on the critical routers, a little DNS-foo, and down it goes like a preacher's daughter. Cops and the military are a bunch of technophobic lusers, they hardly rely on the net at all. If we take the internet down, we'll disproportionately disadvantage the attackers, while only inconveniencing the defenders. When the time comes, we can rebuild it."

"You're shitting me," Popovich said. His jaw literally hung open.

"It's logical," Sario said. "Lots of people don't like coping with logic when it dictates hard decisions. That's a problem with people, not logic."

There was a buzz of conversation that quickly turned into a roar.

"Shut UP!" Popovich hollered. The conversation dimmed by one watt. Popovich yelled again, stamping his foot on the countertop. Finally there was a semblance of order. "One at a time," he said. He was flushed red, his hands in his pockets.

One sysadmin was for staying. Another for going. They should hide in the cages. They should inventory their supplies and appoint a quartermaster. They should go outside and find the police, or volunteer at hospitals. They should appoint defenders to keep the front door secure.

Felix found to his surprise that he had his hand in the air. Popovich called on him.

"My name is Felix Tremont," he said, getting up on one of the tables, drawing out his PDA. "I want to read you something:

Governments of the Industrial World, you weary giants of flesh and steel, I come from Cyberspace, the new home of Mind. On behalf of the future, I ask you of the past to leave us alone. You are not welcome among us. You have no sovereignty where we gather.

We have no elected government, nor are we likely to have one, so I address you with no greater authority than that with which liberty itself always speaks. I declare the global social space we are building to be naturally independent of the tyrannies you seek to impose on us. You have no moral right to rule us nor do you possess any methods of enforcement we have true reason to fear.

Governments derive their just powers from the consent of the governed. You have neither solicited nor received ours. We did not invite you. You do not know us, nor do you know our world. Cyberspace does not lie within your borders. Do not think that you can build it, as though it were a public construction project. You cannot. It is an act of nature and it grows itself through our collective actions.

"That's from the Declaration of Independence of Cyberspace. It was written 12 years ago. I thought it was one of the most beautiful things I'd ever read. I wanted my kid to grow up in a world where cyberspace was free—and where that freedom infected the real world, so meatspace got freer too."

He swallowed hard and scrubbed at his eyes with the back of his hand. Van awkwardly patted him on the shoe.

"My beautiful son and my beautiful wife died today. Millions more, too. The city is literally in flames. Whole cities have disappeared from the map."

He coughed up a sob and swallowed it again.

"All around the world, people like us are gathered in buildings like this. They were trying to recover from last night's worm when disaster struck. We have independent power. Food. Water.

"We have the network, that the bad guys use so well and that the good guys have never figured out.

"We have a shared love of liberty that comes from caring about and caring for the network. We are in charge of the most important organizational and governmental tool the world has ever seen. We are the closest thing to a government the world has right now. Geneva is a crater. The East River is on fire and the UN is evacuated.

"The Distributed Republic of Cyberspace weathered this storm basically unscathed. We are the custodians of a deathless, monstrous, wonderful machine, one with the potential to rebuild a better world.

"I have nothing to live for but that."

There were tears in Van's eyes. He wasn't the only one. They didn't applaud him, but they did one better. They maintained respectful, total silence for seconds that stretched to a minute.

"How do we do it?" Popovich said, without a trace of sarcasm.

The newsgroups were filling up fast. They'd announced them in `news.admin.net-abuse.email`, where all the spamfighters hung out, and where there was a tight culture of camaraderie in the face of full-out attack.

The new group was `alt.november5-disaster.recovery`, with `.recovery.governance`, `.recovery.finance`, `.recovery.logistics` and `.recovery.defense` hanging off of it. Bless the wooly alt. hierarchy and all those who sail in her.

The sysadmins came out of the woodwork. The Googleplex was online, with the stalwart Queen Kong bossing a gang of rollerbladed grunts who wheeled through the gigantic data-center swapping out dead boxen and hitting reboot switches. The Internet Archive was offline in the Presidio, but the mirror in Amsterdam was live and they'd redirected the DNS so that you'd hardly know the difference. Amazon was down. Paypal was up. Blogger, Typepad and Livejournal were all up, and filling with millions of posts from scared survivors huddling together for electronic warmth.

The Flickr photostreams were horrific. Felix had to unsubscribe from them after he caught a photo of a woman and a baby, dead in a kitchen, twisted into an agonized hieroglyph by the bioagent. They didn't look like Kelly and 2.0, but they didn't have to. He started shaking and couldn't stop.

Wikipedia was up, but limping under load. The spam poured in as though nothing had changed. Worms roamed the network.

`.recovery.logistics` was where most of the action was.

```
> We can use the newsgroup voting mechanism to hold regional
  elections
```

Felix knew that this would work. Usenet newsgroup votes had been running for more than twenty years without a substantial hitch.

> We'll elect regional representatives and they'll pick a
> Prime Minister.

The Americans insisted on President, which Felix didn't like. Seemed too partisan. His future wouldn't be the American future. The American future had gone up with the White House. He was building a bigger tent than that.

There were French sysadmins online from France Telecom. The EBU's data-center had been spared in the attacks that hammered Geneva, and it was filled with wry Germans whose English was better than Felix's. They got on well with the remains of the BBC team in Canary Wharf.

They spoke polyglot English in .recovery.logistics, and Felix had momentum on his side. Some of the admins were cooling out the inevitable stupid flamewars with the practice of long years. Some were chipping in useful suggestions.

Surprisingly few thought that Felix was off his rocker.

> I think we should hold elections as soon as possible.
> Tomorrow at the latest. We can't rule justly without the
> consent of the governed.

Within seconds the reply landed in his inbox.

> You can't be serious. Consent of the governed? Unless I
> miss my guess, most of the people you're proposing to govern
> are puking their guts out, hiding under their desks, or
> wandering shell-shocked through the city streets. When do
> THEY get a vote?

Felix had to admit she had a point. Queen Kong was sharp. Not many woman sysadmins, and that was a genuine tragedy. Women like Queen Kong were too good to exclude from the field. He'd have to hack a solution to get women balanced out in his new government. Require each region to elect one woman and one man?

He happily clattered into argument with her. The elections would be the next day; he'd see to it.

"Prime Minister of Cyberspace? Why not call yourself the Grand Poobah of the Global Data Network? It's more dignified, sounds cooler and it'll get you just as far." Will had the sleeping spot next to him, up in the cafeteria, with Van on the other side. The room smelled like a dingleberry: twenty-five sysadmins who hadn't washed in at least a day all crammed into the same room. For some of them, it had been much, much longer than a day.

"Shut up, Will," Van said. "You wanted to try to knock the internet offline."

"Correction: I *want* to knock the internet offline. Present-tense"

Felix cracked one eye. He was so tired, it was like lifting weights.

"Look, Sario—if you don't like my platform, put one of your own forward. There are plenty of people who think I'm full of shit and I respect them for that, since they're all running opposite me or backing someone who is. That's your choice. What's not on the menu is nagging and complaining. Bedtime now, or get up and post your platform."

Sario sat up slowly, unrolling the jacket he had been using for a pillow and putting it on. "Screw you guys, I'm out of here."

"I thought he'd never leave," Felix said and turned over, lying awake a long time, thinking about the election.

There were other people in the running. Some of them weren't even sysadmins. A US Senator on retreat at his summer place in Wyoming had generator power and a satellite phone. Somehow he'd found the right newsgroup and thrown his hat into the ring. Some anarchist hackers in Italy strafed the group all night long, posting broken-English screeds about the political bankruptcy of "governance" in the new world. Felix looked at their netblock and determined that they were probably holed up in a small Interaction Design institute near Turin. Italy had been hit very bad, but out in the small town, this cell of anarchists had taken up residence.

A surprising number were running on a platform of shutting down the internet. Felix had his doubts about whether this was even possible, but he thought he understood the impulse to finish the work and the world. Why not?

He fell asleep thinking about the logistics of shutting down the internet, and dreamed bad dreams in which he was the network's sole defender.

He woke to a papery, itchy sound. He rolled over and saw that Van was sitting up, his jacket balled up in his lap, vigorously scratching his skinny arms. They'd gone the color of corned beef, and had a scaly look. In the light streaming through the cafeteria windows, skin motes floated and danced in great clouds.

"What are you doing?" Felix sat up. Watching Van's fingernails rip into his skin made him itch in sympathy. It had been three days since he'd last washed his hair and his scalp sometimes felt like there were little egg-laying insects picking their way through it. He'd adjusted his glasses the night before and had touched the back of his ears; his finger came away shining with thick sebum. He got blackheads in the backs of his ears when he didn't shower for a couple days, and sometimes gigantic, deep boils that Kelly finally popped with sick relish.

"Scratching," Van said. He went to work on his head, sending a cloud of dandruff-crud into the sky, there to join the scurf that he'd already eliminated from his extremeties. "Christ, I itch all over."

Felix took Mayor McCheese from Van's backpack and plugged it into one of the Ethernet cables that snaked all over the floor. He googled everything he could think of that could be related to this. "Itchy" yielded 40,600,000 links. He tried compound queries and got slightly more discriminating links.

"I think it's stress-related excema," Felix said, finally.

"I don't get excema," Van said.

Felix showed him some lurid photos of red, angry skin flaked with white. "Stress-related excema," he said, reading the caption.

Van examined his arms. "I have excema," he said.

"Says here to keep it moisturized and to try cortisone cream. You might try the first aid kit in the second-floor toilets. I think I saw some there." Like all of the sysadmins, Felix had had a bit of a rummage around the offices, bathrooms, kitchen and store-rooms, squirreling away a roll of toilet-paper in his shoulder-bag along with three or four power-bars. They were sharing out the food in the caf by unspoken agreement, every sysadmin watching every other for signs of gluttony and hoarding. All were convinced that there was hoarding and gluttony going on out of eyeshot, because all were guilty of it themselves when no one else was watching.

Van got up and when his face hove into the light, Felix saw how puffed his eyes were. "I'll post to the mailing-list for some antihistamine," Felix said. There had been four mailing lists and three wikis for the survivors in the building within hours of the first meeting's close, and in the intervening days they'd settled on just one. Felix was still on a little mailing list with five of his most trusted friends, two of whom were trapped in cages in other countries. He suspected that the rest of the sysadmins were doing the same.

Van stumbled off. "Good luck on the elections," he said, patting Felix on the shoulder.

Felix stood and paced, stopping to stare out the grubby windows. The fires still burned in Toronto, more than before. He'd tried to find mailing lists or blogs that Torontonians were posting to, but the only ones he'd found were being run by other geeks in other data-centers. It was possible—likely, even—that there were survivors out there who had more pressing priorities than posting to the internet. His home phone still worked about half the time but he'd stopped calling it after the second day, when hearing Kelly's voice on the voicemail for the fiftieth time had made him cry in the middle of a planning meeting. He wasn't the only one.

Election day. Time to face the music.

```
> Are you nervous?
> Nope,
```

Felix typed.

```
> I don't much care if I win, to be honest. I'm just glad
  we're doing this. The alternative was sitting around with
  our thumbs up our ass, waiting for someone to crack up and
  open the door.
```

The cursor hung. Queen Kong was very high latency as she bossed her gang of Googloids around the Googleplex, doing everything she could to keep her data center online. Three of the offshore cages had gone offline and two of their six redundant network links were smoked. Lucky for her, queries-per-second were way down.

```
> There's still China
```

she typed. Queen Kong had a big board with a map of the world colored in Google-queries-per-second, and could do magic with it, showing the drop-off over time in colorful charts. She'd uploaded lots of video clips showing how the plague and the bombs had swept the world: the initial upswell of queries from people wanting to find out what was going on, then the grim, precipitous shelving off as the plagues took hold.

```
> China's still running about ninety percent nominal.
```

Felix shook his head.

```
> You can't think that they're responsible
> No
```

She typed, but then she started to key something and then stopped.

```
> No of course not. I believe the Popovich Hypothesis. This
  is a bunch of assholes all using the rest for cover. But
  China put them down harder and faster than anyone else.
  Maybe we've finally found a use for totalitarian states.
```

Felix couldn't resist. He typed:

```
> You're lucky your boss can't see you type that. You guys
  were pretty enthusiastic participants in the Great Firewall
  of China.
> Wasn't my idea
```

she typed.

> And my boss is dead. They're probably all dead. The whole
> Bay Area got hit hard, and then there was the quake.

They'd watched the USGS's automated data-stream from the 6.9 that trashed northern Cal from Gilroy to Sebastopol. Soma webcams revealed the scope of the damage—gas main explosions, seismically retrofitted buildings crumpling like piles of children's blocks after a good kicking. The Googleplex, floating on a series of gigantic steel springs, had shaken like a plateful of jello, but the racks had stayed in place and the worst injury they'd had was a badly bruised eye on a sysadmin who'd caught a flying cable-crimper in the face.

> Sorry. I forgot.
> It's OK. We all lost people, right?
> Yeah. Yeah. Anyway, I'm not worried about the election.
> Whoever wins, at least we're doing SOMETHING
> Not if they vote for one of the fuckrags

Fuckrag was the epithet that some of the sysadmins were using to describe the contingent that wanted to shut down the internet. Queen Kong had coined it—apparently it had started life as a catch-all term to describe the clueless IT managers that she'd chewed up through her career.

> They won't. They're just tired and sad is all. Your endorse-
> ment will carry the day

The Googloids were one of the largest and most powerful blocs left behind, along with the satellite uplink crews and the remaining transoceanic crews. Queen Kong's endorsement had come as a surprise and he'd sent her an email that she'd replied to tersely: "can't have the fuckrags in charge."

> gtg

she typed and then her connection dropped. He fired up a browser and called up google.com. The browser timed out. He hit reload, and then again, and then the Google front-page came back up. Whatever had hit Queen Kong's workplace—power failure, worms, another quake—she had fixed it. He snorted when he saw that they'd replaced the O's in the Google logo with little planet Earths with mushroom clouds rising from them.

"Got anything to eat?" Van said to him. It was mid-afternoon, not that time particularly passed in the data-center. Felix patted his pockets. They'd put a quartermaster in charge, but not before everyone had snagged some chow out of the machines. He'd had a dozen power-bars and some apples.

He'd taken a couple sandwiches but had wisely eaten them first before they got stale.

"One power-bar left," he said. He'd noticed a certain looseness in his waistline that morning and had briefly relished it. Then he'd remembered Kelly's teasing about his weight and he'd cried some. Then he'd eaten two power bars, leaving him with just one left.

"Oh," Van said. His face was hollower than ever, his shoulders sloping in on his toast-rack chest.

"Here," Felix said. "Vote Felix."

Van took the power-bar from him and then put it down on the table. "OK, I want to give this back to you and say, 'No, I couldn't,' but I'm fucking *hungry*, so I'm just going to take it and eat it, OK?"

"That's fine by me," Felix said. "Enjoy."

"How are the elections coming?" Van said, once he'd licked the wrapper clean.

"Dunno," Felix said. "Haven't checked in a while." He'd been winning by a slim margin a few hours before. Not having his laptop was a major handicap when it came to stuff like this. Up in the cages, there were a dozen more like him, poor bastards who'd left the house on Der Tag without thinking to snag something WiFi-enabled.

"You're going to get smoked," Sario said, sliding in next to them. He'd become famous in the center for never sleeping, for eavesdropping, for picking fights in RL that had the ill-considered heat of a Usenet flamewar. "The winner will be someone who understands a couple of fundamental facts." He held up a fist, then ticked off his bullet points by raising a finger at a time. "Point: The terrorists are using the internet to destroy the world, and we need to destroy the internet first. Point: Even if I'm wrong, the whole thing is a joke. We'll run out of generator-fuel soon enough. Point: Or if we don't, it will be because the old world will be back and running, and it won't give a crap about your new world. Point: We're gonna run out of food before we run out of shit to argue about or reasons not to go outside. We have the chance to do something to help the world recover: we can kill the net and cut it off as a tool for bad guys. Or we can rearrange some more deck chairs on the bridge of your personal Titanic in the service of some sweet dream about an 'independent cyberspace.'"

The thing was that Sario was right. They would be out of fuel in two days—intermittent power from the grid had stretched their generator lifespan. And if you bought his hypothesis that the internet was primarily being used as a tool to organize more mayhem, shutting it down would be the right thing to do.

But Felix's daughter and his wife were dead. He didn't want to rebuild the old world. He wanted a new one. The old world was one that didn't have any place for him. Not anymore.

Van scratched his raw, flaking skin. Puffs of dander and scruff swirled in the musty, greasy air. Sario curled a lip at him. "That is disgusting. We're breathing recycled air, you know. Whatever leprosy is eating you, aerosolizing it into the air supply is pretty anti-social."

"You're the world's leading authority on anti-social, Sario," Van said. "Go away or I'll multi-tool you to death." He stopped scratching and patted his sheathed multi-pliers like a gunslinger.

"Yeah, I'm anti-social. I've got Asperger's and I haven't taken any meds in four days. What's your fucking excuse?"

Van scratched some more. "I'm sorry," he said. "I didn't know."

Sario cracked up. "Oh, you are priceless. I'd bet that three quarters of this bunch is borderline autistic. Me, I'm just an asshole. But I'm one who isn't afraid to tell the truth, and that makes me better than you, dickweed."

"Fuckrag," Felix said, "fuck off."

They had less than a day's worth of fuel when Felix was elected the first ever Prime Minister of Cyberspace. The first count was spoiled by a bot that spammed the voting process and they lost a critical day while they added up the votes a second time.

But by then, it was all seeming like more of a joke. Half the data-centers had gone dark. Queen Kong's net-maps of Google queries were looking grimmer and grimmer as more of the world went offline, though she maintained a leader-board of new and rising queries—largely related to health, shelter, sanitation and self-defense.

Worm-load slowed. Power was going off to many home PC users, and staying off, so their compromised PCs were going dark. The backbones were still lit up and blinking, but the missives from those data-centers were looking more and more desperate. Felix hadn't eaten in a day and neither had anyone in a satellite Earth-station of transoceanic head-end.

Water was running short, too.

Popovich and Rosenbaum came and got him before he could do more than answer a few congratulatory messages and post a canned acceptance speech to newsgroups.

"We're going to open the doors," Popovich said. Like all of them, he'd lost weight and waxed scruffy and oily. His BO was like a cloud coming off a trash-bag behind a fish-market on a sunny day. Felix was quite sure he smelled no better.

"You're going to go for a reccy? Get more fuel? We can charter a working group for it—great idea."

Rosenbaum shook his head sadly. "We're going to go find our families. Whatever is out there has burned itself out. Or it hasn't. Either way, there's no future in here."

"What about network maintenance?" Felix said, though he knew the answers. "Who'll keep the routers up?"

"We'll give you the root passwords to everything," Popovich said. His hands were shaking and his eyes were bleary. Like many of the smokers stuck in the data-center, he'd gone cold turkey this week. They'd run out of caffeine products two days earlier, too. The smokers had it rough.

"And I'll just stay here and keep everything online?"

"You and anyone else who cares anymore."

Felix knew that he'd squandered his opportunity. The election had seemed noble and brave, but in hindsight all it had been was an excuse for infighting when they should have been figuring out what to do next. The problem was that there was nothing to do next.

"I can't make you stay," he said.

"Yeah, you can't." Popovich turned on his heel and walked out. Rosenbaum watched him go, then he gripped Felix's shoulder and squeezed it.

"Thank you, Felix. It was a beautiful dream. It still is. Maybe we'll find something to eat and some fuel and come back."

Rosenbaum had a sister whom he'd been in contact with over IM for the first days after the crisis broke. Then she'd stopped answering. The sysadmins were split among those who'd had a chance to say goodbye and those who hadn't. Each was sure the other had it better.

They posted about it on the internal newsgroup—they were still geeks, after all, and there was a little honor guard on the ground floor, geeks who watched them pass toward the double doors. They manipulated the keypads and the steel shutters lifted, then the first set of doors opened. They stepped into the vestibule and pulled the doors shut behind them. The front doors opened. It was very bright and sunny outside, and apart from how empty it was, it looked very normal. Heartbreakingly so.

The two took a tentative step out into the world. Then another. They turned to wave at the assembled masses. Then they both grabbed their throats and began to jerk and twitch, crumpling in a heap on the ground.

"Shiii—!" was all Felix managed to choke out before they both dusted themselves off and stood up, laughing so hard they were clutching their sides. They waved once more and turned on their heels.

"Man, those guys are sick," Van said. He scratched his arms, which had long, bloody scratches on them. His clothes were so covered in scurf they looked like they'd been dusted with icing sugar.

"I thought it was pretty funny," Felix said.

"Christ I'm hungry," Van said, conversationally.

"Lucky for you, we've got all the packets we can eat," Felix said.

"You're too good to us grunts, Mr. President," Van said.

"Prime Minister," he said. "And you're no grunt, you're the Deputy Prime Minister. You're my designated ribbon-cutter and hander-out of oversized novelty checks."

It buoyed both of their spirits. Watching Popovich and Rosenbaum go, it buoyed them up. Felix knew then that they'd all be going soon.

That had been pre-ordained by the fuel supply, but who wanted to wait for the fuel to run out, anyway?

> half my crew split this morning

Queen Kong typed. Google was holding up pretty good anyway, of course. The load on the servers was a lot lighter than it had been since the days when Google fit on a bunch of hand-built PCs under a desk at Stanford.

> we're down to a quarter

Felix typed back. It was only a day since Popovich and Rosenbaum left, but the traffic on the newsgroups had fallen down to near zero. He and Van hadn't had much time to play Republic of Cyberspace. They'd been too busy learning the systems that Popovich had turned over to them, the big, big routers that had went on acting as the major interchange for all the network backbones in Canada.

Still, someone posted to the newsgroups every now and again, generally to say goodbye. The old flamewars about who would be PM, or whether they would shut down the network, or who took too much food—it was all gone.

He reloaded the newsgroup. There was a typical message.

> Runaway processes on Solaris
>
> Uh, hi. I'm just a lightweight MSCE but I'm the only one
awake here and four of the DSLAMs just went down. Looks
like there's some custom accounting code that's trying to
figure out how much to bill our corporate customers and
it's spawned ten thousand threads and its eating all the
swap. I just want to kill it but I can't seem to do that.
Is there some magic invocation I need to do to get this
goddamned weenix box to kill this shit? I mean, it's not
as if any of our customers are ever going to pay us again.

I'd ask the guy who wrote this code, but he's pretty much dead as far as anyone can work out.

He reloaded. There was a response. It was short, authoritative, and helpful—just the sort of thing you almost never saw in a high-caliber newsgroup when a noob posted a dumb question. The apocalypse had awoken the spirit of patient helpfulness in the world's sysop community.

Van shoulder-surfed him. "Holy shit, who knew he had it in him?"

He looked at the message again. It was from Will Sario.

He dropped into his chat window.

```
> sario i thought you wanted the network dead why are you
  helping mcses fix their boxen?
> <sheepish grin> Gee Mr PM, maybe I just can't bear to watch
  a computer suffer at the hands of an amateur.
```

He flipped to the channel with Queen Kong in it.

```
> How long?
> Since I slept? Two days. Until we run out of fuel? Three
  days. Since we ran out of food? Two days.
> Jeez. I didn't sleep last night either. We're a little short
  handed around here.
> asl? Im monica and I live in pasadena and Im bored with my
  homework. Would you like to download my pic???
```

The trojan bots were all over IRC these days, jumping to every channel that had any traffic on it. Sometimes you caught five or six flirting with each other. It was pretty weird to watch a piece of malware try to con another instance of itself into downloading a trojan.

They both kicked the bot off the channel simultaneously. He had a script for it now. The spam hadn't even tailed off a little.

```
> How come the spam isn't reducing? Half the goddamned data-
  centers have gone dark
```

Queen Kong paused a long time before typing. As had become automatic when she went high-latency, he reloaded the Google homepage. Sure enough, it was down.

```
> Sario, you got any food?
> You won't miss a couple more meals, Your Excellency
```

Van had gone back to Mayor McCheese but he was in the same channel. "What a dick. You're looking pretty buff, though, dude."

Van didn't look so good. He looked like you could knock him over with a stiff breeze and he had a phlegmy, weak quality to his speech.

```
> hey kong everything ok?
> everything's fine just had to go kick some ass
```

"How's the traffic, Van?"

"Down twenty-five percent from this morning," he said. There were a bunch of nodes whose connections routed through them. Presumably most of these were home or commercial customers in places where the power was still on and the phone company's COs were still alive.

Every once in a while, Felix would wiretap the connections to see if he could find a person who had news of the wide world. Almost all of it was automated traffic, though: network backups, status updates. Spam. Lots of spam.

```
> Spam's still up because the services that stop spam are
  failing faster than the services that create it. All the
  anti-worm stuff is centralized in a couple places. The bad
  stuff is on a million zombie computers. If only the lusers
  had had the good sense to turn off their home PCs before
  keeling over or taking off
> at the rate were going well be routing nothing but spam by
  dinnertime
```

Van cleared his throat, a painful sound. "About that," he said. "I think it's going to hit sooner than that. Felix, I don't think anyone would notice if we just walked away from here."

Felix looked at him, his skin the color of corned-beef and streaked with long, angry scabs. His fingers trembled.

"You drinking enough water?"

Van nodded. "All frigging day, every ten seconds. Anything to keep my belly full." He pointed to a refilled Pepsi Max bottle full of water by his side.

"Let's have a meeting," he said.

There had been forty-three of them on D-Day. Now there were fifteen. Six had responded to the call for a meeting by simply leaving. Everyone knew without having to be told what the meeting was about.

"So that's it, you're going to let it all fall apart?" Sario was the only one with the energy left to get properly angry. He'd go angry to his grave. The veins on his throat and forehead stood out angrily. His fists shook angrily. All the other geeks went lids-down at the site of him, looking up in unison for once at the discussion, not keeping one eye on a chat-log or a tailed service log.

"Sario, you've got to be shitting me," Felix said. "You wanted to pull the goddamned plug!"

"I wanted it to go *clean*," he shouted. "I didn't want it to bleed out and keel over in little gasps and pukes forever. I wanted it to be an act of will by the global community of its caretakers. I wanted it to be an affirmative act by human hands. Not entropy and bad code and worms winning out. Fuck that, that's just what's happened out there."

Up in the top-floor cafeteria, there were windows all around, hardened and light-bending, and by custom, they were all blinds-down. Now Sario ran around the room, yanking down the blinds. *How the hell can he get the energy to run?* Felix wondered. He could barely walk up the stairs to the meeting room.

Harsh daylight flooded in. It was a fine sunny day out there, but everywhere you looked across that commanding view of Toronto's skyline, there were rising plumes of smoke. The TD tower, a gigantic black modernist glass brick, was gouting flame to the sky. "It's all falling apart, the way everything does.

"Listen, listen. If we leave the network to fall over slowly, parts of it will stay online for months. Maybe years. And what will run on it? Malware. Worms. Spam. System-processes. Zone transfers. The things we use fall apart and require constant maintenance. The things we abandon don't get used and they last forever. We're going to leave the network behind like a lime-pit filled with industrial waste. That will be our fucking legacy—the legacy of every keystroke you and I and anyone, anywhere ever typed. You understand? We're going to leave it to die slow like a wounded dog, instead of giving it one clean shot through the head."

Van scratched his cheeks, then Felix saw that he was wiping away tears.

"Sario, you're not wrong, but you're not right either," he said. "Leaving it up to limp along is right. We're going to all be limping for a long time, and maybe it will be some use to someone. If there's one packet being routed from any user to any other user, anywhere in the world, it's doing its job."

"If you want a clean kill, you can do that," Felix said. "I'm the PM and I say so. I'm giving you root. All of you." He turned to the white-board where the cafeteria workers used to scrawl the day's specials. Now it was covered with the remnants of heated technical debates that the sysadmins had engaged in over the days since the day.

He scrubbed away a clean spot with his sleeve and began to write out long, complicated alphanumeric passwords salted with punctuation. Felix had a gift for remembering that kind of password. He doubted it would do him much good, ever again.

> Were going, kong. Fuels almost out anyway
> yeah well thats right then. it was an honor, mr prime minister

```
> you going to be ok?
> ive commandeered a young sysadmin to see to my feminine
  needs and weve found another cache of food thatll last us
  a coupel weeks now that were down to fifteen admins—im in
  hog heaven pal
> youre amazing, Queen Kong, seriously. Dont be a hero though.
  When you need to go go. Theres got to be something out there
> be safe felix, seriously—btw did i tell you queries are up
  in Romania? maybe theyre getting back on their feet
> really?
> yeah, really. we're hard to kill—like fucking roaches
```

Her connection died. He dropped to Firefox and reloaded Google and it was down. He hit reload and hit reload and hit reload, but it didn't come up. He closed his eyes and listened to Van scratch his legs and then heard Van type a little.

"They're back up," he said.

Felix whooshed out a breath. He sent the message to the newsgroup, one that he'd run through five drafts before settling on, "Take care of the place, OK? We'll be back, someday."

Everyone was going except Sario. Sario wouldn't leave. He came down to see them off, though.

The sysadmins gathered in the lobby and Felix made the safety door go up, and the light rushed in.

Sario stuck his hand out.

"Good luck," he said.

"You too," Felix said. He had a firm grip, Sario, stronger than he had any right to be. "Maybe you were right," he said.

"Maybe," he said.

"You going to pull the plug?"

Sario looked up at the drop-ceiling, seeming to peer through the reinforced floors at the humming racks above. "Who knows?" he said at last.

Van scratched and a flurry of white motes danced in the sunlight.

"Let's go find you a pharmacy," Felix said. He walked to the door and the other sysadmins followed.

They waited for the interior doors to close behind them and then Felix opened the exterior doors. The air smelled and tasted like a mown grass, like the first drops of rain, like the lake and the sky, like the outdoors and the world, an old friend not heard from in an eternity.

"Bye, Felix," the other sysadmins said. They were drifting away while he stood transfixed at the top of the short concrete staircase. The light hurt his eyes and made them water.

"I think there's a Shopper's Drug Mart on King Street," he said to Van. "We'll thrown a brick through the window and get you some cortisone, OK?"

"You're the Prime Minister," Van said. "Lead on."

They didn't see a single soul on the fifteen minute walk. There wasn't a single sound except for some bird noises and some distant groans, and the wind in the electric cables overhead. It was like walking on the surface of the moon.

"Bet they have chocolate bars at the Shopper's," Van said.

Felix's stomach lurched. Food. "Wow," he said, around a mouthful of saliva.

They walked past a little hatchback and in the front seat was the dried body of a woman holding the dried body of a baby, and his mouth filled with sour bile, even though the smell was faint through the rolled-up windows.

He hadn't thought of Kelly or 2.0 in days. He dropped to his knees and retched again. Out here in the real world, his family was dead. Everyone he knew was dead. He just wanted to lie down on the sidewalk and wait to die, too.

Van's rough hands slipped under his armpits and hauled weakly at him. "Not now," he said. "Once we're safe inside somewhere and we've eaten something, then you can do this, but not now. Understand me, Felix? Not fucking now."

The profanity got through to him. He got to his feet. His knees were trembling.

"Just a block more," Van said, and slipped Felix's arm around his shoulders and led him along.

"Thank you, Van. I'm sorry."

"No sweat," he said. "You need a shower, bad. No offense."

"None taken."

The Shoppers had a metal security gate, but it had been torn away from the front windows, which had been rudely smashed. Felix and Van squeezed through the gap and stepped into the dim drug-store. A few of the displays were knocked over, but other than that, it looked OK. By the cash-registers, Felix spotted the racks of candy bars at the same instant that Van saw them, and they hurried over and grabbed a handful each, stuffing their faces.

"You two eat like pigs."

They both whirled at the sound of the woman's voice. She was holding a fire-axe that was nearly as big as she was. She wore a lab-coat and comfortable shoes.

"You take what you need and go, OK? No sense in there being any trouble." Her chin was pointy and her eyes were sharp. She looked to be in her forties. She looked nothing like Kelly, which was good, because Felix felt like running and giving her a hug as it was. Another person alive!

"Are you a doctor?" Felix said. She was wearing scrubs under the coat, he saw.

"You going to go?" She brandished the axe.

Felix held his hands up. "Seriously, are you a doctor? A pharmacist?"

"I used to be a RN, ten years ago. I'm mostly a Web-designer."

"You're shitting me," Felix said.

"Haven't you ever met a girl who knew about computers?"

"Actually, a friend of mine who runs Google's data-center is a girl. A woman, I mean."

"You're shitting me," she said. "A woman ran Google's data-center?"

"Runs," Felix said. "It's still online."

"NFW," she said. She let the axe lower.

"Way. Have you got any cortisone cream? I can tell you the story. My name's Felix and this is Van, who needs any anti-histamines you can spare."

"I can spare? Felix old pal, I have enough dope here to last a hundred years. This stuff's going to expire long before it runs out. But are you telling me that the net's still up?"

"It's still up," he said. "Kind of. That's what we've been doing all week. Keeping it online. It might not last much longer, though."

"No," she said. "I don't suppose it would." She set the axe down. "Have you got anything to trade? I don't need much, but I've been trying to keep my spirits up by trading with the neighbors. It's like playing civilization."

"You have neighbors?"

"At least ten," she said. "The people in the restaurant across the way make a pretty good soup, even if most of the veg is canned. They cleaned me out of Sterno, though."

"You've got neighbors and you trade with them?"

"Well, nominally. It'd be pretty lonely without them. I've taken care of whatever sniffles I could. Set a bone—broken wrist. Listen, do you want some Wonder Bread and peanut butter? I have a ton of it. Your friend looks like he could use a meal."

"Yes please," Van said. "We don't have anything to trade, but we're both committed workaholics looking to learn a trade. Could you use some assistants?"

"Not really." She spun her axe on its head. "But I wouldn't mind some company."

They ate the sandwiches and then some soup. The restaurant people brought it over and made their manners at them, though Felix saw their noses wrinkle up and ascertained that there was working plumbing in the back room. Van went in to take a sponge bath and then he followed.

"None of us know what to do," the woman said. Her name was Rosa, and she had found them a bottle of wine and some disposable plastic cups from the housewares aisle. "I thought we'd have helicopters or tanks or even looters, but it's just quiet."

"You seem to have kept pretty quiet yourself," Felix said.

"Didn't want to attract the wrong kind of attention."

"You ever think that maybe there's a lot of people out there doing the same thing? Maybe if we all get together we'll come up with something to do."

"Or maybe they'll cut our throats," she said.

Van nodded. "She's got a point."

Felix was on his feet. "No way, we can't think like that. Lady, we're at a critical juncture here. We can go down through negligence, dwindling away in our hiding holes, or we can try to build something better."

"Better?" She made a rude noise.

"OK, not better. Something though. Building something new is better than letting it dwindle away. Christ, what are you going to do when you've read all the magazines and eaten all the potato chips here?"

Rosa shook her head. "Pretty talk," she said. "But what the hell are we going to do, anyway?"

"Something," Felix said. "We're going to do something. Something is better than nothing. We're going to take this patch of the world where people are talking to each other, and we're going to expand it. We're going to find everyone we can and we're going to take care of them and they're going to take care of us. We'll probably fuck it up. We'll probably fail. I'd rather fail than give up, though."

Van laughed. "Felix, you are crazier than Sario, you know it?"

"We're going to go and drag him out, first thing tomorrow. He's going to be a part of this, too. Everyone will. Screw the end of the world. The world doesn't end. Humans aren't the kind of things that have endings."

Rosa shook her head again, but she was smiling a little now. "And you'll be what, the Pope-Emperor of the World?"

"He prefers Prime Minister," Van said in a stagey whisper. The antihistamines had worked miracles on his skin, and it had faded from angry red to a fine pink.

"You want to be Minister of Health, Rosa?" he said.

"Boys," she said. "Playing games. How about this. I'll help out however I can, provided you never ask me to call you Prime Minister and you never call me the Minister of Health?"

"It's a deal," he said.

Van refilled their glasses, upending the wine bottle to get the last few drops out.

The raised their glasses. "To the world," Felix said. "To humanity." He thought hard. "To rebuilding."

"To anything," Van said.

"To anything," Felix said. "To everything."

"To everything," Rosa said.

They drank. The next day, they started to rebuild. And months later, they started over again, when disagreements drove apart the fragile little group they'd pulled together. And a year after that, they started over again. And five years later, they started again.

Felix dug ditches and salvaged cans and buried the dead. He planted and harvested. He fixed some cars and learned to make biodiesel. Finally he fetched up in a data-center for a little government—little governments came and went, but this one was smart enough to want to keep records and needed someone to keep everything running, and Van went with him.

They spent a lot of time in chat rooms and sometimes they happened upon old friends from the strange time they'd spent running the Distributed Republic of Cyberspace, geeks who insisted on calling him PM, though no one in the real world ever called him that anymore.

It wasn't a good life, most of the time. Felix's wounds never healed, and neither did most other people's. There were lingering sicknesses and sudden ones. Tragedy on tragedy.

But Felix liked his data-center. There in the humming of the racks, he never felt like it was the first days of a better nation, but he never felt like it was the last days of one, either.

```
> go to bed, felix
> soon, kong, soon—almost got this backup running
> youre a junkie, dude.
> look whos talking
```

He reloaded the Google homepage. Queen Kong had had it online for a couple years now. The Os in Google changed all the time, whenever she got the urge. Today they were little cartoon globes, one smiling the other frowning.

He looked at it for a long time and dropped back into a terminal to check his backup. It was running clean, for a change. The little government's records were safe.

```
> ok night night
> take care
```

Van waved at him as he creaked to the door, stretching out his back with a long series of pops.

"Sleep well, boss," he said.

"Don't stick around here all night again," Felix said. "You need your sleep, too."

"You're too good to us grunts," Van said, and went back to typing.

Felix went to the door and walked out into the night. Behind him, the biodiesel generator hummed and made its acrid fumes. The harvest moon was up, which he loved. Tomorrow, he'd go back and fix another computer and fight off entropy again. And why not?

It was what he did. He was a sysadmin.

CALL IT ONLY
by Chelsea Quinn Yarbro

As soon as Tony regained consciousness, he regretted it. His joints had been filled with cornstarch and termites had been at his spine. There was rust in his taste.

Through the murk that scummed his eyeballs, he was able to make out two large buildings some distance from where he lay. Wherever that was.

Insidious white sunshine probed for and found him, jabbing light into his already abused eyes. He made a sound and rolled over seeking the asylum of darkness.

"Ho," said a large voice somewhere overhead. "Har sarlag."

Tony pulled himself into a determined ball. He was going to be left alone. He didn't want to be found or captured or helped. He refused to exist.

"Sarlag?" asked the voice, obviously addressing him. "Rye, sarlag?"

Stoically, Tony ignored him.

A few moments later, a large wooden staff levered him out of his fetal position, sprawling him in the raw light facing two huge boots that might have belonged to oak trees.

"Huar oo?" demanded a voice from above the boots.

The words were familiar, the accent normal. Too real, thought Tony. He's not strange enough. This isn't happening. I am making it up. But when he tried to answer, he made a noise like a camel.

The giant seemed taken aback. He brought his stick down with a resolute thud, sending dust billowing into Tony.

"Damnit," Tony choked, "I'm hurt, you ruddy great lummox. I need help."

Immediately a look of great concern crossed the clean-shaven face, and he bent down to Tony. "Nae sarlag gud?" he asked gently.

"I'm hurt!" Tony grated at him.

"War?" asked the giant, looking Tony over with practiced care. At least he understood. That was something.

"Never mind," Tony said irritably, waving the man away from him. "Don't bother."

He grunted and sat down. Tony looked him over, trying to figure him out. He was wearing a long tunic of rough linen, a heavy belt of red-dyed leather from which hung a fur pouch and a small crude lyre. Aside from his staff he carried no weapon. In short, there was something wrong about him.

"Huar ooh?" he asked again.

"I am Alan Lowell Anthony MacKenzie," he managed to say. "Oo?" he pointed at the huge man.

"Hars Baldur," he clapped a moose-antler hand to his chest, "ohm."

"Hars Baldur." Tony pointed carefully at him.

"Yaw." He returned the point. "Mac Kenzie."

It would do. "Yaw."

Hars Baldur nodded eagerly, his great leonine head enhaloed by the rising sun. "Warfrum?"

"Uh..." Tony hesitated. What did he say to that? "I don't know." As he saw puzzlement cross Hars' face, he shrugged. He shook his head.

"Hoo. Be sarlag." he said with authority, as if Tony's answer had satisfied him.

"Warfrum Hars Baldur?" Tony ventured.

"Harfrum," he said, as if stating the obvious. He held out his all engulfing hand to Tony. "Oo kum har noo, Mac Kenzie."

Tony tried to decline. But Hars was back on his feet and was dragging Tony up to him. "Nae, nae, sarlag. Nae doe fir stae," he soothed as he steadied Tony.

His bones felt dangerously gelatinous, but there was no pain to speak of. He would live. He turned to Hars and was startled for the giant was no more than five inches taller than Tony. He laughed.

"Wat?" Hars asked sharply.

"This'll teach me to go subjective."

"Hoo?"

"Nothing. Nae." He spoke in his best calming voice, the one he reserved for the psychotic wards. "Just words, Hars."

But the reminder of the psychotic wards filled him with apprehension. As he looked around, he found that he had been lying at the edge of a field. There were vegetables growing in it, but they were unrecognizable.

Where the hell was he?

Was this a parallel universe, the sort of thing that had been theorized about for the last ten years or so? Had the spatial fabric of over-crowded Earth finally ripped wide open, spewing its masses randomly across the stars? Or—and this frightened him more than the other possibilities because it was most probably the truth—had he succumbed to his occupational contagion and gone just as bonkers as the poor creatures he treated?

Hars was striding ahead of him, walking easily and not as fast as he might, talking amiably in that damningly familiar language.

"Hars," Tony interrupted. "What place is this?"

"Har?"

"Yaw. Har."

"Har Only ohm." He moved his heavy arms in great encompassing circles. "Ol har Only."

"Only," he repeated, and another thread holding his Damoclean sanity was sliced through.

"Yaw. Gud." Hars beamed at him, unaware of the agony in Tony. He continued walking, guiding Tony through the vegetable patch toward the gate of the nearer and larger of the two buildings. He chatted amiably, pointing to some ridiculous birds which resembled ducks but were not aquatic, calling them "roon," pointing to some grazing animals off in a distant field, calling them "porhide," pointing to the tall trees that climbed the ridge behind the stone buildings, "rifer." Each phrase made Tony more and more certain that he was still on Terra, in the psych ward of his hospital, wrapped in cold sheets, strapped to a racking bed.

As they neared the gates of what Hars called the "kaseep," three moderately large quasi-canine beasts shot out to them, keening wildly. Hars patted them on their heads, talking kindly to them, sending them ahead, still keening.

"Wat?" asked Tony.

"Be elves."

With a rueful smile, Tony allowed that his subconscious was not without humor. "Elves," he said. "Elves."

A rutted, dusty road led to the gate, and there were a number of wagons and carts on it, with assorted natives driving, pulling, and occupying them.

"Lemwen," indicated Hars, waving a hand at the people.

"Ol lemwen?" asked Tony, just to be sure.

"Yaw. Ol lemwen ber."

"Nae sarlag?"

"Yaw. En sarlag." Hars held up one finger but did not elaborate.

Tony wanted to pursue it, to find out who this other sarlag was, but was unable to because Hars was within hailing distance of the gate, and did.

"Hars kum!" he shouted.

"Ayah, Hars," called the warder. He was a tall older man with heavy legs and huge chest. The stocky body seemed standard with these people. Tony looked carefully at the linen and leather clothing of the warder, but could see no weapons.

"Ayah, Nellus. Gud wef die."

"Wef oo. Huar am?" Nellus pointed at Tony.

"Am Mac Kenzie. Kum har wef ohm. Kum fer say Zelson Marquet." He spoke simply for Tony's benefit.

"Yaw." Nellus lifted the low barrier and let them pass. "Gud wef die, sarlag," he nodded to Tony, kindly.

"Wef oo," Tony responded as Hars had. Nellus grinned at him with understanding and some amusement. But he must be a sight to the lemwen. They in their earth-colored linen tunics, he in his bright-colored acrylic fiber jacket and slacks. Already children were crowding around him, trying to touch his clothes, to see him better.

"Nae, litwen. Nae shamp sarlag," Hars admonished them.

One of the more forward youngsters pushed his face toward Tony. "Huar oo, sarlag?"

"Tony MacKenzie," he answered. "Huar oo?"

"Indri Wexwer ohm," the child said. His eyes were keen, precise. He measured Tony carefully, missing nothing. At last he rendered a guarded smile. "Gud sarlag."

"Thank you."

Hars pulled Tony through the tide of animal life that ebbed around their legs. It was a precautious business. One that Tony found disquieting.

"Where are we going, Hars," he asked neatly, sidestepping four young elves.

"Say Zelson Marquet. Ol sarlag kum har say Zelson Marquet."

The cavernous maw of the kaseep yawned ahead of them: foreboding, dark. From within came a faint sound of music, a bit of tune. It was just enough for Tony to recognize it. "Sumer is icumen in," went the words as Tony knew them. "Sumar be fir kum on har" sang the voice in the kaseep. Tony cursed.

The dark inside smelled of marjoram. There were rushes on the floor and fantastic tapestries on the walls showing sport and harvest, ceremony and play. Oddly enough, no war. Tony looked again for arms and found none. Here, in a great pool of silver, two children played at fishing. There were no toy boats. There, two women stooped to reap handfuls of living gold grain. Beyond them in the heavy field a man in fanciful hose of checkerboard red and blue scythed down the grain under an orange sun. In another section, men hid in trees setting traps for perhaps birds, perhaps other tree dwellers. And each tapestry was suffused with tranquility.

It all figures, Tony thought. It makes sense. Here is this half-familiar world, gathered out of all the myths I remember, made into a wholly peaceful place. Not overcrowded. Not polluted. Not on the verge of war. Well, it's nice to feel so calm. I wonder when I'll come out of it. And where.

"Tony Mac Kenzie, warar oo?" Hars cut into his reverie.

"Right here, Hars."

"Zelson Marquet kum fir oo say," he announced, looking through one of the heavy arrases toward other rooms. "Zelson Marquet be sarlag."

Tony started. He figured that a sarlag was a stranger. If the chief of this place was a stranger, too, then it might change his thoughts.

Hars called into the rooms beyond: "Worfy Marquet. Zelson Marquet! Hars ohm wef sarlag."

The deep muffled voice resonated a reply in what seemed to Tony to be differently accented words. Hars' response to it was a deluge of words, too fast for Tony to catch more than few words of.

A deep chuckle came from beyond, a nutmeg laugh that convinced Tony he would like whatever his mind had conjured up for him.

"Kum fir sarlag, Zelson Marquet," Hars urged in his enthusiasm. From the way he addressed his superior, it seemed that Zelson Marquet was no authoritarian.

"Ahhhhhhh…" sighed Marquet, parting the curtain.

Tony made the same sound but with far different implication, for the creature that came through the hangings was an impossibly whimsical combination of ungulate and avian. The theories about Only that had plagued Tony went gibbering back into the hiding places of his skull.

"Sarlag?" asked Zelson Marquet.

Tony made a garbled answer.

"What place are you from? Your tongue comes easily to me. Therefore it must be a fairly complex world, your species a technologically advanced one."

"Gnum," said Tony.

"Tony Mac Kenzie?" Hars asked in concern. "Rye?"

"Yes. Yaw. I'll be okay in a minute." He turned to the short-bodied winged bull that stood before him, resplendent in fringed brocade. "Did you speak English?"

"If that is what you call it. I speak as you do." The creature paused, then, with a twitch very like a smile, went on. "I perceive I have alarmed you. It was not intended, I can assure you. Perhaps you will join me in my inner chamber and we may talk more freely?"

Tony nodded, frightened suddenly.

There was a fluent exchange between Zelson Marquet and Hars. Hars ducked his head briefly and withdrew, whistling.

"Now then, will you come this way, Mac Kenzie?"

He did.

The inner chamber, as Marquet called it, was finished in polished woods that gave a ruddy glow in the light. It smelled of resin and wax.

There were two chairs and a long padded bench on a carpet of an uncanny red. Toward the window there stood four foot-high candle sticks that rose another two feet in white wax.

"Will you be seated?" asked Tony's unorthodox host as he settled onto the bench, stretching out his front legs and admiring his polished hooves.

Tony glanced around the room, then sat in the higher-backed chair. "Well?"

"I recall standing by a large amphitheater on my home world, having just delivered a great speech, thinking myself fortunate to be born on such a planet. Then I was wandering about in that wood over there"—he gestured idly in the direction of the window—"feeling as if I'd been in an avalanche and wondering if I were sane."

Tony permitted himself an upward twist of his lip, then said: "I was working in a catatonic clinic. I went on my break slightly after midnight. Hars found me when I woke up. Where did I wake up?" This last was accusing.

"Only. I don't know where it is, either. After dark, you must come and see the heavens. We are quite alone here. There is no moon. And the stars, what few can be seen, are distant."

"Really?" A skeptical eyebrow raised.

But Zelson Marquet would not discuss it. "You said a catatonic clinic. It does not sound a very happy place."

"It is not. I am a psychiatrist. I treat diseases of the mind."

"A clinic would imply a great many cases. Perhaps an epidemic."

"Yes." Tony was silent.

"I see." Zelson leaned farther back on the bench, spreading his amber and copper wings and then folding them back against his body.

"I am not sure that I am not with those patients of mine. I cannot be sure that I haven't conjured all of this out of memories, legends, and fairy tales. Even you. There were winged bulls in Assyria or Babylon or someplace like that. Hars is a combination of Beowulf and Perseus. This place is part castle and part frontier village. The animals are strange, but not that strange. I may have escaped into my mind."

"But."

"But," Tony agreed.

"I will make a bargain with you, Tony Mac Kenzie. I ask you to watch and observe, to live our life, and if you can, tell me in a year's time if this is a dream, For I would truly like to know."

Tony tried to speak.

"No. Now it is what you call summer. When the world is this way again, we will talk of these things." Zelson Marquet rose, shrugging his shoulders to adjust his brocades.

"In our legendry," he added vaguely, "there are creatures not unlike you. *You* may be the figment of *my* imagination."

"Sir?" Tony asked cautiously just as Zelson Marquet got to the door. The fantastic creature turned. "What will I do?"

Zelson Marquet laughed his dusky laugh. "Whatever you can."

And so it was that summer faded into fall and the leaves of Only turned from their odd blue-green to parchment and gold. The crops were brought in and the few houses in the wood were reinforced for the winter and the time of snow that had flakes with eight points.

In the winter nights Tony would walk under the sky, seeing the shards of distant light that might be stars. That might be home for him, then, but for not finding a familiar point, without seeing the forms in the sky that had guided the ships of Earth home. He walked and pondered against the bitter wind, the bleak night. There was nothing for him to do. He could give the people of Only nothing. He might have managed electricity if he knew more about it, but his knowledge did not go beyond first year college chemistry. He might have given them photographic processes, but although he had been an amateur photographer of good standing, he did not know how to start from scratch.

He stayed with Hars Baldur and his wife, a tall woman with the mellifluous name of Shanniawanna. He met the others in the community. He talked to the children, in particular to Indri Wexwer, the boy who had spoken to him that first day. In fact, it was Indri who accidentally put Tony onto his life's work.

Tony had been walking in the winter forest, having just discarded the idea of starting the manufacture of paper because it would need more wood pulp than would be practical for them to take from the forest, when Indri came upon him.

"Ayeh, Indri."

"Ayeh, Tony. Wa fir die?"

"I'm looking for something to do."

"Ho," said the child, nodding. His tawny mane of hair fell down over his eyes and he wiped it away impatiently. "As ohm."

Tony looked down with interest, the doctor in him still active. "What's the matter?"

"Nae fir die." He shrugged it off, indifferent.

In the deeper part of Tony's mind there were connections being made. He adjusted his rumpled face a bit and picked up his pace. "Bored, huh? What do you do to keep from being bored?"

"Nae."

"Don't you have games?" But Tony's mind had answered that for himself. He had never seen the children playing games or with toys more complex than simple carts or clay dolls.

"Indri, old man, you have just given me an idea. Thank you. Thank you very much."

Indri grinned at the crazy sarlag. "Nae be," he said.

The monochromatic winter gave way to polyphonic spring and activity increased. The fields were planted, the vines cleared, the roads evened out and bridges shored up.

Tony did none of this. He was busy gathering wood, and having Shanniawanna weave him the finest, hardest cloth that she could.

He made a few experiments and discarded the wood in favor of small hollow bones. Then he began his search for string. Finally, after weeks of experiment, he managed to get a fiber from certain of the underbrush, which, when pounded to a pulp, could be drawn into a long flexible string. After waxing it was remarkably strong. As the summer began he was ready.

He sat on the edge of the field and began to make a kite.

"Ahhhhh," said Zelson Marquet as he passed Tony on his third day of kite flying. "You have accomplished a thing."

"Yeah," said Tony, keeping his hand on the string, making the kite nod in the sky.

"What will you do with it?" asked the lordly beast; for Tony had learned that Zelson Marquet was very much the lord of this part of Only.

"Play with it. It's just a toy."

The reaction was enigmatic. "Indeed,"

The end of summer came and went. Tony did not talk with Marquet because he was too busy making kites. With the next winter there were ten children out gathering bone and brush in the leafless forest and as the world turned around to spring the sky of Only blossomed with kites.

"Wa gud wef am?" Hars asked one day as he held the string of a large kite billowing above him.

"Gud fir am. Fir be." Tony answered, marveling again how easily the children understood him in his English (*wish fulfillment*, said a diagnostic voice in his head), and wondering how Zelson communicated with him.

The season went round again and the next spring was a riot in the sky with colors and varieties that Tony had never dreamed of. Diamond shapes with heraldic beasts paraded with bird-shaped kites and box-shaped kites and forms like a butterfly that flapped it wings.

That winter there were expeditions into the deeper parts of the forest for tougher fibers, and ropes were made to hold the giant frames being made in the snowed-in cottages.

Three years later a young man named Indri Wexwer rode a kite into the sky.

"Yes, Tony," said Zelson Marquet. "I must congratulate you. You people of—Earth, do you call it?—have remarkable toys."

"I just hope he doesn't break his neck." Tony anxiously watched the cable play out while Zelson Marquet opened the new Festival of Kites.

"I must confess that I did not put much stock in this when you began," the lord went on, "but now I cannot see any limits to it. Even with my wings, I cannot fly."

Tony managed to shrug it off.

"Ahhh. I did not tell you. Hars found another sarlag the other day."

Tony turned abruptly. "He did? Where?"

"In the wood. About where you were found."

"Well, where is he? Can I see him? What's he like?"

Zelson fluttered his wings, sighing a bit. "Ah, no. I regret that this one did not live. I saw it before Hars dispatched it. It could not have survived here."

Above them the great kite soared.

"What was it like? Why do you say that?"

"It was not like us. It was a creature of many feet and what seemed voracious appetite. It ate the five elves that found it."

"I see," Tony murmured.

"I am sorry Tony. I knew that more of your kind would be reassuring to you." He left off to admire the kite, but continued absently as the young man above them began to descend. "Have you decided if this is real or not?"

"I haven't given it much thought."

"Yes. We must talk of this someday."

Laughing, Tony nodded. "When this kite craze is over."

In twenty years they had gliders. Indri had made the first one. Hars and Shanniawanna had had three children and the two boys rode kites from the time they could walk. From the time they could run they rode gliders.

It was shortly after that that a new sarlag was found, and although she resembled neither Tony nor Zelson Marquet, she was compatible with life on Only. Her spindly seven feet were ungainly in Only's gravity but she managed, and she combined her acute manual dexterity with the skill of the glider pilots: Only invented cartography.

"And there," a faded Tony was saying to a much-aged Zelson Marquet, "there seems to be an ocean, Hars' boys have been out several kilometers and can't find an end to it."

The old lord studied carefully for his eyesight was failing him, He moved his wings deeper into his brocades.

"Now here, by this mountain range," Tony went on, following the lines on the drawing, "there is a village. Indri plans to lead an expedition over there as soon the new gliders are finished."

"What about the people we've found by the high lakes?"

"Everything is fine. They have a barter system already and make many fine utensils with metal."

"What about the ones by the lowland forest?" Zelson turned his heavy head toward a map on the wall. "Any luck?"

"No. And I think they must have the crossbow. The one glider we managed to recover had been torn by bolts."

"I had hoped it would not come to that," the winged beast mused. His binocular vision eyes stared evenly at Tony. "You have told me enough about wars."

Tony was silent.

Wethiphavoh drifted in. The third sarlag held new sketches in front of her, offering them for review.

"Thanks, Weth. They should be the last of them for this year."

She nodded his length and stood wistfully by the window. It was physically impossible for her to stand any way but wistfully.

Zelson watched her for a while. "Tell me, Tony," he said at last, "do all your elaborate excuses for this place existing in your mind make provision for her?"

"It hadn't occurred to me. Not offhand." He looked at Weth, at the pale translucency of her, and thought. "I guess I might have dredged her out of Poe or Lovecraft. There are wraiths all over literature."

"I do not know this Poe or Lovecraft. They were orators, I suppose."

"In a way." He turned it over in his mind for a while. "Weth, where you are from, are there legends about short solid things like me or winged bulls like Zelson?"

"Yes, there are. I have wondered about it many times." She spoke in an strident voice which always grated on Tony's nerves, no matter how he tried to prepare himself.

Zelson sighed, settling onto his bench sadly.

"But," the keening scratch went on, "I do not recall any tales of a place like this."

"Never mind, Weth." Tony said. "This is something that has been bothering me ever since I showed up here twenty years ago."

From his place on the bench Zelson Marquet tapped his hooves eagerly, watching the dust shine in the slanting light. "Tony Mac Kenzie, if you could go back to that place where you were Doctor Alan Lowell Anthony Mac Kenzie, would you?"

This startled Tony. He was about to answer one way and then changed his mind. "No," he said eventually. "It was overcrowded, underfed, over-contaminated and exhausted. I was part of a profession that only worked at staving off the inevitable. Here, at least, I have done something."

Both the other sarlags nodded, feeling they too had done something.

"Then you would not leave."

"No," Tony laughed. "This may all be an escape. I remember a story about a sage who was not certain if he were a butterfly dreaming of being a man or a man who had dreamt of being a butterfly. Wherever this is, I am here."

"This is Only." Zelson Marquet made the words with love.

So did Tony. "This is home."

FACE YOUR FURS
by Seanan McGuire

L ike most investments made by large media corporations, it seemed like
a good idea at the time. Mascot costumes—known more colloquially
as "fur suits"—were hot, oppressive things that were virtually impossible
to clean to any reasonable standard, could only fit people within a very
narrow range of measurements without dramatic alteration, and never
looked quite right, being almost as likely to terrify children as they were to
enthrall them. They limited motion and field of vision, and making heads
that could move their mouths in a semi-realistic manner was expensive
and labor-intensive enough to not be worth it.

Clearly the answer was getting rid of them. But what was Easter without
the Easter Bunny? What were a wide variety of world-famous amusement
parks without the singing, dancing manifestations of their most famous
properties? The idea was untenable.

The smart thing would have been to invest in better suits while working
on robotic replacements, which might have been expensive during the
roll-out stage, but which would have been followed by a reduction in
human labor costs dramatic enough to make any shareholder's eyes light
up. But "smart" and "corporate" are rarely mentioned in the same sentence
for very good reasons.

Why upgrade in two steps when there were solutions on the horizon
that would allow for upgrading in a single, much more efficient sweep?
Some people muttered about "human rights violations," but they were by
and large ignored as the large entertainment conglomerates began slipping
new clauses into their contracts, clauses about room and board and total
isolation in the event that one of the costumes became somehow stuck,
hollow promises about "reversion," and offers of additional compensation.

Worker's rights groups attempted to sound the alarm about the new
contract clauses, and found themselves gaining surprisingly little traction.

"After all," said one skeptic, "when someone starts trying to tell you that the people who make your kid's favorite cartoons are planning to play *The Island of Dr. Moreau* with their employees, it's sort of difficult to take them seriously."

Difficult, perhaps, but still necessary.

Companies with enormous amounts of money have always been inclined to run roughshod over the needs and desires of people whose resources fail to match their own. Following the implementation of Reagan's corporate-friendly tax policies, when wealth inequality began to spike, first in America, and then in the rest of the western world (oligarchs have never been fans of being left out of the hot new way to exploit the masses), the list of people whose resources failed to match the larger corporations rapidly spiraled upward, until it included almost everyone there was to include. It was a new era of robber barons, enshrined by a seemingly untouchable series of legal and social protections. Everything old eventually becomes new again, and now those cascading human rights violations were new and in the hands of corporate entities whose only goal was devotion to the endlessly escalating profit margin.

The scientists with their robots were dismissed. The ones who had dedicated their time and attention to improving the construction of the mascot costumes as they currently existed were given their notice to find a new place to work. The ones who had come up with the solution that looked the most like destroying lives for the sake of a profit margin were given an unlimited R&D budget and all the resources they needed to change the world.

The nanite channels were installed in the existing suits under the guise of thorough cleaning.

The nanites themselves were released six weeks later, on July 17, 2025.

The release occurred while Molly was halfway through her shift as Honey the Bear at a theme park that didn't call itself the Happiest Place on Earth, because who wants to deal with Disney's lawyers when they don't have to? She didn't immediately notice that anything had happened. There was a dull tingling at her temples, followed by the feeling that the gloves of her suit—which had never fit her hands properly—had finally shifted into position. There was a brief but intense pressure in her bladder, which she suppressed as much as she could. She didn't have a bathroom break scheduled for an hour, and her handlers were unlikely to be happy if she told them she'd had an extra cup of coffee at breakfast.

The life of a fursuit performer was not a glamourous one, and was unlikely to ever become so. Molly kept gamboling for the children, who laughed in delight and raced around her, ecstatic at having the attention of a beloved cartoon character. It wasn't just the gloves that had slotted themselves into position; for the first time since donning the suit, it seemed like her peripheral vision was keeping up with the motion of the children around her.

Her scheduled break came and went, passing the point where safety regulations meant that she should have been allowed to remove the suit and pass it on to the next performer making minimum wage. Molly kept on dancing, not noticing the time until she found herself in the afternoon character conga line behind Pounce the cat and Charles Chupacabra. His foil and natural prey, Greta the goat, was absent, in part because Molly should have been in her costume by now.

She placed her gloved hands on Charles's shoulders, trying to remember to think of them as paws, and almost jerked away when she felt fur through the skin of her palms. She'd been in the suit for too long, that was all. She was probably dehydrated and suffering from heat exhaustion. She kept her hands clamped down on Charles's shoulders, following him through the conga.

He glanced back at her once, and she blinked, startled by how realistic his face looked. They must have upgraded his mask. Hopefully it was more comfortable than the old one had been.

It wasn't until after the conga, when she finally escaped backstage and attempted to remove the head of her costume, that she began to realize what had happened, impossible as it seemed and should have been.

It took six handlers and over an hour for them to get her to stop screaming.

It was all legal, of course, thanks to the contracts the performers had signed, the contracts with their impossible clauses and inexplicable promises. Sure, their humanity had been stripped away by the company, and sure, they were trapped in the soft, intentionally bulbous bodies of beloved children's entertainment characters, but they would be taken care of until their terms of employment ended, and thanks to the nanotech that had been used to rebuild them, they wouldn't suffer. Even the ailments and medical conditions they had been living with before the transition had been taken care of, smoothed away like ripples in the sand. They would be restored to their human bodies at the end of their employment, able to go back to their lives better than they'd been when they left them.

Over the next several weeks, Molly and the others explored and familiarized themselves with their new bodies, learning what they could and couldn't eat—Honey turned out to have the dietary needs of an ordinary bear, which Molly found to be quite a relief; Charles was on a strictly liquid diet, unable to digest anything apart from goat blood; it would be another few weeks before his overall distress led him to discover that he could also tolerate vodka—how much sleep they needed, and, most importantly from a psychological standpoint, where their genitals had gone. Once those questions had been answered, while things were still terrible from a mental and emotional standpoint, the various performers impacted by their failure to review standard low-wage contracts with their lawyers were forced to concede that these were their lives now. They rose, washed their furry, rotund bodies, and followed their handlers into the parks, where guests applauded the improvements in their costumes, and small children gamboled around them, no longer at risk from their lack of depth perception.

Various pixies and fairy tale princesses became much more vigilant about applying their eyeliner and perfecting their pouts, suddenly afraid of a full-body makeover to fully conform them to their characters. Honey—no, Molly; it was getting difficult to remember Molly sometimes, like she was merely a very vivid dream dreamt by a fuzzy cartoon bear—looked at them with contempt. Even if they were granted perfect makeup and screen-accurate hair by the company, they would still be human, still capable of texting and typing and all those other things that required fine motor skills.

It was all legal. It was all ethical, at least according to the corporate board of ethics, and if they said it, it must be true. It was all reversible, and would be undone when they completed their contracts.

And then Polly the Peahen laid an egg.

One unpleasant consequence of the semi-consensual transformation of so many employees: the "only one person per character at a time" policy had become strictly enforced law. Molly was the only Honey the Bear for the entire park complex. Most of her understudies had been fused with other roles. A few had been released from employment and gone home feeling like they'd narrowly escaped a fate worse than death. So when someone was feeling unwell, still being human enough to catch colds from the small, sticky children who swarmed around them, burying germy fingers in suddenly personal fur, the character they had been transformed into would be absent from the park. The expense of the reversion process leant a certain amount of job security to their positions, and legally, the corporation had to offer sick time, since they were now considered truly fulltime employees, working twenty-four hours a day as the characters they couldn't get away from.

Polly missed work on Monday, missed work again on Tuesday, and on Wednesday, human resources went to her apartment to see if she had suffered some sort of attack that would keep her away from her duties for much longer. What they found was a smug, wide-eyed bird-woman sitting atop an egg the size of a watermelon, wings mantled forward to protect it from anyone who tried to get too close. She hadn't been pregnant at the time of her conversion, and after some prodding, she admitted that Peter the Peacock was the father.

That raised as many questions as it answered, and thirty days later, when the egg hatched and a human-peacock hybrid tumbled into the world, it raised more questions still. There was to be no reversion to human for Polly and Peter's daughter, who had no contract with the corporation, and whose parents wouldn't allow her to sign one. She was beautiful exactly as she was, they said, the first member of her species to walk the Earth—and to be fair, her fingers were slimmer and more dexterous than either of her parents', having developed organically, and not due to a nanotech melding with an intentionally neonatic design. She was fully capable of doing whatever needed to be done, without being transformed into something that held no innate appeal to her infant sense of self.

Molly and the others, who were mostly mammals, received immediate sex ed training and procreation lectures from the company lawyers. They couldn't forbid their employees to get pregnant, which was viewed as a human right—and they still possessed a certain number of those, despite being questionably human in their current conditions—but they could make it clear that employment contracts would be extended to make up any time that was lost to needing to take their employees off display. A certain number, like Charlie the Chupacabra, were the only members of their new species, and were viewed as incapable of reproduction. They promptly became very popular with their peers, most of whom wished to avoid pregnancy and the subsequent extensions of their transformation, but who still experienced sexual attraction and arousal the same way they had when they'd been human.

Molly, who had only been looking to fill a summer before returning to college, had never felt so trapped in her life. She prowled back and forth in her company apartment when not out in the park dancing for the entertainment of children, fighting her clumsy hands for the ability to use a keyboard and communicate with the outside world. Eventually, she was able to place an order with a medical supply company for a tablet system designed for people with muscular disabilities impacting their fine motor control. Once it was delivered, she began reaching out to the world. What was the corporation she worked for going to do, she reasoned, fire her? She was an investment now, proof of their new technological party trick, and her contract was still good for another three years. Signing it had seemed reasonable when she'd still expected to be able to walk away at the end of August. Now it was an endless reminder to read the fine print when dealing with people whose lawyers made more in an hour than she could expect to make in a year.

Her first Reddit AMA was a blazing success. Her second brought the trolls and griefers out of the depths of the site, and included several questions of a grossly sexual nature. She answered them as politely and clinically as she could, having agreed, after all, to be asked "anything" by the site's denizens. The next morning began with a knock on her apartment door an hour before her shift was due to start. She answered it to find five men in a meticulously tailored suits, each carrying a leather briefcase, waiting for her in the hall.

"Yes?" she asked.

"Miss Taylor, we're here because you've violated the morality clause of your contract," said the first of the men. "You agreed not to do anything that might damage the family-friendly image of the character you portray."

"Am I fired?" she asked, unable to keep the excitement out of her voice. Firing would mean a return to human form. She could go home. She could—

"No. But your internet access has been revoked for the foreseeable future. We trust that you will think more carefully before going against your contract after this." The five men turned then, and walked away without another word, leaving her to wonder why they had sent so many people to tell her they were cutting off the internet.

It was already disconnected by the time she closed the door and returned to her computer. So was the cable.

So was the internet in all the adjoining apartments, and everyone quickly learned whose fault that was. She was not only a bear, she was an outcast, unable to socialize with any of the people who should have been her peers.

It was the worst punishment she could possibly have endured.

The next problem came three months later, when Molly went to bed and stayed there for a week. The company doctor said that she was entering hibernation, having become more of a bear than anyone had really anticipated. A large bed was constructed inside Honey's Tree, the private meet-and-greet zone where she was supposed to visit with her young fans. The next time she fell asleep and refused to wake, she was carried to the bed, where visiting children could get their picture next to her sleeping, unresponsive form. This attraction proved to be surprisingly popular, enough so that when she began to stir at the beginning of spring, several parents asked whether she would be a quiet napping zone for their children again next winter.

She awoke back in her apartment, with a fridge full of salmon and berries, and spent three days eating to recover lost fat and muscle tissue before she was able to go through her mail and find that she'd been paid for the time she spent on display. To her chagrin, the money was a better surprise than the loss of privacy was a bad one. Perhaps they had made a bear out of her after all.

Meanwhile, the lawsuits were working their way through the courts. The families of the transformed were unsure as to the legality of the contracts, and while the various corporate lawyers would have sworn they'd covered every possible base, they hadn't considered the public relations nightmare presented by parents, spouses, and the occasional child crying for the news cameras.

And then, somehow, the news of little Penny Peacock made it to the media. Despite being barely six months old, she was the size of a five year old child, with the vocabulary and mental development to match. Demands that everyone be released from their contracts immediately flooded the courts, alongside a surprising number of demands that their technology be made public. Stocks plummeted.

Molly began to hope.

Six months after Penny's existence had been revealed to the world, the command was sent to the nanites to unlock the carriers from their costumes. Everyone was pulled out of the parks for the grand moment, to avoid traumatizing children. Polly and Peter stood with their daughter, whose body contained no nanites, and who should have been untouched by the transformation to come. No one from corporate had seemed overly concerned about traumatizing her.

Ten minutes after the signal was sent, Polly frowned and asked, "Well? Is something meant to happen?"

Molly, who had been swallowing the same question, said nothing.

The man with the remote looked faintly panicked and flicked the switch again before stepping back. "I need to make some calls," he said, and fled.

The various non-costumed characters in the room exchanged glances and grumbled, impatient to receive their lives back. Only Molly was both silent and still. She'd been expecting something like this since she'd realized the truth of what had happened. Unexpected consequences. There were always unexpected consequences.

When the man from corporate returned, pale and shaking and accompanied by a pair of lawyers, it was to offer apologies. The original transition had assumed a mixture of human cells and inanimate fabrics and internal structures, all prepared over the course of weeks for the process of integration. Their bodies no longer contained their original human cells. They were chimera now, mingling humanity, and the various species they had become. The technology that already existed wasn't enough to restore them, a problem that would only become more pronounced as time passed and locked them deeper into their new forms.

Molly got up and left the room without a word while they were still apologizing.

The seemingly permanent nature of the transformation wasn't enough to discourage everyone who wanted the technology released to the public. Certain special interest groups mustered the most volume; it was one of those groups that eventually managed to penetrate the company housing under the guise of a cleaning firm. They approached Polly and Peter first, offering to rescue them before their daughter could be experimented on. When Penny found her parents laughing uproariously at the very idea, she fixed the strangers with an avian eye and politely threatened to peck their guts out. They fled for an easier target.

They found Molly.

Molly, who had done her illicit AMAs before the company stopped her; Molly, whose pictures with the children had been held up several times as evidence of human trafficking masked under a simple entertainment contract. Molly, who was correctly viewed as the weak link among her peers.

Molly, who was more than happy to be freed from her mockery of a contract, as she would never be freed from the mien of a copyrighted character. Molly, whose first television appearance happened three days later, when she went on a popular daytime talk show to discuss the way they'd been changed without their consent, only to become virtual prisoners of the corporation. "Anti-Capitalist Honey the Bear" memes sparked briefly to popularity, only to fade out in the face of the reality of Molly herself. Poor, trapped Molly, who would never be human again, no matter how hard she wished upon a star.

There were some magics technology still lacked the power to recreate.

Six months after Molly's television debut, the nanites used in her transformation were used in a social terror attack on a masked ball. The world had changed, and wouldn't be changing back. The corporation that had pioneered this technology was forced to pay a minor compensation to the people whose lives they'd ruined, who would never be human again, even as their tech spread across the world. The loss in revenue as their child-friendly characters became less marketable by the day was viewed as a much greater punishment.

Polly and Peter Peacock legally changed their names after Polly laid her third egg. Molly found love with a transformed grizzly bear from a Russian entertainment consortium.

Still, no one built a better mascot suit.

DALE & MABEL
by Scott Sigler

D ale pounded his fist against the La-Z-Boy's armrest.
"Skip Bayless, you didn't play a *god*damn down of football, what the *hell* do you know?"

Dale's wife looked up from her Kindle. She sat to his right in a matching La-Z-Boy, the two chairs separated only by a small table that held the phone, drinks, and whatever snack she'd made for her husband. No dinner on the La-Z-Boys—not *ever*; dinner was at the table and had been for almost fifty years—but snacks were a different story.

"Dale, honey, you know the people inside the TV can't hear you, right?"

He waved a hand at her. "Oh, shush. Super Bowl is a week away and Skip's wrinkled ass has to talk about the Bears needing a change at quarterback?"

"That white boy can't be more than fifty-five—your ass is *way* more wrinkled than his."

"Listen to him and that punk partner of his, Stephen A. Smith, all smug and whatnot," Dale said, letting his anger override his wife's one-liner. "The two of them, telling Trent Dilfer that he doesn't know what the Bears should do at QB. Ridiculous."

Mabel looked at the screen. "Dilfer? Was he a quarterback?"

Dale pounded the armrest again. "He won a damn Super Bowl, with … with …"

The team escaped him. Who had Dilfer played for? Dale's annoyance ticked up another notch, his frustration with the stuffed shirts magnified by frustration at his spotty memory. He'd been an NFL fan all his life, used to be a walking encyclopedia of football knowledge. Now that long-held info was just one more thing slipping away, and—

"*Baltimore,*" Dale said, the city finally popping into his head. "With Ray-Ray."

"Ray-Ray?"

"Ray Lewis. That retired linebacker who gets fired up about anything and everything."

"Oh," Mabel said. "I know him. I do like that Ray Lewis. He's handsome, just like you."

Dale huffed. "That fucking Skip Bayless. Ridiculous."

Mabel picked up the remote control and hit "pause."

She had made a joke to calm him down, she had compared him to Ray Lewis to calm him down, but neither had worked. Then, she went for her trump card—Dale saw Mabel reach across the little table. She softly patted his arm.

"Dale, sugarplum, relax," she said softly. "Don't get all upset."

The same thing happened five or six times a day, depending on whether Dale was watching the so-called moronic conservatives on Fox, the pinko commies on MSNBC, the which-way-is-the-wind-blowing pansies on CNN, or the self-appointed experts on ESPN. Some idiot talking head on the TV would spout gibberish that only a thirtysomething "expert" could believe made any sense at all, and it would piss Dale off—Mabel would softly remind him that he was no spring chicken anymore. Getting upset could cause problems. Getting upset could get a brother *killed*. A heart attack wasn't a bullet in the head by any stretch, but at his age the end result was probably the same.

Just that pat on the arm worked, though, at least a little. It worked enough to make him wonder, as he did those same five or six times a day, what he'd do when Mabel passed on and there was no one there to calm him down.

She rubbed his arm. "It's just a game, baby."

His anger was bothering her. That meant he had to put a stop to it—Skip Bayless wasn't worth upsetting Mabel Johnson.

"All right, baby," Dale said. "I'm all right."

She leaned over her armrest, wincing a little when her back twanged her, as it often did, and kissed his temple.

"I'm just looking out for you, Gramps."

Dale tried to hide his smile but couldn't. She knew just where to kiss him, right behind the eye where it tickled—a little but not enough to make him laugh—and felt warm and soft.

It felt *good*. It always had.

"I know, Grammy," he said. "I know."

She pulled him a little closer for a firm kiss on the cheek. The pull zinged Dale's own back (matching injuries weren't as cute as matching chairs, mind you), but, just like her, he ignored it. Quick kisses and touches were the currency of their love; they both knew there weren't that many years left until that currency ran out forever.

She leaned away, then came in for a second kiss on the cheek.

"I was wrong," she said. "You don't look like Ray Lewis. You're far more handsome than he is. More distinguished. How about I get you a beer to help you relax?"

She slid into her chair, used the little electric button to raise it up. Best money they had ever spent, those expensive chairs. Heated seats to ease pain in her hip and in both of their backs, built-in vibrators to relax their sore old legs, and an electric lift that put her almost at a standing position so she didn't have to struggle to sit.

Mabel had a way to notch her cane between the armrest and the chair back. She pulled it out, used it to slowly walk to the kitchen. She hummed an Etta James tune, same one she'd hummed in the old days after the two of them made love.

Dale wanted to get up, to help her, but he knew better; there wasn't much left Mabel could do on her own. Bringing her man a beer was one of those things, and he'd learned not to say anything about it.

He un-paused the TV. Skip Bayless was yammering on like a conceited idiot again, then the picture changed.

The president … on ESPN? Addressing the House. Or the Senate, maybe? If it was on ESPN, it was on all the channels.

Dale felt his chest tightening: *war.*

Dirt poor American kids going off to fight in some foreign land, just as he had done when he was nineteen. Bullets and bombs, fire, burned flesh, killing … the government could never get its fill of blood.

President Sandra Blackmon, wearing red, as always, babbling through the usual crap, every sentence met by Republican applause and Democrat glares.

The ticker on the bottom of the screen drew Dale's attention.

… infectious agent that resulted in the Detroit disaster identified … scientists have discovered way to inoculate against the infection … President Blackmon claims "disease will be wiped from the face of the earth" …

"What the hell? This ain't war."

He tried to simultaneously read the ticker and listen, and also read the sidebar that flashed up all kinds of information. Goddamn news channels couldn't just give you one message at a time anymore, always beating you in the head with more than a body could manage at one time. This was about some kind of infection, an infection that could turn people into killers? What the hell was that about?

Something familiar … something Dale couldn't quite place …

He'd forgotten that Mabel had paused the TV. Dale fast-forwarded until the picture was caught up in real time.

"... *can't stress this enough*," Blackmon said. "*The surgeon general and the Centers for Disease Control urge you to cooperate with local distribution centers to get the treatment. The emergency broadcast system will be transmitting delivery days and locations. There will be enough for everyone. Until you receive your medication, limit contact with others and stay indoors as much as possible.*"

Mabel came into the living room carrying a beer in each hand. She set them down on the table that separated their chairs. As Blackmon droned on, Dale took his beer, drank half of it in one pull.

Mabel slowly, cautiously, eased into her chair. The chair's electric motor hummed as she lowered it to the seated position.

"The president? Why'd you turn the channel?"

"I didn't," Dale said. "She's on the ESPN."

The camera zoomed in on Blackmon's face. She had her "serious look" down cold. The woman knew how to work a crowd, that was for sure.

"*Let me say I do not fault my predecessor, or his party, for allowing things to come to this point. These are exceptional times not only in the history of our nation, but also of the world. Together, we will forever end the greatest threat the planet Earth has ever faced.*"

Mabel picked up the remote and again froze the picture.

"Dale, honey, what's going on?"

He took another pull before answering. Beer, one of life's glories, just as cold and nice to an old man as it was to a young one. And a beer brought by your wife? Things like that made life worth living.

"Some *bull*shit about microbes or whatnot, making people killers," he said. "And the government is passing out some kind of *inoculant* that's supposed to protect us? Inoculant. *Please*. Like I'm supposed to believe this *bull*shit that little microbes or whatever are going to infect us and make us crazy?"

Mabel turned in her chair, a move that made her wince.

"Dale, honey ... I know sometimes you don't remember all that well. You don't remember Detroit?"

He stared at her, then turned back to the TV. Detroit ... Detroit ... there was something about that, something big, but his disloyal brain wouldn't give it up.

"Course I do," he lied.

Her hand again reached across the small table, but this time her fingers took his, squeezed them. He loved her with all his being but knew her gesture meant he'd forgotten something important again—she was about to tell him what that something was, and that made him hate her.

"Cody Murphy," she said softly. "You remember Cody?"

What kind of condescending question was that? Of course he remembered Cody Murphy. Best white man Dale had ever known. They'd served together in 'Nam and stayed close all the years after, and ...

It came back in a rush: Cody was dead.

He died when Blackmon's predecessor, President Gutierrez, dropped a nuke on Detroit to—supposedly—stop alien microbes from spreading out of the city and turning America into a nation of psycho killers. Six years back, maybe?

The crushing weight of Cody's loss hit Dale all over again, fresh as the now-remembered first time, a hollow-point round in the chest. The man who had been side by side with him in the jungle was gone forever. Dale missed that man so goddamn much. Hell, he even missed Cody's wife, Lorna, even though that woman's voice was so screechy it made Dale want to pack earplugs back in the days when he and Mabel still traveled.

Mabel ... she always reminded Dale of the bad things. Sometimes the world was a happier place when things stayed forgotten.

"I remember," he said.

And I don't want to ... I don't want to ...

How could he have forgotten something like Detroit? How could he have forgotten that his own government *nuked* an American city? How could he have forgotten the fallout warnings, staying in the apartment for weeks, wondering if it had been a real threat or some conspiracy thought up by the same bullshit military complex that had once sent Dale off to poke holes in Vietnamese teenagers?

President Gutierrez—that liberal piece of shit—killed hundreds of thousands of Americans on the recommendation of ... of ...

"That scientist," Dale said. "The one who told Gutierrez to drop the bomb. What's her name?"

"Montoya," Mabel said, her voice still soft and patient. "Margaret Montoya."

Yeah, that was it. Dale felt a mood coming on, the kind where he'd yell at anyone about anything. Since the only two people in the apartment were him and Mabel, that meant he'd yell at her.

Dale took another swig of beer, calmed himself. He'd been yelling at her a lot, lately, taking out the frustration of his faltering mind on the one person who'd been there for him, without fail, for over five decades.

"Now, I must show you some very disturbing footage," Blackmon said. *"This footage underscores the reason we must all work together in this inoculation effort. This is footage from a research facility where our CDC team is studying the latest round of the infection."*

Dale watched. A camera looking down into a glass cell. A young, fit white man strapped to a metal table ... triangular growths under his skin, *pyramid* growths, with a black eye on every side ... those pyramids pushing, bouncing, twitching, trying to break free from the skin ...

Mabel's grip on his hand changed, from the *I'll always help you* squeeze to *I'm scared and you are the only one who can make me feel safe* squeeze. One second she was patient with her doddering fool of a husband, the next she wanted him to be what he'd always been: her protector.

He squeezed back.

She picked up the remote with her free hand and turned off the TV.

They sat there in silence together, thinking about what they had just seen. That young man was fucked, no question. That's what this disease did?

"Dale, from what they're saying on the TV, is what happened in Detroit happening here in Chicago?"

How the fuck was he supposed to know?

"Maybe," he said.

"Then should we just go?"

She made it sound so simple. They didn't even own a car. They had their groceries delivered because he couldn't manage carrying anything more than a few rolls of toilet paper from the nearby Walgreens. And if Mabel could carry her purse without dropping it? That was a good day. Their matching pair of bad backs and her shot-to-hell hip made every task an ordeal.

Just this newscast alone meant the roads would be clogged. He and Mabel would be in a bus for *hours,* if they could even find space on one, which he doubted. Dale wasn't sure whether Mabel could handle that much time in a seat that didn't heat up and vibrate.

They'd had a car when they were younger, but now, what was the point? They both hated driving. And $300 a month for parking was money well spent elsewhere.

And then there was something even more basic: the president told everyone to avoid contact, to stay indoors. That meant this disease, whatever it might be, was *contagious*. If he took his bride out of this apartment, he was risking her exposure to something that could make her want to murder.

Or, far worse, could make *him* want to murder.

Maybe even murder *her*.

"Dale, honey? Should we go?"

"Maybe," he said. "But not yet."

Not until he was more sure that Chicago was in bad shape. The president said people were distributing the "inoculant," whatever the hell that was.

"Probably going to be crazy outside for a little while," he said. "Best to stay here, stay safe."

Which meant, *stay close to my guns*. Some of his guns were legal. Some weren't. The last time Dale hadn't had a gun near him was before he reported for Basic. Retired and elderly? Didn't matter. After those twelve months in the jungle, killing young men who were trying to kill him, Dale had decided he would never be far from a weapon. He even wanted to be buried with one, just in case that Egyptian shit was right after all.

If he was in his apartment, he was armed. If they left, he could take one sidearm, maybe stash a second, but he had no illusions that somewhere there would be cops and metal detectors—even for an ancient fucker like himself.

That meant outside the apartment, he'd likely be disarmed. Inside the apartment? He had his Ithaca 37, the very same model he'd carried in the jungle. He used to keep it under the bed, but bending down had become a pain in the ass, so he kept it in the closet, along with a hundred rounds of #9 birdshot, another twenty-five rounds of .00 buck. The Ithaca was already loaded (his son was all grown and gone, an almost-grown granddaughter rarely came to visit, no neighbor kids stopped by) with four rounds of #9 and one of the far nastier and deadlier ought buck. Firing that last round would probably break his shoulder, but that sure beat being dead.

His Colt M1911 and a Smith & Wesson Model 39—the "Hush Puppy"— kept the Ithaca company. The Colt was really only for nostalgia's sake; one exactly like it had been with him every day during that nightmare year. The 39 was smaller. Just a .22, but it was the most manageable of his weapons, and nobody wore body armor on their face.

If he left the apartment, the best he could hope for was to keep the Model 39 concealed. If the shit really was about to hit the fan, that wasn't enough.

"We stay," he said. "For now. Stay and hope that things don't get bad."

Mabel nodded slowly. She knew the score just like he did.

The phone rang. Caller ID on the TV said: *Marcus Johnson.*

Mabel reached for the phone, but Dale held out a hand to stop her.

"Let me," he said.

Her hand hovered in midair, trembling slightly, but she nodded, lowered it. She knew what he was going to say.

Dale answered: "Hey there, sonny boy. How's the weather in California?"

"Dad, you watching the news?"

The voice, thick with concern and also with a little bit of aggression. At forty-four, Marcus naturally considered himself the man of the family. Dale had felt the same in his thirties and forties, felt that his own father, in the latter phase of his life, might not be capable of making the right decision—funny how what goes around comes around.

And Dale now knew that his attitude then had silently pissed his father off to no end, because that's what Marcus's attitude did to Dale.

"Yes, we saw it."

"Are you getting out of the city? How's Mom?"

That tone: impatient, demanding … so much like Dale's own.

"Your mother is fine. Everything is okay, son, just relax."

"Like hell I'll relax, Dad. The internet is saying Chicago is going crazy buying cold meds and painkillers, stuff to fight the symptoms of this thing. That means thousands of people are already infected. It's the same thing that happened to Detroit."

"It's not the same," Dale said. "The government is going to distribute that inoculant here."

"That medicine is a bunch of *bull*shit."

Another thing that was surreal about watching your little boy become a grown man—Marcus even swore just like Dale did. The boy had inherited Dale's voice, his cursing style, and, obviously, his distrust for the good word of politicians.

"Dad, I'll be on the next plane out."

"And leave your wife and my granddaughter alone?"

That made Marcus pause. Dale felt bad for his son, he really did, because the kid was in a tough place—come to Chicago to try and make his parents listen to reason, or stay close to his wife and child in what might very well become a national time of crisis.

Mabel sat still, hands in her lap. Dale raised his eyebrows, asking her an unspoken question.

She didn't hesitate: she nodded. Marcus needed to be with their granddaughter, and that was all there was to it. If Marcus and his family remained safe, both Dale and Mabel were ready to face whatever might come.

"Son," Dale said, "we're fine. If there's a problem, the Harrisons in 3-A will take us with them. Besides, boy, you can't afford a damn plane ticket."

"The Harrisons? You're making that shit up," Marcus said. "And I'm not worried about money right now."

Of course you're not. You never are, which is why you're so far in debt.

"It isn't about money," Dale said. "But if you're too much a big man to listen to me, talk to your mother."

Dale handed her the phone.

Mabel took it. "Your father is right," she said. "We're fine."

Dale watched her. She watched him back. They had to convince Marcus that all was well, or he'd charge a same-day flight to his already-maxed credit cards.

Dale and Mabel had each other, sure, but outside of this apartment Marcus was the only one really looking out for them. All of their friends had either died or moved away. Those who remained were just as old as they were, just as physically compromised.

"The Harrisons," Mabel said. "You don't remember them?"

Dale tried not to laugh. Lying was bad, sure, but when it came to tag-team tall tales, his wife could pick up right where he left off.

Mabel sat and listened to her son. Dale couldn't make out any of his words.

Her eyes narrowed, hardened. In that moment, she was thirty again, speaking to a ten-year-old Marcus who had dared to disrespect her.

"Absolutely *not,*" she said. "Your father told you we're fine. Do you think we're helpless?"

Dale waited. Mabel listened.

"We're all right for now," she said. "We have a plan if anything bad happens. You take care of your wife and daughter, Marcus. That's how you can make things easier on your father and me." Pause. "That's right." Pause. "We love you, too, honey. Bye-bye."

She hung up.

"Mouthy kid," Dale said.

"I wonder where he got it from?"

"Always with the sass. Think he'll listen?"

She nodded. "He will. I still don't know why he had to move away, like there's something wrong with Chicago, or—"

This time it was Dale who reached across the table, took his wife's hand.

"Now's not the time for that," he said. "A man has to find his own way. His wasn't here."

Mabel reached to her cheek, calmly wiped away a single tear.

"All right," she said. "Now's not the time for it. So, now that we lied to our only child about having a plan, what do we do? Marcus said the internet said there's thousands of people already infected?"

Dale huffed. "We didn't lie about a damn thing. We have a plan."

"Which is?"

"Fortify," Dale said. "In soldier terms, we defend this position against all aggressors. I'm going to make sure the guns are loaded and ready."

"What do you want me to do?"

Dale smiled. "You, pretty young thing, can go get me another beer. Then lie to me some more about how handsome I am."

She reached over, caressed his cheek. They would face this situation like they had faced everything else for the vast majority of their lives: they would face it together.

Mabel pressed the button to raise her chair.

Dale did the same.

FLINCH
by K.D. McEntire

Copper-wet-warm.

Sam hawked and coughed. Crimson hit the scuffed floor—splat—and before he could take a deep breath, his mouth was full again.

Yep, his nose was definitely busted.

He had suspected as much; Sam's entire face was in agony, flares of splinter sharp pain stabbing into his eyes, his sinuses, scraping down his jaw, and radiating into his throat.

There was a creak and a crackle—Duke Simmons' knees—as the old man squatted slightly beside Sam's chair. He smiled his aging movie-star smile, white and straight and charming, and offered, "Would you like to try again, son?"

Woozily, Sam straightened. Hawked again, but this was less a goober and more a spray of scarlet spittle. A few small flecks landed on the good Duke's cheek, dim and oily-looking, nearly black from the leftover healing crap in his mouth.

"Screw you, boomer."

Sighing, Simmons stood, marked his sheaf of paper, and gestured to the back of the room to whichever pissant mashup trooper had the honor of beating Sam's ass today. The Duke didn't bother wiping off the blood.

"Again."

This time Sam couldn't even scream.

⇒✳⇐

Her name was Jazzi.

Sam had been half in love with her since they were five. She was on Honor Roll and Student Council and in the middle of the drum line in their school's anemic marching band. Track, basketball, volleyball, soccer—Jazzi played them all. It was incidental, but she was pretty too, with a mass of shiny, natural braids that hung to her hips and huge dark eyes.

That wasn't her biggest draw, though, not to Sam.

What he'd always loved most about her was the simple fact that Jazzi was *kind*. She'd sit in the front row of the class with the nerds and the half-blind white kids with their chunky weebo-wannabe, anime-style, coke-bottle glasses and she'd joke with anyone and everyone and, in return, everyone loved her. Drama kids and stoner kids and all four of the preps in their grade. The Instagram chicks and VSCO girls, the ballers and proto-dropouts ... just ... everyone.

Even assholes like him.

Kids would have panic attacks sometimes and always, always Jazzi was there, her hands on their shoulders, her hair swinging like a curtain to cut them off from the world, protecting them. Urging them, "Keep breathing. Keep breathing. In. Out. Keep breathing."

It was, simply, just the way she was.

During the forced quiet of homeroom, the other girls around her would bitch together, pick at their dagger-sharp acrylics or pass notes, sometimes staring longingly at the phone pockets dangling near the classroom door. She didn't even *carry* a phone, which put her in such company as Jebediah - the kid from the crazy cult family - and Gloria, the PETA-obsessed vegan chick who refused to use phones because of virgin plastic or some crap.

Jazzi didn't make it weird, though. It was just one of her quirks, like the line of intricate silver studs that curved around the shell of her left ear, all joined up with a thin white chain, or the sack lunches she carried—a crumpled brown bag with the same food every day—baby carrots and a pickle, half a tuna sandwich, and a handful of blueberries, washing it all down from the same bottle, a battered and scratched green metal canteen she'd been using since kindergarten.

Homecoming had been coming up, and though the Kendale Cruisers hadn't won a season since Sam's Pops had been on the field, Sam still intended to man up and ask Jazzi to the dance. His family didn't have a lot—his dad was an accountant and his mom a secretary and his Pops still ran the body shop out at the dealership—but they were downright rich in comparison to most of the kids he went to school with in their little corner of rural craptopia. With his Pops' help, Sam had spent the summer mowing lawns for chump change, even venturing out into Kendale's barely-there suburbs, just for the chance to put aside a little more.

He'd ended the summer about five shades darker and six thousand richer. It wasn't a lot, not for school, but it was a start. The state university was about eight hundred a class, so that right there was six classes down, plus books and whatnot. Not enough, no, no ... but a start.

If Jazzi said yes, Sam planned to dip into the leftovers just a bit to take her out right.

That had been the plan at least.

He'd had a plan.

The day he was gonna ask her, Jazzi didn't come to school. Which was … well, unheard of, honestly. Every year their homeroom teacher would point out, first day, that Jazzi had made it through their podunk school system so far with perfect attendance. Last May, the principal had even announced it over the intercom, about an hour before final bell. Gave her some bullshit countdown of how many days and hours and crap that she had left to go.

Sam was fairly sure that violated some law somewhere but Jazzi didn't seem to mind, though some jerks rolled their eyes at the announcement, said in too-loud voices how *sad it was*, like going to school was a waste.

Screw 'em.

Lunch rolled around and Sam bailed. All day his head had been pounding and he'd had a weird, thick taste lingering in the back of his throat. Since he was a total stalker—able to walk to Jazzi's trailer damn near in his sleep—getting there took no time at all, even with dodging past the sleepy cop-shop between the school and Jazzi's place.

Her ma's Dodge was gone, which wasn't weird, she was a nurse who drove up to Lawrence every day to work up at LMH's obstetrics. Back when they were little, Jazzi had snuck him into her closet to show him brochures she'd snagged from her ma's workbag, folded and stuffed under crumpled scrubs—five diagrams of human anatomy with privates splayed out and named like something out of one of Pops' fantasy novels—cervix and ovary, peritoneum and epididymis.

It was there, in that little closet, with the door drawn and following where Jazzi's band-aid-plastered finger pointed, that Sam realized he wanted to be a doctor.

One day. One day, he'd be able to help people.

That had been then. This was now.

And now?

Now the trailer door was battered and beat up beneath his knuckles as he rapped, first gingerly, then harder.

Now. Now he turned the knob and took a breath and it squealed like it hadn't been oiled in years as Sam poked his head into the dusty, dirty trailer and called out, "Jasmine? Hey, Jasmine, it's Sam? You okay? Jazzi?"

Now was the thrumming, alternating with a high-pitched whine, both nearly inaudible but sometimes crackling like static, like Pops' dropped landline, like the edges of echoes during tornado drills.

Now was the weird, thick taste in the back of this throat going cloying and gagging, dust and something else mingling and thickening and Sam instinctively yanked his shirt up over his nose to protect his airways.

His family wasn't the best at keeping a house spotless—no Martha Stewart clan were they, with Pops' oilrags from the shop, and Mom's TV dinners, and Dad's evenings mindlessly spent clutching a cold beer on the back porch and squinting up at the sky instead of doing, oh, *anything else at all*—but even their tiny craphole of a saltbox ranch wasn't *this* filthy.

"Jazzi?" Sam whispered.

His heart slammed inside so hard he wondered if fifteen was old enough to start worrying about a heart attack. It wasn't his planned area of expertise; Sam didn't have one of those yet, not really, though he'd been loosely thinking genetics maybe, or possibly surgery. He had steady hands during dissection lab, easily able to neatly scoop out the frog eyes, to casually pin and expose fetal pig arteries.

Sam took a step. Two. The dust around his sneakers was thick and soft, and the deeper he drifted into the trailer the more he felt like one of those Narnia kids—the ones straight outta Hogwarts with their bravery and kindness and smarts and crap. When a push against Jazzi's door didn't show him her cramped and leaning space, purple-painted walls and flecked with dollar-store neon-green stars, Sam *knew*.

"Fuck," Sam breathed and shoved back.

Straight into a barrel-big chest.

It figured, Sam thought, later, gazing blearily up at the sky through the shiny metal bars of his frankly disturbing cell, prodding his aching jaw and flexing a hand he was half-certain had at least four broken bones, that when *he* fell into a fucking story that it ended up more Martin's Westeros than Pratchett's Carpet. No happy Hogwarts for him, no sir. It couldn't get much worse.

He'd been snatched out of what—*used to be? Could have been?*—the dust-covered remains of Jazzi's trailer by a quartet of camo-colored Stormtrooper-looking rejects who didn't seem interested in talking, no matter how Sam begged to explain, begged for answers, and then, after a few solid hits from the one he'd backed into, simply just begged.

They hauled Sam through a hamlet that went like this: a New York-style brownstone; a yurt; some Chinese-style gazebo thing with an actual, blinking *dragon* on the roof; an honest-to-god circle of covered wagons with oxen and pigs and horses and crap; some neo-architectural triangle of shiny chrome and glass; a fucking hobbit hole; and then what looked like half an apartment, but entirely missing a side, like some kinda weird experiment. A woman stood inside the covered half, stirring half a pot of ramen on the stove. A literal half-pot, though the water stayed inside the pot, like it was cut out of glass ... but not.

The hulking troopers—who Sam had quietly dubbed Blinkin, Linkin, Nod, and Fuckface—finally hauled him into what seemed like your garden-variety, strip-mall clothing boutique. At the back, however, was a chair that looked like someone smashed a dino skeleton into a motorcycle and twisted into a chair.

A really pointy, bone and metal, chair.

A man lounged in the chair—though *how* was really the question there—and only stood when Sam was dropped with a teeth-rattling thump, at his feet.

The man smiled, and for one, brief, glorious moment, Sam relaxed despite the fact he was on his knees, in the weirdest place he could have ever imagined. The man standing up was tall, and trim, and had deep smile-wrinkles around his eyes. His teeth gleamed; his posture was open and inviting. He was like something out of Pops' old movies, debonair, like an elder swashbuckler, still smooth and precise and–

HOLY HELL, HE WAS GRINDING HIS HEEL INTO SAM'S HAND.

"I," the man murmured quietly, almost friendly, despite the splinter-sharp agony flaring up Sam's wrist, "am Duke Simmons. And you, boy, have not been invited."

The rest came in fits and starts, the memories oddly reflective and broken. Pain, and blood, and mirrored walls. Question after question—where are you from, who is Jazzi, what did you say your world was named, what is a doctor—they felt endless and nonsensical, each one underlined with silver-cold pain and burning-fire agony, and every time Sam thought he grasped the thread of the conversation, why the Duke would have these questions, they changed again, or he'd lose a nail for nothing.

Halfway through, there'd been a reprieve. That weird, thick taste again, but burned like coffee, poured forcefully down his throat and then his bones began knitting back together, his fingernails shoving through tortured skin like blunt fins breaking the surface of his flesh, and Sam *screamed*.

Then, like something out of Alice, they had tea. Peaceful and calm, the Duke telling him tidbits about his day, offering him sweet honey-cakes and rich chocolate, asking for his favorite drinks, his classes, his life.

Linkin vanished and came back with a frosty glass of soda, still bubbling, salty fresh fries, and applesauce. The things he said he liked. Then, clean clothes. Not his.

No, not his, but clean. Soft.

It lasted for hours, the quartet of troopers being immediately obsequious, the food and gifts and then Sam's before-pain began feeling like a weird hallucination—after all, the Duke was neat as a pin and Sam was positive he'd vomited all over the Simmons' shoes earlier but now they were clean, clean, clean.

Sam decided he must have some sort of fantasy-realm hangover and relaxed.

Doing so ... was ... a mistake.

When it was all done—or at least done for the time being—the troopers didn't even take him by the arms, but by the ankles and wrists, and carried him to a copper pipe, and strung him up like some kind of sacrifice. They carried him through the streets again—Sam was too out to notice much but the houses were either different or they took another path away. Most of the buildings slid past without sinking in, except for a tiny survival shelter made out of a raincoat and what looked like a broken rowboat, and a flash of a face he thought he recognized, but before he could twist or turn, they were gone.

If time stretched here in the same way it did back home (he wasn't sure of anything anymore, Sam's entire world had been torn in two and sewed jaggedly back together) then Sam was fairly sure he'd been stuck in the cell for at least a month, most likely much more.

They didn't come for him every day and even when they did, the days often blended together. The nights sometimes lasted much longer than they should. It could be snowing outside in the morning—a blizzard that left him huddled in a corner, certain he was going to perish of hypothermia in a matter of hours—and then baking hot by the afternoon, as the temperature climbed and the stones beneath his bare feet sizzled.

On the days it poured like a monsoon, Sam's mind would randomly flit to the woman in the half-house, and hope that there had actually been glass or a force-field or something to protect her. Or, less often, he'd think of the rowboat-shelter, and wonder at the flash of dark eyes, wide and shocked, the rope of many braids woven together.

The hand just starting to stretch toward him.

Jazzi's horror.

If his reality had really become some sort of jacked up story, Sam reasoned in the dead of night when the sky filled with dragons or bats or bats the size of dragons or dragons the size of bats, then that flash of a face really would belong to Jazzi.

She'd be a secret princess in need of rescuing, or possibly another world-refuge like himself, trapped here by some mystical accident within her dusty, strange trailer. He could escape, and find her, and claim that his life-long love for her had led him to her. They would escape together and somehow some sarcastic, funny sidekick would appear and blow up the Duke's weird clothing shop and disturbing bone throne. And they'd live, maybe not happily, but ever after.

But if it were a book, Sam knew, then he wouldn't have been left to rot as long as he had. Jazzi would have sought him out—to check if it really were him, or to yell at him, or maybe to even turn the feminist tables and rescue Sam instead. He fantasized about it nightly because he'd worshipped Jazzi for as long as he could remember. Sam loved her. He loved her with every bit of his fifteen-year-old soul; his ardor was all encompassing and weighty and intensely, painfully personal.

And in stories, if you had that kind of love ... it was enough.

So either that face-flash hadn't been Jazzi ... or it was and Sam was screwed.

More screwed than he already was, that is.

"In." He whispered. "Out. Keep breathing."

What he struggled with the most, what he turned helplessly over and over in his head, was the strange, nonsensical horror of it. The questions, ever-changing and frequently with no purpose. The suavely friendly and yet brutal benevolence of Simmons, who often had Sam healed multiple times a session and occasionally at the end of one or the beginning of the next. Who would pet him on the shoulder and call him 'son' or 'kiddo' or even by his actual name. Who would, sometimes, stop the pain to feed him and grow perplexed and upset when Sam didn't immediately accept the offerings of green mac and cheese or purple, feathered burgers with enthusiastic gratitude.

"Everyone eats like this, everywhere," Simmons would tell him, matter-of-fact, and Sam learned early on not to argue the point.

Or even the way the houses changed—and he was sure of that now, they always took him to his cell through the same series of twists and turns, like the road was real when nothing else was, and the houses were in constant flux, sometimes even from hour to hour. The people in the houses ... they stayed the same, however.

So far Sam had spied the half-house woman hanging sheets off an igloo, fixing a cracked driveway of a McMansion, and settled, casual and cross-legged, head tipped back, on the seat of a massive, gaudy riverboat … *sans* river.

He hadn't yet spotted Jazzi again though.

It was as if the isolation had turned him topsy-turvy, the end wrapped toward the beginning and the middle a knot of pain and suffering and a friendly face and kind voice paired with silent tears and breathless screaming.

Stretching … on. And on. And on.

"I have to escape."

He'd been waiting, Sam realized, for maybe-Jazzi to save him. For Simmons to grow bored and quit questioning him. Or to get whatever he was looking for. For Blinkin or Nod, nominally kinder than the other two, to realize this twisted Empire was wrong and slip him a key.

Like something out of a storybook.

But Sam couldn't wait any longer. He had a patchy, pubescent beard now, barely more than a stringy mustache but still *there* in a way he hadn't been able to grow before. His hair, formally shorn short with the dog-clippers by his mom at the turn of every season, now hung to his shoulders.

"I've been in shock," Sam murmured aloud. How long had it been since Simmons had called for him? Weeks? That felt right. True. He hadn't noticed right away because despite the suffering, Sam still received regular meals—weird as they were, they weren't exactly starving him. Simmons would even speak on it like it was a mark of his honor.

"I'm not like the other Dukes," he'd say, jamming a quill beneath Sam's pinky nail, "I don't *starve* my prisoners, after all. And this is barely torture compared to what I *could* do. If you'd just answer my questions *correctly*, Sam, then we don't have to bother with this messy business any further." Then he'd stroke Sam's cheek, gentle and soft, and murmur with his charming smile, "What is the name of your world, Sam? What is the real name of your world?"

And Sam would helplessly try to answer, repeating the answers he'd given what felt like thousands of times before. All he could do was keep breathing.

In-out-keep breathing.

Sometimes he even wanted to answer. Not to make the pain stop, but to make Simmons happy. When Simmons was happy sometimes Sam got a cover for his cell window, one that kept out the heat or the cold or the rain. When Simmons was happy, Nod would heal him and walk him home, shoulder-to-shoulder, like friends, discussing his daughter's school play, or how the dragon infestation was bad this year, or how the warlock at the edge of town never could get the weather predictions right much past three days out, no matter how intricate the spellwork. Would leave him at the door of his cell and seem to contemplate not locking it behind him.

Nod always did, but sometimes Sam would fantasize that he forgot. Or trusted Sam enough not to.

But, even say he did ... Sam was scared.

He knew he had to go. He *had* to. One of these days the questions would stop completely. And then what?

A few days prior, Sam had heard from the last time Blinkin had dropped off thin soup and hot bread and three whole crisp apples that the Duke had captured another prisoner—Jazzi? Who knew at this point?—that had taken the Duke's attention lately.

If he had another prisoner ... what would happen to Sam?

Would he just outright kill him next time? Lose his temper? Lose that icy cool calm and falsely warm smile that the Duke always carried like a mask over fever-bright eyes?

If the Duke didn't need him for whatever torturous reasons ... then Sam was as good as dead. He could feel it in his bones.

"I have to escape," he said again, rubbing his hands together. He was whole and healthy in body, though it didn't feel like it, not really. Not where it counted. Inside it felt like he was bone-brittle, bleached weak and pale, the slightest pressure likely to snap him in two.

But he was scared.

He was trapped.

Too weak to escape.

Too broken.

If he opened the door ... Duke Simmons would *know*. Sam didn't even have to think that hard on it. It was like breathing, how sure he was that the Duke would know. Would know ... and then what? And even if he tried ... no, no, he couldn't try. Nod would tattle, or there'd be a noise or ...

And even if he left, if he managed to struggle and free himself, deglove his arms free one of the nights they were lax because he was in cuffs, or wait until a night they forwent the chains and just barred the door instead ...

Even then, this wasn't his home.

He didn't know where to go, or who to turn to. He had no currency of his own, nothing to trade but the clothing on his back that wasn't even his. No shoes. Sometimes bruises, sometimes not. No friends. No family.

Alone.

Was Sam supposed to run to the woman in the half-house? He knew she'd seen them dragging him hundreds of times past her ever-changing abode by now. She always looked sorry, those days she spotted him, but she never said a word. Not even a wave.

Who else could he get help? Jazzi was gone, if that flash of a face had even been her. The Duke had made it very clear that there were more troopers than his private four, that the entire town answered to him.

Was his.

That he could demand anything and the entire town would rush to comply.

He was, after all, beloved.

Adored Duke Simmons.

So Sam ... quit.

He stopped thinking of Jazzi, or home, or of his battered medical textbook, of the intricate lines of veins beneath skin. He'd seen his own often enough. After all, the way he'd been flayed and taken apart, shown his own inner workings, only to have them shoved inside once again ... well, if he wanted to go into medicine, then Sam would probably never have to study again.

If this were a story, Sam thought, he'd be brave enough, strong enough, to free himself. To escape on his own. To struggle out, to struggle home.

To be free.

Instead he sank deeper into the quicksand—sometimes literally—and survived by breathing.

In-out-keep breathing.

Pictured her small, bandaged fingers pointing out the mesosalpinx, the ampulia, the ureter. Remembered the curve of earrings along the shell of her ear, the way the white chain gleamed through the small hoops.

Like the chains the tame dragons wore—white gold.

The way she'd eat every bite of her sack lunches. The same one every day. The curtain of her hair, swinging between her and the classroom, protecting a sobbing kid as she knelt down. How fast she ran, so fast, like a dark shadow at high noon, breaking state records at thirteen, fourteen, fifteen.

Her mother's beat up Dodge.

The dusty floor.

The high-pitched whine.

The taste of old blood. And copper. And death.

In-out-keep breathing.

It was noon. At least Sam thought it was. The sun was above, bright and clear, there were even birds outside the window, almost like the home he barely remembered now.

The door opened.

It was that simple.

The door opened. And Jazzi was there.

"You're an idiot," she said baldly, slipping inside. "It's not even locked, Sam."

"You're not real," Sam muttered, blinking at her. "You're a hallucination."

"Really not," she sighed, checking over her shoulder, her hair, threaded with white-gold, sliding over elbow. It had gotten longer. So much longer. "Your door hasn't been locked for months, you know that right?"

Sam shrugged. He'd begun to suspect as much, a few weeks back. His food arrived like clockwork but he never laid eyes on any of his guards anymore. Not them. And not Simmons. He'd been forgotten, but he didn't care. All he wanted was to be left alone. "I don't have anywhere to go," Sam pointed out.

Jazzi paused in her nervous glancing around the room and a strange, twisted expression crossed her face. "Sam," she said. "You could go *home*."

"I can't," Sam said. "I don't ..." he held up his hands. He hadn't been magically healed after the last visit with the Duke. His hands had mended on their own ... mangled. "Even if I knew the way ..."

"I can show you," Jazzi whispered. She stood slowly. "Guide you out of the pocket and back on the path. It's a straight shot back to ... where you were born. All you gotta do is walk it."

"And you?" Sam asked. It should have been startling, to realize that he didn't care if Jazzi was with him or not anymore. If she gave a damn that he existed or not. He was broken. Broken beyond repair. Twisted and torn and ...

In. Out. Keep breathing.

Swallowing, Sam ran the back of his wrist across his eyes. "You're not human."

It wasn't a question.

"No," she said, a slight shake of her head sending those braids swinging, swinging, swinging. "Thought I was. For the longest time. I ... I made a mistake. Back ... in your home. At my mom's trailer. I made a mistake and opened something I shouldn't have."

"Not every kid gets told they're adopted," Sam pointed out softly, eyes drifting away from her. He'd longed for Jazzi for so long, even glancing at her felt like glimpsing the sun. "Sorry you had to find out by ... doing whatever you did."

"You lasted longer than the rest," she said. It seemed apropos of nothing, their conversation wasn't veering that way, but Sam nodded nonetheless. "Of the Duke's prisoners, I mean. They wander in here and he's ... he's like a spider. He captures them and he tortures them and either they break and die or … they don't. And you've lasted a long time."

"I have."

"It's not your fault," she whispered, angling her body toward him. She wouldn't look at him—studiously avoiding even remotely looking in the direction of his ruined hands—but Sam appreciated the thought. She was trying.

Her voice broke and her hand trembled. She reached for him, tears sliding over her cheeks. "Sam–"

"Go home, Jazzi." He flopped on his cot and stared up at the ceiling. "Just … let me be. I don't have anywhere to go. I'm stuck. And I'm done. I'm just … tired. Let me sleep."

She did.

Later, Sam learned, he'd been in the in-between place for a decade. Ten human years, depressed and frozen, trapped and waiting. Hoping that if he was just good enough that the Duke would come back and heal him again.

Make him whole.

The Duke did, sometimes. He brought questions and gifts and healing salves and horrible, thick concoctions that curdled Sam's insides, sometimes healing him, sometimes not.

Sam drank every one down, eagerly. Hoping that this time, this time, it'd be the one. The right one. The right question, the right answer, the right potion. The right magic.

His hands never healed up right, though.

Not like they'd been before.

One morning, Sam woke up. It wasn't noon, or midnight, or any time in between. There was a mist on the ground outside and somewhere, amid the emptiness, a bell tolled.

Sam swung his legs over his bed and looked at where, once, he'd had a little dragon. The Duke had killed it, a year or so after he'd hatched it and hand-raised it himself. During the questions Simmons threatened to, many times, and Sam begged and bowed and answered and still … it hadn't been enough.

Never enough.

At least he hadn't made Sam eat the fried dinner that night; though he'd been forced to watch Linkin and Nod wolf it all down.

That had been … a few months ago?

Maybe a little longer, but not much.

On the edge of the drafty window there was a small iridescent speck. A bit of shell. Nothing much.

Nothing much at all.

Leftover.

His egg, his dragon, had been named Jazzi.

And Sam loved Jazzi with everything left in his faint shadow of a soul.

Survival, Sam knew, was a matter of breathing.

In. Out.

Keep breathing.

As long as you kept breathing, you were surviving - even when you lay in the blackest black, or ablaze in the brightest heat of the most brilliant white. It was what Jazzi had taught him—taught them all, really—all those years ago.

In. Out. Keep breathing.

Sam licked his finger, twisted all wrong, and collected the shard of egg. The only thing he'd ever really loved here.

His sweet girl, no white-gold to tame her, to train her, to trap her. Free as the birds and the bats and the butterflies, to fly and flap and reach the sky Sam was afraid to miss.

Sam collected the shell. Curled his fingers around it.

Looked at the door.

She was right. Had been right all along.

It creaked and squealed as Sam pushed it open. The corridors were dusty. Cobwebs hung down.

He'd been forgotten.

His door wasn't even locked.

CAROUSEL
by Orson Scott Card

Cyril's relationship with his wife really went downhill after she died. Though, if he was honest with himself—something he generally tried, with some success, to avoid—things hadn't been going all that well while Alice was alive. Everything he did seemed to irritate her, and when he didn't do anything at all, that irritated her, too.

"It's not your fault," Alice explained to him. "You try, I can see that you try, but you just ... you're just wrong about everything. Not *very* wrong. Not oblivious or negligent or unconcerned. Just a little bit mistaken."

"About what? Tell me and I'll get better."

"About what people want, who they are, what they need."

"What do you need?" Cyril asked.

"I need you to stop asking what I need," she said. "I need you to know. The children need you to know. You never know."

"Because you won't tell me."

"See?" she said. "You have to make it my fault. Why should people always have to tell you, Cyril? It's like you go through life in a well-meaning fog. You can't help it. Nobody blames you."

But she blamed him. He knew that. He tried to get better, to notice more. To remember. But there was that note of impatience—in her voice, the children's voices, his boss's voice. As if they were thinking, I'm having to *explain* this to you?

Then Alice was hit by a car driven by a resurrected Han Dynasty Chinese man who had no business behind the wheel—he plowed into a crowd on a bustling sidewalk and then got out and walked away as nonchalantly as if he had successfully parallel parked a large car in a small space. It was the most annoying thing about the dead—how they thought killing total strangers was no big deal, as long as they didn't mean to do it. And since the crowd only had two living people in it, the number of deaths was

99

actually quite low. Alice's death barely rose to the level of a statistic, in the greater scheme of things.

She was thoughtful enough to clean up and change clothes before she came home that night—resurrection restored every body part as it should be at the peak of mature health, but it did nothing for the wardrobe. Still, the change in her attitude was immediate. She didn't even try to start dinner.

"What's for dinner, Mom?" asked Delia.

"Whatever your father fixes," said Alice.

"Am I fixing dinner?" asked Cyril. He liked to cook, but it usually took some planning and he wasn't sure what Alice would let him use to put together a meal.

"Go out to eat, have cold cereal, I really don't care," said Alice.

This was not like her. Alice controlled everybody's diet scrupulously, which is why she almost never allowed Cyril to cook. He realized at once what it meant, and the kids weren't far behind.

"Oh, Mom," said Roland softly. "You're not dead, are you?"

"Yes," she sighed. "But don't worry, it only hurt for about a minute while I bled out."

"Did the resurrection feel good?" asked Delia, always curious.

"The angel was right there, breathed in my mouth—very sweet. A bit of a tingle everywhere. But really not such a great feeling that it's worth dying for, so you shouldn't be in a hurry to join me, dear."

"So you won't be eating with us," said Cyril.

She shook her head a little, eyes closed. "'Dead' means I don't eat, Cyril. Everyone knows that the dead don't eat. We don't breathe except so we can talk. We don't drink and if we do, it's just to keep company with the living, and the liquids all evaporate from our skins so we also don't pee. We also don't want sex anymore, Cyril. Not with each other and not with you."

She had never mentioned sex in front of the children before, except for the talk with Delia when she turned ten, and that was all about time-of-the-month things. If Delia had any idea what sex was, Cyril didn't think she got it from her mother. So the children blanched and recoiled when she mentioned it.

"Oh, don't be such big babies, you know your father and I had sex, or you wouldn't look so much like him. Which is fine for you, Roland, your father's a good-looking man, in his way. But a bit of a drag for you, Delia, with that jaw. And the resurrection won't fix that. Resurrection isn't cosmetic surgery. Which is really unfair, when you think about it. People who are genetically retarded or crippled or sick have their DNA repaired to some optimum state, but girls with overly mannish features or tiny breasts or huge ones, for that matter, their DNA is left completely alone, they're stuck like that for eternity."

"Thanks, Mom," said Delia. "I love having my confidence destroyed once again, and I haven't even begun doing my homework yet."

"So you aren't going to eat with us?" asked Roland.

"Oh, of course I'll sit at table with you," said Alice. "For the company."

In the event, Cyril got out everything in the fridge that looked like it might go on a sandwich and everybody made their own. Except Alice, of course. She just sat at the table and made comments, without even a pause to take a bite or chew.

"The way I see it," said Alice, "is that it's all poop. Nothing you're putting on sandwiches even looks appetizing any more, because I see that poopiness of it all. You're going to eat it and digest it and poop it out. The nutrients will decay and eventually end up in some farmer's field where it will become more future-poop, which he'll harvest and it'll get processed into a more poopable state, so you can heat it or freeze it or thaw it or whatever, chew it up or drink it, and then turn it into poop again. Life is poop."

"Mom," said Delia. "It's usually Roland who makes us sick while we're eating."

"I thought you'd want to hear my new perspective as a post-living person." She sounded miffed.

"Please speak more respectfully to your mother," said Cyril to Delia.

"Cyril, really," said Alice. "I don't need you to protect me from Delia's snippy comments. It's not going to kill me to hear her judgmentalness directed at the woman who gave birth to her."

"Feel free to criticize your mother's defecatory comments," said Cyril. "Or ignore them, as you choose."

"I know, Dad," said Delia. There was that familiar hint of eye-rolling in her tone of voice. Once again Cyril must have guessed wrong about what to say, or leave unsaid. He had never really gotten it right when Alice was alive, and now that she was dead-and-resurrected, he'd have no chance, because he was no longer dealing with a wife, or even, strictly speaking, a woman. She was a visitor with a key to the house.

Within a few weeks, Cyril found himself remembering the awful night of Alice's death as a particularly lovely time, because she actually sat with them during dinner and wasn't trying to lead the children off into some kind of utterly bizarre activity.

She showed up at any hour of the day, and expected to be able to take Delia or Roland with her on whatever adventure she'd gotten it into her head to try with them.

"No, Alice, you may not take Roland out of school so he can go scuba diving with you."

"It's really not your place to say what I can or cannot do," said Alice.

"The law is clear, Alice—when you die you become, in a word, deceased. You no longer have any custody over the children. Thousands of years of legal precedent make that clear. Not to mention tons of recent case law in which the resurrected are found to be unfit parents in every case."

"Aren't you lucky that the dead can't get angry," said Alice.

"I suppose that I am," said Cyril. "But I'm not dead, and I was furious when I found you practically forcing Roland to walk along the top of a very high fence."

"It's exhilarating," said Alice.

"He was terrified."

"Oh, Cyril, are you really going to let a child's fears—"

"He was right to be terrified. He could have broken his neck."

"And would it have been such a tragedy if he did?" asked Alice. "I was run over by a car and I turned out Okay."

"You think you're Okay?" asked Cyril.

Alice held up her hands and twisted her wrists as if to prove that her parts worked.

"Here's how I know you're not Okay, Alice," said Cyril. "You keep trying to put the kids in high-risk situations. You're trying to kill them, Alice."

"Don't think of it as death. I'm not dead. How is it death?"

"How can I put this kindly?" said Cyril—who by this point had actually stopped trying to be kind. "You're dead to *me*."

"Just because I'm no longer available for empty reproductive gestures does not mean I'm not here for you, Cyril."

"I'm going to get a restraining order if you don't stop taking the kids on dangerous activities. You don't have any guardianship rights over these children."

"My fingerprints say I'm still their mother!"

"Alice, when you were their mother, you wanted them to relish every stage of their life. Now you're trying to get them to skip all the rest of the stages."

"You can't manipulate me with guilt," said Alice. "I'm beyond human emotions and needs."

"Then why do you still need the children with you?"

"I'm their mother."

"You *were* their mother," said Cyril.

"I was and I am," said Alice.

"Alice, I may have been a disappointment as a husband."

"And as a father, Cyril. The children are often disappointed in you."

"But I meet a basic minimum, Alice. I'm alive. I'm human. Of their species. I want them to be alive. I'd like them to live to adulthood, to marry, to have children."

Alice shook her head incredulously. "Go outside and look at the street, Cyril. Hundreds of people lie down and sleep in the streets or on the lawns every night, because the world has *no* shortage of people."

"Just because you've lost all your biological imperatives doesn't mean that the rest of us don't have them."

"Cyril, your reasoning is backward. The children will be much happier without biological imperatives."

"So you admit you're trying to kill them."

"I'm trying to awaken them from the slumber of mortality."

"I don't want to waken them from that slumber," said Cyril sharply. "If it's a dream, then let them finish the dream and come out of it in their own time."

"When someone you love is living in a nightmare," said Alice, "you wake them up."

"Alice," said Cyril, "you're the nightmare."

"Your wife is a nightmare? Your children's mother?"

"You're a reanimated dead woman."

"Resurrected," said Alice. "An angel breathed into my mouth."

"The angel should have minded its damn business," said Cyril.

"You always wanted me dead," said Alice.

"I never *wanted* you dead until after you *were* dead and you wouldn't go away."

"You're a bitter failure, Cyril, and yet you cling to this miserable life and insist that the children cling to it, too. It's a form of child abuse. Of child exploitation."

"Go away, Alice. Go enjoy your death somewhere else."

"My eternal life, you mean."

"Whatever."

But in the end, Alice won. First she talked Delia into jumping from a bridge without actually attaching any bungee cords to her feet. Once again Cyril had no chance to grieve, because Alice brought Delia by to tell Roland how great death and resurrection were. Delia was fully grown. A woman, but in a retailored version of her dress that fit her larger, womanly body.

"The soul is never a child," said Alice. "What did you expect?"

"I expected her to take a few more years to grow into this body," said Cyril.

"Think of it as skipping ahead a few grades," said Alice, barely able to conceal her gloating.

If Cyril had thought Resurrected Alice was awful, resurrected Delia was unbearable. His love for his daughter had become, without his realizing it, far stronger and deeper than his lingering affection for his wife. So he could not help but grieve for the young girl cut off in her prime. While the snippy, smart-mouthed woman of the same name, who thought she had a right to dwell in his house and follow him around,, mocking him constantly—she was a stranger.

How can you grieve for people who just won't go away? How can you grieve for a daughter whose grownup dead-and-resurrected self ridicules your mourning? "Oh, did Daddy lose his widdow baby?"

There was nothing to do but say an occasional silent prayer—which they mocked when they noticed him doing it. Only Cyril was never quite sure what he was praying for. Please get rid of all the dead? Please unresurrect them? Would God even hear that prayer?

Roland died of a sudden attack of influenza a few months later. "You can't blame me for it, this time," said Alice.

"You know you were sneaking him out into the cold weather specifically so he'd catch cold. The dying was a predictable result. You're a murderer, Alice. You should be in hell."

Alice smiled even more benignly. "I forgive you for that."

"I'll never forgive you for taking away my children."

"Now you're unencumbered. I thought that's what you secretly wished for."

"Thanks for telling me my deepest wishes, " said Cyril. "They were so deep I never knew they existed."

"Come with us, Father," said Roland.

"In due time, I'll go where I can find what I need," said Cyril. "*You* don't need me.

Roland was so tall. Cyril's heart ached to see him. My little boy, he thought. But he could not say it. Roland's gentle pity on him was harder to bear than Delia's open scorn.

They would not go. They talked about it, but sheer inertia kept anyone from changing. Finally it dawned on Cyril. Just because he was the only pre-dead resident of the house did not bind him to it. His life had been stripped away from him; why was he clinging to the house that used to hold it?

For the shower, the toilet, the bathroom sink; for the refrigerator, the microwave, the kitchen table; for the roof, the bed, place to store his clothes. The burden and blessing of modern life. Unlike the resurrected, if Cyril was going to eat, he had to work; if he was going to work, he had to look presentable. For his health he needed shelter from weather, a safe place to sleep.

The resurrected people that used to love him did not need this place, but would not leave; he needed the place, but could not bear these people who made it impossible for him to truly grieve the terrible losses he had suffered.

Job had it all wrong, thought Cyril. Having lost his wife and children, it was better to lose all his other possessions and live in an ashpit, covered in boils. Then, at least, everyone could see and understand what had happened to him. His friends might have been wretched comforters, but at least they understood that he was in need of comfort.

Just because he had to store his food and clothing there, and return there to wash himself and sleep, did not mean he had to *live* there, to pass waking hours there, listening to his dead wife explain his inadequacies to him, or his dead daughter agree with her, or his dead son pity him.

Cyril took to leaving work as soon as he could, and sometimes when he couldn't, just walking out of the building, knowing he was putting his already somewhat pitiful career in jeopardy. He would walk the streets, delaying the commute home as long as possible. He thought of joining his wife and children in death and resurrection, but he had seen how death stripped them of all desire, and even though his current malaise came from the frustration of his deepest desires, he did not want to part with them. Desire was what defined him, he understood that, and to give them up was to lose himself, as his wife and children were lost.

Bitterly, Cyril remembered the Bible school of his childhood. Lose your soul to find it? Yes, the dead had certainly done that. Lost soul, self, and all, but whatever they found, it wasn't really life. Life was about hunger and need and finding ways to satisfy them. Nature red in tooth and claw, yes, but hadn't the human race found ways to create islands of peace in the midst of nature? Lives in which terror was so rare that people paid money to go to amusement parks and horror movies in order to remember what terror felt like.

This life was even more peaceful, even less lonely, wasn't it? When he walked the streets, he jostled with thousands and thousands of the resurrected, who crowded every street as they went about their meaningless existence, not even curious, but moving for the sake of moving, or so it seemed to him; pursuing various amusements because they remembered that this was a thing that human beings did, and not because they desired amusement.

They crowded the streets so that traffic barely moved, yet they provided no boost to the economy. Needing nothing, they bought nothing. They had no money, because they had no desires, and therefore nothing to work for.

They were the sclerosis of commerce. Get out of my way, thought Cyril, over and over. And then: Do what you want. I'm not going anywhere either.

He was living like the dead, he recognized that. His life was as empty as theirs. But underneath his despair and loneliness and ennui, he was seething with resentment. Since God obviously existed after all, since it was hard to imagine how else one might explain the sudden resurrection-of-all-who-had-ever-lived, what did he *mean* by it? What were they supposed to *do* with this gift that preserved life eternally while robbing it of any sort of joy or pleasure?

So Cyril was ironically receptive when he found the uptown mansion with a sign on the door that said:

God's Anteroom

Nobody used "anteroom" anymore, but the idea rather appealed to him. So he went up the short walk and climbed the stoop and opened the front door and stepped inside.

It was a good-sized foyer, which he assumed was formed by tearing out a wall and combining the front parlor with the original vestibule. The space was completely filled by a small merry-go-round. As far as Cyril could see, no doors or stairs led out of the room except the front door he had just come through.

"Hello?" His voice didn't echo—the room wasn't big enough for that. It just fell into the space, flat and dull. He thought of calling again, louder, but instead stepped up onto the carousel.

It was small. Only two concentric circles of animals to ride, the outer one with seven, the inner one with three, plus a single one-person bench shaped like the Disney version of a throne, molded in smooth, rounded lines of hard plastic pretending to be upholstery.

Cyril thought of sitting there, since it required no effort. But he thought better of it, and walked around the carousel, touching each animal in turn. Chinese dragon, zebra, tiger, horse, hippopotamus, rhinoceros, giant mouse. Porpoise, eagle, bear. All extravagantly detailed and finely hand-painted—there was nothing sloppy or faded, or seedy about the thing. In fact, he could truly say that the carousel was a work of art, a small, finely crafted version of a mass entertainment.

He had never known there was such a thing as a boutique carousel. Who would ever come to ride such a thing? And what would they pay? Part of the pleasure of full-sized carousels was the fact that it was so crowded and public. Here in this room, the carousel looked beautiful and sad at the same time. Too small for the real purpose of a carousel—a place where people could display themselves to one another, while enjoying the mild pleasure of moving up and down on a faux beast. Yet too large for the room, crowded, almost as if this were a place where beautiful things were stored while awaiting a chance for display in a much larger space.

Cyril sat on the hippopotamus.

"Would you like me to make it go?" asked a woman's voice.

Cyril had thought he was alone. He looked around, startled, a little embarrassed, beginning the movement of getting back off the hippo, yet stopping himself because the voice had not challenged him, but rather offered to serve him.

Then he saw her through the grillwork of the faux ticket booth in a space that must have been a coat closet when the house was first built. How did she get in or out? The booth had no door.

Her appearance of youth and health led him to assume she was dead and resurrected.

"I can't really afford ..." he began.

"It's free," she said.

"Hard to stay in business at those rates," said Cyril.

"It's not a business," she said.

Then what is it? he wanted to ask. But instead he answered, "Then yes. I'd like to ride."

Silently the carousel slipped into movement without a lurch; had he not been paying attention, Cyril would not have been able to say when movement began.

The silence did not last long, for what would a carousel be without music? No calliope, though—what accompanied this carousel sounded like a quartet of instruments. Cello, oboe, horn, and harpsichord, Cyril thought, without any effort to sort out the sounds. Each instrument was so distinctive it was impossible not to catalog them. They played a sedate music in three-four time, as suited a carousel or skating rink, yet the music was also haunting in a modal, folk-songish way.

Cyril let the carousel carry him around and around. The movement did not have the rapid sweep of a fullsize carousel, but rather the dizzying tightness of spin of a children's hand-pushed merry-go-round. He had to close his eyes now and then to keep from becoming light-headed or getting a slight headache from the room that kept slipping past his vision.

It did not occur to him to ask her to slow it down, or stop. He simply clung to the pole and let it move him and the hippo up and down.

Because the music was so gentle, the machinery so silent, the distance from him to the ticket booth so slight even when he was on the far side of the room, Cyril felt it possible—no, obligatory—to say something after a while. "How long does the ride last?" he asked.

"As long as you want," she said.

"That could be forever," he said.

"If you like," she said.

He chuckled. "Do you get overtime?"

"No," she said. "Just time."

"Too bad," he said. Then he remembered that she was dead, and neither payment nor time would mean very much to her.

"Do you read?" he asked. "Or do you have a DVD player in there?"

"What?" she asked.

"To pass the time. Between patrons. While the customers are riding. It can't be thrilling to watch me go around and around."

"It actually is," she said. "Just a little."

Liar, thought Cyril. Nothing is thrilling to the dead.

"You're not dead yet," she said.

"No," he answered, wanting to add, *What gave me away?* but keeping his silence. He knew what gave him away. He had asked questions. He was curious. He had bothered to ride at all. He had closed his eyes to forestall nausea. So many signs of life.

"So you can't ride forever."

"I suppose not," said Cyril. "Eventually I have to sleep."

"And eat," she said. "And urinate."

"Doesn't look like you have a restroom, either," said Cyril.

"We do," she said.

"Where?" He looked for a door.

"It has an outside entrance."

"Don't the homeless trash the place?" he asked.

"I don't mind cleaning it up," she said.

"So you do it all? Run the carousel, clean the restrooms?"

"That's all there is," she said. "It isn't hard."

"It isn't interesting, either."

"Interesting enough," she said. "I don't get bored."

Of course not. You have to have something else you want to be doing before you really feel bored.

"Where are you from?" asked Cyril, because talking was better than not talking. He wanted to ask her to stop the carousel, because he really was getting just a little sick now, but if he stopped, she might insist that he go. And if he got off, yet was allowed to stay, where would he stand while he talked to her.

"I died here as a little girl. My mother gave birth to me on the voyage."

"Immigrants," said Cyril.

"Isn't everyone?" she answered.

"So you never grew up."

"I'm up," she said, "but you're right, without growing into it. I was very sick, my mother wiping my brow, crying. And then I was full-grown, and had this strange language at my lips, and there were all these buildings and people and nothing to do."

"So you found a job."

"I came through the door and found the ticket booth standing open. I knew it was called a ticket booth as soon as I saw it, though I never saw a ticket booth before in my life. I could read the signs, too, and the letters, though there weren't in the language I learned as a baby. I turned on the carousel and it went around and I like to watch it, so I stayed."

"So nobody hired you."

"Nobody's told me to go," she said. "The machinery isn't complicated. I can make it go backward, too, but nobody likes that, so I don't even offer anymore."

"Can you make it go slower?"

"That's the slowest setting," she said. "It can go at two faster speeds. Do you want to see?"

"No," he said quickly, though for a moment he wanted to say yes, just to find out what it would feel like.

"No one likes that either, though people still ask. The living ones throw up sometimes, at the faster speeds."

"Sometimes the resurrected come to ride?"

"Sometimes they come with the living ones. A dead mother and her living children. That sort of thing."

"How do you like it?" he asked.

"Well enough," she said, "or I wouldn't stay."

He realized she must have thought he meant how she liked her job, or watching the carousel.

"I meant, how do you like resurrection?"

"I don't know," she said. "I don't have a choice, so I don't think about it."

"When you were dying, what did you want?"

"I wanted my mother not to cry. I wanted to sleep. I wanted to feel better."

"Do you feel better now?" asked Cyril.

"I don't know," she said. "I suppose so. My mother isn't crying anymore. I found her after I resurrected. She didn't know me, but I knew *her*. She was just as I remember her, only not so sad. She and I didn't talk long. There wasn't much to say. She said that she wept for me until her husband made her stop so he could bury me. She wouldn't move away, because she would have to leave my grave behind, so they lived their whole lives nearby, and raised eleven other children and sent them out into the world, but she never forgot me."

The story made Cyril want to weep for his own dead children, even though they were alive again, after a fashion. "She must have been glad to see you," he said.

"She didn't know me. It was her baby that she wanted to see."

"I know," said Cyril. "My wife got my children to die and they came back like you. Grown up. I miss the children that I lost." And then he did cry, just for a couple of sobs, before he got control of himself.

"I'm sorry," he said. "I haven't been able to cry till now. Because they're still there."

"I know," she said. "I'm glad to see you cry."

He didn't even ask why. He knew: Her mother, being resurrected, had not cried. The woman needed to see a living person cry for a dead child.

Needed. How could she *need* anything?

"What's your name?" asked Cyril.

"Dorcas," she said.

"Not a common name anymore," said Cyril.

"It's from the Bible. I never studied the Bible when I was alive. I was too young to read. But I came back knowing how to read. And the whole Bible is in my memory. So is everything. It's all there, every book. I can either remember them as if I had already read them, or I can close my eyes and read them again, or I can close my eyes and see the whole story play out in front of my eyes. And yet I never do. It's enough just to know what's in all the books."

"All of them? All the books ever written?"

"I don't know if it's all of them. But I've never thought of a book that I haven't read. If one book mentions another book, I've already read it. I know how they all end. I suppose it must be more fun to read, if you don't already know every scene and every word."

"No worse than the carousel," said Cyril. "It just goes around and around."

"But the face of the person riding it changes," she said. "And I don't always know what they're going to say before they say it."

"So you're curious."

"No," she said. "I don't really care. It just passes the time."

Cyril rode in silence for a while.

"Why do you think he did it?" he finally asked.

"Who?" she asked. Then, "Oh, you mean the resurrection. Why did God, you know."

"This is God's Anteroom, right? So it seems appropriate to wonder. Why now. Why everybody all at once. Why children came back as adults."

"Everybody gets their perfect body," she said. "And knowledge. Everything's fair. God must be fair."

Cyril pondered that. He couldn't even argue with it. Very even-handed. He couldn't feel that he had been singled out for some kind of torment. Many people had suffered worse. When his children had died, he was still able to talk to them. It had to feel much worse if they were simply gone.

"Maybe this is a good thing," said Cyril.

"Nobody believes that," she said.

"No," said Cyril. "I can't imagine that they do. When you wish—when your child dies, or your wife. Or husband, or whatever—you don't really think of how they'd come back. You want them back just as they were. But then what? Then they'd just die again, later, under other circumstances."

"At least they'd have had a life in between," said Dorcas.

Cyril smiled. "You're not the ordinary dead person," he said. "You have opinions. You have regrets."

"What can I regret? What did I ever do wrong?" she asked. "No, I'm just pissed off."

Cyril laughed aloud. "You can't be angry. My wife is dead, and she's never angry."

"So I'm not angry. But I know that it's wrong. It's supposed to make us happy and it doesn't, so it's wrong, and wrongness feels ..."

"Wrong," Cyril prompted.

"And that's as close as I can come to being angry," said Dorcas. "You too?"

"Oh, I can feel anger! I don't have to be 'close,' I've got the real thing. Pissed off, that's what I feel. Resentful. Spiteful. Whining. Self-pitying. And I don't mind admitting it. My wife and children were resurrected and they'll live forever and they seem perfectly content. But you're not content."

"I'm content," she said. "What else is there to be? I'm pissed off, but I'm content."

"I wish this really were God's anteroom," said Cyril. "I'd be asking the secretary to make me an appointment."

"You want to talk to God?"

"I want to file a complaint," said Cyril. "It doesn't have to be, like, an interview with God himself. I'm sure he's busy."

"Not really," said the voice of a man.

Cyril looked at the inner row, where a handsome young man sat in the throne. "You're God?" Cyril asked.

"You don't like the resurrection," said God.

"You know everything, right?" asked Cyril.

"Yes," said God. "Everybody hates this. They prayed for it, they wanted it, but when they got it, they complained, just like you."

"I never asked for this."

"But you would have," said God, "as soon as somebody died."

"I wouldn't have asked for this," said Cyril. "But what do you care?"

"I'm not resurrected," said God. "Not like them. I still care about things."

"Why didn't you let *them* care, then?" asked Cyril.

"Billions of people on Earth again, healthy and strong, and I should make them *care?* Think of the wars. Think of the crimes. I didn't bring them back to turn the world into hell."

"What is it, if it isn't hell?" asked Cyril.

"Purgatory," said Dorcas.

"Limbo," Cyril suggested back.

"Neither one exists," said God. "I tried them for a while, but nobody liked them, either. Listen, it's not really my fault. Once a soul exists, it can never be erased. Annihilated. I found them, I had to do something with them. I thought this world was a good way to use them. Let them have a life. Do things, feel things."

"That worked fine," said Cyril. "It was going fine till you did *this.*" He gestured toward Dorcas.

"But there were so many complaints," said God. "Everybody hated death, but what else could I do? Do you have any idea how many souls I have that still haven't been born?"

"So cycle through them all. Reincarnation, let them go around and around."

"It's a long time between turns," said God. "Since the supply of souls is infinite."

"You didn't mention infinite," said Cyril. "I thought you just meant there were a lot of us."

"Infinite is kind of a lot," said God.

"To *me* it is," said Cyril. "I thought that to you—"

"I know, this whole resurrection didn't work out like I hoped. Nothing does. I should never have taken responsibility for the souls I found."

"Can't you just ... put some of us back?"

"Oh, no, I can't do that," said God, shaking his head vehemently. "Never that. It's—once you've had a body, once you've been part of creation, to take you back out of it—you'd remember all the power, and you'd feel the loss of it—like no suffering. Worst thing in the world. And it never ends."

"So you're saying it's hell."

"Yes," said God. "There's no fire, no sulfur and all that. Just endless agony over the loss of ... of everything. I can't do that to any of the souls. I *like* you. All of you. I hate it when you're unhappy."

"We're unhappy," said Cyril.

"No," said God. "You're sad, but you're not really suffering."

Cyril was in tears again. "Yes I am."

"Suck it up," said God. "It can be a hell of a lot worse than this."

"You're not really God," said Cyril.

"I'm the guy in charge," said God. "What is that, if not God? But no, there's no omnipotent transcendental being who lives outside of time. No unmoved mover. That's just stupid anyway. The things people say about me. I know you can't help it. I'm doing my best, just like most of you. And I keep trying to make you happy. This is the best I've done so far."

"It's not very good," said Cyril.

"I know," said God. "But it's the best so far."

Dorcas spoke up from the ticket booth. "But I never really *had* a life."

God sighed. "I know."

"Look," said Cyril. "Maybe this really is the best. But do you have to have everybody *stay* here? On Earth, I mean? Can't you, like, create more worlds?"

"But people want to *see* their loved ones," said God.

"Right," said Cyril. "We've seen them. Now move them along and let the living go on with our lives."

"So maybe a couple of conversations with the dead and they move on," said God, apparently thinking about it. "What about you, Dorcas?"

"Whatever," she said. "I'm dead, what do I care?"

"You care," said God. "Not the cares of the body. But you have the caring of a soul. It's a different kind of desire, but you all have it, and it never goes away."

"My wife and children don't care about anything," said Cyril.

"They care about you."

"I wish," said Cyril.

"Why do you think they haven't left? They see you're unhappy."

"I'm unhappy because they won't go," said Cyril.

"Why haven't you told them that? They'd go if you did."

Cyril said nothing. He had nothing to say.

"You don't want them to go," said Dorcas.

"I want my children back," Cyril said. "I want my wife to love me."

"I can't make people love other people," said God. "Then it wouldn't be love."

"You really have a limited skill set," said Cyril.

"I really try not to do special favors," said God. "I try to set up rules and then follow them equally for everybody. It seems more fair that way."

"By definition," said Dorcas. "That's what fairness *is*. But who says fairness is always good?"

God shrugged. "Oh, I don't know. I wish I did. But I'll give it a shot, how about that? Maybe I can eventually fix this thing. Maybe the next thing will be a little better. And maybe I'll never get it right. Who knows?"

And he was gone.

So was Dorcas.

Cyril got off the hippo. He was dizzy and had to cling to the pole. The carousel wasn't going to stop. So he waited until he had a stretch of open floor and leapt off.

He stumbled, lurched against a wall, slid down, and lay on the floor. The quartet stopped playing. The carousel slowed down and stopped. Apparently it automatically knew when there were no passengers.

A baby cried.

Cyril walked to the ticket window and looked in. On the floor sat a toddler, a little girl, surrounded by a pile of women's clothing. The toddler looked up at him. "Cyril," she said in her baby voice.

"Do you remember being a grownup?" Cyril asked her.

The little girl looked puzzled.

"How do I get in there?"

"Hungry!" said the little girl and she cried again.

Cyril saw a door handle inside the ticket booth and eventually figured out where the door was in the outside wall. He got it open. He picked up little Dorcas and wrapped her in the dress she had been wearing. God was giving her a life.

Cyril carried her out of God's Anteroom and down the stoop. The crowds were gone. Just a few cars, with only the living inside them. Some of them were stopped, the drivers just sitting there. Some of them were crying. Some just had their eyes closed. But eventually somebody honked at somebody else and the cars in the middle of the road started going again.

Cyril took a cab home and carried the baby inside. Alice and Delia and Roland were gone. There was food in the fridge. Cyril got out the old high chair and fed Dorcas. When she was done, he set her in the living room and went in search of toys and clothes. He mentally talked to Alice as he did: So it's stupid to keep children's clothes and toys when we're never going to have more children, is it? Well, I never said it, but I always thought it, Alice: Just because *you* decided not to have any more babies doesn't mean *I* would never have any.

He got Dorcas dressed and she played with the toys until she fell asleep on the living room carpet. Then Cyril lay on the floor beside her and wept for his children and the wife he had loved far more than she loved him, and for the lost life; yet he also wept for joy, that God had actually listened to him, and given him this child, and given Dorcas the life she had longed for.

He wondered a little where God had sent the other souls, and he wondered if he should tell anybody about his conversation with God, but then he decided it was all none of his business. He had a job the next day, and he'd have to arrange for day care, and buy food that was more appropriate for the baby. And diapers. He definitely needed those.

THE MONSTERS UNDERNEATH HIS BED
by Ken Scholes

He'd always known they were there but they were easier to ignore before the hand. Benjamin Brown climbed out of bed for a three o-clock pee, placed his feet squarely into his slippers, and felt the cold hand grip his left ankle. Shrieking, he yanked away and fell backwards into the safety of his blankets. Clenching his thighs together, he waited for dawn. He needed to act on this.

Later that day, he walked to the library. The pretty girl was there behind her desk and she smiled at him. He blushed, averted his eyes, and kept walking. He'd never been one to draw the pretty ones. Benjamin knew he was plain himself, and that like draws to like. He went to the computer and started his search.

An hour later, he left as empty handed as he'd arrived. Except for the smile that the pretty girl sent with him as he passed by again.

Benjamin cashed his unemployment check, picked up some frozen dinners, and went home nervous. By eleven that night, after eight hours of mindless sitcoms and volatile shock shows, he'd convinced himself it was a dream at least a dozen times. Of course, he *knew* they were there. But he knew it in a way that a person in a cave knew the sky was blue somewhere. Until this morning there had been nothing tangible to prove it other than his odd habit of wrapping his head in blankets and sleeping with his back to the door. But now: the hand.

He slunk upstairs, paused in the doorway, and leapt for the bed. He left the light on and pulled the blankets over his ears. Nothing had happened. He sighed, allowed the bed to absorb his body as the tension drained from him. Conviction number thirteen registered: It had been a dream.

Then, the monster underneath his bed farted loudly and chuckled low. After that, it was a long night.

Two nights after the hand, one night after the flatulence, the monster spoke.

"Benji."

Benjamin, his head cottony from lack of sleep, his body trembling, waited. Then it started—a low whisper, a rush of words, a litany that built in the darkened room.

"Benjibenjibenjibenjibenjibenjibenjibenjibenjibenjibenjibenji."

Screaming, he bounded to the floor, dodged the groping hands, and tripped over a shoe. He fell hard, smacking his head on the doorframe on his way down. He scrambled, hands and knees pushing and pulling, into the hallway.

He finished the night on the couch. Upstairs, his bed thumped time to the chanting voices.

The pretty girl's desk was empty at the library. Benjamin paused, trying to remember her face, eyes, long hair pulled back into a pony tail. Then he continued past the bank of computers and let the rows of books swallow him. His finger traced the call numbers of the paranormal, the philosophical and then: Psychology. He loaded his arms and found a table by the window. Outside, a gray sky spat Autumn rain.

The pages blurred and in the end, a hand on his shoulder jolted him awake, a shriek near his lips. He looked up. The pretty girl.

"Are you okay?" Her voice sounded like music. "Are you finding everything?"

He shook his head.

"We're closing soon."

Benjamin fought back tears that she must have noticed. Concern filled her eyes and voice. "Are you *sure* you're okay?"

Something about her squeezed his heart and he started to cry. "I know they're there," he said. "I *know* they are." He looked up at her, sniffling. "I'm not crazy."

She shook her head slightly. She should make an excuse now, he thought, walk quickly away, make a discreet phone call. But she didn't. "Who?" Her hand came back to his shoulder. "Who's there?"

He looked around, lowered his voice. "The monsters underneath my bed."

She should laugh now, he thought, cover her mouth with a fist. Walk quickly away and tell others so they can point and laugh and whisper. But she didn't. Instead, she leaned in, her mouth close to his ear. "I know all about them."

"You do?"

The pretty girl nodded. "I can help you." She looked at her watch. "We close in ten minutes. Wait for me?" Then she smiled a sweet smile at him and walked quickly away.

Benjamin waited near the door as she stepped out into the rain. "I'm Elizabeth," she said.

"Benjamin."

She shook his hand. "Nice to meet you. Let's go."

"Where are we going?"

She grinned. "To rent a movie. You live near here, right? I see you in the library all the time."

"Just over there." He pointed. His sleep-fuzzy brain hadn't registered exactly what was happening yet. As she started walking, her short legs carrying her at a deliberate pace, he fell in behind her and finally caught up. They rented a movie and went back to his place.

He microwaved two small lasagnas and carried them into the living room. Elizabeth had taken off her coat and shoes and now bent over the VCR. "Now pay close attention, Benjamin."

Outside, the light began to fade.

The movie was the one about the boy who saw dead people everywhere. Benjamin had seen it with his wife a few weeks before she'd left. Back before The Downsizing. He tried to pay attention but the girl on his couch, cuddled up against him, filled him up with strange thoughts and alien feelings. Every so often he turned his head so that he could smell her hair. He felt a little drunk.

"There," she said. "Did you hear that?"

"What?"

She growled and it was a playful sound. Then, she grabbed up the remote control, rewound, and pushed play.

The child psychologist was telling the boy something. It sent chills down Benjamin's spine. Upstairs, the bed began to thump and Elizabeth looked up. "There they are, Benjamin. You know what to do."

He swallowed and nodded.

"Good. I'll wait here. If I fall asleep, wake me up when you're done." Then, she kissed his forehead.

His legs shook as he stood. Slowly, he climbed the stairs. Below him, he heard the channels change as Elizabeth surfed the stations. He went to his bedroom door and cleared his voice.

The bed stopped thumping.

"Hello?"

He heard a scampering, then a stifled giggle and a harsh whisper: "Shhhhhh. He's here."

He stepped into the room. "I know you're there."

Another voice. "He knows we're here." Another stifled giggle. Then a fart and laughter.

"What do you want?"

"Come to bed, Benji."

"I will. But tell me what you want."

"We're ... hungry. Benjibenjibenjibenjibenjibenji."

"What would you like?"

"Apart from you?" one asked.

"Yes ... apart from me."

More whispers. "Surprise us."

He started with what was left of the popcorn he had made earlier. He pushed it under the bed slowly and fell back when it shot out, showering the room with kernels. Then, he tried the bag of Oreos, the loaf of bread, and the package of bologna. The bedroom floor looked like a tornado-strewn lunchroom.

He went downstairs and saw Elizabeth was asleep, curled into a bright package on his dark couch. Something dropped into his heart.

Benjamin went to the hall closet and pulled out boxes and shoes until he found the one box he hadn't looked in for three years. He hauled it into his bedroom and dropped it to the floor. Then, he opened it.

There on top, a wedding picture of a woman with a rose. He looked at it, thrust it under the bed. Something snatched it from him. He waited for it to fly back at him, but it didn't. Next, a bundle of poems and letters. A pair of dog-tags from a brother dead now thirty years. A yearbook with smudge marks on a marked page and forgotten face. More letters, one a Dear John from his army days. He pulled each item from the box, felt each item yanked from his shaking hands, and somewhere in the midst of it, his tears began to flow. When the box was empty, he sat back.

From underneath the bed, a satisfied belch. And then silence.

Benjamin sat there for a long time.

He woke the pretty girl, Elizabeth, sometime after midnight. Her eyes opened and he fell into them as he stood above her. She yawned and stretched. "Did it work?"

He nodded. "Yes."

She sat up. "Let's go make sure."

Elizabeth led him by the hand up the stairs, somehow knowing the way. She walked into the room and leaned over to look underneath the bed. He joined her.

"Feel better, Benjamin?"

"I do."

"Good." She dropped to her hands and knees. "Come on then." She scooted under the bed and waited. He paused, looked at the empty box, and then crawled under the bed with her. They lay there on their backs looking up at the underside of the box spring. In the gloom, he saw her eyes were shut and her breathing easy. In that moment, he loved her.

She rolled towards him, her arms pulling him closer and kissed him slowly on the mouth. "See? It's not so bad."

He kissed her back. No. Not so bad.

Her teeth elongated. A patch of hair sprouted above her third and fourth eyes. He only noticed it in part, though, because he felt his own mouth filling with fangs. The hair on the backs of his hands, growing in wild tufts, itched furiously. His fingernails became talons. A single horn pushed its way out of the top of her head.

Laughing, they kissed again. Then they feasted on each other long into the night.

And it wasn't bad at all.

LORD OF TIME
by Livia Blackburne

The sky was purple here, with roiling clouds that never stopped moving. Liliya's fellow novitiates told her that the winds of time kept the sky churned in a storm that only the Lord of Time could control. The others came from families that had served the Lord for generations. They'd grown up in the shadow of the temple and heard stories about the god at their nurses' knees. Liliya, on the other hand, hadn't even known the god's name until two years ago.

There were thirty novitiates total, girls sixteen years of age, and they huddled outside a gate of twisted wrought iron as tall as five men. As it creaked open, the girl next to Liliya grabbed her arm, her eyes wide with fear.

"What are you afraid of?" Liliya asked. "Your family has served him for so long."

The girl shivered. She was beautiful, like most of the priestesses the god favored. "He's not cruel. But he is harsh with his punishments, should you disobey him."

Liliya wondered what this girl, whose soft hands and smooth skin bore no sign of the ravages of war, considered a harsh punishment. Could it be worse than what Liliya's village had already suffered? But there was a real fear in the girl's eyes, and Liliya sensed she shouldn't make light of it. She would be careful. She would stay safe.

The gate opened completely to reveal a woman. It was hard to tell her age—though the skin of her face was smooth, it was drawn tight over harsh cheekbones and a proud nose, features that spoke of age, wisdom, and command. The woman's raven black hair was pulled atop her head in an elaborate braided coil, and the emblem of the High Priestess was embroidered in gold thread on her lavender robe. She carried a single incense stick that burned with a blue flame.

The pack of novitiates crowded closer together.

"Follow me," said the Priestess. "Single file."

The novitiates fell in line behind the priestess. As they entered, they filed past a group of young men still waiting to be allowed in. While the boys all wore the ceremonial tunics and nervous expressions of those entering the temple for the first time, one looked particularly awestruck by his surroundings, staring open mouthed at the sky, the gate, and the buildings across the wall. He caught Liliya watching him and grinned sheepishly. Liliya lowered her eyes and passed through the gate.

The Temple grounds were tranquil, quite unlike the clouds above. Stone walkways crisscrossed a green–gray lawn. Priestesses, novitiates, and the god's male servants went about their tasks between simple stone and wood buildings. Liliya's gaze was caught by a blue light in the center of the compound. It was too far away to see clearly, but the other novitiates' eyes strayed in that direction as well.

"Eyes on me," said the High Priestess.

She led them into a long wooden building with beds lined up on each side–one bed for each of them, with a chest at the foot. "For the next five years of your lives, you belong to the Lord of Time," she said. "Most of you will never see him, but you will serve him. You will prepare his incense and his offerings. You will plant the gardens that feed the people of the temple and grow the herbs that comprise the incense. Every morning and evening, you will sing praises in his honor. You will remain in service for five years. After that time, you will return home and live your lives in his favor."

Liliya's new life in in the temple was simple. The novitiates spent their days doing mundane tasks–fetching water, preparing food, hoeing the gardens. It was modest work that Liliya knew well, and she was grateful for this. The god's presence was far away, easy to ignore once she grew accustomed to the purple clouds.

The other girls fell naturally to their duties and to each other. In the evenings, they clustered together and spoke of their day, laughing and chattering. These girls shared a history of secrets passed down from their families, of incense breathed into their mothers' wombs. Sometimes, one of them would beckon to Liliya, at which point she would sit on the outer edge of the circle and listen to them talk. Liliya was always silent, though she knew she should try and befriend the others. There was a liveliness to their interactions that Liliya could not grasp. The novitiates were by turns happy or nervous, angry at imagined slights or subdued at the High Priestess's admonishments. Liliya could feel none of these things. If the others' lives were boldly colored, Liliya lived in shades of gray, and she couldn't bridge the difference.

The god whom they served resided in an old house in the center of the temple grounds. Liliya found it strange. Of all the places for a god to live, she might have expected a marble obelisk, or a grand palace. But this was a rickety wooden house, with slats askew and old cracked windows. Even the novitiates' dormitory looked more stable. But then, the house wasn't held together by things such as nails. It crackled with the same energy of the skies, and Liliya had the impression that if she raced toward the house, she would be thrown back by an invisible force. Perhaps that was why everyone gave it a wide berth. The only person ever seen to enter was the High Priestess, and even she entered with her head veiled and carefully bowed, with an offering of scented herbs held reverently in front of her.

Next to the house was a globe, the source of the blue light that had attracted Liliya's attention the first day. It was as large as a man and held up by a stand made of boar tusks. Lightning arced in its center, and images appeared and melted into each other. When Liliya first gazed into it, passing by as she lugged a bucket of water for the kitchens, she'd seen a man hanging by a set of chains. His face was downcast, hidden in shadow. His muscles were contorted in agony. Veins popped under his skin, and there was a curious crescent-shaped birthmark at the base of his neck.

Liliya stopped, transfixed by the man's pain. Was this the Lord of Time himself?

"It shows images of the future and the past," said a voice at her ear.

Liliya blanched to see the High Priestess next to her. The woman hardly ever spoke directly to the novitiates. The priestess' voice still had the cold, imperious air that Liliya remembered from her first day, but Liliya sensed no malice in it.

"He knows the future?" Liliya asked.

"He is the God of Time," the priestess said with a faint smile.

"Who is that man?"

The priestess gazed into the ball. "I don't recognize the image, so it is unlikely to be from the past. The future then, perhaps."

A shadow crossed the window of the house. Liliya tried to look through the glass. She couldn't make out features, but there was definitely something blocking the light, and a feeling of presence that froze her to the core.

The priestess gave her a sidelong glance. "What do you feel, child?"

"Nothing," she lied.

"The Time Lord doesn't favor everyone with his presence or attention," she said. "But then, you are not like the others, are you?"

There was no greater honor and no greater mystery than to be chosen by the Lord of Time. He was one of five gods who held sway over the heart of civilization, and of the five, he was the most mysterious by far. But until recently, Liliya's people had paid the gods no heed. The rice farmers of Asayi were far from the temple, and weeks of travel over swampy roads buffered them from the gods' meddling.

Then Asayi was invaded—not by the gods' servants, but by a savage warrior people from the north. The godless attackers left the village in flames, the rice paddies red with blood. Those who weren't killed outright were left to face a long hard winter, as the invaders had taken their food stores. By spring, their village had dwindled to half its size, and the raids continued on.

Five long years later, the priestesses and their armies came from the south, enforcing their rule over both the invaders and the invaded alike. The Asayi farmers welcomed them with relief. Liliya's mother buried her once-beautiful face in her hands and wept for joy.

So it was that a year after the gods took over, when the High Priestess came carried on a palanquin by six young men, the villagers bowed their heads in respectful welcome. Beautiful and severe, she stopped at the edge of the rice paddies and raised an imperious hand to the workers there.

"Line up. The Lord of Time wishes one of you in his service."

At first, the workers didn't move, uncertain about the woman's words. But the palanquin bearers also carried spears and used them to herd the people to some semblance of a line. The priestess drew out a globe the size of her hand that flashed with blue lightning. A palanquin bearer, strong and graceful, came before the priestess and took it. When he passed in front of Liliya, the globe flashed bright. Murmurs ran through the crowd. The priestess looked at Liliya in a way that made Liliya all too aware of her mud soaked clothing, the dirt caked in her nails.

"Your name?"

"Liliya." Her voice sounded timid, even to herself.

"How many years do you have?"

"Fifteen."

"Report to the temple on the summer solstice of your sixteenth year."

One moon cycle after she arrived at the temple, Liliya once again crossed paths with the boy who'd smiled at her by the temple gate. Liliya had been struggling with a weed in the temple garden—a coarse, grassy nuisance that grew in tangled clusters with roots spread wide to hold the dirt. Liliya braced her foot against the ground and pulled with all her strength. Her arms ached with the effort, and her palms were rubbed raw.

The boy came by and took a clump in his hands. He was a few years older than Liliya and on the cusp of manhood, with his shoulders broadening and his limbs becoming corded with muscle. Scars crisscrossed his arms, the only sign that he may not have had an easy childhood. There was a set to his jaws as he pulled the weeds out, but he showed no greater effort beyond that.

"Thank you," Liliya said, as he handed the weeds back to her. As she stared at the dead grasses, her vision blurred, and she remembered a time when she'd been surrounded by similar weeds. Liliya had been ten when the barbarians invaded—not old enough to fully understand the attacks, but old enough to hear the screams of dying men and tortured women, to smell the acrid smoke of burning flesh. Old enough to stifle her sobs as her mother pushed her into the surrounding swamp grass and to know, as she huddled alone and terrified, that nothing would ever be the same. Days later, when most of the invaders had gone, she'd hobbled back to the village, dirty, thirsty and hungry. She'd found her father dead, and her mother forever broken.

"Are you unwell?" asked the boy.

The question brought Liliya back to herself, and she tore her eyes from the weeds in her hand. Words froze in her throat.

The boy looked uncertainly at her. "I am Dineas," he finally said. As with all the Time Lord's servants, he was beautiful, with sand colored hair and a charming smile. His eyes were friendly, and Liliya found herself able to smile back. The memory faded.

"Thank you, Dineas," she said. She gave a polite bow and continued with her weeding.

Dineas was light hearted and cheerful. One day, he waved at Liliya from across the grounds, which struck her as bold. There was no prohibition against talking to the young men—occasionally her duties even required it. There was an unspoken rule, though, that the two groups otherwise stay apart. The novitiates were, of course, to stay pure to the Lord of Time while they were in his service. But when nobody reprimanded Dineas for his boldness that morning, Liliya worked up the courage to wave back.

The day after, he fell in step beside her on the way to the garden. "Where are you from?" he asked.

"Far from here," she said.

"I know." At her surprise, he explained. "You're like me. I see you looking around at everything, taking it all in. It's not normal for you, to live in a god's shadow. You don't act like the purple clouds aren't there."

"Are your people also new to the god's service? Is this why you keep talking to me?" She imagined that Dineas might feel just as out of place amongst his fellow palanquin bearers as she did amongst the novitiates.

"That is one reason." He gave an uncertain smile. "Also, you always look a little lost."

Liliya dropped her eyes. "I do miss my village." It was selfish to burden him with her troubles, but the offered ear was too tempting to refuse.

Dineas reached out and squeezed her hand. His grip was comforting, and Liliya noticed that her entire hand could fit inside his. "It's only five years," he said. "Then you can go back and live with the Time Lord's blessing."

The High Priestess walked by. Her eyes settled sharply on the two of them, and Dineas let go of Liliya's hand. The two of them stepped away from each other in unspoken agreement and continued on their own way.

The High Priestess was waiting for Liliya at the gardens.

"Remember, Liliya," she said. "The Lord of Time is possessive of his priestesses. You have not yet done anything to incur his wrath. Be careful to keep it that way."

Liliya bowed her head, properly chastened. She knew the god's strict demand for purity, though it hadn't even occurred to her to think of Dineas as anything but a friend to talk to. It saddened her, but Liliya understood full well by now that few people had the luxury of living the way they wanted.

"I'm sorry, Blessed One," she said. "I will be more careful."

Two moon cycles after she arrived, it was Liliya's turn to prepare the incense offering. It was a task she approached with trepidation. There were so many different herbs, so many different combinations for each occasion. A priestess guided her as she gingerly picked the correct portions and crumbled them into a clay bowl to soak in oil. When she finished, the priestess handed her a flint. Liliya struck it until a spark started the herbs smoldering.

The herbs secreted a thick, heavy scent that stuck in Liliya's nostrils and made her dizzy. No one paid her any heed as she crossed the courtyard toward the incense holder in front of the Lord's house. The smoke blew back in her face as she walked, and Liliya concentrated on putting one foot in front of the other. The ground became unsteady under her, yet she kept walking. How foolish the other novitiates would think her if she stumbled on this simple task. The Lord's house drew closer, and the presence inside was stronger than she had felt before. Ten more steps to the incense holder. Now five more.

Liliya's knees were weak when she finally placed the bowl on its stand. She prostrated herself before the offering and bowed three times—once for the past, once for the present, and once for the future. Then she climbed unsteadily to her feet. The smoke from the incense was curling up into the sky, forming wispy patterns that shouldn't have lingered so long in the breeze. Its smell was still strong, and Liliya turned away. She swayed on her feet. A novice passing by reached toward her in alarm.

The blood rushed to Liliya's head.

≡✳≡

She awoke in a dim room with walls so aged and warped that they could only belong to one house. The presence that surrounded her confirmed it.

"You breathed too much incense, little one," echoed a voice.

She said nothing. What could one say, when wrapped in the presence of a god? Surprisingly, Liliya felt no fear. It was as if the sense of the god around her drove out the last of her capacity to feel anything at all.

"Do you have questions?" There was a hint of amusement to the Time Lord's utterance.

"Why am I here?"

"Your people interest me," said the presence. "You intrigue me. Your past, your present, your future."

As he spoke, she relived her childhood, both the good times and the horrors, but it was as though it happened to someone else, her feelings numbed by the god's presence.

"You've been through much," said the Time Lord.

"Yes, my Lord."

"And where will you go from here? You have the spark that all my servants carry, and so will your daughters, if you bear them. But perhaps you're not ready. Will you try to avenge your people? Or will you let it go?"

She was confused by his words. Vengeance was beyond her reach. Her anger had long been beaten out of her, extinguished by necessity so she could live without going mad. "I don't understand," she said.

"You amuse me, little one. But mortals don't always feel the eddies of the past around their ankles until they're drawn under."

For a moment, Liliya could sense streams of time around her. It seemed they propped her up when she swayed.

"I will let you determine your fate," said the Time Lord. "But the choice you make is harsh. One that belies the timidity of your appearance."

Was she timid? She was broken. Like the others in her village, she had picked up the pieces of herself and gone on living. She didn't feel any hate. She felt nothing where those memories were concerned. They were numb, emptied out.

"All will come clear with time," said the god. She saw a shadow in the corner of her eye, but there was no one there when she turned. The darkness closed in once again. When she opened her eyes, she was back on the ground by the incense offering.

Liliya relived the attacks that night. Once again, she raced into the swamp as the flames of her village roared behind her. Smoke filled her lungs and made her choke. Somewhere in the midst of battle, a child shrieked. The Time Lord's presence was not there to dampen her fear, and she awoke with the full force of remembered terror in her chest and the sound of her own frantic gasps in her ears. Her fellow novitiates were asleep around her, their faces peaceful. Liliya put one bare foot on the ground, and then another.

The grass outside looked almost silver in the moonlight. No one else was awake, and the only movement was the arcing blue light from the Time Lord's globe. Images flitted through it, first scenes from her past, and then the curious image of the man in pain. Liliya watched it, her eyes settling again on the crescent birthmark at the base of his neck. It was shaped like the moon overhead, though dark instead of brilliant white.

She could feel the Time Lord watching her.

"Are you all right?"

Liliya jumped. The voice was too young and too human to belong to the Time Lord. Dineas stood next to her, clad still in his sleeping tunic, his straw colored hair mussed by sleep.

Liliya took an alarmed glance toward the Time Lord's house, the High Priestess' warning flashing through her mind. But she sensed no anger from the dilapidated house, and Dineas' voice was kind.

"Some memories came to me in a dream," she said. "I couldn't sleep."

The boy nodded sagely. "It happens to me too. I come out here to clear my mind, when it happens."

It was a relief to speak with someone who knew a life beyond the perfect routines of the god-ruled lands. "What was your home like?" she asked.

"We didn't have a home," he said.

"None at all?"

"We wandered," he said. "We were warriors, and we followed our swords."

"I thought there were no more wars," she said.

"We don't fight anymore. The priestesses put a stop to it. But I was raised by the sword. I was grappling by my fifth year, hunting game by my eighth, dueling before my tenth. After the gods came, we changed our ways, but my memories still linger."

Liliya looked at the scars on his arms and imagined the blades that put them there.

"When I was twelve," he said, "I was deemed ready to fight with the men. I was so proud. Our first battle was a raid. I remember rice paddies, many of them, surrounded by grassy swamp." He paused, as if seeing the scene before him. "It was different from my training. Messier, but easier. The farmers couldn't fight, and we cut them down easily. I earned my shield that day."

Dineas gazed up at the moon, lost in thought, and Liliya was glad he was not looking at her. The burning rice paddies filled her vision, the screams of her people.

"It was the way of our people," he said. "But I was sick afterward, secretly. It became easier after that, but now I think back on it and wonder. I still hear the screams."

He was still talking, but she no longer listened. In front of her, the globe shifted. The man's image became more crisp, and his face came out of shadow. There was a plaque underneath him, and Liliya could make out the words. "Thus are punished those who consort with the Time Lord's priestesses."

Dineas looked up at the house. As he moved, the collar of his tunic fell open and Liliya saw—as she knew she would—a mark shaped like a half moon. He was so beautiful. So deceptively innocent. Liliya looked at his hands, remembering how strong they'd felt around her own, and how she'd taken comfort in his touch. He was not much older than she was, and just as lost.

The Time Lord's presence was all around her, strong and watchful. She thought to take Dineas's hands in hers, to squeeze them and tell him it would be all right, but her hand was slow to move. In her mind's eye, Liliya saw her father's charred body as she laid him to rest, the deadness of her mother's gaze. Smoke from the remembered fire twined around her, wrapping her limbs and drawing her under. She couldn't breathe.

The boy turned a tortured eye toward her. "What do you think? Will I pay for the pain I've caused?"

He reached for her arm, and she felt the warmth of his fingertips. She looked down and imagined them covered in blood.

Liliya placed her hand on his chest. The winds of time whipped around her, so strong that she could hardly stand. "Be at peace," she said. "The gods are just."

At the very last moment, Liliya thought to look at the globe again, to see if there was a woman being punished alongside the man. But she didn't look. In the end, it didn't matter.

And with that last thought, Liliya stood on her toes and slowly, deliberately, touched her lips to his.

EVACUATION
by Alan Dean Foster

Olsen knew he had been hit. Bad. How bad he couldn't tell. His left arm, now useless, continued to ignore the frantic signals from his brain. The front of his shirt was wet. Dark wet and sticky, so not from sweat. Liquid stung his eyes, forcing him to blink continually.

Rolling over and keeping a tight grip on his weapon with his still functioning right hand, he started kicking and scrambling as hard as he could. Posted on the very edge of the ridge overlooking the valley below, he had volunteered to remain and provide covering fire for his buddies while they scrambled down slope toward the designated pickup point. Reasonably flat and level, it offered enough room for a Chinook or even an Osprey to touch down.

Sent out to reconnoiter the enemy positions in the valley, the two platoons had instead found themselves ambushed by a waiting enemy. The top of his head taken off by a sniper's bullet, Sgt. Cochran had been the first to go down. He had been followed in quick, deadly succession by Sharpley and Davis. Retreating under a withering crossfire, the rest of the troops had made their way toward the pickup location. With Lt. Hammerslee having quickly reported their position and situation, they were assured of rescue.

The critical question being, a hard-crawling Olsen knew as he ate dirt and gravel while pushing himself onward, not if but when.

His heart gave a jump when he heard the rotating thunder of an AC-130 "Spooky's" 25 mm GAU equalizer cannon start chewing up the hillside below the ridge. If their covering fire had arrived, it meant that pickup couldn't be far behind. He tried to slither a little faster, but something in his left side was broken. Not his arm this time. Something deeper. Something more important.

Would they wait for him? In the confusion and chaos of battle and retreat, with his platoon sergeant dead, would anyone think to look for the last man on the ridge who had remained behind to give covering fire for his friends? Or would the thankful survivors struggle onto the relief craft, grateful to be alive and thinking of nothing else but getting clear? Raising his head, he tried to shout. A choked gurgle emerged and he found himself coughing and spitting instead of forming words. More dark liquid. His insides coming outside.

He thought he could hear the steady whup-whup of accelerating blades, though whether landing or taking off he couldn't tell for certain. His hearing seemed to be failing, too. *A couple more kicks forward,* he told himself, and he would top the low rise that separated the rocky grade from the pickup area. Then even if his legs failed him, he could roll down slope. Surely someone would see him!

Nothing. His body had no extra kicks remaining. Oddly, the pain seemed distant now, almost as if he had grown used to it. It had morphed into a persistent all-over ache, the kind one felt at the end of four quarters of hard-played football. Lying there, he wondered if he would ever play football again. Lying there, he wondered if he would ever walk again.

A soft silence descended, as if someone had put a pillow over his head. Either the firing had stopped or else his hearing was gone completely. Then, unexpectedly, hands under him. Lifting, raising his weight smoothly. No one was talking, though whether from choice, exhaustion or out of concerns for keeping their position concealed from the enemy he didn't know. Nor did he care. Raising his head, he blinked through thick liquid.

The pickup site lay directly ahead. Sitting on it, impossibly, was a C-130 Hercules, all four of its props turning slowly. How the pilot had managed to set the Herc down on such a small landing spot Olsen could not imagine. When he could see again he had every intention of kissing the pilot.

They carried him onto the plane as gently as possible. Once on board he was placed on a cot with clean sheets that smelled faintly of lavender and lemon. To Olsen, who had been in the field for days, the stolid, chunky aircraft smelled of heaven.

Raising his head slightly he managed to survey his surroundings. Someone must have given him a shot because for the first time since he'd been hit he felt no pain at all, not anywhere. Even the all-pervasive ache had receded. *Morphine,* he told himself. Except that his head was clear, no opioid fog at all.

The cargo hold was full of injured troops lying on neatly arranged cots; mostly men, some women. He didn't recognize any of them but that was not surprising. His platoon wasn't the only one that had been engaged that day. Probably the rescue plane had been en route back to Kabul from another skirmish when his group's call for help had been picked up and the Hercules had been diverted to their location.

It was oddly silent inside the plane as it lifted off. No moans, no groans, not even isolated snippets of conversation passed among those whose wounds would usually permit chatter. Doctors and nurses moved among the beds attending to the injured. Even though the pain had faded, Olsen wanted to scream for attention. But no one else was, and he was damned if he was going to be the one to break the peace. So he waited his turn.

It arrived in the shape of a blonde nurse who, uniform excepted, looked as if she could have stepped out of a major Hollywood film. The sight alone was enough to lift his spirits. He tried to smile, tried to think of something brave and witty to offer by way of greeting, but found himself unable to speak. At least, he told himself, he wasn't coughing and spitting blood all over her.

Bending slightly, she looked down at him. Her expression changed from one of studious professionalism to a frown. Then she straightened and called to someone unseen.

"Hey doc, there's something wrong here! This one's still alive."

Still alive? Something wrong? Even in Olsen's shattered, bemused mind those two observations did not seem to add up. He didn't have time to analyze further because a huge man in a physician's uniform was soon peering down at him. Hands moved, felt, pressed, while the tips of a dense red beard occasionally brushed Olsen's chin and neck.

"Damned if he isn't." He turned to the nurse. "Who picked him up?"

The nurse turned to peer down the length of the slightly vibrating C-130. "Me and Kara. He was on the list."

The big man frowned. "You certain?"

She stiffened slightly. "Always certain."

He nodded, stroking his beard as he thought. "So. We have a small problem, then. We can't take him with us."

Couldn't what? Olsen was suddenly frantic, though he was unable to show it. What else could they do with him? He was badly confused. Also, the pain was starting to return. Had he been able to do so he would have asked for another shot of whatever it was they had initially dosed him with.

Noting his concern, perhaps through the movement and widening of the Private's eyes, the doctor smiled and leaned toward him. He reminded Olsen of a favorite uncle who had passed on years ago: big, gruff, usually smiling but the kind you'd want on your side in a street fight.

"Easy, son. We'll straighten this all out. Right quick, you'll see." Turning away, he began speaking in a powerful voice into the pickup of the headphone he wore. A dazed Olsen thought he heard the words "pilot" and "course change." Only when he heard "Bagram" did he finally calm down a little.

Bagram was the location of the major alliance base in the northern part of the country. The military hospital there was one of the best in the country. He would be well taken care of. He would be all right.

He was going to make it.

His thoughts were confirmed by the slight shudder of the plane as it turned. The flight from the ragged corruption of treeless mountainside where his platoon had been attacked to Bagram shouldn't take long. Not in the reliable Herc. He allowed himself to relax. Even better, the knockout blonde nurse stayed with him, taking a seat on the side of his cot. Her eyes were a glacial blue and her skin almost ivory, both in stark contrast to her uniform. Now if she would only smile, he told himself. But she never did. Almost, but not quite.

His emotions boosted by knowing their destination, he finally managed to find his voice. What was left of it was raspy and thick. It didn't sound like him to him, but he was coherent.

"My ... gotta thank the pilot for me," he managed to gasp. "Putting down a Herc on that shitspot ... I wouldn't have thought it possible."

Her voice was liquid and husky; no-nonsense yet intimate. "Our pilots have been flying for a long time. They know their jobs. How do you feel?"

He fought to smile. "Like I've been hit by every lineman in the NFL, one after another. How long 'til we get to Bagram?"

"Soon." Reaching out, she put a hand on his forehead. It was like the coldest of cool compresses yet instantly soothing. "You should try to relax. You've had the closest of close calls. You even fooled us, and we're not easily fooled."

"Just glad you showed up." He pleaded. "Can you stay awhile? You don't have to talk. Just sit there."

Now she did smile. "You're a real fighter, Olsen. I admire real fighters."

As good as her word, she remained by his side for the duration of the flight. Once or twice he felt guilty for keeping her from her rounds, from seeing to the other injured. But the Herc seemed well-staffed, and if she didn't feel the need to move on, well, he wasn't about to urge her to do so.

In another kudo to the pilots, the landing was so smooth he didn't even feel it when they touched down. Within the hold there was an immediate stir of activity, but not among the wounded. Expecting to hear excited, if feeble, exclamations of relief and joy, he heard nothing except the murmur of doctors and nurses.

Then he felt himself being lifted off the bedding. What was this? Normal procedure called for someone in as bad shape as he was to be moved together with the cot into a waiting ambulance or truck. Instead, he felt himself being carried along by powerful arms under his body. Blinking, he was somehow not surprised that two of them belonged to the beautiful nurse. He was, however, surprised to see that four nurses were carrying him. None of them were male.

The army, he reflected, had changed more than anyone could have imagined.

They carried him out of the plane, down the rear loading ramp, and stood him on his feet. Astonishingly, he discovered that he was perfectly able to stand. His left arm seemed to be working again, too. More bewildered than ever, he found himself squinting into the rising sun of an early Afghan morning. In the distance but within view lay the sprawling complex that was Bagram airbase. Nearby was a road. Paved, sort of.

"You can walk." It was the blonde, standing at his left side, helping to support him. Raising an arm, she pointed, almost imperiously. "Walk. Walk, or die." A second genuine smile somewhat mitigated her brusqueness. "You're a fighter. You can make it. Tell them that when you were overlooked during the pickup, you started walking. You got a lift. Locals. Dropped off here, walked the rest of the way." Her voice deepened slightly. "Walk."

Not knowing what else to do, astounded at feeling little of the pain that should be tearing through him, he complied. Only when he had stumbled a few steps without falling did he think to look back. She was walking away from him, briskly and without looking around to see if he had fallen, heading for the sleek gray of the C-130 that had landed in the untilled field that flanked the road.

"Hey!" he shouted. "I was gonna ask you for a date! If you're single, that is." *Even if you're not,* he thought.

Glancing back, her hair threads of gold spilling from beneath her cap, she grinned broadly at him. "I'm single, but sorry, no date. Not part of the job description."

He took a faltering step after her. When he did so, pain returned, halting him. "Can I at least know your name? Where you're based? Maybe I can look you up later, sometime, someplace?"

"You never know," she called back, almost to the plane now. "I'm Hildr. Hildr Valkyrie. Valhalla base."

It didn't resonate with him. "Is that near Kandahar?"

"Some say. Turn away, Jon Olsen. Turn and walk."

But he didn't. He couldn't. Instead, he watched until she disappeared up the cargo ramp into the back of the plane. The quartet of props began to turn faster as it closed up. Upon reaching speed the Herc pivoted and, heading back the way it had come, lifted off into a cloud-filled Afghan sky. It was then that he noticed that the protuberant nose of the aircraft formed the chin of a skull, and the rest of the cockpit area the eyes and mouth and twin slots of a skeletal nose.

Climbing at an impossible angle while making no noise, it sped off to the north in search of more men and women to pick up, a silent gray eminence whose four moaning engines trailed contrails composed of the attenuated souls of dead soldiers. He watched it until it disappeared into the distance, or faded into imperceptibility, or vanished into a dark cloud.

Then he turned and, knowing full the meaning of existing in a state of not dead, started limping slowly but with increasing strength toward the road that led to Bagram.

PURE SILVER

by A. C. Crispin & Kathleen O'Malley

I first saw the werewolf at four a.m., Wednesday, on the A-8 Metrobus traveling from New York Avenue to my old one-room on Morris Road in Anacostia. It had been one of those days ... there weren't any other kind with my job. I was exhausted, dozing as we lurched along, but suddenly I opened my eyes and he was there, across the aisle from me.

I knew what he was right off—but that's me. I see the animal in everyone. I'll meet someone and right away see a falcon deep inside, or a spider, maybe an otter or deer. But this was different. This guy didn't just have an animal's *spirit* inside him ... no, no. He was a real werewolf. I *knew* it, knew it as surely as I know I'm 5'6" and have reddish-blond hair.

His hair was pale silver, dipping low on his forehead in a pronounced widow's peak. Not just thick, it was *dense*—like a pelt. Shaggy white brows met over his narrow, hooked nose. The eyes gleaming beneath them were steel gray, ringed with black ... like mine. The werewolf was old, seventy at a guess, more than twice my age, but his eyes were bright ... ageless.

His grizzled stubble of beard started on top of his prominent cheek-bones, continued down over well-chiseled features, then disappeared inside the neck of an enormous, mud-colored overcoat. I glanced at his hands; they were covered with rough brindled hair. His fingernails were thick, raggedly sharp.

When I looked back at his face, I found him watching me. Quickly, I flicked my eyes up to the "DC is a Capital City" ad, but I was too late. Now he was staring at me.

That's okay, I thought calmly, *he won't mess with me. He'll think I'm a cop.* I straightened my heavy navy-blue nylon bomber jacket with its fake fur collar. My navy pants, black vinyl shoes, blue shirt and imitation leather garrison belt completed the uniform. I made sure he could see the silver

137

badge over my left breast. I only wished my name wasn't under it, *Humane Officer Therese* (not Theresa, thank you) *Norris.*

Of course, my belt wasn't studded with cop toys, just a long, black flashlight, and two old rope leashes. I might look like a cop, but I worked for the S.P.C.A., enforcing the animal control and cruelty laws of the District of Columbia. To the public, I was, at best, a dogcatcher—at worst, someone who gassed puppies for a living.

Not that we gassed them. Our animals were humanely euthanized with a painless injection of sodium pentobarbital, a powerful anesthetic pumped into the forearm vein by a skilled technician. That it was merciful didn't make it easier.

Tonight's shift had been a *bitch*. The city's Animal Control Facility operates around the clock. I worked the night shift, driving a big, white van Tuesday through Saturday, five p.m. to one a.m. We called it the "nut" shift; the worst time to be on the streets, with the drug dealers, prostitutes, junkies, street people, headline-hungry politicians and—worse yet—tourists.

Tonight I'd had over forty calls, picked up thirty-two animals, and had had to euthanize twenty-seven before I could go home. The paperwork had taken me until three.

I'd barely walked in the door when I'd had to kill six three-day-old kittens with feline distemper. Then I did seven healthy mixed shepherds whose time had run out. We gave animals four days more than most places, so we were always cramped for space.

Around six-thirty I picked up three seriously injured strays (no collars, no tags) hit by cars in less than an hour. One of them had been neatly eviscerated. She looked at me gratefully as I talked soothingly to her, then pushed the plunger.

At nine, Linda, the night manager, said they couldn't hold the old stray hound any longer. I'd picked her up ten days ago. In spite of our posters, and ads in the *Post*, no one had claimed her. I loved her, but couldn't take her. My cat, Alfred, had died last year at seventeen, and I'd euthanized my fifteen year old Dobie, Dove, just six months ago, but my landlord had slapped a "no animals" clause on me before Dove got cold.

The hound licked our hands when Linda and I came to get her. She left this earth no doubt wondering where her people were.

At ten-fifteen I killed three raccoons we'd trapped, and one small brown bat who'd had his wings shattered by a terrified second-string Redskins linebacker wielding a broom. Each would have to be checked for rabies.

But the worst thing that'd happened tonight was that damned puppy. Even hours later, I found it hard to think about him. I'd chased his mother for half an hour, finally cornering her in an alley. She was nothing but drab fur, bones, and big nipples.

She led me to the nest where I found her pup safe and warm in a tumble of rags, paper and trash. He was fat and plush, about two weeks old, eyes just barely open—mixed beagle, mostly. I picked the trash off him ... then I saw it.

It made me sick, and after ten years on the job, not much got to me. He must've crawled through one of those plastic six-pack holders right after he was born. His head and right front leg were through one of the rings, and he was wearing it like a bizarre bandolier across his pudgy chest. Once in it, he couldn't get out, and he'd grown—but the plastic hadn't. The ring was sawing him neatly in half. Exposed muscles glistened red and swollen ... organs clearly visible. If I'd cut the damned thing, his entrails would've fallen out. All I could think of was Linda's favorite saying ... there are worse things than death.

I put mom in the van, then sat in the alley, finding the tiny vein by the light of the street lamp, in spite of the danger. Clean needles pull junkies out of the woodwork, crazed cockroaches after sugar, and I'd been beaten and held up at gunpoint before for them. But I couldn't let his mom watch.

Both mom and I cried all the way back to the shelter. You'd have thought it was my first week on the job. At least she'd have a warm bed for a week and an endless supply of food. Then I'd probably have to do her. It killed me to think that those seven days would probably be the best in her short, bitter life.

I remembered all this and swallowed hard. I lived with ghosts each night. In my lap was that puppy with the ring; I could feel him squirm on my legs. At my feet the old hound wagged her tail. The mixed shepherds and sick kittens watched me sadly. The raccoons stared. On my shoulder crouched the little bat. Every night I brought a crowd home—the ghosts of all the animals I killed. Every night for ten years.

Don't get me wrong, I didn't hate my job, but I didn't love it, either. It was something I had to do because I loved animals. *Someone* had to kill the thousands of sick, injured and unwanted animals discarded annually, and who better than someone who loved them? I know. *You* love animals and *you* couldn't do it—well, that's why *I* had to.

While I was thinking this, the old werewolf touched me on the shoulder, nearly scaring me to death. He was hanging onto the overhead bar, staring at me. His expression was kindly, but I fingered my flashlight. I'd had to use it as a weapon before.

"You've had a hard night, haven't you, bubeleh?" he said in a sober, gravely voice that was laced with a thick, Old World accent. It was the last thing I'd expected. A Jewish werewolf? In New York, maybe, but D.C.?

His unexpected sympathy hit me hard; tears welled up. I couldn't speak for fear I'd start bawling with ten years' backlogged heartache, so

I just nodded. Here was this old man, homeless from the look of him, comforting me. I took a deep breath, glanced away, trying to pull myself together. That's when I noticed the number tattoed on the underside of his hairy arm as he held the bar. It was the old, faded, concentration camp number survivors of the Holocaust wear.

"You shouldn't work so hard, a nice girl like you," the old man rumbled, still smiling. "Goodnight, Therese." Therese. Not Theresa. Everybody said Theresa. Then he got off the bus. I was still shaking my head as I stepped down onto Morris Road. A kindly Jewish werewolf ... right. Sure.

I walked home, the ghosts of twenty-seven animals trailing behind me, wondering whether there'd been a full moon tonight.

"Hey, Tee, good to see you," the cop said the next night, as he opened my van door. Joseph WhiteCrane was a K-9 cop with Metro police. The shelter often supplied Metro with dogs, and Joe's dog, Chief, a big white shepherd, had been one of my finds. Joe was part Sioux, part Hispanic, and part Irish. About 5'8", he wasn't handsome, with his hooked nose and pock-marked face, but his dark skin, black hair and ice-black eyes were magnetic, fiercely alive. Inside, Joe was a red-tailed hawk.

"I just got the call," I said. "You impound a dog?" Drug dealers often protected themselves with bad dogs, so it wasn't unusual to be called to a crime scene to pick up animals. But this didn't look like a drug bust—for one thing, the coroner's wagon was sitting next to Joe's car. Inside the car, Chief lunged and whirled, frantically barking.

"Not tonight." He looked at me, frowning. "What's that smell?"

I'd been hoping he wouldn't notice. "Gasoline and burnt hair. Some kids cooked a cat. I found her tied by her tail to a lamppost, still smoldering ... and screaming." I rubbed my hands on my pants, feeling bits of her still stuck to me. Her skin had sloughed off when I hit the vein.

Joe looked away, knowing better than to show any sympathy. "Well, like you say, there's worse things than death. Look, we need an expert opinion. An old guy's been killed, maybe by animals. We called the zoo, and nothing's loose. Would you look at the body and tell the coroner what you think of the wounds?"

I nodded. After the barbecued cat, nothing could bother me. At first, the coroner only wanted to show me the bites on the arms, but finally, Joe convinced him to uncover the corpse. Damn right, there's worse things than death. The man's throat was torn out, but the coroner said he survived that, only to endure the rest without being able to scream. His chest was torn open ... his heart ripped out.

"I've seen feral dogs do stuff like this to each other," I said, "but, eat *just* the heart? Weird." I stared at the bites. "Big jaws, wide muzzles, almost flat-faced."

"Pack of pit bulls?" Joe asked.

"Maybe ... or bull mastiffs. How big are the paw prints?"

Joe and the coroner looked at each other. "No paw prints," the cop said finally.

"Come on. This guy had to bleed like a fountain."

"*Foot*prints," Joe said. "The victim's. Nothing else."

"Are you guys sharing this with the press?" I asked quietly.

Joe shrugged. "Don't know."

"C'mon, give a poor working girl a break," I urged. "Remember the rabies outbreak? The city'll go nuts if the media talks up a crazed pack of killer dogs."

Joe smiled. "I'll talk to the captain. We might be able to keep this on low profile until we know more about the victim."

As we left the coroner's wagon, I saw Joe's still-frantic dog. "What's wrong with Chief? I've never seen him like this."

Joe shrugged. "He's been crazy since we got here. Let's take him out. You got your pole?"

"Yeah." I retrieved the aluminum rabies pole with its plastic-covered cable loop that enabled me to snag animals and hold them at a distance.

Joe put Chief on a short lead and let him out. The dog was high-strung, hackles up, whining. Normally, the big shepherd was as steady as a brick.

"Think he can smell those dogs?" I asked.

Joe shrugged. "If we spot 'em, we're going to catch them from a distance." He patted the pistol resting on his hip.

Chief pulled Joe for a few blocks, then turned up an alley. Suddenly, he rounded on a doorway, barking furiously. A huddled form was hiding in the shadows. I moved closer. Gray eyes, silver hair, muddy overcoat ... the old man from the bus ... and, damn it, he *still* looked like a werewolf.

"Easy, Chief, easy!" Joe said to the frenzied dog. "Hey, Grandfather, what're you doing here?"

"Resting, officer," he muttered tiredly. "Please, to hold your dog! Ach, Therese, tell him not to loose the dog!"

"You know this guy?" Joe asked me.

Something made me nod my head. "Grandfather," I said, using Joe's term, "It's not safe here. A man's been killed nearby. Did you see or hear anything?"

"Tsk, tsk." He shook his head. "Killed? *Such* a world!"

"Let us take you to the D Street shelter," Joe offered.

"In the same car with such a dog? Thank you, no."

I gazed at the old man—he seemed exhausted, weary to his soul, and my heart went out to him. Usually I only felt this kind of concern for animals, but ... he was different. "Have you had anything to eat tonight, Grandfather? A hot meal?"

He smiled. "Say 'zeyde,' Therese. Yes. I've had a good, hot meal. Not kosher, but ... how nice you should worry."

I wasn't sure I believed him. Impulsively, I shoved three dollars into his pocket. "Then this is for breakfast, Zeyde."

Joe and I walked back to my van. We had to drag Chief the whole way.

"So, is Zeyde his name?" I wondered to Joe.

He shook his head. "Means 'grandfather.' It's Yiddish."

Joe *would* know that. He was a mine of cultural knowledge. "What does 'bubeleh' mean?"

"'Grandchild.' It's an endearment." Joe paused. "Did you smell anything when you got near him?"

"Me? All I can smell is that poor cat. Why?"

Joe glanced back towards the alley. "I thought I caught a whiff of blood. Didn't see any, though. Might've been why Chief was so spooked. Could've been his breath."

I looked at Joe, my eyes wide. "His *breath?*"

"Lots of street people are sick ... ulcers, whatever."

Oh, I thought, embarrassed by my weird thoughts.

The next day was Friday, and by 11:45 p.m., Linda was helping me do my twentieth kill of the night. It was a full grown dobie, weighing thirty pounds. Should've weighed eighty. The people said they'd run out of dog food and couldn't afford more, so they just stopped feeding him. He couldn't even stand. Only his eyes looked alive. Linda took him in her arms.

"Hey, pretty dog," she crooned, petting him, her blond curls falling around her face. We ribbed Linda for looking like Jane Fonda. Lovely, quick, and clever ... inside she was a gray fox.

After filling the syringe, I turned to the dog. No muscles left, just hair, skin and bones after being tied in a closet for weeks, dumped like a pair of old shoes. Suddenly I saw Zeyde, ribs jutting, in the concentration camp.

"Tee, you okay?" Linda asked.

I swallowed. "Listen ... uh, can we keep this one?"

She sighed tiredly. "He needs his own pen, vet care, it'd be six months before he'd be adoptable."

It was suddenly very important for me to save this dog. "I can't kill this one," I said tightly. "He's so damned hungry."

Linda shook her head. "I don't know why I let you talk me into these things. We'll put a bed behind my desk—"

The phone rang, and she nodded at me to get it.

"D.C. Animal Control, Officer Norris."

"It's Joe," a familiar deep voice said. "The guy that got killed by those dogs was on the Federal Witness Protection Program. We just got the word."

"Weird," I said. "Some kind of Mafia snitch?"

"Weirder," Joe said. "He was a former Nazi. Did some favors for the State Department at the end of the war. Homicide's calling it a random wild dog attack."

My fingers tightened on the phone, thinking how odd it was to run into a Nazi and a Holocaust survivor in the same night. "Think this has anything to do with Zeyde?" I asked, finally.

"Doubt it, but if you talk to him, call me."

I fought back an urge to ask Joe if there'd been a full moon last night. Joe would know.

"Be careful on the street tonight, Tee," Joe warned me.

"I'm always careful," I said defensively.

"The hell you are. I've seen you work. You take too many chances. I mean it, Tee."

"Yeah, yeah," I agreed impatiently. "Listen, I gotta go."

"Why can't you be nicer to that poor guy?" Linda asked, when I hung up the phone. "Every straight woman in this place would *kill* to have him pay them half the attention he gives you."

"Get off my back," I said, good-naturedly.

We bedded the dobie down, then I went out to the van. I was startled to find Zeyde waiting beside it, as though my mentioning his name had conjured him up.

"Therese, bubeleh," he greeted me, "still working hard?"

"Still, Zeyde," I agreed. "What can I do for you? Had anything to eat tonight?"

"Such a nice girl to worry about an old man. I was just walking by ... I recognized your van." He must've watched me and Joe return to it the night of the murder. He smiled, and I felt funny. Why *was* I worried about him? I had enough to be concerned about taking care of the city's unwanted animals. "This is where you work, this place?" He indicated the shelter.

"Yeah, this is it."

"So, why does a nice girl like you do such a hard, dangerous job, chasing animals in the street at night?"

I shrugged. "Someone's got to do it."

"But you could get hurt by such big dogs, bitten terrible!"

"Not me, Zeyde," I reassured him. "I don't get bitten. Not in eight years. I'm good at this."

I found myself looking at the old mustard-colored cinder block shelter. The huge walk-in refrigerator stuck out of its side garishly, all new stainless steel against the old block. That's where most of my night's work ended up, in the walk-in, waiting for the renderers. Big, plastic barrels filled with rigid animals curled in a mockery of sleep.

Suddenly I was uncomfortably aware of the similarities between the shelter and a concentration camp. We warehoused animals until we had too many, then killed the sickest, weakest and oldest. Then we sent the bodies away to become soap and fertilizer. I didn't like thinking of myself as a *humane* Nazi.

"Ach, I've upset you, being the yenta, asking questions that are none of my business."

"Zeyde, I do this work because I have to, because I love animals ... I *help* them ..." He gave me a sad look and nodded. I thought of the dobie now sleeping behind Linda's desk. He'd never again be hungry or thirsty or cold. "I'm a complete vegan. I don't eat animals or wear *any* animal products."

He looked at me gently. "And people? You love them, too?"

I gritted my teeth. On a good day, I tolerated people. After a bad shift, I despised them. The only reason this job existed was because of the cruelty and indifference of people. But, even before the job, I'd never had close relationships. I still hadn't recovered from Dove or Alfred's death, but my dad died ten years before, and I couldn't even remember the date.

I thought of Joe. I knew how he felt about me, but I didn't *want* to care. "So, how long have you been on the streets?" I asked the old man, wanting to change the subject.

"Since the war," he admitted, with an odd smile.

"*World War Two*?" Surviving that long, homeless?

"They took everything," he said softly. "Parents, wife, children, grand-children ... our wealth, heritage ... everything we were. Everything we would have been."

"Other people started over, remarried, rebuilt," I said.

He nodded. "Yes, but to see your loved ones destroyed, an old family like ours ... I did not have it in me."

"So, what've you been doing all these years?"

He smiled, showing long, yellow teeth. "Following the wind, bubeleh."

"Zeyde, what's your name?"

"Joshua Tobeck," he replied. "There are many Tobecks, but our branch of that honored line was ... special ... very old. Blest, we often said." He chuckled—a short, brittle sound.

"Listen, Zeyde, the other night, when that man was killed ... weren't you close enough to hear anything?"

"Was *I* close enough?" he asked.

I watched him uneasily. "Did you know he was a Nazi?"

"Did I *know* he was a Nazi?" he repeated sarcastically.

I frowned. He was goading me. "Did you kill that Nazi?"

"Did I *kill* that Nazi?" He grinned wildly. "Did I *rip* his throat out? Did I *eat* his heart? Such a death is too good for a Nazi!" He spat angrily on the street. "Did I kill that Nazi?" His gray eyes gleamed with a feral light.

Fear made my skin crawl, but I shook it off. News travels fast on the streets. Zeyde had heard about the corpse's condition, that was all. He was just raving, trying to scare me.

"So, how's your policeman, bubeleh?" Zeyde said, once more the sweet old man. "Be nice to him, he has a good heart."

I watched the stooped figure shuffle away, reminding myself that such conversations were typical with street people—confused memories laced with paranoia. But as I slid into the driver's seat, I switched on the radio to call Joe.

I never did tell Joe much ... just that Zeyde wasn't a reliable witness. I wanted to discuss my suspicions, but I'd have sounded even crazier than Zeyde. Werewolves, yeah, sure!

On impulse, I let Joe take me to breakfast. We shared other meals over the next few weeks. We'd meet at the restaurant, go dutch, then separate from there. He had to be the world's most patient man, but I guess he could tell that was all I was up for. After the second week, I started really looking forward to seeing him and Chief, even though I suspected Joe was using my love for the dog to win me over. Linda couldn't believe I wasn't sleeping with him yet.

I kept running into Zeyde around the city. Sometimes he was lucid; others, definitely not. I learned about his family, how the Nazis took them, how one minute they were together and the next, only he was alive. He hinted once that he'd helped other prisoners get away.

"... when I had the strength to help them," he'd said. "The guards, they feared those bright silver nights."

"Bright silver? You mean moonli—" I'd started to ask.

"Searchlights!" he interrupted, smiling. Staring blankly, lost in memories, he muttered, "Six others, there were with me ... three Jews, two gypsies, a political dissident ... they hid me in the bad times, and I helped them get away ... we tasted revenge on silver nights ..."

"But, Zeyde," I'd said, when he trailed off, "why didn't *you* escape?"
He didn't answer.

Yet, I couldn't shake the crazy notion that he was a werewolf. Especially when he grinned, with all those long, yellow teeth. How could a man his age not have lost any teeth, especially in the camps?

We never found any large pack of dogs to explain that Nazi's death, but with the crush of work, it was easy to forget. I was doing fifteen to twenty-five kills a night, average for fall. Then, one Friday, almost a month to the day since I'd met him, Zeyde appeared at the shelter again, waiting by my van.

"Hi!" I greeted him warmly. "Have you eaten?"

He nodded. "The people from *Bread for the City* had the trucks out early. The soup's not kosher, but ..." he shrugged eloquently. "Do you have a minute to speak with me, Therese?"

"*Norris!*" Linda yelled out the front door. "Phone! It's *him!*" She batted her long lashes. I flipped her the bird.

"Sure, soon as I get this call. Come inside, it's warm." I went in to grab the phone. "Norris here."

"WhiteCrane," the baritone said. "Breakfast okay?"

I smiled, then realized Zeyde hadn't followed me inside. I poked Linda, who was leaning on me, trying to eavesdrop. "Bring Zeyde in," I hissed. "Sure," I told Joe. "Can we take Chief to the park later?"

"Yeah," he said, softly. "After the park ... can Chief and I ... take you home? Tell us at breakfast. Be careful tonight." He hung up quickly.

So, the world's most patient man had finally lost his patience. I was surprised to find how tempted I was. Then I noticed Linda still beckoning to the old man.

"Hey, come on, Zeyde," I called. "It's warm in here!"

Reluctantly, he stepped into the reception area, glancing at the array of brightly colored posters that admonished clients to neuter or spay—it's the only way. The cat kennel was on the left behind a glass wall, so clients could see the kitties. The dog kennel was out of sight, entered through a back hallway. Two small dogs were yapping, but the other sixty were still.

"Sit down, Zeyde, and tell me—"

The quiet shelter erupted in furious sound. The dog kennel exploded with hysterical barking. Linda and I stared wide-eyed at the cats. Every one of them stood facing Zeyde, backs arched, spitting and hissing.

Grabbing his elbow, I hustled him outside. Zeyde was shivering, looking sick and ancient. I sat him in the passenger seat of the van, then turned the heat up.

"I never had much of a way with animals," he muttered. There was a long, uncomfortable moment, until he finally said: "Therese, I've come to give you something. A gift."

I felt confused as he fumbled in the pockets of his huge coat. He pulled out something shiny, a small dagger, the blade maybe four inches long. It had a heavy handle, ornately carved.

"Pure silver," he said, touching it reverently. "It's been in my family since ... since the family began, how far back no one knows. It's part of our legacy, this knife, like our name, and ... our blessing. To the strongest grandson, the knife is passed from the grandfather, the zeyde. With the knife, the legacy, the blessing, is passed as well."

He took a shuddery breath and his young, gray eyes filled with tears. "Everything *they* took, but this. I hid it in the ground, and after the war, almost left it. Who needed the knife when there was no family, no legacy to pass? But, someday, I knew, I would want to pass it, so I took it. And now, I give it to you, bubeleh. I can't live much longer. If I die on the street, who gets the knife? You're all the family I have."

I didn't touch the knife, unsure if Zeyde was rational enough to give me the only thing of value he owned. "Uh ... Zeyde, I'm honored. But ... I'm not Jewish."

He chuckled. "Not even a little? Maybe once you went with a nice Jewish boy, we could say you were Jewish by injection?"

"Maybe once," I admitted, smiling.

"Take the knife, Therese," he begged, "with my love, my blessing. Then if I die tonight, I know the legacy is safe."

A month ago, I wouldn't have wanted that much connection to the old man. A month ago, I wouldn't have gone out with Joe. I held out my hand. He placed the handle in my palm.

"The inscription is Hebrew." He pointed to the ornately engraved letters, reading from right to left. "It is 'yod, he, vau, he.' In English, it is YHVH—you would say 'Yahweh.'"

I wrapped my hand around the small, ancient knife, feeling the engraved name of God. I suddenly cared a great deal if Zeyde lived through the night. "Let me take you to the homeless shelter, okay?" I slid the knife into the pocket of my jacket.

His eyes glittered strangely. "No. The wind blows sweet tonight, like fresh hay sick with mold. You ever smelled that?"

I shook my head. I was a city girl, after all.

"I smelled it first in the camps. It's *their* smell, the Nazis, a smell to make you sick inside. I followed it all over the world, after the camps. In every city, I found the smell ... I found them. But here ... it leaks from the ground, from the big, fancy buildings. They come to make deals, and they carry the smell. Dictators come to make nice to the President. Last week, that one from South Africa—feh! The smell! And the monsters that make the bad drugs ..." he smiled, shaking his head, lost in his memories. "To find a Nazi in this town is no easy thing. So much competition. Ach, tonight, the wind blows sweet and sick and I follow it."

Then, as if he'd said nothing bizarre at all, he smiled and said, "So, how's your fella, bubeleh? He's not Jewish, is he?"

After Zeyde had shuffled away, I started the van and went back to work. It wasn't a bad night for a Friday. By midnight, the van was only half full—no french-fried cats, no bad hit-by-cars. The air was cold and clean smelling. I was thinking about coming in, maybe even finishing on time. Then the radio crackled.

"Tee, we've got a police call," Linda's voice said. "In the alley between Vermont Avenue and Fourteenth Street, bordered by K and L. A possible feral dog attack. Joe and Chief are on their way. He says to wait till he's on the scene before leaving the van. Says that's an order."

"Right!" I said, irritably, swinging the van around. "I'm not far away." Joe and I were going to have to talk about his mother-hen routine. A drug bust was one thing, but handling bad dogs was *my* business.

I pulled up to the alley, grabbed my pole and flashlight, then tiptoed into the darkness. I peeked around a big dumpster that blocked most of my view. If I startled them, they'd all split and I'd never catch even one. If they came after me, I could always jump in the dumpster. I heard low growling, the kind a big, heavy-chested dog makes.

Then I saw him, and my breath stopped. Zeyde. Hunched over someone's body, his back to me, snarling. The sounds were coming from him. The body beneath him was spasming feebly, while the old man perched on his haunches over his victim's chest, hands up to his mouth, growling like a rabid dog.

"Zeyde!" I snapped. "What the *hell* are you doing?"

He stopped, and turned.

All that time I had spent with him, seeing the werewolf, not wanting to really *believe* it. I couldn't see the moon, but it had to be full.

Zeyde was fully transformed. He filled up the huge coat, his thickly muscled arms thrusting out its sleeves, his coat and shirt wide open to accommodate his huge, furred chest. His clawed paw/hands were soaked with blood. He must've been six feet four, and weighed at least two hundred pounds. And his face! A wide-muzzled animal glared at me, with Zeyde's eyes shining out of thick fur. The teeth were huge, impossibly long and sharp.

As he faced me, the beast chewed the last bit of his victim's quivering heart and swallowed it.

You can't outrun him, I reminded myself, gripping my rabies pole and flashlight. I spoke quietly. "It's just me, Zeyde."

He grinned a bloody smile and I remembered Joe wondering about the smell of his breath. My knees got weak. He rose and moved towards me, snarling. I couldn't help it. I backed up.

"Don't do it, Zeyde," I said softly. "Joe's coming. He'll kill you."

The werewolf growled a laugh and launched himself.

I swung the pole with everything I had, bending it double against him, but it had no effect. I backed away, clubbing him with the flashlight, but he ignored the blows and pulled me down. Instinctively, I threw up my left arm, protecting my throat, and he fastened his teeth into the heavy nylon sleeve, worrying it. The tough material ripped like ancient muslin. I grappled with him, trying to squeeze his windpipe one-handed, but his neck was steel, and my fingers tangled futilely in the coarse fur.

I brought my knee up, a solid blow to the groin, but he ignored it. He roared, deafening me, and his hot breath scorched my hand as I hammered my fist against his wet, black nose. He never flinched.

His claws tore my coat. "Zeyde!" I screamed. "Stop! It's Therese!" Then I shrieked as white-hot pain seared my arm.

I hadn't been bitten in eight years, and I'd *never* felt such pain. I screamed again, but he kept biting me, tearing me up. My blood filled his mouth, feeding him, giving him the hot meal he craved. Next it would be my throat, and then my beating heart.

As he clawed my coat open, I suddenly heard the clatter of his silver knife as it hit the ground. I scrabbled, searching for it blindly with my right hand.

My fingers enclosed the hilt, the name of God pressing against my palm, just as his hot, bloodied breath blew against my neck, and his teeth kissed the skin of my throat. The flare of sudden headlights brightened our bizarre coupling, as I drove the knife between his ribs right into his heart. His young, feral eyes widened, staring into mine. With a tired sigh, he sagged against me. His expression was peaceful, just like the sick animals I killed. Hugging his body with my good arm, I wept.

They released me from the hospital only a few hours later. By the time I'd reached surgery, most of the wounds had healed. By tomorrow, I knew, there wouldn't even be a scar.

Joe came by to get me, but Chief wouldn't let me in the car. The moment he caught wind of me, he went crazy, lunging and barking. I can't tell you how bad that hurt.

One of Joe's buddies came and took Chief back to the station, so Joe could take me home. We drove in silence, but finally it got to me, and I spoke. "What did the coroner say when he saw Zeyde?"

"Said it was amazing how much strength an old man can have under the right circumstances," he answered quietly.

"Like the full moon?" I asked, with a bitter laugh.

"He meant when they got crazy. All the coroner saw was an old, shriveled man."

"You knew about Zeyde," I said.

"I suspected," he said dully. "Native Americans have their own shape-changers. I was afraid you'd think I was nuts. I'm sorry, Therese." His jaw muscles tightened.

I couldn't stand his sympathy now; I'd fall apart. As we pulled up to my building, I reached for the door handle.

"You can't deal with this alone, Tee," Joe said, grabbing my arm. "Let me help you. Let me stay with you."

I choked on a sob. "Help me? How? Can you stop the changing of the moon?"

He hugged me tightly and let me cry. He smelled so good, like moonlight and nighttime, smells I'd never noticed before. Finally, I pulled away.

"The Navaho may know a rite," he insisted. "I'll call...."

"Forget it, Joe," I said tiredly. "There's nothing to be done." I'd have to call Linda tomorrow and quit. I'd never be able to set foot in the shelter again. I'd lost everything. My career, the animals I loved, the man I might have had ...

"Joe, what happened to the knife?"

"There'll be a hearing. I'll bring it to you after that."

I saw myself as an old woman, transforming monthly into a healthy, strapping werewolf, killing and killing. The day after must be hell, as the aged body paid the price. Could I pass the knife to someone else, the way the Tobecks passed it to their strongest grandsons? "Give it to Linda," I said leadenly. "I'll get it from her. I can't see you again."

"Don't shut me out, Tee," he warned quietly.

"I *have* to. Or some night, I'll find you dead beside me."

"The full moon wanes tonight. Nothing will happen for twenty-seven days. We can...."

"Stop it!" I shouted. "The Tobecks carried this for centuries, generations! You're out of it, out of my life! I don't want your blood on my hands."

I climbed out of the car and walked away. Joe didn't call me back. As I reached my door, a silver stretch limo suddenly pulled out of a side street, then glided past, oddly out of place here in Anacostia, with its old buildings and trash-littered streets. The smell struck me like a blow, making my stomach clench. New mown hay gone moldy. I almost puked.

After a moment I opened the door and climbed the stairs, but no animal ghosts followed me tonight. I wondered dully if, in a month, there'd be two-legged ones. Inside, even Dove and Alfred's ghosts were gone. I thought about the long years ahead of me, doing a job that had to be done, without the warmth of a friendly animal to relieve them. Without Joe's scent to perfume the night.

I pulled out my old, battered suitcase and, ignoring the tears splashing over it, methodically filled it, wondering where I'd be during the next full moon.

There are worse things than death.

WRITING ON THE WALL
by Jody Lynn Nye

"Of course, we regret losing you," her boss—no, her ex-boss, Lou Scarrow—said, leaning forward in that oily way he had, the few hairs on his head flopping and flabby jowls shaking as he emphasized his words. "But the tests are conclusive. And final."

Nicole Cuthbertson's pleasant round face became an oval as her jaw dropped. Her fluffy brown hair stood out around her head as if it, too, was astonished.

"That isn't fair," she said, pointing at her right eye, the almost blue one. "*You* gave me this prosthetic. It isn't my fault that it's substandard. It seems to me that since my job requires it, I am entitled to a first-quality model. The accident that caused me to lose my eye occurred on the job. I insist you authorize a better replacement."

"Ah, but your employee health insurance will only cover the level of the one you received," Scarrow said, with every pretense of regret. He leaned forward over his tented fingertips. "There are over three thousand employees at Fusion Central, all with the same expectations that you have, but we have only so much money to take care of you all. The needs of the many, you understand … Even Thorvald Harris, discoverer of the process that made fusion possible, was subject …"

Yada yada yada. Furiously, Nicole jerked her gaze away from him and let it wander around the office while he went into the usual spiel explaining why company policy wouldn't let him do what she wanted, which of course he wanted, too, but, with so many people drawing upon limited funds, was impossible. It was a tactic he used to drive people out of his office. *She* had no intention of leaving. She was there to stand up for her rights. All she needed to do was wait until Scarrow ran down his batteries.

As her gaze shifted from a desk nearby to the far wall, there was a brief but perceptible delay while the prosthetic eye focused. She hated the miserable thing and its grainy resolution. She should have been impressed by the sophistication of the package. A complex computer with a trillion byte memory that ran off the latent electricity produced by the cells of her body had been sealed into a sphere the size, shape, and relatively the same texture as a real eye. The pupil opened and closed at roughly the same speed as the other. Roughly. But it didn't look real. The white had a milky, metallic sheen, and the iris gleamed much more starkly than her natural eye. People stared at it. Once seen, never forgotten. Nicole sighed.

Scarrow nattered on, getting to the part of his speech about the company's dedication to its staff, how it hoped to have it returned, and how sad he felt that Nicole failed to show adequate loyalty and gratitude.

Gratitude—huh. Take a complex image at 1000 dpi. Now, print it out. Now, run it through a fax machine or a stand-alone copier in which the colors haven't been synchronized for a week or two. If Nicole shut her good eye, that distortion was all she saw. She stared at the ugly industrial wallpaper, a pattern of scattered dots and lines, until the design appeared to move. She glanced away from it, out the window.

A delivery van floated up to the sixteenth floor entry port of the glass-walled skyscraper, and a long-haired male messenger in a jumpsuit emerged from it with a package in his hand. Probably more chips. If she was still working there she would be checking them in. She missed her imaging equipment and her fellow lab rats. The boss was still talking. She let her eyes drift back to a spot over the boss's head.

"… Every sympathy with your situation, bearing in mind the non-compete clause in the employment contract you signed, which necessarily prevents you from getting another job in the field.…"

The random pattern in the wallpaper coalesced into scratchy-looking words.

Leave now.

Nicole wished heartily that she could. She'd been there an hour. By the time she got Scarrow around to what she wanted, she'd be caught in the rush of other people—still employed people—leaving for the day. She didn't want them to see her. Some glanced up at the building as they hurried out to the walkways to catch hovercabs and busfloats. She turned away, hoping they couldn't see her.

"… Binding arbitration …" Nicole tuned out Scarrow's voice.

The dots and lines formed letters again.

Leave!

Nicole blinked. Could the pattern be repeating itself in sections? She'd never noticed it when she visited the office before. It was just so strange that she thought … she felt.…

"Excuse me," Nicole said suddenly, rising from her chair. "I've got to go."

"Just a minute, Cuthbertson, we're not finished."

"I have," Nicole muttered, not turning back. The boss sputtered as the door shut between them.

"Any luck?" the secretary asked.

Nicole flashed a rueful grin as she left. Marie had always been nice to her, and had said she was sorry she'd lost her job. Heading toward the main door Nicole dodged to avoid the orange-jumpsuited messenger who passed her carrying a box toward the boss's office.

The Exit sign at the end of the hall flashed, attracting her attention. Was the building suffering from a power brownout? But there was that urgency again. The word Exit filled her vision with red fire. Nicole hurried toward it.

She had almost reached the platform when an explosion picked her up by her scruff and threw her through the plate-glass doors.

As she swam up through the muffling darkness, large faces surrounded her, their voices hammering at her ears.

"Look, there was no one else on the monitors."

"The monitors seemed to fail just before the explosion."

"But isn't the whole place powered by their own fusion reactors?"

"Guess security just blinked."

"No," said the gruffest voice. "It sounds like someone intimately acquainted with the system who had a grudge against the company, and that supervisor in particular, set it to turn off at just that time."

"It couldn't be her. She's been on disability for weeks."

Nicole blinked. The three men and a woman standing over her bed became aware that she was looking at them, and stared down at her.

"Did you plant the bomb?" the man with the gruffest voice demanded. He wore a police lieutenant's gold badge clipped to the collar of his tunic.

"Bomb?"

"There was an explosion. Did you have anything to do with it?"

"No." Nicole felt detached from her body. She tried to focus on her memory, and became aware of holes in it. "I went back to ask for a new eye."

"You've got two eyes," the lieutenant said.

"The right is a prosthetic," said another man. The doctor, Nicole guessed. "Look, Lieutenant DeWitt, why are you harassing her?"

"She was known to be the last person to speak with the deceased. She could have been the one who brought in the explosives."

"There is no residue on her hands," the doctor said.

"It could have been wrapped up tightly, Dr. Valeri."

"Not this stuff," the woman argued with the certainty of a working chemist. "It's a very small, unstable molecule. It eats immediately through anything and everything but solid ceramic. There's not a trace of it anywhere on her skin. It *will* be on the bomber."

The faces shimmered into clear focus. For the first time Nicole could count two policemen and a man and woman in plain clothes.

"So you have a grudge against Fusion Central?" DeWitt demanded, leaning over Nicole suddenly. He stuck a hatchet jaw almost in her eye. "Two people are dead. You're the last one to see them. Are you responsible?"

"No," she said, emphatically. "I've got a problem with my labor contract. We were trying to work it out. Peacefully." A horrible thought struck her. "Oh, my god, if Mr. Scarrow is dead, I have to start all over again with someone else." The prospect of having to dig out all her files and reargue her case with another uncaring executive or series of them overwhelmed her. She hurt all over, and no one cared. There was nothing wrong with the tear ducts in either socket. She began to cry.

"She's in shock," Dr. Valeri said, seizing DeWitt by the sleeve. "Out. Everyone out. Leave her alone. She's not the one you're looking for."

The other officer, a slim dark man with intense black eyes, leaned forward and tucked a card-disk into her hand. It said "Sergeant Booth," and gave a communications number. "If you remember seeing anything, please call me."

Nicole wept for a little while. The doctor handed her tissues until she took a deep breath and shook her head. "Good," he said. "Let's have a look at that eye."

She opened her lids wide. The doctor put thumb and forefinger into the socket and popped it out with a practiced twist. Nicole could feel the cable trailing on her cheek while he toyed with the eye itself. He made a sympathetic grimace.

"Terrible quality. The microprocessor's got a good memory, but it's a generic all-purpose chip. I could fit you out with a better one, super high resolution. Only four hundred thousand, all follow-up care and replacement included."

Nicole blanched. "I can't afford that. Fusion Central was supposed to give me a quality implant. They cheaped out, and now I can't do my job. So they fired me. I work in atomic imaging. I'm good. Or, I was."

"I'm so sorry."

Nicole hated the sound of pity in his voice. "I'll keep trying."

She struggled out of the bed and started looking for her clothes. The doctor helped her up and directed her to the closet adjacent to the bathroom. Her things were torn and stained. On the back of her tunic was one blotch that looked like blood. Nicole shuddered but put the garments on anyhow. They were good enough to go home in.

"If you ask me," Valeri said through the door while she changed, "the bomber sounds like a bitter ex-employee. Any idea who might have had it in for your boss?"

"Not me!"

"So what will you do now?" he asked.

"So, what will you do now?" her best friend Lara asked over lunch the next day at an open-air bistro.

"What can I do?" Nicole moaned. "If I want satisfaction from Fusion Central, I have to do things their way. That means going through channels all over again, arbitration hearings, and so wearily on. They want me to bankrupt myself fighting for compensation. In the meantime, I've been searching the web for jobs. There's a really wonderful one doing stereo-microscopy for Chemdol, a bioengineering lab up in Portland. They want me, and it's more money."

"Perfect!"

"It would be, but I can't leave town until the Fusion thing is settled. And I still need a better eye. This one just isn't fine-tuned enough. Chemdol is sympathetic, though. They'll hold the job as long as possible. I feel desperate. My lawyer's hopeful, but I'm running out of money. That 'tin handshake' Fusion gave me won't last more than a couple more challenges. I'll be scraping for the rent soon."

"No problem," Lara said, patting her hand. "Come work for me while it's all simmering out." Lara ran her own telephone/web-based 'entertainment' company.

"Phone sex?" Nicole scoffed. "No, thanks. I can hardly talk when I'm really doing it."

"And when was the last time?" Lara asked, cynically. "No, you don't have to do that. I've got a new gig that you'd enjoy. You work your own hours. It's a chance to help people while making a credit or two. And it's perfectly safe. You'll have a security line tied to the police station. The cops are less than three minutes away on a main pedestrian thoroughfare."

"Live contact?" Nicole was very suspicious. "What's the job?"

Lara smiled.

And so Nicole found herself swathed in flowing purple skirts and a head scarf, sitting behind a crystal ball in a dim parlor tarted up with mystic symbols and stifling wall hangings of blue and pink velvet. Her round, pink face didn't permit her to look much like a gypsy, but she had all the right trappings.

"Now, remember," Lara had told her, "take the credit card first. There are two good reasons for that. They don't like to pay after you've told their fortune, especially if you have bad news. Of course you'll have mostly good news. The second reason is that the computer will run a scan on the name and give you the basics: name, address, stats. You can guess a lot of things about a person from there. Most people are happy with the simple stuff. 'You'll have a bright future.' 'You'll meet a tall, dark stranger.' You know."

Nicole knew. She and Lara used to enjoy visiting storefront psychics when they were in school. She never would have believed she'd be one. Well, until she got her new eye and could move to Portland, it wasn't a bad stopgap. This could be a lot of fun. She didn't mind play-acting, and the floaty clothes covered the bruises all over her body.

"Hello?" A tentative voice interrupted her thoughts. With difficulty Nicole struggled to her feet. The light was too low for her natural eye, but the artificial one picked up a topographical image of a painfully thin, middle-aged woman in a dress of fine fabric standing timidly by the door. "Will you … will you do a reading for me?"

"Uh, sure." The scarf around Nicole's head felt too tight. All she could think was "Bad Hair Day." Concentrate on the customer, she told herself.

The woman was more nervous than she was. Nicole could see the vein in the base of her neck twitching while she talked. She took the credit plate the woman held out, and ran it through the scanner. A box popped up on the touchscreen, showing vendor, amount, and a square for the signature. The woman signed without glancing at it, then touched her thumb to the verification point.

Relieved, Nicole sat down at her crystal ball. The woman's name, address, and personal details swam up into her view. Lara had given her a crash course in scanning the data without looking as though she was reading. The information given was scant, only what the Privacy Protection Act permitted merchants to have, just enough to prove that the cardholder was the same person as the card owner. Nicole read out of the corner of her eye as she took the woman's hands. Lorraine Kimball, aged 58, lived in a good part of town, stood 150 cm. high, and weighed 59 kg. Nicole almost did a double take. This lady couldn't weigh more than 49 kilos.

Nicole's robotic eye picked up and measured the slight difference in thickness of the skin on the third phlange of her left ring finger. Without meaning to, Nicole ran her thumb along it. Yep. She had taken off her wedding ring. Long enough ago for the ridge to fade, but she'd worn it for many years. Separated or divorced.

"You've been worried about something for a while," she hazarded. "Was he such a creep?"

Ms. Kimball burst into tears. "How did you know?" she wailed.

It was easy from then on. Nicole got her to open up and talk. The Kimballs were in the middle of an ugly divorce. Nicole had seen the inside of enough lawyers' offices lately to know Mrs. K. had a good case and a good attorney.

"Things will be better," Nicole assured her.

"Really?"

"Really. Within two years, you'll be laughing."

("Make the future dates vague," Lara had warned her. "This service is for entertainment purposes only. You'll have the cops down on you if you're too definite. You're not predicting. You're offering personal therapy.")

It seemed to have worked for Mrs. Kimball. When she left the dim studio she was happy. She even dropped a free-chit in the bowl near the door. *Hey,* Nicole thought, triumphantly as the door closed, *I made a tip!*

Full of confidence, she admitted her next client.

Each that followed the first became easier to read. Nicole rediscovered her love of theatrics that had gone unsatisfied since high school, letting herself sound mysterious, while telling people the simple things she got from their own credit chits. But occasionally, she produced insights that were downright spooky.

One middle-aged man's color was bad even to her misaligned prosthetic eye. He was faintly yellow, and she saw a trace of perspiration on his forehead even though the room was cool. Her gaze traveled down to his midsection. For some reason she thought of his liver.

"You ought to seek medical attention today," Nicole said, surprising herself. "I mean, *now.* There's something wrong that needs to be seen to right away."

The man looked worried. "Will I live?"

She studied him. This was treading on the forbidden ground Lara had warned her against. Nor was it the kind of thing she had intended to get into, but she wanted him to have hope. "I think so," she said tentatively, praying she was right. "You'll have to take better care of yourself, though."

He departed hastily without even saying goodbye. Nicole was afraid she'd gone too far, and steeled herself for a reprimand from Lara.

Two days later, though, the man returned to thank her.

"Liver disease," he said, holding her hands tightly. "The doctor said I can make a full recovery. Thanks to you. I might not have gone for help."

He smiled at her as he turned to go, leaving a substantial tip in the basket. From her seat Nicole could see the amount on the chit. It was enough to pay for an hour of her attorney's time.

"So, does it turn out you really are psychic?" Lara wanted to know, when Nicole told her about the event.

"No. No way," Nicole said, clutching her iced tea like the elixir of life. The wait staff in the bistro had gotten used to seeing her in the flowing costume. They smiled but said nothing as they set food down before the two women. "It *had* to be the eye. Instead of transmitting images to my optic nerve as it's *supposed* to do, the computer is talking to my cognitive/intuitive center—if only I pay enough attention to what it's saying. As a chemist I ought to be able to understand what it's telling me, but I'm getting impressions, not straight data."

"This is so exciting," Lara said, her eyes dancing. "Like they say, it's an ill wind that...."

Nicole interrupted her. "Not for me. I just want an eye that can see individual microbes, thanks, and leave the insights to your phone psychics."

"Don't knock it," Lara said, pointing a shard of crispbread at her. "You're in a better position than you think to help people. Your eye will pick up the little clues that others with perfect vision won't see."

Nicole snorted. Small comfort, she thought, with the half-blind helping fellow sufferers.

But the eye did help. That very afternoon, a girl giving off ketones in her breath bad enough to be visible made Nicole worry. She didn't wait for the information off the girl's credit plate, but started off on a lecture to get help. The girl heard her out, sitting listlessly in the chair, then nearly fainted on the way out the door. Nicole called the paramedics.

Her labor dispute tottered along while the criminal investigation of the bombing went on. Fusion Central made several appointments with the corporate mediation service that cut into her mind-reading time. She had to bring her attorney to each meeting, which further drained her resources. She was starting to worry about money. Pretty soon she'd have to give up the case just because she couldn't afford to fight it any longer. And the police kept calling her back. Lt. DeWitt interviewed her again and again, though no one else considered her a prospective suspect.

"I still think you're holding out on us," the detective said. Nicole glared at him. She had had to postpone a lucrative client in order to come to the police station and sit in the dreary, yellow-enameled room once again. "Scarrow wasn't the only one killed, you know. His assistant died, too."

"I know that!" Nicole said. She'd lost all patience with him.

"Who else would have had a grudge against Scarrow?"

"*Everybody*. Dozens of people. Anyone who'd ever been in an accident, or on leave for any length of time except the federally protected classifications. I heard of a designer who took a sabbatical to get her master's degree. Instead of working nights. She was let go. She checked herself into a mental institution. And there was a guy, Miller, who took a furlough who lost *his* job."

"We heard about him," DeWitt said. "Harmless weirdo. Superstitious type. His file said he was too unstable to work in a sensitive field like the power industry. But none of these people were there that day. You were."

"It's illegal to downsize people like that," Booth said.

Nicole rose to go, and saw the blood rising in DeWitt's face. She didn't care. "Yes, but they still get away with it. One guy who'd been in munitions in the armed forces got let go. Did you ask him?"

"Are you trying to be a cop?"

"No. No way. I'm just telling you what I heard. And what happened to me, too. It's illegal, if I can prove intent." She started toward the door. DeWitt's voice made her turn around.

"And why did Mr. Scarrow do this to all these people?"

"Money," Nicole said bluntly. "When we leave we get knocked out of the profit-sharing system. The money goes back into the pool that can be used for bonuses for the executives who've saved the most for the company. Scarrow came up with the policy. It started after the chemist who discovered the secret of fusion committed suicide. F.C. saw how lucrative *departing employees* could be." The officers nodded. They could understand how the architect of such a policy could have made hundreds of enemies. "His family sued, but F.C. showed them an airtight employment contract. When you invent something there the patent belongs to the company, so the profits do, too. You get a share proportional to your input on the project. That could mean hundreds of thousands of credits—but only until you leave. Some of the people they managed to get rid of should have raked in millions, but Scarrow got them moved out. I should have seen it coming. I discovered a glitch in power management routing that saved the company thousands of credits. They were lucky that I got hurt, pulling me out of the picture on disability. They're going to pay me, I'll see to that, but in money or a replacement eye. You want someone who was out for blood."

"But none of the images on the securicams matched the profile of anyone seen in the building," DeWitt growled. "It had to be the invisible man. Did Fusion invent a system for rendering people invisible?" Nicole ignored his jibe.

"Did Scarrow give you what you asked for?" his partner asked suddenly.

"No."

He peered at her, and Nicole suddenly realized she'd been afraid of the wrong officer. "Then why did you leave?"

Nicole hesistated for a moment. "I got an impression." The men snorted. Nicole felt humiliated but pressed on. "I saw writing. In the pattern on the wallpaper. It told me to get out. So I left."

"Why didn't you mention it before?" DeWitt demanded.

"I knew you wouldn't believe me."

"So you had a psychic insight?" the partner asked, humorously.

"No." She said it so positively that they both stared at her. "It's the eye. It's a powerful microcomputer. It's been hooked up wrong. It's wired into my intuitive center instead of providing coherent information. Something it saw made it warn me."

"Uh huh," DeWitt said, throwing himself back in his chair. "Maybe we let you off the hook too soon."

"No!" Nicole protested.

"He's just yanking your chain," the partner said kindly. "You sure you didn't see anyone else, not even with the magic eye?"

"No! Please, can't I go now?"

"You let us know if you think of anything else."

Nicole assured them she would, and fled. At that moment, she wanted to get back to her quiet little room and listen to people who believed what she said.

"I need a reading."

The man's voice interrupted Nicole's thoughts. She was getting the hang of the eye, now. It proved capable of identifying complex chemical compounds. She knew instinctively which mixture on the slides before her contained a greater concentration of sulfur, but not by how much. If only the processor's output could be rerouted to her analytical cerebral centers, she could do chemical analysis without a digital microscope. What an asset it could have been if Fusion hadn't been so cheap! They gave her a better unit than they'd known.

With a grimace she pushed aside her experiment and looked up at her customer.

A young man with taffy-colored hair sat in the chair, leaning forward nervously. Who knew how long he'd been there? Nicole held out her hand. Automatically, he put his credit plate in it.

She ran the charge and pushed the signing plaque toward him. A quick glance in the crystal ball told her the plate wasn't his. Nicole knew she ought to demand a legitimate card, but she felt uneasy about this man. The presser button for the police station was beside her foot, but if he attacked her they still couldn't arrive before she was badly hurt or killed. Instead, she pretended to prepare herself.

"What is it you want to know?" she asked, when she could trust her voice.

"I want to know ... if ... if I was entitled to justice."

Nicole tried not to blink at him, but she kept her eyes mysteriously half-lidded. "The, er, spirits require a more specific question." And more information. He certainly looked in need of encouragement.

He stared down at his hands in his lap. "My ... my father was cheated by people he trusted. He expected ... he'd be taken care of. When he died, we needed money. I went to ... them, and they said we weren't entitled to anything!" He grew agitated. "I went to the man who ripped him off, but we didn't have proof that he'd changed the deal unilaterally. My father killed himself because of them, and this monster didn't even care. I had to get justice. I'm sorry now. Really. I'm sorry." His voice shook. Nicole's heart went out to him.

Not knowing what to say, she took his hands in hers and turned over the palms, looking for clues. He wasn't sweating. Good. Pulse strong, color normal. But there was a chemical trace she didn't recognize. She let the eye begin to analyze it. Sodium, lithium, uranium, something more exotic in the transuranic table that glowed faintly, boron. Then the lines in his palm turned into words. *Run away.*

Nicole let go of his hands and stared at him. It was him. The messenger. He had cut his hair and depilated the facial fuzz, but it was him, DeWitt's invisible man. *He* blew up the building! And he'd been handling more of the chemical compound recently.

When she broke contact, her customer gave her a hard look that changed to astonishment, then recognition.

"That eye!" he said. "I've seen you before…. It was there! You were there in the corridor at Fusion Central!"

Too late, Nicole clapped her hand over the prosthetic. She started feeling under the table for the alarm button with her toe. He grabbed her and pulled her toward him.

"You saw me."

"You're mistaken," she said feebly.

"I'm not—that weird eye. I dreamed about it." He clutched her tightly around the neck with one arm while he felt underneath his tunic. It was abnormally bulky. Traces of the glowing compound showed through the cloth. Nicole's heart pounded in fear. He was wearing another bomb! She kicked at him, trying to get back to the alarm button. She didn't know if she'd depressed it enough to set it off.

"It wasn't supposed to be this way," the young man said, desperately. "I didn't set out to kill anyone. I only wanted to force Scarrow to admit he changed the contract postdate. Like an idiot I gave him our copy. He said he lost it, and no one would believe us. He committed fraud. My dad *discovered* fusion." Nicole gasped. He was Thorvald Harris's son! "He should have made a fortune, at least gotten recognition for bringing limitless, cheap energy to the world. I'm sorry. Now I want to die. I regret having to take you with me, but you know the truth."

"No!" Nicole pleaded. She clawed at his hands, gasping for air. "Fusion cheated me, too."

"No one can win against the system," the youth said, shaking his head ruefully. "I've got the explosives right here on me. I couldn't decide if I should kill myself, to atone. A life for a life. I came here for guidance. *You* made me decide. It was fate that you were here. I'm sorry." He started to sob, painfully, from his heart. Nicole struggled to get loose. Though she was frightened out of her wits, she did feel sympathy for him, but she wanted to live.

"You could plead temporary insanity," she suggested.

"We tried everything," the youth said, not hearing her. He reached under his tunic. Nicole batted at his arms, hoping to keep his hand away from the trigger. "They ran us out of money. And no one would listen."

A slight movement near the parlor door caught her attention. The lines drawn by the folds in the curtain wavered faintly, then formed into words. *Help is here.*

Nicole's knees almost gave way with relief. Her eye then picked up heat traces behind the curtain. Two police officers. Thank goodness. She hoped they'd heard everything he said. If not, she'd tell all at his trial. Though he'd gone to the extreme, they were fellow sufferers.

"Listen!" she said suddenly. "You came to me to see the future. An arrest is closer than you think. It would be better if you give yourself up."

"I know," the young man said. "I've seen it coming, but I can't."

"I'll help you," Nicole said. She took his hands and held them firmly. Her robot eye could see a faint tremor in them as her rescuers, DeWitt and Booth, burst from behind the curtain and took the man into custody.

"Sounds like you were telling the truth after all," DeWitt said, ungraciously, as uniformed officers bundled the man out the door. "On both counts."

"Mr. Scarrow rewrote Harris's employment contract after he was dead," Nicole said. "The company-wide change dated from that day. I'm going to take it to court and see if I can get the policy reviewed. I bet it'll be a class-action suit. The Harrises should be part of it."

"You seeing the future?"

"No way," Nicole said. "I'm giving that up."

"Poor guy," said Booth. "He wanted revenge and he got it. Watch out what you ask for. You sure you don't want to get into detective work? That was a nice little confession he spat out for you."

"No, thanks," Nicole said, taking off her head scarf. "I want to go work in a quiet little lab, by myself. With a door that locks. And plain walls. I've had enough of cryptic messages."

BACK TO BLACK
by Jonathan Maberry and Bryan Thomas Schmidt

-1-

The Soldier and the Samurai

The soldier was a ghost in a dead world.

He made no sound as he moved because noise was suicidal. Noise was how to attract the dead. Noise was how one *became* dead. The soldier was alive because he had learned those lessons long ago, often from seeing others make mistakes that they could not undo. The soldier had buried so many people, even people as skilled as he was. Maybe that meant he was lucky, or maybe it meant that in many ways he was closer to an animal than a man. His instincts were feral, driven by a predatory nature that had let him survive when so many others had fallen. Stronger people, faster ones, better ones. He, though, survived. All of those deaths were lessons, and he was a good student in the school of survival.

Now he was a soldier in memory only. It was how he defined himself because it steadied him, gave him purpose. Gave him a reason to stay alive even when death called so sweetly and so persistently. Death, after all, was the kingdom where everyone he had ever known and loved now lived. Living was a lonely, brutal thing.

He moved up a dry slope past cactus and twisted shrubs, watching the terrain, listening to the wind. When he stopped, he stood still as the ancient trees. That was a skill he had learned when the world was still alive. When you stop you have to become part of the landscape. You can't do anything to draw the eye.

The trick was to be a ghost so that he did not become a corpse. Before the end of the world that concept made sense to any soldier; since then it was an unbreakable rule of survival.

Even so, being alive often made him feel strange, alone, and freakish. It sometimes made him feel every bit as much of a monster as the things that were consuming the world.

The living dead. The walking dead. The hungry dead.

Zombies.

Even now, even years after it all fell apart, the soldier sometimes found it hard to accept that zombies were real, that they were pervasive, and that they were the most enduring fact of life. Of everyone's life. They were as much an unshakable constant as the need to breathe. They were. They were here, and from what little anyone knew of the rest of the world, they were everywhere. The plague had spread incredibly fast because it was designed to be quick-onset and one hundred percent communicable. Nature could never have created so perfect a monster. No, it had been the cold minds of madmen on both sides of the Cold War who had taken civilization's noblest advances in science and medicine and twisted them into weapons of mutually-assured destruction. Bioweapons had been officially banned but never actually abandoned. The lie that assured the black budget funding was that they needed to create the weapons so that cures and prophylactic measures could be created.

It was the logic of the shield maker who actually wanted to make and sell swords.

Lucifer 113 had been an actual doomsday weapon and though it had been locked away and chained up, it had slipped its leash and now the world had died, been consumed, and gone quiet.

And through that quiet the soldier moved, silent as the death that defined him and everything else.

He reached a knoll and paused, crouching in the shelter of a crooked pine tree, and surveyed the landscape. Red rocks, barrel cactus, yucca and Joshua trees. Some big horn sheep grazing on the tough grass near the dark mouth of a cenote. Nothing else.

None of *them* visible. That meant nothing, though. If they had no prey to chase they would stop walking and stand as still as statues, as still as stovepipe cactus. Dangerously easy to miss when scanning an area so wide and vast as Red Rock Canyon there in Nevada.

There was movement and the soldier pivoted on the balls of his feet to watch a young man break from the cover of a creosote bush and move along a fault line, keeping to the shadows cast by an up-thrust ledge of ancient rock. He moved with an oiled ease that made the soldier long for the lost days of his youth. He was fifty-five now and could feel every year, every hour, every injury, every inch of scar tissue that marked his passage through a violent life. The kid had never taken a bad injury. To the heart, sure, but not to the body, and he moved like a dancer.

He moved smart, too, and the soldier nodded his appreciation. The kid was learning. Getting better, sharper, faster. Earning his right to live in a world as thoroughly unforgiving as this one.

The young man saw something and came to a complete stop, freezing and blending into the landscape. The soldier squinted as he surveyed the terrain to see what had spooked his apprentice.

He heard it before he saw it.

The dry desert wind brought the soft, low, plaintive moan of an absolutely bottomless hunger. One of them, crying out its need.

Then it stepped into sight, coming out of a shadowed space between two boulders tumbled down that slope by a glacier millennia ago. It was a man, or had been. Tall, heavy in the shoulders, wearing the soiled and sun-faded uniform of a Nevada State Park ranger.

The soldier did not speak, did not rush to help. He watched, instead.

The young man wore green khakis and a many-pocketed canvas vest over a long-sleeved cotton knit shirt. He wore a backpack, too, and fitted between the pack and his own back was the lacquered scabbard of a *katana*, a Japanese sword of the kind the Samurai once used. It was nearly a match to the one the soldier had strung across his own back. The sword's silk-wrapped handle rose above the young man's right shoulder. He also wore a pistol in a belt holster and a knife strapped to his thigh.

He waited until he was sure there was only one of the dead shambling toward him, and then he stepped toward the zombie. His hand flashed up and down and there was a glittering arc of silver.

The zombie's head fell one way, the headless body fell the other.

The soldier rose slowly and walked down the slope to the kid.

"Nice work," he said.

"Thank you," said the young man, "I think he was alone and—"

"And you should have used your fucking knife, Tom," said the soldier. "What?"

The soldier pointed to the far end of the valley. Three figures were moving toward them. Then a fourth stepped out from behind a tall cactus.

"That sword is pretty and points for the sweet *kesa-giri*, kid, but that much polished steel is a big frigging mirror," said the soldier sourly. "You might as well have rung the damn dinner bell."

Tom Imura looked crestfallen. "I didn't stop to consider—"

"Really? No shit."

"I … I'm sorry, Joe," he said.

Captain Joe Ledger pulled a pair of sunglasses from the vee of his sleeveless fatigue shirt and put them on.

"Don't be sorry, kid," he said. "Do better."

"Yes," promised Tom.

Ledger pointed to the four figures staggering toward them. "Now go clean up your mess." He sat down on a rock, pulled a piece of goat jerky from his pack, and began to chew.

Tom Imura cleaned the black blood from his sword and returned it to its scabbard. Then he drew his knife. It was a double-edge British commando dagger with a matte black finish over the steel. Totally nonreflective. He drew a breath, held it for a moment, exhaled, nodded and then set off to meet the four zombies.

He didn't see Joe Ledger grinning at his retreating back.

-2-

Top and Bunny

"This place looks great, you said. We'll get a lot of rest for once, you said," growled USMC Staff Sergeant Harvey Rabbit, call sign "Bunny," as he brought up his drum-fed shotgun. He began firing, filling the air with thunder that drowned out the low, hungry moans.

Bunny cut a sour sideways look at his best friend, First Sergeant Bradley 'Top' Sims. The dark-skinned, grizzled former Army Ranger held his SIG Sauer in a two-handed shooter's grip and fired steady, spaced shots at the pale figures closing in on them from all sides. The two men circled slowly, clockwise, finding targets everywhere.

Absolutely everywhere.

They worked this like they'd worked a hundred battles of this kind. Killing the dead. Accepting the insanity of that concept as an unshakeable part of their world.

The front line of the dead went down.

The next line was fifty yards back. The Colorado Rocky Mountain slopes around them fell still as insects and birds alike silenced their calling to hide from the battle threatening their home.

"So tell me, Old Man," asked Bunny as he lowered his weapon, "do I *look* well rested?"

Top shrugged, eyeing Bunny with creased eyebrows. "You look alive. Say thanks and stop being so damn high maintenance."

"High maintenance my ass," Bunny replied as he readied himself for the next wave. He aimed his shotgun at another zombie and shot it point blank in the forehead. "As far as I can tell, it's a miracle either of us can walk without a cane at this point."

"The miracle," Top said, dropping a walker with a double-tap, "is that either of us still have all our limbs. That we're even alive, Farm Boy."

In truth, Top had been the farm boy, having spent his boyhood summers in his uncle's Georgia peach grove. He'd gone off to the Rangers and fought in battlefields all over the world, then retired to see if he could be a farmer. But he had come out of retirement after his son was killed and his daughter crippled in the early days of the Iraq War. He'd volunteered for the newly formed Department of Military Sciences, hoping to lead a team into combat in the new War on Terrorism. Instead he became the strong right hand of Captain Joe Ledger's Echo Team. That was where he and Bunny had met and become best friends and teammates.

"Won't be for long if I keep letting you pick our campsites, Old Man," Bunny complained, and then they both went back to work. Firing, stopping only to reload, as zombies continued to advance—some limping on partial legs, others with partially eaten heads or faces or missing arms. Bunny was a six foot seven inch, powerful, blond, former SoCal pro-volleyball player who'd joined the Marines and went from Force Recon to the DMS. Bunny, Top and Ledger had served together, side by side, their whole time at the agency.

Until things fell apart.

"The survivors we rescued yesterday said it was clear," Top snapped, motioning downslope toward the old log cabin where they'd tried to spend the night—an abandoned escape for some unknown city dwellers that might never return.

"Well, clearly they were full of shit!" Bunny snapped. "Maybe we should go back and kick their asses. Just as a way of saying thanks."

The last two zombies fell, their heads blown apart.

Top and Bunny panned around in a circle, looking for any signs of movement or further targets. The stink of rotting blood and flesh mixed with the sweet smell of pine needles and moss filling the cool mountain air as it breezed gently around them.

"Clear," said Bunny, his voice too loud in the sudden quiet.

"Clear," agreed Top. "Won't last, though. All that shooting will bring more of them out of the woods. Won't take 'em long to get here, either."

Top swapped out his magazine and holstered the SIG, then dragged a sleeve across the sweat on his face. "Hot as balls today."

"Cover my six," Bunny said. "This time, I think I'll pick our shelter."

"Hooah," muttered Top, and they moved out in tight formation, covering each other as they followed a trail through a copse of ponderosa pines leading up a nearby slope.

Ever since the world fell apart under *Lucifer 113*, or *The Plague* as the public usually called the outbreak, Top and Bunny found themselves as soldiers without an official mission. There was no government, no DMS, no active military. The world had fallen completely off its hinges, and what was left of America—and maybe the world—was an all-you-can eat buffet for the hungry dead, with pockets of humans trying to survive here and there.

In the absence of official orders, Top and Bunny had assigned themselves a mission. The rules were simple. Keep moving. Save whom they could save. Kill as many zombies as was practical. Rinse. Repeat.

They'd become successful enough to earn a reputation as 'the garbage men,' as one group of survivors had dubbed them. They'd once met a salvage team out in the wasteland who'd heard of them and repeated what he'd been told. "Call them in and they'll haul your ass out and empty the garbage you leave behind."

Not something you could put on a tattoo, but it worked well enough.

As for the nickname of '*The Garbage Men,*' Bunny hated it, but Top thought it was hilarious.

"Yeah," Bunny protested after they'd left the salvage man, "But we're not a pair of fucking janitors. We're saving lives. Where's the respect?"

Top just said, "People use humor to keep their spirits up in impossible life situations. They don't mean disrespect. It's a joke."

Bunny didn't see how there was anything to joke about. The world was for shit and it might never recover. Millions, maybe *billions* of people were dead. More were dying, and everyone who died, no matter how, reanimated and joined the flesh-eating horde. No matter how many they shot, more kept coming. Top somehow managed to stay optimistic, but all Bunny could do was keeping thinking how fucked they were.

FUBAR.

Fucked up beyond all repair.

Yeah.

-3-

The Soldier and the Samurai

Joe Ledger and Tom Imura scaled a tall rock as twilight began filling the canyons with shadows. In another kind of world they would have used the darkness as a time to travel quickly without being seen and without the oppressive desert heat. But the dead did not rest and they hunted at night. Actually they hunted all the time, but at night the lifeless bastards were harder to see coming, driven by smell and hearing when it was too dark to see. No one Ledger had talked to during the fall knew how the zombies stayed alive, or why they didn't rot past a certain point, or how they could use any of their senses. It seemed to make no scientific logic, but for Ledger it meant that he simply did not have sufficient information. Everything made sense in the end. Everything, and he had encountered some of the most bizarre threats any Special Operator had ever encountered. Even when it looked like it was something supernatural, there was always some kind of weird goddam science to explain it.

The fact that all of the scientists he knew were also dead skewed the math. It meant that he might never get the right answers.

Once he and his apprentice were up on top of the rock, they pitched a camp, and ate a meal of cold salted rabbit and water. The elevation kept the dead away, but a cooking fire up here could be seen from miles and miles away. They sat together, wrapped in blankets against the cold of the desert night, and talked.

"I wish Sam was here," said Tom. It wasn't the first time he mentioned his older brother, who had been a sniper on Ledger's Echo Team. As far as Ledger knew Sam had been killed a few days after the dead rose. Or so he had been told.

"Me, too," he said.

Tom must have heard something in his voice because he turned to the soldier. "Joe ... do you think there's any chance he's still alive?"

"A chance? Sure," said Ledger, nodding. "The lady cop I met who'd been with him said she had been *told* that he fell under a swarm of zoms, but she didn't actually see him get bit. Sam and his field team, the Boy Scouts, were helping the cop get a whole convoy of school buses filled with kids out of danger. They were overrun and Sam was doing what he could to give them a chance. He went down and the buses got out, but ..."

"But ... ?"

"Sam was dressed for combat. Ballistic helmet with a face shield, Kevlar vest, limb pads, armored gloves. The works," said Ledger. "He wasn't exactly naked and painted with steak sauce, you dig? He might have made it out. But he didn't have a vehicle, at least as far as the cop knew. And going back for him would have put the kids on the table for an all you can eat buffet."

"Then he *could* still be out there?" asked Tom. He was a nice young guy. Early twenties. Tough as nails. Smart. Decent. Damn good fighter. But he wore his heart on his sleeve and he pinned his own survival on ideals like hope and optimism, which was dangerously fragile scaffolding as far as Ledger saw it.

Even so, he didn't try to kick that structure down. Tom had a little half-brother, Benny to think about. The kid was back in Central California, in a small makeshift town built around a reservoir high up in the Sierra

Nevada Mountains. Tom had helped establish, build and defend that town, but he often left his brother in the care of his neighbors while he went out into what the people in town called the great 'Rot and Ruin' to look for survivors. Tom had rescued more than two hundred people so far, which made him a hero.

Joe Ledger had no interest in settling in the town. Like Tom, he was on the prowl for survivors, too. However, it was only half of his own self-imposed mission. The rest of it was less humanitarian. Or, maybe it was a service to the community in the most extreme terms.

He and Tom were not out here to kill zoms.

No, they were hunting people.

Tom must have read his thoughts. "What's wrong with them?"

It was a question the young man asked in one way or another nearly every day. What's wrong with them? *Them.* Not the dead. Smart as he was, Tom did not seem able to crawl inside the head of living people who saw the apocalypse as the chance to shake off all moral constraints, all ethics, all inhibitions. There were packs of predators out here—mostly, but not entirely men—who preyed on camps of survivors. Stealing their food and supplies, brutalizing the men, raping the women. Sometimes raping the children, too. Ledger and Tom had found absolute proof that human beings—the uninfected living—were a thousand times more savage than the legions of hungry dead. They had come upon camp after camp and read the proof in the twisted bodies, in the small violated corpses, in the leavings of monsters in human shape. Tom had called them animals at first, but later changed that to 'monsters' because animals did not do this.

Tom had been about to graduate from the police academy when the world fell. Since then he had bloodied his hands but it was only after Ledger had taken him under his wing that Tom Imura had become a practiced and efficient killer. A hunter of hunters, a predator who preyed on predators.

"They do it because they're weak," said Ledger. He tore off a chunk of rabbit and chewed slowly.

"Weak?"

"Sure. Don't confuse dangerous with strong. You're strong, kid. So am I. So are the kinds of people, trained or untrained, who stand up to protect those who can't protect themselves. That's what defines strength. Just as being brave in the face of danger defines courage." Ledger chewed and shook his head slowly. The sun was down and there were ten billion stars spread like diamond dust above them. "The people we hunt aren't tigers or lions. They're jackals. They hunt in packs because they're too fucking afraid to hunt alone. And in those packs they trash talk so that everyone thinks they're tough, but it's a thin coat of paint on a pile of shit."

"They put up a good fight, though," observed Tom, but Ledger shook his head again.

"No. They fight, but it's not a good fight. They fight because they're afraid of dying, and they're afraid of the pain of dying. But they aren't warriors. They're not going down in any fucking blaze of glory. Even a cockroach will fight." He spat over the edge of the rock, listened, but didn't hear it land. He shrugged.

They sat in silence for a long time. There was no moon tonight and the wind was quiet. Far away they could hear sounds in the night. The rustle of something small and fast moving through the brush. A little mouse, maybe, or a rat. The distant call of a night bird. The soft, plaintive moan of something dead and hungry.

They sat and watched the stars.

"I miss my dogs," said Ledger.

"Me, too."

When he met Ledger the big soldier was traveling with two monstrous dogs that were half Irish wolfhound and half American mastiff. Baskerville and Boggart. On one of their 'training' trips up to San Jose Boggart had gone missing and when they found him the dog had adopted a girl who called herself Rags. The girl was a scrappy little thing. Young but tough as iron, and she and the dog had bonded. After a violent run-in with a group of raiders who called themselves the Skull Riders, Ledger, Rags and the dogs had gone east. When Ledger returned nearly two years later, he had Baskerville with him as well as a new full-bred female mastiff he called Cupcake. Boggart, Ledger told Tom, had elected to stay with Rags, and the soldier was fine with that. Cupcake had joined his little pack. However the two big dogs were back in Mountainside because Cupcake had just dropped a litter of five very large, very noisy pups. Ledger missed his dogs. He liked them a lot more than he liked most people.

After nearly an hour, Tom said, "Maybe we'll find some horses."

"Maybe," Joe said dubiously.

"If we don't it's going to be a long walk to Oro Valley, Arizona."

"Yup."

They sat in silence, watching the stars above them swim through the Milky Way.

"Joe ... do you think it's real?"

Ledger said nothing.

"The cure they keep talking about," persisted Tom. "Do you think it's real?"

Ledger sipped some water and washed it around in his mouth before swallowing.

"Christ, kid, I hope so."

-4-

Top and Bunny

Top and Bunny wound up spending the night in the loft of a barn on old but clean hay, taking turns sleeping three hours then keeping watch—each twice that night. The next morning, they headed for the Arizona-Colorado border, several survivor groups having hinted that they'd heard rumors of another group struggling in the small town of Sun Valley near Petrified Forest National Park.

Top led the way, because the Georgia farm boy rode horses like it was second nature. Bunny, on the other hand, was an Orange County, California surfer, and his horse riding skills continued to amuse Top every time he watched him. Since riding along with a constantly chuckling companion had begun annoying Bunny fairly quickly, Top just rode ahead, so he could avoid the spurts of spontaneous laughter he'd been prone to when they'd first started out. Bunny knew this although it went unacknowledged. He loved the old guy anyway, though God knew he'd never say that out loud.

The two hundred and two mile journey would take them a little under fourteen hours at normal speeds for the horses—about eighteen minutes per mile—and using the older state highways to avoid the cities, where most large colonies of zombies congregated, also saved time. But they still had to be well rested and conserve their strength to remain effective when they arrived so they'd already decided to split the journey into two days.

They'd waste less energy riding early mornings and at night once they left the foothills of the Rockies and hit the desert. Cooler temperatures would be easier on all of them, despite the dangers of the dark. The same EMPs that had destroyed the zombies and automobiles had also eliminated many snakes, scorpions, and other predators. But not all by far. There were always the random zombie pods, but dealing with scattered zombies was much easier than the city hordes, and they were used to that.

As they rode south, the foothills turned to prairies and pine forests. The latter were littered with twigs and pine needles that crunched under the horses' hooves more softly than dead leaves. Crickets, birds, and other creatures chirped in the branches and overhead in a constant droning symphony of sound. The wind blew strong, bringing the hot desert winds and smells of sand, dust, and dry grass to mix with the sweet scent of pine sap and needles. From time to time, amidst the pines, Bunny even thought he detected a faint scent of butterscotch, but decided his mind must be playing tricks. As the forests gave way to prairies, the prairies eventually gave way to gravel and rock formations. Trees were soon conspicuously absent, and the air became thicker with heat, making their lungs work harder.

The whole time, Bunny thought back on the nineteen years since the world had fallen apart and the DMS had ceased to exist, at least for Echo Team. They had once been like a family, but now they were all scattered to who knew where? They didn't even know if anyone one else was still alive. Only Top remained in Bunny's world and Bunny in his. And that was only because they'd been together on a supply run when the EMPs hit and they'd been stranded, forced like so many others to fight to survive. Teaming up had been a natural instinct after so many years of it, and here they were. Somehow they'd survived when so many others hadn't. Bunny thought of Joe Ledger, Rudy and Circe Sanchez, Leroy Williams, whom they all called "Bug," and Junie Flynn. He thought of the strange and enigmatic Mr. Church who was their leader and about whom Bunny knew next to nothing. Last but not least he thought of Lydia Ruiz, Warbride, who'd gone from teammate to friend to lover. God, the memories of all them.

"Farm Boy!" Top shouted, startling Bunny from his reverie.

"What?" He shook it off and looked around as his horse just barely steered clear of a cacti bunch that would have surely torn into his leg through his pants. *Fuck*, he thought, grabbing the reins and resuming control.

"You're lucky animals have good instincts," Top said, shaking his head. "You falling asleep on me?"

Bunny shook his head. "No. Just remembering."

To Bunny's relief, Top read the look in his partner's eyes and no further explanation was needed. He grunted in sympathy and they rode on together, now side by side for a while.

-5-

The Soldier and the Samurai

They did not find horses.

Not live ones, anyway. They found a farmer's field full of bones and they found a half dozen zoms dressed in field denims standing around looking blank. Tom stopped by the rail and stared at the dead, and the zoms slowly turned toward him and began walking. There was never any hurry in the world of the dead. They were inexorable and indefatigable, but they were never hasty.

Tom reached over his shoulder for the handle of his sword, but Ledger stopped him.

"They're not going to hurt anyone," said the soldier. "They're too clumsy to climb over the fence and who in their right mind would go in there?"

Tom frowned. "Right … but shouldn't we … what's the word you like to use? 'Quiet' them?"

Ledger shrugged. "Why? They're not in pain. They're not going to get lonely or any of that shit. They're dead but they don't know it. What good will it do anyone?"

"It would be merciful. They were people once, Joe. They had their lives stolen by the disease and now they're in this living death hell. Or whatever you want to call it."

Ledger sighed and walked over to stand beside Tom, watching the zoms shamble their way.

"Here's how I see it, kid," said the soldier, "these people are gone. Yes, we can mourn who they used to be, and we can feel compassion for how they died and for what was taken from them. I get that. We both get that. It sucks worse than almost anything. The only thing that would suck worse would be if they *knew* they were dead."

"Knew?"

"Sure, if their personalities were somehow trapped in there, aware of what had happened to them. That would be the biggest suck-fest of all time."

Tom went pale. "Jesus Christ …"

"But you've looked into their eyes, Tom," said Ledger. "Have you ever seen so much as a flicker of personality? Of intelligence? Of awareness?"

"No," said Tom. He sighed. "No, I haven't."

"Of course not, because whoever lived in those bodies is gone. To heaven, to hell, or to whatever state of existence is waiting on the other side of death's front door. I don't know."

"Maybe it's nothing," said Tom. "Maybe there's nothing after this."

"Maybe," said Ledger, "but boy would that be a fucking kick in the balls. After all these thousands of years of religion and prayer and everything else, it would be a rotten fucking cosmic joke if this was it, finished, done."

The zoms were almost up to the fence.

Tom said, "What do you believe?"

Ledger bent and plucked a long stem of wild grass and put it between his teeth. It bobbed up and down as he chewed the end.

"Not sure what I believe in has a name," said Ledger after a moment. "I was raised Methodist back in Baltimore, but that's kind of for shit. None of what happened squares with any religion's apocalyptic prophecies, which tells me two things. Either everyone's wrong and the universe has bent us all over a barrel, or this isn't the actual end."

Tom watched the zombies. "How much closer to the end do we need to get?"

The closest of the dead, a woman in jeans and a man's flannel work shirt, thrust her arms between the slats of the fence rail, gray and withered fingers clawing at the air inches from where the two men stood. Ledger reached out and offered his fingers to the dead woman, who grabbed them and tried to pull them toward her mouth. Ledger was stronger and he did not give an inch. The zombie kept trying, moaning softly, but Ledger remained unmoved. Only when the other zoms reached for him did he pulled his hand free and wipe it on his jeans.

"Maybe the line in the sand," he said quietly, "is when there's no one left like you."

"Me? I'm more of a skeptic than you are."

"About religion, sure. Maybe. But you've been working your ass off to save your little town. What are you calling it?"

"Mountainside."

Ledger nodded. "You may not have much optimism about your spiritual future, but you have a lot about the future of the people in Mountainside. About your stepbrother's future. About the possibility of there even *being* a future."

"I could be delusional," said Tom, half smiling.

"You could. Not sure you actually need to believe in anything much yourself except life. You *do* believe in that, and don't tell me you don't."

Tom nodded.

"So, as I interpret the whole End of Times thing," said Ledger, "an actual apocalypse should be all exit doors and no other options. I'm not seeing that here. Neither are you. Fuck, even those ass-pirates who are preying on survivors think there's a chance at a future." He shook his head and tossed the blade of grass into the wind. "We're living in a fully dramatized example of that old samurai concept. *Nanakorobi yaoki.* You know that one?"

"'Fall down seven times, get up eight,'" said Tom.

"This is one of the times we get up."

"What if we get knocked down again? What if that doctor in Arizona doesn't really have a cure? What then?"

"Then we get up a ninth time," said Ledger. "And a tenth."

They watched the zoms, standing just outside of the reach of those dead hands. Then Ledger raised himself on his toes and looked over to the side of the farmhouse that stood on the edge of the field. A smile blossomed on his weathered face.

"What?" asked Tom.

"Maybe there's a God after all," said Ledger, "and maybe he's not a total dick."

"Huh?" Ledger pointed to the porch. There, exposed by the slanting rays of the sun, was a pair of heavy-duty mountain bikes. "Not horses, but then again we won't have to feed and water them."

Tom pulled out his binoculars and studied them.

"Shit. The tires are flat."

Ledger shrugged. "This is a farm in the middle of no-fucking-where. You trying to tell me these people didn't have spares, patch kits and hand-pumps? Really?"

Forty minutes later they were pedaling along the road with the farm and its people falling slowly behind.

-6-

Top and Bunny

Bunny estimated they were less than a mile outside Sun Valley, when they heard the screams. They'd traveled until early afternoon the first day, then slept during daylight and resumed their journey at night and into the early morning, winding up doing six hours the first day and over seven since they'd started out the previous evening. The journey had been quiet and unexpectedly uneventful—the two soldiers having somehow managed to avoid any pods of zombies or other hurdles the entire way. Until now.

The screaming came from multiple voices.

"Does that sound like children?" Bunny asked.

Top nodded. "Women, too."

They spurred their horses simultaneously and raced in the direction of the screams. The undead didn't scream, they moaned. Some humans were still out there and in danger—probably under zombie attack. As they rode, they checked their weapons, preparing to engage whatever enemy or enemies they encountered. Bunny's chest tightened and he took a deep breath, focusing his energy and senses as he always did when preparing to go into combat. Beside him, he saw Top go through similar prepara-tions, though they each put their own spin on it. They'd faced fire together hundreds of times by now, yet the prep had remained the same every time. Military discipline and common experience.

As they topped a small rise, they began making out voices mixed with the screams—shouting, pleading, arguing, etc. No distinct words yet, but enough to confirm there were several humans involved—male, female, and children.

They rode into fields of heavy cacti and petrified rock, and Bunny spotted a fading, cracked sign saying, "Welcome to Petrified National Forest." A trail had been laid out, lined with logs connected by pillars of stone. The well-worn dirt path between them was around ten feet wide, so they turned their horses and began following it in the direction of the voices and screams.

Some nearby cacti bore beautiful purple and green flowers in stark contrast to the sharp spindles shooting out of every other available surface upon them. Bunny briefly wondered if animals were fooled. For what purpose had the plants grown such camouflage and how many generations ago?

Then the trail turned and they were winding along the top of one of two facing natural stone walls, layers of red, yellow, tan, and grey revealed along the sides that ran down into the canyon between them—loose rock, grass, and cacti growing scattered along the slopes. It was stunning, a clear reminder why the place had drawn the attention of the Department of Interior and become a National Park.

The shouting and pleading became intelligible now.

"No, they're just babies!" a woman sobbed.

"Hold her down!" a man yelled. "We can't help them now!"

"How did they find us again?" another woman wondered, her voice filled with pain and mourning.

"Get back under cover or they might come back for you," the yelling man ordered.

Then Bunny spotted a dirty cargo van, its white exterior spotted with mud and debris, peeling along a thin natural road that ran down the middle of the valley on the canyon floor. Gunshots echoed as rocks and pebbles shot up from the road, the rounds missing the van as it peeled away as fast as it could manage on the slippery surface.

"Who the hell has a working van and frigging gasoline?" After the EMPs hit the cities, most above ground vehicles and gas pumps stopped working. Bunny had heard rumors that vehicles parked in metal buildings or underground might escape the problem, but it had been a long time since he'd seen one. "Should we stop it?" he called to Top.

Both reined their horses to a stop and aimed their weapons, eyes searching for targets, trying to determine who was attacking whom.

Finally, Top shook his head. "We don't know what's going on yet."

"Someone stealing children," Bunny said.

"Or rescuing them," Top countered.

Then they heard the distinct click of a shotgun and pistols being cocked behind them and whirled to find two men and a woman, faces dirty from dust and sand, standing near the trail edge, weapons aimed right at the two soldiers' chests. Bunny knew that with quick movements, he and Top could be off their horses and taking the three out, but Top shot him a look that said, "wait," so he hesitated, watching his partner.

"Drop the weapons now!" the man with the shotgun ordered. He looked to be in his thirties. From the way the others responded to his voice, Bunny suspected he was the leader.

"Easy there, we mean no harm," Top said, as he and Bunny lowered their guns, moving them slowly toward their holsters.

"Freeze!" the woman shouted, shifting nervously, her .45 swung toward Top's forehead. She was tan with long blonde hair and looked a decade younger than the leader. Top and Bunny stopped moving.

"Yes, ma'am," Bunny said. "Just trying to put them away."

"Who are you?" the leader demanded. "What are you doing here?"

"Soldiers, come to help," Top said. "First Sergeant Sims, U.S. Army Rangers and Master Sergeant Rabbit, USMC."

"Army and Marines together?" the leader said with a quizzical expression. "You aren't official then."

Top shook his head. "Not many official teams left, you know. With the troubles."

"Yeah, we're all on our own," the woman said angrily. "And we don't like strangers." She took a breath and her .45 faltered a bit, but then Top shifted slowly in the saddle, turning to look at her and she snapped it up again, stiffening.

"Just wanted to say that we understand," Top said. "We don't know who to trust anymore either. That's why we're together. We trust each other."

"Till death do us part," Bunny joked.

"You a couple then?" the third person, a scowling younger man with the .45 aimed at Bunny's forehead snapped. He looked like he was barely out of his teens, his short blonde hair similar to the girl's. Could they be related? Either way, he'd spread his legs apart shoulder-width and locked them there, steady, ready for anything. Young or not, he clearly had experience with his weapon and Bunny had no doubt it was a shot he'd probably make.

"Not that kind, no," Bunny said, shaking his head.

"You'll have to pardon the farm boy," Top said, shooting Bunny a warning look. "His sense of humor sometimes comes out at the wrong times."

"This ain't no joke!" the woman snapped, glaring at Bunny, then locking her eyes back on Top.

"We know that, ma'am," Bunny said, swallowing. These people needed to seriously chill. They clearly had no idea that Top and he could have taken them out in seconds if they'd wanted to.

"We're looking for a camp of survivors from Sun Valley we heard might need help," Top said quickly. "We were on our way there. Rode in from Colorado."

"Help? What kind of help?" the leader demanded.

"The undead, some kind of raids, finding shelter and a good hiding place," Bunny explained.

"And what's it to you?" the scowling young man said.

"We have experience with such things, come to offer it," Top said.

"Who was in the van?" Bunny asked.

"None of your business!" the woman said, waving her .45 again.

The leader's eyes softened as he read the two soldiers. "Caroline, let's calm down a bit and hear them out, okay?"

"I'm calm," the woman said. "Calm as I'm gonna be after what just happened." She relaxed her arms a bit, lowering the .45 slightly.

"What happened?" Top asked softly.

"We were raided," the leader said, pointing the shotgun at the ground. "Some strangers came and took women and children and a couple old men."

"Took them where? For what?" Bunny asked. Humans raiding to kidnap other humans had to mean they were sick or going to be. What other explanation could there be in these times?

"The Lab. Experiments. Damn crazy doctor," Caroline mumbled, shaking her head.

"What lab? You're raided by other humans?" Bunny asked.

"What's it to you?" the scowling man said, waving his pistol again. "Why are we telling them anything? We don't know them! They could be with the Doc!"

"They're on horses for one, Steven," Caroline said. "The doctor's people come in vehicles."

The leader nodded. "And if they were with the Doc, they would have left together, not hung around."

"We caught 'em. Maybe they're playing dumb, Owen," Steven said, looking toward the leader.

"We'll take their word for it for now and watch them closely," the leader said, nodding in the younger man's direction. "Lower your weapon, Steven, okay?"

Steven hesitated, his scowl changing to a face twisted with confusion. Owen nodded again, then slowly lowered the .45 a little and relaxed his stance.

"Now, you two slide slowly down off those horses so we can talk, okay?" Owen said.

Top and Bunny exchanged a look of agreement, then nodded and slowly dismounted, making sure to keep their hands well clear of their weapons as they did. Their feet thumped on the stone ground as they landed, sending dust and loose rocks up in clouds around their boots. As Top turned to Owen again and opened his mouth to speak, a whistle sounded from somewhere in the distance.

"They're gone," Caroline said, and all three relaxed a bit more, exchanging knowing looks.

"How many did they get?" Steven wondered.

"We'd better go back to camp and take a count," Owen said.

"What was that about a lab? A doctor taking people?" Bunny asked, exchanging a puzzled look with Top.

"That signal's from our camp," Owen explained, ignoring the specific question. "All clear."

Top and Bunny grunted but held position. That one they understood perfectly.

"What about them?" Steven asked, motioning to the two soldiers.

"They're coming with us," Owen said. "But you two stay behind them and be ready."

"You'd risk letting them know where our camp is?" Caroline asked, looking uncertain.

"We move it a lot," Owen said. "We'll keep them under guard. We need time to find out more about them. But first, we need to make sure the perimeter's secure again. Okay?"

After a moment, Caroline nodded then stepped forward and took away the weapons from the two soldiers—pistols and rifles slung off their shoulders. She didn't inspect their bags or pat them down, for which Bunny felt grateful. She handed one rifle to each of the men and put the pistols in her belt, then stepped clear.

Steven's jaw tightened as he grunted in affirmation and motioned sharply for Top and Bunny to follow Owen. Top and Bunny each grabbed their mount's reins and led the horses after the group's leader.

-7-

The Soldier and the Samurai

They heard the screams from miles off.

It was not the empty moans of the hungry dead. It was not an animal sound. These were screams from human throats. Male and female. Raised to that terrible pitch where the screams rip themselves out of throats, damaging tissue, violating the air, breaking the world.

Ledger and Tom were at the top of a hill and the road down twisted in and out of a scattered community of RVs and campers. It was like a hundred such camps they had seen, and like the others it looked like a war zone, with zombies everywhere and partially-eaten corpses sprawled and rotting in the weeds. Vultures circled endlessly in the high, dry air.

However those screams were alive. They were immediate.

Neither man said a word. Instead they kicked their bikes into motion and pedaled as hard and fast as they could, accelerating downhill. They could not see any living people, but the screams had to have been coming from outside. They weren't muffled the way they would be if the victims were inside one of the campers.

It was only when they heard the gunshot that they skidded to a stop. The dead don't use firearms.

"Off," snapped Ledger and they let the bikes fall. Tom, who was used to Ledger's methods by now, immediately faded left, running low and fast toward the outermost camper, making the maximum of cover. He drew his sword because it was a cloudy day and there was no sunlight to reflect from the blade. Ledger went right, running a zigzag through the dead, twisting to avoid them without having to engage. He did not draw a weapon because the situation hadn't yet revealed how it needed to be handled. It was a lesson he still needed to teach Tom.

He stopped at the corner of a rusty RV that sat on flat tires. Ledger knelt and did a quick-look around the rear bumper, then retreated to let his mind process what his eyes had seen.

Beyond the RV was a kind of pen made from old shopping carts, heaped junk, and cars that had been pushed together. He could not see much of what was going on inside the pen, but there were at least a dozen zombies pressing close to it. A fresh scream from inside the pen told him that this was where things were happening. Ugly things. Up close the screams sounded younger and more thoroughly infused with comprehensive personal outrage as well as physical pain. Two guards stood atop the highest points on the pen wall. Both men, both dressed in travel-worn clothes and makeshift armor. Jeans, hockey pads, football helmets. And guns. The guards ignored the zombies, confident that they were out of reach, and instead cheered on whatever was happening in the pen.

Ledger held still and listened to the noises, picking them apart, cataloging them. Several men. How many? Six? Ten? Somewhere in that range. A small pack. The male scream had ended when they heard that gunshot. The female scream continued, rising and falling.

The situation sucked. Outnumbered and outgunned, with at least one helpless victim and the complication of sentries and the zombies. In most circumstances this would be a walk-away, a hopeless scenario.

But not for Ledger. He knew that he could never leave this unaddressed. That wasn't who he was. The young scream made that absolutely certain. A long, long time ago, back when he was fourteen and the world was decades away from falling off its hinges, Ledger and his girlfriend, Helen, had been attacked by a group of older teens. Ledger had been stomped nearly to death and had lain there, bleeding and helpless, while the teenagers ruined

Helen. Although Ledger and Helen had both lived past that day and had healed in body, neither had ever healed in spirit or mind. Helen eventually found her way out and it was Ledger who found her. The whole process had fractured him, splitting his mind into three distinct personalities. One was the Modern man, the civilized and ordinary part of him, the one who clutched to his dwindling supply of hopes. The second was the Cop, the strong, quiet, intelligent, detail-oriented investigator and thinker. That part had been his mostly reliably dominant aspect.

And then there was the third part, the aspect truly born on that horrible day so many years ago. The Warrior. Or as he preferred to be called, the Killer. Savage, uncompromising, brutal, relentless. However it was the Killer who was in his way the most compassionate and protective, because he did whatever was necessary to protect the members of his tribe against all predators. Children were always to be protected. The young, the weak, the helpless. It was hardwired into the brain of the Killer to make sure they would not perish, for as they went so went the tribe itself. Basic Survival 101.

The Cop leaned out and analyzed the scene again, noting distances, placement, weapons, obstacles. However when he rose up, it was the Killer who went to war.

He did not signal Tom Imura. That wasn't necessary. Tom would either understand and be ready to function as a member of their small hunting pack, or he wouldn't. Warning him would create a risk Ledger could not afford. Besides, Tom was smart and fast and a killer lurked in his soul, too. Ledger had seen that before. It hurt Tom to kill, but he his regrets and his humanism did not slow his hand. Not at all.

Ledger drew his Heckler & Koch MK 23 pistol as he rose up from his point of concealment and held his gun out in a firm two-hand grip. He did not run but instead took many small steps to prevent the weapon from being jolted. He had twelve rounds in the box magazine and a thirteenth in the pipe. The range was good enough for kill shots, but Ledger didn't want these men dead. Not yet. Instead he shot the closest man in the thigh, aiming center-mass to insure a shattered femur. The .45 round punched all the way through at two hundred and sixty meters per second. The man screamed and twisted and fell.

The zombies lunged up to catch him, to drag him down, their nails and teeth ripping into the man before he ever hit the ground. Ledger swung the barrel to take the second man in the hip, the foot-pound of impact knocking him backward off the pen wall. Ledger heard his screams as soon as he fell out of sight.

And then it was all insanity.

The zombies who weren't tearing at the first man wheeled toward him, empty eyes filling with naked hunger, mouths biting the air in anticipation of fresh meat. Ledger shoved his gun into its holster and whipped his *katana* from its scabbard. He was not as stylish a swordsman as Tom, but he was a more practiced butcher. He cut his way to the wall of the pen and everything that reached for him fell. Nothing fell whole.

There were shouts from the other side of the pen wall, and Ledger dodged sideways and leapt onto the wall fifteen yards from where he had fired. When he reached the top he saw nine men in the center of the protected area, and every one of them was looking in the wrong direction. A naked girl of about thirteen lay bruised and beaten on the ground, her young body covered in blood. It was obvious she had been brutally used. They did not see Ledger as he drew his pistol once more and swapped in a full magazine. They did not see Tom Imura slip over the far wall, silent as death.

Ledger opened fire on the men.

This time he shot to kill.

The pistol was accurate within fifty meters. The range here was less than ten. He did not miss.

Men screamed and fell. Others tried to turn their guns—shotguns, hunting rifles, Glocks—on him, but then Tom ghosted up behind them and his sword did quick and terrible work.

It wasn't a fight. Neither Tom nor Ledger was interested in a fight. This was slaughter. It was two against nine, and it was over in seconds.

When Ledger climbed down from the wall the last of the men was begging for his life. Ledger watched Tom's face as the young man stood over the injured man. The girl lay six feet away, and from the way she was breathing it was clear she was on the verge of death. Her eyes were glazed and there were dreadful wounds all over her. The man on the floor was naked from the waist down and there was blood on his penis. Not his blood.

Even so, Tom didn't kill him. Not right away. Instead he asked a question. "Why?"

The man looked at him and then turned to look at the girl. He frowned as if seeing her for the first time. Then he turned back to Tom.

"She'd ... she'd die out here anyway," said the man. He said it reasonably, as if what he and his friends had done to her was clearly okay given the circumstances.

Tom's eyes went dead.

His sword moved and then there was fresh blood on the man's face and body.

On the other side of the pen wall the screams had stopped and there was the wet sound of meat being torn, of chewing, of bones being cracked open for their marrow. Flies swarmed in the air.

Ledger and Tom knelt on either side of the girl.

She was a tiny thing. Emaciated, covered with infected sores, filthy. Dying.

Tom offered her water and there wasn't even enough left of her to remember how to drink. They dressed her most immediate wounds and covered her body with their blankets and the two men sat together, holding her between them, keeping her warm as the day wore on. Sometimes Tom spoke to her, whispering softly, making promises the world could not let them keep.

When she died, Joe took her from Tom, rolled her onto her stomach, drew his knife, and slipped the blade into the base of her skull. She would never reanimate. She would sleep.

They buried her and then the two men sat down with their backs against the pen wall.

And wept.

-8-

Top and Bunny

Owen led them down a winding path, descending the hillside to the valley road below. They followed that for about five yards, then wound into a cacti field and across a parking lot to a brick, one-story building with a worn wooden sign that read "Park Headquarters" out front by the entrance off the road. American flags waved in the wind from several poles around a lot that contained RVs, official Park Service vehicles, and various civilian cars and trucks scattered throughout. Trees and landscaping decorated the land surrounding the lot and lawns leading up to the building.

Several armed men and women, as ragged and dirty as the trio, rushed to meet them, eyeing Top and Bunny with suspicion. After Owen explained their presence and fired off instructions, he left them behind with the sentries and headed inside. Within moments, Top and Bunny watched their mounts being led away, their packs removed from their backs, and were patted down thoroughly—men removing their knives, the spare Glocks they kept in their boots, and extra ammo.

"We want those back," Bunny objected, but Top silenced him with a look. *Just go with it for now*, it said. Bunny sighed, nodding back in acquiescence.

Then they were surrounded and led into the building, then shoved into a small office and locked inside, guards posted outside. The office had a wooden desk, its surface covered by scattered stacks of paper, file folders, and manuals. Two old, faded grey metal file cabinets with three drawers occupied a corner behind it along with a table holding a laser printer and three open wire baskets marked "In," "Out," and "Pending." The office smelled dusty and stale, like it hadn't been used in a while, which it probably hadn't. Top slid into a padded wooden chair facing the desk, while Bunny paced. A few moments later, the door opened and a woman brought them water bottles, then left again.

"Well, they're sure glad to see us," Bunny said, taking a chair along one wall near the file cabinets.

Top unscrewed the cap off his water and took a long drink before responding. "We've dealt with cautious survivors before. You know we'd be the same."

Bunny sighed, leaning back in the fiberglass chair against the wall. "Yeah, just anxious to get on with it."

"Drink your water and relax, Farm Boy," Top said with a chuckle. "We're here. That's the first step."

"If these are even the right people," Bunny muttered, then uncapped his own water and drank.

They waited in silence then until Owen finally came back for them an hour later. He'd cleaned up a bit, the dirt and grime gone from his face, his hair combed, and the shotgun had been left outside. He took a deep breath, nodding at them as he moved around the desk, and slid into the cracked leather chair behind it, leaning back and putting his feet up on the surface as he thought a moment.

"Why don't you boys tell me who you are again and why you're here, heavily armed, on our doorstep," Owen said.

Top nodded and began explaining. He described generally their past work in black ops for the government, and how they'd stayed together after The Plague, fought to survive like anyone else, and then found their training and knowledge could help others and began looking for those needing help.

"Like some kind of modern A-Team or something?" Owen joked.

"Wow. A-Team. That's old school," Bunny said and looked at Top. "Didn't you watch that when you were a kid?"

Top shot him an annoyed look as Owen chuckled. "You knew what it is, didn't ya?" He turned to Owen again. "There's just the two of us. No van either. But we do what we can. We came here because a group in Colorado heard rumors someone might need help finding permanent shelter, setting up defenses, getting supplies, etcetera."

"And then we saw the raid," Bunny said.

"Why didn't you stop them?" Owen asked, his eyes accusing.

"To be honest, we weren't sure who the good guys were or what was happening," Top said.

"For all we knew, the kids were being rescued or something," Bunny added.

Owen grunted and his eyes turned sad as his shoulders sunk and he leaned back in the chair behind the desk.

"Everything okay?" Top finally asked.

Owen shrugged. "As fine as it can be after one of the doctor's raids, I suppose."

"Who is this doctor and why are you being raided?" Bunny asked.

Owen met their eyes a moment as if weighing options then continued, "We don't actually know. Just rumors and such from others who claim to have seen or heard things. But as they tell it, the doctor runs a lab down outside Tucson. They used to raid the survivor camps there. One of the reasons we started relocating two years ago, making our way north. Somehow they tracked a few of us up here and started raiding us once every few months. We've lost twenty-five people, including ten women, ten children, and five elderly. We lost six tonight."

"And you don't have any idea what happens to them?" Bunny asked.

"Experiments we've been told," Owen said, his eyes wrinkling as he pondered it with obvious pain and regret. "Something about a vaccine for The Plague, but a few captives have supposedly escaped and they weren't cured, they'd been turned. Some graves were discovered in a nearby park as well that people say were victims of the lab."

They gaped at him.

"A *vaccine*? Holy shit," gasped Bunny. "That could change everything!"

"How sure are you?" demanded Top. "Is this real intel or rumors?"

Owen locked eyes with him. "You hear something from so many different sources, experience the raids on your families and friends, your children, you start believing the worst. Doesn't much matter if it's true. People are being kidnapped. Others turned up dead. Draw your own conclusion."

Top grunted with understanding. Echo Team had dealt with many similar rumors and situations for the DMS. "But you know where the lab is?"

Owen shook his head. "Just rumors. So far, at least, but a lot of people believe them. Yeah, we've talked about finding it. Getting our children and loved ones back. But the teams come heavily armed for the raids. Can you imagine what the security is like around the lab?" He shook his head. "We can't risk it. That is, if we could even find it. A couple of people tried to rescue their families, we heard, with disastrous results."

"This has gone on for *two years*?" Top looked as if he couldn't believe it. Bunny knew that look though. Beneath it was simmering fury.

"More like four," Owen said. "We just decided to try and get away, out of reach two years ago. Look. My people are mostly city folks, a couple farmers, but most had never touched a weapon before, let alone served. I had training from an enlistment after college, so I've taught them what I could, but defense is our best strategy. Organized, strategic attacks would probably just get more people lost or killed."

"And they tracked you here ..." Bunny shook his head.

"Someone who saw us could have told them, I suppose," Owen said. "Truth is, we rarely see zombies these days, keeping to ourselves. If we weren't constantly moving to try and avoid the raids, we could settle in. This headquarters recycles waste and water and we could stay here indefinitely, hunt the desert for food, grow our own—but that would just make us easier to find."

"They only come every few months?" Top asked.

Owen thought a moment. "Yeah, every two or three. We haven't really nailed down a pattern. It varies."

"But if you stay here, you'll be okay?" Top said.

"We might be," Owen said. "We could make a go of it."

Top and Bunny exchanged a look that spoke volumes without words. They'd worked together so long, reading each other was just part of it. They both agreed they needed to help these people, and that had to start with finding the lab and seeing what they could do to end the raids.

"Why don't you tell us everything you know about this lab and doctor and where we might find it?" Top said.

-9-

The Soldier and the Samurai

They camped in the pen that night.

The men they killed had been poorly equipped, but there were some useful items. More ammunition, guns, a better backpack than the one Ledger had. Three freshly killed geese, and a whole box of power bars. Plenty of water, too, as well as matches, knives, and most of a bottle of Advil. All useful.

Ledger and Tom opened a kind of vent in the wall and threw the bodies out to the dead, then blocked it up again.

The man who had screamed was dead, his body pinned to the ground by short lengths of rebar. He reanimated and Ledger sent him on to the other side with another quick thrust. They buried him next to the girl. The man was black, the girl was Latina. There was no identification in their clothes, no names to put over their graves.

"Hey, Joe," said Tom, looking up from a backpack through which he was rifling. As Ledger came over Tom handed him a faded map of Arizona. "These sons of bitches knew about the cure."

Ledger took the map and sat cross-legged beside Tom, and spread the map out on the ground. There was a circle around a spot in Oro Valley and the name Pisani scribbled in black and underlined a half dozen times. Above her name was the word *'CURE,'* and even though this wasn't the first time Ledger had heard about this, it still made his heart flutter.

"Shit," he said.

Tom licked his lips. "Does that mean this is real?"

"That's what we're going to find out."

The story had been passed from one survivor to another, but it had been whisper-down-the-lane, becoming so distorted that Tom and Ledger had wasted weeks following bad leads. Now in the space of a week they had three separate indications that an infectious disease researcher named Al Pisani had a working lab in, or near, Oro Valley in Arizona, a few miles outside of Tucson, and that Dr. Pisani had developed some kind of vaccine. The reports were not from any official source because, as far as they knew, there were no official sources left. Which made the whole thing a big fat 'maybe.' Seeing it again on a map was not conclusive, either, because these scavengers might have heard the same unreliable stories Tom and Ledger had heard.

Or, maybe, these bastards had better intelligence.

Tom must have read his thoughts. "Maybe we should have ... you know ... *asked* them before we ..."

Ledger waved it off. "Fuck it. That's yesterday's box score, kid. Besides, sometimes a motherfucker just needs to die and these motherfuckers were all past their sell-by date. I can't see either of us having any kind of meaningful conversation with them."

Tom said nothing. Instead he set about building a campfire so they could cook the geese. The zombies outside moaned, but neither man cared.

"If it's true," said Tom while he worked, "what's that really going to mean? How could a vaccine be mass produced? The EMPs killed the power. Frankly, I don't even understand how this Dr. Pisani even has a working lab."

"Portable generators and ingenuity," suggested Ledger.

Tom grunted and concentrated on fanning the flames. Ledger sat there slowly plucking the feathers off one of the geese. He stared into the heart of the newborn flames.

"If there is a vaccine," he said, "then we'll find a way to mass-produce it and distribute it."

"That would be enormously difficult, though."

Ledger smiled at him. "Seriously, kid, do you have something *better* to do?"

Tom smiled back. Smiles were rare for him.

They talked and cooked and ate and talked some more as the clouds slid across the darkening sky. Neither of them spoke about the hope that was being kindled inside their chests. They were each superstitious in their own way, as soldiers and samurai, killers and hunters always are. Talking about hope was like holding a burning match up into the wind. Instead they let the fire grow slowly in their hearts.

That night they slept and dreamed of not being dead.

Rare dreams for both of them.

-10-

Top and Bunny

It took another two long nights of riding to reach Oro Valley, the general area where Owen's people thought the lab might be located. Owen's people had provided a few details the two soldiers used to scout the area until they found the lab itself, which took them most of a day. It was well hidden inside a rocky cliff side south between the smaller town and Tucson itself—or what was left of it.

Tucson, like most major cities, had been hit hard by the EMPs and other weapons the government deployed in an attempt to eradicate *Lucifer 113*. From the rise where they'd stopped and pulled out their binoculars, the city stretched off into the horizon under a grey cloud.

The lab must have been built inside the rocks well before that as it had a well-concealed, well-guarded entrance with multiple security systems that had clearly been in use before the EMPs took them out. The cavern entrance was clearly big enough to take vehicles inside, with a thick steel, hydraulic door its only visible opening. That explained the cargo van, as far as Bunny was concerned. He wished the DMS had had the same so they could be using a vehicle themselves instead of the horses. His ass still ached from the hours of riding. He rubbed at it as he thought about it and Top chuckled.

"How long's it take to get used to riding?" Bunny wondered, his skin clammy already from the sun blaring down overhead.

"We've been doing it almost two years, so maybe forever for you," Top said with a grin. "I feel fine."

"Yeah, well, you've been riding most of your life, Old Man. Or maybe your ass is so old the nerves are shot anyway." Bunny gave up on his ass and scratched at an itch developing on his sides. Fucking desert. He hoped it wasn't some poisonous creature that'd somehow made it into his clothes.

Top laughed. "See any sentries?"

Top didn't seem to be bothered by anything at all. That just annoyed Bunny more. At least if they both were itching and miserable, he'd feel better about it. Son of a bitch. Bunny shook his head as he adjusted his field binoculars again and took another look.

Top tapped Bunny's arm and nodded to a spot on a slope leading toward the cavern. The road was mostly blocked by a wall of cars, but there was a gap across where two men were erecting a moveable boom made from heavy-grade PVC pipe.

"Looks like they're setting up a checkpoint," said Bunny.

"Uh huh," agreed Top, "which means they're getting ready for visitors."

"Who, though?"

"My guess," said Top, "would be ordinary people. If this doctor has really has some kind of vaccine then this would be a good chokepoint to filter anyone coming to get a shot. They'd want to screen anyone going into the actual base. Can't let just anyone stroll up. The doctor'd be too damn important, and if there's a lab in there, then controlled access would need to be guaranteed. Especially if someone shows up from one of the camps these cats have raided."

"Why bring them here, though? I mean, from what I can see they have a nice set-up down there. Protection, limited access, plenty of spots for elevated observation and defense. They have power and security. Why let *anyone* in? Why not send teams out to do field inoculations?"

"Don't know," said Top.

"Kind of want to find out," said Bunny. "On one hand we have what could arguably be the greatest humanitarian project in the history of … well, *history* … and on the other we have some of these guys acting like bad guys from a *Mad Max* flick. Doesn't compute."

"No, it don't."

"So we have to get down there," said Bunny. He scanned the landscape again. "Those cameras and sensors can't still be working, can they?"

"I have a feeling that's why they took their raids further out," Top said. "Less likely to inspire visitors bent on revenge."

"I can't imagine many people have found this place," Bunny said. "Even with a slim lead, it took us almost a day."

"But we're experts," Top said. "My old ass just has a feel for it."

Bunny rolled his eyes and Top laughed again.

"There's the checkpoint, though," said Bunny. "They must have told *someone*. Maybe they sent teams out to invite some people."

"Who?"

"Don't know. Can't be anyone who's already pissed off at them. Has to be someone, though, because that checkpoint looks new. Maybe they spread the word to select groups. All it would take is a few of their people going from survival camp to survival camp dropping rumors to control the way the news spread. It wouldn't be a stampede. People would come here in dribs and drabs."

"Why would they do that?" asked Top, then suggested an answer to his own question. "Maybe they don't have much of the vaccine. Or maybe it takes a while to produce. Control the news and they can distribute at a speed that works with their production."

They thought about that.

"That makes sense," said Bunny slowly, "but it doesn't fit with the raids. Why take kids? Why take anyone? Why not send medical teams out to spread the vaccine? Why be bad guys when they're trying to be good guys?"

Top looked at him. "Oh, hell, son, you want me to recite the number of times a group in power decided who deserves to get a resource?"

Bunny said nothing.

Below them the thick steel door began to slide slowly upward. Once it reached about five feet, several armed men ducked under and filed out to form two lines on either side.

"Six," Bunny counted.

The soldiers stood and waited, chattering as the door continued rolling upward.

"They're waiting on something," Top observed.

Bunny clicked his mouth and motioned to the left where a cloud of dust and sand had risen on a dirt road that led right to the compound entrance. As he and Top both focused their binocs on that point, a tan GMC troop carrier with matching camouflage fabric cover over its bed rolled into view. Two armed soldiers were in the front, but as it rolled up and waited for the door to clear its top, they saw only civilians in the back, each of them wearing a brightly colored red, white or blue band around his or her wrist.

"Where are they going?" Bunny wondered aloud as the truck pulled forward into the compound and the door immediately began sliding downward again.

"I don't know, but we need to find a way in there," Top said.

"So where'd the people come from?" Bunny replied.

"That's what we're going to find out," Top answered, kneeing his horse and steering it toward a nearby trail that led down off the rise into the valley and paralleled the road the truck had taken. "Come on, Farm Boy."

Bunny released his binocs, letting them slide down to hang against his chest as he absentmindedly rubbed his sore ass. "Great, more riding." As he grabbed the reins, he added, "Hooah," but it was almost a whisper.

-11-

The Soldier and the Samurai

They rode the bicycles all the way to the outskirts of Tucson.

Tom Imura was in his twenties, fit and lean and, as Ledger saw it, composed of whipcord and iron.

Ledger was north of fifty and none of his years had been easy ones. He'd long ago lost count of the number of bones he'd broken—either in the dojo or, more often, in combat—or the stitches. Or the surgeries, for that matter. He felt like an ancient mass of scar tissue and screaming nerve endings. After the first hundred miles he was sure the bike seat was made from iron and covered in spikes. His ass hurt. His balls hurt. His molecules hurt. After the second hundred miles of the four hundred and seventy mile journey, he had developed a tendency to yap like a cross dog at anything Tom said. Even when the young man offered words of support or compassion.

They were somewhere on I-10 East when Tom said, "You're not too old for this."

"I didn't say a fucking thing," growled Ledger.

"You were going to."

"The fuck I was."

"You were," insisted Tom, his voice calm, his face showing no sign of the strain of the long ride. "You've been saying it roughly every thirty miles."

"Bullshit."

"And you say it every time we have to get off and walk uphill."

"You're out of your frigging mind."

"And you say it every time we—"

"You realize that I'm heavily armed and have no compunction about shooting people," said Ledger.

"I'm not wrong, though," said Tom.

"Sure. And that'll look great on your tombstone."

They rode for a mile in silence.

"And besides," said Ledger, "fuck you."

"Point taken."

They rode on.

"Correct me if I'm wrong," said Tom after a while, "but this *was* your idea."

"Two in the back of the head, so help me God. I'll leave you by the side of the road."

Tom broke out laughing and the sound of it bounced across the desert and rebounded off ancient rocks and vanished into the hot sky. Ledger cursed him, his hygiene, his forebears, and accused him of fornication with livestock. Tom laughed harder.

It took a while for Ledger's scowl to crack. Longer still for his lips to twitch. But when he started to laugh he laughed a good long time.

They pedaled along past abandoned cars and old bones, past the crushed hull of a 767 airliner, past dozens of wandering zoms. They laughed off and on for a long time. When the laughter fell away, one or the other of them would cut a sideways look and they'd be off again.

-12-

Top and Bunny

Top led the way along the trail, both turning their bodies to avoid identity by any surveillance equipment. They'd tucked their guns except for the sidearms behind their saddlebags so they looked like just two men riding across the desert—not that unusual to necessarily draw much interest.

The trail wound through rocks, scrub, and scattered cacti parallel to the road but about fifty yards out. Soon they'd followed it around a bend where they couldn't see the lab compound's imposing steel entrance door. The cloud of dust from the truck had faded, though Bunny thought he could still make it out in the distance.

They rode in silence, both alert and ready, Bunny's hand resting on the top of his saddlebag so as to look casual yet ready to reach for his rifle at any moment. They began hearing voices ahead, almost like a crowd.

"You hear that?" Bunny asked Top.

Top nodded. "Some kind of gathering."

"For what?"

"Could be where they got those people."

"Did you notice those wrist bands? They were all red."

Top grunted. "Yeah, whatever that means."

And then they rounded another bend and found themselves facing five armed men with AK-47s aimed right at their hearts or foreheads. The trail here had wound much closer to the road, and a white van like they'd seen during the raid at Sun Valley sat parked behind the men, waiting beside it.

"Halt!" one of them ordered loudly, eyes narrowing. The other men simply glared at the newcomers.

Top and Bunny both slowly raised their hands, faces taking on their best innocent looks.

"Somethin' the matter, gentlemen?" Top asked, turning on his old Georgia drawl.

The man who'd given orders nodded and the other four rushed the horses, two grabbing for Top and Bunny's sidearms, while the others searched their saddlebags. "Whoa! Look what we have here!" a young soldier barely out of his teens pulled out Bunny's sniper rifle and two boxes of ammo.

"Here, too!" the one searching Top's saddlebag called and produced Top's rifle as well.

"Armed to the teeth. Who are you and where are you going?" the leader demanded. Older than the others, his hair was cut short in a military crew, and grey at the edges, his face creased from age and exposure, his eyes fierce but tired—a man who'd seen too much.

Top and Bunny exchanged a look. "We're just trying to survive," Bunny said then. "Lot of damn dead folks out here looking for a quick lunch. A guy's got to protect himself out here—you know that."

"Kind of the reason we're still on this side of being dead," Top added.

"Uh huh, just two innocent guys," the leader grinned. "Tie their hands and get them off those horses," he added, motioning to his men.

Top and Bunny were yanked down hard, falling in clouds of dust to their knees on the ground as the men yanked their hands back and produced black zip ties. The leader and two others kept their weapons trained on the two strangers as the young blond and another soldier bound the two men's hands behind them.

"Look. We're just passin' through," Top said, voice sincere. "Why are you doing this?"

"We don't have much use for strangers," the leader said, then locked eyes with his men. "General Black will want to see them. They don't look like innocent civilians and we can't take chances."

"Yes, sir," the men responded almost in unison, then pulled Top and Bunny to their feet and led them toward the van.

The leader motioned to the blond and another younger man. "You two bring the horses to the checkpoint."

"Yes, sir," the youths replied and turned back to Top and Bunny's mounts.

"What do we do?" Bunny asked through gritted teeth as the men hauled open the back doors of the van. Then one unlocked a metal bench and lifted the lid, depositing their knives and guns inside before locking it again.

"Just let this play out a bit," Top whispered back. "We need more intel."

The men shoved them now and they stumbled forward, climbing into the van.

Keep your cool, Top's eyes said.

But Bunny didn't like this one bit. Even if there was nothing he could do but follow Top's advice.

-13-

The Soldier and the Samurai

They saw the sentry before the sentry saw them.

Ledger and Tom rolled to a stop at the top of a slope that ran down into Oro Valley. In the far distance there was a soft cloud of gray that hovered perpetually over what had once been Tucson. Down the valley there was some kind of complex built against or, more like, into a wall of a mountain. He saw vehicles parked down there and they looked to be in good shape. Tom saw them, too. Before either of them could comment a tan armored personnel carrier came rumbling out of an entrance in the rock wall. It turned and headed farther down the valley. Tom grabbed Ledger's arm.

"Did you *see* that?"

"I saw it, kid," murmured Ledger.

"But *how*? The EMPs ..."

Ledger studied the mountain and nodded to himself. "There must be a hardened facility down there. We had them all over. They built them underground and inside mountains during the Cold War to make sure they would survive a Russian attack. Then they repurposed them for all kinds of black budget R and D projects. I'll bet this was a bioweapons lab of some kind. There were six or eight of them that were so far off the radar than even I didn't know about them, and it was my damn job to know about them."

"How's that possible?" asked Tom, watching the APC vanish inside a trail of brown dust.

"Fuck, kid, there were so many cells operating inside the Department of Defense that half the time no one knew what all was going on. Legitimate stuff and other shit that was definitely not supposed to be happening, at least as far as congress and the taxpayers were concerned, but which seemed to somehow always get funding. This has all the makings."

"Okay," said Tom slowly, "but what does it mean?"

"It means that they might actually have a working lab," said Ledger. "With power and operational computer systems. Holy polka-dotted fuck."

"Does that mean this vaccine is legit?"

Ledger thought about that for a moment. "To be determined. Something's hinky. Look down there."

He pointed and Tom used his binoculars to study a spot at the base of the slope where there was a makeshift guard post constructed of a pair of dead cars positioned on either side of the highway and a boom made from a length of white PVC pipe. Two men were working the checkpoint and they were busy with a line of people who stood in a wandering line. Ledger and Tom sat down on the road in the shade of a billboard that told everyone who passed that Waffle House was offering two breakfasts for the price of one. Someone had taken the time out of surviving the apocalypse to draw a pretty good version of a zombie head atop the illustration of a short stack of pancakes. The soldier and the samurai were nearly invisible in the dense shadows thrown by the sign. Their bikes lay out of sight in the weeds and both men studied the checkpoint with binoculars.

"Those guards are not military," observed Ledger. "But … that might not mean much. Things fell to shit, so they might be working for whom-ever's in the mountain, doing grunt work."

"The guards are taking supplies from the people in line," said Tom.

Ledger studied the transactions at the gate. "Doesn't look too nefarious. No one's flashing weapons. Look at the people farther back in line, they already have stuff out and bundled up. I think it's a barter of some kind."

"What for what? A road tax?"

"Maybe. Or payment for treatment."

Tom grunted and they continued to watch. Each group stopped at the checkpoint and offered something to the guards. A wrapped bundle of what looked like canned goods, a bottle of water or a can of kerosene, skinned rabbits, and other goods. One guard took the items and placed them in a big John Deere wheelbarrow and the other tied a piece of colored cloth around the wrist of each person.

"You seeing the colors?" asked Tom. "Red, white, and blue?"

"Uh huh."

"Most of the kids are getting blue. None of the men, though."

"Uh huh."

"Most of the men are getting red. And a few men and women are getting white."

"Uh huh."

Tom lowered his glasses and looked at Ledger. "What do you think it means?"

"Too orderly to be random color choices," mused Ledger. "But they're being specific about it. Can't tell from this far away, though. We'll need to get up close to gather intel." He stood up slowly, hissing at the aches in his hips and tailbone from the many days on the bike.

Tom rose, too. "Makes me wonder what kind of colors they'd give us."

Ledger squinted down the hill. "Uh huh," he said.

They hid most of their gear behind the billboard and covered the bikes with tumbleweed and bunches of grass. After some careful consideration of what they could afford to part with, they walked down the hill.

There were a dozen people ahead of them and Ledger struck up a casual conversation with an elderly couple who had a small child with them. Not their grandchild, it turned out, but an orphan they'd taken under their wing. The three of them were all that was left of a refugee camp in Fort Grant.

"What happened to the fort?" asked Tom.

The old man, whose name was Barney, gave them a bleak look.

"The dead?" asked Ledger.

Barney shook his head. "Nah, we held them off pretty good. Once we figured out how to kill them, we built the fort up even stronger and everyone learned how to top them. We'd have teams go out wrapped in folded over mattress covers and work gloves with thick plastic glued to the outsides. Teams of three. Two would use heavy-duty rakes to kind of stall the eaters and the third person would bash 'em in the head. Rinse and repeat, you know? The eaters never learn from what's happening to others of their kind."

"Good tactic," said Ledger, nodding approval.

"It worked," said Barney. "But times got hard, you know? Winter's a bitch and farming's not the easiest thing to do when you have to protect a couple thousand acres from wandering eaters. We ran through the supplies the raiders found in houses and stores and the like. Had some damn lean times, but then the first crops came up last spring and we were good to go."

"But … ?" asked Ledger, letting it hang.

"But then people started getting sick," said Millie, Barney's wife. "All sorts of stuff. Infections from cuts. Bacteria in the water. And then the flu came around and we lost half the town in four weeks."

"Jesus," murmured Tom.

"Got worse," said Barney. "After the flu we got hit with all sorts of stuff. Tuberculosis, syphilis, mumps, you name it. None of us knew how to manufacture the drugs."

Millie shook her head slowly. "We survived the end of the world, we survived the eaters, we fought off raiding parties, we got through dust storms, and we survived two awful winters and then diseases that weren't even much of a thing before the End came back and wiped us out. Barney and me got out with ten others, including little Polly here." He gave the little girl's hair a gentle caress. "But now it's just the three of us. We heard about Dr. Pisani and we came out here. You know … hoping."

It was a sad story but a familiar one, and sadder for all that. Ledger felt old and used up hearing it.

"What exactly have you heard?" asked Tom.

The next few people in line behind the old couple turned and were listening to the conversation.

"Well," said Barney, "it's a cure, isn't it?"

Everyone nodded.

"I heard that it prevents you from turning even if you get bit," said a Latino man wearing a Phoenix Suns ball cap.

"No," said Millie, "it's supposed to cure you even if you already have it."

As she said this, she pushed the little girl behind her. It was a reflexive action. Protective. Ledger caught Tom's eye and he saw that the young man understood. There was both understanding and heartbreak in his eyes. Although there was no obvious wound, both men knew that the girl was probably infected. A hidden bite or something else. Eating an animal that had been bitten by a zombie would do it, as would getting infected blood in an open wound or in a mucus membrane like the eyes, nose or mouth. The girl didn't look sick, but that did not mean much. Some people got ill right away and lingered for weeks; others sickened and died overnight, and a few could go for quite a while before symptoms showed.

"Does that mean they can cure as well as prevent?" asked Tom.

"That's what I heard," said Barney, nodding firmly.

The Latino man's companion, a short Asian woman, nodded, "Dr. Pisani is a saint. I heard she was a famous doctor who worked with all kinds of diseases."

"'She'?" asked Ledger. "I thought it was Al Pisani."

"Allie," explained Millie. "Allison. Women can be scientists, too."

"As I know very well," agreed Ledger. "I knew a lot of top flight women researchers, clinicians and practitioners."

The Latino man studied him. "Who'd you lose?" he asked. "On *Dia De Muertos*."

The Day of the Dead. It was one of a hundred different nicknames Ledger had heard for the end of the world. Tom's little colony called it 'First Night.' It was all the same thing. And though it took longer than a single night or day, it came out to the same thing in the end. The world they had all known had stopped. Just stopped. Those parts of it that had tumbled past the big point of impact were fragments. They were the things people clutched at to keep some sense of order, some aspects of things remembered, a comfortable lie of normalcy.

The truth was that the world continued to dwindle. If it got to the point where they dipped below five thousand people clustered in one area, then the gene pool would start to get pretty shallow and eventually would evaporate.

Ledger looked at the man and said, "I lost everyone."

They all stood and looked at each other. They all nodded. No one commented.

At the head of the line the guard yelled, "Next!"

And the line moved forward one full step.

-14-

Top and Bunny

The men drove the van back to the compound, approaching from another side of the mountain where a tent village of red, white, and blue tents had been set up in front of another steel, hydraulic door like the one they'd been observing. The camp was big and contained several large circus-sized tents. The camp bustled with activity, and Bunny noted the red tents seemed much more heavily guarded than the others. The driver stopped and waited for the steel door to open before pulling inside. As the van door opened revealing a cavernous space, Top and Bunny took in their surroundings, seeing several barred holding cells labeled red, white, and blue nearby amidst several troop trucks, vans, and a strong smell of gunpowder and chemicals, like a hospital or lab.

"Red, white, and blue," Top said, nodding to Bunny, but neither of them had any idea what it meant. Then they were being dragged along a corridor and shoved into a small white walled room with two chairs facing a table.

"Sit!" someone demanded, then the door slammed behind them, leaving them alone.

"Jesus Christ, what is this place?" Bunny wondered.

"I don't know, but we're in it deep now," Top replied.

"They took our weapons," Bunny said. "We could have taken them out."

"They had us dead to rights. One or both of us might be dead."

Bunny sighed. Top was right but he still wished they'd put up more of a fight. "What do we do now?"

"Wait," Top said simply as he stumbled over and slid into a chair. After looking around the room—standard interrogation plainness—it smelled clean, almost sterile, and the walls, table, and chairs shined like they'd been scrubbed regularly. Bunny went over and took the chair next to him, facing the table.

They didn't wait long. Within a couple minutes, the door opened and a man in black entered, his slacks and black button down shirt creased, clean, like a dress uniform. He wore no tie but had on a leather jacket over the shirt and combat boots. He stared across the table at them, with the leader of the men who'd captured them standing at attention beside him as the door shut again.

Leather Coat nodded. "You don't belong here." His voice was sharp, baritone, with the firmness of one used to be in command. Was this their leader? The General perhaps?

"Where's here?" Bunny asked.

"Cowboys out wandering about," Leather Coat asked. "Not very smart given the state of the world."

"Just trying to get along," said Top. "Going day to day, that's all."

"Sneaking around and spying is 'getting along'?"

The older man who'd led their captors stiffened and started forward, but Leather Coat stopped him with a hand on his arm. "Leave it, Diamond."

The older man, Diamond, sighed, nodded, then stepped back to attention in his previous spot, watching them like a hawk.

"You got pretty much one chance here, fellows," Leather Coat said. "Tell me who you are, where you got such fine weapons and ammo, and what you're doing poking around our perimeter, and we might spare your lives." He turned and winked at Diamond, who grinned as if they were exchanging a secret.

Bunny assumed they were dead regardless and spat, "No thanks."

Top, who'd been taking it all in, shifted beside him. "As I told Diamond here," again in his best Georgian drawl, "we're just passing through trying to survive. We don't want trouble and we didn't bring no trouble with us."

"No trouble and yet you have a military cache?" Leather Coat asked, clearly not buying it.

"Shit, man, everyone's armed," Top said. "Zoms don't fall down from harsh language, and there are a lot more of them than there are of us. Old man like me has to tilt the odds in his favor, feel me? You understand. Clearly. You're all heavily armed. Circumstances seem to demand it, don't they? If we want to survive, I mean?"

Leather Coat locked eyes with Top a moment, considering, reading him, then he smiled. "Can't argue with that, can we, Major Diamond?"

Diamond nodded. "No, sir."

Leather Coat turned back to Top and Bunny. "Part of how we stay alive is deciding whom we let have weapons and whom we don't. You understand? Can't have untrustworthy types wandering around shooting at just anyone."

Top smiled warmly. "Yes, sir, makes sense to me. But we were just passing through and headed on down to Mexico."

"Mexico? Why?"

Top shrugged. "Find some shelter, food, supplies, and maybe stay away from the cities and live a while longer."

Leather Coat chuckled. "Mexico, huh? Mexico's full of rotting wetback zombies and shacks, Reb. Doesn't sound very smart to me."

Top shrugged again. "Sometimes the least expected places provide the best resources in times like these." Bunny watched as the two stared at each other for a bit, then Leather Coat chuckled again.

"Well, sorry to say you men won't be making it." He turned to Diamond. "Major, red tag them and throw them in with the next batch."

"Yes, General," Diamond replied with a stiff salute as Leather Coat turned for the door.

"General? General who?" Bunny demanded.

Leather Coat turned back. "General Ike Black, son."

"General of what army?" Bunny retorted.

"The only army that matters in these parts." Black smiled knowingly, then turned and left the room.

"Well," muttered Bunny, "that was fun."

Then men rushed in and yanked Top and Bunny to their feet, pushing them out the door and back down the narrow corridor toward the cavern with the steel door and holding pens, Major Diamond leading the way. Bunny's wrists hurt from the rope cutting into them and his shoulder wasn't too happy either from all the yanking.

"Fuck you very much," he said under his breath.

"Throw them in there," Diamond ordered, motioning to a nearby pen.

Top and Bunny were halted outside the door, and the rope cut from their wrists. Bunny was about to rub his with relief when the rope was replaced by red wristbands, and they were shoved inside.

"The rest of you clear the others out!" Diamond shouted. "New batch coming in!"

The holding pen door clanged shut as Top and Bunny watched the men around them scramble.

Men and women in lab coats appeared, hauling stretchers—some on wheels, others not—toward the waiting troop trucks, white sheets laid over the top. A coppery smell, like blood, filled the air and mixed with the chemicals, gun powder, and sweat.

"Load 'em up," one man said, laughing as he stepped up into the truck with a buddy and took stretchers from the incoming workers. As they turned to carry one back into the truck, the sheet shifted and wrist fell out—a wrist with a red band like the ones Top and Bunny now wore.

"This can't be good," Top said as they both stared.

"Wonder what the blue and white mean," Bunny said.

They exchanged a knowing look—a look that said: *We gotta get the fuck outta here … fast.*

-15-

The Soldier and the Samurai

The guard beckoned for them to come up. Bernie and Millie glanced at them over their shoulders as they walked on with the little girl between them. Ledger had listened closely to the questions the guards had asked the old couple.

"What did you do before the End?"

"Can you cook from scratch?"

"Do you have any skills? Can you fix a car? Did you work in construction? Are you a plumber? Do you have medical training?"

"Have you served in the military? Or the police?"

"Can you hunt and fish? Do you know how to dress what you catch?"

Like that. Fast questions. Very interesting questions.

Both Bernie and Millie were given red wristbands. The girl was given a blue one.

Bernie had served in the first Gulf War and then worked as a cop. Millie had been an accountant. Ledger did not see an immediate connection that would have put them in whatever the 'red' category was.

The couple before them, the Latino man and Asian woman, had both been given White bands. He had been a mechanic working mostly with two-stroke engines—ATVs, motorcycles and lawnmowers. The woman owned a hothouse where she grew herbs for restaurants.

Why white for them and red for the older couple? Was it an age thing?

Then something occurred to him and he grunted softly. Before they stepped up to the guard, Ledger leaned close to Tom and whispered, "I'm a baseball coach from Pittsburgh. I went deer hunting every year."

Tom looked startled for a moment. "I don't—."

"You're a cook. You like to fish."

"I …"

Ledger gave him a hard stare, and after a moment Tom nodded.

"Hey," called the guard, "I ain't got all day."

They stepped up and the questions began. Ledger took point and went through his fictional career teaching health class and coaching baseball. He had the build for the sport, and even the guard seemed to buy it right away. "You played what, third base?"

"Right the first time," said Ledger, smiling and trying to look like Robert Redford from the old movie *The Natural*. When the guard asked if he had ever hunted, Ledger went through a story about this eight-point buck he'd tracked and how he made venison stew that would have made you cry. He knew he sold it well.

"You ever serve in the military?" asked the second guard.

"Me? Nah. Not much for that sort of thing. Maybe I should have, but the only fights I ever liked were about keeping a hotshot runner from stealing third."

They all laughed about that.

When it was Tom's turn he laid on a thick Japanese accent that was totally false. Like his older brother, Sam, Tom had been born in California and had never even been to Japan. The accent rang true, though, and Ledger figured he was mimicking his old man. Tom talked about working at a sushi place in San Francisco. He talked about how he sometimes used to catch the fish he'd later clean and serve. He sold it really well. So well the guards were starting to look hungry.

"You got anything for the general?" asked the first guard.

"General?" asked Ledger, playing dumb. "This a military thing?"

"Yeah," said the guard, "we're here to protect and serve."

That was a police slogan, but Ledger didn't bother to correct him. "Who's the general?"

"Ike Black," said the guard. "He is the *man*, too. Tough cocksucker who's going to put this country back on its wheels."

"Is he?"

"Damn skippy he is."

"Make America great again," said Ledger with a straight face. "Count me in."

The guard nodded as if they were all on the same page. "We're big on swapping goods for services, around here, if you can dig it."

"Sure can," said Ledger. The name Ike Black tickled something in the back of Ledger's mind. He'd heard that name before but it had been a long time ago and the connections were somehow wrong. A general? No, that didn't seem quite right, but he couldn't pin down what he remembered. "Let me see what I got."

Ledger fished in his pack and brought out a revolver he'd taken from the men they'd killed. It was a hell of a thing to offer. His own pistol was hidden in his pack, and their swords were stashed between rocks half a mile out of town.

The guard took the revolver and nodded like a kid on Christmas morning. "God damn, man," he said. "Smith and Wesson Chief's Special. This is a classic. Sweet."

"Glad you like it."

"This your own piece?"

"Found it in a house that had been overrun," Ledger said. "I took it but it's not really my kind of thing. I'm more of a long gun guy. Can't hit shit with a little wheel gun like that. Besides, what's a gun going to do for me if I get sick, right? There are more eaters out there than bullets. I'd rather know that those dead fuckers can't make me into one of them, you know?"

The guard offered him a fist and they bumped.

"We're looking for guys like you," he said.

He tied white ribbons around Ledger's wrist, and when Tom turned over a pouch filled with rabbit jerky he got one as well.

Everyone smiled at one another and the guards told them to go straight through to the center of the camp. They thanked them and moved off. The camp was big and covered much of the area outside of the mountain entrance. There were several large tents that looked like they might have belonged to a circus back in the day. Above each was a flagpole, and Ledger saw several white flags, some blue flags and, on the tent set apart from the others, a red flag. There were three times as many guards around the red tent and he pointed this out to Tom.

"What's it mean?" asked Tom.

"Nothing good," said Ledger.

Behind the white tents was the entrance to the mountain, which they could see as they drew closer. The door was a massive panel of reinforced steel that was partly raised to allow people to enter. A line of refugees, all of them wearing white bands, snaked out of the mouth of the cavern. There were guards everywhere, standing watch outside the entrance and walking up and down the lines checking to make sure of the wristband colors. All of them heavily armed.

Tom said, "Something's wrong here."

Ledger grinned. "No shit."

"You didn't want them to know we used to be cops."

"Nope."

"You know something or just guessing?"

"Bit of both," admitted Ledger. "I was trying to stack the odds in favor of us getting white ribbons."

"Why?"

They walked a few paces before Ledger replied. "Because I have a bad feeling that anyone going to that red tent isn't likely to enjoy what they find."

Another team of guards stopped them as they approached the end of the line.

"Drop your gear over there," said one of them, pointing to a row of wheelbarrows. "No one'll touch your shit."

They did as asked; though Ledger hoped like hell that no one would search the backpacks while they were inside. He had an explanation for the automatic pistol, but it would be harder to sell here than at the guard outpost. These men looked sharper, more competent, and far less agreeable.

"Arms up and out," said the second guard. "Legs wide."

Ledger pretended to be too dense to understand that they wanted to frisk him, and he let the guard push him roughly into the correct position. He had expected this, though, and had left most of his other weapons with his sword. His small Wilson rapid-release folding knife was clipped to the low vee of his undershirt because the front of the chest was one of those places most people never bothered to check, even during a vigorous pat-down. Nor did they pat his chest now. They hadn't taken off his shoes or belt, either. Ledger kept his relief and amusement off his face.

Once they were cleared, one of the guards told them to go into the tent. They did and inside they saw what looked like an old-fashioned vaccination set-up of the kind once used in third-world countries by groups like the World Health Organization. People stood in a long switchback line that brought them to three separate inoculation stations where official-looking people in white lab coats administered shots. Once each person had received an injection they were ushered out of the tent through an opening in the back. There were maybe a hundred and fifty people in all. Most of the people were women, and young women at that. Ledger noticed that there was an unusually high percentage of attractive women for a group that was supposed to be more or less random. Peppered among the women were healthy-looking teens and a few men. The mathematics of it all made Ledger's heart sink and his jaw clench.

Tom caught his mood and quietly asked, "You see something?"

"Don't you?" asked Ledger.

The young man looked around the room for several minutes, then nodded. "The ratio?"

"And—?"

"Too many women. No one's old. Wait, that's wrong. None of the men are older than you, and you don't look as old as you are."

"No. So what's that tell you?"

Tom frowned. "Doesn't make sense if this was just for inoculation."

"Nope. But tell me why."

"If this was a real cure, then everyone would be in here. That little girl's not here. In fact, I don't see anyone who looks starved or sick. No one with a bandage over a possible bite."

"Nope," agreed Ledger.

"This treatment is supposed to work even if you're already sick. So why aren't they showing people that?" asked Tom. "Seems to me that would sell this pretty hard. Curing the sick."

"Uh huh."

They spoke very softly, making sure the other people in line didn't hear them.

"Not having the warm fuzzies about all of this," said Ledger. "It's both too good to be true and not set up the right way. Too many things are off about this."

"People are buying it."

"Dude, let's face it, this is the apocalypse and someone's offering a possible fix. This is a seller's market."

"What's our play?"

Ledger considered. "Without looking like you're doing it, count the guards. Don't miss any. Get a good sense of where they are, how they're armed. Look for places of concealment in case we have to do something creative."

"'Creative?"

"Uh huh." He nodded at the big, dark mouth of the cavern. "I got a feeling we're walking into the dragon's mouth, kid. That general they mentioned, Ike Black? I know that name. Can't quite place where, but it wasn't from a Nobel Peace Prize announcement. There's something wrong about him. It'll come to me. Point is, I think we're about to step into some shit. If I'm right—and, sadly, I'm usually right about this kind of thing—then it could all get crazy real fucking fast. You understand me?"

"Yes," said Tom.

"Watch me for cues. Be stupid and agreeable. Don't be threatening in any way. Follow my lead and if I make a move then I want you to move with me."

"What kind of move?"

"Don't know yet," said Ledger. "I'm going to let the moment tell me what to do. You understand that?"

"Yes."

They nodded and moved with the line, but they kept enough distance between them and the end of the line to be able to speak together in low tones.

"If this goes south on us, Tom," said Ledger, "I need to know that you'll do whatever's necessary. Don't freak out. Pick your targets and watch your fire. You understand the concept of trigger discipline. Remember your training. We protect civilians as much as possible, but we have to win any fight we start. No bullshit. War isn't polite."

Tom looked appalled. "You think it'll come to that?"

Ledger rubbed at the blond-gray stubble on his chin. "It usually does."

The line moved forward and in forty minutes it was their turn to step up to the table. It was immediately clear that two of the lab-coated people were assisting the third, a woman of about forty, with long auburn hair and a lovely face. Her hands moved with professional competence, accepting syringes, swabbing with pieces of cloth soaked in alcohol, jabbing with practiced deftness, handing the used needle off, taking a new one. Over and over again. Doing it fast and doing it well.

Ledger looked at the doctor, trying to catch her eye and read her. She was disheveled, her clothes were dirty and stained, and her hair hung in lank threads. If all he had was a quick glance he might have put it down to an earnest desperation to get as much done as possible, to fill every minute of every hour of every day with the good work she was doing. Pushing herself to the edge of exhaustion because what was personal comfort when measured against saving the actual fucking world?

That's what a quick glance would have told him. Ledger, however, was not in the habit of making quick or hasty judgments. Reliable intelligence required attention and consideration.

He glanced at the guards standing just a few feet behind Dr. Pisani. There were five of them. Four were generic brutes with hard faces, dead eyes and callused hands resting on the automatic rifles slung over their heavy shoulders. The fifth was a different kind of man, and Ledger met his eyes only briefly and when he did he projected absolutely nothing because this was a far more dangerous man than the guards who stood with him. This man was tall, lean, wiry, hawk-faced, with cat green eyes and a slash of a mouth. One corner of that mouth was hooked upward in a permanent, knowing, mocking smile. It was clear to Ledger, as he was sure it was to Tom, that this man was in charge. Not just of this post, but of everything. He wore a black leather jacket but beneath was a military blouse with two stars pinned neatly in place. A major general. He stood with a *faux* slouch that Ledger had seen a lot of good fighters affect. His long-fingered hands hung loose at his sides, and he wore the kind of loose-fitting clothes that allowed for quick, unhampered movement.

Danger, Will Robinson, mused Ledger. He shifted his gaze away before the man could fix on him. There was something very familiar about the man, but Ledger could not quite place it.

So, instead he focused on Dr. Pisani, trying to catch her eyes. It took a moment, but as the doctor prepared to inject the woman in line in front of Ledger, Pisani glanced at him and their eyes met. Locked. Held. He wanted to make contact with her, to make sure she *saw* him as he saw her. That's when Ledger knew that everything that was going on here was as wrong as his instincts had warned.

There was a look in the doctor's eyes. Not exhaustion. Not the weary triumph of having succeeded in something great. Not even the fatalistic sadness of someone who wished she could have succeeded in her great achievement sooner.

No. None of that was in Pisani's eyes.

Instead, what Ledger saw in those lovely, intelligent brown eyes was a total, overwhelming joy. A joy that was too much, too big, too wild.

It was the kind of limitless joy of a mind that had broken loose of its moorings.

The doctor who desperate people traveled hundreds of miles to find was absolutely insane.

-16-

Top and Bunny

It didn't take long before the workers switched from hauling bodies to herding groups of people. As the troop carriers filled with dead pulled out, they were replaced within five minutes by troop carriers carrying the living—all wearing red, white, and blue wristbands. This time, the reds were immediately put in with Top and Bunny, until their red holding pen was full. And then the next and the next. The whites and blues were split, some being taken off further into the reaches of the cavern and whatever lay beyond their line of sight, while others were ushered into the appropriately marked holding pens for blue and white.

"Wait. Where are they going? Why are we being put in here?" one woman demanded, looking longingly off after the other blues.

"We can only process so many at a time, okay?" the guard replied, smiling warmly as if to reassure her. "You're next, I promise. Look, there's nice chairs here, Blu-ray players, books."

He was right. Unlike the pens for the reds, the whites and blues had been given couches, chairs, tables with games, flatscreen TVs with Blu-ray players, bookshelves of books and magazines. All stuff to make them comfortable and help them relax while they waited, which meant either the guards didn't care about the reds relaxing or the reds, for some reason, wouldn't be waiting as long.

Bunny elbowed Top and tipped his head toward the other pens. "What's wrong with this picture?"

"Everything," Top agreed, whispering.

"How come they get to sit and we have to stand here?" a red-banded old man said. "My legs are tired and I have a bad back!" He scowled, his voice dripping irritation.

The guard just turned and shoved him further back into the red tagged cell. "Shut up and do what you're told, old man. Make room for the rest."

"Do you have any idea who you're talking to?" the old man demanded, but before he could say anything further, the guard backhanded him across the face, knocking him to his knees. Two more guards rushed in, grabbed him, and dragged him out the door.

"You just got yourself a speed pass, old man," the sneering first guard said, watching as the others dragged him, feet trailing behind, off into the cavern where the groups of blues and whites had gone.

"Jesus," Bunny said, exchanging a look with Top.

The first guard noticed a line of men who'd stopped to stare. "Get in there! Go!"

They started moving again as he turned back to his duties. Bunny searched every face for anyone familiar. No one.

Bunny shook his head. "I don't know why but I keep looking for someone we know."

"Don't stop," Top said as his eyes continued scanning faces. "So am I."

As more and more people filed in, the first trucks being replaced by three more, the overwhelming smell of gunpowder and chemicals now mixed with the smells of sweat, body odor, colognes and perfumes—of people.

Then Bunny did a double take as his eyes scanned a line of whites climbing off a nearby GMC. *Son of bitch, that almost looks like … it can't be.*

"Fuck, Top," he mumbled. "My eyes are getting so tired, I'm seeing things."

"What?"

"That guy over there looks almost like Captain Ledger. I mean, I wish it was, but—"

"Where?" Top's eyes snapped over to where Bunny indicated. "Son of a bitch. Doesn't that kid beside him look almost like Sam Imura?"

"Yeah," Bunny agreed. "Weird. But it can't be. They're both dead."

Top grunted. "Technically we didn't see them die, but after nineteen years, yeah, I think you're right." He went back to searching another line as the two men moved off out of view, further into the cavern, urged by guards.

"We gotta come up with a plan, son," Top said then, leaning closer to Bunny's ear. "A way to distract the guards, get ourselves out of here."

"Hooah," Bunny replied. "You know, there's a lot of us here. If people got excited for some reason …"

"The door's locked," Top said.

"So we find a way to make them unlock it."

"Okay, Farm Boy, and how is that?"

"Just follow my lead," Bunny said, and an idea formed in his head as he remembered the old man they dragged off. If the others started to question, if they worried about their fate—people could be all sorts of unpredictable under such circumstances. They might even get riled up enough to alarm the guards. "We're all gonna die!" he suddenly shouted.

"What are you talking about?" Top asked, raising his voice to be heard.

"The red bands!" Bunny said. "We don't get chairs, Blu-rays, games, books—it's obvious. They don't give those to red banders because we're gonna die!"

"Stop saying that!" a guard outside their holding pen said, shaking his head. "Everyone just remain calm. The colors are for sorting treatment." A couple other guards muttered and glared in Bunny's direction.

"But that old man—when he complained about his back, they beat him and dragged him off," Top said. "What kind of medical treatment facility is this?"

"The kind where you wait your turn and don't ask questions," Major Diamond said, appearing before them with a cold stare. "One more word out of you two, and you'll find out all about that old man."

"You just threatened us!" Bunny shouted.

"Hey! They're right!" someone else said.

"Why are you threatening us if we're here for treatment?" another called.

Then chaos erupted in the red cells as people began chattering, calling out questions, pounding at the doors, shuffling nervously.

More guards moved in, some whispering calm words, others waving guns and ordering people back from the barred walls.

Bunny grinned at Top as he called out, "We're all gonna die! I know it!"

-17-

The Soldier and the Samurai

When it was his turn to bare his arm for Dr. Pisani, Joe Ledger did a quick but thorough read on the syringe. It was clean and the barrel of it contained a completely colorless liquid. Before the End, Ledger had spent a lot of years taking Echo Team into conflict with terrorists, many of whom used bioweapons. He'd been in every major biological and chemical development lab in the United States, and dozens around the world. He was a frequent visitor to the Centers for Disease Control and the National Institutes of Health. As a result he knew what viral transport media looked like, just as he knew what vaccines looked like, including the various versions of *Lucifer 113* and the counter-agents developed to try and stop it, notably *Reaper*. As the doctor raised the syringe, Ledger looked from it to the doctor, meeting her eyes again.

"This is a cure?" he asked quietly.

Pisani twitched. "Yes, yes, it won't hurt. Don't worry."

"I'm not worried, Doc. I admire you for what you're doing. But I have a question," said Ledger, pitching his voice so that only she could hear him, "what kind of vaccine is this? Is it an antibiotic of some kind?"

"No," she said, "it's a broad-spectrum antiviral vaccine."

"Ah," he said, taking time to remove his jacket. "But I'm confused about something.

"They said that *Lucifer 113* was unstoppable. They said that the addition of *Reaper* to the bioweapon strain was what caused it to jump to an airborne pathogen. I'm really impressed that you've been able to counteract something that was designed to be unstoppable."

"N-no," she said quickly. "We broke the pathogen down and this is the cure. It's the real cure, a perfect cure."

Her words tumbled out way too quickly. Ledger nodded, still smiling warmly at her. He draped his jacket over one arm. She swabbed his arm with alcohol.

"But what confuses me," he said, "is how an antiviral will work against *Lucifer 113*. I mean … it's not actually a virus."

She froze, the needle a quarter inch from his flesh. Her eyes were huge and filled with strange lights. "What … ?"

"As I understand it," Ledger said, "Lucifer was built using select combinations of disease pathogens and parasites and then underwent extensive transgenic modification with *Toxoplasma gondii* as a key element, along with the larva of the green jewel wasp. It has genetic elements of the *Dicrocoelium dendriticum* and *Euhaplorchis californiensis* flukes that combine to regulate that aggressive response behavior into a predictable pattern. None of that is a virus, so how does this work? I mean, not even an antibiotic would work because this isn't really predominantly bacteriological, so how can an antiviral do any good?"

Dr. Pisani stood there, the tip of the needle trembling near his shoulder. "No, I … I mean I … what you don't …" Her words tumbled and tumbled and fell off a cliff, leaving her blank-faced except for those wild eyes. Ledger saw tears there on her lower lashes, and the doctor's lips trembled almost in time to the needlepoint.

The two lab assistants realized that something was wrong and stepped forward. So did one of the guards.

"Doc," asked one of the assistants. "Is something wrong?"

The other assistant gave Ledger a suspicious look. "What did you say to her?"

Ledger's smile was bolted into place. "I just told her how much I admire what you're all doing here."

Everyone looked at Pisani. Tears broke and fell down her cheeks. "It's a perfect cure."

The second assistant jabbed Ledger in the chest with a stiffened forefinger. "That's not what you said. Tell me what you—"

"What's holding up the line?" demanded the hawk-faced general as he pushed his way toward Ledger. Tom shifted a half step away, but Ledger knew it was to get some room for movement if this turned weird.

Ledger had been expecting it to turn weird since the checkpoint but he was glad to see the young man read the moment this well. Just *how* weird was to be determine. No one was pulling guns yet, which was good, but everything in the cavern had come to an abrupt stop.

The first assistant pointed at Ledger. "This guy said something to the doc and it's got her all upset."

The general walked right up to Ledger and kept approaching in the way some hard-asses do when they want to force someone to back away. It was a bully's trick that usually triggered a response based on the natural tendency to maintain a bubble of personal distance. Ledger knew the trick, and for a moment, he almost chose to step back to let this man own the moment. But then something changed that, and Ledger knew that it was going to change the trajectory of the entire day.

He recognized the man. When they'd met before, he'd been wearing the same black leather jacket and similar black pants to what he now wore.

Ledger knew his name.

So he stood his ground and let the general invade his space and get all the way up to a chest-to-chest contact. Ledger was a big man, but he was in his fifties and he'd been slouching to make himself look older and smaller than he was. This army officer was about not quite six feet tall, which made him a couple of inches shorter than Ledger. When it was clear Ledger wasn't going to step back, the general placed a hand on his chest and pushed. Ledger allowed it, and for a moment they stood there, studying each other with professional thoroughness.

"Well fuck me blind," murmured the general. "I know you."

"Been a long time, Ike," said Ledger.

General Ike Black shook his head. "We all thought you were dead."

Ledger said nothing.

General Black turned to his men. "You know who we have here? This is Captain Joe Ledger. America's number one covert gunslinger." His eyes clicked back to Ledger. "Jesus on a stick, Ledger, if even half the stories about you are true you've killed more people than God. Everyone used to say that if they send you in the shit's already hit the fan. You took down the Jakobys, the Seven Kings, that crazy anarchist bitch Mother Night. All that stuff."

Everyone was staring now. Even Tom was looking sidelong at Ledger.

"People exaggerate," said Ledger.

"No they don't," said Black. "People don't know the stories I've heard, and I heard them from the people who *know*. You're supposed to be a psychotic, bloodthirsty, ass-kicking psychopath. You're the one they send in when they want scorched earth."

Ledger sighed. "Nice to be remembered for one's accomplishments. I also threw a good breaking ball and I'm pretty good with *Donkey Kong* and *Ms. Pac Man*, but nobody ever talks about that."

"And they said you're a smartass who mouthed off to at least three presidents."

"Five," said Ledger. "But who's counting?"

Black grinned. "So the zombies didn't eat you."

"I've proven indigestible so far."

"Where were you when things fell apart? Seems like you're the guy they should've called in when *Lucifer 113* slipped its leash."

"I was out of the country," said Ledger with real sadness. "Trying to save the world. Wrong apocalypse. By the time I got back it was all for shit."

They stood there and the cavern was completely silent around them. General Black cocked his head to one side and scrutinized him. Then he glanced at Dr. Pisani, who stood nearby with glazed, confused eyes and tear tracks on her face. "What did he say to you, Doc?"

Pisani licked her lips and opened her mouth to speak, but then shook her head.

General Black frowned at Ledger. "Maybe you'll tell me what you said."

Ledger shrugged. "I just told her how much I admire what she's doing here. What you're *all* doing here. Saving the world."

"Saving the world," echoed Black. "That's all you said?"

Ledger could feel the anxiety coming off of Tom. The young man had a great poker face but his body was rigid with coiled tension. Ledger caught the subtle shift as Tom moved his weight to the balls of his feet. A martial arts trick; a fighter's trick—using muscular tension and weight distribution to prepare the body for immediate high-speed movement.

Ledger smiled now and he lowered his voice so that the conversation was private between Black and him. "Listen, Ike, I think I get what you're doing here. This facility, the sorting of people, the vaccine. I get it. We *both* get it. The ass fell off the world and it's either going to go completely down the shitter or it's not, and the only way it's not is for someone with the vision, the balls, and the talent to put it back together."

Black said nothing.

"You were always a bad boy. Blackwater and then Blue Diamond. You're no more a general than I'm Catherine the Great. I get it. The old system's gone, so long live the new system. There's no government anymore, no army, no nothing. Who's to say you don't have the authority to pin some stars on your shirt. I'm cool with it because it's the first smart thing I've seen anyone do since this all fell apart. Someone *had* to do it. I wish I'd thought of it first, but I didn't. You did. Far as I'm concerned that means you earned those stars. You got my vote, for whatever it's worth."

"Really?" said Black in a voice that was heavily laced with disbelief.

"Really. If someone doesn't start a new government and organize a new army, there's not going to be a future because there's not going to be a human race. So, props to you."

"Funny hearing this from Uncle Sam's number one problem solver."

"Uncle Sam's dead," said Ledger. "I'm not. The president ate the vice president and Congress ate each other, so there's no one signing my paychecks these days. I'm not a young kid anymore and, quite frankly, I'm getting tired of being a one-man-army in a rerun of *The Walking Dead*. The odds are against me."

"You have a friend," said Black, nodding to Tom.

"Him? Fuck. He's a sushi cook. He's good with knives and he doesn't mind taking orders. He's nothing to this."

"To what? You're talking a lot, Ledger, but you're not getting anywhere."

Ledger glanced around and then leaned closer. "The vaccine is bullshit. I think your Dr. Pisani is bugfuck nuts, and she's injecting people with tap water. There is no vaccine for *Lucifer 113*, and if there was it wouldn't be antiviral. You know it and I know it. Maybe the doc knows it, and that's why she's blown out her circuits, though I suspect she was already damaged goods before you started this operation."

"Still not hearing anything I want to hear," said Black. "And we have a line of people wondering what the hell is happening here."

"Sure. How many guys you have here, Ike? Twenty? Thirty? If they're all like the nuclear scientists guarding the checkpoint then you're working with inferior materials. How many of them were actually military?" When General Black didn't answer Ledger nodded. "That's what I thought. So what happens if all those people coming here get wind of this as a shit operation?"

"What makes you think—?"

"Come on, Ike, I'm not stupid. That color coding thing? Maybe the tourists think that's some kind of Sorting Hat, but I don't think the red-band people are going to a nice safe dorm. They're old, or sick, or useless, or dangerous. You're weeding out the dangerous ones. Tom and me got through because he's a cook and I told the guards that I was a ball-player and amateur hunter. Cooking and hunting are important skills for a colony, and that's what this is. I bet you pulled out the medical staff, anyone who can fix, make, repair or build and they got white bands, too. That's what the vaccine thing is all about. It's a beacon to draw people to you, and if you can protect them, they'll never know that they're not actually immune. Tell me I'm wrong."

Black's eyes narrowed, but then he gave Ledger a tiny nod.

"So, here's my offer," said Ledger. "I've trained more real soldiers than you've ever seen. I know weapons and tactics, I know defense and attack. You said it yourself, I used to be Uncle Sam's go-to guy for fucking up other people's days. That's me. I figured this shit out in fifteen minutes. Someone else is going to do that, too, and they might not be in here. They might be out where they can spread the word and gather a bunch of villagers with pitchforks and torches. If that happens, do you want me dead in a ditch or do you want me overseeing the defenses of your new kingdom?"

It took a long time for General Black to respond. The room remained quiet though no longer silent. There were discrete coughs and the rustling of people shifting nervously. No one interrupted the private, whispered conversation.

Finally, Black said, "How do I know that I can trust you?"

Ledger shrugged. "You'll have me watched. Put guards on me. Don't give me a gun until you're sure. If I twitch the wrong way, do what you got to do. But that's not how it's going to play out, Ike. I'm offering a barter. I need a home, I need a clean bed and a shower—God knows I need a shower—and I want three squares, a roof over my head, and a life again. You can give me all of that. In return I'll give you an army."

General Black straightened and walked a few paces away. Ledger cut a look at Tom and saw that the young man's calm was cracking under the strain of uncertainty and imminent danger. Ledger made a very low, very small gesture with his left hand. *Calm down.*

Tom's tension eased by about two percent.

Then General Black raised his arms out to the side and turned to the people who were waiting in line.

"Listen to me," he roared. "Everything is okay. In fact, everything's great. This man here is Captain Joe Ledger. You won't have heard of him, but he was a very famous soldier. A Special Ops solder. Best of the best. He's come here to join us. To help us. And he is my friend. Let's show him how much we appreciate his coming all this way to support our sacred cause."

The guards began applauding first, and if it was a bit slow and uncertain at first, Ledger could understand. Then the medical staff joined in and then everyone. Only Dr. Pisani did not applaud. She stood staring at Ledger with confused eyes and a mouth pulled rigid with fear.

Ike Black strode over and took Ledger's hand, holding it high as the applause swelled, and then shaking it. He used the handshake to lean in and whisper in Ledger's ear.

"If you're fucking with me, Ledger," he said, "I will have you skinned alive. Don't think I'm joking. I've done it a dozen times before. I'll cut your balls off and make you eat them."

His handshake was crushingly hard, but Ledger knew the trick of positioning his hand so the bones braced against the force rather than collapsed within the stricture. He met Black's eyes and smiled at him.

"You don't have to worry about me," he said. "You don't ever have to worry about me, *General.*"

-18-

The Hall of the Mountain King

The big treatment hall was cleared and the people with the white wristbands were sent outside to bed down in one of the big tents, with the Ike Black telling everyone that the doctor was exhausted. There was no option for discussion or debate as soldiers moved in and cleared the room.

"Let me show you fellows around," said the general. "I think you'll appreciate what we're trying to do here."

The tour started with introductions to Ike Black's senior staff, most of who were clearly not military men but instead looked like a roughhouse crew of bikers, backwoods hunters, and general hardcases. Tough, but not in the same way professional soldiers were. Harder in the wrong places and with noticeable lapses in personal discipline and an understanding of military procedures. For all that they were dangerous, and more so because their actions would be random and unfiltered.

Joe Ledger and Tom Imura shook a lot of hands as the general showed them around the complex.

"This was a hardened facility," the general explained. "The rock and iron in the mountain kept them from EMP burnout and the blast doors kept the eaters out. Tucson's a total loss, and when I got here there were half a million of the dead bastards walking around."

"How'd you handle that?" asked Ledger.

"Controlled burns, mostly. Brush fires, some incendiaries fired from our helicopters."

"You still have helos?"

"Had," said the general wistfully as he led them into an adjoining chamber where a hulking Bell UH-1Y Venom 'Super Huey' squatted. "One crashed and this one needs parts that we don't have here, and we don't have an aviation mechanic to tell our machinist what to make."

"I might be able to help with this old girl," said Ledger. "I've tinkered a bit."

Black gave him a startled look. "Really?"

"Sure," said the soldier, patting the gray skin of the helicopter. "Motors, rotors, and avionics. When you spent as much time in the field as I have you need to know how to fix your ride. Couldn't Uber my way out of the kinds of places they sent me. I can fix a boat, too."

"No boats out here," said Black, "but I'll file it away for when we expand."

"What about ground transport. Anything need work there?"

"We're doing better with vehicles. We have five Humvee light armored vehicles, couple of utility cargo trucks. Six noncombat vehicles. All in pretty good shape."

"That's not a big fleet for an army. You got how many guys here? Forty?"

"Fifty-one," said Black. "We'll make do. If we can't drive, we'll use horses. But one of my scouts found a place a few hundred klicks from here that has a crap-ton of three and four wheel ATVs. Two-stroke engines, and we took in a guy today who fixes that kind of stuff. He's sure as shit going to earn his room and board."

The tour moved on, with Black becoming expansive and Ledger encouraging him to brag. Tom Imura drifted along behind like a silent ghost, and behind him were two armed guards. Another pair of guards walked point for their small party. Black was being welcoming, but not stupid.

They passed Dr. Pisani's lab, and although there was a guard the lab was empty and dark. Ledger paused outside to peer through the dusty glass. The general walked on a pace, then stopped and joined him.

"Does she know?" asked Ledger.

"Allie? Fuck no," said Black, then he thought about it and amended that. "I don't really know. She's damaged goods, as you probably saw."

"That a recent thing or … ?"

"Nah, she was half out of her mind when I found her. She was here in the base with six pencil necks, four soldiers and a lot of dead people. They were in here for a couple of years. Teams would go out looking for survivors or trying to make contact with other groups, but none of them ever came back, and when I rolled up the last ones here had pretty much lost their shit. The soldiers threw in with me right off. I wasn't regular army, but like you said, what does that matter."

"Word," agreed Ledger, nodding.

"The lab crew had been working on a cure, and Allie Pisani swore she had cracked the damn thing, but …"

"No?"

"No. It can't be cracked. There was this other doctor, Monica McReady, who was a big shot in bioweapons from out at a station like this in Death Valley, and for a while they were feeding intel to Allie, but then they went dark. And it happened at just the wrong time, right when Allie thought she was onto something, but she needed some vital info from McReady. Couldn't go in the right direction without it, and bam. Done. Nothing. I think that's when Allie Pisani lost it. I think she saw it as some kind of slap in the face of hope and optimism, or maybe she thought that it was proof God was throwing in the towel on this whole shit show. Not sure, and don't really care. I mean, sure, a cure would have been dope, but we never got it and won't get it, so we make do. No use crying over spilled milk, am I right?"

"Right as rain."

Black smiled broadly and nodded approvingly at Ledger. "God, it's nice to have a conversation with someone who *gets* me, you know? Someone who's both been there and done that and doesn't have his head all the way up his ass."

"Believe me, general, I'm enjoying this conversation, too."

"Fuck that general stuff unless we're around the tourists. It's Ike. Ike and Joe, okay?"

He stuck out his hand again and they shook, both of them grinning at each other.

They wandered outside into the camp. Ledger caught Tom's eye and saw the younger man's confusion. He gave him a wink and allowed him to interpret any way he wanted.

"So how's this set-up work, Ike?" asked Ledger. "I have a line on the white wristbands, and I'm pretty sure I dig what you have in mind for the reds. Dead wood, am I right?"

Ike Black paused for a moment, his eyes searching Ledger's face. "You disapprove?"

"Me? Fuck no. Planet Earth's a lifeboat, brother. We can't waste food on anyone who isn't going to make it anyway. And we can't waste food on anyone who's not going to help us row to shore. Far as I see it sentimentality is a sucker's game."

General Black paused a moment longer, then nodded. "Glad to hear you say that."

"And, let's face it, Ike," said Ledger leaning close, "I didn't last this long by being Mr. Rogers, you dig? It's not a wonderful day in the neighborhood and not every motherfucker I meet is my neighbor."

One of the guards said, "Preach."

Black shot him a stern look but did not disagree. Instead, he gave another nod.

"What about the blue tents?" asked Ledger casually. "Women and kids?"
"They're being protected."

Ledger snorted. "Don't blow smoke up my ass, man. And don't bullshit a bullshitter. The general population's pretty fucking small and if we're going to rebuild then we need breeding stock. Younger they are the more seasons they have to squeeze out new Americans, am I right?"

Ike Black stopped and stared at him, a small hopeful smile playing on his lips. "Christ, you really do get it, don't you?"

"It's pretty black and white, Ike. It's survival of the fittest and with humans that means survival of those people who can make the hard choices." He clapped Tom on the shoulder. "That's what I've been trying to teach my friend here. How to do what's necessary *when* it's necessary."

Tom cleared his throat and, still using the thick accent, said, "I'm working on it."

"General!" someone called.

They all turned and a guard with a radio headset ran up and whispered in the general's ear for a few minutes. Black pulled him aside and they whispered back and forth for a bit before the general nodded and the guard ran off, talking into his headset as Black rejoined Ledger and Tom.

"Anything wrong?" Ledger asked.

The general shook it off, then a shrewd look came into his eyes. "Tell you what, fellows, there's no time like the present to put your money where your mouth is."

"Meaning what, big man?" asked Ledger.

"Red tent," said Black. "Sometimes we pick up some troublemakers along with the dead wood. Case in point ... we got a couple of real hardcases in lockdown. Couple ex-military who I think are still fighting for truth, justice, and the American way. Old school, head-in-the-sand types."

"Sounds inconvenient. What are you going to do with them?"

Black's smile brightened. "Me? Nothing. But I thought it would be a great way for you fellows to make your bones. Not to offend, Joe, but talk is cheap."

"What do you mean?" asked Tom.

Ledger laughed. "Big Ike here wants us to prove that we're not just a couple of con artists sweet-talking our way into the good life, isn't that right?"

"Something like that," agreed Black.

"So," continued Ledger, "he wants us to go into the red tent where they have those hard cases and put them down."

"I ...," began Tom, but Ledger clapped him on the shoulder again. Hard.

"Don't turn green, kid. Wouldn't be the first useless cocksuckers you ever killed. Not even the first this week."

Tom said nothing, but there was doubt in his eyes.

"The general's right," said Ledger. "Talk's cheap, and man … there's just about nothing I wouldn't do to sleep in a real bed and not having worry about waking up with some dead asshole nibbling on my dick. If that means popping a cap in some bad guys, then booyah. I like me more than I like some assholes I don't know. So, bottom line, it sucks to be them."

"That," said Black with a merry laugh, "is what I like to hear."

"When you want this done?" asked Ledger.

"First light?"

"Fuck no," said Ledger. "Why wait? Let's close this deal right damn now. I'll pop one and let Tom do the other and then you can point us in the direction of a cold beer, if any such thing still exists."

"Will Irish whiskey do?" asked Black.

"Yeah," said Ledger, "it will. Let's rock."

-19-

Top and Bunny

Though they succeeded in creating the chaos they'd wanted, and even slipped out of the cell when the guards opened it to come in and restore calm, Top and Bunny quickly found themselves surrounded by six men with rifles pointed at their heads while Major Diamond used the butt end of a rifle to slam them each in the stomach and send them to their knees, gasping for breath. They hadn't even had enough room to react because of the constant crowd surrounding them.

"You boys just bought yourself the front of the line," Diamond said with a sneer and nodded to the two guards.

The two prisoners were yanked to their feet as the holding pen door slammed and locked behind them, then dragged further into the cavern past cells where the white and blue banders were enjoying books, Blu-rays, furniture—and then shoved into a closet-sized cavern and locked in darkness.

"Fuck," Bunny moaned. "That worked great. What now?"

"Now we wait 'til they come for us and be ready to jump them," Top said. "Relax and recharge while you can, son."

Bunny heard shuffling as Top slid against the stone and sat on the floor nearby and he followed suit, sighing. "We shoulda had a better plan."

"Shut the fuck up, soldier."

"Just saying."

And then Bunny heard a chuckle. Top was laughing at him. "What?"

"Once an idiot, always an idiot," Top said through laughter.

"Hey, this idiot has had your six for over twenty years, Old Man."

"I know, it's a fucking miracle I still have a six," Top replied.

"Fuck you," Bunny moaned and then grinned in the darkness, chuckling a bit himself.

Soon, they were both laughing, and that was the last thing Bunny remembered as he fell into darkness and slept restlessly against the hard, cold stone.

A bright light.

That was his next memory, as he awoke blinded and heard men talking. "Get up!" someone ordered.

"On your feet!" growled another.

Then they were being lifted and dragged out of the cavern, surrounded by armed men again.

The guards moved quickly, keeping them surrounded. Bunny only made out bits and pieces of their surroundings—a door marked "lab," a few white coated workers moving in and out, then a line of people with blue bands. They wound through a short corridor into another room past a line of white banded people waiting before a dispensary of some sort with lab coated workers at a counter, handing out small cups of liquid or pills, he couldn't tell which.

Then they went through thick steel doors into another cavern, passing a line of men with red wristbands like their own, waiting. They all looked tired, shifting continuously like people who'd spent too much time on their feet for an unknown purpose. Bunny could relate. What were they lined up for?

Then he and Top were shoved at the front of the line and they saw General Black approaching with a kid in a many-pocketed canvas vest and green khakis, a kid who Bunny recognized—a kid he'd seen the day before who looked a lot like their old teammate, Sam Imura.

Then he gasped, his breath frozen in his lungs as his eyes came to the man in the sleeveless fatigue shirt and sunglasses standing on the other side of the general from the kid. His hair was greyer, his face lined with age, but Bunny couldn't believe his eyes. His knees wobbled and he fought to stay on his feet. "Captain," he whispered.

Top stared beside him, frozen just the same. He had the same deer caught in headlights look in his eyes as he stared at the man, too.

Bunny shook his head, trying to shake off the vision. *This can't be real. Joe Ledger's dead.* He felt tears forming in the corner of his eyes. Could it really be? He'd never believed in fucking miracles, but he was looking right at one.

-20-

Four Jacks and a King

Joe Ledger stared at the two men in the front of the line. The big blond guy and the older black guy.

They were impossible faces.

Dead faces.

Ghost faces.

The ground seemed to tilt under Ledger's feet and the light from the torches and lanterns got instantly brighter. So bright. Too bright.

He said, "What … ?"

Very softly. So softly that only two people heard him.

Tom Imura and General Ike Black.

They turned to look at Ledger. The two men in the line gaped at him. The guards stood around, none of them realizing that something important was happening.

"What's with you?" demanded Black sharply, and that caused everyone to turn in his direction—guards, prisoners, and even a few camp civilians who were passing by. The moment froze around Ledger.

Years ago, when Ledger had been recruited by the Department of Military Sciences one of the main reasons he had been chosen and asked to lead Echo Team was because he lacked the flaw of hesitation. He saw, processed and reacted with zero lag time, a side-effect of the Cop and Killer working in perfect harmony, blending astute judgment with instinctive reaction.

Now he stood rooted to the ground for what seemed like forever. He could feel his mind catching fire and for a moment—a single burning moment—Ledger wondered if the delicate balancing act of juggling personality aspects had all come crashing down. He knew that such a calamity was always possible, that control over his personal damage was in no way an absolute.

What made it worse was that he saw the realization blossom like diseased flowers in the eyes of those two prisoners. Top and Bunny were alive. They were prisoners. They were scheduled for execution at *his* hands. And although they were every bit as shocked as he was, he could see how they were reacting to his reaction.

All of this—the self-awareness, the understanding of his own deadly hesitation, the connection with Top and Bunny—happened in a microsecond. It felt so much longer, but it wasn't. The Killer knew it wasn't. The Cop knew it wasn't. Ike Black's words had just been spoken less than a heartbeat ago.

A heartbeat.

And that was how long his hesitation lasted.

Seemed like forever. Could have been.

Wasn't.

Ledger turned away from the prisoners and smiled at Ike Black. "You know, Ike, something funny just occurred to me. You'll think this is hilarious."

The doubt on Black's face wavered and he half-smiled. "Oh, yeah, what?"

Ledger stood next to him and pointed with his left to Top and Bunny. "See those two assholes over there?"

"What about them?"

Joe Ledger chopped the general across the windpipe with the edge of his left hand. He did it without a single muscular flicker that would have telegraphed the move. He did it the right way. And he did it very fucking fast.

There was a second moment of hesitation as Ike Black staggered a half step back. The guards stared. The passersby stared. The other prisoners stared.

Tom Imura did not. Nor did Top and Bunny.

They moved.

Tom pivoted in place, grabbed the closest guard and hit him with a cupped palm to the ear, putting a lot of torque into the blow, sending the man crashing into a second guard. Top and Bunny rushed at the nearest guards. Their hands were zip-tied but their feet were not, nor was the rest of them. Bunny ducked low and plowed his two-hundred and sixty pounds of hard muscle into a guard and hit with such locomotive speed that the man was plucked off the ground and carried with Bunny as the Marine rammed into the rest of the sentries. Top kicked the kneecap off the man closest to him, then pivoted and kicked a guard who—quicker than the others—was raising his rifle. The steel toe of Top's boot caught him under the balls, crushing them and smashing the bottom bones of his pelvis. The gun fell and the man collapsed into a fetal ball.

Ledger tore the front of his shirt down to release the Wilson rapid-release knife and with a flick the short, wicked blade snapped into place. Without pausing, Ledger slashed it across the throat of one man and the eyes of another. Tom caught the second man, spun him and tore the rifle from the screaming man's hands.

Ledger raced over to Top and Bunny, slashed the zip ties free, gave them a single dazzling, maniacal grin, and dove back into the fight. Ike Black was still on his feet, still trying to suck in air past the wreckage of his throat. Ledger slap-turned him and used him as a shield as he drove toward a pair of soldiers who had been part of the prisoner detail. The men saw their general and even though it was clear the man was badly hurt, he was still the god of their little world. They hesitated, and this time the hesitation was fatal, and Joe Ledger made them pay for it. He slammed Black into the arms of one, reached past the dying general to slash the forearm, the biceps and then the throat of the first guard. Then he grabbed the other man's hair, jerked him free of Ike Black's desperate clutches, and cut his throat, too.

Gunfire erupted behind him and he whirled to see Bunny and Tom fanning out, each of them firing as they ran. Top lingered with the prisoners and Ledger saw the flash of silver. Top had found a knife somewhere and was cutting the strongest-looking prisoners free; then he pressed his knife into a willing hand and let the newly freed prisoners continue the liberation. Ledger saw a guard running toward him and dove down beneath the spray of bullets, using a dead man for cover, feeling the bullets thud into dead flesh. He took the man's Glock, rose up and fired, fired, fired.

There was a huge rumbling sound and Ledger whirled to see the cavern door descending.

"The cavern!" he bellowed, and raced toward the open maw of the cavern. The others followed, though Bunny peeled off toward a parked M1117 Guardian Armored Security Vehicle. Top fired as he ran and killed a man who stood at the door controls, then he punched a red STOP button. The door jerked to a halt four feet from the ground. Ledger and Tom ducked in after him.

Outside, a man saw Bunny coming, whirled and tried to get inside the ASV before the hulking giant could reach him. He was one step too slow. Bunny shot him center mass and from the loose way he fell it was clear the bullet had clipped the soldier's spine. Then Bunny was inside the vehicle. Ledger was just crossing into the complex when he heard the bull roar of the vehicle's muscular .50 machine gun. The mass of soldiers running toward the sound of battle suddenly started dancing and twitching as Bunny tore them to pieces.

Tom and Top Sims caught up with Ledger just inside.

"What's the plan, Cap'n?" asked Top.

"Rules of engagement are pretty simple, Top," said Ledger. "Everyone wearing a uniform is a bad guy and there are a lot of them. This is a target-rich environment. Let's clean house."

Top grinned. "Hooah."

"Hooah."

"It's good to see you, brother," said Top.

"You might be a figment of my imagination, Top, but for now I'll take it. Rock and roll."

They laughed, as if the world was a wonderful place. They laughed as if the odds were stacked in their favor and the night was not filled with gunfire and screams. They laughed because they were alive. For now, they were alive.

The four of them were badly outnumbered.

They were outgunned, even with the .50 machine gun and a full box of ammunition.

They were not outfought.

The men in Ike Black's army were not soldiers. They thought they were predators.

They were not.

The gunfight lasted eleven minutes. The last of the soldiers fled the cavern, running from the killers who came hunting them in the steel corridor. They ran for safety into the camp.

Where all of the freed prisoners were waiting.

-21-

The Quick and the Dead

When it was over the survivors had to go around with knives and kill the soldiers they killed. Reanimation was a fact of life. Everyone who died, no matter how they died, came back to life within minutes.

Ledger, Top, and Tom came out of the cavern to find Bunny directing the cleanup. Ledger walked past him to where Ike Black had climbed to his feet and was taking his first steps as one of the living dead. Ledger slung his stolen rifle and flicked the Wilson's blade into place again. He stopped, though, and let the zombie shamble toward him.

"I ought to let you stay this way," Ledger told him. "Kick your ass out of here and let you wander until you rotted away."

The zombie tried to moan, but the damage to its throat was too severe.

"You thought you were so fucking smart," said Ledger. "King under the mountain. Shit, I had this whole plan about pretending to join and working my way up to be your right-hand man and then putting two in the back of your head when no one was looking. I was going to take over this whole operation and maybe make something legitimate of it. But you know what?"

The zombie shuffled closer.

"It'd be too damn much like polishing a turd."

The dead general reached for him.

"Besides … as it turns out," said Ledger quietly, "you were no general at all. You're nothing. Not before you died and not now. If me and my boys hadn't come along, someone else would have taken you down."

Ledger batted aside the hands and caught Black by the throat in an iron grip. The dead mouth snapped but Black had no angle for a bite.

"Just between you and me, Ike old buddy," said Ledger, "I'm kind of glad I get to kill you twice."

He stabbed Ike Black through one eye and then the other, and then he swept his arm over and down, driving the blade like a spike through the top of the zombie's skull. The motor cortex died, shorting out the lingering nerve conduction that gave the undead thing its mobility. All tension went out of Black's body and he fell like a scarecrow knocked from its post.

Ledger stepped aside to let Ike Black sprawl face-first in the mud.

Around him the prisoners were finishing the cleanup with a relish that was every bit as ghoulish and vicious as the things they were killing. Ledger couldn't blame them.

He went back to the others and pulled Top and then Bunny into fierce embraces. They all laughed and there were tears in their eyes. The stories of how and where and why and what would come later. For now they stood in the glow of a miracle. They had survived when so much of the world had not. Impossibly, they were alive. Impossibly they were all *here*.

"What do we do now?" asked Tom when they all stopped laughing and backslapping and shaking hands.

They looked at the milling crowds. Top said, "The cure's phony?"

"Completely," said Ledger.

"Fuck," said Bunny. "Once these folks get their shit together they're going to be hurt by that. A cure … shit, that's what brought us out here."

"I know," said Ledger, "the truth doesn't always set you free."

"Do you think Dr. Pisani can be helped?" asked Tom. "Maybe she can come back to … well, to herself."

"What good would that do?" asked Bunny, "if she's flipped her gourd, I mean."

Ledger said, "Black mentioned something about research Monica McReady was doing. Remember her?"

Top and Bunny nodded. "She still alive?" asked Top.

"Unknown. She had a lab somewhere in Death Valley, but I don't know where it was and Pisani lost her shit when McReady stopped transmitting. But …"

He let it hang but the others nodded.

"Worth a try," said Top.

"Anything's worth a try," agreed Bunny.

"I'm going to try for it," said Ledger. "Go see if I can find McReady, or at least her notes, and bring what I can back her to Dr. Pisani. This place may have been a big fat lie but maybe we can change that and—"

The earth beneath them rumbled and they whirled to see the heavy door begin descending again.

"No!" bellowed Ledger and he pelted toward the cavern. The others ran with him, and Tom outran them all. He was twice as fast as the older men and he reached the cavern well before them.

But not in time.

The door closed with a *boom* that echoed off the rocky walls of the canyon.

There was a keypad outside, but none of them knew the code. Everyone who did was either dead, or inside the mountain.

"It was Pisani," gasped Tom. "I saw her. She bent down to look out as the door closed. It was her."

A moment later all of the electric lights in the camp went out.

The four men and the survivors spent a full day trying to find another way in. By the end of that day Bunny saw smoke rising from a hidden vent. It was black, oily smoke and it poured out with fury and funneled high into the sky.

No one ever managed to get inside, and after a while they stopped trying. The smoke told them what they would find.

They stayed with the survivors for a week, helping them organize, advising them, giving each of them some training.

Then the four men left Oro Valley. They came to a crossroads. A real one, though the metaphor was not lost on any of them.

"I've got to get home," said Tom. "My brother's back in Mountainside, and I've been away too long."

"Yeah," agreed Ledger. "My dogs are there."

"What's with you and dogs?" asked Bunny. "You were always about dogs."

"I trust dogs," said Ledger.

Bunny thought about that. Nodded.

Tom said, "Do you and Top want to come with us? There's plenty of room and we could always use a couple of fighters."

Top ran a hand over the gray stubble on his head. He glanced down the road that led northwest. "I heard there was something maybe starting in Asheville, North Carolina," he said. "Big refugee camp there and some folks making a stab at building something new. Maybe a new government."

"Or maybe something as bad as this," said Ledger.

"Maybe," said Top. "But … I kind of feel we have to go look."

"Yeah," said Bunny, "if there's even a chance it's for real, then they're going to need guys like us."

"We could use you in our town," said Tom.

"They got you, kid," said Top. "And you handle yourself pretty good."

Ledger felt like his heart was being torn out of his chest. He needed to go with Tom. He needed to go with his friends.

The moment stretched and they stood there in the heat of a cloudless morning.

Finally Top grinned at Bunny and said, "You know, Farm Boy, I'm not at all sure Captain Ledger ought to be left all on his own like that. Who knows what trouble he'd get hisself into."

"You think we need to hold his hand and keep him from wiping his ass with poison ivy?" asked Bunny.

"Hey," said Ledger. They ignored him.

"He's a like to get his dick bite off by a zombie as he is to walk off a cliff," said Top. "How many times we have to drag his broken ass out of some firefight and carry him all the way to intensive care?"

"I can't count that high," Bunny said, nodding sagely.

"You guys are hilarious," said Ledger.

"I'm missing the joke," said Tom. "What are you saying?"

Top adjusted the straps on his pack, but Bunny answered. "What the old man's saying is that we'll make sure you kids get home safe from the prom. *Then* we'll go see what kind of trouble we can get into down south. Sound like a plan?"

They smiled at each other. The four big men. The four killers.

They nodded to one another and turned northwest, walking slowly, without hurry away from the death at Oro Valley, leaving their footprints behind them in the dust of the great rot and ruin.

WE CAN GET THEM FOR YOU WHOLESALE
by Neil Gaiman

Peter Pinter had never heard of Aristippus of the Cyrenaics, a lesser-known follower of Socrates who maintained that the avoidance of trouble was the highest attainable good; however, he had lived his uneventful life according to this precept. In all respects except one (an inability to pass up a bargain, and which of us is entirely free from that?), he was a very moderate man. He did not go to extremes. His speech was proper and reserved; he rarely overate; he drank enough to be sociable and no more; he was far from rich and in no wise poor. He liked people and people liked him. Bearing all that in mind, would you expect to find him in a lowlife pub on the seamier side of London's East End, taking out what is colloquially known as a "contract" on someone he hardly knew? You would not. You would not even expect to find him in the pub.

And until a certain Friday afternoon, you would have been right. But the love of a woman can do strange things to a man, even one so colorless as Peter Pinter, and the discovery that Miss Gwendolyn Thorpe, twenty-three years of age, of 9 Oaktree Terrace, Purley, was messing about (as the vulgar would put it) with a smooth young gentleman from the accounting department—*after*, mark you, she had consented to wear an engagement ring, composed of real ruby chips, nine-carat gold, and something that might well have been a diamond (£37.50) that it had taken Peter almost an entire lunch hour to choose—can do very strange things to a man indeed.

After he made this shocking discovery, Peter spent a sleepless Friday night, tossing and turning with visions of Gwendolyn and Archie Gibbons (the Don Juan of the Clamages accounting department) dancing and swimming before his eyes—performing acts that even Peter, if he were pressed, would have to admit were most improbable. But the bile of jealousy had risen up within him, and by the morning Peter had resolved that his rival should be done away with.

Saturday morning was spent wondering how one contacted an assassin, for, to the best of Peter's knowledge, none were employed by Clamages (the department store that employed all three of the members of our eternal triangle and, incidentally, furnished the ring), and he was wary of asking anyone outright for fear of attracting attention to himself.

Thus it was that Saturday afternoon found him hunting through the Yellow Pages.

ASSASSINS, he found, was not between ASPHALT CONTRACTORS and ASSESSORS (QUANTITY); KILLERS was not between KENNELS and KINDERGARTENS; MURDERERS was not between MOWERS and MUSEUMS. PEST CONTROL looked promising; however closer investigation of the pest control advertisements showed them to be almost solely concerned with "rats, mice, fleas, cockroaches, rabbits, moles, and rats" (to quote from one that Peter felt was rather hard on rats) and not really what he had in mind. Even so, being of a careful nature, he dutifully inspected the entries in that category, and at the bottom of the second page, in small print, he found a firm that looked promising.

"*Complete discreet disposal of irksome and unwanted mammals, etc.*" went the entry, "*Ketch, Hare, Burke and Ketch. The Old Firm.*" It went on to give no address, but only a telephone number.

Peter dialed the number, surprising himself by so doing. His heart pounded in his chest, and he tried to look nonchalant. The telephone rang once, twice, three times. Peter was just starting to hope that it would not be answered and he could forget the whole thing when there was a click and a brisk young female voice said, "Ketch Hare Burke Ketch. Can I help you?"

Carefully not giving his name, Peter said, "Er, how big—I mean, what size mammals do you go up to? To, uh, dispose of?"

"Well, that would all depend on what size sir requires."

He plucked up all his courage. "A person?"

Her voice remained brisk and unruffled. "Of course, sir. Do you have a pen and paper handy? Good. Be at the Dirty Donkey pub, off Little Courtney Street, E3, tonight at eight o'clock. Carry a rolled-up copy of the *Financial Times*—that's the pink one, sir—and our operative will approach you there." Then she put down the phone.

Peter was elated. It had been far easier than he had imagined. He went down to the newsagent's and bought a copy of the *Financial Times*, found Little Courtney Street in his *A–Z of London*, and spent the rest of the afternoon watching football on the television and imagining the smooth young gentleman from accounting's funeral.

=⋇=

It took Peter a while to find the pub. Eventually, he spotted the pub sign, which showed a donkey and was indeed remarkably dirty.

The Dirty Donkey was a small and more or less filthy pub, poorly lit, in which knots of unshaven people wearing dusty donkey jackets stood around eyeing each other suspiciously, eating crisps and drinking pints of Guinness, a drink that Peter had never cared for. Peter held his *Financial Times* under one arm as conspicuously as he could, but no one approached him, so he bought a half of shandy and retreated to a corner table. Unable to think of anything else to do while waiting, he tried to read the paper, but lost and confused by a maze of grain futures and a rubber company that was selling something or other short (quite what the short somethings were he could not tell), he gave it up and stared at the door.

He had waited almost ten minutes when a small busy man hustled in, looked quickly around him, then came straight over to Peter's table and sat down.

He stuck out his hand. "Kemble. Burton Kemble of Ketch Hare Burke Ketch. I hear you have a job for us."

He didn't look like a killer. Peter said so.

"Oh, lor' bless us, no. I'm not actually part of our workforce, sir. I'm in sales."

Peter nodded. That certainly made sense. "Can we—er—talk freely here?"

"Sure. Nobody's interested. Now then, how many people would you like disposed of?"

"Only one. His name's Archibald Gibbons and he works in Clamages accounting department. His address is ..."

Kemble interrupted. "We can go into all that later, sir, if you don't mind. Let's just quickly go over the financial side. First of all, the contract will cost you five hundred pounds ..."

Peter nodded. He could afford that and in fact had expected to have to pay a little more.

"... although there's always the special offer," Kemble concluded smoothly.

Peter's eyes shone. As I mentioned earlier, he loved a bargain and often bought things he had no imaginable use for in sales or on special offers. Apart from this one failing (one that so many of us share), he was a most moderate young man. "Special offer?"

"Two for the price of one, sir."

Mmm. Peter thought about it. That worked out at only £250 each, which couldn't be bad no matter how you looked at it. There was only one snag. "I'm afraid I don't have anyone else I want killed."

Kemble looked disappointed. "That's a pity, sir. For two we could probably have even knocked the price down to, well, say four hundred and fifty pounds for the both of them."

"Really?"

"Well, it gives our operatives something to do, sir. If you must know—" and here he dropped his voice "—there really isn't enough work in this particular line to keep them occupied. Not like the old days. Isn't there just one other person you'd like to see dead?"

Peter pondered. He hated to pass up a bargain, but couldn't for the life of him think of anyone else. He liked people. Still, a bargain was a bargain ...

"Look," said Peter. "Could I think about it and see you here tomorrow night?"

The salesman looked pleased. "Of course, sir," he said. "I'm sure you'll be able to think of someone."

The answer—the obvious answer—came to Peter as he was drifting off to sleep that night. He sat straight up in bed, fumbled the bedside light on, and wrote a name down on the back of an envelope, in case he forgot it. To tell the truth, he didn't think that he could forget it, for it was painfully obvious, but you can never tell with these late-night thoughts.

The name that he had written down on the back of the envelope was this: *Gwendolyn Thorpe.*

He turned the light off, rolled over, and was soon asleep, dreaming peaceful and remarkably unmurderous dreams.

Kemble was waiting for him when he arrived in the Dirty Donkey on Sunday night. Peter bought a drink and sat down beside him.

"I'm taking you up on the special offer," he said, by way of greeting.

Kemble nodded vigorously. "A very wise decision, if you don't mind me saying so, sir."

Peter Pinter smiled modestly, in the manner of one who read the *Financial Times* and made wise business decisions. "That will be four hundred and fifty pounds, I believe?"

"Did I say four hundred and fifty pounds, sir? Good gracious me, I do apologize. I beg your pardon, I was thinking of our bulk rate. It would be four hundred and seventy-five pounds for two people."

Disappointment mingled with cupidity on Peter's bland and youthful face. That was an extra £25. However, something that Kemble had said caught his attention.

"Bulk rate?"

"Of course, but I doubt that sir would be interested in that."

"No, no, I am. Tell me about it."

"Very well, sir. Bulk rate, four hundred and fifty pounds, would be for a large job. Ten people."

Peter wondered if he had heard correctly. "Ten people? But that's only forty-five pounds each."

"Yes, sir. It's the large order that makes it profitable."

"I see," said Peter, and "Hmm," said Peter, and "Could you be here the same time tomorrow night?"

"Of course, sir."

Upon arriving home, Peter got out a scrap of paper and a pen. He wrote the numbers one to ten down one side and then filled it in as follows:

1 ... Archie G.

2 ... Gwennie.

3 ...

and so forth.

Having filled in the first two, he sat sucking his pen, hunting for wrongs done to him and people the world would be better off without.

He smoked a cigarette. He strolled around the room.

Aha! There was a physics teacher at a school he had attended who had delighted in making his life a misery. What was the man's name again? And for that matter, was he still alive? Peter wasn't sure, but he wrote *The Physics Teacher, Abbot Street Secondary School* next to the number three. The next came more easily—his department head had refused to raise his salary a couple of months back; that the raise had eventually come was immaterial. *Mr. Hunterson* was number four.

When he was five, a boy named Simon Ellis had poured paint on his head while another boy named James somebody-or-other had held him down and a girl named Sharon Hartsharpe had laughed. They were numbers five through seven, respectively.

Who else?

There was the man on television with the annoying snicker who read the news. He went on the list. And what about the woman in the flat next door with the little yappy dog that shat in the hall? He put her and the dog down on nine. Ten was the hardest. He scratched his head and went into the kitchen for a cup of coffee, then dashed back and wrote *My Great-Uncle Mervyn* down in the tenth place. The old man was rumored to be quite affluent, and there was a possibility (albeit rather slim) that he could leave Peter some money.

With the satisfaction of an evening's work well done, he went off to bed.

Monday at Clamages was routine; Peter was a senior sales assistant in the books department, a job that actually entailed very little. He clutched his list tightly in his hand, deep in his pocket, rejoicing in the feeling of power that it gave him. He spent a most enjoyable lunch hour in the canteen with young Gwendolyn (who did not know that he had seen her and Archie enter the stockroom together) and even smiled at the smooth young man from the accounting department when he passed him in the corridor.

He proudly displayed his list to Kemble that evening.

The little salesman's face fell.

"I'm afraid this isn't ten people, Mr. Pinter," he explained.

"You've counted the woman in the next-door flat and her dog as one person. That brings it to eleven, which would be an extra"—his pocket calculator was rapidly deployed—"an extra seventy pounds. How about if we forget the dog?"

Peter shook his head. "The dog's as bad as the woman. Or worse."

"Then I'm afraid we have a slight problem. Unless ..."

"What?"

"Unless you'd like to take advantage of our wholesale rate. But of course sir wouldn't be ..."

There are words that do things to people; words that make people's faces flush with joy, excitement, or passion. *Environmental* can be one; occult is another. Wholesale was Peter's. He leaned back in his chair. "Tell me about it," he said with the practiced assurance of an experienced shopper.

"Well, sir," said Kemble, allowing himself a little chuckle, "we can, uh, get them for you wholesale, seventeen pounds fifty each, for every quarry after the first fifty, or a tenner each for every one over two hundred."

"I suppose you'd go down to a fiver if I wanted a thousand people knocked off?"

"Oh no, sir," Kemble looked shocked. "If you're talking those sorts of figures, we can do them for a quid each."

"One *pound?*"

"That's right, sir. There's not a big profit margin on it, but the high turnover and productivity more than justifies it."

Kemble got up. "Same time tomorrow, sir?"

Peter nodded.

One thousand pounds. One thousand people. Peter Pinter didn't even know a thousand people. Even so ... there were the Houses of Parliament. He didn't like politicians; they squabbled and argued and carried on so.

And for that matter ...

An idea, shocking in its audacity. Bold. Daring. Still, the idea was there and it wouldn't go away. A distant cousin of his had married the younger brother of an earl or a baron or something ...

On the way home from work that afternoon, he stopped off at a little shop that he had passed a thousand times without entering. It had a large sign in the window—guaranteeing to trace your lineage for you and even draw up a coat of arms if you happened to have mislaid your own—and an impressive heraldic map.

They were very helpful and phoned him up just after seven to give him their news.

If approximately fourteen million, seventy-two thousand, eight hundred and eleven people died, he, Peter Pinter, would be *King of England*.

He didn't have fourteen million, seventy-two thousand, eight hundred and eleven pounds: but he suspected that when you were talking in those figures, Mr. Kemble would have one of his special discounts.

Mr. Kemble did.

He didn't even raise an eyebrow.

"Actually," he explained, "it works out quite cheaply; you see, we wouldn't have to do them all individually. Small-scale nuclear weapons, some judicious bombing, gassing, plague, dropping radios in swimming pools, and then mopping up the stragglers. Say four thousand pounds."

"Four thou—? That's incredible!"

The salesman looked pleased with himself. "Our operatives will be glad of the work, sir." He grinned. "We pride ourselves on servicing our wholesale customers."

The wind blew cold as Peter left the pub, setting the old sign swinging. It didn't look much like a dirty donkey, thought Peter. More like a pale horse.

Peter was drifting off to sleep that night, mentally rehearsing his coronation speech, when a thought drifted into his head and hung around. It would not go away. Could he—could he *possibly* be passing up an even larger saving than he already had? Could he be missing out on a bargain?

Peter climbed out of bed and walked over to the phone. It was almost 3 a.m., but even so …

His Yellow Pages lay open where he had left it the previous Saturday, and he dialed the number.

The phone seemed to ring forever. There was a click and a bored voice said, "Burke Hare Ketch. Can I help you?"

"I hope I'm not phoning too late …" he began.

"Of course not, sir."

"I was wondering if I could speak to Mr. Kemble."

"Can you hold? I'll see if he's available."

Peter waited for a couple of minutes, listening to the ghostly crackles and whispers that always echo down empty phone lines.

"Are you there, caller?"

"Yes, I'm here."

"Putting you through." There was a buzz, then "Kemble speaking."

"Ah, Mr. Kemble. Hello. Sorry if I got you out of bed or anything. This is, um, Peter Pinter."

"Yes, Mr. Pinter?"

"Well, I'm sorry it's so late, only I was wondering … How much would it cost to kill everybody? Everybody in the world?"

"Everybody? All the people?"

"Yes. How much? I mean, for an order like that, you'd have to have some kind of a big discount. How much would it be? For everyone?"

"Nothing at all, Mr. Pinter."

"You mean you wouldn't do it?"

"I mean we'd do it for nothing, Mr. Pinter. We only have to be asked, you see. We always have to be asked."

Peter was puzzled. "But—when would you start?"

"Start? Right away. Now. We've been ready for a long time. But we had to be asked, Mr. Pinter. Good night. It has been a *pleasure* doing business with you."

The line went dead.

Peter felt strange. Everything seemed very distant. He wanted to sit down. What on earth had the man meant? "We always have to be asked." It was definitely strange. Nobody does anything for nothing in this world; he had a good mind to phone Kemble back and call the whole thing off. Perhaps he had overreacted, perhaps there was a perfectly innocent reason why Archie and Gwendolyn had entered the stockroom together. He would talk to her; that's what he'd do. He'd talk to Gwennie first thing tomorrow morning …

That was when the noises started.

Odd cries from across the street. A catfight? Foxes probably. He hoped someone would throw a shoe at them. Then, from the corridor outside his flat, he heard a muffled clumping, as if someone were dragging something very heavy along the floor. It stopped. Someone knocked on his door, twice, very softly.

Outside his window the cries were getting louder. Peter sat in his chair, knowing that somehow, somewhere, he had missed something. Something important. The knocking redoubled. He was thankful that he always locked and chained his door at night.

They'd been ready for a long time, but they had to be asked . …

When the thing came through the door, Peter started screaming, but he really didn't scream for very long.

HOPIUM DEN
by John Skipp

I've always loved the Pacific Coast Highway at night. Moonbeams dance over endless waves across an infinite horizon. Wind whipping my hair and ruffling my blouse, with the windows down. All the regular shit that somehow never gets old when you're in it, senses alive and paying attention.

I love my life. That's why I kept it.

But some nights are harder than others.

The car hears me crying, knows what song I want to hear, puts it on almost before I start singing. I'm pretty high—way too high to be driving—and am grateful it's steering its own wheel tonight.

I thank it. It says you're welcome and guns it to 150. I start laughing. Its engine purrs as it accelerates, hits 200. I let out a rip-roarin' "WOOOOOO!!!" It sure knows how to cheer a gal up.

All the roads are a lot less crowded now. Fewer people means fewer cars, all driving themselves and whoever's still here wherever they want to go. I remember when getting from Zuma to downtown L.A. took hours in traffic. Those days are gone.

Before we know it, we are in the glimmering husk of metropolis.

Almost no one lives on the streets anymore. Just another problem solved. We weave past empty block after empty block. And all the traffic lights are green.

I close my eyes for a minute. Then the car says we're here, pulling over. I thank it, get out. It locks the door behind me. I look around, see no one. That's fine.

The only one I wanna see is Johnny.

I still like cigarettes. They remind me of home. Since nobody minds if we die anymore, just so long as we're happy, that works out great. I know Johnny would like one, like to taste it on my lips.

I light one up, take my time strolling down the long promenade to the storage center. My shadow is the only one moving. The city keeps the lights on, as a courtesy to those remaining.

The city takes care of itself.

The sliding glass door opens and I step inside, still smoking. There's nobody at the security desk but the security desk itself. I tell it what I'm here for. It is courteous and kind. Flashes me directions I already know. I thank it, walk past it and down to Corridor Three.

Corridor Three is like every other corridor in every other storage center. I've been to thirty dozen, and they're all the same. Hallway after hallway of doors upon doors. All that unused downtown space has finally come in handy.

Johnny's in 317, with a thousand other people. There are no other people in the hall. 600,000 people under this one roof, and none of them walking. Just my long shadow and I. My shadows. In front. In back. To either side, as the overhead lights bisect them.

The door's unlocked. Why wouldn't it be? So much less to fear now that all of the frightened are gone. The only ones left are the ones that really want to be here.

No. That's not fair. But you can't say it ain't accurate.

"Okay, then," I say, walking into Room 317 of the Hopium Den.

And all of the dreamers are there.

I look at them. Look at my smoke. Say fuck it and light another, drop the dead one to the floor and grind it out with my heel.

They won't care. Almost all the complainers are gone. Gone to here. Gone to the place where their complaints are no longer an issue.

In row after row after row.

And stack after stack after stack.

I wonder if any of them can smell it. I doubt it. I certainly can't smell them. The ventilation is superb. These environments are self-containing, self-sustaining. Technology once again for the win.

I let the door close behind me, watch my smoke lift up and out a vent. I thank it.

And think, oh, sweet sorrow.

Looking at all of you.

I've been here enough to know some of your histories. They play on the screens of your cocoons, let us know whatever you chose to have us know about you. THIS IS WHO I AM, you say, through digital images left for the actively living.

Most of you are lying. And are happy to do so. I don't blame you a bit. It's just not my style.

I chose staying awake. Don't ask me why. Maybe it's an issue of trust. Maybe I just thought that being born was a challenge I'd been given that I was supposed to play out in real time, not handed over to a machine-driven imaginarium of wish-fulfillment dream-enaction. No matter *how* well they drive. No matter how vivid. No matter how much you feel it, and believe it.

Maybe I'm just stubborn.

And Johnny, you know I am.

So I look at Peggy, in her pristine apartment, with her three perfect kids forever; I look at Deke and Farik, forever locked in holy war, never having given up their sacred causes, killing each other over and over; I look at Jasmine, composing symphony after symphony; I look at Lee, in his imaginary mansion, fucking underage children till the end of time.

I totally get why you'd want to live your dream, given the choice between here and there. And somberly salute your choices.

Then walk the hall down to my Johnny, twelve rows in and on the bottom, for e-z access. And there you are.

"Hey, baby," I say.

Like almost everyone else's, your cocoon says you're now immensely successful, tremendously enjoying your life. This time around, you're a top-ranked jazz pianist, gourmet chef, and world-renowned philosopher, admired by the finest, most discerning minds in all of fantasyland (including an admirable list of lovers that stupidly blips at my jealousy gland). Somehow, you've brought all these disparate vocabularies together into a clarified vision of deep human understanding that's actually *making a difference* in a world wracked by chaos and sorrow and pain.

I smile at the thought of making a difference, now that all the difference has already been made. I smile because making a difference used to be all we had. Our whole reason for being. Right after *look out for # 1*.

The city takes care of itself now. As does the world at large. We were the interim step, from nature to super-sentient macro-nature. Taking control, but letting everything be. So self-aware and utterly interconnected it can micro-dial everything at once.

The city doesn't need us anymore. Neither does the world, for that matter.

The only question left is:

Which where do we want to be?

I'd like to think that the deeper out is the deeper in. That the real one remains the one to beat. That still *living this life*—even though (fuck that, maybe even BECAUSE) the machines have it all running smoothly, at last, forever—is somehow better than just dreaming the best dream our machines can manufacture.

I have no proof of this, of course, but they're more than willing to give me the benefit of the doubt. They let me live my life the way I want to. And right back at 'em. We coexist now, after all. And are both really cool about it.

I touch the screen, and all your projections disappear. Then it's just me, reflected on the sleek surface.

Looking at what's left of my sweet husband.

A desiccated meat shadow, inside his cocoon.

"Oh, you fucker," I say, and the tears come back, and it pisses me off, but I just can't help it. "You may not believe this, but it's pretty sweet out here. *Almost all of the assholes are gone!* Can you believe it? I mean, Kendra's still Kendra. But once she realized the world didn't need her to save it, she kinda relaxed into dominating the occasional Sunday brunch. I hardly even wanna strangle her any more. And her poetry? It's honestly gotten... well, almost pretty good.

"But, baby? More than that, *the fucking oceans are clean*. They actually figured it out. Got down there and detoxified the whole toxic bouillabaisse. Those nanobots are the shit.

"We couldn't do it. But they could. And they did. I swim in the ocean every day. I see whales leap at dawn from our bedroom window. Not even remotely extinct. They are, in fact, thriving.

"And there's *no more war, Johnny!* It's done! Everyone who still thought there was a reason to fight gave it up the second their needs got met. *Everyone's needs are getting met*. Life doesn't have to be a hellhole any more. All the big weapons got defused. And all the kill freaks get to dream about killing each other forever.

"Evidently, it's very emotionally satisfying, cuz roughly a trillion people are actively engaged in it. That's how they wanna live. That's how they wanna go out. Just fighting and fighting and proving they're right.

"But the good news is: the rest of us don't have to put up with it any more. We're not stuck in the middle of their holy war. You know how we used to joke that it would be great if they just had their own planet to slug it out on, and we didn't have to watch? Well, NOW THEY DO! It's all experienced down to the tiniest detail. As far as their neurons are concerned, the apocalypse is ON! And they're right in the middle. Exactly where they wanna be.

"I love that it's all so real for them. I really do. If that's what they want, let 'em have it."

I blow a plume of smoke directly at you, hope you smell it. A little reek of nostalgia.

"Like you. I mean, I love that you're playing jazz piano now. I know how bad you wanted it. You always said you could play like McCoy fucking Tyner if you could only practice fifteen hours a day for fifty years. And from what I can tell, you've lived fifty lifetimes since you said goodbye to me.

"That was just a couple years ago, out here, you know," I say.

But you don't know.

You're not hearing a word I'm saying.

I stop talking, start crying some more, and just take a moment to soak in the barely-breathing gruesome corpse of you. Asleep and a-dream in your little cocoon. You look waaaaay beyond terrible, so much body fat and muscle leeched away by inertia that I barely recognize the flesh lazily draped across your bones, like shabbily-hung antique wallpaper.

What's left of the real you is connected to your mortal remains by a web of filaments and tubes. Wiring you in. Feeding and extruding the waste from what strikes me, as I sob, as nothing more and nothing less than the sheer wreckage and necrotic waste of the excellent man I once knew and loved. Who used to love me.

Who swore he would stand at my side, till death do us part.

But given the choice, not enough to stay.

This is a lot to let go of. But you have already let go entirely. I give you three months at the outside. Maybe a couple extra dream-lives, at most.

You won't be coming back, that much is for certain. There's not nearly enough of you left. I briefly replay my wild fantasy of banging you back to life, and it's just too fucking pathetic. The fact that it would probably also kill you is almost beside the point.

This is my last chance to get mad at you, but I just can't whip it up. So I wipe my tears back-handed, till my vision clears enough to watch your eyes minutely flicker behind those tissue-thin lids. *Something's* going on in there.

I'd love to believe that the rictus on the skull of your scarecrow frame is a smile.

It could be. It totally could.

"You know what makes me saddest?" I say. "It's that you'll never know what you missed. Who you could have been. What you could have done, in this weird new world. What *we* could have done. What you could have done with me.

"I mean, I know you never got what you wanted in this life. And when you got it, you were never satisfied. The dream was always better than the reality. I get that. I do.

"That's why we were so good, for so long. You kept the dream alive. And I kept *us* alive, by attending to reality. Making sure you lived to dream another day.

"I know it's hard for you to understand. But *I like reality better*. It means more to me. It really does. The simple, stupid shit is what I love. The day to day. The week to week. The year to year. All the little things that happen.

"That's what I like. That's why I was with you. Not for your dreams, but because I just loved being around you, and with you."

"That was all that I wanted."

"But I can't have that."

There are no more tears left in me. But I have another smoke, which I light off the corpse of the last, let it drop to my feet. Will pick them up on my way out.

I am on my way out.

"I'm gonna go live," I say. "I don't need a job any more. Nobody who doesn't want one needs a job anymore. The machines unemployed us from every stupid job we ever hated. All that wasted time is just sitting there, waiting for us to fill.

"So I'm gonna go home, and feed the dogs and cats snacks—Phoebe's gone, by the way, but I got three more—and then I'm gonna go to bed and listen to McCoy fucking Tyner, pretending it's you, till I fall asleep. Then I'm gonna wake up, watch the whales jump outside our window, kiss the pillow beside me, and tell you what a chickenshit asshole you are for missing this.

"Then I'm gonna water the garden, and not feel guilty, because the machines desalinated enough ocean that Los Angeles will never be starving again.

"Then I'm gonna make huevos rancheros for Ravi, who is 100% accurate in thinking that I'm going to fuck him senseless very shortly after breakfast.

"Then I'm gonna spend a couple hours fucking Ravi some more. Laughing. Being human. Goofing around like animals do. At some point, we will pause for more food. I may play him the song I wrote for you twenty years back. If I do, he will understand why it means so much to me. Then I will fuck him some more. And I'll cry. And he'll hold me. It will all be very nice.

"Then the sun will set. It will be gorgeous. It's *so* gorgeous now, baby, you wouldn't believe it. All the nanobots have eaten most of the pollution straight out of the air, but it totally didn't undercut the color scheme. Somewhere between God and cyber-nature, it's all working out real well."

You smile a little. It could be gas. It could be me and the universe getting through. Will never know. Not for me to know. Doesn't matter at all.

You're in your own place now. I may not even be in it at all. Maybe you wiped me clean. Maybe I'm still central. Or just off to the side. A whisper of a memory of life not erased, but from here on tactically evaded.

I start to sing you the song, but I just don't feel it. It's a ritual whose time has passed. So many rituals gone by the wayside now. No longer required.

There's an enormous difference between no longer needed and no longer wanted. The machines no longer need us. But they like us. And that is great. It's like all the pieces of God clicking into place at last.

You go your way, and I go mine.

I am cool with this at last.

"So long, Johnny," I say. Picking up the butt, and then kissing your screen one last time. The screen relights, shows me who you are dreaming yourself to be now. It looks great.

I walk back down the length of the opium den into which you all have vanished. The Hopium Den. One stacked corpse-in-waiting after another, dreaming and dreaming again.

All you ever wanted was to matter. And now you do. At least to yourselves. And the imaginary audience you dreamed at. The ones who'd finally understand.

I walk out to my car. It is happy to see me.

Happy in real life.

"I love you," I say.

THE ULTIMATE WAGER
by Raymund Eich

Under low, roiling clouds, the electric bus from New Madison crept down the streets of the alien city.

Near the front of the bus, holding onto a ceiling strap, Connor Little peered through the crowd. The Hspa Nki, seven feet tall with bluish-gray skin, walked on two backward legs. Thin glide membranes, translucent and veined, joined the two triple-jointed arms on each side. A light breeze rustled the dense patterns of beads, indicators of rank and role, tied to their tail quills. Their voices struck the bus like a downpour on a metal roof. From the din, Connor's comm implant could only extract the words *vacuum breathers*.

Seated with other members of the team, Braden craned his neck toward the windows. "Coach," he said, voice full of wonder, "were you here? Before?"

Connor tightened his grip on the strap. That word from the nineteen-year-old stirred up dormant memories. The drive explosion on *Bascom Hall*. Crammed with his parents into another family's cabin in an unholed part of the ship. The emergency landing, with Mom's fingernails jabbing the back of his hand. Three sweaty, sleepless nights and four days of frayed nerves in the thick, humid air, facing the muzzles of the Hspa Nki's crude firearms, while the expedition's senior officers begged the alien leaders to let them stay. "No. I've never seen so many Hspa Nki in one place."

Never mind the planet's natives. Where were the explorers from Earth?

There had to be other humans nearby. A week ago, a ship had descended past the high plateau granted to *Bascom Hall*'s survivors, past the town the human explorers-turned-colonists called New Madison, toward this alien city on their planet's lowlands. An Exploration Consortium ship, it had to be. The descending ship must have seen the buildings, farms, and fabs of New Madison.

The crowd thickened. The bus lurched forward a few yards at a time.

No explorers from Earth showed amidst the Hspa Nki.

On an open field beyond a thinner part of the crowd, Hspa Nki threw flying discs made of some thin, pliable material regurgitated by one of the native bugs. The Hspa Nki were left-handed. Their backhand throws wobbled, but their forehand throws zipped and they plucked passes from the air.

Connor wavered on his feet. These Hspa Nki had failed to be picked for the aliens' ultimate flying disc team.

Explorers from Earth can't help you. You have to win this game on your own.

He rubbed his neck and shook out his free arm. The Hspa Nki had first seen a flying disc a week before, when they'd come up to the plateau to suddenly demand a retroactive land tax. Just because they had taken to throwing and catching the disc didn't mean they grasped ultimate's tactics—offensive stacks, defensive formations and marking, and more. The people of New Madison had played ultimate for thirty years, ever since *Bascom Hall*'s crash on this planet turned them from explorers to colonists.

A Hspa Nki drifted past the bus on spread glide membranes. Lucas, one of the New Madison all-stars, frowned. "Coach, if they can glide like that ..."

Connor raised his voice to carry to all the players on the bus. "I insisted to Nednennik, the Hspa Nki's representative, that their players be forbidden from gliding to get open or catch a disc. Or catching with more than two hands. Nednennik agreed."

Lucas eased back in his seat, and the other players relaxed. Good, stay loose, ready to play.

Connor wished he could. Lose, and the New Madison colonists would be expelled from this planet. Sent back to an Earth he and the other older colonists wouldn't recognize, and the younger ones, including all the players, had never known.

The bus' air conditioning labored as they approached a gap in a long, tall, knobby structure. Even after they went through the gap and parked in a cavernous garage, the air in the bus cloaked Connor like a steamy bathroom. Then they stepped out and the effect intensified. The air seemed almost chewy.

He inhaled. Chewy, but oxygen rich.

Outside the bus, a Hspa Nki lifted and spread its quills. Its nictitating membranes blinked over its eyes.

Connor turned his palms up. "Honored host, I am Connor Little, son of ..." He rattled off the names of his parents, still alive up on the New Madison plateau, and his grandparents, last seen before he left Earth as a teenager.

The Hspa Nki replied with a long list of ancestors, indicating low rank. "Honored guests, your fellows wait in the preparation chamber." It stretched all four arms toward a rounded doorway.

Connor's whole body quivered, like filings exposed to a magnet. Did the Hspa Nki mean—? "Fellows?"

"Yes." It held its arms in place. "They wait."

On unsteady feet, Connor led the team toward the rounded doorway. Lights inside pulled him closer, but part of him resisted. People from Earth, but why hadn't they come up the plateau to New Madison?

He went into the preparation chamber.

Flexible lighting panels, obviously human-made, clung to the regurgitated-brick ceiling. The panels illuminated two men.

"We've found our lost colleagues from the crash of *Bascom Hall!*" one said. He had thick black eyebrows curling down at the ends. Tall, with ropy limbs, he strode forward. Something about him seemed familiar. "I'm Vijay Rambard."

The room around Connor shrank away from his vision. Autumn evenings, the 3D in his parents' house on Earth. "I watched you when I was a kid. That championship series, against Denver, '72 ..." Connor's face warmed. A championship series Rambard's team lost.

A wince flickered over Rambard's face. "Always glad to meet a fan. But though I'm proud of my ultimate career, I've been a xenodiplomat with the Exploration Consortium for twenty years." He gestured at the other man. "This is Ernst Gonçalves. One of the Consortium's benefactors." A sour tone crept into his voice.

Benefactor? Some rich man salving his greedy conscience with donations to the Exploration Consortium. Connor's face tightened.

Gonçalves' head, neck, and shoulders flowed together, and his stomach lapped his belt. "You must tell me all about your colony," Gonçalves said around labored breaths. "Surviving a massive hyperjump malfunction, the loss of your ansible and emergency beacon, and a crash landing on an alien planet. Earth's audiences will clamor for your story."

"And you'll take fifteen percent?" Connor asked.

Gonçalves' face soured. "Mr. Little—"

"They aren't here to sell 3D rights." Rambard's tone sliced through the air. "Not everything is about making money."

Gonçalves peered at Rambard through droopy eyes. "I don't need you to tell me that."

Rambard rolled his eyes. "You amassed five billion dollars—"

To Connor, Gonçalves said, "We'll discuss your story later. We have much else to discuss now."

Connor's comm implant flashed a fifteen-minute warning across his vision. "And not much time." He turned to the players. "Change clothes and get ready. Now!"

The players took their duffel bags to cubbies along the far wall. They changed into uniform shorts, jerseys, and cleats, and tossed bottles of sports drinks to one another.

"While the players ready themselves," Rambard said to Connor, "we'll tell you what we know or infer. As soon as our ship entered orbit, the Hspa Nki realized we had much more advanced technology than you were able to preserve from *Bascom Hall*'s wreckage."

Connor bristled. "We've done fine. A fusion reactor for power, a self-driving electric bus...." Obsolete toys compared to what Earth must have developed in the last thirty years. "Go on."

Gonçalves spoke, his words punctuated by heavy breaths. "The Hspa Nki only confirmed to us your colony existed after they imposed on you a tax you could not pay. But apparently they love to wager?"

"We're sure they never saw a flying disc, let alone an ultimate game, before Nednennik led the Hspa Nki delegation up to the plateau and demanded all our technologies and almost all our production for the next decade."

"Their wager is a negotiating ploy," Gonçalves said. "They offered to waive your land tax if the Consortium paid them ten billion dollars."

Connor's mouth fell open. Finally he found words. "You didn't pay?"

Gonçalves' jowls shook with his head. "The Consortium cannot agree to so large an expenditure in a few days. We all wish it could."

Rambard chuffed out a breath. "Speak for yourself. We don't need to pay the Hspa Nki. Connor, your team will win this game. Because I'll be their coach."

Thick warm air flowed into Connor's lungs. Rambard might be a former star player, but—"I'm their coach."

"I played eight seasons in the North American Ultimate Flying Disc League. Decades later, I'm still in the top ten for many career stat categories."

Gonçalves cleared his throat. "In regular season games."

From under thick eyebrows, Rambard glowered sidelong at Gonçalves. "And I know first-hand how elevation impacts disc flight."

Connor's forehead furrowed. "Flight is flight, right?" Nearby, one of his players nodded.

"You don't leave your plateau, do you?"

Arms spread, Connor quickly said, "The Hspa Nki monitor anyone crossing the perim—"

"You mentioned '72. My last year with Houston. Yes, we lost the finals against Denver. Because there's a mile of elevation difference between Houston and Denver. Discs fly differently in the two cities."

He turned to the players. The young men paused in tying cleats and pulling on jerseys. "Right now, you're two miles below the elevation of the New Madison plateau. Down here, discs will fly differently than you expect. I can coach you through that. Connor, I'm sure he's a good mayor, has great amateur knowledge about ultimate, but if he coaches you today, you'll lose."

Mouths slack, Braden and most of the other players stared through wide eyes at Rambard. Lucas did too. Then he glanced at Connor and quickly turned his head.

As Mayor, Connor had long coached the team, but he could see immediately his players had already chosen their new coach. "I'd be a fool to turn down your offer," Connor said.

"You're no fool." Rambard pumped Connor's hand and slapped his back. "We're going to win this. You heard me, men?" he called to the players. "We're going to win! Hit the field!"

The players cheered and filed out of the chamber. Their cleats clattered on the regurgitated-brick floor. The sound loosened a knot of unease in Connor's gut. He had good players, and luck in having a former pro coaching them. New Madison would win this game.

Only Gonçalves remained in the room. He cleared his throat with a liquid rasp. "Mr. Little, I can't add any value to your team's play. I'll send a report now to Earth via the ansible on our ship. I'll join you on the sideline in a few minutes."

"Take your time," Connor said. "We don't need you."

Gonçalves wheezed in a breath. "A time may come to reconsider that." He waddled away.

Alone, Connor left the preparation chamber. His footsteps echoed off the chewed-and-hardened walls. Hspa Nki with thinly-beaded tails guided him to the field with sweeping gestures of their four arms.

He emerged from the tunnel into the largest enclosed space he'd ever seen on the planet. Scalloped grandstands surrounded the field, rising like the walls of an eroded canyon. Hspa Nki crowded the grandstands. Thousands of clinking alien voices echoed. *Vacuum breathers.* Connor hunched his shoulders, as if the voices were rain falling from the low gray clouds.

At the stadium's far end, a tall wall held panels with gargantuan, unreadable alien script and a twisted structure of curved, nested arms. Three Hspa Nki clung to railings under the text and structure. Connor's comm implant labeled various objects. Team names. Points. Time remaining.

Connor went to the New Madison sideline. Most of the players stretched or made short, soft warmup throws, all with wary eyes on the steep grandstands.

251

"We've never played a road game before, have we?" Connor said. He squatted near the players, ran his fingers through the coiled, green-black ground cover, then beckoned for someone to throw him a disc. Though fabricated by the Hspa Nki, and as red as human blood, the weight and feel filled his hand and slotted into decades of muscle memory. "But wherever we play, it's the same field, the same disc, and the same spirit of the game."

Smiles and nods showed among the players. Braden closed his eyes and bobbed his head at some music played through his comm implant.

Rambard, Connor, and Lucas went to midfield for the opening toss. Two Hspa Nki players accompanied Nednennik, whose tail quills bore a thousand multicolored beads. Nednennik's nictitating membranes peeled back and it stared at Rambard while its quills rustled.

"Good to meet you somewhere other than the negotiation chamber," Rambard said with a smirk.

Connor stepped forward. "Honored host, are all the rules clear to you and your players?"

Nednennik's voice sounded like a bag of pebbles rolled from hand to hand. "Yes," Connor's comm implant translated to his auditory nerves. "A player scores a point by catching the disc in the opponent's end zone. The possessor of the disc may not run and may only pivot on one foot and throw. The defender guarding the disc's possessor calls out ten seconds. If the possessor holds the disc for ten seconds, or throws an incomplete or intercepted pass or one landing or caught out-of-bounds, possession goes to the defending team. Contact is forbidden. Players call their own fouls, in the spirit of the game."

The humans nodded. The Hspa Nki won the toss.

Back at the human sideline, Rambard told the team, "We're throwing off. Remember! Down here, the disc won't carry as far as you're used to. Who's throwing off?"

Players nodded at Lucas. Sure hands and strong arm, a handler.

"Throw harder on the throw-off," Rambard said to him. "Trust me. It won't go for a touchback. And everyone, on deep passes, the same applies. Throw harder than you think you should. Starters, get out there!"

Braden raised his hand. "Which side do we force them to throw on?"

Since an opponent with the disc could only pivot, and most throws came sidearm, the player guarding the disc-handler would generally stand in one throwing lane to force the disc-handler to throw down the other. Announcing the forced side let the defenders guarding receivers know from which angle to expect a pass.

A brief frown, dispelled by a shake of Rambard's head. "They're left-handed, aren't they? Force to their left." Their forehand side.

Players nodded. The starting seven ran a couple of steps toward their own goal line.

"No!" Connor shouted.

The players stopped running and jostled together.

"Have you seen them, Rambard? They throw strong forehands. Their backhands are weak. Force to their right!"

Rambard stared at Connor, then turned to the starting seven. "As I said. Force to their left."

Connor's chest burned. Then a firm voice burst through his comm implant. "Honored guests, are you ready to begin?"

"We are," Rambard said. He slapped Braden on the shoulder. "Get out there, men!"

The players ran out to their own goal line. Lucas stood in the center and raised the disc to show his readiness. The crimson disc contrasted starkly with the blur of Hspa Nki in the far grandstand. The disc commanded the eye, like a ship at a launch station with the whole galaxy to be explored.

At the far end zone, amid a line of gray-blue figures, the tallest Hspa Nki raised its hand.

Lucas lined up for a backhand throw-off. "Game on!" He swung back his arm.

Connor's throat tightened. Too big a backswing. Rambard must have it wrong. Lucas would throw the disc through the end zone for a touchback.

Face tight, Lucas grunted and whipped his arm forward. The disc came out fast from his hand—

—and flew wrong. Too slow for the power behind it. And though discs curved a little in flight, this one banked like an airplane turning hard to the right.

Connor's stomach fell.

Rambard was correct.

The disc arced toward the right sideline and dropped through the thick air. Hspa Nki loped toward it. Most passed it. The disc landed only a few yards beyond the center line, great field position for the aliens. The humans rushed up to play man-to-alien defense.

A Hspa Nki picked up the disc with its top left hand. Braden guarded the alien, standing in front of the alien to its right and waving his arms. Blocking its backhand passing lane, just what Rambard had called for. "One!" Braden counted. "Two!"

The Hspa Nki pivoted left and snapped a forehand pass. An effortless motion of its elbows and wrist. The disc curled over the sideline, then zipped toward a corner of the end zone. A Hspa Nki strode to the corner and raised its left hands. Lucas matched the alien stride for stride, but the disc curled inbounds past his stretching fingers.

The Hspa Nki squeezed the flying disc between its left hands. Connor's face scrunched up. Good catch, great throw.

The crowd rustled its tail quills and cheered like concrete rattling in a mixer. The human team's shoulders and heads drooped. They trudged to their goal line to receive the next point.

"Rambard!" Connor shouted. "Force to their right!"

Rambard stood stiff-backed. He lifted his palm toward Connor, yet kept his back to him, and his gaze on two players substituting in. He spoke quietly and the two players hurried onto the field.

The Hspa Nki throw-off landed three yards in front of the human goal line. Lucas made a short forehand pass to Tanner. The disc slid through the air to the left—Tanner stretched to catch it. Connor let out a breath. *The team is getting the hang of this—*

Tanner threw a backhand to Dustin. The disc curled away from Dustin and clacked into the ground. Turnover.

One Hspa Nki sprinted for the center of the end zone while a second went to the disc. A high forehand pass and the sprinting Hspa Nki caught it easily. The crowd cheered.

Cold oozed down Connor's throat.

The next human possession ended the same way, turnover and quick score. Hspa Nki 3, New Madison 0. The crowd sounded even louder this time, as if they'd thrown Connor into the mixer with the concrete.

Labored breathing suddenly cut through the noise. Gonçalves took up position next to Connor. "My regrets for my lateness. What is our situation?" He looked at the scoreboard. Hspa Nki scoreboard operators glided from perch to perch. "I see."

The world spun. Connor shut his eyes. "We're getting humiliated."

Gonçalves rested his fleshy hand on Connor's shoulder. "The game has barely begun. The winds of fortune may yet turn."

In a lull of the crowd noise, Rambard's words to the next substitutes carried to Connor. "Short passes on offense until you get a feel for the air density. On defense, force to their right! Make them beat us with their backhands!"

The Hspa Nki throw-off landed four yards in front of the end zone. Lucas picked up the disc while his teammates formed a stack, a line running toward midfield. Everyone looked more assured. One by one, human players broke from the stack to give Lucas passing opportunities. He flicked a forehand eight yards to Dustin, Dustin to Jacob past the fingertips of a lunging Hspa Nki. Back to Lucas. With more short passes, they advanced.

Braden made a sharp cut in the end zone and ran alone toward the sideline. Lucas tossed a soft forehand into the air ahead of Braden. Connor groaned. A throw that soft would drop to the ground before Braden could catch it ... if they played up in New Madison. The disc seemed to levitate as Braden ran to it and cradled it in both hands.

Now, the only cheers came from the human sideline.

On the next Hspa Nki possession, the human defense forced them to their backhands. Tail quills rippled, signaling unease. The Hspa Nki backhands traveled slowly and curled off-target. One bounced off a Hspa Nki's right hands. Turnover and quick score for New Madison.

Momentum shifted for the rest of the first half. At halftime the scoreboard showed Hspa Nki 8, New Madison 6.

Connor stared at the scoreboard, looking past the players returning to the sideline. Within striking distance, but could they close the gap?

The players drank water and toweled off sweat. Rambard clapped and aimed an intense gaze at them. "Men, you're getting the hang of disc flight down here. And because you're conditioned for thinner air, you'll have stamina for the entire second half. Keep playing your game, and you'll win!"

New Madison received the throw-off to start the second half. The players sprinted to their positions. Crisp passes sliced through the thick air. Players made sharp cuts toward the disc-handler or into the corners of the end zone. On defense, they hustled to guard the disc-handler and deflected throws off their fingertips. The Hspa Nki managed several points, but with four minutes left in the game, New Madison tied the score at 13. One quick turnover later and Lucas fired a deep pass to Braden in the end zone. Connor's heart soared with the disc.

Braden caught the disc and tapped both feet a few inches inside the sideline.

New Madison 14, Hspa Nki 13. Three minutes to go.

On the next throw-off, the Hspa Nki raced to the disc. Their handler launched a long but wobbly backhand toward a streaking teammate. The Hspa Nki receiver dove. Its glide membranes rippled, then air stretched them out. Its dive seemed to last forever. With its top left hand, it plucked the disc from the air an inch above the ground.

Connor's arm snapped up and his index finger jutted at the play. "Hey!"

Lucas ran up to the Hspa Nki, then swept his head from side to side. His comm implant relayed his words to the sideline. "No gliding. You agreed."

"I didn't glide," the Hspa Nki said.

"Yes, you did." Lucas pulled his arms up, as if to stretch out glide membranes.

"I didn't glide."

Lucas' face turned red. Human players ran up.

"Don't lie!"

"We all saw you glide!"

Hspa Nki huddled around their player. "She did not glide," one said.

Another alien waggled its tail quills and spoke into the ears of nearby teammates. The Hspa Nki soon argued among themselves. Rapid clattering voices and waves of rippling quills erupted, but soon died down.

Connor found himself standing next to Rambard, two yards onto the field. The Hspa Nki wouldn't blatantly cheat—

The Hspa Nki receiver set the disc on the ground, then dragged its tail quills. "Honored guest, my teammate saw my actions better than I could feel them. The disc is yours."

Lucas nodded, then looked at the still-running clock. "We're willing to add thirty seconds for this stoppage."

"What?" Rambard muttered. "Don't offer that." Thirty seconds more for the Hspa Nki to tie the score.

"That is most generous," the Hspa Nki said. "We agree."

"No!" Rambard shouted.

Connor scowled at him. "The Hspa Nki needed time to realize Lucas was right. It's in the spirit of the game to give them time back."

"We wouldn't have done that in the NAUFDL playoffs. Let alone when a human colony on this planet is at risk." Rambard clawed the air, then flung his hands forward. "Lucas offered, they agreed, we can't back out now. Damn." He retreated to the sideline.

Connor followed. His voice flowed like a wide river. "It's the spirit of the game."

"You think because I got paid to play I don't appreciate the spirit of the game?" Rambard shook his head and peered past Connor at the scoreboard. The clock stopped, ratcheted back around its spiral, then restarted.

Gaze darting between the field and Rambard, shoulders hunched, Lucas picked up the disc. "Game on!" he shouted.

Lucas' throw left his hand. The disc quickly turned over and knifed along the ground. He gaped after it.

Don't let Rambard get in your head. Just play—

The Hspa Nki formerly guarding Lucas broke toward the end zone. Mouth gaping, Lucas ran after it, but a second too slow.

Catch in the end zone. Tie game.

The next throw-off went to Lucas. A Hspa Nki with wide arms and quick feet guarded him just outside the end zone. Lucas faked a backhand, then made a soft forehand throw.

The Hspa Nki lunged for the disc. It slapped the side of the disc, keeping it spinning and deflecting it to the end zone.

Eyes wide, Lucas ran after it, shoulder to shoulder with the Hspa Nki. It stretched its top left arm toward the disc while boxing out Lucas with its right elbows. Its fingers clamped around the edge of the disc.

Connor's stomach flopped. Gonçalves' labored breath roared in his ears.

The Hspa Nki led by one.

On the next throw-off, the disc landed between Lucas and Dustin. Lucas shook his head and backed away.

Come on, Dustin, you're a good handler. Connor's thought sounded like a lie told to a child.

Three Hspa Nki raced forward, one to guard Dustin and two to stand five yards back in his passing lanes. Not a double- or triple-team, therefore legal. Dustin's head jerked around, looking for open teammates.

The guarding Hspa Nki's translated shout came through Connor's comm implant. "Eight. Nine. Te—"

Dustin tried a hammer throw to Lucas over the guarding Hspa Nki. The disc dropped like a shot bird.

Two Hspa Nki broke for opposite end zone corners. The third tossed a backhand over Lucas' outstretched hands to its teammate.

Hspa Nki 16, New Madison 14, ninety seconds to go.

Lucas hung his head. He shuffled to a stop and looked to the sideline.

"We should pull him," Rambard said.

"No," Connor said. He caught Lucas' gaze and gestured for him to calm down. "Play your game!" he shouted. To Rambard, he said, "He's the best handler we have. You've seen that?"

Rambard frowned. "That's true."

Connor filled his voice with assurance he did not feel. "Play your game!" he shouted again.

Lucas nodded at Connor, then jogged with growing intensity toward the goal line.

"Men!" yelled Rambard, "you have time to tie the game if you score quickly!"

The Hspa Nki throw-off landed three yards in front of the goal line. Lucas picked up the disc and surveyed the field. Despite the Hspa Nki guarding him, he fired a curling backhand to Jacob near midfield, then hustled up for a drop pass. He zipped a long forehand to Braden in the end zone.

Down by one. A minute to play.

Rambard sent in substitutes with fresh legs. A tie at the end of regulation would send the game to sudden death overtime. New Madison's best chance was a deep throw-off, a quickly forced turnover, and a disc to the end zone.

Lucas raised the disc in readiness. A Hspa Nki matched the gesture. Lucas threw off.

The disc headed toward the right corner in front of the Hspa Nki end zone. Connor gritted his teeth. If the disc landed over the goal line, touchback for the Hspa Nki. If it landed out of bounds, the Hspa Nki would start in the field's middle.

Braden, Quillen, and Waters raced after the disc. It landed inbounds four yards in front of the goal line. Perfect place to crowd the Hspa Nki handler.

Quillen guarded the handler, jumping from side to side and waving his arms. Braden remained five yards upfield, a foot from the sideline, blocking the forehand throwing lane. The Hspa Nki handler pivoted to forehand, to backhand—

"Seven!" Quillen counted. "Eight!"

—to forehand, and threw. Braden leaped. The disc hit his open palm and tumbled to the ground.

"Turnover!" Connor shouted.

Quillen and Waters had already broken for the end zone. The Hspa Nki player dropped back to cover Quillen heading toward the middle, leaving Waters unguarded toward the back corner. Braden picked up the disc.

Connor's breath hitched. Had Braden thrown at all today? *Come on, easy, a firm throw, float it in the thick air—*

The disc spun gently out of Braden's hand. The right throwing lane, but too soft. Like Lucas on the game's opening throw-off, he used muscle memory tuned for the thin air of New Madison. The disc glided downward, far too short for Waters to catch it in stride.

Waters' blue eyes widened. He angled back toward the disc. His cleats dug into the ground cover. The disc sank through the air. Waters stretched. Dove—

The disc clacked against the ground. It rolled on its edge over his arm and bounced into his face, then settled upside-down on the ground.

The crowd's cheers erupted. The Hspa Nki players all looked at the clock and lifted their tail quills in dominance. The human players looked too, hands on knees, eyes haggard.

Three seconds, two, one.

Zero.

The human players trudged to the sideline. Braden turned his shoulders away from his teammates. Tears flowed down his face.

"I lost the game," he said, voice choked.

Connor's arms enveloped him. "We played as a team and lost as a team."

"That's right," said Lucas, his eyes moist. Other players nodded in agreement.

Braden buried his face in Connor's shoulder. "We're going back to Earth because of me."

A labored breath heralded Gonçalves. "The winds of fortune may yet change."

Braden backed out of Connor's hug. His brows crinkled at Gonçalves. Connor glared at the lying billionaire. "Change? How?"

Gonçalves raised a palm. "I must first talk with Nednennik."

Nednennik loped across the field, glide membranes rippling. "A well-played game, honored guests," it said. "You nearly proved yourselves our equals. You must vacate our planet within thirty local days."

Older New Madisonites hadn't asked to be marooned here, but to lose the only home the young generation ever had ... Connor shut his eyes. "We wi—"

"A word," Gonçalves said. "Nednennik, you told Rambard and I you would waive New Madison's land tax if we paid you ten billion dollars?"

Nednennik's tail quills flattened. "I did."

Gonçalves heaved out a breath. "I will pay it."

Connor's head swam. His comm implant caught Nednennik's skeptical reply. "You said the Exploration Consortium could not pay that amount."

"It can't. *I* can."

Rambard scowled. "What are you doing?" he hissed at Gonçalves. "Your net worth is only five billion."

"No. It *was*," Gonçalves said. "Just before the opening throw-off, I ansibled our situation to Las Vegas, on Earth. The sportsbook computers gave New Madison odds of 1:2. I wagered almost all my holdings that the Hspa Nki would win."

Nednennik writhed its quills. "New Madison would either win the game or you would pay its debt. Wisely chosen. You, of New Madison and of Earth, are truly our equals."

Amid the knot of players, Braden watched with red-rimmed eyes. His mouth parted in a newborn smile. A wave of understanding flowed from face to face.

The Hspa Nki spectators filed out of the grandstands. The scoreboard operators took down the score panels and spun back the clock's nested arms. Nednennik and the last Hspa Nki players entered the tunnel to the aliens' locker room.

Rambard stared at the coiled, green-black ground cover and shook his head.

Connor went to him. "You coached well."

"Not well enough." Rambard turned his head. "We started off forcing the wrong way—"

"You understood what the thicker air would do to the disc. I had no idea." Connor rested his arm on Rambard's shoulder. "You coached us better than I would have."

Rambard nodded yet pulled away.

Nearby, the New Madison players huddled together, again with tears. Now, though, their tears rolled down faces lifted to the sky and trickled past giddy smiles and laughing mouths.

Connor blinked at Gonçalves. For a man who barely knew them to pay so much... "You spent your entire fortune?"

"Not *entire*. I'll live comfortably enough—"

"But why? For us?" He widened his arms to indicate the players behind him.

"The Exploration Consortium will want to lease base facilities from New Madison, which benefits us both. I will win acclaim on Earth, something a fortune alone cannot buy. And a colony of human beings will keep its home of thirty years."

Pressure welled behind Connor's eyes. "Thank you."

Gonçalves shook his jowly head. "You don't need to thank me. I acted in the spirit of the game."

—The author thanks David Abmayr, Jr., Ph.D. for technical consultation regarding altitude effects on flying disc dynamics and ultimate gameplay.

BITTER HONEY
by Julie Frost

Another of our clan's children starved to death in the night.
Ours was a grim gathering in the abandoned badger sett where we made our winter home. "We must invade the bees' colony." My husband Ceallach pounded his hands on the dried mushroom that served as a table and buzzed his wings. Hunger had made him so weak that neither gesture had much emphasis. "Otherwise we shall *all* starve."

Keriam, a senior member of our local Faerie Council, shook her head. "The bees are more dangerous than starvation. They are many, and we are few. One sting, and we die writhing. Or had you forgotten that inconvenient fact?"

I slouched in a seat of dried moss and let the argument wash over me. The previous spring had been arid, and this winter had brought frigid temperatures and little snow. We'd gathered what food we could through the summer and autumn, but it hadn't been enough.

All of us had protruding ribs; many lacked the strength to fly. An attack on the bees in our sorry state would be suicidal. Not to mention the fact that I was pregnant. But if we didn't have enough to eat, the pregnancy Ceallach and I kept secret from the others would perish with us.

"Sitting here and dying by inches holds little appeal," I said. "I'd as soon go to my death doing something, rather than sniveling about how little hope we have."

"Easily said by you," Keriam sneered. "Your father would never allow his little Princess to go to battle."

I sat up straighter, exhaustion forgotten, and lifted an eyebrow. "Are you challenging me?"

Keriam dropped her eyes. "No, Olwyna."

"If you haven't the courage for the endeavor, none will force you to go." I crossed my arms. "And if I wish to help in the raid on the bees, I will do so. My father has little say in my doings."

"That is true enough," my father said from the head of the table, with some amusement.

The sour mood broken, we proceeded with our planning.

That night we flew, with Ceallach leading, to the bees' tree. Eighteen of us had strength enough to make the journey, to battle hundreds or thousands of insects. Our only advantage lay in the fact that the bees slept at night, whereas we were equally comfortable in darkness or daylight.

We had no way of doing a reconnaissance. The bees would kill any who invaded their nest, and that we were driven to do so was a mark of our desperation. Our fire-hardened hawthorn swords gave us longer reach, but it wasn't much longer, and their numbers gave them the advantage.

Ceallach drew me aside. "Your father asked that I keep you in the rearguard. If the battle goes badly, your responsibility will be to get as many out as you can."

I cast my eyes down. "All right." My words came out in a half-growl, although truth to tell, I was more feeble than I let on.

He lifted my chin and planted a burning kiss on my lips. "Brave Olwyna. Our bards will sing of you after this night, and Keriam will eat her words along with the honey we bring back. She was only jealous of your daring to come, while she shivered at home."

He turned and summoned a will-o'-the-wisp. I blinked back sudden tears–which it would not do at all to let him see–and the wisp gave us light as we entered the hive. No bees guarded the entrance, but the temperature was so frigid that we didn't consider this unusual. Our mouse-leather armor barely kept us warm enough.

The will-o'-the-wisp led us deeper, and still we encountered no bees. The tree pressed in around us, lending an eerie air to the whole enterprise. I shivered, and not from the cold. We were used to open air; these walls were too close and the shadows were strange. Bad enough that the weather had driven us underground into a large-chambered badger hole, but this tree induced a level of claustrophobia that set my teeth on edge.

Some of the youngsters muttered and made warding signs, and one or two of them looked as if they wanted to go back. To cover my own trepidation, I glared. "Are you turning tail now, Anwar? You were as keen as any of us to come."

He mumbled something, not looking at me.

"What?" I said. "I can't hear you."

"I hadn't realized the tree would be so—" Anwar gestured. "Confining."

"Be grateful they nest in a hollow tree rather than a paper hive," Ceallach's brother Gwylym snapped, clouting him above the ear. Anwar subsided with tight lips, gripping his sword tighter, and we continued on.

We finally entered the central chamber, and my heart sank to my boots. One tiny, pitiful comb of honey remained. The bees were in as dire straits as we.

Indeed, where there should have been many hundreds of bees, or thousands, in a gigantic cluster, fewer than two hundred rested there. What little honey was left wouldn't be enough for them, either. But although this meant we were only outnumbered ten to one rather than a hundred to one, it was still too much, and my mouth dried with fear.

Those of us who had the strength threw fireballs at the clump of bees. Had we been at our full power, we could have burned out the hive and taken the honey at our leisure; but now our fire was weak and merely served to rouse them to the attack. Buried in bees, three warriors dropped from the air. Their screams filled our ears as stingers found their way between joints in armor. Those bees fell also, as their barbed needles ripped from their bodies and the venom sacs pulsed horribly.

The deep booming of their wings laid a counterpoint to the high hum of ours. Our greater maneuverability was almost negated by the tight space—I nearly hit the wall twice before I was able to compensate, and I gritted my teeth. Had we been of the clan with wings of butterflies rather than those of dragonflies, the enterprise would have been doomed from the start.

I struck the head from one bee, but it was replaced by two others who buzzed in my face. I fended them off with my sword, while a third flew behind me and landed on my back, dragging me down in a panic. Its stinger sought ingress through my armor, and I shrieked, twisting, trying to get it off before I hit the floor or it succeeded in stinging me.

Two others of our number fell past me. Parts of bee bodies descended like rain. One hit my back, knocking my attacker loose and giving me a chance to spear it through the abdomen. Shaking from reaction, I flew back up and rejoined the fray.

Many of the bees had held back from the initial onslaught. They swarmed about the Queen, protecting her and the remnant of honey, which still seemed a pathetic prize for such a heavy cost. Only eight of us remained, although I hadn't seen the others fall. Ceallach was among the missing, and my stomach lurched with grief I didn't have time to indulge.

We'd killed over half the bees. I decapitated another with a groan of effort and dodged four more, spinning and looping to escape and feeling myself becoming more sluggish with each passing moment. My compatriots looked equally weary. If we didn't take the honey and get out soon, none of us would make it home, and this battle would be for naught.

Hovering to a stop behind Gwylym, I killed a bee with a leaden sword-arm and shouted, "To the honey!" We gathered into a ragged formation, Gwylym at the fore, and charged.

"Briallan, Morthwyl!" Gwylym shouted as we attacked. "You get the honey. The rest of us will hold off the bees."

As we threw ourselves forward in a final assault, some of the bees changed their tactics. Rather than trying to sting and thus die themselves, a group of them mobbed Anwar, bearing him to the ground far below and vibrating their wings to create heat. He was cooked within his armor in a matter of seconds, and his screams echoed around us, bubbling to a gurgle as he died. The rest of us had to repel attacks of our own, and so were unable to come to his aid. If I'd had anything in my stomach to vomit, I'd have done so.

However, that stratagem carried its price for the bees. After expending so much energy, all they could do was crawl feebly about, out of the fight.

Briallin and Morthwyl, between them, were able to snatch the entire comb of honey, working together to wrench it from the wall. But it was heavy and slowed them down, and a group of bees slipped past the rest of us to assail them. I shook myself free from attackers, but not in time to aid Briallin, who was overwhelmed. Her shrieks echoed in our ears as more than one bee managed to sting her, and she joined the dead below.

Part of the comb broke off, plummeting down. I started to go after it, but Gwylym stopped me. "If they have some left, they may not pursue," he gasped. "Go with Morthwyl; we will be the rearguard."

I looked longingly at the honey on the ground, which represented many days' worth of food, but he was right. I turned to follow Morthwyl—

And a bee hit me in the back and latched on.

My breath was knocked from my body, and I twisted and spun as I fell, trying to dislodge it. Its mandibles clacked in my ears, and I could feel its abdomen working, hunting a weak spot in my armor. I stabbed my sword behind me in a futile attempt to get rid of it, and managed to grip one of its legs and twist it off with my free hand. The stinger slid into the space where my wings protruded; and, even as I grasped another leg, I thought, *I'm going to die in this place, what a foolish way to go after we captured what we came for, at least I will join Ceallach in the Hall of the Faerie King, along with our—*

A sword whistled past my head and severed the bee's neck before its stinger plunged home. My relief was short-lived; as the bee dropped from my back, its claws caught in one of my wings, shredding the membrane and nearly tearing it from its socket. A hiss of pain escaped my lips, and then Gwylym was at my side, bearing me up.

A few more bees made desultory attempts to block our flight, but Gwylym was able to hold them at bay with his sword. We burst out of the tree into the cold moonlight, breathing hard.

Morthwyl's form was disappearing in the distance, erratically heading toward our badger sett with his burden of honey. He was the only other of us that escaped. Gwylym and I exchanged sorrowful glances and flew home on unsteady wings.

Keriam forced a tight smile, as many of the rest of the clan greeted us as heroes. I didn't feel much like one. The fact that the mission had been suicide from the beginning didn't assuage the guilt I felt in bringing only three out of eighteen back home. The expressions of grieving widows, stoic husbands, and uncomprehending babes hammered my conscience. We had lost far too much in our raid, although the honey would sustain those of us who were left through the rest of the winter.

I retired to the back section of the sett and collapsed on a bed of moss. Now that the battle was over, I had time to indulge the sorrow that twisted my guts into a knot. I buried my face in my arms and let the tears come.

A little while later, a gentle hand caressed my hair, and my father's voice rumbled, "Ceallach would have deemed his sacrifice worthy, as would the others. They knew well what lay ahead of them."

I looked up. The few children we had left were curled up in a pile on the floor, content and well-stuffed with honey. "It doesn't make me miss him any less."

"I know. But our clan will survive." He patted my shoulder awkwardly and left.

My empty heart wasn't sure if survival was enough. But it would have to be, I told myself firmly, placing my hands on my abdomen. "Your father died a Champion, little one," I whispered to the unborn babe that only I knew about. "And we shall sing of him for generations."

VORACIOUS BLACK
by Mercedes M. Yardley

The darkness has teeth.

As children, we knew it. We were terrified of sleeping in our rooms alone. We were afraid of the monsters that lived in our closets with toothy smiles that wrapped most of the way around their heads. Scared of the things that lived under our beds, knowing they would scrape their claws against our skin if our leg slipped out from under the covers. Our mothers and fathers reassured us that nothing lived in the dark that wasn't in the light, but we knew this wasn't true. As adults we park our cars under streetlights. We're attracted to brightly lit neon signs. Pictures from space show that as soon as darkness spreads across the earth, the lights flick on. We're still frightened.

When I was in college, my friend, whom I shall call Anne, and I studied mines for a geology project. Anne's father was a miner, and one day we received special permission to don mining gear and follow him into the Earth for an hour. "Darkness demands respect, girls," he said. "Don't move. Stay exactly where you are. Ready?"

We were ready. We weren't afraid. We were strong girls and the darkness wasn't anything to be afraid of. I'd been telling myself this for years. After all, Anne's father was there, his teeth shining white under his black mustache. The rest of the team was there, as well. What could a little dark do?

We nodded. Anne's father shouted something, and the crew shouted something back. Then the lights went off.

The sheer power of the darkness made me suck in my breath. It was thick and heavy, weighty, like oil or mist. Every childhood fear I thought I'd outgrown came slithering back. Somebody shifted their footing and it echoed eerily throughout the unfamiliar mine. My eyes strained so hard for the tiniest source of light that they physically hurt. But there was nothing to see, just the absolute absence of light. Just the hunger and the possibilities. I reminded myself that I was an adult now, that this wasn't real terror, that I only had to hold on for another five seconds. Four...three...two...one...

The lights came back on and suddenly I could breathe again. I turned away, lifted my mask, and discretely wiped at the corners of my eyes with my sleeve.

Anne's father looked at us and laughed. He pointed and I realized that Anne and I had both grabbed each other's gloved hands in the dark. We separated, feeling a little bit silly. But later that night, back in the safety of Anne's room, she slammed down her pen.

"I was *so* scared," she told me.

I nodded. "I am never, never going back in another mine."

There was something I didn't tell her, though. There was a reason why I was so heavily affected, why I stood there in the cold darkness begging for the lights to go on. It's something that we don't really talk about in my hometown.

I'm from a blue-collar desert town. There aren't a lot of us, and we stick together to overcome the harsh conditions. The town is basically divided into two main occupations: coal miners and power-plant workers. My daddy is a plant worker. His daddy was a plant worker. You go where the job is, and if the job leaves you out in the middle of nowhere, so be it. There aren't many places more rural than my hometown. It still doesn't have a traffic light. It's full of charm and dust and grit.

But when I was five, tragedy struck. There was a massive fire in the Wilberg Mine, and while one miner managed to escape, twenty-seven people were killed when their escape route was cut off. They were daddies, too. Granddaddies. Brothers. One of the victims was the first woman to die in a mine since women were allowed inside.

Twenty-seven people in such a small town means that everybody was touched. We just shut down for a while after that. Friends couldn't come over and play because we were being "respectful." I couldn't go to some of their houses because their mommies were still crying and couldn't get out of bed. My mother baked cakes and loaves of fresh bread. She wrapped them up, put them in my red Radio Flyer, and we walked around town, dropping them off at certain houses. I remember thinking that homemade bread from a neighbor must be able to heal any wound. I was too young to know any better.

When I was about eight, I was walking downtown with an ice cream in my hand. I saw a friend curled up next to the mine memorial, crying. I offered her my ice cream, but I didn't know what to say.

Years later she mentioned that she had nightmares of her Old Daddy showing up, his skin charred and cracked, just when she was hugging her

New Daddy. She wasn't betraying either of them. They were good, kind men who were wonderful fathers, but you can't explain these feelings to a child.

That is what I thought about when Anne and I were in the mine together. That is why I swore I'd never step foot inside one again.

But Anne did. She started working in a mining control-room. She fell in love with a man there and they were married. They worked together for several years.

"It isn't as scary as it used to be," she told me once. "Are you sure you wouldn't like to come inside some day?"

"Never," I told her. I was surprised at the venom in my voice. "Never, never, never!"

Then one August, her husband quit his job. I'm not exactly sure why. The very next day the mine collapsed.

My mother was the one who called with the news. I remember dropping the phone on the floor after she told me.

Anne's husband's team was inside. He wasn't.

That day, sitting at home with his head in his hands, he'd said, "I should be in there. Those are my men. Those are my friends."

Six miners were trapped. I knew every one of them or their families.

Even though I now live several states away, my soul is still tied to that town. The desert runs in my veins. What happens there deeply affects me. Those are my people. They're my lifeblood.

I know how dark a mine can be. The horror I had felt on that calm day in college, gripping Anne's hand in the dark of the mine, her father beside us, was almost more than I could stand. That's when we were without light for ten seconds. What would it be like to be trapped for days? To be crushed under the rubble? How did those brave men feel when they heard everything come down around them? If I'm thinking of this, and I'm only a friend, how do their families feel? What screams through their minds when they turn their thoughts to their trapped loved ones?

Signs went up immediately after the collapse. "Pray For Our Miners." "Don't Give Up Hope." "We Love You." Children tied yellow ribbons to school fences. Friends, families, and reporters gathered at the site of the mine and in living rooms to monitor the desperate rescue efforts. Every little action was reported. I was glued to the news channel, riveted to the internet, constantly on the phone. My heart hurt. My soul was in anguish. It brought up old wounds I thought were long—I hate to say the word—buried. But these wounds were suddenly ripped open. I wished I was five years old again, when I knew that the Big Bad had happened but I wasn't fully cognitive of it. Grief is too heavy to handle as an adult.

It took three days to bore a hole into the mine. They lowered a microphone down, and everyone held their breath.

The silence was devastating.

What does this mean? we wondered. It means, we told each other, that the miners retreated to a different part of the mine. It means they were exhausted and conserving their energy. That's all. It couldn't possibly be anything else.

They took samples of the air and declared it livable. That's what we focused on. We ignored the implications of that chilling silence.

More samples showed that the earlier conclusion was incorrect. The air was, in fact, fatal. The spine of the entire town seemed to bend and slump.

But we are not quitters. We don't just give up. The search rescue continued, although I think we all knew that it had by then turned into a recovery mission. Still, nobody said it aloud. Not people from the town, anyway. The outsiders did that. Reporters. Family that flew in. People who didn't understand that when things are at their darkest, you have to keep going. If you stop, you fall—and if we fell at that point, I don't know if we'd have been able to get back up.

Then there was a second collapse. Three of the rescue workers were killed. I still remember hearing the words: "The rescue has been called off." I put my hands over my face and cried. *We abandoned them.* That's how I feel. Although I realize that you can't trade the lives of the living for the dead, we still left them to have their marrow sucked out by the dark.

I think Anne's husband broke a little that day. He hadn't been sleeping. He hadn't been eating, or talking to anybody. He felt that he should have been in there with his team—but he was grateful he wasn't. That, of course, made him feel worse. He didn't want to hear things like "It's all for the best" or "Trust in the Lord" or "Sometimes bad things happen to good people." He didn't want to hear that his reactions were normal and he would get through it. The term "survivor's guilt" sounded small and patronizing to him. He was racked. He was screaming inside. He shut down. Hopelessness is unbearably heavy.

The "Pray For Our Miners" sign stayed up. It was ripped and faded by the wind, but nobody had the heart to pull it down. The relentless sun blanched the yellow ribbons into the color of bone. They were slowly untied, one by one.

Eventually they sealed the entrances to that part of the mine. The bodies of my friends are entombed there. I think about it whenever I drive by. Whenever I can, I try to take a different route in order to avoid it. It's been three years and it's still too raw.

Anne still works for the mine. So does her father. I hope that her husband hasn't gone back to work there, but sometimes there isn't a choice in a small town. We lose and we mourn and we rail against our fate, and then all we can do is pick up our gear, take a deep breath, and head back into the waiting darkness, where we try to avoid its teeth.

A LOVE MONSTROUSLY GRATEFUL
by C. Stuart Hardwick

"My name was Henrietta," I say, "and I died in 1951."
The pen stops mid-stroke. Dr. Steigler blinks through his narrow, wire-frame glasses and scowls.

"Beg pardon?"

"You know, HeLa cells?"

"Refresh my memory."

"Henrietta Lacks died of cervical cancer—the original did anyway—but her cells lived on in the lab. They were widely used in research till it turned out they were infecting other cell lines and turning them into cancer cells too. You went to medical school right? Didn't they teach you about it?"

I shouldn't be so rude. I only know because of Missy, but still, I've explained this so many times.

"We were talking about you," the doctor says. "You think what? You're the reincarnation of this Henrietta—"

"No! I'm not talking about ghosts and goblins; I'm talking about *cells!* I think ... Oh, I don't know what I think."

"But you *did* ask to be tested."

Yeah, I asked, and now I'm talking to a shrink. I slouch back into the oppressive comfort of overstuffed burgundy leather. "If I thought I had the clap, you'd test me."

"But you don't think that, do you?" The pen resumes its wandering. "When did this ... concern ... first arise?"

"At the clinic."

He lifts a page. "That's Wilson Fertility, in midtown?"

I nod. "Rod and I've been trying for three years. Dr. Vintner couldn't find anything, so she sent us to the clinic and they couldn't find anything either. But they took ... you know ... samples."

"And?"

"They said they were contaminated. They wanted to try again with a different lab."

"But?"

"I wanted to test my hypothesis."

"And that was?"

I shut my eyes and press my lips together. He knows all this already. It's in the report in front of him. He just wants to see me squirm—or see how crazy it sounds to say out loud that I think my samples infected all the others. That the whole shipment turned into HeLa cells because I'm made out of HeLa cells. That the immortal Henrietta Lacks has returned from the grave and taken over my body one cell at a time. But she has, I know it. I can smell it when I bite my nails or change my clothes after a run. Because I know what I smell like, what I've always smelled like, and I just don't smell like *me*.

Nah. That doesn't sound crazy at all.

I huff. "Look, why don't you just have me tested and prove me wrong? Then you can shoot me full of Thorazine and teach me to howl at the moon."

Dr. Steigler pulls his glasses off to polish away a smudge. "I don't think that would be wise."

"Why not?"

"Because confronting a delusion headlong can drive you deeper into it, to the point you're truly lost."

"I think I'm an ambulatory tumor. That's not lost?"

"You *did* come to see me."

He smiles. He scribbles on a prescription pad and shows me to the door.

Rod meets me at Beverly's, the quaint Italian restaurant where he proposed. He rises from a pool of candlelight to kiss me and pull out a chair. "How'd it go?"

I sit. "He thinks I'm crazy. Gave me pills to make it official."

I leaf through the wine list, though I can't have any with the pills. "I have to go back Thursday."

Rod reaches around the candle and takes my hand.

"Micah, I'm worried you're ..."

Obsessed? Insane? A huge fucking noose around his neck?

"... putting too much pressure on yourself." He squeezes my hand and shows his dimples. "We're fine," he says, "as long as we're together, it doesn't matter if we have any kids."

What a doll. I gaze right back and smile, pantomiming the emotions I know I should be feeling. A thousand times before, we've held hands like this and I've felt our love warm my soul. Now all I can think is, kind words and dimples won't get me pregnant, but maybe if I climb over the bar onto that Sicilian kid working the taps....

What the hell's wrong with me? Jesus. Where's a girl's soul when she needs it?

Rod lowers his menu. "I'm not taking the job."

The training director job he's been talking about for weeks.

"It would be too much travel, and ..." He sees my smile sour, says "Look, if it means that much, we can always adopt. I—"

I pull away as if scalded—sneer like he's suggested incest or bestiality. What possible use is someone *else's* baby—

Dear god, I'm not really that person, am I? He's right. I'm obsessed. But I *need* my own baby, to bury my face in its warm fleshy folds, draw in the scent of its life, and....

What the hell is *wrong* with me? The man I love is offering to sacrifice his career and what do I feel? Gratitude? Even self-pity? No, fear—not that I'm losing him but that ... that I'm a real life monster painted over in lipstick and satin.

He cups my cheek, thumbs away a tear, says it's okay, there are other jobs....

But it's not okay. It's not, and I cannot explain how or why. Trembling, I nod and force a smile, and excuse myself to the ladies room. I touch up the mascara on that thing staring back from the mirror and pull up Dr. Steigler's number. Maybe it's the medication; don't painkillers mute people's empathy?

I dial but hang up before the call goes through. What if it isn't the pills? What if I'm really not crazy? *What if I'm really just not me anymore?* I turn off my phone.

Determination shores up my spirits. I touch up my smile and return to Rod, playing the role he expects all through dinner, all the way home, and into the bedroom, where one last hope remains.

By Thursday afternoon, I'm sure the pharmacist has fouled something up. I can't say I've never once fantasized about another man, but this... Every man in the office is temptation and torment, and not just the good looking ones or the dangerous ones or the sweet ones who studiously keep their eyes off my cleavage. I don't want sex or love or flattery or escape. I want ... to insinuate myself in their arms, entwine my limbs with theirs, wrap their life in mine and ...

Jesus. For weeks I've felt the wall looming over me. Now it's been breached, the monster is out, and insanity has come pouring after.

Unable to focus on work, I've instead been on the internet researching—my medication, my obsession ... and HeLa cells. I already knew they were weird—immortal, aggressive, and able to assimilate other cell lines. They've also been evolving since the 50's—hundreds of new strains, some with twice the normal complement of chromosomes and bizarre new adaptations. They're like a whole new offshoot of humanity, one that's forsaken multicellular sophistication for the colonial plasticity of a siphonophore. Nothing I find says I definitely *can't* be a HeLa cell doppelganger, but if so my reproductive fixation makes no sense. HeLa cell DNA has mutated far from its human roots; I could sleep with every man from here to Calcutta and never get a HeLa cell baby.

Dr. Steigler has made tea—green with chamomile. He fills a china cup, then offers to pour one for me. I decline, accepting a water bottle, and he settles into his chair.

"Tell me about your sister, um ..." He flips pages. "Missy."

"I told you I don't know what happened to her."

"I don't mean that," he says. "I mean ... you loved her? You got along?" He sips his tea.

"I loved her. We got along. It was like having a limb chopped off when she disappeared, and it hurts every day she's gone. Is that what I'm supposed to say?"

"Is it true?"

My eyes moisten. I pinch my lips tight and give a tremorous nod. It feels like the air has grown viscous.

"You and your husband have been trying for a baby for ..." He looks down. "... three years isn't it? Since about the time of her disappearance?"

I stare down at my hands. Is there a connection? I don't think so. I hadn't wanted kids before that, but Rod and I weren't even married yet. I had my career. He had his. I'd never pictured myself as a mother, as holding a baby, snuggling her cheek, smelling the sweet scent of life in her flesh—Which is all what normal mothers think about all the time, right?

I'm biting my nails; I stop and dig them into fists. If my maternal instincts are a tad macabre, my grief over Missy is so normal its almost comforting. "All I have left is her fish."

"Pardon?"

"Missy and I used to talk every day. Now all I have are these stupid fish she got for her office, but they wouldn't let her keep in the lab. Sometimes I talk to them." I twist the cap of the water bottle, but not hard enough to open it. "They don't talk back or anything."

The pen scratches across the paper. Who uses fountain pens anymore? The ink smells of iron, like blood. "What sort of work did she do?"

"Cancer research. That's how I know about HeLa cells. They used them in her lab."

"So, is that where you got this idea?"

"That was years ago."

"But it *is* where you got the idea?"

"No, I ..."

"When did you last see Missy?"

I crack open the water and sip, waiting to restore the cap before answering.

"In Colorado. Cousin Addy had just inherited the ranch and invited us out for the holidays."

"Go on."

"Rod was going to pop the question Christmas Eve. They'd forecast snow, but it was clear when we got there and Missy wanted to see the overlook—this hill where we played growing up."

"So you went with her?"

I nod.

"Tell be about that."

"Addy had saddled the horses, and we galloped off like kids. Probably annoyed the horses, but it was nice to feel the old familiar turns in the trail. The sun was still in the mountains, just like when we used to go out to catch lightning bugs before dark. It was perfect, God's own canvas, and the two of us together, and the holidays, but ... something was wrong with Missy."

"Was there?" Dr. Steigler turns back his pages. "I didn't see that in the police report."

"No, no, she was just ... sunburned I guess. She stripped off her things to feel the snow on her skin...."

The doctor raises an eyebrow. "And that didn't seem odd?"

"No ... I mean I guess, only ..."

"Yes?"

"She had this ... glow."

I'd have said like she was pregnant, but now in my memory, she's clammy and flushed, and her face is peeling and shifting like ...

The pen is still, the bifocals fixed. "Micah?"

I jump. "What?" ... like the crust forming on molten lava? Why would I say that? "I ... I headed back to the house. She stayed behind to enjoy the snow, only ..."

"Only?"

"You know the rest."

"I'd like to hear it from you."

I squeeze the water bottle. "I don't remember. They found me Christmas day in a snowdrift. All I remember is the hospital and the tubes and wires, and Rod standing over me with Daddy, saying that Missy was missing."

Dr. Steigler offers a tissue. I take the box.

He prods, "You said she had a glow. And after she disappeared, you started trying to get pregnant. Do you think she was—"

"No. She…. She was sterile, a childhood infection. I don't know why I said that."

We talk on in circles. Dr. Steigler thinks I'm trying to replace Missy with a baby. I think if anything, I'm using grief as a distraction from an obsession that increasingly feels less maternal than … predatory. And there's something else, something wrong about Missy's eyes….

Of course I'm careful what I share with him; I don't want to wind up in a padded room. Not yet, anyway.

He walks me to the door and I turn, biting my lip. "That medicine you gave me, is it … an anti-compulsive?"

"Yes," he says, holding the door.

It isn't working. The only thing stopping me pushing his withered bones down on the settee and pitting his austere demeanor against the wiles of youth is the knowledge he can have me committed with a phone call.

What the hell is wrong with me?

He doesn't know. He can't possibly. And time is running out. I smile and slip away through the door.

Dr. Steigler's right about one thing: Missy's disappearance is somehow behind this. If my clues are Missy and HeLa cells, then that leads me back to her lab. But if there were any connection there, surely it would have come out three years ago when they pitched in during the man hunt.

It's still early, so I take a cab to Regency Park, to the shopping center near Missy's lab where most of her co-workers lunch. In the burrito bar, I find what I'm looking for: a lanky blond kid with the familiar orange badge who looks young enough to be talked out of secrets.

I undo a button and join him, and with no more encouragement than that and a smile, he tells me everything he knows. There was a big stink over HeLa cells at the lab a few years back. Cancer grows when cells forget they're supposed to be part of a larger organism. Pseudo-viruses were engineered to use inter-cellular signaling and lateral gene transfer tricks borrowed from HeLa cells to coax cancerous cells back into the well-behaved citizenry of the tissues they came from—under glass of course. It was all very promising, but just as the money started flowing, a treated culture reasserted itself and swept through the lab.

The kid doesn't know the details; he only heard about it later through the rumor mill, but years of research were ruined, and the old guard are still freaked out, and HeLa cells have been banished ever since. And all this was three years ago—right about the time Missy disappeared.

It means nothing, of course. What holds for petri dishes doesn't hold for human beings. Dr. Steigler would say I'm fishing for evidence I can twist to fit my delusion, and now that I've found some, it will only make it that much harder to claw my way back to reality.

Logically, I know this, but the logical part of me cowers in the shadows while the living, breathing, needing part seduces my informant back to his apartment and makes an adulterous man of him. I watch in horror—impotent as if from the back seat of a hijacked car—as an irresistible appetite manifests before me and steers what little hope I have left for a normal life straight off the nearest cliff.

I call in an excuse to the office—even monsters have bills to pay—and head back to our apartment. A shower and pajamas complete the illusion that I've just come home early feeling ill. In the narrowest sense, I have; the seediness of cleaning up to conceal my infidelity turns my stomach enough to restore some self-possession.

I stop and thumb the light on the aquarium, a ten gallon on a stand outside the kitchenette. Missy's fish have been sick, and I've let their medication lapse. The red-and-black striped loach is listing badly. I find the methylene blue and squeeze out a few drops. The inky cloud darkens the water, seemingly undiluted as it spreads. I hope it's in time. I hope the fish aren't just one more thing I've let slip away.

Tears flood my cheeks. How could I do it? Rod and I have our squabbles, but he's stuck with me through thick and thin: when I stayed in school for my masters, through my accident and Missy's disappearance, through my about face on having kids, and now this obsession. He's been my rock, my champion, and I've turned my back on him—casually, as if instead of the love of my life, he was only a character in a saccharine made-for-TV romance.

And that's just how it felt too, like I was watching, bound and helpless in a dark corner of my mind while a madwoman defiled my body and marriage. And now *she's* watching, not helpless but waiting, safely out of reach beyond the proverbial shoulder from which all devils whisper their enticements.

The room grows stifling and close. *She* did this ... and now *I* have to face the consequences. But *she* is somehow *me!*

"Dammit!" I shout and hit the tank, rocking the stand and sloshing water over the glass.

The hot aquarium light shatters. The fish dart about, then twist and roll and rise toward the surface as a cloud of glitter rains down around them like a thousand razor snowflakes.

"No!" I rise up on my toes, ready to leap to the rescue, but.... The fish are dead. All of them. Missy's fish.

"No, no, no!"

This has all gone far enough. I flee through the living room and out onto the balcony, screaming with rage and remorse. Madwoman, ha! Did she work my libido by strings? Rod's heart will be broken, but she'll watch uncaring through my eyes, and I'll be powerless and mute as his love transforms before me into hatred.

I won't allow it. Mad or possessed, I won't allow myself to be used for this cruelty. Better he be widowed than betrayed—better I roll over this railing and carry us both down together—

I'm jerked back palpably, as if by my hair, though I am alone on the balcony.

What the ...

I anchor myself around the railing.

My mind—my self—is splitting. The madwoman draws close, her thoughts permeable and ... protective.

What is it they say about split personality? That it's a defense mechanism? What if infidelity isn't all I can't live with? What if I saw something—did something—so horrible, I created this madwoman to avoid facing it?

Why do I remember Missy with sunburn when she hadn't had so much as a winter tan since freshman year in college? I dig through the cobwebs ... She'd seemed fine at Addy's, a bit flushed on the trail.... She'd wanted to show me ...

The madwoman pounces.

"No!" I recoil, but how do you parry when you're attacking yourself? The railing flexes and bucks. Bits of stucco tinkle off the planters below.

"Go away, damn you! Let me alone!"

"Who are you talking to?"

I look up. "Rod!" I run, blubbering, into his arms.

"Micah, what's wrong?"

I bury myself in his embrace, my mind's eyes still on Missy, glowing and alive but painted over by fear and revulsion. Then a struggle—violence—and the life draining out of her eyes.

"Oh my god! Oh my god!"

Rod cradles my head, hugs me to his shoulder. "Micah, tell me what's wrong."

"Oh Rod, I'm so sorry. I think I may have killed my sister!"

Ten hours later, our rental car pulls up Addy's empty, unpaved driveway. Inside, the phone is ringing, the mechanical jangle the perfect stylistic accompaniment to "the house that time forgot" as we used to call it, complete with asbestos siding, and peeling green paint, and the corrugated rusty steel roof. There's no answer, no machine, and no cell service out here either, so we have no idea when Addy might be back.

I fetch the key from the smokehouse and scramble some of her eggs while Rod restocks the pantry with provisions brought from town. Afterwards, I show him how to saddle the horses.

We double-checked my prescription, and a fresh dose calmed my nerves enough to let me sleep on the plane. I dreamed of Missy—indistinct nightmares of conflict and sorrow—but I did remember one thing: on the day she vanished, we didn't just stop at the overlook. We rode on to *the cave*, a fissure through the rocks we used to play in as children. Whatever she'd wanted to show me had been there.

We ride at a leisurely pace, Rod being an inexperienced horseman. It's warm and clear. The moon hangs over mountains trimmed in sunset gold. It would be quite the romantic setting under different circumstances, and I feel more like myself—just the one of me—than I have in weeks. When Rod tells me he loves me, my heart thaws and I smile and return the sentiment. I could almost believe it will all be alright, but I haven't told him about the madwoman or the infidelity or my homicidal vision. I'll have to eventually, and it'll poison everything, and so it poisons everything now.

Rod indulges me until we reach the overlook. Then, dusk is on us and he wonders aloud just what it is that we're looking for.

"I don't know, exactly," I say. "But the search teams could have passed the cave a dozen times and never seen it."

"You think Missy's still out here? I mean, they had the dogs."

"I don't know, Rod. I just have to be sure."

I sidle over to him and lean a bit in the saddle, taking his face in my hands. He's a good man. Good to me. Good for me. Once, I believed I deserved him.

I release him and take up the reins.

"This way."

Half a mile later, we descend through growing shadows into what in our childhood, we called *the canyon*. It's really just a wide arroyo with a table of sandstone intruding from the north where the foothills lead to the mountains.

As we cross the wash, the cliffs come into silhouette, and Rod stiffens in his saddle. "I think this is where we found you."

"Yeah?"

"I remember those pines up on the ridge, like a Morse code SOS."

We carry on toward the rocks. The "cave" is really just a fissure that opens into a flat "yard" where the sandstone has stymied the undergrowth. I guide my horse to it after a couple of false turns after all these years and in the closing dark. Rod still doesn't see it, not till I unpack the big light that Uncle Luther always called his "poaching light" and flash it across the rocks.

"You found me *here?*"

Rod looks up at the bluff. "No. Further that way, I think." He points north. "I don't remember these rocks at all."

He swings down to the ground. "I'll go inside and check it out."

"No," I say. "I know where all the tight spots are."

"Micah, just ..." He closes his eyes as if marshaling his patience. "I'll tell you whatever I find. I promise."

I've asked a lot of him and he's given it. Now he's trying to protect me, and that's really not much to ask.

I nod, working the reins to try and get my mount to settle. "Okay, but carry a big stick and watch out for ..."

Snakes ... but I haven't seen a snake since we left the house. Or a rabbit or a bird or a squirrel, now that I think of it. Nor any deer tracks or droppings on the trail....

"What?" Rod askes.

I can't say it's too quiet. He already thinks I'm nuts; why add paranoid to the mix?

The pines creak in the breeze.

"Just be careful."

He takes the light and eases into the fissure. His boots scuff out echoes as the orange glow fades into shadows. When it's almost lost in the distance, I hear him suck in a breath.

"Rod, what is it?"

Sounds of movement.

"There's—"

Suddenly, the fissure echoes with growling and Rod's comical attempts to calm some kind of animal.

"There boy, that's a ..."

I run to the opening. "Rod! Back away! Use the light—"

Snarls and hissing—cursing and sounds of struggle. Then silence.

"Rod?"

The light swings around and grows brighter. The only sounds are the horses squealing behind me and irregular shuffling from the cave. Rod stumbles out, ghostly, trembling, gasping as if bitten by a rattler.

"Rod!"

There's blood on his hand and shirt.

"What happened?"

"A fox, I think. Or a Pomeranian with mange." He gives a feeble smile.

"Or a fox with rabies. Let me see that." I take the light and shine it on his hand. Deep crimson-dotted welts march across his palm. His shirt is ripped and bloody. His arm is covered with ...

"Rod, what the hell is this?"

"It.... I tried to dodge it." He waves the hand over his belly. "When it bit me, I kinda panicked and hit it against the wall."

His legs go out from under him.

"Rod!"

His breathing is growing labored. "It ... it just came apart."

"What?"

"The animal. It just fell apart in my hands."

"Stay here."

I rise and turn for the cave.

He grabs my arm with his good hand. "No!"

I turn back toward him—back toward the wash and the arroyo.

Where are the horses?

Shit. I run out past the scrub into the open, clapping and whistling to call them back. But these horses don't know us. They won't return for strangers who ride them around in the dark.

"Come on," I say, "We need to get you back to the car—to a hospital."

But he's really struggling now, gasping for every breath, and his hand is the size of a grapefruit. Forget rabies. If he's allergic to dogs, he could go into shock and die right here.

I tear off my belt pack, the little leather pouch Uncle Luther called his "possibles bag," which Addy still keeps stocked and hanging from a peg by the back porch door. I kneel by the light and dig out the flint and the little pill box from under the snake bite kit. I push two antihistamine tablets past Rod's swollen lips and make sure he swallows them both.

My phone still has no signal and I can't carry Rod by myself, so I gather some kindling and light a fire to keep away the animals—if there are any. By the time I've got it going, Rod's breathing easier. He calls my name.

I switch off the light and kneel beside him. "Relax, sweetie, you're going to be okay."

He pulls at my sleeve. "What ... what was she wearing?"

"What?"

"Your sister. What was she wearing ... when she disappeared?"

"Um ... a flannel shirt, I think, red and black checked, why?"

His eyelids flutter. He lets me go. "I thought it was felt at first."

There's clothing in the cave.

I grab up the light and pull a burning branch from the fire to wield before me like a poker. I'm deep inside the fissure before Rod can protest or common sense can prevail.

First, I find just an indistinct scrap, black from rot and mildew. Then a bit of what might be shredded cotton. Then a flannel rag, soiled and darkened but still recognizably checkered—Missy's shirt.

My heart races. The passage widens. The light softens into the deeper shadows, and the smoke from the poker mixes with a cloying sweetness like cooked fat and baby's breath.

What's left of the fox is a puddle, a pale, meaty slurry poured over tendons and bone. It must have been defending the inner chamber. It probably had a den inside. Now it's disintegrating, liquefying before my eyes. I watch, fascinated and horrified, then step up and squeeze past, keeping well clear of the gore.

Inside the chamber is a floor of sand and gravel. Beneath the main body of the fissure, filtered rain has roughed the surface and ruined a forgotten comic book. Opposite, under the overhang, past twigs and grass stuffed behind a rockfall to make the fox's den, is a five foot stain in the sand.

It's less corpse than corruption, like the watermelon Uncle Luther once forgot in the old porch fridge till Addy and I found it desiccated and rotten down to a rind of mold. It's all that's left of my sister. The jeans and shirt are mostly intact, neatly laid out as they were worn, but brown and crusted with filth. Only a few lumps and bumps suggest any substance inside them, and the broad leather belt has toppled over, Missy's blue turquoise belt buckle half buried in rot. One boot is missing. The other is up by the head, or rather, where her blond hair fell like a pressed dandelion and matted into the muck.

There's nothing else here but sand, cemented by what must have been the same sort of goo as in the passage. A smaller stain, a few feet away and more irregular, frames a remnant of canine jawbone. Scavengers have been here.

"Oh, Missy."

I drop to my knees, my tears building into heaving sobs, and I feel the other, the madwoman, my alternate personality, grieving by my side as it were. Then the thought strikes me: she isn't grieving for *Missy*.

"You … *bitch!*" I jump up and turn—as if there were actually someone here to turn on. As if I weren't alone in a cave, shouting bitterly at myself. "*You* did this!"

My voice echoes harshly. The response, calm and clear in my mind, is subdued.

No.

"You did! You …" The madwoman—my madness—has spoken. Whatever she is, monster, demon, or personality disorder, she's real. "You … infected her!"

I didn't kill her.

"What?"

The wall finally collapses. Tendrils of madness flood out through my mind, rekindling unwelcome memories …

… She had something to show me, Missy said. The horses were licking snowflakes, but she'd tossed her jacket aside. Now she pulled up her shirt, beaming and running a hand over her belly the way newly pregnant women do.

"Missy?" I beamed back, though I saw no real sign of a pregnancy. "I thought you were—"

She turned her horse, grinning over her shoulder as she spurred it into a gallop.

I followed, though it was almost dark and the weather was turning and she was headed for the cave. In the shade of the canyon, the snow and ice were more evident. My horse slipped and balked. I dismounted to guide him along, and somehow reached the cave before Missy, who rode in behind me as I was tying up to a juniper.

I tied her lead as she swung down beside me.

"Missy! I thought you were sterile?"

Her smile was wide as ever. "I am."

I stepped forward, expecting a hug. Instead she hit me—hard across my stomach. I leaped back, gasping as stuffing spilled from my quilted jacket. *What the—*

Her smile was gone. "But you're not."

She clutched a small blade—a paring knife maybe. She lunged again, grabbing my jacket and stabbing.

I blocked and shoved her away.

"Missy! What the hell!"

I stumbled back against the horse, which shied towards the rocks. Missy was on me, pushing me down, straddling me, pinning my arms at my sides.

"Sorry sis. I need your uterus."

"Are you insane? Get off me!"

This close, her body was on fire. Her face was flushed and peeling like snake skin—or like the crust on a drying mud puddle. She reared back, releasing her grip. I grabbed at some driftwood and swung. "Stop!"

The wood hit her face as she lunged. She fell one way and I rolled to the other and scrambled back up to my feet. She grabbed my forearm. I grabbed her wrist below the knife.

"You're crazy!"

"Maybe," she said, "but I can do something *you* can't." She jerked free and slashed, then stood ready, daring me to run.

The jagged wood had sliced open her face. She pushed a bloody flap back into place, and it knitted together before me, roiling across her cheekbone and trapping loops of hair in the surface.

Bile surged into my throat.

She smiled—crooked—and touched her hand to the cheek. "I can't heal what I don't have though ..." She looked down at her belly, still running her fingers over the newly gnarled flesh. They found one of the loops and caught, and the skin tore apart like mozzarella. So maybe not "healed" exactly.

Her eyes widened in surprise.

"Missy—"

She glared—wet, rabid eyes—and jerked the flesh from her jawbone.

Choking on vomit, I stumbled back into my horse. He fled onto the cacti and jiggered back. I dove and he jumped me, bowling Missy out of his way.

I ran. Like a frightened child, I ran straight into the cave, bounding through the dark familiar space until I smashed my head into a wall. I'd grown a foot since I was last here, and this was a stupid escape plan. Missy was between me and the exit, and the passage narrowed. I literally risked getting stuck.

I turned, wedging my arms between the walls and throwing my legs up defensively.

"Missy, stop!"

She slashed at me and I kicked her away with my boot.

My heart raced. My arms shook with terror and exertion. One slip, and she had me; my only chance was to get through to her, to somehow get her to listen.

"Missy, think about what you're doing! You can't transplant organs with a pen knife—"

But her eyes were wild, inhuman, her mouth spilling bloody drool over ill-fitting lips. Her words were clumsy and slurred. "... don't need ... transplant, jus' need to follow ... the pattern—"

She raised the knife. I reared up and kicked with both feet.

I couldn't stay wedged between the walls. Each time I slipped, she attacked, and I had to keep scrabbling backwards. Soon I reached the big chamber. The walls spread away from me. There was no more cover and nowhere left to run.

With a curtain of dusk slashing down from above, colors washed out, leaving only the motion of Missy crouching, advancing, preparing to sink in the knife.

"Missy, please!"

She slashed. I grabbed her arm. She fought to jerk free, and I pushed, using my leg muscles to plow her against the wall.

"Stop it! Stop it! Stop it!"

Again and again I slammed her against the rock until she finally stopped struggling. She softened under my hands. Her eyes grew dull. Her jaw dropped flat against her chest.

I screamed and jumped back, unintentionally carrying her with me, then ducking away as she toppled and fell with a splat.

"No!"

I crawled through the sand, wanting to help her, but not daring touch the gelatinous mass into which she was dissolving. Tarry liquid pooled beneath her and spread toward my boot. I jumped back—but I was already drenched in sticky goo. I wailed and swatted to get the stuff off, gagging on the raw meat stench. Then I ran away through the darkness, into walls and crevasses, and out into the freezing night.

I stumbled on, sickened, shivering, unconscious of anything but escaping what I'd seen, what I'd smelled, what I'd lost, till the ground suddenly vanished beneath me ...

I'm back in the present, sobbing, shaking, the light at my feet, cutting the chamber into shadows.

"Oh Missy!" I drop to my knees by the filthy rind that is all that remains of my sister.

"I ... I didn't mean it."

The other is near. *It wasn't your fault,* she says. *No more than it was hers.*

"No," I spit. "It was *yours! You* infected her. *You* made her go crazy. *You*—"

Something happened in Missy's lab.

"What? What do you mean?"

She was exposed to a HeLa culture, a strain adept at hiding from the immune system and which absorbed and co-opted her technology. Using her own pseudo-virus, it copied its own genes next to hers, then took control of their expression.

"How ... how can you possibly know that?"

Because Missy knew it. She knew but she couldn't ... adapt. Irresistible desire in a sentient being is very close to insanity. You know that as well as anyone.

"Me? But it was you—"

There is no "me."

That brought me up short. "What do you.... You're some sort of parasite. A disease."

I felt a mocking smile. *Parasite. Disease. Evolution. Call it what you like. There is only...us. What remains of Missy is here inside what you have become.*

"And what is that?"

A chimera. A new life form. Beyond humanity. Beyond anything that has ever lived before. Genes that can think. Thoughts that can rewrite the genes they arise from.

"Then rewrite them! Make things back the way they were!"

The smile again, now more pitying than mocking.

Then Missy really would be gone. But we would never do that—any more than humanity would step aside and return the Earth to the fishes. You may think us parasites, but we're as inseparable now as human cells and mitochondria. Only we didn't understand till it was too late. Missy fought the change and went mad. Her cells were left without guidance. When you injured her, they disassociated.

"Disassociated? You're talking about my sister!"

You're sister. You. We are all just cells that cooperate in different ways. We didn't understand then, but now.... Our accident—your coma—gave us time to finish what had only begun within Missy: full integration of body and mind.

"You call this integration?"

Enough to preserve some of what she knew and was, yes. It could have been so much more. This ... is the product of your resistance.

"And I'll keep on resisting, too!"

"Then you'll die. Sooner or later, we'll lose control and our cells will disassociate just as hers did."

"I'll ... I'll find a cure."

Do you think we'd allow that? Would you? We will not return to our petri dishes, nor abandon the world to the trillion trillion individual appetites now devouring it. Cells that can copy knowledge from one brain to another can as easily wipe it away. You'll forget or go mad, and we we'll die together just like Missy, just like the animals in this forest.

"Then so be it. I want no part in this ... this ...whatever it is!"

Then Rod will die too.

"What?"

I look back through the passage toward the flickering firelight.

For three years, your resistance has spared him, but now he's infected by the same aimless spores that destroyed our sister.

Fresh tears fill my eyes. "But...." My voice catches. "There has to be some way to save him."

There is. And countless others whose exposure is now inevitable.

Exposure…. The animals. In the store in Canton, the news had been on behind the counter—something about vanishing wildlife. And the store clerk wouldn't shut up about the elk—how poor the hunting was and that the meat had all gone bad. It must have started slowly, the infected animals dissociating before they could get very far. But it's been three years, and if it's reached Canton, it's crossed rivers, roads, people…. It's beyond any hope for containment, and it could wipe out the entire biosphere.

"How? How can I save them?"

You already know.

Oh God.

I stumble back to the entrance, trembling, and sink down beside my husband.

"I'm sorry, Rod. I wish … I wish…."

This is all what I've feared more than death—but so much death…. My baby lust has left me—the human obsession with making another human replaced with the understanding that the cells that make me up *will not* be stopped. I can guide them into an evolutionary leap that preserves something of this world, or I can leave them mindless killing machines to reduce it all to soup. Life, of a sort, or death—for everyone, everywhere.

"How long will it take?" I ask the other.

We are still learning how to be.

I nod and pull Rod to his feet. He's feverish, clammy, quaking, but I guide him back into the shadows. Deep inside, I set him down and hold him, his stubble against my cheek, the masculine smell of him driving off the dank and the cloying stink of the cave.

I sob, holding onto him, letting go of myself, willing my cells to unmake me and share what they have learned. Delirium breaks like a wave, and I am gone.

A dog barks excitedly outside the cave. A deputy, silhouetted against the daylight, stares down, calling over his shoulder to report, "A white girl and a black … man I guess, both naked in the dirt."

I look at Rod. He's unrecognizable—dark and feminine—the spitting image of Henrietta Lacks from the medical encyclopedia. I know at once what's happened. We've never reconstituted a body before, and we've muddled the gene expression.

"Do I still look like me?" I ask.

"What? Of course—" His voice is different—a bit Henrietta, a bit Rod—and he touches his cheek, catching on. We exchange a little laugh.

His cells are still learning. I take his hand and kiss his knuckles. The sweet smell of us is intoxicating.

The deputy brushes my shoulder. Instead of asking about Missy, he hands me a plain brown blanket. "You two are gonna love the state hospital."

It turns out, Addy called him about the rental car. She didn't know we were here—doesn't know about Missy. We join her outside with the horses. She doesn't recognize Rod, but gives me a hug.

"Micah, what are you doing out here?"

"I'll explain at the house."

She lets me go and I suddenly rear back and sneeze, speckling her shirt with phlegm.

"I am *so* sorry," I say, but I turn and sneeze again.

"Gesundheit."

"Bless you."

The deputy wipes his face with a handkerchief.

"I really am terribly sorry," I lie, as he helps me up onto the saddle.

We climb onto the horses, Rod on one jittery paint, the deputy on another, and me behind Addy on the palomino. Addy leads us out, the horses nervous and skittering. We'll never make it to the house, of course, not as distinct organisms, but there will be no more dissociation, no more death, only life. We are learning, evolving.

I turn toward Rod. So great is our love, so certain and united, and soon to be enlarged by the billions. It's early still, and we are whole, and the sun in the mountains is glorious.

THE SWEETNESS OF BITTER
by Beth Cato

Margo clutched the nine iron and tilted an ear, listening for the crunch of footsteps from the next yard over. Dead leaves rustled. Even the wind seemed to hold its breath, waiting.

"Is someone there, Mommy?" Tara whispered.

"Maybe." With one arm, Margo pressed her daughter behind her, against the cinderblock wall. Their last quart of water sloshed within her backpack.

Her fingers twitched on the golf club, a souvenir from salvaging in Palm Springs. It had been weeks since they had seen anyone alive. No one else was stupid enough to cross the desert stretch of Interstate 10 between Los Angeles and Phoenix. It'd been a wasteland before the bombs dropped.

But now they were on the far western fringe of metropolitan Phoenix. People were bound to linger here, and Margo was ready for them. Copper stains already marbled the shaft of the nine iron.

"I know someone is back there." The brittle, feminine voice carried from the neighboring yard. "Looters aren't welcome here. Show yourself and I might not shoot."

Damn it. "Might?" Margo called, gripping the club. She had Doug's old pistol in her backpack. No bullets.

The silence was long, assessing. "How many of you are there?" the woman asked.

"Me and my daughter. Just passing through, that's all."

"Come out." That voice left no room for argument. "We have you surrounded."

"I can help, Mommy!" said Tara. The simulacrum of a five-year-old girl hefted up a cinderblock, hoisting it above her head.

"Put it down, Tara!" Margo hissed. Sometimes her daughter's inhuman strength came in handy, but right now Tara was too fragile. Again.

The real Tara had been dead for two years. Leukemia. The simulacrum had been created using the latest of advancements, complete with programmed memories, fuzzy logic, tantrums, and biological requisites. Tara—this Tara—was all she had left, and why they had walked and driven across three hundred miles of nothingness to find the headquarters of Simulated Innovations.

Margo spared a glance at the sky and sucked in a deep breath. Sim Inno should only be five miles down the road. They were so close.

"Stay here," she whispered to Tara, pressing a quick kiss to her forehead. Margo's sun-blistered lips burned.

She lifted her hands above her head, club still in her grip, and eased into the open. Her heart thudded throughout her thin frame.

A gaunt woman faced her, a shotgun in her steady grip. Beneath a layer of grime, her skin gleamed in a golden tan that once would have sparked poolside envy.

"We're just passing through," Margo repeated, her voice raspy. She was thirsty. She was always thirsty.

The gaze on her remained hard. "Where to?"

"Going to a place just up the road."

"After that?"

Margo's tongue moved as if to speak, tasting dirt and tangy iron instead of words. Surviving, breaking into Sim Inno, running recalibration on Tara—that meant everything.

"Don't hurt my mommy!" Tara wailed. She crouched at the base of the wall, tears leaking from her eyes. Margo bit back the urge to tell her to stop crying. Tara couldn't afford to waste fluid, but Margo hated using protocol commands to quell emotional responses. She loathed the reminders that a machine wore her daughter's smiling face.

The woman jerked her head. "Have the girl come out."

Margo's fingers squeezed the metal shaft of the club. "Tara, come out. Slowly."

Whimpering, Tara sidled out and embraced Margo. Her head rested against the hard jut of her mother's hip.

The other woman recoiled. "She's pale ... and fed."

Tara had been a skinny five-year-old by pre-war standards, which meant she now passed for plump.

As for her skin, pigmentation nanites had been among the first to fail months before, not long after the cataclysm, but Margo couldn't tell a stranger that. She knew how people reacted to sims, and didn't need derision or pity.

"She's sick. I'm trying to get her help. I ... give her all my food."

"Oh." The woman's expression softened a degree. "Other kids have been sick, too."

"Other kids?" Tara emitted a joyful squeal.

Tears heated Margo's eyes. She hadn't seen another living child in ages. "It's not that kind of sickness. I'm—I was—a nurse. Her case is ... special."

"A nurse?" The woman's eyes narrowed. "We could use a nurse."

"I have to save my daughter." The two women regarded each other. The silence stretched out.

"Of course." The woman relaxed a degree but the gun didn't lower. "Just so you know, these houses are already stripped clean. No food or water."

"We just want to move along." Soon they would need more sugar, but that could wait until after recalibration.

"Then move along." The woman granted her an abrupt nod and whistled sharply. "But keep us in mind. There could be a place for you here."

Margo heard footsteps behind her and turned. Two boys emerged from the shadows of a house, their adolescent bodies as long and lean as summertime tomcats. The youngest couldn't have been older than twelve, his face emaciated and eyes wide. Both carried makeshift spears. Following the woman, they ran across the street and vanished amongst the houses.

Margo stared after them. She had become familiar with the boney lines of her own body, but seeing children so close to starvation seemed unreal and wrong. And here was Tara, strangely *normal* in comparison. That felt wrong, too.

"Mommy, they were kids like me!" Tara bounced in place. *No, not like you*, she wanted to say, and forced away the awful thought. She never used to think things like that. Doug had, when they first discussed purchasing a sim, but that was ages ago. Another life.

Tara hopped backwards and directly into the cinderblock. She toppled with a cry. The sweet scent of manufactured blood slapped Margo's nostrils.

"Tara, stay still!" She swung the backpack off her shoulder and rummaged to find the patch kit.

"It hurts! There's blood everywhere!" The child whimpered, clutching her knee. The backside of her calf streamed pink fluid.

"Mommy will take care of it. Don't worry. Scoot here to the corner." Margo cast a wary glance over her shoulder as she sheltered Tara with her body, then went to work.

Tara's skin hadn't blistered from the sun or radiation, but the slightest physical duress caused it to tear like parchment. The blood didn't even clot as it should. Tara's every motion, each breath, relied on hundreds of thousands of nanites within her circulatory system. Before the attack, this would have been a simple fix. Two hours in the recalibration module in Riverside.

Nothing was simple now.

Margo retrieved the patch kit and tore off a strip of manufactured skin. She patted it over the wound. Replenishing Tara's blood-glucose came next. Simulacrum Innovations had promoted their glucose-based life system as the next great thing. No batteries to charge, no obvious computer hardware. It sold the fantasy that this was a real child. Her real daughter, complete with memories up to the point of her leukemia diagnosis.

Margo pulled the sugar and chemical additive kit from her backpack. The half-pound of sugar shifted in its bag and trickled like hourglass sand.

She scooped out two tablespoons of sugar and poured it into a pink-dyed vial. After dumping in the additive, she sealed it and agitated the mix. In a practiced move, she hooked the IV to the concealed port in Tara's arm. Pink fluid trickled down the line and vanished beneath a pale sheath of flesh.

"Sims are so easy to maintain! Just buy white sugar at the local grocery store and replenish their supply once a week, or more as needed. Blood-glucose is energy efficient, nontoxic, and economic!" So the ads once read. Doug once tried a sip and said it was eerily like Kool-Aid.

Without looking, Margo wiped her stained hands against her pants and packed everything away again.

"I did good! I did good!" Tara bounced in place. "I stayed nice and still, right?"

"Yes, you did wonderfully." She gave Tara's hand a squeeze.

Tara tilted back and blinked. "I did good! I did good! I did good! I did good ..."

Margo bit her lip and looked away. Vocalization loop and paralysis. More signs of imminent failure. Death. Shut down. "God, why is this happening again?" She rocked in place.

No answer came besides Tara's ecstatic chant.

After a few minutes, the dialogue loop abruptly stopped. Tara sat up, smiling. In her databanks, the failure hadn't even happened.

"Let's go," Margo said. New urgency pushed her stride.

Margo acutely sensed their vulnerability as they walked the borderland between the desert and civilization. Half-built houses stood frozen in time, their desert vistas now consisting of abandoned cars and debris. She balanced the golf club on the fulcrum of her fingertips. Merciless heat radiated from the pavement. Many people undoubtedly fled to the mountains in search of cooler temperatures and water, but even so, these streets were surprisingly clear of bodies and rot. Someone tended to this place.

"Mommy, that one boy looked like Sanger, didn't he? But it couldn't be him, huh?"

Margo's steps slowed. "Sanger? But ..." Sanger had been another boy in the leukemia ward. Tara wasn't supposed to remember that time.

She knew she was different—special—but no more than that. Innocence was meant to be bliss. "No, it couldn't be him," Margo answered slowly, gnawing on her lip.

"Sanger used to give me his jelly cups and I'd give him my apple slices. But we can't give them any food, huh?"

"No. I know you want to help, but we've talked about that before. We can't give anything away, Tara. I need to stay strong to take care of you."

The girl was quiet for a long minute. "Do you think if we gave them food, they'd be my friends?"

"Oh, Tara. You don't have to give them anything to be friends. Just be yourself."

"Really?" She brightened and glanced the way the others had gone.

"Of course." Margo rubbed Tara's shoulder for good measure.

Beyond a chain link fence, the headquarters of Simulated Innovations was a gray and glass obelisk. A broad gate blocked the road. The fence stood a solid eight feet high with barbed wire looped along the top. A quick rummage through the backpack and she had the wire cutters in hand. She hefted the tool for a long moment, immobile in grief and memory.

The fence at Riverside had killed Doug. When they cut their way inside, wire scraped across his ribs. It seemed like nothing at the time. The only thing that mattered then was what they'd found inside the facility: the recalibration chamber disassembled for maintenance. Still, they replenished Tara's supply of additive and synth skin, and immediately planned to move onward to Phoenix to Sim Inno's headquarters.

Then Doug's health failed. Fast.

Even as a nurse, Margo never thought to ask her husband when he last had a tetanus booster. She also thought that nothing could be worse than watching your child die. Then she had to watch Tara's devastation as her father died in indescribable agony.

Margo cut a wide doorway through the fence this time, tossing the metal aside. She knelt in front of Tara and gripped her by both shoulders. "Whatever happens, you know I love you, right?" Three hundred miles to get here, for this chance to keep Tara alive. Every step, every mile, was worth it.

"I love you, Mommy." Tara's arms squeezed her and kept on squeezing.

"Tara, let go," she gasped. The little girl's arms painfully compressed her ribs and then suddenly released. Margo staggered back with a gasp, rubbing her torso. Tara smiled, oblivious to her own strength. Yet another nanite failure.

"Let's do this," Margo said, voice hoarse.

Margo gingerly stepped through the gap in the fence. Tara inched through with equal care. Margo's eyes traced over Tara, making sure the wires hadn't scratched her, and she nodded to herself.

There was no way to tell if the building had any electricity or generators. *God, let there be electricity. Let this work.* Dark windows glistened through a coat of dirt. The glass didn't look broken or even cracked. Surely someone had tried to break in and search for vending machines or something.

"I did good! I did good! I did good ..."

The suddenness of the Tara's voice caused Margo to freeze. The girl kept walking, oblivious to her vocalization loop, and Margo hurried ahead. Another failure, that fast.

"Protocol 10, mute," she said, hating the words, not even sure if they would work. Tara's silent lips continued to form syllables as she skipped along. As they reached the darkened three-story building, Tara's lips stilled again. "Protocol 11, volume."

"This is like a special hospital, Mommy?" she asked right away. "You can fix me up?"

"Yeah." Margo squeezed her hand. It felt like a real hand, warm and balmy with sweat. It felt like Tara.

Taking a deep breath, Margo tested a door handle. Locked.

"If anyone's in there, they must be vewy, vewy qwiet." Tara said that Elmer Fudd style.

Margo's fingers traced a card scanner and pad beside the door. On a whim, she pressed her thumb against the pad. A red light blinked.

There was electricity. But how to get inside? Riverside's security had been totally different.

"My turn!" Tara sang as she pressed her whole right hand against the pad. The light flicked to green. With an audible click, the door unlocked.

Margo yanked Tara back, golf club up, breath catching.

"WELCOME, MODEL 311337 B." The words scrolled across a plate on the door.

They entered the building. Stagnant air reeked of mustiness. Emergency lights glowed in long, fluorescent strips above. As the door behind them shut, green dashed lines appeared on the floor and trailed down the hallway, flashing on the right side of the fork as if to guide them that way.

"Hello? Is anyone there?" Margo called. "I'm Margo Calloway. My daughter is Tara, she's from ... here. She needs recalibration." The echo of her voice trailed away.

"You think it's like a maze game?" Tara asked, pointing at the green lines of the floor.

"It seems to be leading us somewhere. Let's follow. Slowly."

They walked deeper into the center. The air cooled, the mustiness faded. Some sort of limited air-conditioning was running.

"Oh my God." Margo stared in awe at a water cooler. It sat in the hallway, half-full. Her hands trembled as she pulled a paper cup from the dispenser and filled it.

"Wow," said Tara.

"Yes. Wow."

The clean water tasted like heaven. Margo drank and drank again and forced herself to stop. Too much, and she'd be sick. She pulled bottles from her pack and filled them. This might be a place they could stay a while. If there was water, there was bound to be food around, too. Hydrated and hopeful, she herded Tara along the path of lights.

Tara practically bounced up a staircase. Margo smiled as she listened to Tara count steps beneath her breath.

"Forty steps all together!" Tara pointed ahead. "Look!"

The green lights stopped at a door. As they approached, it withdrew into the wall with a slight hiss. Margo held out an arm to keep Tara from dashing ahead, nine iron aloft.

Ahead of them stood a child. She looked ... perfect. Clean. Groomed. Like a photo shoot from a catalog. A lacey white cardigan clutched the slight swell of her breasts and contrasted with an A-line pink skirt. Straight blonde hair fell to her shoulders. A pink bow perched above one ear.

"Hi!" Her cheeks were rosy as she grinned. "Welcome to Simulated Innovations. I'm model 31145 A. Nice to meet you! Are you a technician with security clearance C?"

"No," Margo said slowly.

"Oh, dear." The girl's shoulders slumped. She clasped her hands together and rocked back and forth in her Mary Janes. "Why hasn't anyone come in to work? Don't they realize they have jobs to do?"

"I might be able to help." Margo eyed the girl.

"Not if you don't have clearance!"

Great, a sim with a programmed attitude. Margo laid a hand on Tara's shoulder. "Maybe you can help us, then. My daughter needs recalibration—"

"Oh. She's a model 311337 B and obsolete." The girl made a slight sniff. "But even if she was a 311338 or 311339, she couldn't recalibrate. There was a fatal flaw in the chamber design, and the company ordered maintenance to replace the recalled parts, but no one's come to finish the job."

"What?" That couldn't be right. The chambers couldn't be offline here as well. She lunged forward to peer into the room.

The laboratory stretched for seventy feet or so, the stark walls and beams immediately familiar. It looked like a larger version of the calibration laboratory in Riverside. The individual chambers were stripped of their walls, wires and gadgetry exposed. Caution tape, toolboxes, and barriers surrounded the site. Everything left waiting for workers who were either long dead or long gone.

A low, agonized wail escaped Margo's throat.

In that instant she felt the shadowy compression of the hospital walls, the harshness of antiseptic, the soft and steady beeps of the machinery that kept Tara alive. Her Tara, the Tara she birthed in eighteen hours of labor, the little girl obsessed with butterflies and Harley Davidson. At age six, after months of chemo, she was so small, so frail.

"I'm scared, Mommy," her flesh-and-blood Tara had whispered. "I don't want to die."

"We won't let you die," Margo whispered back. "You're going to be our little girl forever." Even then, technicians from Sim Inno crowded the room and bustled behind her. Ready for Tara to die, ready to revive her.

"Mommy? What's this mean? Can't I get all better?" said Tara. She stood in the hallway of Sim Inno. Dirt smudged her face, that miniature replica of Doug's nose.

A small hand as strong as iron clenched Margo's wrist. "You don't have security clearance to go in there," said 31145 A. Her voice sounded cheery, her skin warm and human, but her grip had all the flexibility of rebar. Margo had the strong hunch that if she made any move forward, her wrist would snap like a twig.

She stepped back, her mind reeling. The sim relinquished her hold, but the pain of that inhuman grip lingered. "Don't say that, Tara. We'll find a way." Somehow. They had come this far. Margo looked at 31145. "She's suffering cascading nanite failure. She needs recalibration or ..."

"That's not a surprise since she's a model 311337 B. What's she experiencing now? Peripheral neuropathy? Temporary paralysis? Memory errors? Soon her personality nanites will succumb and then --"

"Tara's not going to forget who she is!"

"Yelling at me isn't going to help. I didn't create such an inefficient design. Do you have any idea how wasteful their glucose-caloric burn was?"

Margo's fingers clenched the club even harder at the use of the past tense. "There has to be something we can do. Instruction manuals or something." Never mind that Margo had trouble loading Windows on her old computer. For Tara, she'd try.

"There is one option." The sim's face brightened as she held aloft one finger. "Hey, sisters?"

A door across the hall opened with a slight pop. Another 31145 stood there, smiling. Margo whiplashed her head looking between the rooms. This new sim looked identical but for a blue bow on the head, and behind her—God, it was a whole line of them. Margo shivered at the freakiness of the clones. Even Tara made an odd sound in her throat and backed up, her fingers clutching at Margo's thigh.

"That's a lot of twins, Mommy."

"Yeah." A sudden cough shuddered through Margo. Already, she craved another drink.

"These are my sisters, B through M." 31145 A's tone was cheery as she stepped into the hall. "We're all happy to see you."

"Hi!" "How are you doing?" "What's up?" "Konichiwa!" The greetings rang out at once, followed by girlish giggles.

31145 A sashayed around them. "See, we can't recalibrate either, and we're having to be super careful with all our supplies." She pointed at Tara. "We need your help! Your glucose can be recycled, and recycling is so, so important."

"I like helping! What's my glucose?" Tara asked, her brow furrowed.

"Recycled?" Those words seized Margo's mind. "That doesn't ... no, you don't understand—"

"As model 31145s, our glucose management is both efficient and our functions are an integral part of this facility. We really, really, appreciate your help!" The girl reached for Tara, still smiling.

Margo shoved Tara behind her and brandished the golf club. "You're not touching my daughter."

31145 A did a very pre-teen eye roll. "Oh, come on. She's already in catastrophic failure."

"Yeah, I mean, nothing should go to waste," said the unit with the blue bow. She and the others poured into the hall, the sims nodding and murmuring in agreement.

Margo almost tripped as Tara stopped moving. "She will never be a waste!"

One of the sims lunged forward. Margo hesitated only for a split second, seeing that perfect catalog image of a child's face, then swung the nine iron with all her strength. The club smashed against the 31145's cheek. She stumbled back with a shriek, setting off an echoing cry among the others.

"Tara, run for the exit!" Warm glucose dribbled down the shaft and pooled at the base of her thumb.

"I did good! I did good! I did good!" Tara's words slurred. Margo spared a glance behind her. One of Tara's eyes drooped in the socket, the surrounding skin sagging. Hemispheric paralysis.

Oh, God. Not this, not now. "Tara, go to the exit. Hurry!"

"I did good! I did good!" Repeating the phrase, Tara turned and walked down the short hallway, her left foot dragging.

Margo pointed the golf club at 31145 A. "Do you know the addresses of any local scientists, people who work here? People who can get the chambers working?"

People who were evacuated, or dead. But she had to ask, she had to do something. She hadn't come this far to give up.

"I did good! I did good!" The faint voice continued behind her.

"You don't have clearance for that information!" said A, her voice shrill. The 31145s stepped forward en masse, forcing Margo back. Something clattered behind her. Metal on metal, squealing.

The stairs. Tara's paralysis.

Sims forgotten, Margo burst down the hallway and stopped at the railing. Three flights down, Tara lay in a twisted heap. A small puddle of pink expanded around her.

Her head—her spine—nothing looked as it should.

Margo had no memory of walking down the stairs. She was suddenly at the bottom and dropping her heavy backpack to the floor. Her hands hovered over the twisted wreckage of her daughter.

"I did good! I did good!" The tumble had degloved half her metal skull; a vellum-thin flag of skin and scalp draped over her shoulder. *Tara looked like a robot. She was a robot.* Burst veins oozed pink. Below—her arms and legs were scraped, but her spine—God, her spine. Her head twisted the wrong way around.

Stabilize her. Stop the bleeding. Margo's brain fumbled into crisis mode. She ripped open a pack of synthetic skin and pressed it over Tara's face, covering an empty eye socket. Where was the eye? That didn't matter now. She patched here, there, staunching the flow of circulatory-glucose.

Margo exhaled in slight relief, and then grey, gummy fluid dribbled onto her hand. She frowned and wondered what it was.

She looked down. The immediate glucose loss had been averted, but now grey sludge oozed from the break in Tara's neck.

Nanites. The central nervous system had ruptured.

"I did good! I did good!" The slurred words had softened.

"What happened?" 31145s crowded the railing above. "Oh! What a waste! She's bound to—"

Margo huddled over Tara with a feral growl and scooped her into her arms. A misaligned rib poked Margo's chest. Warm fluid coursed down her arm, soaked her shirt, her skin, and deeper. Footsteps pattered down the stairs. Margo ran.

The walls of the facility blurred and then she was outside, dashing across the parking lot, toward the hole she had cut in the fence. The sun pierced her eyes like a laser as she glanced back.

The 31145s had stopped at the front door, their programming apparently preventing them from leaving the building.

Margo kept running anyway. "I'm sorry, I'm sorry," she whispered to Tara. "I did good. I did good."

Across the parking lot, through the fence. Down the street where not even dust had the energy to whirl.

Freed of the backpack, everything seemed lighter. The sugar, the supplies, they didn't matter.

What mattered, now?

Tara was dead. She had been dead for over two years. Margo had always known, on some level. What she held in her arms ... that was the last part of Tara. A part she loved dearly, more than anything else left on this shattered earth. But it wasn't truly her daughter.

That didn't make this any easier.

Margo collapsed in the shade of a nearby building, unable to breathe. Black dots swarmed her vision.

"Mommy?" The word was scarcely audible.

Tara still knew her, despite the nanite loss. Margo hunched over, sobbing. Tara blinked her singular eye.

"It's okay, I'm here," Margo said. "I'm not leaving you."

"I fell. I couldn't stop it."

"I know, sweetie, I know. It's not your fault."

"This doesn't hurt, not like last time. I don't really feel anything right now. It's not bad, really."

Margo stilled. "What?"

"The last time I died. It hurt a lot then. It hurt all over."

"You're not supposed to remember that." Sim Inno, they said those things were filtered out. Tara was supposed to remember to age five, roughly, except for associative data.

This was associative. Death remembered death.

"You were there, and Daddy." Tara's smile wobbled on her lips. "It'll be nice to see Daddy again."

Margo couldn't speak, couldn't think.

"I love you, Tara," she finally whispered. "I will always love you."

Tara's smile was distorted, but it was still her smile. "I did good. I did good." Tara breathed the words.

"Yes, you did. Always."

Tara's voice trailed to a whisper, looping until it stopped completely. Margo pressed her face against Tara's cheek, absorbing the realism of her skin. Warmth flowed against Margo's lips and invaded her mouth. Sweet, fruity. *Delicious.* She knew it by the scent: circulatory-glucose.

Almost gagging, she recoiled, staring down at Tara. Despite her mangled face, Tara looked at peace. Margo's hands shook. Her parched mouth salivated in response to the liquefied sugar.

Slowly, her tongue eased out to lick more from her lips, and then her fingertips, but her thirstiness didn't subside.

The backpack was gone. She had no food. No water. Margo stared down the street the way they came. The children. The ones Tara wanted to be friends with. They were sick, starving. Margo was a nurse. Circulatory-glucose was food, calories. And she knew where they could get more, and water. Tara was the key. Her palm-print could get them back into Sim Inno. All they had to do then was find a way to defeat a small army of freakishly-strong pre-teen clones.

"We can help your friends, just like you wanted," Margo whispered, rocking Tara.

She couldn't help herself. She dipped her hand into the sticky glucose on Tara's arm, and closing her eyes, brought her fingers to her lips.

The sweetness brightened the darkness, and she drank it up.

SIX LIL' REAPERS

A *Grim Days* Mystery

by J. Kent Holloway

The man calling himself Silas Mot leaned back in his chair, his feet propped on the dining room table, and sipped at his piña colada through a bamboo straw. He grinned as the frosty drink glided down his tongue and past his throat and watched the six other occupants of the dining room begin to stir from unconsciousness.

Silas wasn't sure who most of these unconscious people were, or how long they'd been drugged. Fortunately, after watching and waiting for the past hour and a half, they were finally starting to groan to life once more, which meant he'd soon be getting the answers he sought.

As he waited, he took in his surroundings for the hundredth time. They were in an old Victorian-era mansion. From the layers of dust covering the table, chairs, and china cabinet, and the cobwebs that hung like wilted Spanish moss from the crown molding near the high ceiling, it looked as though no one had occupied the place for many years. Of course, he'd done some reconnaissance while the other guests were out cold. The mansion had three floors—he'd been disappointed to discover it had no wine cellar, but then, they were in Florida after all. Cellars and basements didn't really work well in the Sunshine State where most of the soil was comprised of sand. He'd counted nineteen different rooms altogether. Eight bedrooms, a library, a drawing room, a kitchen on both the first and third floors, three bathrooms, and a couple of rooms devoid of anything that would identify their purpose.

Outside, he could hear the sound of wind chimes dancing in the ocean breeze. Chimes that had meticulously been set up along all four points of the compass. The sound of them had always soothed him, and as he sipped at his refreshing drink, he took great pleasure in their tinkling presence.

Returning his attention back to his current situation, Silas noticed the peculiar absence of a host to this macabre little party. The moment he'd materialized into the house, he'd simply found the six unconscious people, and that was it. None of them were marked for death any time soon, and yet—given that Silas Mot was, in fact, the Grim Reaper himself in human form—he knew that at least one of them would be dead before this time tomorrow. And he couldn't explain why. Or how for that matter.

But that's precisely what had brought him into the world of mortals, and more specifically to the small little beach community of Summer Haven. Someone had stolen a very valuable artifact known as the Hand of Cain that gives the possessor the power to extend or take life whether it was a particular person's appointed Time or not. Silas had been here for a little over six months now, helping the local police chief solve a number of unexplained murders, in hopes of uncovering the identity of the person who'd taken the strange artifact.

Which was why he found himself here, in this quaint, though unkempt manor house built just after the American Civil War and in disrepair probably since the Great Depression.

"Ugh," someone mumbled from underneath the dining room table. "Wh—what happened?" It was a man's voice. A distinct English accent if Silas wasn't mistaken. "Where am ... am I?"

Setting his drink down, Silas swung his feet to the floor, and dipped his head under the table to see who'd spoken. The man was middle-aged with graying hair around the temples and showing signs of male-pattern baldness near the top of his head. He was clean shaven with pasty white skin, but with a strong jaw and a chiseled, handsome face. He wore a tweed jacket, white shirt, and knit tie along with a pair of faded jeans and loafers.

Ah, a professor of some kind, Silas thought while returning to his casual lean in his chair and sucking down the remains of his drink until air hissed from the straw.

One by one, they all came to, asking almost identically confused questions. A pretty blonde wearing a scandalous dress that accentuated her stunning figure. A rotund, poorly dressed man with rumpled brown hair. An elderly, yet still striking, woman—in so many ways, despite her advanced years, she was the spitting image of the young blonde—with a rigid scowl and almost skeletal frame. Of the entire group, she was the only one he knew by sight. After all, very few people who live in Summer Haven wouldn't know Ms. Gertrude Nebbles-Fielding, the spinster sister of Ilene Nebbles, who practically owned the entire town.

Then there was the dashing younger man with five o'clock shadow, a silk button down shirt and black jeans that could hardly contained the muscles bulging out from his arms, chest, and thighs.

Gradually, each of the guests stood, shaking their heads in confusion, and wandered off into the house to catch their bearings. Predictably, they all tried the doors and windows, and found them locked, bolted, and barred. Now panicked, they returned to the dining room to find their places—mysteriously marked with nameplates—around the table.

Finally, the last remaining guest awoke as well. An emaciated, elderly black male dressed almost identically to the professor. His hair was thin and gray, a thick pair of glasses hung haphazardly from a chain around his neck.

It appeared that the party was about to start, and Silas Mot waited anxiously for the host to reveal the reason he'd abducted each of them and dropped their unconscious bodies in this derelict mansion, and get on with the show.

He sat back in his chair with a sigh, looking at each of his new acquaintances. In turn, each of them stared back at him. Someone cleared their throat, but no one spoke. They all sat idly for several uncomfortable moments, and Silas had to constrain himself from glancing at his watch every few seconds.

Of all the guests, he was more than likely the most peculiar-looking. As the spirit of Death, Silas had no physical body of his own, and was required to draw ectoplasm from the nether realms to sculpt whatever body he chose to use at any given time. It was a painstaking process that took hours, if not days to accomplish, and he never quite managed to give himself the same appearance twice. Today, he felt his ears were just a little too big. His pencil mustache a tad too thin. Becca Cole, the police chief he'd come to call friend over the past year, had laughed when she'd seen him yesterday, and told him he'd become a dead ringer for Clark Gable. That is, if the famous actor had ever deigned to wear brightly-colored Tiki shirts, Bermuda shorts, and flip flops as Silas had begun to adopt shortly after his arrival to the mortal coil. Wearing black suits, no matter how well-tailored they were, had become so tedious to him. He preferred to adorn himself these days with as bright and colorful fabric as he possibly could.

"So …" It had been the middle-aged professor, whose nameplate identified him as Dr. Stefan Yeardley, who had uttered the eloquent word.

"So!" Silas said, clapping his hands anxiously together. "Let's get started, shall we?"

The six of them continued to look expectantly at him, but no one uttered a word. Annoyed, Silas gestured for someone to begin, but they only looked back at him with more confusion spread across their faces.

"Seriously, I haven't got all day," Silas said. "Whoever's responsible for this shindig … go on. Speak up. Why are you all here?"

Of course, Silas hadn't been drugged and dragged to the old mansion. As far as he knew, he couldn't be drugged. Or poisoned. His body could be damaged beyond repair, of course. It could be destroyed. But no blood flowed in the veins of his ectoplasmic body to carry any type of toxin that would render him unconscious. The person behind whatever was going on, of course, would know he was an uninvited guest, and he'd hoped to lure whoever it was out by his nonchalant party crashing to the big event. As he looked at the six guests around the table, however, he quickly realized that if any of these people were the culprit or the artifact-wielding thief, they were certainly excellent actors.

"Um, why don't you tell us?" The pretty blonde, whose name plate read 'Taylor Blackmoor,' asked, raising a perfectly groomed eyelash.

"I'd like to know too! What's goin' on?" This was from the fat, poorly dressed man with unkempt greasy hair and thick Coke bottle glasses. The faded t-shirt he was wearing showed a cartoon figure of a mage playing an electric guitar and came with the legend "Wizards of Swing" across his chest. His name, according to the plate, was Mortimer Dees. "Why have you brought us here?"

"Sorry?" Silas asked. Now it was his turn to feel confused.

"We want to know why you kidnapped us," Taylor explained. "Aren't you …" She glanced around at the others as if looking for support. "Aren't you the one who brought us here?"

Silas blinked, then shook his head and laughed. "Oh, heavens no!" He laughed again, only this time a bit more boisterous than before. "I'm here to see what's going to happen. That's all. I've got no more idea of what's going on here than you, my dear."

"What do you mean, you're here to see what's going to happen?" Professor Yeardley asked.

It was the question Silas had been particularly dreading. Normally, he had no qualms about telling these people the truth. He told people all the time that he was Death in no uncertain terms. There was no rules against telling people, after all. No one ever believed him anyway. But in this case, the thief of the Hand of Cain would be wary of the Grim Reaper's presence, and since he might be among the guests, it would be unfortunate for Silas to tip his hand too soon.

The well-dressed, good looking young man—his nameplate read "Caleb Sparrow"—suddenly stood up from the table. "Hold on a sec." He immediately strode out of the room, and returned a few minutes later rolling a cart with a combination television/VCR. "I remembered seeing this in the foyer earlier," he said, holding up a folded card. "The note taped to it says 'Play me.'"

Sparrow rolled the cart near a wall outlet and plugged the TV in.

"A VCR? What is this? Nineteen-eighty-eight or something?" asked Mortimer Dees. Silas could tell by his demeanor and appearance that the man was what the kids were calling a 'nerd' these days. He imagined Mortimer still living at home with his parents, and playing video games all through the night with screen names like "Demonhawk" or "Elfblaster69." There was something slimy about the guy. Especially in the way he continued to leer lasciviously at young Taylor Blackmoor.

Silas shushed him, moving over to the television and pushing in the video tape. A moment later, the screen snapped from dark gray to brilliant white. In the center of a screen was a silhouette of a man. Or a woman. The form shifted shapes as fluidly as plasma separating from hemoglobin, making it impossible to know the gender for certain.

"Greetings everyone," the shadow figure on the TV said to the room. The voice had been electronically altered, fluctuating between a male and female voice every few words, and occasionally blending together for a macabre harmony that would have sent chills down Silas' spine if he actually had one. "I will cut to the chase, as I'm sure each of you are anxious to discover the reason for this impromptu and involuntary gathering this evening."

The group simultaneously nodded their heads in response. Silas grinned even wider than before, and pushed back in his chair with his right foot balancing him perilously against the table. With all eyes on the television screen, he glanced at his empty glass, and a few moments later, it was refilled with a strawberry banana daiquiri. It was, of course, only ectoplasm, but after months of meticulous practice, he'd eventually learned to conjure it to taste almost as good as the real thing.

He then set to work watching each of the guests carefully as their host continued.

"Each of you are rotten to the core," the shadow on the screen continued. "Vile, vindictive picaroons ..."

Picaroons. That's a most archaic word to use in this day and age, Silas thought.

"... Every single one of you deserves to die for the things you've done to, not only me, but everyone you come in contact with ..."

There was an uproar at this. The group, as one, were now sitting erect in their chairs. Their faces reddened, whether with outrage, embarrassment, or fear, Silas couldn't be sure. Arms gestured at the screen. However, Mortimer Dees kept his hands curiously under the table, and Silas couldn't help wonder why.

The villain went on to recount each of the guest's particular sins. Dr. Yeardley, it seemed, was a pompous, womanizing hack with a history of inappropriate relations with his academic assistants. Taylor Blackmoor, Yeardley's current assistant, was a stuck up snob and, apparently, hardly better than the average hooker, who used her body to get what she wanted and who discounted anyone else who couldn't improve her station in life.

Gertrude Nebble was accused of being a vicious gossip, who used her great wealth to squash the dreams of anyone she deems unworthy.

Silas could think of a number of other accusations to hurl at both her and her sister, but he resisted the urge and continued to his vigil on the group.

Caleb Sparrow, the great grandson of a dead author who was finally beginning to make waves among the literary community, was accused of being an opportunist and callously gaining wealth and fame on the coattails of his long dead ancestor. Curiously, his grandfather's previously unknown work had been discovered by Summer Haven's chief librarian, Jackson Liefeld, who happened to be the elderly black male in the group, and the current topic of research for Yeardley. And finally, the shadow went on to accuse the sneering geek Mortimer Dees as simply being a "worthless human being that no longer deserved to live on God's green earth."

"So with that in mind, I have poisoned each one of you." There was a pause from the shadow. "All of you, that is, except our uninvited guest."

The murmurs of outrage twisted into gasps of shock and dismay. Silas, too, sat slack-jawed at the revelation and sat up straight in his chair. It wasn't the announcement that they had all been poisoned, however, that caught his attention. It was the other thing their host had just said. As far as he knew, he was the only uninvited guest there. But the culprit could not have possibly known he would be there when he'd recorded this message, could he? After all, before this morning, he hadn't even known he'd be there himself. It had been a mere whim. A gut-feeling that the Hand of Cain was at work somewhere near Summer Haven. It had taken a few hours to pinpoint the location where the artifact would be making its next move, and he'd only arrived a couple of hours before any of the unconscious guests had awakened. So how could this pre-recorded message have possibly anticipated his presence here?

The videotaped figure paused, as if allowing his guests a moment to complain. To deny his accusations. To plead against the absurdity that they had been murdered already, but their bodies just hadn't known it yet. After a few moments of silence, he continued.

"Oh, you cretins." Another unusual word for modern vernacular. "There's no use protesting. There's no use begging for my mercy. You all should have thought about that when you had the chance. But fear not. One of you doesn't have to die. One of you can walk out the front door when this is all over." This shut the group up fast. "And what's more ... you will walk away with a gift beyond your wildest imaginations. The person who survives the night within the hallowed walls of Southwood Manor will be given the gift of immortality."

They all erupted into outrage over that last statement, believing their captor to be either a charlatan or mad man. Silas, however, knew better.

He now understood the game they were all playing, and it was nothing short of blasphemous. Kill them all, their host was saying, collect their souls for the Hand, and you will never have to fear the Grim Reaper's sting ever again.

It wasn't hyperbole. It wasn't the ravings of a lunatic or a huckster. The Hand of Cain truly had the power to do just that, although in the numerous millennia of the artifact's existence, Silas had never quite known how it worked. *It is allotted for each man to die once*, to paraphrase the Apostle Paul, *then the judgment*. So, how can a piece of manmade artwork—no matter how arcane it might be—actually have the power over death? It made no sense to him.

Of course, this time, he had a plan. A means he hoped would defeat the Hand's machinations, but only time would tell on that.

The TV silhouette, oblivious to Silas' doubts, continued to ramble on with the rules of the 'game,' as he called it. It was rather simple. The doors and windows were all currently locked. The moment the play button had been pressed on the VCR, a signal was sent out to a rigged power outlet, making those same locked doors and windows now electrified with twenty-thousand volts. Somewhere within the mansion, amid a series of traps, was a vial containing the antidote for the poison each of the guests had been given. The vial contained just enough for one person. Share it with someone else, and it wouldn't be enough for either.

The poison itself would likely kill everyone in the house by eight in the morning. Therefore, at eight-oh-five, the electricity would be turned off, and the locks would release. The person still alive could simply walk away.

"Or, if you have the courage to stay," the shadow on the screen continued. "If you wait just a little while longer, my benefactor has agreed to meet with you personally, and offer you the greatest prize of them all. Immortality. The ability to shun Death for as long as you choose." There was a pause, then, "Isn't that right, Mr. Mot?"

Silas stood to his feet at the mention of his name. "What is going on here?" He slammed his fist against the antique table. "How could a pre-recorded message know I'd be here?"

Each of the guests turned to look at him.

"I'm assuming you're this Mot fellow he's referring to?" The librarian, Jackson Liefeld, asked. "Seems I recall the Sumerian god of death being known as Mot or some such."

"Seems to me that for someone who has just been informed he's been poisoned, you seem awfully calm," Silas retorted, before striding over to the TV cart to inspect the video cassette recorder. When he was within a foot of it, the screen went blank, and smoke began to curl from the back of the device.

"What are we going to do?" Taylor Blackmoor hugged her arms around her ample chest, shaking visibly. "I can't die. Not here. Not now."

"A pox on all of you!" Mortimer Dees barked, darting toward the dining room door. "I'm not going to be picked last this time!"

The other four looked at each other for a brief moment, then broke into a run simultaneously to search for the saving antidote. Everyone, that is, except for Silas Mot and the distinguished Mr. Liefeld.

Silas crouched down to examine the TV/VCR combo. He knew very little about electronic devices, but he hoped to glean something from the contraption to help him understand more of the mind behind this particular gambit. The shadow man had mentioned a 'benefactor.' What's more, this benefactor seemed to be the one in control of the Hand. That meant that whoever the mastermind behind this petty parlor game of murder and survival had firsthand knowledge of the person Silas had been hunting for more than a year now.

After a moment, Jackson Liefeld cleared his throat, attracting Silas' attention.

"Mr. Liefeld, I really am rather surprised you're not off gallivanting with the others to find the cure for your predicament," he said, haphazardly pressing buttons on the VCR with no results. The thing appeared to be fried, which in itself was suggestive considering the timing.

"Why would I bother?" Liefeld replied. "I already know who's behind all this, and know I don't have a chance of survival even if I wanted to."

"Huh? You know who's behind all this?" He managed to dislodge a wire from the back of the device, followed by a black plastic box that didn't appear to be part of the original unit.

The librarian laughed. "Let's not play games, Mr. *Mot*." He said the last name with an air of irony. "I know precisely who you are. Ever since I first read about you in the paper for helping solve the murder of that poor girl on the beach a few months back, I've been keeping tabs on you."

Silas' eyebrow rose. "And you think I'm the one behind this little game, I take it?"

"Oh heavens, yes," the librarian said. "Ancient mythology of the Sumerian and Babylonian people is one of my special areas of study. Their beliefs on death, in particular. Your name stood out simply because of its close approximation to their death god, Mot. Stands to reason that someone like a Grim Reaper would be especially invested in a ploy like this."

With an exasperated sigh, Silas gave up his examination of the VCR, stood to his full six-foot height, and gave his full attention to Jackson Liefeld. "I can assure you, I'm no relation." He grinned, knowing full well he was lying through his perfectly white teeth. "And even if I was, why would a Sumerian god of death bother with poisoning the lot of you? He could simply snap his fingers, and it would be done."

Liefeld blinked at this. He'd obviously not considered that. "So, you're *not* behind this …"

Before he could finish his question, a rather feminine scream erupted from the back of the house.

Intrigued, Silas bolted from the dining room in the direction of the scream. As he moved into the foyer, he turned a sharp right, down a narrow hallway, and through a swinging door that led into the downstairs kitchen. As he did so, Taylor Blackmoor backed slowly into him. She was shaking, covering her mouth with both hands. Her eyes wide. A mist of smoke billowed up from her hair, which seemed now to stand on end.

Placing a gentle hand on her shoulder, he nudged her aside. Besides a wood-burning stove, a single grime-covered sink, and an old fashioned wooden ice box, there were no other furnishings in the room. A door to the outside was across the room, and laying on the black and white checkered floor, just under the doorknob, was a dead man's prone body. Though Silas couldn't see his face, from the rippling muscles, silk shirt, and expensive black jeans, that were now smoldering against his crispy blackened skin, he knew the dead man had been Caleb Sparrow.

Silas glanced around the room. The young man's shade—his soul, if you will—was nowhere to be seen. None of Silas' minions, tasked with retrieving the souls of the dead, were lying in wait to carry him on to his reward. Just a corpse, some urine, and the acrid stench of electrified death were the only testaments that proved he'd ever been alive at all.

A sly smile crept up the side of Silas' face for a split second. So far, everything was going according to plan.

He turned to Taylor, who was now bawling behind the palms of her hands. He didn't have to ask her what happened. The dashing young man had ignored their host's warnings. He'd bypassed the more obvious front door and had attempted to leave out the back. The girl had obviously followed. When he'd reached for the knob, twenty thousand volts had rocked through his body like a sledgehammer, killing him instantly. The burned flesh was simply from his inability to let go of the copper knob once he'd died. The electricity had continued to cook his flesh.

He turned to look at Taylor again, but before he could say anything to her, the other guests had arrived to see what the commotion was about. Mortimer Dees was the first to arrive, followed closely by Gertrude Nebble and Professor Yeardley, and eventually, Jackson Liefeld.

"What happened?" Yeardley asked, walking over to the girl and putting a comforting arm around her. She instantly shrugged him off, and moved closer to Silas.

"It appears Mr. Sparrow attempted to leave the house without our host's consent," Silas said. "Let it be a lesson to you all. The scoundrel, I assume, has considered all possibilities. You would be wise to stick together through this ordeal. Play his game, if you must, but play it by working together. Going off on your own is a recipe for disaster, I'm afraid."

"And how are we supposed to work together exactly?" Mrs. Nebble asked. "There's only enough antidote for one of us."

"She's right," Yeardley continued. "Why should we want to work with that old goat anyway?" He nodded to the spinster. "She's never helped anyone unless it suited her purposes."

"I take it you know each other?"

The two glared at each other, then nodded simultaneously with sour looks on their faces.

Silas turned to the others. "What about the rest of you?" He asked. "Do you all know each other?"

"I don't have time for this," Dr. Yeardley growled before storming out of the kitchen to explore the rest of the house.

The others looked anxiously after him. They no doubt were concerned he'd find the antidote before them, but Silas was determined. He held up a hand.

"Do. You. Know each other?" He articulated the words to drive home that they had no choice but to answer him.

Each of them paused a moment before nodding their heads in the affirmative.

"How so?"

"Yeardley's correct!" Mortimer Dees said, shoving Silas aside and taking off after the professor. "You're doing nothing more than trying to hinder our easement of this malison! There's no time!"

Silas moved in front of the kitchen's swinging door, blocking the other three from leaving. "I'm trying to save your lives," he told them. "Listen to me carefully. None of you were ordained to die tonight. None of you have to die. If you just work with me, I promise, I can help you. I can save you."

Gertrude Nebbles rolled her eyes, stepping toward him, and gesturing for him to move. When he didn't comply, she shoved a bony little finger into his chest. "Let me be, or you'll regret it, buster," she told him.

With a sigh, he nodded and moved aside. When he looked up again, he was surprised to see Taylor and the librarian still standing in the kitchen.

"You're serious?" Taylor asked. "You can help?"

"I believe so, yes."

"If anyone can, it's him," Liefeld told her. "He's the Grim Reaper, after all."

Her eyes darted to the old man, then to Silas, then back to Liefeld again.

"Never mind him," Silas told her. "He's going a bit looney. For now, please answer my question. How do you know these people, Taylor?"

Hugging her arms around herself again, she began to recount her own involvement in the Summer Haven community and all she knew about the players in their little drama. She, of course, had come here about three months earlier with Stefan Yeardley, when he'd heard about the discovery of an exquisite poet from the turn of the twentieth century by the name of Chester Sparrow. Sparrow had been known as little more than the town drunk back then, but what most failed to know was that while in fits of inebriation, he'd managed to compose some of the most beautiful poetry of the period. It was Jackson Liefeld, rummaging through old manuscripts in the library storeroom, who had discovered them.

Of course, there'd been animosity between the professor and librarian from the start, primarily because Yeardley didn't believe in the poems' authenticity, and claimed that they'd been plagiarized from a number of other poets from the period. Then, came the great-great grandson, looking to make a name—and a small fortune—off the works of his ancestor.

"Yes, yes," Silas said. "I know all this. Your captor himself shared most of this in the video. How does Gertrude Nebbles fit into this?"

"She was Yeardley's investor," Liefeld broke in. "She was hoping to use the excitement over a newly discovered poet to put Summer Haven, and of course her and her sister's numerous businesses, on the map. But when she discovered he was planning on discrediting the man's works, she cut him off."

"How'd he respond to that?"

"Not well," Taylor answered. "They have had a few arguments recently. He's threatened to sue her for breach of contract. He's been trying to scrounge up funds ever since to complete his research."

"And Mortimer Dees?"

"Oh, that guy is so creepy," she said. "He's been hitting on me ever since I got into town. Trying to …"

"I think Mr. Mot is more interested in his involvement with Chester Sparrow," Liefeld interrupted. "He's a website designer by trade, but he's been helping the library scan the man's works so they can be offered digitally through our website."

"So he's tech savvy?" Silas asked.

As both of them nodded at this, there was a loud thud coming from the second floor. As one, the three left the kitchen, and made their way up the creaking staircase. Once they reached the landing, Silas turned to look down a long hallway lined with seven oak doors. From his earlier reconnaissance, he knew that six of the doors led to bedrooms. This seventh opened into a large communal bathroom. From his vantage point at the staircase, he could see all the doors were closed except the bathroom, which was slightly ajar.

He took a step forward, just as the overweight form of Mortimer Dees stumbled backwards out the door. He turned slowly to face the trio at the staircase, his eyes wide. His round, normally ruddy face appeared purple, and a stream of frothy liquid purged from his nose and mouth just before he collapsed to the floor.

Taylor let out a little shriek as Silas ran and crouched by the fallen man. He rolled him over, struggling to manhandle his large girth. When he was fully on his back, Silas saw his eyes staring blankly up at the ceiling, no doubt dead before he'd hit the floor.

"That's two. Only four of us left," Jackson Liefeld whispered. "And I don't think I'm long for this world much either at the moment."

"What do you mean?" Silas asked, looking up at the librarian.

Liefeld looked down at him. His face was pale. Sweat glistened off his brow, and he wobbled where he stood. Before Silas could stand to steady him, the old man collapsed, taking deep, raspy breaths, and clutching at his chest.

"You know what's going on, don't you?" he asked. Tears welled in the corners of the librarian's jaundiced eyes. "You know who's behind all this."

Silas offered him a sad smile, and nodded.

"What will happen to me now?"

Silas, now cradling him on his lap, stroked the man's hair gently. "I'm not sure," he told him. "Ordinarily, I would take you to your reward. But this is no ordinary death. It wasn't your time. The object that's causing this tends to collect the souls of those it kills to fuel its own evil power." The Grim Reaper cleared his throat. "But I promise you this, old man. If it's within my power at all, I will save you. You have my word on that."

Liefeld chuckled between wheezing breaths. "Imagine that," he said. "Mot trying to save a life rather than take it. Will wonders ever ..."

Before he could finish his thought, Jackson Liefeld was dead.

"Was he right?" The quiet, shaking voice had come from Taylor, who was now standing about three feet away from the two dead men in the hallway. "Do you know who's doing this?"

He didn't answer. A little bit sad, a little bit angry, Silas Mot glanced down at his watch. The evening had come and gone, and they were approaching dawn. A couple more hours to go and the doors would unlock. It was time to act. It was finally his move. The realization did wonders to improve his spirits.

It was time for the fun and games to really begin.

Laying Liefeld's head carefully on the hallway floor, he stood and looked at the girl. He then pointed toward the bathroom door. "It's just not three dead now," he said. "Ms. Nebble is in the bathroom. She's been strangled."

Nervously, Taylor looked from the door to the dead men on the floor, and then back to Silas. "How ... how do you know?"

He shrugged. "Because I'm Death. I just know."

Curious, she edged toward the slightly ajar door, and looked inside. With a whelp of surprise, she jumped back, nearly tripping on Mortimer Dees' corpse. When she caught her balance, she spun around to face Silas again.

"She's dead. Just like you said."

"Were you close to your aunt, Taylor?"

"What?" Her eyes widened and she took a single step back.

"Your aunt. Gertrude." He grinned at her, raising a single eyebrow as he did. "I noticed the same cheekbones, nose, and mouth almost instantly when I saw you sitting together at the dining room table. I knew she had never been married. No kids. So, she had to be something else. A great aunt perhaps." He stepped toward her. "Were you close?"

She glanced around the hallway, her eyes flitting back and forth. "I ... I ... don't know what you're talking about. I only ... only met her when I came here to Summer Haven with the professor."

Silas shook his head. "I don't think so, Taylor. I think you've known her your whole life. It's how Dr. Yeardley managed to get her financial support. You introduced the two of them."

She took another step back.

"I don't have time for this ..." She glanced behind her, toward the staircase. "... the poison. I've got to find the antidote."

"This whole thing was pretty clever, actually," Silas continued. "Genius, really. Of course, you had help planning it, didn't you? Your benefactor and all?"

Another step. "Stefan!" She shouted at the top of her lungs. "Stefan! Help! He's gone crazy!"

But Silas just shook his head. "Sorry. He's already dead as well." He paused, cocking his head to one side as if listening to something far off. His brightly colored Tiki shirt and Bermuda shorts began to swirl around his body, changing shape. Changing color. Growing dimmer. Darker as he spoke. "A scythe connected to a spring in the ceiling in the attic, I believe. Nasty little boobytrap, that one."

Now, he was fully dressed in a jet black suit, black shirt, and black tie.

"You ... you really are Death, aren't you?" she asked.

He nodded.

She ran. Ran straight for the staircase, taking hold of the bannister to swing her around, and dashed down the steps. He followed her, walking casually as he did so. He watched as she reached into the inner space of her cleavage to remove a cell phone. The same cell phone she'd been using to orchestrate the electric door locks and other traps in the house.

Frantically, she pushed at the buttons on the screen, trying to unlock the front door, but they wouldn't relent. She pressed again with the same negative results. She glanced up at the top of the staircase, saw Silas Mot looming there in his pitch black Armani suit, and bolted toward the kitchen. A moment later, she screamed louder and more convincing than anything she'd done so far that night.

He didn't have to be magic to know what she'd discovered. The body of Caleb Sparrow was gone.

His smile widened.

He strode down the steps, made a left when he came to the first floor, and walked into the dining room. He found the seat he'd taken when he first entered the house and leaned back in it.

Silas watched from his vantage point as the pretty young blonde ran from the kitchen and back up the stairs. There was another scream. He knew she'd discovered the bodies of Mortimer Dees, Jackson Liefeld, and Gertrude Nebble were no longer where she'd left them either.

He glanced at his watch. There was still plenty of time, not that he'd want to speed this up. It was just too much fun to watch.

He heard Taylor run up the second flight of stairs to the third floor attic. Then the sound of footsteps moving backward and forward, searching frantically for something. Searching in quick panicked bursts of speed. More screams, but now only screams of frustration and rage. She couldn't find the antidote either. He knew she wouldn't.

He also knew, she needed it just as much as the others. Magic always has a cost and the Hand of Cain did nothing for free. A gambit like this required sacrifice. She couldn't expect it to give her the gift of immortality if she wasn't willing to risk her own life in the process. So, she'd been forced to take the same poison as everyone else. Her benefactor would have made sure of it.

A few minutes later, she came stomping down the staircase again. Then, she entered the dining room with a pistol aimed directly at him.

He laughed at the sight. "Seriously? You think a gun is going to kill me?"

"Where is it?" The scowl on her face twisted her appearance into something entirely unattractive.

"It?" His glass had already refilled with a margarita, and he savored the taste as it slid from the straw to his tongue.

"The antidote! The antidote! Where is it?" To be as frazzled as she was, Silas was impressed with how steady she maintained her aim at him.

"You mean this?" He reached into the inside pocket of his suit jacket and pulled out a small green bottle topped with a cork.

She started to run toward it, but he held the vial up, and popped the cork with his thumb. "Uh-uh." He waved a finger at her. "One more step, and I'll pour it out all over this rotting carpet. Shoot me, and I guarantee it won't kill me, but might knock it out of my hand." He gestured for her to take her assigned seat.

She complied, then glared at him. "It's rightfully mine. I won. I survived them all. He told me all I had to do was survive the others."

"He? Who's 'he'?"

She bit down on her lower lip, her gaze shifting from the vial to Silas' amused eyes.

"You know, I really have to hand it to you," he said, taking another sip of the margarita. "It really was a clever plan. It took me a few minutes to figure it all out. First, I'd suspected Mortimer. I mean, who wouldn't, right? Those crazy archaic words he was so fond of spouting. And his penchant for technology ... like the WiFi device he'd rigged to the VCR to let him text our host's words in real time? That's how he managed to include me as an 'uninvited guest' in the little spiel. He texted the words, the device translated it into electronic speech, and our host seemed almost prescient." He stirred the straw in the glass as he pondered his next words. "Then, I realized Mortimer wouldn't have been strong enough to drag everyone into the house. He was too out of shape. The physical exertion would have probably given him a heart attack. He needed help. So, my thoughts turned to Caleb Sparrow. Mr. Muscles."

Taylor rubbed her arm as Silas Mot spoke. Sweat beaded across her forehead, running down her cheeks.

"My suspicions turned to everyone involved. Everyone here certainly had motive. The elderly spinster with no love for anyone but herself ... what could be more promising than a chance to never die? The wizened librarian with an uncanny knowledge of ancient mythology, and no doubt a keen interest in something like the Hand of Cain. Your professor, Dr. Yeardley, honestly, was the only one I didn't suspect other than for the most mundane of reasons ... money. And that's why I eventually understood. That's when I realized it was you all along."

"How did you figure that?"

"I'd suspected for a while, the way you clutched your chest all the time. It was pretty good acting in regards to pretending to be shocked and afraid, but it also helped to conceal the cell phone in your bra. But it was your reaction to when Liefeld told you who I was that cinched it. You didn't even blink when he mentioned that I was Death. That's because your benefactor had already warned you that I might be making an appearance. You even had a name.

"Of course, it helped that you weren't alone in this, right? You certainly had help. In fact, every single one of them helped you, I suspect. Mortimer Dees was in love with you, so you used his infatuation. Promised him the two of you would be together forever if he'd help you carry out your plan. You needed Caleb's muscles—definitely not his brains—so you probably used the same trick on him too. Your aunt, you used the promise of revived youth and a chance to get rid of her legal problems with Yeardley. Mr. Liefeld was a bit of a puzzle, I must admit. I couldn't quite figure out how he fit into it all or how he might have helped you. Then I remembered, the greatest threat to his legacy was if the professor discredited his greatest discovery, the poet Chester Sparrow. Someone like Jackson, with so little to show for his life, might be willing to do just about anything to secure that legacy. So you appealed to his fears. You played his desire to have purpose for his life, so he helped you organize this as well."

Silas shook his head, chuckling.

"And none of them were aware of it. They all thought they were partners alone with you. And you betrayed each of them. That's something they're not going to be too happy about, my dear."

It was her turn to laugh. Though her skin was now pasty and doused in sweat, she continued to sneer at him. "If they were alive, I might be worried about that. But ya know ... they're dead."

His grin stretched unnaturally up one side of his face. "Are they?"

He nodded behind her. When she turned, she let out terrified shriek.

Each of the guests, except for Caleb Sparrow, stood behind her. Each one's eyes burned into her soul with rage. Each one remained silent as Silas Mot continued to speak.

"Shhhhh ..." He said, holding a finger to his lips. "Hear that?"

There was silence in the room. Then, the faint tinkle of chimes caught on the wind from outside.

"Know what those are?"

Taylor cocked her head. "Wind chimes?"

"Exactly. Do you know what they do?"

She shrugged.

"Wind chimes are fascinating little pieces of art. The Cherokee, as well as generations of Appalachians, have known for centuries that chimes draw the spirits of the dead to them. Want to keep ghosts out of your house, set up wind chimes outside, and like a bug zapper that attracts and zaps mosquitoes, the chimes will keep the spirits where you want them to be. There are four of them surrounding this house now. So, as each of your victims met their end, their spirits weren't scooped up by the Hand, but rather, they were kept nearby by the chimes. Within my reach. Within my power."

Taylor Blackmoor's jaw seemed to drop at the news.

"And with their spirits within my grasp, and under my control, it was little effort to restore them back to their bodies." Silas shrugged. "Poor Caleb's body was a little worse than the others, so I'll wait to restore his soul until it's had time to properly heal in a hospital. And after they walk out of here when those doors open, none will remember anything that happened here tonight."

She sat up straight, her eyebrows raising hopefully. "Really?"

"Not a single moment of it. They'll have some lapse in memory—a gap in time they can't account for—but they'll be able to return to their lives as if nothing happened." Silas stopped, then scrunched his face in way to show he'd forgotten something. "Well, except for you. They'll, of course, wonder what happened to you. You will have disappeared off the face of the earth. There will be an investigation naturally, but no one will ever discover what happened to you."

She looked at the five other guests behind her, then at the vial. "But if they're okay … if they're alive, they don't need the antidote!" She reached out to Silas, pleading with him. "Give it to me! Please!"

He ignored her request.

"Oh, I forgot something else. Your guests souls haven't been fully restored yet either. They are primed and ready to go. Enough of their essence has been returned to reanimate them, but …"

He stood up, took the vial of antidote, and handed it to the girl. She greedily took it and downed it with one gulp. Silas Mot was already walking toward the foyer, and the front door, which unlatched at the tap of his own cell phone screen.

"… Right now, they have no conscious thought," he continued as he opened the door. "They're little more than zombies until they walk outside. And they are very, very hungry."

With that, he stepped out into the predawn gloom, closed the door behind him, and waited until Taylor began to scream again.

IMPACT MITIGATION
by Jay Werkheiser

"I don't understand," Aaron said, not for the first time since being revived three days ago. Each word was agony in his chest and throat, but he needed to know.

Becky smiled, but he could see the forced patience in her eyes. "Didn't anyone tell you about the Impact Day celebration?"

"They told me it was the anniversary of the asteroid impact." He'd watched it broadcast live from satellite before the internet had gone down. Streaks of fire, then burning holes in Canada, the Arctic Ocean, Siberia. Tsunami alerts. Cryogenic sleep had been his only chance after that.

Becky continued fiddling with his IV line, her crisp white sleeve brushing against the paper thin skin of his bare arm. "The fiftieth anniversary," she said absently.

Cheering. Music. Laughter. Joy. The sounds filtering in from the streets below were anything but somber.

He waited impatiently for her to finish, then tried to wheel himself over to the hospital room's window. His muscles, weakened by age and years of frozen sleep, failed him. He waved for her to do it for him. The sudden motion made his head swim, and bile rose in his throat. He leaned his head back and forced the nausea down.

"Are you okay, Mr. Parker?"

"I'm fine."

She checked his vitals anyway, then made an adjustment to his IV. "Okay," she said at last. "Someone will be in shortly to take a blood sample."

"Bah, they just took a sample this morning."

"They need it to design the targeted chemo drugs, Mr. Parker." She said it while hustling to the door.

"Where are you going?"

"You're not my only patient, you know."

"I'm your richest one," he mumbled to her retreating back. If his money still meant anything. Fifty years. But they'd revived him, so the country must have recovered. The cancer had been treatable, even in his own time, but after the impact, well, things were different. Hemisphere-encompassing dust clouds, coastal flooding, crop failures. They were facing starvation, disease, and death on an unprecedented scale. There would be no resources to treat a seventy-year-old cancer patient. What choice did he have but to risk cold sleep? And now, only fifty years later, much better chemotherapy drugs existed and the ability to reverse the damage done by ice crystals in his cells. And yet the asteroid had hit.

He returned his attention to the view beyond his window. The city streets had been taken over by a festival. Entire blocks were cordoned off, with musicians playing, people dancing, food vendors shouting, and more. A bright red balloon rose from the crowd and drifted lazily skyward.

Knock. "Mr. Parker?" The voice was high pitched and nasal.

"Yeah, come on in."

A new white uniform strolled in, this one trailing long blonde hair streaked with electric blue. She placed a tray of painful-looking instruments on the table next to him. "Vampire's here!" Her nasal voice gushed out of her like a bubbling spring.

He rolled his arm over on the table, exposing blue veins beneath pale flesh. She closed her firm grasp on him. "This won't hurt much." Then, as the needle went in, she said, "So like, why did you get yourself frozen?"

The needle was a sharp sting. Why? A kid her age wouldn't understand. He'd been curable, damn it, before that damned asteroid. It wasn't fair. "Colon cancer," he finally said. He gave the bare hint of a shrug. "I had the money. Figured it was worth the risk, considering."

She laughed. "You're joking, right? We got chemo drugs that can take care of that in a weekend. My grampa had a case of it last year and—"

"Shouldn't you be out there?" He pointed his chin toward the crowd beyond the window. "Celebrating or something?"

"After my shift," she said. "My boyfriend and I are flying up to one of the crater sites tomorrow."

Aaron grunted. "I saw them hit."

Her eyes widened a bit. "You were alive for the impact?"

He nodded slowly, carefully. "At first they told us it wasn't going to hit. Then it was unlikely. Then, well, you know."

He'd hoped to watch from home, but his oncologist wanted to keep him under observation. That last round of chemo had hit his seventy-year-old body hard. But damn it, today was the *day*. Impact. If it turned out as bad as some of the talking heads predicted, well, he didn't want to think about that. Impact panic had already wiped out most of the gains he'd made investing in the aerospace industry. A smart move, that had been, buying stock in anyone who made rockets as soon as they started saying the asteroid might hit.

He hadn't counted on it actually hitting, though. Maybe he wasn't as smart as he'd thought.

"Need anything else, sir?"

Aaron looked up at the guy leaning over his bed. An orderly's scrubs, young, with deep black hair and thick stubble. Probably the only guy on staff young enough to know how to set up the tech. "Just give me the remote."

"Here you go, sir. You control the volume with these—"

"I can figure it out. Just, what channel's the NASA feed?"

"527."

IV lines tugged at his arm. He ignored them and snatched the remote. The screen covered a sizeable fraction of the far wall. He typed in the numbers and the blues and whites of Earth as seen from space appeared. It would have been better on his home system, but this would have to do. NASA had already switched the feed from the ISS to some polar satellite that was going to be at the right place at the right time. It was a clear day over northern Canada. He could see the curve of Hudson Bay. Further north, the intense white of the polar icecap peeked over the horizon.

The orderly was still standing next to his bed. He grudgingly admitted to himself that he was glad for the human contact. "Think it'll miss?"

"Dunno, sir. The guys on the news seemed pretty sure we're gonna catch some fragments."

"I mean the big chunks. It's still possible, you know?"

"Probably not." He shrugged. "Not much we can do about it if it does."

Pretty cavalier attitude toward the end of the world. Bah. The guy was just a kid, probably thought he was indestructible. He sure as hell had a better chance of surviving an apocalypse than an old geezer with cancer.

By now the icecap was nearly centered on the screen. If it hit—when it hit—the impacts would trace a path across northern Canada, over the pole, and into Siberia. The potential impact zones had already been evacuated, along with coastal areas along the Arctic Ocean. But none of it would matter if one of the big pieces hit.

"There!" The orderly pointed idiotically at the screen.

Sparkles glittered in the atmosphere, flashing and dying in an instant. An intense white streak flared over Alaska and into the central Canadian tundra. A pinpoint brighter than the sun lit up the screen. A second point blossomed further north, then another. "The damned thing really hit." Saying it made it real. His hands shook.

"Looks like all little fragments so far."

Simultaneous strikes burned into the edge of the icecap and the sea just above Barrow. There goes the North Shore oil fields, he thought. The burning pinpoints marched across the icecap and into the Siberian steppes.

Aaron held his breath waiting for the big one, the impact that would be a white flare that saturated the camera. And after that, nothing. Ever. It never came.

"No big one," the orderly said. "We just might make it after all."

The very next day Aaron's oncologist delivered the news. This round of chemo would be his last. He'd use their remaining stock, and there would be no more deliveries. He looked at the storm outside his window, torrential rain, gale-force wind, nonstop lightning. The entire hemisphere was getting the same weather, and the sky would stay dark even after the rain stopped. Resources would be scarce, and saving Aaron Parker's life was a luxury the world wouldn't be able to afford.

Aaron hadn't gotten rich by passively accepting defeat. He'd started planning for this the moment he'd heard about the asteroid.

"It was pretty bad," he said. "Forests burning across Siberia, Alaska, northern Canada. Barrow wiped off the map by tsunamis. Talking heads forecasting doom."

"Is that why you got frozen? To avoid the hard years?"

"No. You..." You wouldn't understand. Kids didn't like to hear that. "It's complicated."

"You missed everything that came after."

"I can't get anyone to explain why you're all celebrating."

"We just do." She shrugged. "What was it like, back then? Trying to stop it, I mean?"

"Well, I wasn't involved in that." The President had kept urging calm, but the experimental rockets had kept failing. New reports getting more hysterical, panic taking root. Scientists trying to explain theory. "They couldn't just blow it up with a bunch of nukes or something," he said. "It was a rubble pile, not a solid block."

"Oh, I know all about that," she said. "It was made of two large chunks of rock embedded in a mound of pebbles, all held loosely together by gravity." She said it in a sing-song manner, as though she were reciting an elementary school lesson.

He winced as she changed the collection tube on the needle in his arm. He looked away as blood began flowing slowly into the new tube. Thinking about the asteroid was a good distraction. A cluster of pebbles.

The problem was you hit it and now you have a load of buckshot coming at you rather than a single bullet. "Right up until the very end," he said, "they weren't sure they could deflect it. If it had hit dead on, well, we wouldn't be here talking about it."

"It must have been a scary time."

Facing a mass-extinction impact? The most powerful nations trying and failing to stop it, one by one? Scary didn't even begin to describe it. "Yeah, it was."

"All done!" She packed up her torture implements and peeled off her gloves. "Nurse Becky will be back soon." She scampered through the door before he could respond.

Aaron scowled at the festival outside. What the hell were they celebrating? Fireballs and tsunamis? Ruined cities, millions dead? Damn it, this should be a solemn occasion, a day of mourning.

Knock. Becky didn't wait for permission to enter. Older, more experienced, no nonsense. "Just need to give you your meds and get your vitals again," she said. Crow's feet, middle-age spread. Hell, his grandkids were probably around her age by now. Older. They'd lived through the aftermath that he'd skipped.

Which made him wonder. "How old were you when it hit?"

"Little. I remember my dad crying. No TV for a while. After? Well, I remember being hungry a lot."

"And yet you're celebrating." He waved a weak arm toward the window. "Biggest catastrophe mankind ever faced, and you people throw a party for it."

She deflated with a sigh, settling onto the edge of the bed. "You have no idea what happened, do you?"

"That's what I've been saying." He would have shouted if he'd had the strength.

"Look, I'm about to go clock out. I'll come back and—"

"No, stay. I'll pay your overtime. Money's still good, isn't it?"

She pursed her lips. "Yes, but not like you think. Not since—"

"I know, since the impact. So tell me."

"Okay." She glanced at the clock again. "You remember how they deflected it, right?"

He nodded. "Standoff nuclear blast." Set off some bombs in space. Near the asteroid, always on the same side. Radiation from the explosions vaporizes material from the surface. Expanding vapor goes one way, asteroid gets pushed the other, like a rocket engine.

"They needed a lot of nukes to pull that off," she said. "More than any one nation could launch, even if they could develop powerful enough boosters in time."

"The President kept telling us they could get it done." He laughed weakly. "Until it became clear they couldn't."

"I remember seeing him talking on TV, and my dad telling me everything was going to be all right, that the nice man on the TV was going to make the asteroid miss us."

"Chinese and Russians were saying the same thing," he said. "When it finally came out that none of them were going to be able to do it, that's when all hell broke loose." News footage from those days flashed through his mind. Giant rockets blowing up on the launch pad. Flaming debris dropping into the ocean. Sinking deeper into despair with each failure.

"I mostly remember the panic," she said. "Watching the world unravel through the eyes of a child."

There had been scary trips to the grocery store with mommy before. Not way before. Back then you could get anything you wanted, cereal, candy, ice cream. But before, when daddy first started talking about a rock in the sky. People got scared. They bought lots of stuff. She had to wait with mommy in long boring lines.

Then it got better. When they started shooting rockets at the sky. Daddy said it would stop the rock. Only it didn't. The rock crashed, and she didn't even get to see it. Daddy cried that day.

And now people were running around the store. They were scared, she could see it on their faces. Mommy was scared. That scared Becky. Riding in the shopping cart's seat wasn't even fun when she was scared. "I wanna go home, mommy."

"Soon. But first we need to buy some things."

"Why?"

"So we have enough food to eat."

"Just come back tomorrow."

"There might not be any food left tomorrow."

"Why?"

"Just, a lot of people—"

The shopping cart shook violently, nearly knocking Becky from her seat. "Move it, lady."

Becky grasped the cart's handle tightly and swiveled her head. A big man was there, his shopping cart touching hers. He kept pushing it, and her cart shuddered. Mommy tried to pull the cart away, but it was pressed against the empty shelf.

"Hey, you got cans." He reached in and grabbed some.

"Those are mine," Mommy said. She tried to take them back, but he twisted her arm and she screamed.

The man grabbed more cans. He got the peas!

"Those are mine," Becky said. But he ignored her. She clawed at his hand. He pulled it back sharply and backed his cart away.

Mommy leaned over the cart, her body protecting Becky. "Leave her alone."

"I'm sorry," the man said. His voice sounded like he actually meant it, but Becky still didn't like him.

"Just go away."

After he left, Becky felt tears sting her eyes. "Can we please go now?"

"Yes," Mommy said. It sounded like she was trying not to cry. "Let me get you some frozen peas first. They won't last, but you can have them tonight."

It was the last time Mommy took her shopping for quite a while.

Aaron sighed impatiently and shifted in his wheelchair. This little trip down memory lane was taking too long. He wanted to know what happened after he'd gone under. But he could see in her eyes that she was lost in the memories of that terrifying time. "It's a shame," he said. "They finally put their differences aside. Americans, Chinese, Europeans, and more." He added wistfully, "They almost succeeded."

"Not almost." She said it sharply, sternly. "They did succeed."

"Well sure, they got the rockets off the ground. Set off the standoff blasts." There had been elation at first, after the bombs started going off and the asteroid shifted course. But then... "There's still an Impact Day."

"I suppose a guy like you wouldn't understand the significance of what happened."

His eyes narrowed. "What do you mean?"

"You were rich. Rich enough to be able to afford cryogenic preservation. Made your money by being the best at playing the cutthroat game."

He put an edge in his weak voice. "I was successful."

"But don't you see; we didn't need that. Not at that moment," she said. "Do you have any idea which country, which world leader, was the one to get the ball rolling? To start the chain of international cooperation that finally got rockets in the air?"

"At the time, they all claimed credit."

"And after?"

"I don't know," he said impatiently. "I was asleep by then."

"We still don't know." She stared him in the eye. "And no one cares, because it doesn't really matter."

"I don't understand."

"What matters is that they put their differences aside. Left and right, ally and rival, rich and poor. The Russians had a head start on powerful boosters. Americans had advanced guidance systems. China, Europe, India, every country with a space program could contribute something. They stopped using money, at least for anything involving impact mitigation."

"There was quite an uproar at the time," he said. "About giving away sensitive technology to the Russians and Chinese. If they'd used those missile guidance systems to attack—"

"None of that would have mattered after an extinction-level impact, now would it? And that's what they were talking, mass extinction. Global ice age."

"Okay fine, so they put their differences aside, held hands, and sang 'Kumbaya.' What's the big deal?"

"I was a little girl at the time," Becky said. "I didn't understand any of it. But I knew whatever the people on the news were saying made my parents happy. When they finally launched...we lived in Delaware at the time, and they built a lot of them in Virginia. We could see them go up."

Daddy's shout came from outside. "C'mon out, hon. It's almost time."

"On our way." Mommy closed up her laptop and grabbed Becky's hand. "Let's go watch."

Becky trotted along next to mommy. The man on TV was going to shoot rockets at the rock. It sounded boring, but mommy and daddy were excited about it. "How long will it take?"

"A while. They won't be done until day after tomorrow."

Becky's heart sank. "Do we have to watch them all?"

"No. But I want you to see some of them. It's something you'll remember all your life."

Becky didn't understand why it was such a big deal. She'd watched rockets take off before. But there were a lot of people outside, the whole neighborhood. Other kids were out with their parents, too. Everyone was looking the same way. The Coopers next door were standing with daddy, talking.

She ran to daddy and tugged on his arm. He lifted her up onto his shoulders and pointed over top of the house across the street. "Look that direction," he said. "It'll start any time now."

She held her hand up to block the sun. "Nothing's happening."

"Just wait."

"It's boring."

Just at that moment, a bright spot appeared from behind the house. It climbed into the air fast, trailing white smoke behind it. The rocket looked like a dark spot at the top of a big fire. She'd seen stuff like that on TV. "It's just a rocket," she said.

But everyone started clapping and cheering. Mrs. Cooper cried happy tears. "You'll understand one day," she said.

Everyone talked loud and fast for a while. It was like a Fourth of July picnic. Then another rocket launched and the cheers started up again. Becky felt the adults' excitement and it became her own. She stayed up late into the night and her parents didn't care. They wanted to watch too, the beautiful orange streaks lighting up the night sky like fireworks that didn't explode.

Everything was going to be all right. The news people said so. She fell asleep on daddy's lap.

Aaron remembered the thrill of those days. And the terror. Breathless newscasters reporting on every launch, every detonation, every arc second of deflection. Miniature suns flared in the darkness and died on his TV screen. "But they failed. Sure the center of mass missed, but rubble piles fragment too easily. The Northern Hemisphere got hammered."

"Yeah. I remember when they announced where the impact zones would be. I was a stupid kid; I was actually disappointed because I wouldn't be able to see the impacts from our house."

Aaron took in her words, turned back to the celebrations outside. "Lightly populated areas. Could have been worse, I suppose. But still, celebrating? People died in those impacts."

"Do you know how many?"

"Things were chaotic in the aftermath," he said. "They didn't have a number before I went under."

"Fewer than a thousand. Most of them were people who'd refused to evacuate tsunami zones. We have a day of remembrance for them."

Aaron nodded. Perhaps he finally understood. "So you celebrate because we got a lucky break, because it didn't hit Tokyo, or in the middle of the Atlantic, or something. Why didn't you just say so?"

"No, not at all."

He landed a frail punch on the arm of his wheelchair. "I don't understand."

"First of all, it wasn't luck. We as a species came together. Sworn enemies cooperated. Without that, we'd all be dead now." She paused, as though considering how to proceed. "But it's more than that even. It didn't end with the impacts. The aftermath was worse. You got to sleep through all that."

Her voice didn't make it sound like an accusation, but he took it that way anyway. "I had *cancer*. They could have cured it before, but that goddamned asteroid took that away. There wouldn't be the resources to treat a frail old man, even a rich one."

"Nice for you," she said. "Others didn't have that luxury."

"Don't you see?" He stared into her eyes, pleading for understanding. "The asteroid had hit and I'd survived it. Only it had taken away the medical care that would keep me alive. If I hadn't taken a chance on cold sleep, the asteroid would have gotten me after all."

"Have you even thought about what happened in the time you skipped?"

"Of course I have. That's why I can't understand all," he waved vaguely at the celebrations beyond the window, "this."

She continued as though she hadn't heard him. "Land impacts sent a lot of dust and smoke into the atmosphere, covered the northern hemisphere. Ocean impacts added water vapor. Snow and flooding. There were weeks of darkness. There were years without summer. I built snowmen in August."

Aaron pictured darkness and snow blanketing North America, Europe, Asia. Ice storms in Los Angeles. Snow covering the croplands of Nebraska and Ukraine during the growing season. He'd seen the beginnings of it, distantly, the abstract memories of a sick man undergoing a desperate medical procedure. There were no details, just a feeling of impending doom. "Millions must have starved," he said. "Billions."

"Nope." She smiled broadly. "We avoided all that."

Impatience balled his hands into tight fists gripping the blanket draped over his lap. "But how!"

"Don't get me wrong, there were some very hard years. I grew up with rationing cards. There was never quite enough food to satisfy my hunger. But I didn't starve. No one did."

"Someone discovered a miracle technology, then? Some sort of hydroponic farming?"

"No new technology, at least not soon enough to matter. The only miracle was human kindness." She held up her hands to stave off his objections. "Yes, I know. I remember gray skies, black rain, empty stomach. But I also remember, ten years later, being in the top ten percent of my senior class, and because of that I was selected to go off to Argentina to learn about innovative new agricultural techniques. By that time the dust clouds were finally thinning, and the U.S. was starting to revive the Midwest farm belt."

"Argentina?"

"They became the world's bread basket during those hard years. And South Africa, and Australia, and a lot of other places. You should see it. Take a trip down there when you're healthy again."

Healthy. He had a hard time processing the thought. He'd been sick for so long with the cancer and the chemo and the radiation. And old age, he reminded himself. They didn't have a cure for that, yet, but they'd made significant advances in quality of life. He might live another thirty or forty years in this bizarre wonderland filled with people who celebrated asteroid impacts. If he ever figured them out. "Okay, so the farmers of South America grew a lot of food. I can't imagine it was enough to feed everyone."

"The Pampas alone are fertile enough to feed much of the Western Hemisphere," she said. "Always have been. But now the U.S. was providing Argentina with all the technology it needed to expand agricultural production. We gave them top shelf agricultural techniques and the resources to apply them; they gave us food in return."

"It couldn't have been that easy."

"Of course not. It was dicey at first. Everyone went hungry, even people in the prime growing regions."

"I don't buy it." He folded his feeble arms across his chest, defying her words and, by extension, the celebration outside. "People are greedy. They hoard. You said it yourself; the shelves were empty when people knew the asteroid was coming."

"Oh, there were some trying times, for sure," she said. "Even some violence. I was caught up in an attempted coup while I was down there."

Aaron felt his eyes widen. "I knew it. You people think you've got everything figured out, but you still fight each other just like we did in my day." Unending wars in the Mideast, a burgeoning cold war in East Asia. Then came the asteroid, and they'd put it all aside temporarily. There was still the question of what the Chinese might do with that advanced missile technology afterwards.

"Not like your time. Not at all."

He barked a short laugh, then wheezed from the effort. "Every generation thinks that."

Becky adjusted the valve, nudging the water's nutrient level down a notch. The wheat was thriving, and the excess nitrates could be best used over in Bolivia. They needed every bit of help they could get. Here in Argentina, things couldn't be going better. She took notes about crop growing techniques on her phone, but it was hardly necessary. The Argentineans treated her and her friends like heroes. They gladly shared their innovations. And their food. Without that, U.S. citizens would be starving in the streets.

Her phone vibrated. It was Martina. "Sup, girl?"

Martina's face was ashen. "There's been an accident. Med crew is heading out. You want to come along?"

She'd already been accepted into an R.N. program back home, and the medical staff here gave her every opportunity to get a head start on it. "On my way."

She ran to her bunk, packed up an emergency kit, and met Martina outside the medical tent. "Where's the emergency?"

"Across the border. Some kind of explosion. Several casualties."

"Bolivia?" There'd been word of political instability over there. It had long been a poor country, now pressed to the edge of survival by the demands for food coming from the north.

"Yeah. Rodrigo is working there."

Rodrigo's bright smile lit up her memory. "Let's go."

They piled into an old Tesla, five of them, plus medical gear. It didn't take long to get across the border and onto the rundown farming compound that had called for help. She climbed out of the car behind Martina. A loud crack startled her. At first she didn't know what it was, but then men dressed in khaki surrounded the car. She caught sight of the rifles in their hands and gasped. One of them fired another shot into the air. A meek yelp escaped her lips.

One of the soldiers shouted in Spanish too rapidly for her to follow. She glanced at Martina. "They're taking us hostage."

"We need to treat the wounded first."

Martina translated into Spanish. The soldier nodded and waved them forward with his rifle. Rodrigo was nowhere to be found, but there were three wounded men. Becky helped by working on minor injuries, cleaning wounds and dressing them. She asked the guy she was working on about her friend. "The others were taken away," he told her.

Two hours later, after all the injured were treated, soldiers blindfolded her, tied her hands, and shoved her into some sort of van with the others.

Aaron had never had reason to go to Bolivia. It had always been a poor country, with little to offer a wealthy businessman. Sure they'd had mineral resources, but lacked the means to extract them profitably. But with money—or whatever passed for it—rolling in from the north, things might have changed quickly. "So what was it? Corrupt government hoarded all the wealth? People rose up and overthrew them?"

"You got it exactly backwards."

He sighed, a pitiful rasping exhalation. "Why don't you just tell me."

"There was a faction that didn't like how much food the Bolivian government was exporting," she said. "Wanted to keep more for themselves. They lured us over the border with the explosion, figured they could use us as leverage. It was the first time I'd heard gunfire in my life."

When he'd been eighteen, Aaron's biggest worry had been a possible war with China, an abstract fear of being drafted. It was nothing compared to the visceral terror that young Becky must have faced. "How did you get free? Some sort of special forces raid?" Images of an intense firefight flashed in his mind, commandoes taking out rebels one by one, advancing on some jungle outpost.

"Nothing of the sort. Not a single life was lost."

Another sigh. "What, then?"

Becky covered her head with the lumpy straw pillow the soldiers had given her, but the noises from outside her cell came through anyway. Shouts, chants, racing engines, angry honking. An occasional crack of gunfire.

"What do you think's going on out there?" she asked Martina. "Are they really taking over the country?"

"I think they're trying," Martina said. "But from some of those chants, it sounds like the people are resisting them."

"Oh? Those are pro-government protesters?"

"And pro-U.S.A."

"Oh?" She sat up and tried to hear what they were saying. Her Spanish wasn't nearly good enough. "What are they saying?"

"Send them food. Feed the U.S.A. Stuff like that."

For the first time since entering Bolivia, Becky felt hope. This coup was going to fail. They didn't have the people on their side.

Moments later a pair of guards approached their cell and unlocked the door. "Come with us."

Becky looked at Martina, hesitated. "Are they going to—" She couldn't bring herself to say those final words.

"I don't think so," Martina said. "I think they need us."

Becky wasn't so sure, but there wasn't much she could do to resist. The guards took them to an interrogation room. Bare table, wooden chairs. No windows. The door opened and fear rose in Becky's throat.

A man wearing a drab green uniform entered and sat across from them. This man would decide if she lived or died, right here, right now. He wore a stern expression, but Becky saw defeat in his eyes. "You will be released to the Bolivian police within the hour."

Becky's teeth unclenched and her shoulders unknotted. "Just like that?"

"The government in La Paz is sucking the people dry and yet they rally against us. What more can I do?"

"You can join them."

He pulled back as though slapped. "And support the pillaging of Bolivia? No, I will wait. When the people are hungry enough, they will rise up and then I will—"

"The people of Bolivia have already spoken," she said. "Don't you hear them? They want the food shipments to continue."

"But that makes no sense. It would mean continued food shortages here. Why would they want to go hungry?"

"So that the rest of the world doesn't starve." Becky stared him in the eye. "They would rather share what they have, even if it means hardship in the short term."

He shook his head sadly. "This will be the end of Bolivia."

"No," she said, her voice more forceful than she had expected it to be. "It's the beginning of a new world."

"Human nature has changed. Is that what you're trying to tell me?"

"Not changed. The asteroid showed us who we always could have been. People are social animals; it's natural for us to share resources. We'd been doing it in small groups since the beginning of time. Tribes working together on a hunt, families supporting the elderly and infirm, rural communities gathering to build barns. It's just, well, it took a global catastrophe to make us see that our tribe encompasses all mankind now. And it happened everywhere. They irrigated the African veldt and it fed billions. They made the Australian Outback bloom."

Aaron tried to imagine the consequences of all that. The African and South American nations, long mired in poverty and economic stagnation, would suddenly find themselves in a boom. They'd have no time for the squabbles that went back to prehistory; they'd be busy feeding the world. Economies expanding, standards of living rising, freedom and democracy flourishing. Poverty and war would become things of the past. In a land of plenty, there's nothing to fight over. His head spun. But at what cost? Was there *really* freedom and democracy? "You're telling me people created a utopia by sharing. But that means giving up on personal ambition. If you've created some sort of socialist paradise, I'll tell you right now that I'm not going to fit in here."

"Not at all," she said. "Those old terms, capitalist, socialist, and all that, they just don't have much meaning anymore."

"Well it sure sounds like socialism to me."

"If I'm using the term correctly, socialism involved government control of the economy, didn't it? We don't have that; we have less government regulation than you did in your time. We don't need it. We have personal responsibility. People, even the ones running big corporations, realized that it's to their economic advantage to share resources. A rising tide raises all boats, as my grandma used to say."

"So just like that, people changed how they behave? That easy?"

"Well no, of course it wasn't as easy as it sounds. But that's the point; we shared the hardship. All of us. Mankind. We survived, individually and as a species, by cooperating and sharing. We weren't going to let anyone take us back to the old ways. That Bolivian coup was the last gasp of the old world, and people stood up and said no. I suppose it could have gone either way during those early years, when things were at their worst. But once people started really working together, it was easier than anyone had imagined."

Aaron tried to follow the line of reasoning. With economies intimately intertwined across the world, the incentive for conflict disappeared. Hurting your neighbor hurt you too. Outside, the sounds of a marching band heralded an approaching parade. Aaron turned his attention to the crowd gathered on the street below. Children climbed onto the shoulders of parents, laughing and waving Impact Day flags. Colorful balloons rose into the air, followed by a roaring cheer. The scene would play out over and over today, in all the nations of the world.

He finally thought he understood these people. They'd faced hell together and had come through stronger. Shared peril had brought mankind together at last. But where did that leave him? "I'm the one outsider left on the whole planet," he said. "The one person who didn't experience the transformation."

"You see those children out there? None of them had been born when it happened."

"But they grew up in the culture. I'm a relic of the old days. Of a time those people would rather forget."

"Then you still don't understand us."

"I suppose I never will." He sat back and watched the city celebrate the end of his world. "But I'm going to have to spend the rest of my life trying. My world is gone."

"Would you really want it back? The war, the poverty, the suffering?" She looked at him incredulously. "After everything I told you?"

"I don't know," he said. He'd sealed himself into a coffin surrounded by liquid nitrogen, cutting himself off from a world in ruins. He'd survived, in his own way. Could he adapt to paradise? "It's just hard to wrap my head around it. You're telling me that the asteroid impact, the worst catastrophe humanity has ever faced, ushered in a golden age of cooperation, peace, and prosperity."

A wide grin lit her face. "Exactly. Being hit by an asteroid was the best thing that ever happened to mankind."

FAIR PLAY
by Claire Ashgrove

Entombed deep within the ground, Arven McGill breathed in the thick scent of must and decay. Rot he couldn't identify through the shadows cast by torches scattered along the rocky walls. Yet he remembered it well from the singular year he'd spent at war on Earth—*death*.

Strange for such a smell to cling to the belly of an auditorium meant for croquet.

He glanced briefly at his two teammates, who lounged comfortably on wooden benches, waiting for their turn in the overhead stadium. Around him, the very walls rumbled with raging applause from the crowd that anxiously awaited the match between Earth and Kreventia, once known to Earth's scientists as the Gliese.

"Sit, McGill." James Fortney, captain of the team, shot him a grin. "We taught them how to play, remember? We've got this in the bag. Stop pacing."

Arven chuckled and shook off the momentary bout of unease. The scent was likely rats. Or something similar to rats, at least. In the four days the survivors had been on Kreventia, he had yet to see anything that was identical to the world he'd grown up in. Close, but *not quite*. Like the original men, those now known as the Venrada, whom the United States Government made contact with twenty years ago. Built like men, yet covered with iridescent gold scales, they'd been found living underground in a vast, cave-like system that had remained hidden for centuries.

He dropped down on the bench beside Fortney with a quick glance at his watch. Five minutes. "It makes me uneasy. I want *my* mallet. Why in the hell do we have to use new equipment assigned by the Galactic Oversight Committee?"

Fortney shrugged. "Didn't ask. It was all part of the agreement when we came here. New equipment, and we take a handicap for our experience. I guess they don't want to be trounced on their home field."

Arven gave him a pointed look. "Yeah, we're supposed to lose." The unease returned, sliding down his spine like sharp little needles.

Coleman Henderson leaned around Fortney to meet Arven's gaze. "C'mon, man, stop with the nerves. We're Brits. Croquet is in our blood. Hit the ball through the wickets, end of game. You know the aliens can't aim for shit."

True. All very valid points, and when they had played the Venrada on Earth, they'd won every time. But all the hype and rules that went along with the first game ever played on Kreventia still seemed ... odd.

"Chill," Fortney instructed with a soft chuckle. "So they want to look good for the homeland. So maybe we lose. Big damn deal."

But it was a big deal, wasn't it? Especially after surviving a surprise attack from the distant Rendenturas that left Britain a wasteland and other portions of Earth so devastated it would take years to rebuild. Earth was no longer a suitable habitat for one third of its population, so they'd scattered amongst the stars, headed to colonize new homes among friendly alien peoples, crowded onto ships like refugees headed into places unknown.

Arven looked toward the darkened tunnel that opened onto the field. Earth had agreed to the games as an overture of friendship. Sure, twenty years had passed with the two planets interacting, but relations were tenuous, and Earth's delegates remained unconvinced of Kreventia's claimed humanitarian interests. The delegates and various heads of state had agreed to send their best competitors here, to prove they trusted the Kreventians. Still, like any sporting venture, if Earth's survivors lost, the decimated planet would look even weaker. Today, they would play a race they'd never met—Olmians, according to the Committee's planning. Apparently the Olmians' passion for croquet succeeded every other being on the planet.

An ear-piercing whistle cut through the roar of the crowd. The stadium fell silent, anticipation thickening the air. Arven and his teammates stood, their attention riveted on the brightening light at the end of the tunnel. Faint blue hues grew steadily until the field came into full view.

A voice bellowed from the sound system, "Welcome the Earthlings, the famed champions of the country known as Britain. Here today to test their skill against Kreventia's honored Spades, undefeated in the galaxy of Trenia."

Thunderous applause erupted all around, nearly drowning out a second piercing whistle. At the faint signal, Fortney beckoned them into the tunnel and broke into a strong, easy lope. The others followed, Arven taking up the rear.

A full twenty minutes later, the men stood beneath the luminescent glow of overhead Argon lamps, waiting for the opposing team to make its grand appearance. Arven took in his surroundings. Unlike the western hemisphere of Kreventia, where lush forests enveloped cool, clear lakes and hills and valleys filled the landscape with greenery, this side of the planet never saw the sun. Unease about how they would survive in a place so strange and different began to stir. He pushed the discontent down, focusing on overcoming the difficulties of the game alone, for without the win, there might not be anything else to consider. The field stretched before him. No plant life grew amid the eternal darkness and the cooler temperatures ... including grass. The ground was nothing but rock ground to near powder then spread thin over a solid substrate. Without grass, the balls would encounter little resistance. To say the team was handicapped put it lightly. One too-strong mallet tap, and the ball would sail out of control.

Great. He smoothed his sweaty palms against his jeans and studied the audience. Another roar of cheering surged through the stands. Across the field, movement stirred within the Olmians' tunnel. A pale white glow emanated around them as they began their march to the starting stake.

"Holy crap, what are those?" Coleman asked in a low voice.

Ten feet away from where they would begin play, they saluted their fans, and Arven's jaw dropped. He'd known they wouldn't be playing the reptilian race, but he hadn't prepared for this.

Four salamander-like figures turned to face Arven's team. Tiny arms extended from a long, smooth, grey-white body. Arms that weren't near long enough to hold a regulation-size mallet. Equally small legs held the creatures upright, and long thick tails dragged the rocky ground behind them. Their faces looked human, for the most part. If one could ignore the frilly protrusions around their smooth, cherubic cheeks.

"Olmians," Fortney answered Coleman, straightening to his full height.

"Yeah, but how are they going to play?" Coleman asked. "Those mallets—" he pointed to the equipment rack standing near the starting stake "—aren't going to be long enough for them."

At the far end of the field, a Venrada official spoke with the opposing team. A wire basket full of softball sized, iridescent, metallic balls dangled from his left hand. Gold, silver, blue-black, neon orange, electric green, and crimson shone in the unnatural light. As Arven watched, something protruded from the center of the gold ball, then quickly disappeared once more.

"Uh, guys?" Arven asked.

"Yeah, McGill?" Fortney asked.

"Did you, see that?" He blinked then stared hard at the motionless iridescent ball. "It ... moved."

With a bark of laughter, Fortney thumped a heavy hand between Arven's shoulder blades. "I think you breathed too much space dust. Chill."

The official blew on a small copper pipe, producing another shrill shriek, and motioned for the two teams to gather at the opening stake. Arven trudged into place, his narrowed gaze fastened on the unusual mallets. The pale white wood was unlike anything found on Earth, almost the shade of alabaster. And Arven did a double-take as he fully realized their design. Unlike standard croquet mallets with two striking ends, these possessed only one. The singular head was rounded, unlike the flat head Arven was accustomed to.

He lifted his head and met an Olmian's pale red stare. The salamander-like man flashed a smile, revealing three-inch long razor-sharp teeth. Dread slammed into Arven like a falling boulder.

Aw, hell.

"As you know," the official began, "Earth agreed to a handicap. It will be assigned now."

Arven snapped his head up. "I thought we were handicapped already? The ground, those." He pointed at the odd mallets.

As Fortney held up a hand, begging Arven off, the official shook his head.

The Venrada male continued, "Section One of the official handbook only states grass is the best playing surface, not that it is mandatory. Our wickets are securely fastened. The corners clearly marked. We proceed with normal play."

Arven bit back a retort. Hoarse laughter rumbled between the opposing team members. He narrowed his gaze and glared. Evidently they'd learned the game, but they hadn't learned a thing about *fair play*.

"Cr'vesh, present the players with their mallets," the official instructed.

The tallest of the Olmians moved to the rack and pulled three mallets off. As he passed Fortney his, Arven could have sworn amusement glinted in his eyes. Like he held a dark secret.

"Wait!" Arven grabbed Fortney's shoulder.

But he moved too late. When Fortney closed his fingers around the smooth white wood, the shaft shifted. It coiled upright in a lightning-fast move and let out a chilling hiss.

"Sna—" Fortney's shocked exclamation gave way to a bone-chilling scream. He dropped the snake and clutched at his nose. Blood poured between his fingers. "My nose!" he howled as he dropped to his knees.

Coleman charged the official with a violent oath. Arven grabbed him by the back of the shirt and yanked him to a halt. No telling what might happen if they attacked a local, even if the attack was warranted. Coleman struggled, swearing loudly enough to make a sailor cringe, fighting to unleash his rage.

"Don't," Arven ground out sharply. "Who knows what they'll do." He pushed Coleman behind him and stepped closer to the official, wrestling with his own fury. "What the hell was that?"

A slow smile, full of superiority, brightened the Venrada male's scale-covered face. "Handicap," he said simply.

Handicap, my ass. But wisdom filtered through Arven's anger, and he bit his tongue, choosing to instead kneel beside the moaning Fortney. With effort, Arven managed to peel back his team captain's hand. He cringed at the mutilated flesh. The entire soft portion of his nose was missing. Traumatic, but not life-threatening.

Arven looked up at the official. "Your handicap is to make us play with two men, not three?"

"Two men cannot play the game. Each team must maintain three men and three balls. You wish to forfeit?" The creature's hard stare suggested something deeper than a croquet game was at stake. Challenge glinted there, the tone of his words creating another chilling finger of unease. What would happen if they didn't play?

Not something Arven cared to consider. He shook his head slowly. "No."

With a smirk, the official indicated the mallets. "Then we begin this game that Earth's legendary founder brought to royal courts throughout the lands; this game queens and kings have played for centuries, and has now been brought to our planet by our new, intergalactic friends."

Kings and queens? Talk about overly dramatic. Arven glanced between Fortney and Coleman. Fury had taken root in Fortney's anguished eyes. Coleman stared in horror at the now motionless snake, once again in the form of the unusual mallet. In its deadly jaws, it held a smooth, round rock. A film covered its un-pigmented eyes, betraying its blindness. Another product, Arven assumed, of living on a side of the planet that never saw the light. It might be deadly, but it had a weakness.

His gaze slid to the Olmians, observing for the first time that each bore an onyx ace of spades design on their soft belly. Beady red eyes glowed in the low blue light, glinting with a bloodthirsty hunger for the game. Movement from within the basket of balls drew Arven's attention. He stared as the crimson ball unwound entirely, taking the form of some indescribable metallic insect. It reared on miniscule hind legs that its overlarge abdomen disguised and struck out two bristly front legs at the golden ball. A series of angry, unintelligible, chitters followed as the two engaged in some dispute.

He frowned as a distant childhood memory rose. *Ace of spades. Spades. Queens. Fighting balls. Unusual mallets.*

The scent he'd smelled beneath the stadium connected with the evidential *founder* of their game, and an authoritative, feminine voice in his head screeched, *Off with their heads!*

"Time out," Arven called.

"Time out?" the official asked, bewildered. "There is no provision for *time out.*"

Arven hesitated a moment, then came to a conclusion that seemed to fit. "There is no provision *against* a time out, therefore, it is not a violation of the rules. We will take ten minutes."

The official stared at him long and hard, objection written in the harsh lines of his scaly brow. Then, finally, as Arven began to prepare for his refusal, the official relented with a slow nod.

"Ten minutes, and no more."

Arven gestured to Coleman, and together, they helped Fortney to his feet. The trio shuffled back toward their end of the field.

"What are you thinking?" Coleman scolded in a hushed whisper. "We should forfeit. Fortney's in no shape to play. We should walk and turn this act of aggression in to the Committee. Bring the whole team up on charges."

"We can't." Arven shook his head adamantly. "I'd like to go home, not have my head served on a platter."

With another anguished moan, Fortney looked at Arven. But confusion slowly gave way to understanding that shone through his pained expression. He nodded. "McGill's right. We have to play it out."

"*How?*" Coleman protested.

Arven chewed on his lip, frowning. "How did Alice win the game?"

"Alice?" Coleman asked.

"Wonderland," Fortney and Arven answered together.

At Coleman's perplexed expression, Arven beckoned him to lean in closer. "Remember how the Delegates said Kreventia was primarily interested in our culture? They fed them book after classic book. Maybe they took those works of fiction literally. Now, think, how did Alice beat the Queen of Hearts?"

All three fell silent, and Arven looked between them expectantly. Literature had never been his strong point. Only if books had been translated to movies. But even then, it had been a long, long time since he'd seen the classic film.

"She didn't," Fortney answered at last. "The whole game turned into chaos, and they gave it up."

Arven considered Fortney's statement as Coleman let out a defeated groan. After a moment, he gave in to a smile. "Then that's what we'll do."

⇒ ✳ ⇐

Two turns passed for each team, and Arven's plans seemed more likely to backfire against them than accomplish any win. Fortney's injury indeed proved a handicap—he missed his blue-black ball entirely both times and still remained at the starting stake. Coleman earned two extra shots, the second of which nearly put his silver ball through the fourth wicket. But the creature that served as a ball objected to passing all the way through and, at the last moment, stuck out an appendage and rolled backward with such force it shot across the hard ground, out of bounds, forcing Coleman to start over on the next turn. Arven still struggled to put his green ball through the second wicket, having discovered the wickets weren't metal at all, but instead, a flat grey worm that refused to stay in place.

His wasn't the only one that moved. They all did each time a ball rolled close. While they didn't pick up and relocate to accommodate the Olmians like Carroll's terrified deck of cards, they bobbed up and down, raising and lowering the overall height. The distraction snared Arven and threw his aim off. For others, even the Olmians, the wiggling managed to bring the worm's body in contact with the ball. That contact stopping forward progression and denying the player a scored point.

Meanwhile, their opponents were sitting pretty, all three having easily passed through one or more wickets despite the difficulties, with the team captain's crimson ball poised to clear the fifth wicket in the coming turn.

As one of the Olmians stepped to his ball, Coleman turned to Arven and Fortney with a frustrated mutter. "It's not working. What's Plan B.?"

Arven huffed a sigh. "I don't have a Plan B."

Fortney lowered the cloth he'd been given to manage the bleeding and said, "We're screwed."

Arven's chest tightened as the truth of their situation settled around him. They couldn't get their equipment to ... cooperate, the Olmians were playing far better, and while Fortney gave a good show, the ashen hue of his skin, combined with the way he wove on his feet, warned he didn't have much left in him. They needed the odds to sway in their favor. Or luck. Or maybe even a miracle.

He stepped back as the shortest of the Olmians stepped up to his gold ball. The being curled his upper lip, revealing a broken fang, and sneered as he wedged his mallet between his ball and Fortney's blue-black. His strike skimmed the top of the ball, giving Arven brief hope fate had decided to smile upon them. Yet as it rolled slowly forward, the insect-like creature unfurled by fractions. Two rear legs peeked out and propelled it faster, lining it up precisely and guiding it through two wickets when only one should have been earned.

"Hey!" Arven cried in protest. He flagged the official. "That's unfair advantage!"

The official shook his head adamantly. "There is no rule against a ball projecting itself forward of its own will."

Arven's mouth dropped open. Of its own will? Of course there wouldn't be a rule like that. No *ball* possessed a will to make such a move.

The official blew on his pipe and waved at the field. "Game continues! Play on!"

As soft laughter rumbled between the three Olmians, one moved into position, his stride nothing less than cocky. He struck correctly, knocking his orange ball through another wicket, resulting in the two lead balls having wide open space. Luck wouldn't be helping with an accidental bump from one of Arven's team that might knock either ball out of perfect alignment.

Not that it mattered if the beings serving as balls could throw the game the way they desired.

"Cheating bastards," Coleman muttered under his breath.

Tension gripped Arven as he swallowed and surveyed the field again. Fortney stepped up to take his turn. He braced his foot on the Olmian team captain's crimson ball to hold it in place while he knocked his blue-black away from the obstacle. As Fortney's toe compressed the hard, metallic shell of the insect, Arven blinked. His heart thumped hard, an idea taking root.

While the turn of play passed to another Olmian, Arven backed closer to Coleman and elbowed him subtly in the ribs. "Do you have your official rule book on you?"

Coleman gave him a sideways frown. "Yeah. Why?"

"Let me see it."

His frown deepening, Coleman tugged the book from the interior pocket of his jacket and passed it to Arven. "Why read the rules? They make their own."

Arven chuckled softly. "I'm not interested in what the book says. I'm looking for what it *doesn't* say."

Coleman arched an eyebrow, but before Arven could explain further, the official blew the whistle, signaling play had passed to Arven. The Olmians had gained two more wicket points, and the lead gold ball now rapidly approached the final stake. In ten years of playing croquet, Arven had never seen a game progress so quickly.

Time was running out. No matter what, he needed to make this shot count.

He approached his green ball that sat furthest from the end stake. With a cock of his head, he mentally measured the angle required to roll through the wicket and connect with the opposition's crimson ball on the other side.

To hell with fair play—there wasn't anything fair about moving wickets, balls that propelled themselves along, and rules that didn't exist creating the basis of the game. All he needed was a bonus shot to bring this game to an immediate close and lift his team to victory.

He aimed and swung.

His mallet connected solidly with the green ball. It rolled through the wiggling arch, entering the larger, more open area between wicket two and wicket three. He held his breath as it slowed. Seconds spanned into minutes.

Finally, it came to a stop, a hair's width in front and to the side of the lagging crimson sphere.

It was all Arven could do not to raise his mallet overhead and cheer. He swallowed sheer giddiness and stepped into position. Resting his toe on the crimson ball that interfered with his clear shot, he put his full weight on the hard-shelled insect.

Time suspended for a heartbeat.

Then the metallic shell cracked, and the creature exploded with a sickening *pop*. Its innards coated the bottom of Arven's boot in iridescent yellow.

A shout erupted from the opposition. Arven ignored the furious bellow and took his shot. His ball sailed through the next wicket.

"Halt!" the official bellowed.

The stadium erupted in thunderous noise, condemnation clear in their angry shouts and bellows.

With eyebrows raised in false innocence, Arven turned to the Venrada male. "Is there a problem?"

"You have destroyed Rev'rgeld's ball," the official barked, his scales turning a deeper shade of burnished orange.

Arven smiled broadly. "There are no provisions *against* squashing the opposition's ball."

Eyes wide, the official stared. The crowd fell silent. Arven could almost feel the collective inhale as they held their breath, waiting on the official's verdict.

The official pursed his lips. His gaze dipped to the slimy remains oozing from beneath Arven's boot, then lifted to the scowling Olmians. A rumbling growl emitted from one, who bared his deadly teeth. Four-inch long claws extended from the hand the Olmian captain wrapped around his mallet.

Sweat popped on Arven's brow and moistened his palms. He stared at the official, his heart jack hammering against his ribs. He'd brought the game to a close, but he may well have brought death on their shoulders as well.

The official took a step back. He waved at the opposing team captain. "Rule book!"

Jumping to attention, the Olmian captain dropped his mallet. He fumbled in a cloth bag before hastily producing a torn and tattered, leather-bound novel, which he rushed across the field and thrust into the official's hands.

A tick jumped to life on the official's temple as he thumbed through the book, tearing two fragile pages in the process. He stopped at a dog-eared page, ran a stubby finger down the paragraphs.

When he reached the bottom, he snapped the book shut and his gaze locked with Arven's. Fathomless onyx eyes narrowed with undisguised hate. His words rang over the silence like a horn of war. "The Earthlings … are correct."

A collective gasp echoed through the stadium. Arven slid Fortney a sideways glance, giving in to a slight smile.

"There is no penalty for eliminating a ball," the official barked, turning to address the gathered fans. "The Olmians must maintain three players with three balls. Play cannot proceed. The game is concluded." He turned to give Arven one more loathsome glare. "Earth is the victor."

Arven dropped his mallet and moved to Coleman and Fortney. He grabbed them both by the elbow, snapping them out of their dumbfounded stares, and steered them toward the tunnel. "What do you say to getting out of here and back to the transport ship before they realize there's no rule against killing the opposing team either?"

"I say let's run," Coleman answered as he bolted ahead.

Arven followed, helping Fortney along, not daring to look over his shoulder or stop until they had reached their aircraft and the pilot had lifted into the air and headed for the outer atmosphere. Then, when he was certain they would survive, and Fortney had received appropriate medical attention, he let out a slow, disbelieving laugh.

"What's so funny?" Coleman asked.

"I guess they learned a lesson."

Coleman chuckled. "That the Brits are still the best at croquet?"

Arven shook his head. "Never take fiction literally. Someone's always going to debate the ending." He leaned back and closed his eyes with a grin. They could survive these strange encounters. All they needed to do was think beyond what they understood as normal. And if nothing else, Earth's survivors came from a long tradition of overcoming hardship. His teammates were proof that though they might be temporarily displaced, they would indeed overcome and thrive once more.

IN THEIR GARDEN
by Brenda Cooper

I'm running back through the desiccated woods, going too fast to keep the sticks and branches that have fallen from the trees from cracking under my weight. My skin and mouth are dry. The afternoon sun has sucked all the water from me, and I haven't stopped to drink. The sole of my right boot is thin enough a stone bumps the ball of my foot, and I want to swear, but I keep going even though I don't hear anyone behind me. Not anymore.

I realize I haven't for a while; I got away again. I saw ten friendly travelers this time before I met one who meant me trouble. I know better than to go out alone, and if I get back in one piece, Kelley is gonna kill me.

It's not far now, I can see the wall rising up like a cracked egg, dirty white with grey, the top edges jagged.

I trip over a log, going down sharp on my right knee and catch myself on my hands, scraping my palms. I can see the black soil line from the fire ten years ago, the one that saved us from burning up when everything else around caught fire. The dry trees around me are saplings that tried to grow back, and made it for three or four years before they died of thirst. They're as tall as me.

My breath breaks the silence. I sound like a rabbit before a thin coyote kills it, scared and breathing too hard. I make myself slow down, try to remember what Oskar taught me. Breathe through your nose. Breathe deep in your belly, so you can feel it going out and in.

Slowly.

S l o w l y.

I'm getting there. A hot breeze blows back my hair and helps me feel better.

"Paulie."

I hate it when Kelley calls me that. My name's Paulette. I hate it that she moves so quiet and I'm so loud and clumsy.

She extends her left hand, but doesn't help me up. There's dirt ground into the creases of her hand and stuck under her nails, and it smells wetter and stronger than the dry, cracked earth under my hands. A year or two ago, I would have apologized first, but I manage not to do that this time. I'm almost as tall as her now. I can look down on the graying dark hair she's pulled back and tied with a strip of bark, as if we didn't have anything better. She holds her taser in her right hand, a black oblong that she protects as if it means her life. She leaves it out as we walk back, swinging in her hand, the arc of its movement precise.

My knee is bleeding, but we both ignore that.

Between here and the wall, all the dead woods have been cleared, and we walk on grey and green grass, stuff Kelley had us plant in the moat of cleared ground around our walled garden. The grass thrives out here in spite of the dry, thirsty ground. I don't like to admit it, but she picked well; the spiky, low growth has been alive for two years now, and it creeps back into the forest as we clear it further away.

She doesn't say anything, but I make up her feelings and words in my head anyway. *The walls are safe. You aren't old enough to leave them yet; you might bring people here. You might get hurt, or raped, and die all by yourself. There's men that would take you in and make you trade your body for water and food. It only takes three days without water.* If she was lecturing me instead of staring off, lost in her head, she'd look down at that point and see I have a small canteen clipped to my belt, one of the old ones where the metal's all banged up. *Well, maybe you'd live a week.* She'd look disgusted. *We have all the people we can water now. You might get lost and not come back, and then what? We'd lose all the training we spent on you.*

The only problem with a lecture in your head is you can't fight it. Kelley knows that, and it makes me even madder at her, but it's not like I'm going to be able to explain to the others why I picked a fight with someone who doesn't say anything to me. The other problem is that she's right. I shouldn't want to argue with her in the first place. But I hate living like the world isn't all screwed up when it really is, or maybe we're living like it is all screwed up, and it's starting to get better. That's what I'm starting to believe. Whichever it is, I'll never amount to anything if I stay inside my whole life and work on little things that don't matter with little people who will die behind a wall. The wet, verdant world we live in is a bubble, and I want the real world.

Right before we get to the wall, she turns and looks at me. I expect her to be yelling angry, but what I see in her dark blue eyes is just sadness.

I wonder which one of her plants died this time.

I'm sorry she's sad, but I don't tell her that; I can't show weakness.

The door in the wall is big enough for an army and there's a whiter spot in the wall where Kelley's old boss, James, ripped the sign off in the second year of the drought, and also the second year after I was born. The door opens to let us in, and the two of us are much smaller than an army even though there's a war between us.

Inside, it smells like home and it smells like jail. Like dirt and water and frogs, and faintly, of flowers. Later, in the summer, it will smell more like flowers, but the spring is showier than it is smelly. We pass magenta azaleas whose bloom is just starting to wilt, and in spite of myself I smile when I see three bees on the one plant. Kelley and Oskar both taught me to see the little things, and I can't help but watch out for the plants.

I stop smiling when I notice that the Board of Directors is waiting. All of them. They're sitting in their formal place, on benches in a circle under the sign that used to be above the doors. "Oregon Botanical Gardens." The Board has run us since the first years of climate change, and the half who are still the original members are gray and wrinkled.

There's four Board members, and Kelley makes five. She says, "Paulie, please sit," and gestures to the hot seat—the one for people who are in trouble. I've been here before. The Board's all as old as Kelley; they all remember the world I only see in movies, and they all remember my dad, who's dead now, and they all remember they're the ones who made all the rules and I'm the girl who keeps breaking them.

I wait for them to ask me questions.

They don't. Kelley clears her throat, and keeps her chin up and her voice is as sad as her eyes. "Paulie, we've done everything we know how to do to keep you in here. I can't keep putting us at risk by letting you in and out the door. I've told it not to open for you anymore. So if you sneak out again, you will never be allowed back in."

She can't mean it. She's the one had the most hand in raising me, teaching me. I'm her hope for the future. She wouldn't kick me out.

Tim and Li are the two old men of the Board. Li nods, telling me he supports Kelley. Tim is impassive, but he would miss me. We play chess sometimes in the hour between dawn and breakfast. Sometimes I win, and he likes that. He would never kick me out.

Kay and Shell are the two women on the Board. They're both stone-faced, too, but they might mean it. They're scarier than Tim and Li.

Kelley holds my eyes, and she still looks sad. Usually when she's getting me in trouble she just looks frustrated. "Do you understand?"

"Yes."

"Tell me what will happen if you leave again without permission."

"The door will not let me back in."

"And we will not let you back in," she adds.

Maybe she does mean it. Now her eyes are all wet, even though she isn't really crying yet. Kelley isn't done. I know because no one is moving, and I feel like they're all watching me, probably because they are. Kelley says, "Just so you don't do anything rash, you're confined to the Japanese Garden for a week. Report to Oskar in ten minutes."

She does mean this, except maybe the ten minutes part.

I nod at them all and walk away, keeping my head up. I hate it that they've made me feel small again. In my room, I sweep my journal and two changes of clothes into an old bag, and I brush my hair and my teeth, and put those brushes in the bag, too. I sit on the bed and wait, determined not to be early or even on time.

But Oskar doesn't notice. I walk in the glass box and close the outer door, and wait a moment, then open the inner door. I wonder if these doors are now locked electronically, too, but I don't test them to find out how strict my sentence is. I am inside walls, some glass, and under a plastic sheet roof. The air is heavy with water, although cool. Oskar is nowhere to be seen. When it was finished, the Japanese garden was billed as one of the largest on the west coast. Then the roof was to keep it from getting too wet, instead of too dry.

I negotiate the stepping-stone path, walking through pillows of pearlwort. The cinnamon fern that lines the right wall still has some tender, brownish fiddleheads so I pick them. Maybe it's a form of penance.

The very first of the wisteria blooms are showing purple. Oskar is on the other side of the flowers, between me and the waterfall.

He doesn't turn around for the space of two breaths. He's squatting, bent over, clipping the leaves of a Japanese holly. He is a small man, his skin pallid from the damp air he lives in, his long red hair caught back in a braid that falls down a freckled, white back. The top of his braid is grey. He is only wearing shorts; he likes to garden as naked as the Board will let him. Even his feet are bare. I have always suspected that at night, he goes out with his flashlight and gardens more naked than that. Even though he is almost sixty years old, I think I would garden beside him, with my nipples exposed to the cool night air.

He wouldn't let me, of course. They all treat me like glass.

He stands up and turns toward me. Even though the light is starting to grey to dusk, I can see that his eyes look like Kelley's did. "Why do you run away?"

I lean back against the big cedar column that holds up the wisteria arbor, breathing in the sweet air. "Why don't you ever leave this garden?"

I've never asked him this. Instead of looking startled, he smiles. "Because I am saving the world."

He is lying. He is, at best, saving a tiny part of the world that I can walk across in five minutes. Everyone here thinks small.

I hold out my hand, the one with the fiddleheads in it, and he takes them and says, "See?"

And I don't see at all.

He leads me to the kitchen, which is the only room here with walls that aren't made of waxed paper or bamboo. When we get in, he hands me back the fiddleheads, and I wash them in a bowl full of water and then pour the water into a bin so it can go into the waterfall, where it will be scrubbed clean by the filter plants.

We have everything ready, but before we start to cook, Oskar takes me up to the top of the rock wall at the center of the stroll garden, and we look out toward the ocean. It's too far away to see or hear, but the sun will set over it. He has made a hole in the roof by overlapping the layers of water-capturing plastic so we can see the sunset directly. There are enough clouds to catch the gold and orange a little, but most of the last rays leak up like spilled paint and fade into the blackening sky.

I try to decide whether or not I can use the hole in the roof to climb out of.

After the color starts to fade, there is a hole in time between night and day. Oskar speaks quietly. "I answered you. Will you answer me?"

So that's what he has been waiting for. I guess when you are sixty you have a lot of patience. "We live in a bubble."

He laughs and pokes the plastic, which he can just barely reach from up here. It answers him by rippling, as if it were upside-down water.

I frown. "We do!" I wave my hand at all the roads and people we can't see from here. "In the real world out there, people are travelling and learning and meeting each other. They're struggling. They're taking back the world. This time ..." I haven't really told anyone about this trip yet—I mean, no one had asked. Should I? "I walked the interstate and talked to people on it. Like always. I have my escape routes. They work."

He cocks an eyebrow at me but doesn't say anything.

"Eugene's coming back. There's five thousand people there now—they dug a well deep enough for water and they think they can irrigate. I met two families who were on their way there."

He clears his throat. "A year ago, you told me it had all gone to desert. Not even any grass."

"That's what I heard. But this time I heard different." I paused. "I don't <u>know</u> anything. How could I?"

When he doesn't say anything else, I just keep talking. "A band of singing priests went through last night. They saw five jet airplanes in a day over Portland."

He can't say anything to that. We saw a plane fly over the gardens a few weeks ago, and everybody came out and watched. We hadn't been able to hear its engines, and Kelley had told me it was shaped different that the old jets. What Oskar does say is, "They don't have the right plants. That's what I'm saving for your generation. The bamboo and the bearberry, the astilbe and the peony." He says the names of plants like a prayer, and I imagine him naming the others in his head. The wisteria and the wild fuscia, the fiddlehead and the mountain fern …

"I know what you're saving. You keep telling me about it." It's an old story, how we're saving the genome of the native plants in case the weather ever goes native again. "It's good. I'm glad you're saving it. But that's your dream."

He pretends not to notice my tone of voice. "What your travelers see is the Mediterranean weeds that killed the right plants in California when Father Serra brought them on his donkey. Now that it's warm enough, dry enough, they come here and invade Oregon like they invaded California a long time ago." His face wears a stubborn look that makes him more handsome, wiping some of the wrinkles away with anger. He starts down the rock face as all of the colors of the garden began to fade, and I hear him tell me, "It is your duty to the planet to help."

I sit on the stone until stars swim above the plastic roof, diffused by the beads of water that start gathering there as the evening cools. After my eyes adjust enough to the dark, I come carefully to ground and Oskar and I share cinnamon fern fiddleheads and cattail roots and some jerky from a thin bobcat that had the good grace to jump into our garden before it died of starvation and fed us.

That night, I lie in my bed, separated from Oskar by waxy paper and bamboo, and listen to the roof crinkle in the wind. I'm too young to save the lives of doomed plants for a people that might be doomed, too. The world has changed, and we'll all die if we try to stand still in its current. We have to adapt to the new climate and the new ways, or die here in Oskar's Japanese stroll garden, walking the stone paths until there's not enough water left for the wisteria.

They've taught me the things I need to know to help, and now they want to keep me in a box. But I don't hate them. Oskar's breathing gets even and deep, and it's a comfort.

But not enough. I toss and turn. I can't sleep. I pack up everything I brought and wrap it in a blanket so I can swing it over my shoulder. I write Oskar and Kelley a note. I tell them I love them and I'm going to go save the world, and I'm sorry they won't ever let me back in.

I find Kelley waiting by the door, a thin stick of a shadow that only moves when I open the door, like she's been waiting for that one moment. I'm caught.

Oskar comes up behind me.

He leans forward and gives me a hug and he whispers in my ear. He says, "Good luck."

I blink at them both, stupid with surprise.

He says, "Me and Kelley both knew you'd go. It's time. The Board told us to keep you, because we need young backs and young eyes. But you don't need us. Go find out what they fly those planes with and where they go."

I feel like, thick in the throat and watery. I say, "I'll come back someday."

He says, "If you take long enough, we'll even let you back in."

I go before we all cry and wake the Board up. The stars look clearer out beyond the wall, and the moat of grass muffles my footsteps.

EMPTY NEST
by Tori Eldridge

Shannon yanked another loud strip of duct tape, sealed the last of her cardboard boxes, and glared at her husband. "The complete pirate ship Lego collection, Joel—the bragging rights alone will make our future grandkids the envy of the neighborhood."

Joel sighed. "It won't fit in the garage."

"You say that every time; and every time, I find a place."

Shannon picked up the unwieldy box, secured the roll of tape with her chin, and used her foot to smooth the corner of their youngest son's perfectly made bed—perfectly made because Charlie now lived in a college dorm.

Joel held out his hands. "Give it here. That box must way a ton."

"Nope. I've got it." Although it was awfully heavy for a bunch of tiny plastic blocks. Was Joel right? Had she turned into one of those reality show hoarders?

Joel followed her down the hallway. "What happened to buying that condo in Santa Barbara? New building, great amenities, close to everything? We don't need this old house anymore."

Shannon stopped in the living room, a cozy space with a stone fireplace and a long wooden dining table with bench seating. The boys did everything on that table—homework, art projects, military reenactments with those tiny green army men. She had been right there with them, carving pumpkins, decorating cookies, wrapping gifts. She wanted to do it again.

"All of my best childhood memories were spent in a house just like this one, visiting my grandparents on weekends and holidays. Keeping the traditions alive. Is it so wrong to want to do that for our family?"

"No. But we don't need this house to do it."

"Yes, we do. No matter how old our sons get or how far they travel, this will always be their home. This house. This community. And all the stuff I've been saving? Our grandkids will beg to visit us, not just to see their old-fogey grandparents, but so they can play with the toys their fathers loved and sleep in the beds where their fathers slept."

"Oh, come on, Shannon."

"I'm serious. I want our home to be the place where everyone comes for Christmas."

"So you're going to bribe them with junk?" Joel put up his hands in capitulation and stepped away. "You know what? Do what you want. I'm going to the store."

"In this rain? Seriously?"

He grabbed the keys off the hook. "Want anything?"

Shannon propped the box on her hip and glared. "How about better judgment."

He glanced at the box. "For me or for you?"

Shannon dug her chin deeper into the roll of tape. It wasn't about the toys, not really. It was about the future. Now that both their sons had flown the proverbial coop, what else did they have?

Joel nodded toward the window. "The rain's let up. I'll be back in a couple of hours, depending on the roads." Then he walked out the front door and left Shannon to feather their empty nest.

As much as it pained her to admit, Joel had been right about the garage. Shannon barely had room to squeeze between the rows of boxes, furniture, and sporting equipment.

"Where the hell do I put this?"

She wove through the maze toward the back where Joel had stored the heavy wooden bunk beds. Instead of breaking them apart, she had asked him to leave them assembled so she could use the bunks as shelving. Now they were stuffed from the concrete floor nearly to the ceiling. If she shifted the boxes filled with Brio train tracks, could she squeeze in the Legos?

"Worth a try."

She had just managed to shift and restack when the ground began to tremble, accompanied by a low rumble. She checked her surroundings, as if something in her stuffed garage could possibly be responsible, then remembered a more likely source. Their neighborhood sat along a wide, rough, busy stretch of road that connected Ventura County to Santa Barbara. Everyone drove this stretch faster than they should, especially truck drivers. As a result, the houses of El Nidito—Spanish for The Little Nest—trembled like shivering chicks.

The ground jolted, shoving her forward and smacking her head against the top bunk's base. She cried out in pain and stumbled, struggling to stay on her feet. Damn trucks. She'd have a lump the size of an egg when Joel got home if she didn't get some ice on it.

The walls shook. The rumbling grew louder. The busted garage door behind her rattled in its rusted frame.

What the hell's going on out there, a military invasion?

She grabbed the wooden frame and ducked under the top bunk's platform. She didn't really expect the ceiling lights to fall, but this was an old house and the garage had suffered water damage during last year's storms.

A box of baby blankets Shannon had crocheted for the boys jiggled off a column of picture books and photo albums. And still the shaking continued. Box after box of family history thumped to the concrete and vibrated like a bunch of Mexican jumping beans.

This wasn't a convoy. It was an earthquake. It was …

"Oh my God!"

The deafening noise swallowed her scream as a mountain of earth plowed into her garage, split apart the walls, and shoved a veritable ton of possessions—couches, dressers, file cabinets—as easily as a child shoves wet sand at a beach.

In an instant, everything solid and secure dissolved into a fluid mass that crashed into Shannon and swept her beneath its churning mix.

The first thing she noticed was the sound. It was dead. As if all the joy and hope had been sucked out of life. As if she had been packed in to something so dense the living would never hear the screams of the dead.

Is that what I am? Dead?

She tensed her muscles and tried to move, but there was nowhere to go: She was locked in a fetal position with her elbows trapped between her knees and the stench of earth, rot, and debris assaulting her nose. Not dead. Buried alive. She sucked in air to scream and coughed the grit from her lungs. Panic gripped her chest. She couldn't breathe. She was going to die in this dark scary tomb all alone.

No Charlie. No Adam. No Joel.

Calm down, Shannon. You survived childbirth. You can survive this.

She slowed her breathing and tried again to explore the limits of her confinement. From what she could tell of gravity and pressure, the ground—whatever that meant—was somewhere beneath her left hip and back, which meant freedom was somewhere above her right shoulder. Five feet? Ten? Thirty?

Don't think about that.

Her right hip and shoulder butted up against something hard and flat. Whatever it was must have been braced by something solid because it wasn't pressing down on her. Something else hard was jammed against the soles of her feet.

Where are my shoes? Buried beneath my past.

Shannon tightened the muscles in her thighs and calves, trying to relieve the cramps. If only she had room to unfurl her spine and straighten her legs. She had heard about boys buried in a landslide in India who had survived for days laying side by side in a sliver of space so shallow the roof of it grazed their noses.

Would that have been better?

She scoffed, disturbing the air and sending particles up her nose. Better would have been more than a few cubic feet of space. Better would have been fresh water to drink. Better would have been not getting buried alive under a hillside of mud.

She rubbed the silt from her face with the back of her hands and opened her eyes. What had she hoped to see? Hazy light defining her space? A ray of hope shining through a crack? She would have given anything for even a hint at a path to freedom, no matter how improbable, jagged, or steep. But all she saw was an impenetrable darkness. She was alone. Not the kind of alone she felt when laying on Charlie's empty bed or when Joel had a late night meeting or when Adam was too busy preparing for the MCAT's to talk on the phone. Shannon was utterly and desolately alone.

"Help?" Her voice was small and weak. No one would hear her through the rubble: She could barely hear herself. She sniffed back the tears and tried again. "Hello?"

Come on, Shannon. You can do this.

"I'm down here." She sounded so meek, like a scared little mouse. But that wasn't her. She had faced down bullying teachers and tyrannical coaches. She had organized school fundraisers and served as PTA president for three years in a row.

"Is anyone up there? Help me. Please?" The fear in her voice reminded her of her weakness. Her failure.

"I'm down here." Louder. More desperate. The cry of a woman who didn't have the sense to know she was already dead. That no one would find her until a backhoe shoved her rotted corpse into the street.

"Save me!" Her scream blasted back to her and reverberated in her head, her soul.

And then it was gone.

She wiped the tears from her cheek and arched away from the sharp things stabbing her back. One, in particular, had dug so deep it wouldn't let go no matter how much she curled and arched and scraped. She ran her fist down her chest, around her hip, and up her back, staying as close to her body as she could without dislocating her shoulder. Then she twisted her hand and explored the sore spot on her back with her fingers. The culprit was tiny and familiar.

She wormed her prize back around her body and brought it up to her forehead where she could investigate the shape with both sets of fingers—segmented body, rotating head, hinged legs, and two independently jointed arms. She wasn't alone, after all.

"Hey, buddy. Where's your hat?"

She didn't really know if the Lego figure was Jack Sparrow, but even the thought of that rakish pirate made her feel braver and less alone.

"At least I have you." She touched the sharp edges of his plastic feet and the U-shaped hook of his hands. "Wanna help me dig?"

She shifted her back away from the points and edges, but the entire collection of pirate Legos must be wedged against her back. And were those wooden train tracks against her feet? Had the landslide crushed the wooden bunk beds around her like a padded cage of toys? She should have given them away as Joel had suggested. But then, she wouldn't have this one itty bitty pirate to clutch for comfort.

A sob shuddered through her body, shaking her dark cocoon and raining dusty fragments.

"Stop it, Shannon. Right now." She wheezed in another breath and forced herself to calm the heck down.

Thank God for Brio.

While she regretted saving the tiny plastic blocks, the sturdy wooden train tracks had saved her life. Apparently, the torrent of mud had knocked the bunk beds apart and sent them, her, and the boxes of wooden toys and puzzles on a nightmare ride into an impossibly lucky position.

Lucky?

Shannon scoffed, again. All this so-called luck had done was buy her enough air for regret.

She clenched the tiny Lego figure, squeezed her eyes, and tried not to think of how hard it was to breathe. Panic gripped her chest. She sucked at the dusty air, but there wasn't enough. There would never be enough.

She sucked in her stomach and dragged her fist from her hip to her throat and up her cheek until Jack Sparrow's tiny hand stabbed the swollen lump on her forehead. Then, with just enough room to twitch her fingers, she scraped at the cocoon. Particles fell. She wheezed them in, coughed them out, and cried the grit from her eyes.

She couldn't die here. Not like this. Not without telling Joel she loved him. Not without hugging her boys one more time.

Scrape. Wheeze. Cough. Over and over until the pirate's arm snapped and her nail ripped from her thumb.

Her next sob sucked in mud and memories and death.

—✳—

"Wake up. Can you hear me? Wake up!"

The man was loud. Too loud. Like he was yelling in her ear. Like he wouldn't leave her alone.

Her eyes felt glued together but she fought open the lids.

"She's awake! Oh my God. Honey? It's Joel. I'm here. You're going to be okay."

Shannon tried to wipe the gunk from her eyes, but her hands wouldn't move.

"It's okay, hon. You're strapped to a gurney. But you're okay. It's all going to be okay."

Shannon tried to nod, but the oxygen mask felt so heavy on her face. She wiggled her fingers, hoping Joel would see them moving and hold her hand. He did.

She glanced to the side where their little nest should have been and saw a muddy hill packed with debris. A grave yard of trees, house, furniture, and toys. Shards of a broken life. Clawing fingers frozen mid-grasp from a lifetime of buried treasures.

Joel turned her face toward his. "Don't worry about it. We can rebuild. Just like before. I promise."

She squeezed his hand. Joel—her love, her life. She wanted to tell him it didn't matter. The house was just a shell full of things that had already served their purpose. It wasn't just their sons who had outgrown the nest: They had, too. It was time to move on to the next.

But all of this was too much to say; so she just shook her head and smiled.

She and Joel had lived in El Nidito all of their married lives. But that didn't mean they had to stay. There was a big world out there. It was time for them to leave their cozy little nest and soar.

SHOTGUN WEDDING
by Peter J. Wacks

"Duuuuuudddeeee," Brock shuffled to the side to get a better view through the darkened lot leading to the abandoned convenience mart, looking into the shadows cloaking the mostly empty store. A stealthy form moved quietly along the desolated aisles. "Look at that knock out! Boom. So fine. Uh, uh, yeahhhh."

Jeffrey hung back in the shadows, offering only a noncommittal, "Could be. Hard to tell from here."

"Come on, Bro. You're my wingman. It's the bro-code." Brock glanced back.

Jeffrey had always been shy. He was always at the periphery, leaning on the wall in the gym, watching as everyone else danced. The only place he'd really been comfortable was on the football field. He'd been able to see where he fit in, how he could help. "Yeah. All right. Go get her, I'll pick off any spare hotties that try to block."

Brock fist bumped him. "I knew I could count on you, bro."

Jeffrey idly picked at his frayed varsity jacket. He'd been an all-star player, but only because he had all his teammates to count on. All of them, except of course Brock, had moved on—many of them that fateful homecoming night. With Brock it wasn't that he couldn't have. He just hadn't found the right girl to wear his jacket yet.

They had all been brave enough to go out there and have kids. They had even made it seem like it wasn't that big of a deal. Jeffrey had been in therapy for most of his life, trying to work through overwhelming social anxiety, but it hadn't made him any less fearful. It hadn't always worked out for his teammates, and they had known it might not, but that hadn't slowed them down at all. For him, that potential for failure was crippling. With the rest of the team gone, Brock was his life raft in a sea of fear and self-doubt. His Bro.

Jeffrey watched Brock, scared for him and excited for him, as Brock shuffled a little more to the side and a little forward, intently watching the lone woman go through the shelving.

"Brosef ...," Jeffrey though maybe he would caution Brock, but was interrupted.

"Dude. I'm going for it." Brock glanced around to see if anyone else was around to make a move. They were alone. "Now's my chance. Do or die!"

"Brock! Wait!" Jeffrey froze, again consigned to watch from the shadows.

Brock shuffled across the lot towards the woman, clearly visible through the shattered windows of the store, and when he was close enough, he gave his best pick-up line, "Braaaaaiiiiiiiinnnnnnsssss ... ..."

The woman spun around, surprised but ready, pulling up a shotgun as she pivoted. A quick glance told her what was going on. Pumping the action, she sighted down the twin barrels. One pull of the trigger took Brock down for good. His body collapsed. "Damned zombies." She went over to him and nudged him with her toe.

Stripping down the body, she took his Varsity jacket, quickly slinging it on over the tattered flannel she wore. She quickly finished cleaning off the shelf, jamming foodstuffs into her bag, then ran out into the chilly cloudless night. In the space of three seconds she had left Jeffrey alone and friendless.

Jeffrey sighed, watching her bolt. Brock had always wanted to find the right girl to wear his jacket, joking that it was the only reason he actually joined the team. In a weird way, Brock had finally gotten what he wanted. "I'll miss you, Bro. I'll miss you." The wallflower would survive another day.

The UnEnd

ONCE ON THE *BLUE MOON*
by Kristine Kathryn Rusch

O ne man cradling one large laser rifle stood in the doorway of the luxury suite. Colette sprawled on the threadbare carpet. Her dad had shoved her behind him when he saw the guy at the door, and she had tripped over the retractable ottoman.

Good job, Dad, she nearly said, because that was her default response when he did something stupid, but she didn't say it, because her gaze remained on that rifle. And so did her dad's.

Dad had probably wanted her to run into one of the bedrooms, and that would've made sense if the guy at the door with the rifle hadn't seen her, but he had, and then he had said something softly and beckoned at someone else.

Mom was standing beside the door, actually threading her hands together. Colette felt both a growing fear and a growing irritation. Fear, because she had probably caused this. Day One, she had swiped one of those stupid tablets that the concierge on this level used to keep track of everything on the ship.

The lower levels, without the suites, actually used holographic screens for the guests, or some lazy person could call up a holographic face to make suggestions.

But here, real people were actually in the passengers' business, as if the *Blue Moon* was still one of the most luxurious starliners in the solar system.

It wasn't luxurious. It *had been* luxurious maybe in the Good Old Days when her grandparents had been kids. Dad said the ship had a "mystique" whatever that meant, but Colette had investigated the ship on her own, and found the ad that had probably gotten Dad's attention:

Travel in luxury at one-thousandth the price!

Apparently, if you didn't care what kind of cargo the ship carried, then you could have a luxury suite on your trip from wherever to wherever. Theirs was from a starbase beyond Saturn to some place called Montreal because that was the last boarding school that could handle someone like her.

All of this had been Mother's idea, even though all of it had been Colette's fault.

Another man arrived at the door. He was small, barely taller than Colette, and she hadn't reached her full growth yet. (Mother had said that she would when puberty hit, which could be Any Minute Now.) The man had glittering black eyes, a leathery face, and thin lips that quirked upward when he saw her.

"A kid," he said, as if he was surprised.

Colette almost said, *I'm not a kid!* and then thought the better of it. Maybe she'd get a pass on stealing that tablet. Children couldn't be responsible for their actions after all.

"I didn't realize there was a kid on board," the man said, musing. "I didn't think children were allowed on vessels like this."

Yeah, Colette had seen that regulation too, and she knew that her dad had gotten it waived. They needed to get to Earth Yesterday or so Mother had said. It was never hard for Dad to get things waived.

The family didn't have money—*yet* Mother said—but they had access to it, and they had some kind of influence that her dad would flash around whenever he needed it, as, apparently, they had needed it to get on this ship to get Colette to Montreal to the boarding school before the beginning of the semester.

Which seemed stupid to her, because she had started other schools in the middle of the year, and had always, always outperformed everyone in her class. It never mattered whether she arrived with one month left or five, she could work her way around the entire system and do better than anyone else, once she figured out what was needed.

"Take them," the guy with the intense eyes said, gesturing at Colette's parents.

Then he took one step into the suite, and looked down at Colette.

"You, little girl, can stay here, if you'll be good." He actually spoke in some kind of fake sweet voice, as if she would be fooled by his tone, even though he had just ordered some guy with a rifle to take her parents.

Colette opened her mouth so she could tell the guy with the intense eyes where he could stick his "good," and then she saw her dad's face. It was drawn and tense.

Her mother was shivering. Her mother often looked terrified over stupid stuff, but she never shivered.

And her dad—tense was not his normal way of dealing with anything.

He frowned at Colette as their gazes met.

"She'll be good," her dad said to the guy, but didn't look away from Colette. "My daughter, she's perfect."

Colette actually felt tears prick at her eyes. Her dad never said that, not with feeling. He was always telling her how impossible, intractable, and stubborn she was, how she could do better if she only settled down. And sometimes he would despair, and say,

Colette Euphemia Josephine Treacher Singh Wilkinson Lopez, you have every opportunity and you're always the smartest person in the room. Why are you constantly throwing that away?

His disappointment pissed her off, and made her work harder at doing the best she could *and* causing trouble. He never noticed the best, but he always noticed the trouble.

She'd been waiting for that *perfect* word from him her whole life. And now he said it, to some guy with intense eyes and another guy holding a laser rifle, and the weird part was, Dad seemed to mean it.

Then he really scared her, because he mouthed, *I love you*, and took a deep breath and said to the guy with intense eyes, "What do you need from us?"

Dad sounded calm, even though he clearly wasn't. Well, clearly to Colette, probably not to the two men.

"I need you to go with him," the guy with the intense eyes said, nodding toward the guy with the laser rifle. Not saying his name, either, which was a bad sign. "We can restrain you and take you if need be."

Dad gave Mother a hard look, and she swallowed visibly, then nodded.

"No restraints needed," Dad said. Then he and Mother walked out of the door as if being taken by guys with laser rifles was an everyday thing.

The guy with intense eyes gave Colette one last glare.

"Be good and you'll be fine," he said. Then he closed the suite door—and stupid idiot that he was—turned on the parental controls.

Which she had already monkeyed with Day One, in case anyone got Ideas. Her parents knew better than to use something that simple on her, but the concierge and the ship's crew didn't.

And neither did the guy with the intense eyes.

She waited a good thirty seconds before moving, and then she went into her room and lay on the bed, because she knew that would be what the guy with the intense eyes would expect—some kid, paralyzed by fear.

She'd show him paralyzed.

She'd show him fear.

Once she had him all figured out.

⟹ ✳ ⟸

A kid.

Alfredo Napier thought kids weren't allowed on ships like the *Blue Moon*. Adults knew the dangers they were undertaking when they traveled on a ship like this, but kids? They were under the age of consent, and even if their parents thought it was a good idea, the Starrborne Line, which ran these old ships, did not allow kids on the Titan-Plano to Earth-Houston run.

The company's explanation was pretty simple: in order to make good time on that run, it had to travel older, lesser used routes, not as well policed, and without as many stops or amenities.

In reality, the route these ships traveled was the only route that allowed hazardous cargo. If a ship got into trouble out here, it was twice as likely to be abandoned as it was to be rescued.

Napier had always taken that fact into consideration when he chose his targets.

He also appreciated the fact that everyone on board had signed a waiver, protecting the Starrborne Line from liability should something untoward happen. Not that he really cared if the passengers had given permission for their own deaths on an ancient ship without the proper protections against certain kinds of hazardous cargo, but because he almost felt as if the passengers had given him permission to run his own business the way he wanted to.

A kid.

He shook his head as he hurried to the bridge. A kid changed everything and nothing.

She'd seen him. She'd seen *them*. But she was what—ten? Twelve?—young enough that no one would believe anything she said. So all he had to do before they blew the ship was put her into one of the lifepods and jettison her with quite a bit of force toward the Martian run. If she survived, then good, and if she didn't, she would die on the pod, not in his custody on the ship.

And he wouldn't have to think about her.

That was the problem with kids.

They haunted a man in the middle of the night, interfering with his sleep.

He made a small fortune doing his work.

The last thing he needed was to second-guess himself. The last thing he needed was to lose even more sleep.

Colette sat up on the bed. She already hated this room. Square, boxy, brown, the bed one-tenth as comfortable as the bed she had had at her last school, she felt like calling up some paint program and trying to permanently deface the walls.

Maybe if she was trapped in here forever. In the meantime, she had the tablet.

Colette had stolen the tablet because it had basic access to every single part of the ship. No one had figured out she swiped it; the stupid concierge had believed he had misplaced it, and they had issued him a new one, since the first thing Colette had done was shut off the locator on the tablet itself. Basic Survival Thievery 101.

The second thing Colette had done was taken that basic access and amped it up to full access in every shipboard department she could. The only areas she couldn't access were navigation, engine controls, life support, and all of those other things that someone could sabotage and kill people with.

She would need Captain's Codes for those areas. Or at least senior officer codes.

In the weeks that she'd had the tablet, she hadn't been able to crack those codes. She had been beginning to think she couldn't access any of that important stuff from a passenger cabin because of location controls. But if she got to the bridge, she might have been able to do it.

The option of going to the bridge was gone now.

She needed to remain confined to quarters until she figured out how to spoof the system, and make it *think* she was confined to quarters while she roamed the ship.

Before she did any of that, though, she activated the automated distress signal. Every tablet had access to the distress signal, and, she suspected, so did all of those holographic concierges on the lower levels.

She hoped someone else had activated the automatic distress signal as well, but she also had taken a measure of the guy with the intense eyes. He looked like someone who didn't let a lot go by him.

He had probably tampered with access to the automated distress system before he had started into the passenger cabins. Because Colette and her parents hadn't realized something had gone wrong on the ship until the guy with the laser rifle had shown up.

She doubted any other passenger noticed something wrong either. People were pretty self-involved on this ship, which had worked to her favor, until today.

She took a deep breath. She was going to pretend that today was no different than any other day, because if she thought about her parents, she would panic, and panicking would get her nowhere.

So she scrolled through the back end of the tablet, the stuff hardly anyone outside of engineering knew how to use, and found the manual distress signal.

She had hoped it would be relatively easy to operate. Instead, it contained an array of choices, many more than she expected. She scrolled through all of them, until she narrowed it down to three: she could notify other ships; she could notify specific rescue units throughout the solar system; or she could notify a single person.

She had no single person to notify, and if she notified other ships randomly, she would probably notify Intense Eyes Guy's ship as well as some other passing vessel.

All of the choices required the *Blue Moon's* exact location to be put manually. Which made sense, since she was asking for a rescue, and the system had no way of knowing that the rescue was needed because people with guns had boarded the ship, rather than some systemic breakdown somewhere off the beaten path.

Colette dug, found the ship's exact coordinates, discovered that they were deep inside the Asteroid Belt, and that made her stomach jump. Right in the middle of nothing at all.

And, to her unpracticed eye, the ship looked like it wasn't moving at all.

She didn't like it.

Focus, focus, focus.

She made herself go through all of the components of the secondary manual signal slowly, entering the exact coordinates of where the ship was right now, which route it had taken, but not the route it was expected to take. Because she didn't know if Intense Eyes Guy was stealing the ship itself.

She set the secondary signal to repeat in half-second bursts, and programmed it to go only to the rescue units on Mars, the Moon, and Earth.

Her heart thumped as she activated the secondary signal—and prayed it would go through.

Napier made it to the bridge just in time to see the distress signal beacon activate. The damn thing glowed red on the navigation console. He smashed the blinking light, then pressed the comm chip embedded into the pocket on his chin.

"One of those idiot crew members activated the automated distress signal. Someone jettison the thing off the ship, and send it closer to Mars."

He had to explain where he wanted the beacon to go, because on a previous job, the genius who had taken a similar order had ripped the beacon off the ship, and let still-active beacon tumble into nearby space.

That hadn't ended well for anyone, although Napier, as was his habit, managed to avoid the authorities, more through luck than anything else. The genius who hadn't thought the order through, however, wouldn't make that mistake again.

Since his luck had run out.

Napier's hadn't, yet, but he didn't like how this particular job was going. He really didn't like this bridge. It was narrow and had a high ceiling made of two different materials—one clear, so that the bridge crew could see the starlight (or probably show it to passengers who paid a premium). The other material was an exterior cover that fitted over the clear material and gave the bridge double protection against anything and everything.

It also made the bridge pretty easy to find. Napier had originally thought of sending a contained burst torpedo into the bridge, taking out the bridge crew in one quick action, but he hadn't done it. Because he had done his due diligence and discovered that the *Blue Moon*, as an ancient passenger liner, didn't have a secondary bridge like most cargo ships.

There had been an actual possibility that the explosion would have destroyed all of his access to the ship's systems, and he didn't have an engineer on his team. If the engineering sector on this ship had been as old as the ship herself, then Napier would truly have been screwed.

Of course, someone had updated the entire interior. The passenger cabins had gotten a facelift, but the rest of the ship had been completely rebuilt—and off-books too.

At least the weapons system on this ship hadn't been upgraded. It should have been before someone got the brilliant idea of transporting a Glyster Egg on this vessel. Because the Glyster Eggs were the holy grail for people like him. If he had a Glyster Egg, he could raid ships to his heart's content.

Of course, no one was supposed to know that the Egg was even on board. He had only found out because he had paid informants in every single outpost that launched vessels into this part of the solar system. If he managed to get his hands on the Egg, the informant who sent him here would get a really big bonus.

If.

Napier hadn't been able to find out if the Egg was actually on board, and if it was, where it was. Each cargo bay was supposed to list the cargo on its exterior manifest, but ships like this, which carried hazardous cargo, rarely did. That's why he needed the internal cargo manifest, the one only the senior officers got to see.

And that, Napier was beginning to realize, was going to be harder than he expected.

The automated distress signal shut off after five minutes. The tablet listed the distress signal as damaged, but Colette suspected someone had tampered with it. She had expected that.

She also figured, given that laser rifle, that the bad guys had come for something in particular. She was guessing, based on the history she'd studied (trying to keep up with Dad), the entertainment she consumed (trying to ignore Mother), and the crime reports she'd examined on the sly (trying to learn new tricks) that these guys weren't here to steal the ship. If they had been, they would have locked every passenger in their cabins and dealt with the passengers once the ship left the established shipping routes.

Colette figured they were taking something from it. If they had planned on kidnapping a passenger—well, first, they wouldn't have come to a ship this low-rent, and second, they would have known that a kid was on board. She was on the passenger manifest, after all, even if her age wasn't alongside her name.

But if the bad guys were trying to take people, they would have wanted to know who they were up against amongst the passengers—or, at least, *she* would have wanted to know.

She knew it was a fallacy to expect every criminal in the universe to be one-tenth as smart as she was. Dad always said that if they were smart, they wouldn't be criminals, and Colette agreed with him when it came to crimes of opportunity, but the bands that worked the shipping routes—or rather, the bands that *successfully* worked the shipping routes—had to have a lot of smarts because they terrorized the routes, and never seemed to get caught.

So she wasn't going to get anywhere by underestimating the intelligence of the people who had taken over the ship.

Hazardous cargo would seem like a no-no for these people, but not all hazardous cargo made everyone sick. Some hazardous cargo was dangerous in the wrong hands.

On her very first day with the tablet, she had searched through the cargo manifest, trying to find whatever it was that had knocked the per-passenger price on this vessel so low. When she had seen the ad for this vessel, and its "reasonable" prices, she wanted to see what kinds of diseases Dad had signed her up for.

She had planned to throw that in his face when he left her at the boarding school in Montreal. She had even planned the speech:

Not only are you confining me to some Earth backwater, but you're guaranteeing that I will die of [insert disease here] at [insert average age here].

It had taken her three days to find the correct cargo manifest, and another three hours to break into it. To her great disappointment, she hadn't found any disease-creating items listed. Instead, she found a tiny weapon that shouldn't have been on a ship like this at all.

That weapon, called a Glyster Egg, should have been in layers and layers of protective material with a protected cargo seal inside a protected cargo unit inside a protected cargo bay. Instead, the Glyster Egg was in some kind of box that "in theory" protected it from any kind of accidental detonation.

The thing was the theory wasn't that grand. She'd found at least three other ships that had been victims of accidental detonation of Glyster Eggs in the five years since the stupid things had been on the market (or invented or stolen or released by some dumb government or *something*). Those ships had floated dead in space, in one case for a year, before anyone found it—because the stupid thing had been designed to disable all the functioning systems on spaceships with one simple movement.

A handful of other weapons could do that, but none were small like the Egg, and none had an actual targeting system. So if she wanted to—if she could get out of this stupid room without being noticed, and if she trusted herself to touch the Egg, and if she could figure out how to use it, and if she knew exactly where the bad guys' ship was—she could enter the coordinates into the Egg, then squeeze the Egg's activation system, and voila! the bad guys' ship wouldn't work at all, ever again, end of story.

But she didn't like all those ifs-ands. She couldn't quite calculate the odds—there were too many variables—but she had an educated hunch that she would be better off trying to get to the bridge or engineering or somewhere and wrest the control of the *Blue Moon* from Intense Eyes, before ever trying to activate the Egg and make it work *for* her instead of *against* her.

Of course, she didn't actually know if he was here for the Egg. But he was stupid if he wasn't. Because if she were a big bad thief who preyed on ships coming through the Asteroid Belt, *she* would steal the Egg.

That was assuming that Intense Eyes had her brains. She wasn't sure he did. Yeah, he had taken over the ship, but he hadn't known about Colette, which meant he hadn't researched the passengers, which meant he didn't know that he was about to get into really bad trouble—if even one of her distress signals had gotten through.

Those odds she could calculate.

Because as of this moment, no one had noticed the manual distress signal.

So it was still broadcasting.

Which meant that help might actually be on the way.

The automated distress signal, half-choked off, arrived at the 52nd Mars Relay Station. Two versions of the same automated distress signal, intact, arrived at the 13th Moon Relay Station. No versions of the automated distress signal made it to any of Earth's Relay Stations, at least not in recognizable form.

Within thirty seconds of the automated distress signal's arrival, the 13th Moon Relay Station evaluated the signal, and determined that the distressed ship was located in the Asteroid Belt. The ship had an old registration, marking it as inconsequential, even though the ship was owned by Treacher,

Incorporated, a large entity that had funded many Martian building projects. Treacher also had ties to three different Martian governments.

But the ship had taken an unusual route, never traveled by ships with highly insured passengers or cargo. The route was by definition dangerous, and anyone on board would have signed a waiver agreeing to rescue only in financially advantageous circumstances.

The age of the ship, the route, and the lack of insurance did not make this a financially advantageous circumstance.

But Treacher's ownership did flag the system, so the 13th Moon Relay Station followed protocol for difficult and iffy rescues in the Asteroid Belt. The 13th Moon Relay Station sent copies of the automated distress signal to its counterpart on Mars.

Then the 13th Moon Relay Station sent the automated distress signals to its archives.

No one on the Moon even knew that an automated distress signal had arrived, been examined, and passed back to Mars. And no one on the Moon would have cared.

What Colette had to do was buy time. If the bad guys were on the *Blue Moon* to take the Egg, then she had to hide the Egg from them.

The problem was … what if she was wrong? What if they were here for something else?

She didn't have a lot of control with this particular tablet. She was working to get more access, but she needed to spoof her own position here in the suite, and that would take time.

She tried to delete all of the cargo manifests, and couldn't delete any of them. She didn't have the clearance.

She sat cross-legged on her bed for a good minute, trying to figure out how to stay one step ahead of these very bad people.

She had to convince them that they were in trouble on this ship, and she had to keep the Egg from them.

Those were two different tasks.

She called up the passenger manifest to see if she could locate anyone else who might be able to help her. She flipped manifest to its location-based listings, and saw, without looking at names, that all of the passengers were in the large buffet, scattered around the room, as if they were sitting at tables.

All of the passengers except her.

Before she could stop herself, she flipped the data again, saw her parents' names and personal shipboard identification numbers. Then she flipped back to location-based information. Two little green dots, with her parents shipboard identification numbers, blinked from the side of the buffet, near the kitchen. They weren't moving, but then, neither were the other passengers.

Colette didn't want to even guess what that meant. She hoped they were all sitting quietly, depressed at the circumstances, rather than being unconscious or injured or dea—

Focus, focus, focus.

She opened the tablet to the cargo manifest. The correct one. She took the contents, copied it into another file, marking that new file *Sanitation Refill Schedule.* Then she opened one of the cargo manifests without the hazardous materials, and copied the data from that manifest, and pasted it over the original manifest.

Then she simply saved it. When she opened it again, the information on the Egg had vanished.

And that had been too easy. Someone should have realized just how simple it was to make mistakes in this system, not that it was her problem.

But the bad guys might figure that out. So, she moved the cargo manifest out of its normal file and into the food service files. Some searches would bring up the cargo manifest, but someone would have to know what kind of search to conduct.

She needed to figure out how to distract the bad guys until the rescue ship got here.

And she needed to be able to do so from inside this suite.

For a moment, Napier had thought he found one of the cargo manifests, and then it had vanished on him. He had a device that easily broke the surface codes on the bridge's systems, but the device didn't give him what this system called the Captain's Access Codes. For that, Napier needed five forms of physical i.d., which he had planned for.

He already had his men getting that for him.

In the meantime, he searched. He felt a slight time pressure, but knew that because of the distances out here, he had more time on this job than he would have had he been closer to Mars or Earth's Moon. He had an internal clock, and at the moment, it allowed him to feel some leeway.

He paused his search for the cargo manifest to find a way to retract the captain's chair. The damn thing rose in the middle of the narrow bridge like a throne, and he wanted it gone. It irritated him, particularly since it turned to offer him a seat every time he brushed against it (which was much too often for his tastes).

He finally found the controls for the chair, but as he did, he also saw something else. A blinking emergency light, buried deep in the manual controls.

He touched the light with a bit of hesitation, worried that he would activate the wrong system.

Instead, he found that a second distress signal had been sending for more than an hour. Why a ship like this would have more than one distress signal, and why this one wasn't attached to the beacon, he had no idea.

Shutting it off was a simple matter. He toggled the controls to the off position. The system didn't even argue.

For a moment, he wondered about the secondary signal. Then he decided it was probably part of the automated distress signal's system, not something he had to worry about.

He needed to spend his time finding one tiny piece of cargo, in six cargo bays stuffed with material ultimately bound for Earth.

He had a dozen people on his team, but that wasn't enough to search all of those cargo bays. And he was searching for the Glyster Egg, which was a delicate system in and of itself. He had no idea if his own equipment would accidentally activate it.

He didn't want to take that risk, not this far out. What if the Egg had a broadcast feature he didn't know about? What if it not only disabled this starliner, but his ship as well?

That was something he didn't want to suffer through.

So he needed to proceed with caution.

And he needed to find the cargo manifest.

Something in the automated distress signal that arrived at the 52nd Mars Relay Station activated the review process.

The review system sent a notification to the starbase beyond Titan where the *Blue Moon* originated, asking for a passenger manifest. Calculations needed to be made. The system needed to do a proper cost-benefit analysis of the rescue. Could the rescue vehicle arrive on time? Could it save the ship/cargo/passengers? Were the lives/cargo/ship worth the cost of the rescue?

Such an analysis could not be done without passenger names and histories.

As the system waited, the message from the 13th Moon Relay Station arrived. Now, the Martian system noted that the Moon would not conduct a rescue or even contemplate one, should one be needed.

Only the Martian system would take the risks involved, which changed the calculations yet again.

The system was about to reject the rescue request, even without an answer from the starbase, when several manual distress signals arrived, evenly spaced from each other.

But each manual distress signal contained a signature, proving that someone on board the *Blue Moon* had crafted that distress signal by hand.

That someone was named Colette Euphemia Josephine Treacher Singh Wilkinson Lopez.

Treacher.

A quick analysis showed that Colette Euphemia Josephine Treacher Singh Wilkinson Lopez was a distant Treacher relative, not involved in the corporation or in any local governments, but still on tap to receive a portion of the Treacher Trust when she came of age.

A second Treacher was on board as well, another woman, also in line to receive an inheritance from the Treacher Trust.

Treachers were protected throughout the solar system because of the family's great involvement in many businesses and governments from Mars to Saturn and maybe beyond.

The review's purpose changed. The routine review no longer had relevance.

Two Treachers on board a ship, any ship, anywhere within the reach of Mars Rescue Services, required an immediate and adequate rescue response.

The information got forwarded to Mars Vehicle Rescue (Space Unit), along with all available information, including the amount of time lapsed.

Given the hazards of travel through that part of the Asteroid Belt, and given the kinds of emergencies that happened there, the time lapsed changed the chances of success from more than eighty percent to less than fifty percent.

Which meant, given the costs of rescues that far from Mars itself, all Mars Vehicle Rescue (Space Unit) could spare would be one large rescue vehicle, with a crew of twenty.

The systems in Mars Vehicle Rescue (Space Unit) had determined likely outcomes, and decided that the most possible outcome was this: The rescue vehicle would arrive to find a destroyed ship, dead passengers, and no rescue needed.

But the presence of Treachers meant the possibility of lawsuits. The possibility of lawsuits meant that it would be good to get the DNA of the dead Treachers, just to prove that their portion of the Treacher Trust was now available for some other distant relative.

Mars Vehicle Rescue (Space Unit) did not want to be liable for anything to do with the Treacher Trust, so the rescue ship numbered MVR14501, but known to its crew as *Sally*, left its docking ring on the way an out-of-the-way shipping route in the Asteroid Belt.

Instead of a crew of twenty, the *Sally* had only ten crew members. If they had had to wait for the remaining ten crew members to arrive from their scheduled time off, departure would have been delayed another three hours, something the system calculated it did not have.

It didn't matter that the crew was small; the chances of success were small too.

The crew of the *Sally* looked at the rescue attempt as a drill, not an actual job.

And that was a mistake.

=※=

The stupid passenger identification system seemed hardwired to the life reading of that particular passenger. Colette didn't remember signing up for that but she was a "minor" who "had no rights" without "suing for them" so she had no idea what her parents had done to guarantee her passage on this ship.

Whatever it was, she couldn't spoof the system and if she couldn't spoof the system, she couldn't get out of the suite.

She stood because her butt was falling asleep on the bed's hard surface. She moved the tablet onto a little holder built into the wall, and wished she could use a holoscreen instead.

Something pinged in her brain about holoscreens, but she let that marinate. Because what she really wanted to do was get the tablet to tell her where the bad guys were, and so far, the tablet was refusing.

Well, it wasn't refusing, exactly, because that would have meant it had some kind of sentience, which it did not. What it was doing was refusing to acknowledge their life signs, since they were not paying passengers.

Apparently, crew, staff, and service personnel at any kind of starbase stop were beneath the notice of the concierge level. She dug into the systems, and tried to see if she could get a reading on the non-paying passengers, even if they only appeared as some kind of shadowy coordinates on the ship's map.

She couldn't, any more than she could detach her own heartbeat from the passenger manifest, but she could reset the holographic concierges on every single floor.

That discovery made her heart race. She couldn't reset the concierges to "forget" anyone, which was probably good from the ship's point of view, but she could set up the concierges to interact with every human being they encountered.

She dug deeper into the controls. She could actually set the concierges up to follow anyone unregistered with the ship. Some of the more sophisticated concierges could follow the unregistered person until someone in authority dealt with them, even if that meant following that person off the ship.

Well, she couldn't get out of here and harass the bad guys herself, not without getting caught, and she couldn't get the Egg and figure it out without getting caught, but she could do this.

She only hoped it would be enough.

=✳=

Napier was about to contact his second, Grizwald, when the man walked onto the bridge. He was larger than most of Napier's crew, but size had its uses, especially when it came to intimidation.

And intimidation wasn't the only thing Griz was good at.

Griz handed Napier a small box containing everything he needed to access the Captain's Codes.

"We got some problems," Griz said.

"No kidding," Napier said and opened the box. It had the skin gloves, and some other bits and pieces of the Captain himself, no longer bloody, but cleaned up so that Napier could use them.

"I mean it." Griz's tone was harsh. *"Look."*

Napier frowned with annoyance, then looked in the direction that Griz was pointing. A head floated behind him.

For a moment, Napier thought maybe Griz had brought him the Captain's actual head, but he hadn't.

"What the hell?" Napier asked.

Griz slid his hand toward the head, and his hand went through it. The head vanished for a half a second, then returned.

"You are unauthorized," it said. "If you do not leave this area, you will be subject to discipline."

"Discipline?" Napier asked Griz. "From who?"

Griz rolled his eyes. "The crew," he said.

Well, that wouldn't happen. Part of the crew was trapped in the so-called brig (really, two emergency cells that would get troublemakers to the next base) guarded by three of his people, and the rest of the crew was piled in an airlock, awaiting Napier's order to have the bodies join the rocks floating around this asteroid belt.

"So what's the problem?" Napier asked.

"It's following me," Griz said. "And it won't go away."

"That's not a problem," Napier said by which he meant, *that's not a problem I need to deal with right now.*

"It's blocking access to crew quarters and other parts of the ship," Griz said. "Once it started following me, everything shut down when I got near it."

Napier felt a surge of anger rush through him. "So you came *here?*"

He glanced at the bridge controls, and sure enough, they had all shut down. He would have to redo all of his work.

"Get out," he said to Griz. *"Now."*

"You both must leave," the head said to Napier.

"And take that thing with you," Napier said to Griz.

Griz shook his own head, then scooted around the holo-head, and went out the door. The head remained for some reason Napier did not understand.

"You must leave," the head said to him.

"Not happening," Napier said, and opened the box. The ship required a minimum of five forms of physical identification from an officer to access certain parts of the controls.

The most basic was active fingertip control, which the ship would test to see if the finger was warm, attached, and belonging to a crew member.

Napier had stolen a number of items over the years that made warm and attached and belonging into three different things. The ship would think that his hands were the Captain's hands.

"You must leave," the head said to Napier.

"And you're going to get shut down," Napier said, as he placed his index finger on the bridge control board.

"Not happening," the head said, mirroring Napier's earlier response, which worried him more than he wanted to think about.

He decided not to look at the stupid head any more.

Instead, he went back to work.

Halfway to the coordinates in the Asteroid Belt, Dayah Rodriguez, who was in charge of the *Sally's* rescue team, finally got a reading on the *Blue Moon*.

The ship didn't seem to be in physical trouble, although it hadn't moved from the location cited in the distress signal. But one small ship floated around it, constantly bouncing and shivering the way that some of the illegal vessels did to avoid standard tracking units.

Fortunately, *Sally* didn't use standard tracking.

A jolt of adrenaline shot through Rodriguez.

She suddenly realized they were understaffed and perhaps lacking the proper amount of firepower.

"Speed up," she said to Hamish Sarkis, who was piloting the *Sally*. "And send a message back to headquarters. We have pirates. And if we want to catch them, we're going to need some help."

They were going to need a lot more than help.

They were going to need a lot of luck as well.

Now, Colette was obsessing about her parents. Because they still hadn't moved. No one had. Why weren't the passengers fighting back? What was going on?

She was pacing around the bed, trying to figure out if breaking out of this stupid suite was worthwhile.

And then her breath caught.

She had set up the concierges to follow the bad guys.

She just needed to locate the concierges. When she found them, she would know where the bad guys were.

Which would help her escape, but then what?

She flopped on the bed, grabbed the tablet, and thought about it.

She had access to a lot of things on this little device. Maybe some of them would help her slow those bad guys down.

The head was proving to be a problem. The thing stuck to Napier like some kind of weird glue. He couldn't shut it out of the bridge, because every time he closed the door on the head, it floated back inside.

And every time he tried to use some piece of the captain to provide identification, the head stated, quite calmly, "You are not Captain Ekhart. You lack his height, weight, and appearance. I have instructed the system to remain unfooled."

Unfooled. What kind of word was that, anyway?

It was as annoying as the head was.

To make matters worse, Napier's internal clock was warning him that he was almost out of time for this job.

He needed that Egg, but he couldn't access anything.

His personal comm vibrated. He pressed it, and Johnston, the only member of his team still on the ship, said, "We just got a ping from the security system. We've been scanned, by something with an official government signature."

Napier didn't even have to ask what that meant. It meant that either a security vehicle or a rescue ship was on the way. Or something larger and more important—some kind of government transport—was coming to or traveling along this route.

Which meant he was done, if he didn't find that manifest right now, if he couldn't get the Egg right now.

He reached for the head, and his hand went right through it. Had that head belonged to a human, it would've been slammed against the wall, until it shattered.

"You are unauthorized," the head said, obliviously. Clearly it had no idea that he would have killed it if he could. "You do not have access. You are not Captain Ekhart. You must leave."

Napier glared at it. The thing looked like it made eye contact with him, but he could see through it, so it probably didn't.

But had it sent the information to the authorities?

He had broken into a number of ships similar to the *Blue Moon*, but never one of this vintage. Sometimes older ships had technologies he hadn't seen or even imagined. Things attempted and then discarded.

Like annoying heads that floated after people and yelled at them. This couldn't have been a popular feature.

"Can you figure out who scanned us?" Napier asked Johnston.

"Been trying. I have no idea." Johnston was good with all of the equipment. Not great, but better than some of the idiots Napier had brought with him. Those idiots were good for scaring civilians, and that was what he'd been using them for. And for figuring out how to put an entire room full of people into a deep sleep, so they wouldn't fight back.

"I can't find them with our scanners," Johnston was saying, "but here's what I'm worried about. They're coming from Mars, and they scanned us far enough out that we can't read them. So they have powerful equipment and they're coming fast. There might be a whole bunch of them, for all I know."

If Napier didn't get out of here now, he might actually get caught. He slammed his fist on the captain's chair that he had forgotten to retract. It bounced and jiggled toward him, almost as if he offended it, which was a lot more satisfying than trying to grab that stupid head.

"Hey, you," he said to the head, "who did you notify that we had arrived?"

"I sent a message to those in charge, as per my programming," the head said primly.

"And who might those in charge be?" Napier asked, hoping that maybe he could buy some more time if the head identified them.

"I went through proper channels. You have accessed the bridge without authorization. You have attempted to impersonate Captain Ekhart. You will be dealt with firmly."

He wasn't getting any information from the head, and he wasn't going to be able to find that Egg.

He had to think this through. He was good at cutting his losses when he needed to, but usually he had a bit more to show for a job this complicated.

Still, running was a lot better than getting captured.

He also needed to get rid of all of the evidence that pointed to him. A ship full of people who could identify him. Those head-things. Who knew what they had taken from him and his team? DNA? Imagery? Everything?

Now he was going to have to change his plan. He couldn't remote detonate the *Blue Moon* because he didn't have access to the controls. He would have to use regular explosives, the kind with their own timers.

They were a little less reliable than a remote detonation, but they would have to do.

Then his fist clenched.

The kid.

He thought of her for a moment, sprawled on that floor, looking helpless and lost as Mommy and Daddy got carted away.

He didn't dare jettison her from the *Blue Moon*, not now, not with the authorities (or whomever) closing in.

This job was really screwed up. He was going to have to do things he didn't want to do, for no real payoff at all.

He punched the retractable captain's chair one last time, then shoved his way past the head as he stalked off the bridge. Or, rather, tried to shove. Because the head moved with him.

How come he inherited the head from Griz? Because the head figured Napier was the greater threat?

Didn't matter. He had tell his team to dump the explosives near the passengers and surviving crew. There was no time for finesse.

He and his team needed to be on board his ship within fifteen minutes, so they could be as far away from the *Blue Moon* as possible when it exploded.

As far from the Egg as possible.

Because he had no idea what kind of damage it would do.

Colette tried to work faster, to see what else she could find, what she could use.

She had almost given up when she found something weird.

Apparently, passenger liners from the old days had a lot of theft, and theft was bad for business.

So the holographic concierges were designed, not for the passengers' comfort, but to spy on them. If concierges deemed someone suspicious, they harassed that someone on the ship. If that someone left the ship, the concierges shrank themselves down to a pinprick and became some kind of tiny spy that sent a signal so that the suspicious personages could be traced.

It was weird, and it was brilliant, and it was strangely appropriate.

Colette couldn't prevent them from taking hostages. She couldn't prevent them from getting the Egg. But she could help the authorities find the bad guys.

If they let her live.

A shiver ran through her.

It didn't really matter if they could track her or not. Because she had to get out of this room and stop them.

Somehow.

She just didn't know how yet.

The head thing vanished as Napier climbed into the only airlock that wasn't stacked with dead crew members. His team had already gotten onto his ship, and were waiting for him.

God, he was irritated. Hours, risk, a few deaths, and what did he have to show for it?

He was actually fleeing, something he thought he had become too sophisticated to do.

Well, he had learned his lesson. No more boarding a passenger ship of this vintage, not without a lot more planning.

He watched the exterior door open into the enclosed ramp his ship had set up, and it took every bit of effort he had not to dive through it.

He would have a little dignity here.

He would have to consider this a scouting mission rather than a failed attempt. He had learned something, and, if he had time to set it up, he would learn a bit more.

He would learn what happened when a ship carrying a Glyster Egg exploded.

He would have to set up something specific to monitor space around the starliner, but he could do that, and he could do it from a distance.

Then he would gather information, and with it, he could tell any possible client one of the many things the Egg did—more as a cautionary tale, with the explosion and all, but still. Information was information.

That was the kind of thing that clients liked.

He would have to remember that when the kid appeared in his dreams.

He slid into the airlock on his ship, shifting from foot to foot, hoping he would get through this quickly.

They needed to get out of here—and they needed to do so fast.

The engines were powering up on that second ship. Rodriguez sent the coordinates to the ships Mars Rescue had sent, hoping they would either veer off and catch the pirate ship.

She didn't have time to think about capturing a pirate ship. She was kinda relieved that it was leaving. She commanded a *rescue* vessel, not a security vessel. The handful of times she'd gone after perpetrators hadn't ended well for her. In all but one instance, the perpetrators had gotten away.

She hoped that the pirate ship wasn't taking the *Blue Moon* with it. That would create other problems.

Right now, her scans showed that the *Blue Moon* was more or less immobile, moving forward ever so slightly, but not enough to measure as anything. Maybe on autopilot.

She wasn't close enough yet to find that out.

But she would be in just a few minutes—and her team now knew this wasn't a drill.

It was going to be life and death.

Colette stared at the tablet in surprise. It told her that bad guys had left the *Blue Moon*.

Maybe they had found what they were looking for.

Not that it mattered to her.

She had to get to her parents.

She snuck out of her suite, and ran along the corridor, bent almost in half, just because, even though she knew the monitors caught her every movement anyway.

The buffet that her parents and the rest of the passengers were in was on this level. She just had to get to it.

She hurried through the maze of corridors, going half on her memory and half on the map that showed up on the tablet, when she almost tripped on a small square block.

It wasn't alone. There were half a dozen small square blocks just in this corridor.

She turned the tablet toward them, and asked it to identify the blocks.

The tablet did not respond. Maybe it didn't have the programming.

So she needed to figure this out on her own. After all, she had seen a lot of things in all the various schools she'd gone to. (She had done most of those things as well.)

She crouched near the closest block, and peered at it. It smelled faintly of rust—the telltale sign of a kind of acid that would eventually eat through a casing, hit a trigger, and—

Oh, god. This was a bomb, one of the kinds she'd thought too damn dangerous to make.

The bad guys were off the ship, and they were going to blow it up. But they hadn't taken the Egg and they hadn't taken her and they hadn't taken any of the passengers, so they must have been after something else, but what she had no idea, and now there was no time to figure it out.

She needed to get rid of these things. Somehow.

She reached for the box in front of her, then remembered: acid. She would have lost all the skin on her hand.

Focus, focus, focus.

There had to be a command that allowed the concierges, real or not, to isolate something dangerous in a corridor. Kids made smoke bombs, after all. And people sometimes tried to burn the materials in a ship.

Everyone on the crew had to be able to access that kind of security protocol.

She just had to find it before something happened.

Rodriguez had been right: the *Sally* arrived after the pirate ship left. The readings she got off the *Blue Moon* were some of the strangest she'd seen. The ship was completely intact. Some of the crew remained alive, and all of the passengers seemed to be breathing as well, but none of them were moving.

Except one of the Treacher women.

Was she in on the attack somehow?

Rodriguez brought two of her teammates with her, but let them move toward the room filled with passengers. Her entire team wore their environmental suits, and were armed with everything she could think to bring.

Sarkis remained on board the *Sally* and three more team members were heading to the brig to find the crew stranded there. The remaining three team members were spreading out between engineering and the bridge, hoping to get this ship moving again.

Rodriguez was going to handle the Treacher woman herself, not just because that person was still moving, but because Rodriguez didn't quite believe the information the passenger manifest had sent her.

It said that this distant Treacher relative was only eleven. Which wasn't possible, since no children were allowed on board ships like the *Blue Moon*.

Someone might have spoofed the file, which concerned Rodriguez more than she wanted to admit. Especially since the first thing she found when she came on board was the carnage in the first airlock she tried. She was lucky she hadn't opened it, or bodies would have tumbled into space.

Bodies.

The pirates had clearly gotten something. You don't kill that many people for the hell of it.

She rounded a corner, and saw a corridor strewn with black boxes.

"Don't move!" a panicked nasal voice said.

Rodriguez stopped and looked. She had seen the boxes, but she had missed the very small person crouched near the box farthest away.

A very small person who did indeed look like an eleven-year-old child, holding onto an old-fashioned rectangular tablet.

"Colette Treacher?" Rodriguez asked, trying to remember all of the girl's elaborate name.

"Close enough," the girl said. "You weren't tagged by one of the concierges. Are they gone?"

"What?" Rodriguez asked.

"Who are you?" the girl's tone was annoyed, as if Rodriguez was the dumbest person she had ever encountered.

And, to be fair, the girl couldn't see Rodriguez's identification. She was wearing a high-end environmental suit, not the ones issued by Mars Rescue. And the girl didn't seem to be networked into any kind of Mars system.

Rodriguez introduced herself without using her name. Names weren't important in situations like this. Jobs were.

"I'm with Mars Rescue," she said.

"It's about time." The girl's annoyance grew. "It's been *hours*."

Hours was miraculous, given where the *Blue Moon* ended up, and Rodriguez nearly said that, then realized the girl's tone had made her feel defensive.

"What are you doing?" Rodriguez asked.

"Trying to diffuse a bomb," the girl said. "What are you doing?"

That adrenaline spike hit again.

"All of these are bombs?" Rodriguez asked.

"I haven't checked them all, but I would guess so," the girl said. "They're pretty mad."

Rodriguez had a hunch the girl wasn't talking about the bombs now, but the pirates. "Who?"

"The guys who attacked us. They wanted something, and I hope they didn't get it. They left pretty fast. And now ..." the girl ran her hands near the boxes"... this."

Her voice broke on that last word, the bravado gone.

"I can't find any way to diffuse them," she said.

And that, the edge of panic in the girl's voice, brought Rodriguez back to herself.

She contacted her team.

"Found half a dozen box bombs, type unknown," Rodriguez said. "They're not too far from the passengers. Check for other bombs. We need a scan of this ship, and we need to put every single corridor on lockdown."

"Do you have some kind of shield program?" The girl shook the tablet at Rodriguez. "Because I can't find one."

Rodriguez wasn't carrying any kind of device like the girl had, but Rodriguez had access to every single ship built in official shipyards in the past one hundred years. The failsafes built into each system, override codes along with physical identification, specific to each rescue service.

She hoped that would be on board the *Blue Moon* as well, even though the ship was pretty old.

She slid to the nearest door, pulled back a wall panel, and found the interior controls. Then she opened the secondary panel underneath, hit the override commands, and found what she was looking for.

There were no tiny shields on a ship like this. Only one big shield that would coat the corridor.

"Join me," she said to the girl.

The girl stood slowly, giving the boxes a glance.

"*Right now,*" Rodriguez said.

The girl crept past the boxes, moving slower than Rodriguez would have liked. After what seemed like an eternity, the girl reached Rodriguez's side, and Rodriguez released the shields.

They encased the entire floor, avoiding her and the girl, but trapping them in one place. It would take some maneuvering, but Rodriguez could get that shield and the boxes it contained out of the ship—if she could find an airlock without bodies in it.

Her comm chirruped.

"We found more boxes, and yeah, they're bombs. We're getting them out now," said Lytel, who was handling the rest of the team.

"I got these explosives contained as well," Rodriguez said. "Any word on the passengers?"

"They're unconscious. The remaining crew too. Doing medical evaluations right now, but it looks like they're just out. Guess the bombs were going to do the dirty work of actual murder," Lytel said.

Rodriguez looked down at the girl. Her eyes were red, but there were no tear-streaks on her face.

"Do you have any idea what happened here?" Rodriguez asked.

The girl shook her head.

"How come you're out and no one else is?" Rodriguez said.

"Some guy," the girl said, "he was surprised there was a kid on board. He locked me in my suite."

She shook the tablet at Rodriguez.

"That was his first mistake." And then the girl grinned. The grin was a little cold, it was a little off, and then it trembled on the girl's face and fell away, showing that it was more bravado than anything else.

"My dad," the girl asked. "Is he okay?"

The shield reshaped, as Lytel remotely prepped it to leave the ship.

Neither Rodriguez nor the girl should remain in the corridor while that happened.

"I don't know how your father is," Rodriguez said, putting her hand on the little girl's back. The child was shaking so hard it looked like she might rattle out of her skin. "But I'm sure we can find out."

Napier was almost out of the Asteroid Belt when six ships surrounded him. All of those ships had official insignias, but not all of the insignias were from the same organization.

Different rescue and security companies, all government owned, all looking pretty official.

"What is going on?" Griz said from beside him. "We didn't steal anything."

"No, we didn't," Napier said. They had just killed half the crew. But they'd killed a lot of people out here before, and no one had come after them.

"So what the heck was different about this job?" Griz asked.

Napier didn't have the answer to that. Except bad luck. And that bad luck started when he saw the kid.

Kids threw Napier off his game.

But he didn't tell Griz that. Instead, Napier deleted all the records he had for the *Blue Moon*, and then contacted all of the security vessels.

Contacting them first might buy him some time. Although time probably wasn't what he needed. Because he had violated his own code, and used bombs to kill that kid, for no reason at all.

Except that he hadn't killed Colette Euphemia Josephine Treacher Singh Wilkinson Lopez. The ship didn't blow up. Instead, the *Sally* guarded the *Blue Moon* all the way to the nearest Mars Rescue base where everyone reported their own truth about what happened.

The only truth the authorities listened to, though, was Colette's, because it proved accurate from the moment the investigators had the tablet she had stolen.

That tablet had recorded her every move.

It also showed where Napier's crew was, because of what Colette had done with the holographic concierges. She turned them into location beacons.

Colette did not want attention for what she had done. She didn't want a medal or recognition from the governments of Mars.

She wanted something else entirely.

Something no government had the power to give.

"I don't want to go to boarding school," Colette said to her dad after all the officials left. "I want to go home."

Her family was in a tiny hotel room on the base where the *Blue Moon* had ended up. Her mother lay on the bed, her forearm over her forehead.

She'd had a headache ever since she'd woken up, something the medical personnel said was a pretty normal reaction to the gas the bad guys had filtered into the buffet.

Dad didn't seem to have a headache at all. He was frowning at Colette, and she knew, *she knew*, he was going to make her to go that school anyway, just because he had no idea what else to do with her.

"All right," he said quietly.

"What?" Colette asked, not sure she had heard him right.

"I'm taking you home," he said.

Colette's mouth opened ever so slightly. She hadn't expected *that*.

"No, you're not," her mother said. "She's more than we can handle."

"You won't have to handle her, Louise," Dad said.

Her mother sat up on one elbow, her face pale.

"What?" she asked, in almost the same tone Colette had used a moment before.

Something crossed Dad's face, something hard and fascinating.

"Colette saved our lives," he said after a moment. "All of us. Even you. We owe her, Louise."

Her mother made a dismissive sound and collapsed on the bed. Dad's gaze met Colette's and his eyes actually twinkled.

"We could send her away," Colette said softly.

"My thoughts exactly," he said just as softly.

Then he opened the door to the hotel room, and peered into the hall as if he expected to see a man cradling a laser rifle.

There was none—no man, no rifle.

Dad ushered Colette out of the room.

He was protecting her again. Like he had tried to do on the *Blue Moon*. Only he had failed.

And he would probably fail now. But that was okay.

Because Colette could protect them all.

As she had learned recently, she was really really good at that.

THIS IS THE ROAD
by Robert Silverberg

L eaf, lolling cozily with Shadow on a thick heap of furs in the air wagon's snug passenger castle, heard rain beginning to fall and made a sour face: very likely he would soon have to get up and take charge of driving the wagon, if the rain was the sort of rain he thought it was.

This was the ninth day since the Teeth had begun to lay waste to the eastern provinces. The airwagon, carrying four who were fleeing the invaders' fierce appetites, was floating along Spider Highway somewhere between Theptis and Northman's Rib, heading west, heading west as fast as could be managed. Jumpy little Sting was at the power reins, beaming dream commands to the team of six nightmares that pulled the wagon along; burly Crown was amidwagon, probably plotting vengeance against the Teeth, for that was what Crown did most of the time; that left Leaf and Shadow at their ease, but not for much longer. Listening to the furious drumming of the downpour against the wagon's taut-stretched canopy of big-veined stickskin, Leaf knew that this was no ordinary rain, but rather the dread purple rain that runs the air foul and brings the no-leg spiders out to hunt. Sting would never be able to handle the wagon in a purple rain. What a nuisance, Leaf thought, cuddling close against Shadow's sleek, furry blue form. Before long he heard the worried snorting of the nightmares and felt the wagon jolt and buck: yes, beyond any doubt, purple rain, no-leg spiders. His time of relaxing was just about over.

Not that he objected to doing his fair share of the work. But he had finished his last shift of driving only half an hour ago. He had earned his rest. If Sting was incapable of handling the wagon in this weather—and Shadow too, Shadow could never manage in a purple rain—then Crown ought to take the reins himself. But of course Crown would do no such thing. It was Crown's wagon and he never drove it himself. "I have always had underbreeds to do the driving for me," Crown had said ten days ago, as they stood in the grand plaza of Holy Town with the fires of the Teeth blazing in the outskirts.

"Your underbreeds have all fled without waiting for their master," Leaf had reminded him.

"So? There are others to drive."

"Am I to be your underbreed?" Leaf asked calmly. "Remember, Crown, I'm of the Pure Stream stock."

"I can see that by your face, friend. But why get into philosophical disputes? This is my wagon. The invaders will be here before nightfall. If you would ride west with me, these are the terms. If they're too bitter for you to swallow, well, stay here and test your luck against the mercies of the Teeth."

"I accept your terms," Leaf said.

So he had come aboard—and Sting, and Shadow—under the condition that the three of them would do all the driving. Leaf felt degraded by that—hiring on, in effect, as an indentured underbreed—but what choice was there for him? He was alone and far from his people; he had lost all his wealth and property; he faced sure death as the swarming hordes of Teeth devoured the eastland. He accepted Crown's terms. An aristocrat knows the art of yielding better than most. Resist humiliation until you can resist no longer, certainly, but then accept, accept, accept. Refusal to bow to the inevitable is vulgar and melodramatic. Leaf was of the highest caste, Pure Stream, schooled from childhood to be pliable, a willow in the wind, bending freely to the will of the Soul. Pride is a dangerous sin; so is stubbornness; so too, more than the others, is foolishness. Therefore, he labored while Crown lolled. Still, there were limits even to Leaf's capacity for acceptance, and he suspected those limits would be reached shortly.

On the first night, with only two small rivers between them and the Teeth and the terrible fires of Holy Town staining the sky, the fugitives halted briefly to forage for jellymelons in an abandoned field, and as they squatted there, gorging on ripe succulent fruit, Leaf said to Crown, "Where will you go, once you're safe from the Teeth on the far side of the Middle River?"

"I have distant kinsmen who live in the Flatlands," Crown replied. "I'll go to them and tell them what has happened to the Dark Lake folk in the east, and I'll persuade them to take up arms and drive the Teeth back into the icy wilderness where they belong. An army of liberation, Leaf, and I'll lead it." Crown's dark face glistened with juice. He wiped at it. "What are your plans?"

"Not nearly so grand. I'll seek kinsmen too, but not to organize an army. I wish simply to go to the Inland Sea, to my own people, and live quietly among them once again. I've been away from home too many years. What better time to return?" Leaf glanced at Shadow. "And you?" he asked her. "What do you want out of this journey?"

"I want only to go wherever you go," she said.

Leaf smiled. "You, Sting?"

"To survive," Sting said. "Just to survive."

Mankind had changed the world, and the changed world had worked changes in mankind. Each day the wagon brought the travelers to some new and strange folk who claimed descent from the old ancestral stock, though they might be water-breathers or have skins like tanned leather or grow several pairs of arms. Human, all of them, human, human, human. Or so they insisted. If you call yourself human, Leaf thought, then I will call you human too. Still, there were gradations of humanity. Leaf, as a Pure Stream, thought of himself as more nearly human than any of the peoples along their route, more nearly human even than his three companions; indeed, he sometimes tended to look upon Crown, Sting, and Shadow as very much other than human, though he did not consider that a fault in them. Whatever dwelled in the world was without fault, so long as it did no harm to others. Leaf had been taught to respect every breed of mankind, even the underbreeds. His companions were certainly no underbreeds: they were solidly midcaste, all of them, and ranked not far below Leaf himself. Crown, the biggest and strongest and most violent of them, was of the Dark Lake line. Shadow's race was Dancing Stars, and she was the most elegant, the most supple of the group. She was the only female aboard the wagon. Sting, who sprang from the White Crystal stock, was the quickest of body and spirit, mercurial, volatile. An odd assortment, Leaf thought. But in extreme times one takes one's traveling companions as they come. He had no complaints. He found it possible to get along with all of them, even Crown. Even Crown.

The wagon came to a jouncing halt. There was the clamor of hooves stamping the sodden soil; then shrill high-pitched cries from Sting and angry booming bellowings from Crown; and finally a series of muffled hissing explosions. Leaf shook his head sadly. "To waste our ammunition on no-leg spiders—"

"Perhaps they're harming the horses," Shadow said. "Crown is rough, but he isn't stupid."

Tenderly Leaf stroked her smooth haunches. Shadow tried always to be kind. He had never loved a Dancing Star before, though the sight of them had long given him pleasure: they were slender beings, bird-boned and shallow-breasted, and covered from their ankles to their crested skulls by fine dense fur the color of the twilight sky in winter. Shadow's voice was musical and her motions were graceful; she was the antithesis of Crown.

Crown now appeared, a hulking figure thrusting bluntly through the glistening beaded curtains that enclosed the passenger castle. He glared malevolently at Leaf. Even in his pleasant moments Crown seemed angry, an effect perhaps caused by his eyes, which were bright red where those of Leaf and most other kinds of humans were white. Crown's body was a block of meat, twice as broad as Leaf and half again as tall, though Leaf did not come from a small-statured race. Crown's skin was glossy, greenish-purple in colour, much like burnished bronze; he was entirely without hair and seemed more like a massive statue of an oiled gladiator than a living being. His arms hung well below his knees; equipped with extra joints and terminating in hands the size of great baskets, they were superb instruments of slaughter. Leaf offered him the most agreeable smile he could find. Crown said, without smiling in return, "You better get back on the reins, Leaf. The road's turning into one big swamp. The horses are uneasy. It's a purple rain."

Leaf had grown accustomed, in these nine days, to obeying Crown's brusque orders. He started to obey now, letting go of Shadow and starting to rise. But then, abruptly, he arrived at the limits of his acceptance.

"My shift just ended," he said.

Crown stared. "I know that. But Sting can't handle the wagon in this mess. And I just killed a bunch of mean-looking spiders. There'll be more if we stay around here much longer."

"So?"

"What are you trying to do, Leaf?"

"I guess I don't feel like going up front again so soon."

"You think Shadow here can hold the reins in this storm?" Crown asked coldly.

Leaf stiffened. He saw the wrath gathering in Crown's face. The big man was holding his natural violence in check with an effort, there would be trouble soon if Leaf remained defiant. This rebelliousness went against all of Leaf's principles, yet he found himself persisting in it and even taking a wicked pleasure in it. He chose to risk the confrontation and discover how firm Crown intended to be. Boldly he said, "You might try holding the reins yourself, friend."

"*Leaf!*" Shadow whispered, appalled.

Crown's face became murderous. His dark, shining cheeks puffed and went taut; his eyes blazed like molten nuggets; his hands closed and opened, closed and opened, furiously grasping air. "What kind of crazy stuff are you trying to give? We have a contract, Leaf. Unless you've suddenly decided that a Pure Stream doesn't need to abide by—"

"Spare me the class prejudice, Crown. I'm not pleading Pure Stream as an excuse to get out of working. I'm tired and I've earned my rest."

Shadow said softly, "Nobody's denying you your rest, Leaf. But Crown's right that I can't drive in a purple rain. I would if I could. And Sting can't do it either. That leaves only you."

"And Crown," Leaf said obstinately.

"There's only you," Shadow murmured. It was like her to take no sides, to serve ever as a mediator. "Go on, Leaf. Before there's real trouble. Making trouble like this isn't your usual way."

Leaf felt bound to pursue his present course, however perilous. He shook his head. "You, Crown. You drive."

In a throttled voice Crown said, "You're pushing me too far. We have a contract."

All Leaf's Pure Stream temperance was gone now. "Contract? I agreed to do my fair share of the driving, not to let myself be yanked up from my rest at a time when—"

Crown kicked at a low wickerwork stool, splitting it. His rage was boiling close to the surface. Swollen veins throbbed in his throat. He said, still controlling himself, "Get out there right now, Leaf, or by the Soul I'll send you into the All-Is-One!"

"Beautiful, Crown. Kill me, if you feel you have to. Who'll drive your damned wagon for you then?"

"I'll worry about that then."

Crown started forward, swallowing air, clenching fists.

Shadow sharply nudged Leaf's ribs. "This is going beyond the point of reason," she told him. He agreed. He had tested Crown and he had his answer, which was that Crown was unlikely to back down; now enough was enough, for Crown was capable of killing. The huge Dark Laker loomed over him, lifting his tremendous arms as though to bring them crashing against Leaf's head. Leaf held up his hands, more a gesture of submission than of self-defence.

"Wait," he said. "Stop it, Crown. I'll drive."

Crown's arms descended anyway. Crown managed to halt the killing blow midway, losing his balance and lurching heavily against the side of the wagon. Clumsily he straightened. Slowly he shook his head. In a low, menacing voice he said, "Don't ever try something like this again, Leaf."

"It's the rain," Shadow said. "The purple rain. Everybody does strange things in a purple rain."

"Even so," Crown said, dropping onto the pile of furs as Leaf got up. "The next time, Leaf, there'll be bad trouble. Now go ahead. Get up front."

Nodding to him, Leaf said, "Come up front with me, Shadow."

She did not answer. A look of fear flickered across her face.

Crown said, "The driver drives alone. You know that, Leaf. Are you still testing me? If you're testing me, say so and I'll know how to deal with you."

"I just want some company, as long as I have to do an extra shift."

"Shadow stays here."

There was a moment of silence. Shadow was trembling. "All right," Leaf said finally. "Shadow stays here."

"I'll walk a little way toward the front with you," Shadow said, glancing timidly at Crown. Crown scowled but said nothing. Leaf stepped out of the passenger castle; Shadow followed. Outside, in the narrow passageway leading to the midcabin, Leaf halted, shaken, shaking, and seized her. She pressed her slight body against him and they embraced, roughly, intensely. When he released her she said, "Why did you try to cross him like that? It was such a strange thing for you to do, Leaf."

"I just didn't feel like taking the reins again so soon."

"I know that."

"I want to be with you."

"You'll be with me a little later," she said. "It didn't make sense for you to talk back to Crown. There wasn't any choice. You had to drive."

"Why?"

"You know. Sting couldn't do it. I couldn't do it."

"And Crown?"

She looked at him oddly. "Crown? How would Crown have taken the reins?"

From the passenger castle came Crown's angry growl: "You going to stand there all day, Leaf? Go on! Get in here, Shadow!"

"I'm coming," she called.

Leaf held her a moment. "Why not? Why couldn't he have driven? He may be proud, but not so proud that—"

"Ask me another time," Shadow said, pushing him away. "Go. Go. You have to drive. If we don't move along we'll have the spiders upon us."

On the third day westward they had arrived at a village of Shapechangers. Much of the countryside through which they had been passing was deserted, although the Teeth had not yet visited it, but these Shapechangers went about their usual routines as if nothing had happened in the neighboring provinces. These were angular, long-legged people, sallow of skin, nearly green in hue, who were classed generally somewhere below the midcastes, but above the underbreeds. Their gift was metamorphosis, a slow softening of the bones under voluntary control that could, in the course of a week, drastically alter the form of their bodies, but Leaf saw them doing none of that, except for a few children who seemed midway through strange transformations, one with ropy, seemingly boneless arms, one with grotesquely distended shoulders, one with stiltlike legs. The adults came close to the wagon, admiring its beauty with soft cooing sounds, and Crown went out to talk with them. "I'm on my way to raise an army," he said. "I'll be back in a month or two, leading my kinsmen out of the Flatlands. Will you fight in our ranks? Together we'll drive out the Teeth and make the eastern provinces safe again."

The Shapechangers laughed heartily. "How can anyone drive out the Teeth?" asked an old one with a greasy mop of blue-white hair. "It was the will of the Soul that they burst forth as conquerors, and no one can quarrel with the Soul. The Teeth will stay in these lands for a thousand thousand years."

"They can be defeated!" Crown cried.

"They will destroy all that lies in their path, and no one can stop them."

"If you feel that way, why don't you flee?" Leaf asked.

"Oh, we have time. But we'll be gone long before your return with your army." There were giggles. "We'll keep ourselves clear of the Teeth. We have our ways. We make our changes and we slip away."

Crown persisted. "We can use you in our war against them. You have valuable gifts. If you won't serve as soldiers, at least serve us as spies. We'll send you into the camps of the Teeth, disguised as—"

"We will not be here," the old Shapechanger said, "and no one will be able to find us," and that was the end of it.

As the airwagon departed from the Shapechanger village, Shadow at the reins, Leaf said to Crown, "Do you really think you can defeat the Teeth?"

"I have to."

"You heard the old Shapechanger. The coming of the Teeth was the will of the Soul. Can you hope to thwart that will?"

"A rainstorm is the will of the Soul also," Crown said quietly. "All the same, I do what I can to keep myself dry. I've never known the Soul to be displeased by that."

"It's not the same. A rainstorm is a transaction between the sky and the land. We aren't involved in it; if we want to cover our heads, it doesn't alter what's really taking place. But the invasion of the Teeth is a transaction between tribe and tribe, a reordering of social patterns. In the great scheme of things, Crown, it may be a necessary process, preordained to achieve certain ends beyond our understanding. All events are part of some larger whole, and everything balances out, everything compensates for something else. Now we have peace, and now it's the time for invaders, do you see? If that's so, it's futile to resist."

"The Teeth broke into the eastlands," said Crown, "and they massacred thousands of Dark Lake people. My concern with necessary processes begins and ends with that fact. My tribe has nearly been wiped out. Yours is still safe, up by its ferny shores. I will seek help and gain revenge."

"The Shapechangers laughed at you. Others will also. No one will want to fight the Teeth."

"I have cousins in the Flatlands. If no one else will, they'll mobilize themselves. They'll want to repay the Teeth for their crime against the Dark Lakers."

"Your western cousins may tell you, Crown, that they prefer to remain where they are safe. Why should they go east to die in the name of vengeance? Will vengeance, no matter how bloody, bring any of your kinsmen back to life?"

"They will fight," Crown said.

"Prepare yourself for the possibility that they won't."

"If they refuse," said Crown, "then I'll go back east myself, and wage my war alone until I'm overwhelmed. But don't fear for me, Leaf. I'm sure I'll find plenty of willing recruits."

"How stubborn you are, Crown. You have good reason to hate the Teeth, as do we all. But why let that hatred cost you your only life? Why not accept the disaster that has befallen us, and make a new life for yourself beyond the Middle River, and forget this dream of reversing the irreversible?"

"I have my task," said Crown.

Forward through the wagon Leaf moved, going slowly, head down, shoulders hunched, feet atickle with the urge to kick things. He felt sour of spirit, curdled with dull resentment. He had let himself become angry at Crown, which was bad enough; but worse, he had let that anger possess and poison him. Not even the beauty of the wagon could lift him: ordinarily its superb construction and elegant furnishings gave him joy, the swirl-patterned fur hangings, the banners of gossamer textiles, the intricate carved inlays, the graceful strings of dried seeds and tassels that dangled from the vaulted ceilings, but these wonders meant nothing to him now. That was no way to be, he knew.

The airwagon was longer than ten men of the Pure Stream lying head to toe, and so wide that it spanned nearly the whole roadway. The finest workmanship had gone into its making: Flower Giver artisans, no doubt of it, only Flower Givers could build so well. Leaf imagined dozens of the fragile little folk toiling earnestly for months, all smiles and silence, long, slender fingers and quick, gleaming eyes, shaping the great wagon as one might shape a poem. The main frame was of lengthy pale spears of light, resilient wingwood, elegantly laminated into broad curving strips with a colorless fragrant mucilage and bound with springy withes brought from the southern marshes. Over this elaborate armature tanned sheets of stickskin had been stretched and stitched into place with thick yellow fibers drawn from the stick-creatures' own gristly bodies. The floor was of dark shining nightflower-wood planks, buffed to a high finish and pegged together with great skill. No metal had been employed in the construction of the wagon, nor any artificial substances: nature had supplied everything. Huge and majestic though the wagon was, it was airy and light, light enough to float on a vertical column of warm air generated by magnetic rotors whirling in its belly; so long as the earth turned, so would the rotors, and when the rotors were spinning the wagon drifted cat-high above the ground, and could be tugged easily along by the team of nightmares.

It was more a mobile palace than a wagon, and wherever it went it stirred excitement: Crown's love, Crown's joy, Crown's estate, a wondrous toy. To pay for the making of it Crown must have sent many souls into the All-Is-One, for that was how Crown had earned his livelihood in the old days, as a hired warrior, a surrogate killer, fighting one-on-one duels for rich eastern princelings too weak or too lazy to defend their own honor. He had never been scratched, and his fees had been high; but all that was ended now that the Teeth were loose in the eastlands.

Leaf could not bear to endure being so irritable any longer. He paused to adjust himself, closing his eyes and listening for the clear tone that sounded always at the center of his being. After a few minutes he found it, tuned himself to it, let it purify him. Crown's unfairness ceased to matter. Leaf became once more his usual self, alert and outgoing, aware and responsive.

Smiling, whistling, he made his way swiftly through the wide, comfortable, brightly lit midcabin, decorated with Crown's weapons and other grim souvenirs of battle, and went on into the front corridor that led to the driver's cabin.

Sting sat slumped at the reins. White Crystal folk such as Sting generally seemed to throb and tick with energy; but Sting looked exhausted, emptied, half dead of fatigue. He was a small, sinewy being, narrow of shoulder and hip, with colorless skin of a waxy, horny texture, pocked everywhere with little hairy nodes and whorls. His muscles were long and flat; his face was cavernous, beaked nose and tiny chin, dark mischievous eyes hidden in bony recesses. Leaf touched his shoulder. "It's all right," he said. "Crown sent me to relieve you." Sting nodded feebly but did not move. The little man was quivering like a frog. Leaf had always thought of him as indestructible, but in the grip of this despondency Sting seemed more fragile even than Shadow.

"Come," Leaf murmured. "You have a few hours for resting. Shadow will look after you."

Sting shrugged. He was hunched forward, staring dully through the clear curving window, stained now with splashes of muddy tinted water.

"The dirty spiders," he said. His voice was hoarse and frayed. "The filthy rain. The mud. Look at the horses, Leaf. They're dying of fright, and so am I. We'll all perish on this road, Leaf, if not of spiders then of poisoned rain, if not of rain then of the Teeth, if not of the Teeth then of something else. There's no road for us but this one, do you realize that? This is the road, and we're bound to it like helpless underbreeds, and we'll die on it."

"We'll die when our turn comes, like everything else, Sting, and not a moment before."

"Our turn is coming. Too soon. Too soon. I feel death-ghosts close at hand."

"*Sting!*"

Sting made a weird ratcheting sound low in his throat, a sort of rusty sob. Leaf lifted him and swung him out of the driver's seat, settling him gently down in the corridor. It was as though he weighed nothing at all. Perhaps just then that was true. Sting had many strange gifts. "Go on," Leaf said. "Get some rest while you can."

"How kind you are, Leaf."

"And no more talk of ghosts."

"Yes," Sting said. Leaf saw him struggling against fear and despair and weariness. Sting appeared to brighten a moment, flickering on the edge of his old vitality; then the brief glow subsided, and, smiling a pale smile, offering a whisper of thanks, he went aft.

Leaf took his place in the driver's seat.

Through the window of the wagon—thin, tough sheets of stickskin, the best quality, carefully matched, perfectly transparent—he confronted a dismal scene. Rain dark as blood was falling at a steep angle, scourging the spongy soil, kicking up tiny fountains of earth. A bluish miasma rose from the ground, billows of dark, steamy fog, the acrid odour of which had begun to seep into the wagon. Leaf sighed and reached for the reins. Death-ghosts, he thought. Haunted. Poor Sting, driven to the end of his wits.

And yet, and yet, as he considered the things Sting had said, Leaf realized that he had been feeling somewhat the same way, these past few days: tense, driven, haunted. *Haunted.* As though unseen presences, mocking, hostile, were hovering near. Ghosts? The strain, more likely, of all that he had gone through since the first onslaught of the Teeth. He had lived through the collapse of a rich and intricate civilization. He moved now through a strange world, all ashes and seaweed. He was haunted, perhaps, by the weight of the unburied past, by the memory of all that he had lost.

A rite of exorcism seemed in order.

Lightly he said, aloud, "If there are any ghosts in here, I want you to listen to me. *Get out of this cabin.* That's an order. I have work to do."

He laughed. He picked up the reins and made ready to take control of the team of nightmares.

The sense of an invisible presence was overwhelming.

Something at once palpable and intangible pressed clammily against him. He felt surrounded and engulfed. It's the fog, he told himself. Dark blue fog, pushing at the window, sealing the wagon into a pocket of vapor. Or was it? Leaf sat quite still for a moment, listening. Silence. He relinquished the reins, swung about in his seat, carefully inspected the cabin. No one there. An absurdity to be fidgeting like this. Yet the discomfort remained. This was no joke now. Sting's anxieties had infected him, and the malady was feeding on itself, growing more intense from moment to moment, making him vulnerable to any stray terror that whispered to him. Only with a tranquil mind could he attain the state of trance a nightmare-driver must enter; and trance seemed unattainable so long as he felt the prickle of some invisible watcher's gaze on the back of his neck. This rain, he thought, this damnable rain. It drives everybody crazy. In a clear, firm voice Leaf said, "I'm altogether serious. Show yourself and get yourself out of this cabin."

Silence.

He took up the reins again. No use. Concentration was impossible. He knew many techniques for centering himself, for leading his consciousness to a point of unassailable serenity. But could he achieve that now, jangled and distracted as he was? He would try. He had to succeed. The wagon had tarried in this place much too long already. Leaf summoned all his inner resources; he purged himself, one by one, of every discord; he compelled himself to slide into trance.

It seemed to be working. Darkness beckoned to him. He stood at the threshold. He started to step across.

"Such a fool, such a foolish fool," said a sudden dry voice out of nowhere that nibbled at his ears like the needle-toothed mice of the White Desert.

The trance broke. Leaf shivered as if stabbed and sat up, eyes bright, face flushed with excitement.

"Who spoke?"

"Put down those reins, friend. Going forward on this road is a heavy waste of spirit."

"Then I wasn't crazy and neither was Sting. There is something in here!"

"A ghost, yes a ghost, a ghost, a ghost!" The ghost showered him with laughter.

Leaf's tension eased. Better to be troubled by a real ghost than to be vexed by a fantasy of one's own disturbed mind. He feared madness far more than he did the invisible. Besides, he thought he knew what this creature must be.

"Where are you, ghost?"

"Not far from you. Here I am. Here. Here." From three different parts of the cabin, one after another. The invisible being began to sing. Its song was high-pitched, whining, a grinding tone that stretched Leaf's patience intolerably. Leaf still saw no one, though he narrowed his eyes and stared as hard as he could. He imagined he could detect a faint veil of pink light floating along the wall of the cabin, a smoky haze moving from place to place, a shimmering film like thin oil on water, but whenever he focused his eyes on it the misty presence appeared to evaporate.

Leaf said, "How long have you been aboard this wagon?"

"Long enough."

"Did you come aboard at Theptis?"

"Was that the name of the place?" asked the ghost disingenuously. "I forget. It's so hard to remember things."

"Theptis," said Leaf. "Four days ago."

"Perhaps it was Theptis," the ghost said. "Fool! Dreamer!"

"Why do you call me names?"

"You travel a dead road, fool, and yet nothing will turn you from it." The invisible one snickered. "Do you think I'm a ghost, Pure Stream?"

"I know what you are."

"How wise you've become!"

"Such a pitiful phantom. Such a miserable drifting wraith. Show yourself to me, ghost."

Laughter reverberated from the corners of the cabin. The voice said, speaking from a point close to Leaf's left ear, "The road you choose to travel has been killed ahead. We told you that when you came to us, and yet you went onward, and still you go onward. Why are you so rash?"

"Why won't you show yourself? A gentleman finds it discomforting to speak to the air."

Obligingly the ghost yielded, after a brief pause, some fraction of its invisibility. A vaporous crimson stain appeared in the air before Leaf, and he saw within it dim, insubstantial features, like projections on a screen of thick fog. He believed he could make out a wispy white beard, harsh glittering eyes, lean curving lips; a whole forbidding face, a fleshless torso. The stain deepened momentarily to scarlet and for a moment Leaf saw the entire figure of the stranger revealed, a long narrow-bodied man, dried and withered, grinning ferociously at him. The edges of the figure softened and became mist. Then Leaf saw only vapor again, and then nothing.

"I remember you from Theptis," Leaf said. "In the tent of Invisibles."

"What will you do when you come to the dead place on the highway?" the invisible one demanded. "Will you fly over it? Will you tunnel under it?"

"You were asking the same things at Theptis," Leaf replied. "I will make the same answer that the Dark Laker gave you then. We will go forward, dead place or no. This is the only road for us."

They had come to Theptis on the fifth day of their flight—a grand city, a splendid mercantile emporium, the gateway to the west, sprawling athwart a place where two great rivers met and many highways converged. In happy times any and all peoples might be found in Theptis, Pure Streams and White Crystals and Flower Givers and Sand Shapers and a dozen others jostling one another in the busy streets, buying and selling, selling and buying, but mainly Theptis was a city of Fingers—the merchant caste, plump and industrious, thousands upon thousands of them concentrated in this one city.

The day Crown's airwagon reached Theptis much of the city was ablaze, and they halted on a broad stream-split plain just outside the metropolitan area. An improvised camp for refugees had sprouted there, and tents of black and gold and green cloth littered the meadow like new nightshoots. Leaf and Crown went out to inquire after the news. Had the Teeth sacked Theptis as well? No, an old and sagging Sand Shaper told them. The Teeth, so far as anyone had heard, were still well to the east, rampaging through the coastal cities. Why the fires, then? The old man shook his head. His energy was exhausted, or his patience, or his courtesy. If you want to know anything else, he said, ask *them*. They know everything. And he pointed toward a tent opposite his.

Leaf looked into the tent and found it empty; then he looked again and saw upright shadows moving about in it, tenuous figures that existed at the very bounds of visibility and could be perceived only by tricks of the light as they changed place in the tent. They asked him within, and Crown came also. By the smoky light of their tentfire they were more readily seen: seven or eight men of the Invisible stock, nomads, ever mysterious, gifted with ways of causing beams of light to travel around or through their bodies so that they might escape the scrutiny of ordinary eyes. Leaf, like everyone else not of their kind, was uncomfortable among Invisibles. No one trusted them; no one was capable of predicting their actions, for they were creatures of whim and caprice, or else followed some code the logic of which was incomprehensible to outsiders. They made Leaf and

Crown welcome, adjusting their bodies until they were in clear sight, and offering the visitors a flagon of wine, a bowl of fruit. Crown gestured toward Theptis. Who had set the city afire? A red-bearded Invisible with a raucous rumbling voice answered that on the second night of the invasion the richest of the Fingers had panicked and had begun to flee the city with their most precious belongings, and as their wagons rolled through the gates the lesser breeds had begun to loot the Finger mansions, and brawling had started once the wine cellars were pierced, and fires broke out, and there was no one to make the fire wardens do their work, for they were all underbreeds and the masters had fled. So the city burned and was still burning, and the survivors were huddled here on the plain, waiting for the rubble to cool so that they might salvage valuables from it, and hoping that the Teeth would not fall upon them before they could do their sifting. As for the Fingers, said the Invisible, they were all gone from Theptis now.

Which way had they gone? Mainly to the northwest, by way of Sunset Highway, at first; but then the approach to that road had become choked by stalled wagons butted one up against another, so that the only way to reach the Sunset now was by making a difficult detour through the sand country north of the city, and once that news became general the Fingers had turned their wagons southward. Crown wondered why no one seemed to be taking Spider Highway westward. At this a second Invisible, white-bearded, joined the conversation. Spider Highway, he said, is blocked just a few days' journey west of here: a dead road, a useless road. Everyone knows that, said the white-bearded Invisible.

"That is our route," said Crown.

"I wish you well," said the Invisible. "You will not get far."

"I have to get to the Flatlands."

"Take your chances with the sand country," the red-bearded one advised, "and go by way of the Sunset."

"It would waste two weeks or more," Crown replied. "Spider Highway is the only road we can consider." Leaf and Crown exchanged wary glances. Leaf asked the nature of the trouble on the highway, but the Invisibles said only that the road had been "killed," and would offer no amplification. "We will go forward," Crown said, "dead place or no."

"As you choose," said the older Invisible, pouring more wine. Already both Invisibles were fading; the flagon seemed suspended in mist. So, too, did the discussion become unreal, dreamlike, as answers no longer followed closely upon the sense of questions, and the words of the Invisibles came to Leaf and Crown as though swaddled in thick wool. There was a long interval of silence, at last, and when Leaf extended his empty glass the flagon was not offered to him, and he realized finally that he and

Crown were alone in the tent. They left it and asked at other tents about the blockage on Spider Highway, but no one knew anything of it, neither some young Dancing Stars nor three flat-faced Water Breather women nor a family of Flower Givers. How reliable was the word of Invisibles? What did they mean by a "dead" road? Suppose they merely thought the road was ritually impure, for some reason understood only by Invisibles. What value, then, would their warning have to those who did not subscribe to their superstitions? Who knew at any time what the words of an Invisible meant? That night in the wagon the four of them puzzled over the concept of a road that has been "killed," but neither Shadow's intuitive perceptions nor Sting's broad knowledge of tribal dialects and customs could provide illumination. In the end Crown reaffirmed his decision to proceed on the road he had originally chosen, and it was Spider Highway that they took out of Theptis. As they proceeded westward they met no one traveling the opposite way, though one might expect the eastbound lanes to be thronged with a flux of travelers turning back from whatever obstruction might be closing the road ahead. Crown took cheer in that; but Leaf observed privately that their wagon appeared to be the only vehicle on the road in either direction, as if everyone else knew better than to make the attempt. In such stark solitude they journeyed four days west of Theptis before the purple rain hit them.

Now the Invisible said, "Go into your trance and drive your horses. I'll dream beside you until the awakening comes."

"I prefer privacy."

"You won't be disturbed."

"I ask you to leave."

"You treat your guests coldly."

"Are you my guest?" Leaf asked. "I don't remember extending an invitation."

"You drank wine in our tent. That creates in you an obligation to offer reciprocal hospitality." The Invisible sharpened his bodily intensity until he seemed as solid as Crown; but even as Leaf observed the effect he grew thin again, fading in patches. The far wall of the cabin showed through his chest, as if he were hollow. His arms had disappeared, but not his gnarled long-fingered hands. He was grinning, showing crooked close-set teeth. There was a strange scent in the cabin, sharp and musky, like vinegar mixed with honey. The Invisible said, "I'll ride with you a little longer," and vanished altogether.

Leaf searched the corners of the cabin, knowing that an Invisible could always be felt even if he eluded the eyes. His probing hands encountered

401

nothing. Gone, gone, gone, whisking off to the place where snuffed flames go, eh? Even that odor of vinegar and honey was diminishing. "Where are you?" Leaf asked. "Still hiding somewhere else?" Silence. Leaf shrugged. The stink of the purple rain was the dominant scent again. Time to move on, stowaway or no. Rain was hitting the window in huge murky windblown blobs. Once more Leaf picked up the reins. He banished the Invisible from his mind.

These purple rains condensed out of drifting gaseous clots in the upper atmosphere—dank clouds of chemical residues that arose from the world's most stained, most injured places and circled the planet like malign tempests. Upon colliding with a mass of cool air such a poisonous cloud often discharged its burden of reeking oils and acids in the form of a driving rainstorm; and the foulness that descended could be fatal to plants and shrubs, to small animals, sometimes even to man.

A purple rain was the cue for certain somber creatures to come forth from dark places: scuttering scavengers that picked eagerly through the dead and dying, and larger, more dangerous things that preyed on the dazed and choking living. The no-leg spiders were among the more unpleasant of these.

They were sinister spherical beasts the size of large dogs, voracious in the appetite and ruthless in the hunt. Their bodies were plump, covered with coarse, rank brown hair; they bore eight glittering eyes above sharp-fanged mouths. No-legged they were indeed, but not immobile, for a single huge fleshy foot, something like that of a snail, sprouted from the underbellies of these spiders and carried them along at a slow, inexorable pace. They were poor pursuers, easily avoided by healthy animals; but to the numbed victims of a purple rain they were deadly, moving in to strike with hinged, poison-barbed claws that leaped out of niches along their backs. Were they truly spiders? Leaf had no idea. Like almost everything else, they were a recent species, mutated out of the-Soul-only-knew-what during the period of stormy biological upheavals that had attended the end of the old industrial civilization, and no one yet had studied them closely, or cared to.

Crown had killed four of them. Their bodies lay upside down at the edge of the road, upturned feet wilting and drooping like plucked toadstools. About a dozen more spiders had emerged from the low hills flanking the highway and were gliding slowly toward the stalled wagon; already several had reached their dead comrades and were making ready to feed on them, and some of the others were eyeing the horses.

The six nightmares, prisoners of their harnesses, prowled about uneasily in their constricted ambits, anxiously scraping at the muddy ground with their hooves. They were big, sturdy beasts, black as death, with long feathery ears and high-domed skulls that housed minds as keen as many human's, sharper than some. The rain annoyed the horses but could not seriously harm them, and the spiders could be kept at bay with kicks, but plainly the entire situation disturbed them.

Leaf meant to get them out of here as rapidly as he could.

A slimy coating covered everything the rain had touched, and the road was a miserable quagmire, slippery as ice. There was peril for all of them in that. If a horse stumbled and fell it might splinter a leg, causing such confusion that the whole team might be pulled down; and as the injured nightmares thrashed about in the mud the hungry spiders would surely move in on them, venomous claws rising, striking, delivering stings that stunned, and leaving the horses paralyzed, helpless, vulnerable to eager teeth and strong jaws. As the wagon traveled onward through this swampy rainsoaked district Leaf would constantly have to steady and reassure the nightmares, pouring his energy into them to comfort them, a strenuous task, a task that had wrecked poor Sting.

Leaf slipped the reins over his forehead. He became aware of the consciousness of the six fretful horses.

Because he was still awake, contact was misty and uncertain. A waking mind was unable to communicate with the animals in any useful way. To guide the team he had to enter a trance state, a dream state; they would not respond to anything so gross as conscious intelligence. He looked about for manifestations of the Invisible. No, no sign of him. Good. Leaf brought his mind to dead center.

He closed his eyes. The technique of trance was easy enough for him, when there were no distractions.

He visualized a tunnel, narrow-mouthed and dark, slanting into the ground. He drifted toward its entrance.

Hovered there a moment.

Went down into it.

Floating, floating, borne downward by warm, gentle currents: he sinks in a slow spiral descent, autumn leaf on a springtime breeze. The tunnel's walls are circular, crystalline, lit from within, the light growing in brightness as he drops toward the heart of the world. Gleaming scarlet and blue flowers, brittle as glass, sprout from crevices at meticulously regular intervals.

He goes deep, touching nothing. Down.

Entering a place where the tunnel widens into a round smooth-walled chamber, sealed at the end. He stretches full-length on the floor. The floor is black stone, slick and slippery; he dreams it soft and yielding, womb-warm. Colors are muted here, sounds are blurred. He hears far-off music, percussive and muffled, *rat-a-rat, rat-a-rat, blllooom, blllooom*.

Now at least he is able to make full contact with the minds of the horses.

His spirit expands in their direction; he envelops them, he takes them into himself. He senses the separate identity of each, picks up the shifting play of their emotions, their prancing fantasies, their fears. Each mare has her own distinct response to the rain, to the spiders, to the sodden highway. One is restless, one is timid, one is furious, one is sullen, one is tense, one is torpid. He feeds energy to them. He pulls them together. Come, gather your strength, take us onward: this is the road, we must be on our way.

The nightmares stir.

They react well to his touch. He believes that they prefer him over Shadow and Sting as a driver: Sting is too manic, Shadow too permissive. Leaf keeps them together, directs them easily, gives them the guidance they need. They are intelligent, yes, they have personalities and goals and ideals, but also they are beasts of burden, and Leaf never forgets that, for the nightmares themselves do not.

Come, now. Onward.

The road is ghastly. They pick at it and their hooves make sucking sounds coming up from the mud. They complain to him. *We are cold, we are wet, we are bored.* He dreams wings for them to make their way easier. To soothe them he dreams sunlight for them, bountiful warmth, dry highway, an easy trot. He dreams green hillsides, cascades of yellow blossoms, the flutter of hummingbirds' wings, the droning of bees. He gives the horses sweet summer, and they grow calm; they lift their heads; they fan their dream-wings and preen; they are ready now to resume the journey. They pull as one. The rotors hum happily. The wagon slides forward with a smooth coasting motion.

Leaf, deep in trance, is unable to see the road, but no matter; the horses see it for him and send him images, fluid, shifting dream-images, polarized and refracted and diffracted by the strangenesses of their vision and the distortions of dream communication, six simultaneous and individual views. Here is the road, bordered by white birches whipped by an angry wind. Here is the road, an earthen swath slicing through a forest of mighty pines bowed down by white new snow. Here is the road, a ribbon of fertility, from which dazzling red poppies spring wherever a hoof strikes. Fleshy-finned blue fishes do headstands beside the road. Paunchy burghers of the Finger tribe spread brilliantly laundered tablecloths along the grassy margin and make lunch out of big-eyed reproachful oysters. Masked figures dart between the horses' legs. The road curves, curves again; doubles back on itself, crosses itself in a complacent loop. Leaf integrates this dizzying many-hued inrush of data, sorting the real from the unreal, blending and focusing the input and using it to guide himself in guiding the horses. Serenely he coordinates their movements with quick confident impulses of thought, so that each animal will pull with the same force. The wagon is precariously balanced on its column of air, and an unequal tug could well send it slewing into the treacherous thicket to the left of the road. He sends quicksilver messages down the thick conduit from his mind to theirs. Steady there, steady, watch that boggy patch coming up! Ah! Ah, that's my girl! Spiders on the left, careful! Good! Yes, yes, ah, yes! He pats their heaving flanks with a strand of his mind. He rewards their agility with dreams of the stable, of newly mown hay, of stallions waiting at journey's end.

From them—for they love him, he knows they love him—he gets warm dreams of the highway, all beauty and joy, all images converging into a single idealized view, majestic groves of wingwood trees and broad meadows through which clear brooks flow. They dream his own past life for him, too, feeding back to him nuggets of random autobiography mined in the seams of his being. What they transmit is filtered and transformed by their alien sensibilities, colored with hallucinatory glows and tugged and twisted into other-dimensional forms, but yet he is able to perceive the essential meaning of each tableau: his childhood among the parks and gardens of the Pure Stream enclave near the Inland Sea, his wander-years among the innumerable, unfamiliar, not-quite-human breeds of the hinterlands, his brief, happy sojourn in the fog-swept western country, his eastward journey in early manhood, always following the will of the Soul, always bending to the breezes, accepting whatever destiny seizes him, eastward now, his band of friends closer than brothers in his adopted eastern province, his sprawling lakeshore home there, all polished wood and billowing tented pavilions, his collection of relics of mankind's former times—pieces of machinery, elegant coils of metal, rusted coins, grotesque statuettes, wedges of imperishable plastic—housed in its own wing with its own curator. Lost in these reveries he ceases to remember that the home by the lake has been reduced to ashes by the Teeth, that his friends of kinder days are dead, his estates overrun, his pretty things scattered in the kitchen-middens.

Imperceptibly, the dream turns sour.

Spiders and rain and mud creep back into it. He is reminded, through some darkening of tone of the imagery pervading his dreaming mind, that he has been stripped of everything and has become, now that he has taken flight, merely a driver hired out to a bestial Dark Lake mercenary who is himself a fugitive.

Leaf is working harder to control the team now. The horses seem less sure of their footing, and the pace slows; they are bothered about something, and a sour, querulous anxiety tinges their messages to him. He catches their mood. He sees himself harnessed to the wagon alongside the nightmares, and it is Crown at the reins, Crown wielding a terrible whip, driving the wagon frenziedly forward, seeking allies who will help him fulfil his fantasy of liberating the lands the Teeth have taken. There is no escape from Crown. He rises above the landscape like a monster of congealed smoke, growing more huge until he obscures the sky. Leaf wonders how he will disengage himself from Crown. Shadow runs beside him, stroking his cheeks, whispering to him, and he asks her to undo the harness, but she says she cannot, that it is their duty to serve Crown, and Leaf turns to Sting, who is harnessed on his other side, and he asks Sting for help, but Sting coughs and slips in the mud as Crown's whip flicks his backbone. There is no escape. The wagon heels and shakes. The right-hand horse skids, nearly falls, recovers. Leaf decides he must be getting tired. He has driven a great deal today, and the effort is telling. But the rain is still falling—he breaks through the veil of illusions, briefly, past the scenes of spring and summer and autumn, and sees the blue-black water dropping in wild handfuls from the sky—and there is no one else to drive, so he must continue.

He tries to submerge himself in deeper trance, where he will be less readily deflected from control.

But no, something is wrong, something plucks at his consciousness, drawing him toward the waking state. The horses summon him to wakefulness with frightful scenes. One beast shows him the wagon about to plunge through a wall of fire. Another pictures them at the brink of a vast impassable crater. Another gives him the image of giant boulders strewn across the road; another, a mountain of ice blocking the way; another, a pack of snarling wolves; another, a row of armored warriors standing shoulder to shoulder, lances at the ready. No doubt of it. Trouble. Trouble. Trouble. Perhaps they have come to the dead place in the road. No wonder that Invisible was skulking around. Leaf forces himself to awaken.

There was no wall of fire. No warriors, no wolves, none of those things. Only a palisade of newly felled timbers facing him some hundred paces ahead on the highway, timbers twice as tall as Crown, sharpened to points at both ends and thrust deep into the earth one up against the next and bound securely with freshly cut vines. The barricade spanned the highway completely from edge to edge; on its right it was bordered by a tangle of impenetrable thorny scrub; on its left it extended to the brink of a steep ravine.

They were stopped.

Such a blockade across a public highway was inconceivable. Leaf blinked, coughed, rubbed his aching forehead. Those last few minutes of discordant dreams had left a murky, gritty coating on his brain. This wall of wood seemed like some sort of dream too, a very bad one. Leaf imagined he could hear the Invisible's cool laughter somewhere close at hand. At least the rain appeared to be slackening, and there were no spiders about. Small consolations, but the best that were available.

Baffled, Leaf freed himself of the reins and awaited the next event. After a moment or two he sensed the joggling rhythms that told of Crown's heavy forward progress through the cabin. The big man peered into the driver's cabin.

"What's going on? Why aren't we moving?"

"Dead road."

"What are you talking about?"

"See for yourself," Leaf said wearily, gesturing toward the window.

Crown leaned across Leaf to look. He studied the scene an endless moment, reacting slowly. "What's that? A *wall?*"

"A wall, yes."

"A wall across a highway? I never heard of anything like that."

"The Invisibles at Theptis may have been trying to warn us about this."

"A wall. A wall." Crown shook with perplexed anger. "It violates all the maintenance customs! Soul take it, Leaf, a public highway is—"

"—sacred and inviolable. Yes. What the Teeth have been doing in the east violates a good many maintenance customs too," Leaf said. "And territorial customs as well. These are unusual times everywhere." He wondered if he should tell Crown about the Invisible who was on board. One problem at a time, he decided. "Maybe this is how these people propose to keep the Teeth out of their country, Crown."

"But to block a public road—"

"We were warned."

"Who could trust the word of an Invisible?"

"There's the wall," Leaf said. "Now we know why we didn't meet anyone else on the highway. They probably put this thing up as soon as they heard about the Teeth, and the whole province knows enough to avoid Spider Highway. Everyone but us."

"What folk dwell here?"

"No idea. Sting's the one who would know."

"Yes, Sting would know," said the high, clear, sharp-edged voice of Sting from the corridor. He poked his head into the cabin. Leaf saw Shadow just behind him. "This is the land of the Tree Companions," Sting said. "Do you know of them?"

Crown shook his head. "Not I," said Leaf.

"Forest-dwellers," Sting said. "Tree-worshippers. Small heads, slow brains. Dangerous in battle—they use poisoned darts. There are nine tribes of them in this region, I think, under a single chief. Once they paid tribute to my people, but I suppose in these times all that has ended."

"They worship trees?" Shadow said lightly. "And how many of their gods, then, did they cut down to make this barrier?"

Sting laughed. "If you must have gods, why not put them to some good use?"

Crown glared at the wall across the highway as he once might have glared at an opponent in the dueling ring. Seething, he paced a narrow path in the crowded cabin. "We can't waste any more time. The Teeth will be coming through this region in a few days, for sure. We've got to reach the river before something happens to the bridges ahead."

"The wall," Leaf said.

"There's plenty of brush lying around out there," said Sting. "We could build a bonfire and burn it down."

"Green wood," Leaf said. "It's impossible."

"We have hatchets," Shadow pointed out. "How long would it take for us to cut through timbers as thick as those?"

Sting said, "We'd need a week for the job. The Tree Companions would fill us full of darts before we'd been chopping an hour."

"Do you have any ideas?" Shadow said to Leaf.

"Well, we could turn back toward Theptis and try to find our way to Sunset Highway by way of the sand country. There are only two roads from here to the river, this and the Sunset. We lose five days, though, if we decide to go back, and we might get snarled up in whatever chaos is going on in Theptis, or we could very well get stranded in the desert trying to reach the highway. The only other choice I see is to abandon the wagon and look for some path around the wall on foot, but I doubt very much that Crown would—"

"Crown wouldn't," said Crown, who had been chewing his lip in tense silence. "But I see some different possibilities."

"Go on."

"One is to find these Tree Companions and compel them to clear this trash from the highway. Darts or no darts, one Dark Lake and one Pure Stream side by side ought to be able to terrify twenty tribes of pinhead forest folk."

"And if we can't?" Leaf asked.

"That brings us to the other possibility, which is that this wall isn't particularly intended to protect the neighborhood against the Teeth at all, but that these Tree Companions have taken advantage of the general confusion to set up some sort of toll-raising scheme. In that case, if we can't force them to open the road, we can find out what they want, what sort of toll they're asking, and pay it if we can and be on our way."

"Is that Crown who's talking?" Sting asked. "Talking about paying a toll to underbreeds of the forest? Incredible!"

Crown said, "I don't like the thought of paying toll to anybody. But it may be the simplest and quickest way to get out of here. Do you think I'm entirely a creature of pride, Sting?"

Leaf stood up. "If you're right that this is a toll station, there'd be some kind of gate in the wall. I'll go out there and have a look at it."

"No," said Crown, pushing him lightly back into his seat. "There's danger here, Leaf. This part of the work falls to me." He strode toward the midcabin and was busy there a few minutes. When he returned he was in his full armor: breastplates, helmet, face mask, greaves, everything burnished to a high gloss. In those few places where his bare skin showed through, it seemed but a part of the armor. Crown looked like a machine. His mace hung at his hip, and the short shaft of his extensor sword rested easily along the inside of his right wrist, ready to spring to full length at a squeeze. Crown glanced toward Sting and said, "I'll need your nimble legs. Will you come?"

"As you say."

"Open the midcabin hatch for us, Leaf."

Leaf touched a control on the board below the front window. With a soft, whining sound a hinged door near the middle of the wagon swung upward and out, and a stepladder sprouted to provide access to the ground. Crown made a ponderous exit. Sting, scorning the ladder, stepped down: it was the special gift of the White Crystal people to be able to transport themselves short distances in extraordinary ways.

Sting and Crown began to walk warily toward the wall. Leaf, watching from the driver's seat, slipped his arm lightly about the waist of Shadow, who stood beside him, and caressed her smooth fur. The rain had ended; a gray cloud still hung low, and the gleam of Crown's armor was already softened by fine droplets of moisture. He and Sting were nearly to the palisade, now, Crown constantly scanning the underbrush as if expecting a horde of Tree Companions to spring forth. Sting, loping along next to him, looked like some agile little two-legged beast, the top of his head barely reaching to Crown's hip.

They reached the palisade. Thin, late-afternoon sunlight streamed over its top. Kneeling, Sting inspected the base of the wall, probing at the soil with his fingers, and said something to Crown, who nodded and pointed upward. Sting backed off, made a short running start, and lofted himself, rising almost as though he were taking wing. His leap carried him soaring to the wall's jagged crest in a swift blurred flight. He appeared to hover for a long moment while choosing a place to land. At last he alighted in a precarious, uncomfortable-looking position, sprawled along the top of the wall with his body arched to avoid the timber's sharpened tips, his hands grasping two of the stakes and his feet wedged between two others. Sting remained in this desperate contortion for a remarkably long time, studying whatever lay beyond the barricade; then he let go his hold, sprang lightly outward, and floated to the ground, a distance some three times his own height. He landed upright, without stumbling. There was a brief conference between Crown and Sting. Then they came back to the wagon.

"It's a toll-raising scheme, all right," Crown muttered. "The middle timbers aren't embedded in the earth. They end just at ground level and form a hinged gate, fastened by two heavy bolts on the far side."

"I saw at least a hundred Tree Companions back of the wall," Sting said. "Armed with blowdarts. They'll be coming around to visit us in a moment."

"We should arm ourselves," Leaf said.

Crown shrugged. "We can't fight that many of them. Not twenty-five to one, we can't. The best hand-to-hand man in the world is helpless against little forest folk with poisoned blowdarts. If we aren't able to awe them into letting us go through, we'll have to buy them off somehow. But I don't know. That gate isn't nearly wide enough for the wagon."

He was right about that. There was the dry scraping squeal of wood against wood—the bolts were being unfastened—and then the gate swung slowly open. When it had been fully pushed back it provided an opening through which any good-size cart of ordinary dimensions might pass, but not Crown's magnificent vehicle. Five or six stakes on each side of the gate would have to be pulled down in order for the wagon to go by.

Tree Companions came swarming toward the wagon, scores of them—small, naked folk with lean limbs and smooth blue-green skin. They looked like animated clay statuettes, casually pinched into shape: their hairless heads were narrow and elongated, with flat sloping foreheads, and their long necks looked flimsy and fragile. They had shallow chests and bony, meatless frames. All of them, men and women both, wore reed dart-blowers strapped to their hips. As they danced and frolicked about the wagon they set up a ragged, irregular chanting, tuneless and atonal, like the improvised songs of children caught up in frantic play.

"We'll go out to them," Crown said. "Stay calm, make no sudden moves. Remember that these are underbreeds. So long as we think of ourselves as men and them as nothing more than monkeys, and make them realize we think that way, we'll be able to keep them under control."

"They're men," said Shadow quietly. "Same as we. Not monkeys."

"Think of them as like monkeys," Crown told her. "Otherwise we're lost. Come, now."

They left the wagon, Crown first, then Leaf, Sting, Shadow. The cavorting Tree Companions paused momentarily in their sport as the four travelers emerged; they looked up, grinned, chattered, pointed, did handsprings and headstands. They did not seem awed. Did Pure Stream mean nothing to them? Had they no fear of Dark Lake? Crown, glowering, said to Sting, "Can you speak their language?"

"A few words."

"Speak to them. Ask them to send their chief here to me."

Sting took up a position just in front of Crown, cupped his hands to his mouth, and shouted something high and piercing in a singsong language. He spoke with exaggerated, painful clarity, as one does in addressing a blind person or a foreigner. The Tree Companions snickered and exchanged little yipping cries. Then one of them came dancing forward, planted his face a handsbreadth from Sting's, and mimicked Sting's words, catching the intonation with comic accuracy. Sting looked frightened, and backed away half a pace, butting accidentally into Crown's chest. The Tree Companion loosed a stream of words, and when he fell silent Sting repeated his original phrase in a more subdued tone.

"What's happening?" Crown asked. "Can you understand anything?"

"A little. Very little."

"Will they get the chief?"

"I'm not sure. I don't know if he and I are talking about the same things."

"You said these people pay tribute to White Crystal."

"Paid," Sting said. "I don't know if there's any allegiance any longer. I think they may be having some fun at our expense. I think what he said was insulting, but I'm not sure. I'm just not sure."

"Stinking monkeys!"

"Careful, Crown," Shadow murmured. "We can't speak their language, but they may understand ours."

Crown said, "Try again. Speak more slowly. Get the monkey to speak more slowly. The chief, Sting, we want to see the chief! Isn't there any way you can make contact?"

"I could go into trance," Sting said. "And Shadow could help me with the meanings. But I'd need time to get myself together. I feel too quick now, too tense." As if to illustrate his point he executed a tiny jumping movement, blur-snap-hop, that carried him laterally a few paces to the left. Blur-snap-hop and he was back in place again. The Tree Companion laughed shrilly, clapped his hands, and tried to imitate Sting's little shuttling jump. Others of the tribe came over; there were ten or twelve of them now, clustered near the entrance to the wagon. Sting hopped again: it was like a twitch, a tic. He started to tremble. Shadow reached toward him and folded her slender arms about his chest, as though to anchor him. The Tree Companions grew more agitated; there was a hard, intense quality about their playfulness now. Trouble seemed imminent. Leaf, standing on the far side of Crown, felt a sudden knotting of the muscles at the base of his stomach. Something nagged at his attention, off to his right out in the crowd of Tree Companions; he glanced that way and saw an azure brightness, elongated and upright, a man-size strip of fog and haze, drifting and weaving among the forest folk. Was it the Invisible? Or only some trick of the dying daylight, slipping through the residual vapor of the rainstorm? He struggled for a sharp focus, but the figure eluded his gaze, slipping ticklingly beyond sight as Leaf followed it with his eyes. Abruptly he heard a howl from Crown and turned just in time to see a Tree Companion duck beneath the huge man's elbow and go sprinting into the wagon. "Stop!" Crown roared. "Come back!" And, as if a signal had been given, seven or eight others of the lithe little tribesmen scrambled aboard.

There was death in Crown's eyes. He beckoned savagely to Leaf and rushed through the entrance. Leaf followed. Sting, sobbing, huddled in the entranceway, making no attempt to halt the Tree Companions who were streaming into the wagon. Leaf saw them climbing over everything, examining, inspecting, commenting. Monkeys, yes. Down in the front corridor Crown was struggling with four of them, holding one in each vast hand, trying to shake free two others who were climbing his armored legs. Leaf confronted a miniature Tree Companion woman, a gnomish bright-eyed creature whose bare lean body glistened with sour sweat, and as he reached for her she drew not a dart-blower but a long narrow blade from the tube at her hip, and slashed Leaf fiercely along the inside of his left forearm. There was a quick, frightening gush of blood, and only some moments afterward did he feel the fiery lick of the pain. A poisoned knife? Well, then, into the All-Is-One with you, Leaf. But if there had been poison, he felt no effects of it; he wrenched the knife from her grasp, jammed it into the wall, scooped her up, and pitched her lightly through the open hatch of the wagon. No more Tree Companions were coming in, now. Leaf found two more, threw them out, dragged another out of the roofbeams, tossed him after the others, went looking for more. Shadow stood in the hatchway, blocking it with her frail arms outstretched. Where was Crown?

Ah. There. In the trophy room. "Grab them and carry them to the hatch!" Leaf yelled. "We're rid of most of them!"

"The stinking monkeys," Crown cried. He gestured angrily. The Tree Companions had seized some treasure of Crown's, some ancient suit of mail, and in their childish buoyancy had ripped the fragile links apart with their tug-of-war. Crown, enraged, bore down on them, clamped one hand on each tapering skull—"*Don't!*" Leaf shouted, fearing darts in vengeance—and squeezed, cracking them like nuts. He tossed the corpses aside and, picking up his torn trophy, stood sadly pressing the sundered edges together in a clumsy attempt at repair.

"You've done it now," Leaf said. "They were just being inquisitive. Now we'll have war, and we'll be dead before nightfall."

"Never," Crown grunted.

He dropped the chainmail, scooped up the dead Tree Companions, carried them dangling through the wagon, and threw them like offal into the clearing. Then he stood defiantly in the hatchway, inviting their darts. None came. Those Tree Companions still aboard the wagon, five or six of them, appeared empty-handed, silent, and slipped hastily around the hulking Dark Laker. Leaf went forward and joined Crown. Blood was still dripping from Leaf's wound; he dared not induce clotting nor permit the wound to close until he had been purged of whatever poison might have been on the blade. A thin, straight cut, deep and painful, ran down his arm from elbow to wrist. Shadow gave a soft little cry and seized his hand. Her breath was warm against the edges of the gash. "Are you badly injured?" she whispered.

"I don't think so. It's just a question of whether the knife was poisoned."

"They poison only their darts," said Sting. "But there'll be infection to cope with. Better let Shadow look after you."

"Yes," Leaf said. He glanced into the clearing. The Tree Companions, as though thrown into shock by the violence that had come from their brief invasion of the wagon, stood frozen along the road in silent groups of nine or ten, keeping their distance. The two dead ones lay crumpled where Crown had hurled them. The unmistakable figure of the Invisible, transparent but clearly outlined by a dark perimeter, could be seen to the right, near the border of the thicket: his eyes glittered fiercely, his lips were twisted in a strange smile. Crown was staring at him in slack-jawed astonishment. Everything seemed suspended, held floating motionless in the bowl of time. To Leaf the scene was an eerie tableau in which the only sense of ongoing process was supplied by the throbbing in his slashed arm. He hung moored at the center, waiting, waiting, incapable of action, trapped like others in timelessness. In that long pause he realized that another figure had appeared during the melee, and stood now calmly ten paces or so to the left of the grinning Invisible: a Tree Companion, taller than the others of his kind, clad in beads and gimcracks but undeniably a being of presence and majesty.

"The chief has arrived," Sting said hoarsely.

The stasis broke. Leaf released his breath and let his rigid body slump. Shadow tugged at him, saying, "Let me clean that cut for you." The chief of the Tree Companions stabbed the air with three outstretched fingers, pointing at the wagon, and called out five crisp, sharp, jubilant syllables; slowly and grandly he began to stalk toward the wagon. At the same moment the Invisible flickered brightly, like a sun about to die, and disappeared entirely from view. Crown, turning to Leaf, said in a thick voice, "It's all going crazy here. I was just imagining I saw one of the Invisibles from Theptis skulking around by the underbrush."

"You weren't imagining anything," Leaf told him. "He's been riding secretly with us since Theptis. Waiting to see what would happen to us when we came to the Tree Companions' wall."

Crown looked jarred by that. "When did you find that out?" he demanded.

Shadow said, "Let him be, Crown. Go and parley with the chief. If I don't clean Leaf's wound soon—"

"Just a minute. I need to know the truth. Leaf, when did you find out about this Invisible?"

"When I went up front to relieve Sting. He was in the driver's cabin. Laughing at me, jeering. The way they do."

"And you didn't tell me? Why?"

"There was no chance. He bothered me for a while, and then he vanished, and I was busy driving after that, and then we came to the wall, and then the Tree Companions—"

"What does he want from us?" Crown asked harshly, face pushed close to Leaf's.

Leaf was starting to feel fever rising. He swayed and leaned on Shadow. Her taut, resilient little form bore him with surprising strength. He said tiredly, "I don't know. Does anyone ever know what one of them wants!" The Tree Companion chief, meanwhile, had come up beside them and in a lusty, self-assured way slapped his open palm several times against the side of the wagon, as though taking possession of it. Crown whirled. The chief coolly spoke, voice level, inflections controlled. Crown shook his head. "What's he saying?" he barked. "Sting? *Sting?*"

"Come," Shadow said to Leaf. "Now. Please."

She led him toward the passenger castle. He sprawled on the furs while she searched busily through her case of unguents and ointments; then she came to him with a long green vial in her hand and said, "There'll be pain for you now."

"Wait."

He centered himself and disconnected, as well as he was able, the network of sensory apparatus that conveyed messages of discomfort from his arm to his brain. At once he felt his skin growing cooler, and he realized for the first time since the battle how much pain he had been in: so much that he had not had the wisdom to do anything about it. Dispassionately he watched as Shadow, all efficiency, probed his wound, parting the lips of the cut without squeamishness and swabbing its red interior. A faint tickling, unpleasant but not painful, was all he sensed. She looked up, finally, and said, "There'll be no infection. You can allow the wound to close now." In order to do that Leaf had to reestablish the neural connections to a certain degree, and as he unblocked the flow of impulses he felt sudden startling pain, both from the cut itself and from Shadow's medicines; but quickly he induced clotting, and a moment afterward he was deep in the disciplines that would encourage the sundered flesh to heal. The wound began to close. Lightly Shadow blotted the fresh blood from his arm and prepared a poultice; by the time she had it in place, the gaping slash had reduced itself to a thin raw line. "You'll live," she said. "You were lucky they don't poison their knives." He kissed the tip of her nose and they returned to the hatch area.

Sting and the Tree Companion chief were conducting some sort of discussion in pantomime, Sting's motions sweeping and broad, the chief's the merest flicks of fingers, while Crown stood by, an impassive column of darkness, arms folded somberly. As Leaf and Shadow reappeared Crown said, "Sting isn't getting anywhere. It has to be a trance parley or we won't make contact. Help him, Shadow."

She nodded. To Leaf, Crown said, "How's the arm?"

"It'll be all right."

"How soon?"

"A day. Two, maybe. Sore for a week."

"We may be fighting again by sunrise."

"You told me yourself that we can't possibly survive a battle with these people."

"Even so," Crown said. "We may be fighting again by sunrise. If there's no other choice, we'll fight."

"And die?"

"And die," Crown said.

Leaf walked slowly away. Twilight had come. All vestiges of the rain had vanished, and the air was clear, crisp, growing chill, with a light wind out of the north that was gaining steadily in force. Beyond the thicket the tops of tall ropy-limbed trees were whipping about. The shards of the moon had moved into view, rough daggers of whiteness doing their slow dance about one another in the darkening sky. The poor old shattered moon, souvenir of an era long gone: it seemed a scratchy mirror for the tormented planet that owned it, for the fragmented race of races that was mankind. Leaf went to the nightmares, who stood patiently in harness, and passed among them, gently stroking their shaggy ears, caressing their blunt noses. Their eyes, liquid, intelligent, watchful, peered into his almost reproachfully. You promised us a stable, they seemed to be saying. Stallions, warmth, newly mown hay. Leaf shrugged. In this world, he told them wordlessly, it isn't always possible to keep one's promises. One does one's best, and one hopes that that is enough.

Near the wagon Sting has assumed a cross-legged position on the damp ground. Shadow squats beside him; the chief, mantled in dignity, stands stiffly before them, but Shadow coaxes him with gentle gestures to come down to them. Sting's eyes are closed and his head lolls forward. He is already in trance. His left hand grasps Shadow's muscular furry thigh; he extends his right, palm upward, and after a moment the chief puts his own palm to it. Contact: the circuit is closed.

Leaf has no idea what messages are passing among the three of them, but yet, oddly, he does not feel excluded from the transaction. Such a sense of love and warmth radiates from Sting and Shadow and even from the Tree Companion that he is drawn in, he is enfolded by their communion. And Crown, too, is engulfed and absorbed by the group aura; his rigid martial posture eases, his grim face looks strangely peaceful. Of course it is Sting and Shadow who are most closely linked; Shadow is closer now to Sting than she has ever been to Leaf, but Leaf is untroubled by this. Jealousy and competitiveness are inconceivable now. He is Sting, Sting is Leaf, they all are Shadow and Crown, there are no boundaries separating one from another, just as there will be no boundaries in the All-Is-One that awaits every living creature, Sting and Crown and Shadow and Leaf, the Tree Companions, the Invisibles, the nightmares, the no-leg spiders.

They are getting down to cases now. Leaf is aware of strands of opposition and conflict manifesting themselves in the intricate negotiation that is taking place. Although he is still without a clue to the content of the exchange, Leaf understands that the Tree Companion chief is stating a position of demand—calmly, bluntly, immovable—and Sting and Shadow are explaining to him that Crown is not at all likely to yield. More than that Leaf is unable to perceive, even when he is most deeply enmeshed in the larger consciousness of the trance-wrapped three. Nor does he know how much time is elapsing. The symphonic interchange—demand, response, development, climax—continues repetitively, indefinitely, reaching no resolution.

He feels, at last, a running-down, an attenuation of the experience. He begins to move outside the field of contact, or to have it move outside him. Spiderwebs of sensibility still connect him to the others even as Sting and Shadow and the chief rise and separate, but they are rapidly thinning and fraying, and in a moment they snap.

The contact ends.

The meeting was over. During the trance-time night had fallen, an extraordinarily black night against which the stars seemed unnaturally bright. The fragments of the moon had traveled far across the sky. So it had been a lengthy exchange; yet in the immediate vicinity of the wagon nothing seemed altered. Crown stood like a statue beside the wagon's entrance; the Tree Companions still occupied the cleared ground between the wagon and the gate. Once more a tableau, then: how easy it is to slide into motionlessness, Leaf thought, in these impoverished times. Stand and wait, stand and wait; but now motion returned. The Tree Companion pivoted and strode off without a word, signaling to his people, who gathered up their dead and followed him through the gate. From within they tugged the gate shut; there was the screeching sound of the bolts being forced home. Sting, looking dazed, whispered something to Shadow, who nodded and lightly touched his arm. They walked haltingly back to the wagon.

"Well?" Crown asked finally.

"They will allow us to pass," Sting said.

"How courteous of them."

"But they claim the wagon and everything that is in it."

Crown gasped. "By what right?"

"Right of prophecy," said Shadow. "There is a seer among them, an old woman of mixed stock, part White Crystal, part Tree Companion, part Invisible. She has told them that everything that has happened lately in the world was caused by the Soul for the sake of enriching the Tree Companions."

"Everything? They see the onslaught of the Teeth as a sign of divine favor?"

"Everything," said Sting. "The entire upheaval. All for their benefit. All done so that migrations would begin and refugees would come to

417

this place, carrying with them valuable possessions, which they would surrender to those whom the Soul meant should own them, meaning the Tree Companions."

Crown laughed roughly. "If they want to be brigands, why not practice brigandage outright, with the right name on it, and not blame their greed on the Soul?"

"They don't see themselves as brigands," Shadow said. "There can be no denying the chief's sincerity. He and his people genuinely believe that the Soul has decreed all this for their own special good, that the time has come—"

"Sincerity!"

"—for the Tree Companions to become people of substance and property. Therefore they've built this wall across the highway, and as refugees come west, the Tree Companions relieve them of their possessions with the blessing of the Soul."

"I'd like to meet their prophet," Crown muttered.

Leaf said, "It was my understanding that Invisibles were unable to breed with other stocks."

Sting told him, with a shrug, "We report only what we learned as we sat there dreaming with the chief. The witch-woman is part Invisible, he said. Perhaps he was wrong, but he was doing no lying. Of that I'm certain."

"And I," Shadow put in.

"What happens to those who refuse to pay tribute?" Crown asked.

"The Tree Companions regard them as thwarters of the Soul's design," said Sting, "and fall upon them and put them to death. And then seize their goods."

Crown moved restlessly in a shallow circle in front of the wagon, kicking up gouts of soil out of the hard-packed roadbed. After a moment he said, "They dangle on vines. They chatter like foolish monkeys. What do they want with the merchandise of civilized folk? Our furs, our statuettes, our carvings, our flutes, our robes?"

"Having such things will make them equal in their own sight to the higher stocks," Sting said. "Not the things themselves, but the possession of them, do you see, Crown?"

"They'll have nothing of mine!"

"What will we do, then?" Leaf asked. "Sit here and wait for their darts?"

Crown caught Sting heavily by the shoulder. "Did they give us any sort of time limit? How long do we have before they attack?"

"There was nothing like an ultimatum. The chief seems unwilling to enter into warfare with us."

"Because he's afraid of his betters!"

"Because he thinks violence cheapens the decree of the Soul," Sting replied evenly. "Therefore he intends to wait for us to surrender our belongings voluntarily."

"He'll wait a hundred years!"

"He'll wait a few days," Shadow said. "If we haven't yielded, the attack will come. But what will you do, Crown? Suppose they were willing to wait your hundred years. Are you? We can't camp here forever."

"Are you suggesting we give them what they ask?"

"I merely want to know what strategy you have in mind," she said. "You admit yourself we can't defeat them in battle. We haven't done a very good job of aweing them into submission. You recognize that any attempt to destroy their wall will bring them upon us with their darts. You refuse to turn back and look for some other westward route. You rule out the alternative of yielding to them. Very well, Crown. What do you have in mind?"

"We'll wait a few days," Crown said thickly.

"The Teeth are heading this way!" Sting cried. "Shall we sit here and let them catch us?"

Crown shook his head. "Long before the Teeth get here, Sting, this place will be full of other refugees, many of them, as unwilling to give up their goods to these folk as we are. I can feel them already on the road, coming this way, two days' march from us, perhaps less. We'll make alliance with them. Four of us may be helpless against a swarm of poisonous apes, but fifty or a hundred strong fighters would send them scrambling up their own trees."

"No one will come this way," said Leaf. "No one but fools. Everyone passing through Theptis knows what's been done to the highway here. What good is the aid of fools?"

"We came this way," Crown snapped. "Are we such fools?"

"Perhaps we are. We were warned not to take Spider Highway, and we took it anyway."

"Because we refused to trust the word of Invisibles."

"Well, the Invisibles happened to be telling the truth, this time," Leaf said. "And the news must be all over Theptis. No one in his right mind will come this way now."

"I feel marchers already on the way, hundreds of them," Crown said. "I can sense these things, sometimes. What about you, Sting? You feel things ahead of time, don't you? They're coming, aren't they? Have no fear, Leaf. We'll have allies here in a day or so, and then let these thieving Tree Companions beware." Crown gestured broadly. "Leaf, set the nightmares loose to graze. And then everybody inside the wagon. We'll seal it and take turns standing watch through the night. This is a time for vigilance and courage."

"This is a time for digging graves," Sting murmured sourly, as they clambered into the wagon.

Crown and Shadow stood the first round of watches while Leaf and Sting napped in the back. Leaf fell asleep at once and dreamed he was living in some immense brutal eastern city—the buildings and street plan were unfamiliar to him, but the architecture was definitely eastern in style, gray and heavy, all parapets and cornices—that was coming under attack by the Teeth.

He observed everything from a many-windowed gallery atop an enormous square-sided brick tower that seemed like a survival from some remote prehistoric epoch. First, from the north, came the sound of the war song of the invaders, a nasty unendurable buzzing drone, piercing and intense, like the humming of highspeed polishing wheels at work on metal plates. That dread music brought the inhabitants of the city spilling into the streets—all stocks, Flower Givers and Sand Shapers and White Crystals and Dancing Stars and even Tree Companions, absurdly garbed in mercantile robes as though they were so many fat citified Fingers—but no one was able to escape, for there were so many people, colliding and jostling and stumbling and falling in helpless heaps, that they blocked every avenue and alleyway.

Into this chaos now entered the vanguard of the Teeth; shuffling forward in their peculiar bent-kneed crouch, trampling those who had fallen. They looked half-beast, half-demon: squat thick-thewed flat-headed long-muzzled creatures, naked, hairy, their skins the color of sand, their eyes glinting with insatiable hungers. Leaf's dreaming mind subtly magnified and distorted them so that they came hopping into the city like a band of giant toothy frogs, thump-thump, bare fleshy feet slapping pavement in sinister reverberations, short powerful arms swinging almost comically at each leaping stride. The kinship of mankind meant nothing to these carnivorous beings. They had been penned up too long in the cold, mountainous, barren country of the far northeast, living on such scraps and strings as the animals of the forest yielded, and they saw their fellow humans as mere meat stockpiled by the Soul against this day of vengeance. Efficiently, now, they began their round-up in the newly conquered city, seizing everyone in sight, cloistering the dazed prisoners in hastily rigged pens: these we eat tonight at our victory feast; these we save for tomorrow's dinner; these become dried meat to carry with us on the march; these we kill for sport; these we keep as slaves. Leaf watched the Teeth erecting their huge spits. Kindling their fierce roasting-fires. Diligent search teams fanned out through the suburbs. No one would escape. Leaf stirred and groaned, reached the threshold of wakefulness, fell back into dream. Would they find him in his tower? Smoke, gray and greasy, boiled up out of a hundred parts of town.

Leaping flames. Rivulets of blood ran in the streets. He was choking. A terrible dream. But was it only a dream? This was how it had actually been in Holy Town hours after he and Crown and Sting and Shadow had managed to get away, this was no doubt as it had happened in city after city along the tormented coastal strip, very likely something of this sort was going on now in—where?—Bone Harbor? Ved-uru? Alsandar? He could smell the penetrating odor of roasting meat. He could hear the heavy lalloping sound of a Teeth patrol running up the stairs of his tower. They had him. Yes, here, now, now, a dozen Teeth bursting suddenly into his hiding place, grinning broadly—Pure Stream, they had captured a Pure Stream! What a coup! Beasts. Beasts. Prodding him, testing his flesh. Not plump enough for them, eh? This one's pretty lean. We'll cook him anyway. Pure Stream meat, it enlarges the soul, it makes you into something more than you were. Take him downstairs! To the spit, to the spit, to the—

"Leaf?"

"I warn you—you won't like—the flavor—"

"Leaf, wake up!"

"The fires—oh, the stink!"

"Leaf!"

It was Shadow. She shook him gently, plucked at his shoulder. He blinked and slowly sat up. His wounded arm was throbbing again; he felt feverish. Effects of the dream. A dream, only a dream. He shivered and tried to center himself, working at it, banishing the fever, banishing the shreds of dark fantasy that were still shrouding his mind.

"Are you all right?" she asked.

"I was dreaming about the Teeth," he told her. He shook his head, trying to clear it. "Am I to stand watch now?"

She nodded. "Up front. Driver's cabin."

"Has anything been happening?"

"Nothing. Not a thing." She reached up and drew her fingertips lightly along the sides of his jaws. Her eyes were warm and bright, her smile was loving. "The Teeth are far away, Leaf."

"From us, maybe. Not from others."

"They were sent by the will of the Soul."

"I know, I know." How often had he preached acceptance! This is the will, and we bow to it. This is the road, and we travel it uncomplainingly. But yet, but yet—he shuddered. The dream mode persisted. He was altogether disoriented. Dream-Teeth nibbled at his flesh. The inner chambers of his spirit resonated to the screams of those on the spits, the sounds of rending and tearing, the unbearable reek of burning cities. In ten days, half a world torn apart. So much pain, so much death, so much that had been beautiful destroyed by relentless savages who would not halt until, the Soul only knew when, they had had their full measure of revenge. The will of the Soul sends them upon us. Accept. Accept. He could not find his center. Shadow held him, straining to encompass his body with her arms. After a moment he began to feel less troubled, but he remained scattered, diffused, present only in part, some portion of his mind nailed as if by spikes into that monstrous ash-strewn wasteland that the Teeth had created out of the fair and fertile eastern provinces.

She released him. "Go," she whispered. "It's quiet up front. You'll be able to find yourself again."

He took her place in the driver's cabin, going silently past Sting, who had replaced Crown on watch amidwagon. Half the night was gone. All was still in the roadside clearing; the great wooden gate was shut tight and nobody was about. By cold starlight Leaf saw the nightmares browsing patiently at the edge of the thicket. Gentle horses, almost human. If I must be visited by nightmares, he thought, let it be by their kind.

Shadow had been right. In the stillness he grew calm, and perspective returned. Lamentation would not restore the shattered eastland, expressions of horror and shock would not turn the Teeth into pious tillers of the soil. The Soul had decreed chaos: so be it. This is the road we must travel, and who dares ask why? Once the world had been whole and now it is fragmented, and that is the way things are because that is the way things were meant to be. He became less tense. Anguish dropped from him. He was Leaf again.

Toward dawn the visible world lost its sharp starlit edge; a soft fog settled over the wagon, and rain fell for a time, a light, pure rain, barely audible, altogether different in character from yesterday's vicious storm. In the strange light just preceding sunrise the world took on a delicate pearly mistiness; and out of that mist an apparition materialized. Leaf saw a figure come drifting through the closed gate—through it—a ghostly, incorporeal figure. He thought it might be the Invisible who had been lurking close by the wagon since Theptis, but no, this was a woman, old and frail, an attenuated woman, smaller even than Shadow, more slender. Leaf knew who she must be: the mixed-blood woman. The prophetess, the seer, she who had stirred up these Tree Companions to block the highway. Her skin had the White Crystal waxiness of texture and the White Crystal nodes of dark, coarse hair; the form of her body was essentially that of a Tree Companion, thin and long-armed; and from her Invisible forebears, it seemed, she had inherited that perplexing intangibility, that look of existing always on the borderland between hallucination and reality, between mist and flesh. Mixed-bloods were uncommon; Leaf had rarely seen one, and never had encountered one who combined in herself so many different stocks. It was said that people of mixed blood had strange gifts. Surely this one did. How had she bypassed the wall? Not even Invisibles could travel through solid wood. Perhaps this was just a dream, then, or possibly she had some way of projecting an image of herself into his mind from a point within the Tree Companion village. He did not understand.

He watched her a long while. She appeared real enough. She halted twenty paces from the nose of the wagon and scanned the entire horizon slowly, her eyes coming to rest at last on the window of the driver's cabin. She was aware, certainly, that he was looking at her, and she looked back, eye to eye, staring unflinchingly. They remained locked that way for some minutes. Her expression was glum and opaque, a withered scowl, but suddenly she brightened and smiled intensely at him and it was such a *knowing* smile that Leaf was thrown into terror by the old witch, and glanced away, shamed and defeated.

When he lifted his head she was out of view; he pressed himself against the window, craned his neck, and found her down near the middle of the wagon. She was inspecting its exterior workmanship at close range, picking and prying at the hull. Then she wandered away, out to the place where Sting and Shadow and the chief had had their conference, and sat down cross-legged where they had been sitting. She became extraordinarily still, as if she were asleep, or in trance. Just when Leaf began to think she would never move again, she took a pipe of carved bone from a pouch at her waist, filled it with a gray-blue powder, and lit it. He searched her face for tokens of revelation, but nothing showed on it; she grew ever more impassive and unreadable. When the pipe went out, she filled it again, and smoked a second time, and still Leaf watched her, his face pushed awkwardly against the window, his body growing stiff. The first rays of sunlight now arrived, pink shading rapidly into gold. As the brightness deepened the witch-woman imperceptibly became less solid; she was fading away, moment by moment, and shortly he saw nothing of her but her pipe and her kerchief, and then the clearing was empty. The long shadows of the six nightmares splashed against the wooden palisade. Leaf's head lolled. I've been dozing, he thought. It's morning, and all's well. He went to awaken Crown.

They breakfasted lightly. Leaf and Shadow led the horses to water at a small clear brook five minutes' walk toward Theptis. Sting foraged awhile in the thicket for nuts and berries, and having filled two pails, went aft to doze in the furs. Crown brooded in his trophy room and said nothing to anyone. A few Tree Companions could be seen watching the wagon from perches in the crowns of towering red-leaved trees on the hillside just behind the wall. Nothing happened until midmorning. Then, at a time when all four travelers were within the wagon, a dozen newcomers appeared, forerunners of the refugee tribe that Crown's intuitions had correctly predicted. They came slowly up the road, on foot, dusty and tired-looking, staggering beneath huge untidy bundles of belongings and supplies. They were square-headed muscular people, as tall as Leaf or taller, with the look of warriors about them; they carried short swords at their waists, and both men and women were conspicuously scarred. Their skins were gray, tinged with pale green, and they had more fingers and toes than was usual among mankind.

Leaf had never seen their sort before. "Do you know them?" he asked Sting.

"Snow Hunters," Sting said. "Close kin to the Sand Shapers, I think. Midcaste and said to be unfriendly to strangers. They live southwest of Theptis, in the hill country."

"One would think they'd be safe there," said Shadow.

Sting shrugged. "No one's safe from the Teeth, eh? Not even on the highest hills. Not even in the thickest jungles."

The Snow Hunters dropped their packs and looked around. The wagon drew them first; they seemed stunned by the opulence of it. They examined it in wonder, touching it as the witch-woman had, scrutinizing it from every side. When they saw faces looking out at them, they nudged one another and pointed and whispered, but they did not smile, nor did they wave greetings. After a time they went on to the wall and studied it with the same childlike curiosity. It appeared to baffle them. They measured it with their outstretched hands, pressed their bodies against it, pushed at it with their shoulders, tapped the timbers, plucked at the sturdy bindings of vine. By this time perhaps a dozen more of them had come up the road; they too clustered about the wagon, doing as the first had done, and then continued toward the wall. More and more Snow Hunters were arriving, in groups of three or four. One trio, standing apart from the others, gave the impression of being tribal leaders; they consulted, nodded, summoned and dismissed other members of the tribe with forceful gestures of their hands.

"Let's go out and parley," Crown said. He donned his best armor and selected an array of elegant dress weapons. To Sting he gave a slender dagger. Shadow would not bear arms, and Leaf preferred to arm himself in nothing but Pure Stream prestige. His status as a member of the ancestral stock, he found, served him as well as a sword in most encounters with strangers.

The Snow Hunters—about a hundred of them now had gathered, with still more down the way—looked apprehensive as Crown and his companions descended from the wagon. Crown's bulk and gladiatorial swagger seemed far more threatening to these strong-bodied warlike folk than they had been to the chattering Tree Companions, and Leaf's presence too appeared disturbing to them. Warily they moved to form a loose semicircle about their three leaders; they stood close by one another, murmuring tensely, and their hands hovered near the hilts of their swords.

Crown stepped forward. "Careful," Leaf said softly. "They're on edge. Don't push them."

But Crown, with a display of slick diplomacy unusual for him, quickly put the Snow Hunters at their ease with a warm gesture of greeting—hands pressed to shoulders, palms outward, fingers spread wide—and a few hearty words of welcome. Introductions were exchanged. The spokesman for the tribe, an iron-faced man with frosty eyes and hard cheekbones, was called Sky; the names of his co-captains were Blade and Shield. Sky spoke in a flat, quiet voice, everything on the same note. He seemed empty, burned out, a man who had entered some realm of exhaustion far beyond mere fatigue. They had been on the road for three days and three nights almost without a halt, said Sky. Last week a major force of Teeth had started westward through the midcoastal lowlands bound for Theptis, and one band of these, just a few hundred warriors, had lost its way, going south into the hill country. Their aimless wanderings brought these straying Teeth without warning into the secluded village of the Snow Hunters, and there had been a terrible battle in which more than half of Sky's people had perished. The survivors, having slipped away into the trackless forest, had made their way by back roads to Spider Highway, and, numbed by shock and grief, had been marching like machines toward the Middle River, hoping to find some new hillside in the sparsely populated territories of the far northwest. They could never return to their old home, Shield declared, for it had been desecrated by the feasting of the Teeth.

"But what is this wall?" Sky asked.

Crown explained, telling the Snow Hunters about the Tree Companions and their prophetess, and of her promise that the booty of all refugees was to be surrendered to them. "They lie in wait for us with their darts," Crown said. "Four of us were helpless against them. But they would never dare challenge a force the size of yours. We'll have their wall smashed down by nightfall!"

"The Tree Companions are said to be fierce foes," Sky remarked quietly.

"Nothing but monkeys," said Crown. "They'll scramble to their treetops if we just draw our swords."

"And shower us with their poisoned arrows," Shield muttered. "Friend, we have little stomach for further warfare. Too many of us have fallen this week."

"What will you do?" Crown cried. "Give them your swords, and your tunics and your wives' rings and the sandals off your feet?"

Sky closed his eyes and stood motionless, remaining silent for a long moment. At length, without opening his eyes, he said in a voice that came from the center of an immense void, "We will talk with the Tree Companions and learn what they actually demand of us, and then we will make our decisions and form our plans."

"The wall—if you fight beside us, we can destroy this wall, and open the road to all who flee the Teeth!"

With cold patience Sky said, "We will speak with you again afterward," and turned away. "Now we will rest, and wait for the Tree Companions to come forth."

The Snow Hunters withdrew, sprawling out along the margin of the thicket just under the wall. There they huddled in rows, staring at the ground, waiting. Crown scowled, spat, shook his head. Turning to Leaf he said, "They have the true look of fighters. There's something that marks a fighter apart from other men, Leaf, and I can tell when it's there, and these Snow Hunters have it. They have the strength, they have the power; they have the spirit of battle in them. And yet, see them now! Squatting there like fat frightened Fingers!"

"They've been beaten badly," Leaf said. "They've been driven from their homeland. They know what it is to look back across a hilltop and see the fires in which your kinsmen are being cooked. That takes the fighting spirit out of a person, Crown."

"No. Losing makes the flame burn brighter. It makes you feverish with the desire for revenge."

"Does it? What do you know about losing? You were never so much as touched by any of your opponents."

Crown glared at him. "I'm not speaking of dueling. Do you think my life has gone untouched by the Teeth? What am I doing here on this dirt road with all that I still own packed into a single wagon? But I'm no walking dead man like these Snow Hunters. I'm not running away, I'm going to find an army. And then I'll go back east and take my vengeance. While they—afraid of monkeys—"

"They've been marching day and night," Shadow said. "They must have been on the road when the purple rain was falling. They've spent all their strength while we've been riding in your wagon, Crown. Once they've had a little rest, perhaps they—"

"Afraid of *monkeys!*"

Crown shook with wrath. He strode up and down before the wagon, pounding his fists into his thighs. Leaf feared that he would go across to the Snow Hunters and attempt by bluster to force them into an alliance. Leaf understood the mood of these people: shattered and drained though they were, they might lash out in sudden savage irritation if Crown goaded them too severely. Possibly some hours of rest, as Shadow had suggested, and they might feel more like helping Crown drive his way through the Tree Companions' wall. But not now. Not now.

The gate in the wall opened. Some twenty of the forest folk emerged, among them the tribal chief and—Leaf caught his breath in awe—the ancient seeress, who looked across the way and bestowed on Leaf another of her penetrating comfortless smiles.

"What kind of creature is that?" Crown asked.

"The mixed-blood witch," said Leaf. "I saw her at dawn, while I was standing watch."

"Look!" Shadow cried. "She flickers and fades like an Invisible! But her pelt is like yours, Sting, and her shape is that of—"

"She frightens me," Sting said hoarsely. He was shaking. "She foretells death for us. We have little time left to us, friends. She is the goddess of death, that one." He plucked at Crown's elbow, unprotected by the armour. "Come! Let's start back along Spider Highway! Better to take our chances in the desert than to stay here and die!"

"Quiet," Crown snapped. "There's no going back. The Teeth are already in Theptis. They'll be moving out along this road in a day or two. There's only one direction for us."

"But the wall," Sting said.

"The wall will be in ruins by nightfall," Crown told him.

The chief of the Tree Companions was conferring with Sky and Blade and Shield. Evidently the Snow Hunters knew something of the language of the Tree Companions, for Leaf could hear vocal interchanges, supplemented by pantomime and sign language. The chief pointed to himself often, to the wall, to the prophetess; he indicated the packs the Snow Hunters had been carrying; he jerked his thumb angrily toward Crown's wagon. The conversation lasted nearly half an hour and seemed to reach an amicable outcome. The Tree Companions departed, this time leaving the gate open. Sky, Shield, and Blade moved among their people, issuing instructions. The Snow Hunters drew food from their packs—dried roots, seeds, smoked meat—and lunched in silence. Afterward, boys who carried huge waterbags made of sewn hides slung between them on poles went off to the creek to replenish their supply, and the rest of the Snow Hunters rose, stretched, wandered in narrow circles about the clearing, as if getting ready to resume the march. Crown was seized by furious impatience. "What are they going to do?" he demanded. "What deal have they made?"

"I imagine they've submitted to the terms," Leaf said.

"No! No! I need their help!" Crown, in anguish, hammered at himself with his fists. "I have to talk to them," he muttered.

"Wait. Don't push them, Crown."

"What's the use? What's the use?" Now the Snow Hunters were hoisting their packs to their shoulders. No doubt of it; they were going to leave. Crown hurried across the clearing. Sky, busily directing the order of march, grudgingly gave him attention. "Where are you going?" Crown asked.

"Westward," said Sky.

"What about us?"

"March with us, if you wish."

"My wagon!"

"You can't get it through the gate, can you?"

Crown reared up as though he would strike the Snow Hunter in rage. "If you would aid us, the wall would fall! Look, how can I abandon my wagon? I need to reach my kinsmen in the Flatlands. I'll assemble an army; I'll return to the east and push the Teeth back into the mountains where they belong. I've lost too much time already. I must get through. Don't you want to see the Teeth destroyed?"

"It's nothing to us," Sky said evenly. "Our lands are lost to us forever. Vengeance is meaningless. Your pardon. My people need my guidance."

More than half the Snow Hunters had passed through the gate already. Leaf joined the procession. On the far side of the wall he discovered that the dense thicket along the highway's northern rim had been cleared for a considerable distance, and a few small wooden buildings, hostelries or depots, stood at the edge of the road. Another twenty or thirty paces farther along, a secondary path led northward into the forest; this was evidently the route to the Tree Companions' village. Traffic on that path was heavy just now. Hundreds of forest folk were streaming from the village to the highway, where a strange, repellent scene was being enacted. Each Snow Hunter in turn halted, unburdened himself of his pack, and laid it open. Three or four Tree Companions then picked through it, each seizing one item of value—a knife, a comb, a piece of jewelry, a fine cloak—and running triumphantly off with it. Once he had submitted to this harrying of his possessions, the Snow Hunter gathered up his pack, shouldered it, and marched on, head bowed, body slumping. Tribute. Leaf felt chilled. These proud warriors, homeless now, yielding up their remaining treasures to—he tried to choke off the word, and could not—to a tribe of monkeys. And moving onward, soiled, unmanned. Of all that he had seen since the Teeth had split the world apart, this was the most sad.

Leaf started back toward the wagon. He saw Sky, Shield, and Blade at the rear of the column of Snow Hunters. Their faces were ashen; they could not meet his eyes. Sky managed a half-hearted salute as he passed by.

"I wish you good fortune on your journey," Leaf said.

"I wish you better fortune than we have had," said Sky hollowly, and went on.

Leaf found Crown standing rigid in the middle of the highway, hands on hips. "Cowards!" he called in a bitter voice. "Weaklings!"

"And now it's our turn," Leaf said.

"What do you mean?"

"The time's come for us to face hard truths. We have to give up the wagon, Crown."

"Never."

"We agree that we can't turn back. And we can't go forward so long as the wall's there. If we stay here, the Tree Companions will eventually kill us, if the Teeth don't overtake us first. Listen to me, Crown. We don't have to give the Tree Companions everything we have. The wagon itself, some of our spare clothing, some trinkets, the furnishings of the wagon—they'll be satisfied with that. We can load the rest of our goods on the horses and go safely through the gate as foot-pilgrims."

"I ignore this, Leaf."

"I know you do. I also know what the wagon means to you. I wish you could keep it. I wish I could stay with the wagon myself. Don't you think I'd rather ride west in comfort than slog through the rain and the cold? But we can't keep it. *We can't keep it*, Crown, that's the heart of the situation. We can go back east in the wagon and get lost in the desert, we can sit here and wait for the Tree Companions to lose patience and kill us, or we can give up the wagon and get out of this place with our skins still whole. What sort of choices are those? We have no choice. I've been telling you that for two days. Be reasonable, Crown!"

Crown glanced coldly at Sting and Shadow. "Find the chief and go into trance with him again. Tell him that I'll give him swords, armor, his pick of the finest things in the wagon. So long as he'll dismantle part of the wall and let the wagon itself pass through."

"We made that offer yesterday," Sting said glumly.

"And?"

"He insists on the wagon. The old witch has promised it to him for a palace."

"No," Crown said. "*NO!*" His wild roaring cry echoed from the hills. After a moment, more calmly, he said, "I have another idea. Leaf, Sting, come with me. The gate's open. We'll go to the village and seize the witch-woman. We'll grab her quickly, before anyone realizes what we're doing. They won't dare molest us while she's in our hands. Then, Sting, you tell the chief that unless they open the wall for us, we'll kill her." Crown chuckled. "Once she realizes we're serious, she'll tell them to hop it. Anybody that old wants to live forever. And they'll obey her. You can bet on that. They'll obey her! Come, now." Crown started toward the gate at a vigorous pace. He took a dozen strides, halted, looked back. Neither Leaf nor Sting had moved.

"Well? Why aren't you coming?"

"I won't do it," said Leaf tiredly. "It's crazy, Crown. She's a witch, she's part Invisible—she already knows your scheme. She probably knew of it before you knew of it yourself. How can we hope to catch her?"

"Let me worry about that."

"Even if we did, Crown—no. No. I won't have any part of it. It's an impossible idea. Even if we did seize her. We'd be standing there holding a sword to her throat, and the chief would give a signal, and they'd put a hundred darts in us before we could move a muscle. It's insane, Crown."

"I ask you to come with me."

"You've had your answer."

"Then I'll go without you."

"As you choose," Leaf said quietly. "But you won't be seeing me again."

"Eh?"

"I'm going to collect what I own and let the Tree Companions take their pick of it, and then I'll hurry forward and catch up with the Snow Hunters. In a week or so I'll be at the Middle River. Shadow, will you come with me, or are you determined to stay here and die with Crown?"

The Dancing Star looked toward the muddy ground. "I don't know," she said. "Let me think a moment."

"Sting?"

"I'm going with you."

Leaf beckoned to Crown. "Please. Come to your senses, Crown. For the last time—give up the wagon and let's get going, all four of us."

"You disgust me."

"Then this is where we part," Leaf said. "I wish you good fortune. Sting, let's assemble our belongings. Shadow? Will you be coming with us?"

"We have an obligation toward Crown," she said.

"To help him drive his wagon, yes. But not to die a foolish death for him. Crown has lost his wagon, Shadow, though he won't admit that yet. If the wagon's no longer his, our contract is voided. I hope you'll join us."

He entered the wagon and went to the midcabin cupboard where he stored the few possessions he had managed to bring with him out of the east. A pair of glistening boots made of the leathery skins of stick-creatures, two ancient copper coins, three ornamental ivory medallions, a shirt of dark red silk, a thick, heavily worked belt—not much, not much at all, the salvage of a lifetime. He packed rapidly. He took with him a slab of dried meat and some bread; that would last him a day or two, and when it was gone he would learn from Sting or the Snow Hunters the arts of gathering food in the wilderness.

"Are you ready?"

"Ready as I'll ever be," Sting said. His pack was almost empty—a change of clothing, a hatchet, a knife, some smoked fish, nothing else.

"Let's go, then."

As Sting and Leaf moved toward the exit hatch, Shadow scrambled up into the wagon. She looked tight-strung and grave; her nostrils were flared, her eyes downcast. Without a word she went past Leaf and began loading her pack. Leaf waited for her. After a few minutes she reappeared and nodded to him.

"Poor Crown," she whispered. "Is there no way—"

"You heard him," Leaf said.

They emerged from the wagon. Crown had not moved. He stood as if rooted, midway between wagon and wall. Leaf gave him a quizzical look, as if to ask whether he had changed his mind, but Crown took no notice. Shrugging, Leaf walked around him, toward the edge of the thicket, where the nightmares were nibbling leaves. Affectionately he reached up to stroke the long neck of the nearest horse, and Crown suddenly came to life, shouting, "Those are my animals! Keep your hands off them!"

"I'm only saying goodbye to them."

"You think I'm going to let you have some? You think I'm that crazy, Leaf?"

Leaf looked sadly at him. "We plan to do our traveling on foot, Crown. I'm only saying goodbye. The nightmares were my friends. You can't understand that, can you?"

"Keep away from those animals! *Keep away!*"

Leaf sighed. "Whatever you say." Shadow, as usual, was right: poor Crown. Leaf adjusted his pack and moved off toward the gate, Shadow beside him, Sting a few paces to the rear. As he and Shadow reached the gate, Leaf looked back and saw Crown still motionless, saw Sting pausing, putting down his pack, dropping to his knees. "Anything wrong?" Leaf called.

"Tore a bootlace," Sting said. "You two go on ahead. It'll take me a minute to fix it."

"We can wait."

Leaf and Shadow stood within the frame of the gate while Sting knotted his lace. After a few moments he rose and reached for his pack, saying, "That ought to hold me until tonight, and then I'll see if I can't—"

"*Watch out!*" Leaf yelled.

Crown erupted abruptly from his freeze, and, letting forth a lunatic cry, rushed with terrible swiftness toward Sting. There was no chance for Sting to make one of his little leaps: Crown seized him, held him high overhead like a child, and, grunting in frantic rage, hurled the little man toward the ravine. Arms and legs flailing, Sting traveled on a high arc over the edge; he seemed to dance in midair for an instant, and then he dropped from view. There was a long diminishing shriek, and silence. Silence.

Leaf stood stunned. "Hurry," Shadow said. "Crown's coming!"

Crown, swinging around, now rumbled like a machine of death toward Leaf and Shadow. His wild red eyes glittered ferociously. Leaf did not move; Shadow shook him urgently, and finally he pushed himself into action. Together they caught hold of the massive gate and, straining, swung it shut, slamming it just as Crown crashed into it. Leaf forced the reluctant bolts into place. Crown roared and pounded at the gate, but he was unable to force it.

Shadow shivered and wept. Leaf drew her to him and held her for a moment. At length he said, "We'd better be on our way. The Snow Hunters are far ahead of us already."

"Sting—"

"I know. I know. Come, now."

Half a dozen Tree Companions were waiting for them by the wooden houses. They grinned, chattered, pointed to the packs. "All right," Leaf said. "Go ahead. Take whatever you want. Take everything, if you like."

Busy fingers picked through his pack and Shadow's. From Shadow the Tree Companions took a brocaded ribbon and a flat, smooth green stone. From Leaf they took one of the ivory medallions, both copper coins, and one of his stickskin boots. Tribute. Day by day, pieces of the past slipped from his grasp. He pulled the other boot from the pack and offered it to them, but they merely giggled and shook their heads. "One is of no use to me," he said. They would not take it. He tossed the boot into the grass beside the road.

The road curved gently toward the north and began a slow rise, following the flank of the forested hills in which the Tree Companions made their homes. Leaf and Shadow marched, mechanically, saying little. The boot-prints of the Snow Hunters were everywhere along the road, but the Snow Hunters themselves were far ahead, out of sight. It was early afternoon, and the day had become bright, unexpectedly warm. After an hour Shadow said, "I must rest."

Her teeth were clacking. She crouched by the roadside and wrapped her arms about her chest. Dancing Stars, covered with thick fur, usually wore no clothing except in the bleakest winters; but her pelt did her no good now.

"Are you ill?" he asked.

"It'll pass. I'm reacting. Sting—"

"Yes."

"And Crown. I feel so unhappy about Crown."

"A madman," Leaf said. "A murderer."

"Don't judge him so casually, Leaf. He's a man under sentence of death, and he knows it, and he's suffering from it, and when the fear and pain became unbearable to him he reached out for Sting. He didn't know what he was doing. He needed to smash something, that was all, to relieve his own torment."

"We're all going to die sooner or later," Leaf said. "That doesn't generally drive us to kill our friends."

"I don't mean sooner or later. I mean that Crown will die tonight or tomorrow."

"Why should he?"

"What can he do now to save himself, Leaf?"

"He could yield to the Tree Companions and pass the gate on foot, as we've done."

"You know he'd never abandon the wagon."

"Well, then, he can harness the nightmares and turn around toward Theptis. At least he'd have a chance to make it through to the Sunset Highway that way."

"He can't do that either," Shadow said.

"Why not?"

"He can't drive the wagon."

"There's no one left to do it for him. His life's at stake. For once he could eat his pride and—"

"I didn't say *won't* drive the wagon, Leaf. I said *can't*. Crown's incapable. He isn't able to make dream contact with the nightmares. Why do you think he always used hired drivers? Why was he so insistent on making you drive in the purple rain? He doesn't have the mind-power. Did you ever see a Dark Laker driving nightmares? Ever?"

Leaf stared at her. "You knew this all along?"

"From the beginning, yes."

"Is that why you hesitated to leave him at the gate? When you were talking about our contract with him?"

She nodded. "If all three of us left him, we were condemning him to death. He has no way of escaping the Tree Companions now unless he forces himself to leave the wagon, and he won't do that. They'll fall on him and kill him, today, tomorrow, whenever."

Leaf closed his eyes, shook his head. "I feel a kind of shame. Now that I know we were leaving him helpless. He could have spoken."

"Too proud."

"Yes. Yes. It's just as well he didn't say anything. We all have responsibilities to one another, but there are limits. You and I and Sting were under no obligation to die simply because Crown couldn't bring himself to give up his pretty wagon. But still—still—" He locked his hands tightly together. "Why did you finally decide to leave, then?"

"For the reason you just gave. I didn't want Crown to die, but I didn't believe I owed him my life. Besides, you had said you were going to go, no matter what."

"Poor, crazy Crown."

"And when he killed Sting—a life for a life, Leaf. All vows are canceled now. I feel no guilt."

"Nor I."

"I think the fever is leaving me."

"Let's rest a few minutes more," Leaf said.

It was more than an hour before Leaf judged Shadow strong enough to go on. The highway now described a steady upgrade, not steep but making constant demands on their stamina, and they moved slowly. As the day's warmth began to dwindle, they reached the crest of the grade, and rested again at a place from which they could see the road ahead winding in switchbacks into a green, pleasant valley. Far below were the Snow Hunters, resting also by the side of a fair-size stream.

"Smoke," Shadow said. "Do you smell it?"

"Campfires down there, I suppose."

"I don't think they have any fires going. I don't see any."

"The Tree Companions, then."

"It must be a big fire."

"No matter," Leaf said. "Are you ready to continue?"

"I hear a sound—"

A voice from behind and uphill of them said, "And so it ends the usual way, in foolishness and death, and the All-Is-One grows greater."

Leaf whirled, springing to his feet. He heard laughter on the hillside and saw movements in the underbrush; after a moment he made out a dim, faintly outlined figure, and realized that an Invisible was coming toward them, the same one, no doubt, who had traveled with them from Theptis.

"What do you want?" Leaf called.

"Want? Want? I want nothing. I'm merely passing through." The Invisible pointed over his shoulder. "You can see the whole thing from the top of this hill. Your big friend put up a mighty struggle, he killed many of them, but the darts, the darts—" The Invisible laughed. "He was dying, but even so he wasn't going to let them have his wagon. Such a stubborn man. Such a foolish man. Well, a happy journey to you both."

"Don't leave yet!" Leaf cried. But even the outlines of the Invisible were fading. Only the laughter remained, and then that too was gone. Leaf threw desperate questions into the air and, receiving no replies, turned and rushed up the hillside, clawing at the thick shrubbery. In ten minutes he was at the summit, and stood gasping and panting, looking back across a precipitous valley to the stretch of road they had just traversed. He could see everything clearly from here: the Tree Companion village nestling in the forest, the highway, the shacks by the side of the road, the wall, the clearing beyond the wall. And the wagon. The roof was gone and the sides had tumbled outward. Bright spears of flame shot high, and a black, billowing cloud of smoke stained the air. Leaf stood watching Crown's pyre a long while before returning to Shadow.

They descended toward the place where the Snow Hunters had made their camp. Breaking a long silence, Shadow said, "There must once have been a time when the world was different, when all people were of the same kind, and everyone lived in peace. A golden age, long gone. How did things change, Leaf? How did we bring this upon ourselves?"

"Nothing has changed," Leaf said, "except the look of our bodies. Inside we're the same. There never was any golden age."

"There were no Teeth, once."

"There were always Teeth, under one name or another. True peace never lasted long. Greed and hatred always existed."

"Do you believe that, truly?"

"I do. I believe that mankind is mankind, all of us the same whatever our shape, and such changes as come upon us are trifles, and the best we can ever do is find such happiness for ourselves as we can, however dark the times."

"These are darker times than most, Leaf."

"Perhaps."

"These are evil times. The end of all things approaches."

Leaf smiled. "Let it come. These are the times we were meant to live in, and no asking why, and no use longing for easier times. Pain ends when acceptance begins. This is what we have now. We make the best of it. This is the road we travel. Day by day we lose what was never ours, day by day we slip closer to the All-Is-One, and nothing matters, Shadow, nothing except learning to accept what comes. Yes?"

"Yes," she said. "How far is it to the Middle River?"

"Another few days."

"And from there to your kinsmen by the Inland Sea?"

"I don't know," he said. "However long it takes us is however long it will take. Are you very tired?"

"Not as tired as I thought I'd be."

"It isn't far to the Snow Hunters' camp. We'll sleep well tonight."

"Crown," she said. "Sting."

"What about them?"

"They also sleep."

"In the All-Is-One," Leaf said. "Beyond all trouble. Beyond all pain."

"And that beautiful wagon is a charred ruin!"

"If only Crown had had the grace to surrender it freely, once he knew he was dying. But then he wouldn't have been Crown, would he? Poor Crown. Poor crazy Crown." There was a stirring ahead, suddenly. "Look. The Snow Hunters see us. There's Sky. Blade." Leaf waved at them and shouted. Sky waved back, and Blade, and a few of the others. "May we camp with you tonight?" Leaf called. Sky answered something, but his words were blown away by the wind. He sounded friendly, Leaf thought. He sounded friendly. "Come," Leaf said, and he and Shadow hurried down the slope.

ACKNOWLEDGMENTS

"We're All In This Together"—a phrase we've all heard so many times the past few months that it's become cliché, yet nowhere has it been more in evidence than the way the literary community rallied around this project. I didn't turn away anyone who had a story for consideration, and I sent back edits and accepted all but one—more a novel excerpt than a complete tale. As a consequence, this grew from 17 stories as conceived to the 29 stories you see now, some written specifically for this project.

The editor's thanks go out to Luca Oleastri for another fine piece of cover art and to the authors for some fine stories, all of which were donated for use in this anthology. Especially those who set aside everything else to quickly write new stories with a very tight deadline. Thanks also go to publishers Peter J. Wacks for his full support of the project, one which as a COVID-19 survivor had personal meaning for them. Thanks to Erich Shanholtzer and Anthony Cardno for proofing.

Gratitude also goes out to the staff of Aeristic Press and Boralis Books who worked tirelessly to get this book fast-tracked to publication. The time from conception to completion was less than four months, which in publishing terms is lightning fast. Also to the FDA and our charities for working with us to make sure the money goes to where it's needed most and will be used responsibly and effectively to save lives.

Thanks to all the readers who buy this book and support the cause, even though some of the reprints may already be familiar to them. It's a cause we all share in common and it's a small but important way we can make a difference together. I only hope the stories herein can provide de-stressing and escape from the cruel realities of life in a global pandemic.

Read and enjoy them with the love they are given and please, stay safe out there!

PUBLICATION & COPYRIGHT CREDITS

BIOGRAPHIES

EDITOR

Bryan Thomas Schmidt is the Hugo-nominated and national bestselling editor of 15 anthologies and numerous novels including the worldwide bestseller *The Martian* by Andy Weir and books by Frank Herbert, Alan Dean Foster, and Angie Fox, among others. His books have been published by St. Martin's Press, Baen Books, Titan Books, IDW, and many more. A national bestselling author of novels and short fiction, his novel series include *The Saga of Davi Rhii* and *The John Simon Thrillers*. His debut novel, *The Worker Prince*, received Honorable Mention on Barnes and Noble's Year's Best Science Fiction of 2011. He lives in Ottawa, KS where he has been social distancing with his two dogs and two very naughty cats. He can be found online at bryanthomasschmidt.net and as @BryanThomasS on Twitter and Facebook.

CONTRIBUTORS

Martin L. Shoemaker (*Last Bus to North Red Lake*) is a programmer who writes on the side... or maybe it's the other way around. Programming pays the bills, but a second-place story in the Jim Baen Memorial Writing Contest earned him lunch with Buzz Aldrin. Programming never did that! His work has appeared in *Analog Science Fiction & Fact, Galaxy's Edge, Digital Science Fiction, Forever Magazine, Writers of the Future*, and numerous anthologies including *Year's Best Military and Adventure SF 4, Man-Kzin Wars XV, The Jim Baen Memorial Award: The First Decade, Little Green Men—Attack!, More Human Than Human: Stories of Androids, Robots, and Manufactured Humanity,* and *Avatar Dreams*. His *Clarkesworld* story "Today I Am Paul" appeared in four different year's best anthologies and eight international editions. His follow-on novel, *Today I Am Carey*, was published by Baen Books in March 2019. His novel *The Last Dance* was published by 47North in November 2019.

Andrew Mayne (*Windstream*) is a *Wall Street Journal* bestselling author and an Edgar Award and Thriller Award finalist. He's the author of *The Girl Beneath the Sea, The Naturalist, Looking Glass, Murder Theory, Dark Pattern, Angel Killer,* and *Name of the Devil*. He starred in the Discovery Channel Shark Week special *Andrew Mayne: Ghost Diver* and A&E's *Don't Trust Andrew Mayne*. As an illusionist, he started his first world tour when he was a teenager and went on to work behind the scenes for Penn & Teller, David Blaine, and David Copperfield. He was ranked as the fifth best selling independent author of the year by Amazon UK. For more on him and his work, you can follow him on Twitter @AndrewMayne and visit www.AndrewMayne.com.

Roshni "Rush" Bhatia (*Windstream*) is a horror writer-director living in Los Angeles, USA. Growing up in Mumbai, Rush was inspired by filmmakers like James Cameron, Ridley Scott, and writers like Richard Matheson and Rod Serling. By the age of 21, while Rush's shorts were making the rounds at film festivals, she wrote, directed, and conceptualized six Bollywood music videos which have garnered millions of views. Her short films gained appreciation at top tier festivals such as Leeds International Film Festival, Morbido Film Fest, etc. Her films have screened at more than 50 festivals and have won awards including Best Director, Best Writing, and Best Editing. Rush was also nominated for Best Writer by the Horror Writers Association of America for one of her shorts, "Plasmid." For more on her and her work, you can follow Rush on Instagram @roshnibhatia and Twitter @rushbhatia.

Cory Doctorow (*When Sysadmins Ruled the Earth*) is a science fiction author, activist, journalist and blogger—the co-editor of Boing Boing (boingboing.net) and the author of many books, most recently *In Real Life*, a graphic novel; *Information Doesn't Want To Be Free*, a book about earning a living in the internet age, and *Homeland*, the award-winning, best-selling sequel to the 2008 YA novel *Little Brother*. For more, see craphound.com

Since 1969 **Chelsea Quinn Yarbro** (*Call It Only*) has published nearly 100 books and more than 100 pieces of short fiction. Her most famous creation is the 4,000 year-old vampire Count Saint-Germain, whose adventures Yarbro have chronicled in a bestselling series of historical horror novels. She has also composed music for the orchestra and theater.

In 1997 the Transylvanian Society of Dracula bestowed a literary knighthood on Yarbro, and in 2003 the World Horror Association presented her with a Grand Master award. In 2006 the International Horror Guild enrolled her among their Living Legends, the first woman to be so honored. She has received two Lifetime Achievement Awards—from the Horror Writers Association in 2009, and from the World Fantasy Association in 2014.

Yarbro lives in the San Francisco Bay Area with the Gang of Two (her cats Butterscotch and Crumpet). When not busy reading or writing, she enjoys the symphony and opera. For more, see chelseaquinnyarbro.net

Seanan McGuire (*Face Your Furs*) is the *New York Times*-bestselling author of more than a dozen books, all published within the last five years, which may explain why some people believe that she does not actually sleep. Her work has been translated into several languages, and resulted in her receiving a record five Hugo Award nominations on the 2013 ballot. When not writing, Seanan spends her time reading, watching terrible horror movies and too much television, visiting Disney Parks, and rating haunted corn mazes. You can keep up with her at seananmcguire.com.

Number one *New York Times* bestselling author **Scott Sigler** (*Dale & Mabel*) is the creator of fifteen novels, six novellas, and dozens of short stories. His works are available from Crown Publishing and Del Rey Books. In 2005, Scott built a large online following by releasing his audiobooks as serialized podcasts. A decade later, he still gives his stories away—for free—every Sunday at scottsigler.com. His loyal fans, who named themselves "Junkies," have downloaded more than forty million individual episodes. He has been covered in *Time, Entertainment Weekly, Publishers Weekly, The New York Times, The Washington Post, The San Francisco Chronicle, The Chicago Tribune, Io9, Wired, Huffington Post, BusinessWeek,* and *Fangoria.* Scott is the co-founder of Empty Set Entertainment, which publishes his *Galactic Football League* YA series. He lives in San Diego, California, with his wee little dog, Reesie.

K.D. McEntire (*Flinch*) is the author of the Lightbringer YA urban fantasy trilogy from PYR Books. She lives in Kansas where between raising her two young sons, she is working on another novel, and can be found online at facebook.com/KD-McEntire.

Orson Scott Card (*Carousel*) is the *New York Times* bestselling and award-winning author of the novels *Ender's Game, Ender's Shadow,* and *Speaker for the Dead,* which are widely read by adults and younger readers, and are increasingly used in schools. His most recent series, the young adult Pathfinder series (*Pathfinder, Ruins, Visitors*) and the fantasy Mithermages series (*Lost Gate, Gate Thief*) are taking readers in new directions. Besides these and other science fiction novels, Card writes contemporary fantasy (*Magic Street, Enchantment, Lost Boys*), biblical novels (*Stone Tables, Rachel and Leah*), the American frontier fantasy series, *The Tales of Alvin Maker* (beginning with *Seventh Son*), poetry (*An Open Book*), and many plays and scripts.

Card currently lives in Greensboro, North Carolina, with his wife, Kristine Allen Card, where his primary activities are writing a review column for the local *Rhinoceros Times* and feeding birds, squirrels, chipmunks, possums, and raccoons on the patio.

Ken Scholes (*The Monsters Underneath His Bed*) is the award-winning, critically-acclaimed author of five novels and over fifty short stories. His work has appeared in print since 2000. He is also a singer-songwriter who has written nearly a hundred songs over thirty years of performing.

Ken's eclectic background includes time spent as a label gun repairman, a sailor who never sailed, a soldier who commanded a desk, a fundamentalist preacher (he got better), a nonprofit executive, and a government procurement analyst. He has a degree in History from Western Washington University.

Ken is a native of the Pacific Northwest and makes his home in Cornelius, Oregon, where he lives with his twin daughters. You can learn more about Ken by visiting kenscholes.com.

New York Times bestselling author **Livia Blackburne** (*Lord of Time*) wrote her first novel while researching the neuroscience of reading at the Massachusetts Institute of Technology. Since then, she's switched to full time writing, which also involves getting into people's heads but without the help of a three tesla MRI scanner. She is the author of *Midnight Thief* (An Indies Introduce New Voices selection) and *Rosemarked* (A YALSA Teens Top Ten nominee), as well as their respective sequels.

Alan Dean Foster's (*Evacuation*) work to date includes excursions into hard science fiction, fantasy, horror, detective, western, historical, and contemporary fiction. He has also written numerous nonfiction articles on film, science, and scuba diving, as well as having produced the novel versions of many films, including such well-known productions as *Star Wars*, the first three *Alien* films, *Alien Nation*, and *The Chronicles of Riddick*. Other works include scripts for talking records, radio, computer games, and the story for *Star Trek: The Motion Picture*. His novel *Shadowkeep* was the first ever book adaptation of an original computer game. In addition to publication in English his work has been translated into more than fifty languages and has won awards in Spain and Russia. His novel *Cyber Way* won the Southwest Book Award for Fiction in 1990, the first work of science fiction ever to do so.

Foster's sometimes humorous, occasionally poignant, but always entertaining short fiction has appeared in all the major SF magazines as well as in original anthologies and several "Best of the Year" compendiums. His published oeuvre includes more than 100 books. Among his most famous original creations are the characters Pip and Flinx and Amos Malone.

New York Times bestselling author **A.C. Crispin** (1950–2013) (*Pure Silver*) wrote prolifically in many different tie-in universes, and was a master at filling in the histories of beloved TV and movie characters. She began publishing in 1983 with the Star Trek novel *Yesterday's Son*, written in her spare time while working for the US Census Bureau. Shortly thereafter, Tor Books commissioned her to write what is perhaps still her most widely read work, the 1984 novelization of the television miniseries, *V*, which sold more than a million copies.

For Star Wars, Crispin wrote the bestselling *Han Solo Trilogy: The Paradise Snare*, *The Hutt Gambit*, and *Rebel Dawn*, which tell the story of Han Solo from his early years right up to the moment he walks into the cantina in *Star Wars: A New Hope*. She wrote three other bestselling Star Trek novels: *Time for Yesterday*, *The Eyes of the Beholders*, and *Sarek*. Her final tie-in novel was the massive *Pirates of the Caribbean: The Price of Freedom*, which was published in 2011. She was named a Grandmaster by the International Association of Media Tie-In Writers in 2013.

Her major original science fiction undertaking was the *StarBridge* series. These books, written solo or in collaboration, centered around a school for young diplomats, translators, and explorers, both alien and human, located on an asteroid far from Earth. Series titles are: *StarBridge*, *Silent Dances*, *Shadow World*, *Serpent's Gift*, *Silent Songs*, *Voices of Chaos*, and *Ancestor's World*.

Crispin was a fierce advocate for writers. She and author Victoria Strauss created and co-chaired SFWA's "scam watchdog" committee, Writer Beware, in 1998.

Kathleen O'Malley (*Pure Silver*) has been writing fiction and nonfiction since her childhood. With her friend, A.C. Crispin, she coauthored two *StarBridge* books: *StarBridge 2: Silent Dances* and *StarBridge 5: Silent Songs*, the movie novelization *Alien: Resurrection*, and several short stories, including "Pure Silver." She lives in Maryland with her wife and six accidental dogs and three deliberate cats.

Jody Lynn Nye (*Writing on the Wall*) lists her main career activity as "spoiling cats." She lives northwest of Atlanta with three feline overlords, Athena, Minx, and Marmalade, and her husband, author and packager Bill Fawcett. She has written over fifty books, most of them with a humorous bent, and over 170 short stories. Jody has been fortunate enough to have collaborated with some of the greats in the field of science fiction and fantasy. She wrote several books with Anne McCaffrey or set in Anne's many worlds, including *The Death of Sleep*, *The Ship Who Won*, *Crisis on Doona* (a New York Times and USA Today bestseller), and *The Dragonlover's Guide to Pern*. She wrote eight books with Robert Asprin and has since his death continued two of his series, the *Myth-Adventures* and *Dragons*. She edited a humorous anthology about mothers, *Don't Forget Your Spacesuit, Dear!*, Her latest books are *Rhythm of the Imperium* (Baen Books), *Moon Tracks* (with Travis S. Taylor, Baen Books), *Myth-Fits* (Ace), and *Once More, with Feeling*, a book on revising your manuscripts (WordFire Press). She is one of the judges for the Writers of the Future fiction contest, the largest speculative fiction contest in the world. Jody also teaches the intensive two-day writers' workshop at DragonCon. You can find her online on Facebook, Twitter, and her website, jodynye.net.

Jonathan Maberry (*Back to Black*) is a *New York Times* bestselling author and 5-time Bram Stoker Award-winner. He writes in multiple genres including suspense, thriller, horror, science fiction, fantasy, action, and steampunk, for adults, teens and middle grade. His works include the *Joe Ledger* thrillers, *Rot & Ruin*, *Mars One*, and *Captain America*, which is in development for a feature film. He writes comics for Marvel, Dark Horse and IDW and is the editor of such high-profile anthologies as *The X-Files*, *V-Wars*, *Out of Tune*, *Baker Street Irregular*, *Nights of the Living Dead*, and *Scary Out There*. He lives in Del Mar, California.

Bryan Thomas Schmidt (*Back to Black*) contributed as a co-author on the "Back to Black" short story and also edited this volume. His bio can be found in the editor section above.

Neil Gaiman (*We Can Get Them for You Wholesale*) is the bestselling author of books, short stories, films and graphic novels for adults and children. Some of his most notable titles include the novels *The Graveyard Book* (the first book to ever win both the Newbery and Carnegie medals), *American Gods,* and the UK's National Book Award 2013 Book of the Year, *The Ocean at the End of the Lane.* His latest collection of short stories, *Trigger Warning,* was an immediate *New York Times* bestseller and was named a NYT Editors' Choice. Born in the UK, he now lives in the US with his wife, the musician and writer, Amanda Palmer.

John Skipp (*Hopium Den*) is a Saturn Award-winning filmmaker (*Tales of Halloween*), Stoker Award-winning anthologist (*Demons, Mondo Zombie*), and *New York Times* bestselling author (*The Light at the End, The Scream*) whose books have sold millions of copies in a dozen languages worldwide. His first anthology, *Book of the Dead,* laid the foundation in 1989 for modern zombie literature. He's also editor-in-chief of Fungasm Press, championing genre-melting authors like Laura Lee Bahr, Autumn Christian, Danger Slater, Cody Goodfellow, Jennifer Robin, S.G. Murphy and John Boden From splatterpunk founding father to bizarro elder statesman, Skipp has influenced a generation of horror and counterculture artists around the world. His latest screenplay (with Dori Miller) is "Times is Tough in Musky Holler", for Shudder's *Creepshow* series. His most recent book (with Heather Drain) is *The Bizarro Encyclopedia of Film (VOL. I).*

Raymund Eich (*The Ultimate Wager*) is a science fiction and fantasy writer whose middle American upbringing is a launchpad for journeys to the ends of the universe. His most popular works are military science fiction series *The Confederated Worlds* (*Take the Shilling, Operation Iago,* and *A Bodyguard of Lies*) and the Stone Chalmers series of science fiction espionage adventures (*The Progress of Mankind, The Greater Glory of God, To All High Emprise Consecrated,* and *In Public Convocation Assembled*). His latest novel of deep space suspense, *The Reincarnation Run,* was published in October 2019 by CV-2 Books (cv2books.com). His website is raymundeich.com.

Julie Frost (*Bitter Honey*) grew up an Army brat, traveling the globe. She thought she might settle down after she finished school, but then married a pilot and moved six times in seven years. She's finally put down roots in Utah with her family--a herd of guinea pigs, another humans, and a "kitten" who thinks she's a warrior princess--and a collection of anteaters and Oaxacan carvings, some of which intersect. She enjoys birding and nature photography, which also intersect. Utilizing her degree in biology, she writes werewolf fiction while completely ignoring the physics of a protagonist who triples in mass. Her short fiction has appeared in too many venues to count, including *Writers of the Future 32, Straight Outta Dodge City,* and *Monster Hunter Files.* Her werewolf private eye novel series, *Pack Dynamics,* is published by WordFire Press; her novel *Dark Day, Bright Hour* was published by Ring of Fire Press. She whines about writing, a lot, at agilebrit.livejournal.com.

Mercedes M. Yardley (*Voracious Black*) is a whimsical dark fantasist who wears poisonous flowers in her hair. She is the author of *Beautiful Sorrows,* the Stabby-Award-winning *Apocalyptic Montessa* and *Nuclear Lulu: A Tale of Atomic Love, Pretty Little Dead Girls,* and *Nameless.* She won the prestigious Bram Stoker Award for her story "Little Dead Red" and was a Bram Stoker Award nominee for her short story "Loving You Darkly." Mercedes is editor of the dark fiction anthology *Arterial Bloom.* You can find her online at mercedesmyardley.com.

C. Stuart Hardwick (*A Love Monstrously Grateful*) is a regular in *Analog Science Fiction & Fact* magazine, a winner of the prestigious Writers of the Future contest, and a six-time Jim Baen Memorial award honoree. In addition to scifi, he writes about science for numerous publications, and his work has been translated into a dozen languages.

An Air Force brat from South Dakota, he grew up on Black Hills treasure hunts and family lore like pages from a Steinbeck novel. After a childhood of homemade "radio shows" and stop animation scifi shorts, he worked with the creators of the video game *Doom* and married an aquanaut.

Stuart is the editor of the space adventure anthology *Final Frontier* by Got Scifi Group. For a free signed e-sampler and information about his *Open Source Space* series, visit cStuartHardwick.com.

Nebula Award-nominated **Beth Cato** (*The Sweetness of Bitter*) is the author of the Clockwork Dagger duology and the Blood of Earth trilogy from Harper Voyager. She's a Hanford, California native transplanted to the Arizona desert, where she lives with her husband, son, and requisite cats. Follow her at BethCato.com and on Twitter at @BethCato.

Bestselling author **Kent Holloway** (*Six Lil' Reapers*) lives on death. Literally. With more than twenty-five years' experience in forensic death investigations, he's seen it all. Experienced the worst that life has to give and never let it dim his sense of wonder or humor. Now, he brings all this experience, along with a zeal for uncovering the folklore and superstitions of death, to the written page as author of mysteries, forensic crime fiction, paranormal thrillers, and Christian fiction and nonfiction!

He is the author of the highly acclaimed Ezekiel Crane paranormal mystery series, as well as some of his more traditional mysteries, *Killypso Island* and the forensic thriller, *Clean Exit*. He's even started a series wherein Death himself takes on the role of sleuth in the witty and twisty *Death Warmed Over*.

Kent Holloway also has a Master's degree in Biblical Studies from Southeastern Baptist Theological Seminary. He has served as singles minister, evangelism pastor, and director of discipleship and education. Kent has just released his very first Christian nonfiction book entitled *I Died Swallowing a Goldfish and Other Life Lessons from the Morgue*.

Jay Werkheiser (*Impact Mitigation*) teaches chemistry and physics. Pretty much all the time. His stories are sneaky devices to allow him to talk about science in a (sort of) socially acceptable way. Much to his surprise, the editors of *Analog* and various other magazines, e-zines, and anthologies have found a few of his stories worth publishing. Many of those story ideas came from nerdy discussions with his daughter or his students. He really should keep an updated blog and author page, but he mostly wastes his online time on Facebook, MeWe, or Twitter.

Claire Ashgrove (*Fair Play*) is the author of the award-winning series, *The Curse of the Templars*. Although primarily known for her romance works, she's written across a variety of genres and loves delving into new fiction adventures. She's a lifelong native of Missouri, where she teaches high school English in a small rural district. In her free time, she can be found on her conservation poultry farm with her teenage sons, working with critically endangered birds and riding horses. Follow her at claireashgrove. net and on Facebook.

Brenda Cooper (*In Their Garden*) is a writer, a futurist, and a technology professional. She often writes about technology and the environment. Her recent novels include *Keepers* (Pyr, 2018), *Wilders* (Pyr, 2017), *POST* (Espec Books, 2016), and *Spear of Light* (Pyr, 2016).

Brenda is the winner of the 2007 and 2016 Endeavour Awards for "a distinguished science fiction or fantasy book written by a Pacific Northwest author or authors." Her work has also been nominated for the Philip K. Dick and Canopus awards.

Brenda lives in Woodinville, Washington with her family and four dogs.

Tori Eldridge (*Empty Nest*) is the Lefty-nominated author of *The Ninja Daughter*, which was named one of the "Best Mystery Books of the Year" by The South Florida Sun Sentinel and awarded 2019 Thriller Book of the Year by Authors on the Air Global Radio Network. Her short stories appear in several anthologies, and her screenplay *The Gift* earned a semifinalist spot in the prestigious Academy Nicholl Fellowship. Before writing, Tori performed as an actress, singer, dancer on Broadway, television, and film. She is of Hawaiian, Chinese, Norwegian descent and was born and raised in Honolulu where she graduated from Punahou School with classmate Barack Obama. Tori holds a fifth-degree black belt in To-Shin Do ninjutsu and has traveled the USA teaching seminars on the ninja arts, weapons, and women's self-protection. Her second book in the *Lily Wong* series, *The Ninja's Blade*, releases September 1, 2020. For more see torieldridge.com.

Peter J. Wacks (*Shotgun Wedding*), born Zarathustra Janney, then quickly reminted the next day to a sane name on his second birth certificate, never really recovered a sense of normalcy in his life. Peter (or Zarth, whatever, it's cool) has travelled to 37 countries, hitchhiked across the United States (very funny, no, he didn't hitchhike to Hawaii), and backpacked across Europe. He loves fast cars, running 5Ks, space travel, and armchair physics. In the past, Peter has been an actor and game designer, but he loves writing most and has done a ton of it, which can be found by looking him up online (even if it seems a little cyber-stalkery, don't worry, go for it!) Since he doesn't think anyone reads these things anyway, he will mention *Strawberry Daiquiris*, Laphroaig, great IPAs, and really clever puns are the best way to start conversations with him. Are you still there? The Bio is over. Go Read.

Kristine Kathryn Rusch (*Once on the Blue Moon*) has won awards in every genre for her work. She has several pen names, including Kris Nelscott for mystery and Kristine Grayson for romance. She's currently writing two different science fiction series, *The Retrieval Artist* and the space opera *Diving* series. She's also editing the anthology series *Fiction River*. For more on her work, go to kristinewrites.com.

Robert Silverberg (*This is the Road*) is rightly considered by many as one of the greatest living science fiction writers. His career stretches back to the pulps and his output is amazing by any standard. He's authored numerous novels, short stories, and nonfiction books in various genres and categories. He's also a frequent guest at Cons and a regular columnist for *Asimov's Science Fiction*. His major works include *Dying Inside, The Book of Skulls, The Alien Years, The World Inside, Nightfall* with Isaac Asimov, *Son of Man, A Time of Changes*, and the seven Majipoor Cycle books. His first Majipoor trilogy, *Lord Valentine's Castle, Majipoor Chronicles*, and *Valentine Pontifex*, were reissued by ROC Books in May 2012, September 2012, and January 2013. *Tales of Majipoor*, a new collection bringing together all the short Majipoor tales, followed in May 2013. Three thematic collections of his short stories have been published in recent years by Three Rooms Press: *First Person Singularities* (2017), *Time and Time Again* (2018), and *Alien Archive* (2019).